NIGHT SHADOWS

HEATHER AMES

WELL OF IDEAS PRESS

ISBN (ebook): 978-0-9991359-3-8

ISBN (paperback): 978-0-9991359-2-1

CHAPTER ONE

Driving along the narrow, rutted track between bare-limbed trees and spindly pines brought memories of happier times to Carissa Yates. She relaxed her grip on the wheel as the trees fell away to reveal a white-washed lighthouse and keeper's quarters perched on an outcropping of bare rock facing the ocean.

She pulled up in front of the garage and turned off the engine. After driving more than twelve hours between New York and Maine, her trip punctuated only by stops at gas stations and rest areas, her eyes smarted and her limbs ached. But she had left her problems behind, she reminded herself. Ex-husband Matthew and the persistent paparazzi would have to find someone else to harass. Savoring the silence, broken only by gusting wind and distantly pounding surf, she laid her head back against the seat and closed her eyes.

A sharp knock on the window startled her.

"Ms. Yates...wake up!"

A thin, middle-aged man, his cheeks ruddy with cold despite a heavy woolen overcoat, headgear reminiscent of a World War II pilot and over-sized leather gloves, tapped the glass again. Carissa cracked open the window.

"The name's Al Dyson," he shouted, dancing from one foot to the other. "William Dansinger, your aunt's lawyer sent me over with the keys. I've been waiting close to an hour. I thought you weren't coming."

Carissa opened her door and stumbled out, her legs cramping after too many hours behind the wheel. "My car had a flat. I left Mr. Dansinger a voicemail."

"He's out of town." Dyson shrugged. "No harm done, but I would've left in a couple more minutes. It's close to dusk already."

"I know." Carissa looked at the darkened windows of the keeper's quarters. "I really appreciate you waiting for me, Mr. Dyson. You should have gone in and made yourself comfortable."

He shook his head. "No thanks. I'll see you get inside okay, then I'm heading home." He motioned her to follow him and walked toward the picket fence, his feet crunching over a mixture of gravel and crushed shell. "Call me Al," he said over his shoulder, holding the gate open for her. "Everyone does."

"Okay." She managed to return his smile despite wanting to pull away when he placed one hand on her back to guide her onto the porch.

He was a weird little man, his nose reddened not only from cold but prominent veins. His eyes, murky blue surrounded by yellowed whites, protruded in a disconcerting way. As he fumbled around in his pockets for the keys, Carissa stepped back off the porch and turned her head toward the ocean.

Salt stung her face and the biting smell of the sea cleared the cobwebs from her brain, purging her fatigue. During the five years since she'd visited Aunt Jessica at the defunct lighthouse, very little had changed. The fence needed painting and a large crack in one of the flower boxes beside the worn wooden door had leaked dirt across the concrete, but the neatly printed name on the mailbox still read "Malloy," and a holly bush continued to sprawl over the trellis above the garden gate in its untidy fashion. Beside the door, a much smaller and compact holly bush made her smile. A Carissa Holly, planted by her aunt to celebrate her niece's birth.

Peace, Carissa thought as Al opened the door. A chance to rebuild her shattered self-esteem and calm her nerves in the serenity of Aunt Jessica's beloved home. If only her aunt could have been there to greet her. Tears blurred Carissa's vision; Aunt Jessica's death had precipitated her arrival.

Al flipped the light switch inside the dark hallway. "Damn," he said when nothing happened. "Dansinger told me the power would be on." He glanced back at her. "Not thinking of staying here tonight anyway, are you?"

"I was," Carissa said, doubt filling her. How could she spend the night there without electricity?

"You can follow me down to the Cove. I'll see you get a room at the local inn," he offered, starting to back out of the house. "You shouldn't be here by yourself. The faster you put this place on the market, the better. It gave me the creeps even before your aunt died here."

His proprietary manner angered Carissa. "That's a bunch of nonsense," she said, pushing past him. "I've stayed here several times in the past, and I've never been scared."

Taking out her smartphone, she activated the flashlight. It would run her battery down quickly, but it was better than tripping or running into something. She started walking down the passageway toward the center of the house. "I'm sure there have to be candles or kerosene lamps. My aunt wouldn't have relied only on electricity with the frequency storms blow up around here."

Al grabbed her arm. "All right; if you're so determined, let me help you. Put your phone away before it runs out of juice; I've got a flashlight." He pulled it out of his pocket. "Let me go first."

"Thanks, but I'm probably more familiar with Aunt Jessica's home than you are. I'll lead the way."

She used his flashlight to guide them both into the living-room. Dark shapes loomed at the edges of the beam—furniture shrouded in dust covers. Someone had cared enough to be thorough, presumably William Dansinger. Carissa made her way over to the windows and opened the drapes.

Weak late-afternoon light struggled into the room. Dust tickled her nose. She stifled a sneeze and glanced around, finding everything the way she remembered it, right down to the baby grand piano in the bay window.

"I'm staying," she said.

Al Dyson snorted. "You're making a mistake. The furnace has been off since your aunt's death. You'll freeze."

"I can light a fire. Look, there's plenty of wood."

She pointed the flashlight toward a stack beside the fireplace and a basket filled with kindling. A box of long matches sat on the mantle beside a pair of candles. She struck a match and lit both candles, carrying one to the coffee table. She pulled off the dust cover and set the candle holder in the middle of the Vermont maple Aunt Jessica had purchased in an estate sale during one of Carissa's visits.

"I'll be fine," she assured Al, handing him back his flashlight. "The keys, please." She held out her hand.

Al snorted again but dropped the keys into her palm. Carissa wondered what had happened to the rabbit's foot Aunt Jessica always kept on her key ring.

"Your funeral, I guess." He chuckled hollowly. "Proverbially speaking, of course. If you change your mind, the inn's on Main Street. You can't miss it. The lights are always on."

Carissa followed him back to the front door. He stopped on the threshold, dug into yet another pocket and brought out a handful of crumpled-edged business cards. He thrust one at her. "Here."

She wanted to refuse, but reminded herself he had been kind enough to wait over an hour in the cold. She took the card. "I won't change my mind, but thanks."

Al handed her the flashlight. "You'll need this more than I will tonight. You can bring it to my office when you change your mind about selling." He walked over to the gate, swinging back and forth in time with the wind gusts, looked back at her again before closing it, and gave it a good shake to make sure the latch was fastened. His voice barely carried above the combination of roaring wind and crashing surf. "I already have an interested buyer."

"I won't change my mind." She waved him away and closed the door before he'd reached his car.

Within thirty minutes she'd kindled a fire, removed all the dust covers and piled them in the guest room, taken her bags inside the cottage, locked her Lexus into the garage and brought two oil lamps in from the mudroom. Aunt Jessica kept a camping stove, which Carissa used to heat a can of chicken noodle soup and water for tea after finding several gallon jugs stored in the pantry. She found stale crackers in a tin and a small box of raisins hidden in the back of a cupboard. Taking her meager supper on a tray into the living room, she wrapped herself in one of Aunt Jessica's crocheted afghans and settled onto the couch in front of a cheerful blaze.

Carissa mulled over her conversation with Al Dyson while munching a tasteless soda cracker. He'd imagined she'd be afraid to spend a night alone at the lighthouse, but he was completely mistaken— its isolation had motivated her to make the long trip. Apparitions were among the least of her concerns. The proximity of a very much alive and breathing Matthew Yates in New York had been far more disturbing.

Abandoning the crackers, she finished the soup, placed her tray on the coffee table with the half-burned down candle and drew her knees up to her chin as she stared at flickering flames illuminating the fireplace and the decorative metal fire screen. Logs settled, sparks shooting up the chimney.

For five years Matthew had out-maneuvered her, out-witted her and threatened her. Did she really think she was clever enough to turn the tables now, because she had finally managed to run away? For a moment, she allowed misery to seep back into her consciousness. There could be no escape from Matthew as long as he was alive. *Or as long as I am.*

Carissa threw off the afghan. Grabbing the poker, she pulled the fire screen aside and viciously stabbed the logs while flames crackled in protest. *I'm never going to allow Matthew to rule my life again.*

One of the logs started to roll out and she quickly pushed it back to join its neighbors. *I'm safe now, as long as he doesn't remember Aunt Jessica's lighthouse.*

The room had become noticeably colder. Unsure if more wood was stored in the shed, she decided against adding another log to the fire.

Instead, she draped one afghan over herself, wrapped another around her legs and stretched out with her head on one of her aunt's cross-stitched pillows. *I'll be fine,* she told herself as she tried to relax. *I'll be fine...*

CHAPTER TWO

CARISSA STARTED out of a deep sleep, curled up a fetal ball, her neck bent at a painful angle. Her heart drummed softly in her ears. The once-cheerful blaze in the fireplace had dwindled to smoldering embers. She threw off the afghans, swung her legs off the couch and sat up. Something other than cold or discomfort had awakened her. The remains of a log shifted and she jumped, nerves jangling like exposed wires.

Outside the keeper's quarters, the wind screeched and rattled the casement windows. The old house creaked and groaned in protest. Carissa wondered how long she had slept. She peered at her smartphone: 2:00 AM. She yawned. Time to bank up the fire, and then try to get more sleep.

She stood up, shivered and wrapped an afghan around her shoulders. Why was it so incredibly cold? She pulled the fire screen aside, poked the remains of the fire until a stronger glow returned and added rolled up newspaper, followed by kindling. Smoke blew against the back of the fireplace before disappearing up the chimney. A draft curled around her feet.

Carissa listened. Not only was the wind still roaring around the outside of the building, something was flapping. Flapping with a dull, persistent monotony. She turned Al's flashlight back on but it only gave out a meagre glow. So much for his helpfulness. The batteries needed replacing, and she had no idea if Aunt Jessica kept a supply. She listened, trying to identify the source of the noise. *Outside? Near the kitchen?*

Unless her memory was faulty, outside the back door sat a wood shed and a decommissioned pump. She'd left one of the lamps lit but it barely glowed—the oil had burned away much faster than she had expected. Carissa added more tinder to the fire, coaxing flames with careful use of Aunt Jessica's bellows. To avoid smothering the rekindled blaze, she slowly and carefully added a log.

While she worked, she listened to the flapping. Timed perfectly with the gusting wind, it sounded like a door. Maybe the shed was open.

Whatever the source, it needed to be stopped or she'd get no more sleep. Carissa decided to light the other lamp and take it with her into the kitchen. Her cold fingers knocked the matchbox off the coffee table. She got down on her knees and groveled around on the cold carpet. Perhaps Al was right and she *was* a fool, stubbornly insisting on staying at the cottage instead of spending the night in a nice, warm hotel room.

Why hadn't she made sure all doors and windows were locked before going to sleep? There was no telling what could have happened in the month since her aunt's death. William Dansinger may have had all the furniture covered, but he might not have checked the house for vandalism before going off on his trip. Windows could be broken, and obviously, judging by the sounds coming from the direction of the kitchen, at least one door was unlatched.

Finally locating the matches under the couch, Carissa lit the second lamp and took it with her into the kitchen, where the icy draft intensified. Her breath billowed out into the air and her teeth chattered. The outer door was definitely open, swinging back and forth, banging against the door frame. Carissa placed the lamp on the kitchen table and walked over to face the mudroom.

Maybe William Dansinger *had* checked everything before leaving on his trip, she thought as she put her hand on the door knob. Maybe someone else had left it open. Someone who had broken in and left the door unlocked...or someone with a key. *Someone who might be in the house right now.*

Fear rippled up Carissa's back. Her heart thudded painfully, its rhythm a whole lot faster than the flapping door. Wishing she'd had the sense to bring her phone with her, but refusing to waste time going back for it, she turned the doorknob. First thing's first. If she closed the outer door she wouldn't be so cold. It would also be a lot quieter. If someone else was in the house, she'd stand a better chance of hearing the intruder.

The door flew out of her grasp, crashing back against the wall while the wind slapped her cruelly in the face. The force of it galvanized her into action. She ran into the mudroom, grabbed the swinging outer door, closed both it and the latch, then bolted it top and bottom. The wind tunnel stopped. The noise stopped. She felt rough, frigid concrete beneath her feet. Carissa charged back into the kitchen, slammed the inner door and bolted that, too. She ran into the living-room and jumped under all three afghans, her body trembling with cold.

She had to get warm fast. She put on a second sweater before returning to the kitchen, where she boiled more water and took a jar of instant coffee from the pantry. First thing in the morning, she'd call about the utilities. Once they were all back on, she'd jack up the thermostat and blast the cottage out of its Arctic mode. Deciding safety was even more paramount than a hot drink, she turned off the camping stove and took the poker and oil lamp with her while she patrolled the rest of Aunt Jessica's home. All windows were latched. She had already bolted the front door. The lighthouse tower was locked.

She stopped short of looking under the beds. Anyone hiding there would freeze to death before getting a chance to murder her. She jammed her feet into fuzzy pink slippers she found at one side of Aunt Jessica's bed and draped a thick blue blanket decorated with wandering moose over her shoulders.

Instantly warmer, Carissa returned to the kitchen. Waiting for the water to reheat, her thoughts drifted back to Matthew. He'd once asked what person in her right mind would want to spend the last years of her life on the weather-beaten coast of DownEast Maine. He'd curled his upper lip into an elegant sneer after she told him about her aunt's unique home. Now she hoped he'd forgotten all about Aunt Jessica and Treacher's Cove.

At one point in their marriage, she had feared him. Now she loathed him and blessed the Malloy traits she had inherited: courage and stubbornness. Both had refused to allow Matthew to completely destroy her. He had fought their divorce every step of the way, appearing completely detached while she crumbled under the strain. He remained convinced she would ultimately return to him. All the copyrights for the intricate beading and braiding designs Aunt Jessica had taught Carissa to fabricate were in danger of remaining with the House of Yates. She had to prove infringement. There was even a question of work for hire, since she had brought those designs to the fashion house before her marriage to Matthew. And then there was a question of patents, due to the techniques used to create those intricate designs.

Just thinking about the pending case made her head ache and her stomach churn. She needed Aunt Jessica's original designs, but her aunt had died before sending them. Carissa hoped she would find them somewhere in the keeper's quarters. She already knew Aunt Jessica had not been sufficiently forward-thinking to leave copies with her attorney, William Dansinger.

She tossed a heaping spoonful of instant coffee into her cup. She had used Aunt Jessica's designs on Matthew's creations without protecting them, but she'd never expected them to become such an integral part of his line that they couldn't be separated from the clothes they embellished without serious consequences to the fashion house. When she filed for divorce, she finally realized the full extent of her foolishness.

The kettle's mournful whistle interrupted her painful introspection. Adding water and a spoonful of sugar to her coffee, she warmed her hands on the mug as she carried it into the living room. While she watched flames licking the logs in the fireplace, memories of her life in New York persisted. Taking a sip of the coffee, she decided it tasted as stale as everything else in her life at that moment.

Her thoughts continued to dwell on Matthew, which saddened her. They had been introduced by her best friend and roommate, Lorna. Matthew was an up and coming designer, who was looking for something definitive to take his designs from good to spectacular. Lorna had evidently told him about Carissa's distinctive embroidery and braiding. Matthew had hired Carissa after Lorna brought him to their little apartment and showed him Carissa's work. After she stitched one of Aunt Jessica's seed pearl designs onto the front of a shot-silk jacket, garnering rave reviews and making it the most sought-after piece of his new collection, Matthew gave Carissa her own office.

They started dating, but she refused to sleep with him, worried that her success in his company would come to an abrupt end if she did. Three months into their relationship, he got down on one knee, popped open a jewelry box containing an enormous diamond and asked her to marry him. He had chosen the perfect moment after a perfect evening, and his proposal was equally romantic. Carissa joyfully accepted. She joined the board as soon as they returned from their honeymoon, and Matthew had promoted her to vice president of their overseas interests within six months of their marriage.

Carissa came to suspect he had not only slept with Lorna, formerly one of his marketing managers, on several occasions, but had bribed her to introduce him to her friend, probably with a substantial sum of money after hearing about the 'crafts' Carissa had been fabricating as she worked to perfect Aunt Jessica's patterns before designing her own.

How stupid I was, Carissa thought, adding another log to the fire. When Matthew suggested using more of those designs on his creations, she had been overwhelmingly flattered. Now they were such an integral part of the House of Yates, she was deep in litigation in an effort to reclaim them.

She had trusted Matthew far too much, allowing him access to all her patterns. Aunt Jessica had been justifiably upset when Carissa finally told her what had happened. Those patterns had been a secret she shared only with Carissa. The intricate beadwork, the tapestries, the delicate lacework interwoven with threads of silver and gold had taken years to perfect.

Wearily, Carissa abandoned her efforts to drink the coffee. She could create new designs with many hours of work, but who would want to buy them without the Yates name? Who would believe the patterns were hers if Matthew won the suit?

Carissa knew she had to hunt for the proof of ownership she needed so desperately. She hadn't been able to think clearly with the press following her everywhere. Frequent, highly stressful conferences with attorneys took much of her time. Matthew's hounding, day and night, took a lot more.

First he asked her to sign away her rights to the designs, then he *demanded* she do so. He described ghastly, graphic scenarios of her life if she continued to resist—he'd make sure she ended up penniless, ridiculed and completely abandoned. She would no longer work in the fashion industry she loved. She began to believe him, and her faith in her own attorney, Roland Finch was undermined despite his reputation and his apparent staunch support for her case.

Carissa hoped staying hidden for a while would allow everything to calm down—stop the middle-of-the-night phone calls from either Matthew or reporters that ruined what little sleep she tried to get. She longed to escape the microphones thrust into her face every time she tried to leave her building and the never-ending barrage of hateful emails from social media trolls.

She knew Aunt Jessica had to have kept records of those patterns. Her aunt had laughed and told Carissa one time that she couldn't keep all those techniques and designs in her head. She always made sketches and kept them organized. Wide awake after the adrenalin rush caused by the open door and the caffeine buzz from the horrible coffee, Carissa felt like mounting a search of the keeper's quarters right then, but she knew the middle of the night was no time to start tearing the cottage apart.

Before spending what could be hours, even days on that quest, she needed utilities, heat and food, which she vowed to have by the following afternoon. If she had failed to find patterns, sketches or notebooks filled with designs by the time William Dansinger returned, she would ask him if he knew anything about their whereabouts. If his trip lasted more than a couple of days, she'd contact him through his administrative assistant.

Then she wondered whether a small town attorney would even have an office and an assistant. Maybe he worked from home and used an answering machine instead of a human to field his calls. He hadn't given her access to a cell phone number when he'd notified her about Aunt Jessica's death and they'd made plans to meet at the lighthouse.

If only her aunt hadn't died from such a freak accident, she thought, brushing away tears. Carissa wanted her aunt back for many reasons, most of them emotional, but she also knew her court case would have been resolved a lot faster and easier if Aunt Jessica hadn't tumbled to her death down the lighthouse tower's stairs. Aunt Jessica would have sworn the designs belonged to her and to Carissa. She would have been able to convince any amount of attorneys, because she could have sat in front of them and fabricated many of the designs without consulting any pattern books.

Carissa longed for sleep, but her mind kept racing. How strange that her aunt would have decided to go up those stairs in the first place. Bennett Point Light had been decommissioned some years before Aunt Jessica even bought it and moved into the keeper's quarters. Carissa shifted on the couch and yawned. Perhaps being on the lighthouse stairs wasn't unusual for Aunt Jessica at all. Perhaps she walked up and down the tower steps on a daily basis to get exercise and enjoy the view.

She tried lying down again, two cushions under her head and the blue blanket wrapped around her. She wished she had asked Aunt Jessica to visit more often, but Aunt Jessica and Matthew had quickly formed a mutual dislike. Torn between her husband and her aunt, Carissa knew she had chosen unwisely, neglecting her aunt to be with the husband who ultimately had proved to be unfaithful, controlling, cruel and selfish beyond anything she could ever have imagined.

Her eyelids finally felt heavy. She allowed them to close as she drifted into a light doze. The rhythmic, heavy ticking of the grandfather clock soothed her. She'd worry about everything in the morning, she told herself. Matthew couldn't possibly arrive any earlier than that, even if he had already figured out why she wasn't answering her phone...or her door...

A tiny voice in her head urged caution even as her mind surrendered itself to sleep.

CHAPTER THREE

CARISSA AWOKE to a bitterly cold morning. The fire must have died hours before. A glance at her watch showed her it was 8:00 AM. Weak light struggled through a chink in the drapes. She stretched cramped limbs and carried a pot filled with warmed water into the bathroom. She wanted to bathe and change clothes in the worst way, but stripping naked when she had finally managed to put on enough layers to ward off the cold was too harsh even to think about seriously. She settled for a quick wash of face and hands and brushing her teeth.

She conquered her fear of spiders long enough to run into the basement for a quick look at the furnace. With a sinking heart, she realized the 'Beast' she had both hated and feared still resided there. An antiquated oil guzzler, it had roared whenever she went downstairs to the washer or dryer. She checked the gauge: empty. She decided to move replacing that furnace higher on her to-do list; right after getting the utilities turned on.

Eager to escape the frigid house, Carissa wrapped her cape around herself and left the cottage. Outside was even colder than inside. A biting wind watered her eyes; a keen tang of salt touched her lips and stung her cheeks. Her forest green cape flapped behind her like the mainsail of a storm-tossed ship. She pulled her knitted cap down over her cold ears, but sounds of the surf far below still provided a background roar. Drawing on gloves, she walked to the property line behind the garage, stood on tip-toe and peered over a rugged, gray stone wall. About a hundred yards away stood a house made of the same gray stone.

Sheltered by trees which had grown at an angle due to severe winds, the three-story house looked even older than the lighthouse towering behind her. Smoke curled from the chimney and white lace curtains covered numerous little diamond-paned windows. Carissa noticed a man working outside, cutting firewood beside what must be the kitchen door.

Further down the wall, a half-open gate beckoned. She walked through the gap. Why not introduce herself to her neighbors? After the miserable night she had just spent, there seemed no sense in waiting. If she had more problems, she might be able to turn to someone close-by, if the man was agreeable to helping her. Even if he wasn't, at least someone else knew she was living in the cottage.

"Hello," she said when she was still several yards away from him.

Despite the weather he was shirtless, his muscles bulging with the effort of splitting logs. Deeply tanned, he wore his faded jeans low on his hips, a ragged red bandana hanging from one back pocket. His heavy, battered work boots were heavily stained and coated with dried mud. At the sound of her voice he straightened up like a spring uncoiling. He didn't seem at all surprised to see her.

"'Morning," he offered, leaning on the axe handle. A wayward lock of dark hair curled over his high forehead. His face had the texture of aged leather beneath a thick beard.

"I'm your new neighbor, Carissa Yates." She held out her hand. "Jessica's niece."

"Blake Ulster." He hesitated a moment before shaking hands, looking her over carefully through pale blue eyes that squinted in the daylight.

"I moved into the lighthouse last night," she offered when he didn't say anything else.

"I know. We heard you were coming, my wife and I."

"Oh." Carissa brightened a little. Another woman lived next door. Maybe she'd come over for coffee.

"Blake? Who is with you?" A female voice, heavily accented, drifted to them from the screen door behind Blake Ulster's back.

"Our new neighbor, Mai Ling. Come and be sociable." Blake remained still, one foot propped on a log while he leaned over the axe. His icy eyes continued to watch Carissa's face, unnerving her with their intensity.

The screen door creaked open. Carissa watched a slender Asian girl walk down the steps. She wore a bulky green cardigan over a long fuchsia satin dress with side-slits up to her knees. Her dress and her waist-length black hair swirled around her in the wind. Carissa wondered how she and Blake had met. She looked at least fifteen years younger than her husband and very much out of place.

"Greetings." She smiled and bowed. Uneven teeth spoiled an otherwise pleasant face. Mai Ling's eyes were large, dark and limpid, her nose a tiny button.

"Pleased to meet you." Carissa smiled warmly. "It's good to know I'm not the only woman out here."

"Getting to you already, isn't it? The isolation, I mean." Blake took his foot off the log. "Gets to a lot of outsiders. Most of 'em don't last long." He grunted and grabbed the axe. "We've got work to do, don't we, Mai Ling?" He gave his wife a quick glance from those shuttered, ice-blue eyes. The squint was evidently permanent.

"Yes, Blake." Mai Ling backed quickly away. "Nice to meet you," she said to Carissa before walking rapidly up the steps and disappearing into the house. The screen door slammed behind her.

"We'll have to invite you over when we're not so busy." Blake placed a log on end. With one blow, he severed it in two.

"Great." Carissa took the hint and retreated.

They weren't putting themselves out to be friendly, she thought, quickly retracing her steps. Blake Ulster certainly didn't waste words where strangers were concerned. If first impressions weren't deceiving, she doubted Mai Ling led a very happy life. Carissa resolved to ask the girl over for coffee as soon as living at the lighthouse wasn't like extreme camping. Dear Blake looked like he could make anyone feel unwelcome, including family members.

"Outsiders," she muttered, jerking the garage door open. "What a greeting." She grabbed the door as it tried to slam shut. "Oh, no you don't."

She used a brick she found inside to block the door open and glanced over at her aunt's old dark green Pontiac, sitting on the other side of the 2-car garage and surrounded by patio furniture.

"Sorry, but you'll have to go," she told the car. She got behind the wheel of her Lexus. "I've got to stop talking to myself," she said. If she didn't make friends quickly, she'd hear the villagers of Treacher's Cove whispering behind her back, declaring that living at Bennett Point Light had made her as loony as her aunt.

CHAPTER FOUR

THE VILLAGE of Treacher's Cove lay two miles away. White caps raced for rugged cliffs whenever Carissa caught glimpses of the ocean during the drive down a steep, winding road. Calmer water lapped in the harbor, but the fishing boats still rocked like plastic toys in a child's bathtub. White cottages with black shutters packed narrow streets leading down to the water. Shops with swinging signs announced the presence of antique shops and an inn named The Fisherman's Rest. A sign in one window of the inn announced FULL BREAKFAST UNTIL 10:00 A.M. Carissa's stomach growled in response to the sign. She parked and hurried inside.

Round tables with captain-style chairs crowded the dining room, visible beyond a reception desk. A large bar sported glowing brass foot-rails and regimental rows of liquor bottles lined up on shelves in front of mirrors that reflected their colors. Timbers that looked as old as the town itself supported the rafters and gave an overall appearance of stepping into an English pub.

"Can I help you?" A rich voice boomed from a darkened corner of the bar.

Carissa jumped.

"Startled you, huh?" The voice held a trace of humor. "Sorry about that."

A very tall man in a black cable knit sweater walked out of the gloom. His well-built body dwarfed the low-ceilinged room. She looked up into kindly brown eyes set in a rugged face with features too sharp to be called handsome. His generous Roman nose and stubble-covered cheeks and chin gave him an almost Machiavellian appearance.

"I'm fine," Carissa assured him. "My eyes hadn't adjusted from the brightness outside, that's all." She pulled up her purse strap, which had slipped off her shoulder. "I came in to have breakfast, if I'm not too late."

He flashed her a quick smile. "This way." He led her into the dining room. "Just you, or will someone else be joining you?"

"Just me. I arrived last night. I'm moving into the keeper's quarters at the Bennett Point Light."

He stopped, and she ran into him.

"You're Jessica Malloy's niece?" He sounded excited. "We've all been wondering when you'd come. You're from New York, right?"

"Boston originally, but yes, that's right."

"Welcome." He extended one large hand.

Carissa took off her glove and shook it. "Thank you. I'm Carissa Yates."

"Steve Raymond. I own the inn." He beckoned to a waitress bringing breakfast to an elderly couple seated at a table in front of one of the windows. "Coffee?" He asked Carissa.

"Please." She removed her other glove and started to take off her cape.

"Here, I'll take care of this for you." Steve Raymond swept the cape away and hung it with a couple of other coats on a row of pegs next to the doorway.

"Am I really too late for breakfast?" Carissa looked at a large clock over the entrance to the dining room. It said 10:25 A.M. Her stomach growled loudly.

"Normally I'd say you were, but you're our new neighbor." He smiled. "Hilly," he told the waitress, walking briskly toward them with a carafe in one hand. "Please bring her the Cottager's breakfast."

"Yes, sir." She jogged back to the kitchen.

Carissa wanted to ask what the Cottager's breakfast contained, but she didn't want to seem rude or ungrateful, since he had offered to keep the kitchen open for her. She heard loud grumbling, followed by the clatter of pans. Steve Raymond's smile slipped a little.

Carissa looked around the virtually empty restaurant. A table a little way from the elderly couple was bathed in pale sunlight. She pointed. "Would it be okay if I sat there? The sun's trying to come out, and I was so cold last night, I need all the heat I can get."

Banging from the kitchen was accompanied by loud complaining about the wages, the customers, and the fact that lunch would now be late.

"Of course." Steve strode over to the sun-bathed table and pulled out a chair. "Eva really doesn't mind cooking breakfast," he assured Carissa as she sat. An unmistakable sound of breaking plates interrupted the serenity of the restaurant. "She loves to complain; it's her way." His thick, dark eyebrows almost met as he frowned. "I'll get the coffee. Mind if I join you?"

"I'd like that."

She watched him stop to speak with the elderly couple before going into the kitchen. One more pot clanged before silence took over, louder somehow than the noises. Carissa heard faint traffic sounds until strains of piped-in music filled the air. Sinatra, in his younger days. The elderly couple raised their coffee cups and toasted each other.

Steve returned with a carafe, a jug of cream and two cups. "Sorry about that."

Carissa shook her head at the cream. "I need it black this morning. I'm still only half-awake." She took a sip and hoped the breakfast would be as good as the coffee. "Oh, that tastes so good. All my aunt had was instant. Who even drinks that anymore?"

"No one I know." Steve settled back in his chair. "So, you're a Malloy." He grinned.

"Very much so." She returned the smile. "Irish roots and proud of them. I was born in South Boston...Southie."

Carissa watched him stretch his long legs out to one side of the table and lean back. He certainly knew how to be the charming host. She found the tension inside her dissipating. What a contrast Steve Raymond was to Matthew, who always kept her on-edge. She'd been required to remain well-groomed, witty and good-humored whenever she was around him, regardless of how she felt inside.

He would never have smiled at her the way Steve Raymond did, with warmth in his eyes, if he had seen her dressed in jeans and a baggy sweater, her hair pulled back into a ponytail and no makeup to bring out her "insipid" features as he had called them during one of their frequent arguments. Her pleasure in her inherited Irish coloring of black hair and blue eyes had dwindled. She'd taken to wearing a hat and sunglasses whenever she went out in public.

Away from his influence and able to think rationally, she wondered why she had stayed with him so long. If it hadn't been for the guilt-induced reconciliations, she didn't think she would have lasted a year, much less five.

"So, what in the world are you going to do with that old lighthouse?" Steve asked, bringing Carissa back from yet another sad introspection. "After Jessica died, I thought the place would be boarded up until it got sold for re-development."

"I didn't want anything to be done with it until I tried living there. I set my mind on escaping the rat-race of Manhattan. This is the ideal spot." She stopped herself from expounding further. Secret wounds weren't meant to be shared with strangers, however friendly.

"I see." Steve folded his arms across his chest. "I hope you're not biting off more than you can chew, to quote an old cliché. That place is in pretty bad shape."

"Not really. My aunt had some structural work done ten years ago and a lot of plumbing replaced maybe two or three years ago. I wish she'd decided to get new windows at the same time, but they're leaded and so pretty, I guess she couldn't bring herself to do it. I've got to find someone to install a new gas furnace. The oil burner's outdated and empty. I had no electricity or water last night, either. It was pretty Spartan. I lit a fire and camped out under blankets."

Steve looked shocked. "You should have stayed here."

"That's what Al Dyson told me, but I wouldn't listen. I couldn't get back in my car for anything after the long trip up here."

"I can relate." He smiled again. "I don't want to go anywhere, either, after I finish a long trip." He drained his cup and lifted the carafe. "More?"

"Yes, please."

"I can recommend a good place for a new furnace," Steve said. "But the power company doesn't have an office here. It's in Whitstead, six miles from here, if you needed to talk to anyone in person. Same with the water and landline."

"I'll call about the utilities. If you can send me to someone reliable for the new furnace, that would be great." Carissa shook her head ruefully. "My aunt was a bit of a traditionalist. She called her heater the 'Beast' and refused to update."

"She had her landline disconnected one time," Steve said. "William Dansinger talked her into getting it hooked back up. She had already refused to get a cell phone."

"How could she even think she could stay out at the lighthouse without a reliable way of getting help if she needed it? What if she'd had an accident?"

Carissa stopped abruptly. Aunt Jessica had definitely had an accident. She'd fallen down the lighthouse steps and broken her neck. No one had even known she was dead until her attorney arrived the following day to get her to sign some routine papers.

Breakfast arrived, a very welcome interruption from the direction of their conversation. Plump and sweet-faced, Hilly smiled widely at Carissa before giving Steve the details of the lunch menu and assuring him it would not be served late, as Eva had threatened.

The Cottager consisted of eggs over easy, crisp bacon, home fries and toast. While Steve gave her a quick history of Treacher's Cove and its strong ties to fishing, Carissa cleared her plate and washed everything down with two more cups of coffee and a large orange juice. She felt warmer and a lot less edgy afterward.

"So what do you do when you're in Manhattan?" He asked over his fourth cup of coffee. "Modeling," Carissa hedged.

"With an appetite like that?" Steve's eyebrows raised in disbelief.

He had a mobile face, Carissa thought, clasping her cup with both hands. He could never be called handsome, but when a man was that personable and charming, he didn't need to be.

"I don't model, myself," she told him. "I stay behind the scenes."

She wasn't tall enough, for one thing. Her long legs coupled with a short torso didn't flatter the gowns Matthew designed. Ironically, she had often thought, he designed clothes for other women but never for his wife.

"I'm also lucky enough to have a high metabolism," she told Steve. "It saves me from having to diet but tends to make me jittery when I sit too long." She picked up her purse and took out her billfold. "Speaking of which, I think I've sat here long enough. I'm warm, I'm completely full thanks to the Cottager's breakfast, and I need directions to the store where I can buy my new furnace."

Steve waved to Hilly, who brought Carissa's check. "I'll take you over there and introduce you to the owner. I know he'll give you a fair deal on the furnace. I had to replace the heating and cooling systems when I bought this place."

He fetched her cape while she paid for her breakfast and generously tipped Hilly. While Carissa fastened the cape, he shrugged into a sheepskin jacket and pulled on a knitted cap and gloves.

"You need a better coat," he told her as they walked out of the dining room. "Something that buttons or zips up to the neck."

"Thank you, Miss," Hilly called, her voice filled with surprise, probably at the size of the tip. She followed them as far as the desk, where she stopped to put the money in the till.

"I'll be back shortly," Steve said over his shoulder. "I'm taking Ms. Yates to Chuck's appliance store, then joining Sally for lunch at her apartment."

"Okay, Mr. Steve." Hilly picked up a handful of lunch menus and began pushing them down into stainless steel holders at the center of each table. "I'll keep an eye on the bar."

"No drinking until noon, whoever stops in and tries to talk you into it." Steve opened the front door.

"Yes, sir. I'll tell Mr. Dyson or any of the other regulars who stop by," Hilly called, her voice muffled by the sound of the wind gusting through the open door.

Out on the sidewalk, Steve took Carissa's arm and steered her northward. As they climbed the steeply sloping hill from the harbor, she welcomed his grip. The wind had intensified, howling down the narrow streets and flapping the rigging of sailboats moored beside the jetty. It was impossible to speak and be heard. *Welcome to Maine in the fall.* Maybe she had been crazy to think she could live there.

"Looks like a storm," he shouted in her ear, pointing toward gun-metal gray clouds gathering on the horizon.

She nodded, pulling her cape tighter around herself. She had forgotten her hat and gloves, sitting on the front passenger's seat of her car, in her haste to get breakfast before it was too late.

Steve took a scarf out of his pocket and handed it to her. "Put this on; your ears are turning red."

Carissa gladly took it. He must think her completely unprepared for the weather, and he was probably right. She tied the ends of the wool scarf under her chin. Miss New York, wearing woefully inadequate clothing and talking about living in a deserted lighthouse's quarters. She could have told him she'd left home in a hurry, but that would have opened the door to a conversation about why.

The moving van would arrive soon with her boxes, and then she'd be more prepared for her new life, but she did need a better coat. Right after she took care of the utilities and the furnace, she promised herself. She glanced at her watch: 12:15 P.M. She'd stayed far longer at the inn than she'd planned. Involuntarily, she glanced back over her shoulder. The lighthouse stood white and prominent above the harbor. Matthew would be able to locate her hiding place without any effort on his part if he remembered her connection to Treacher's Cove. Carissa wondered if she should get back in her car and keep driving all the way up to Canada.

"Here's the store," Steve shouted, tugging at her arm.

Carissa abandoned thoughts of running any further when the door opened and warmth hit her face. She walked into a surprisingly large, modern showroom lined with appliances. One corner held televisions, the other a desk with a sign that read: 'Heating and Cooling.'

A short, portly man with a jovial face and full beard came out of the back office, his rolling gait giving him the appearance of a sea-captain who had just stepped onshore after a long voyage.

"Hi, Steve. Nice to see you. Brought a new friend with you, I see." The man beamed like Santa Claus in a toy department at Christmas.

"This is Carissa Yates, Jessica Malloy's niece. She moved into the old lighthouse last night and wants to upgrade the heating system. Carissa, this is Chuck Collins of Chuck's Guaranteed Appliances, Heating and Cooling."

Carissa shook hands. "Nice to meet you."

"Give her a fair deal, Chuck, or she's going to blacklist me and the inn." Steve patted Chuck on the back. "I've got to go," he told Carissa. "If I'm late meeting my girlfriend for lunch, she'll get upset with me again. I run late frequently."

He squeezed her arm, dug a card out of his pocket and handed it to her, a logo of a fishing boat floating above raised printing that announced: *'The Fisherman's Rest. Steve Raymond, Proprietor,'* with the inn's phone number. He'd hand-printed his cell phone number below.

"Call if you need help with anything else. I'm usually at the inn or Sally's Gift Emporium. That's my girl's shop. Her name's Sally Mainard." He smiled, showing big, white teeth before striding away.

Carissa wondered if he had another set of cards without the added cell number inside his other pocket. But she had found no reason to think he was anything but friendly and hoped Sally wasn't the jealous type. Steve was someone she would really like to become a friend.

She explained her problem to Chuck and arranged to meet him at the lighthouse at two o'clock, so she had time to call about the utilities and stock up on groceries.

CHAPTER FIVE

CARISSA ARRIVED BACK at the keeper's quarters with three bags of food, more candles and several flashlights. No more fun and games like the previous evening.

The garage door was closed. Annoyed, she opened it and searched for the brick, but it had disappeared. She couldn't imagine any wind strong enough to pick up a brick and move it out of sight. She found an old can filled with dried paint at the back of the garage and used that to prop open the door while she drove into the garage. She tried taking all three grocery sacks with her, but they were too heavy. She'd have to make two trips, whether she wanted to or not.

Grocery sacks in both arms, she walked quickly over to the house, her head bowed against the buffeting wind. She didn't know if she would ever get used to living on a cliff, exposed to all the elements. Some people would find it invigorating. Carissa knew she wasn't one of them.

Balancing both sacks between her hip and the door frame, she managed to unlock it and step inside. She butted the door closed. Icy cold cloaked her. A draft curled around her ankles. An oddly familiar draft. Carissa walked into the kitchen and dropped the bags. The mudroom door stood wide open. So did the back door.

CHAPTER SIX

CARISSA'S first impulse was to run back to her car, drive away and never look back, but she had never been a quitter. Not until Matthew, anyway, she thought, taking Aunt Jessica's rolling pin out of a drawer.

Stepping over her spilled groceries, she walked into the mudroom. A blast of arctic proportions almost took her breath away, but she seized the outer door as it swung back toward her, wrestled it closed, locked it and shot the bolts home. She locked the inner door, dragged the solid oak kitchen table across the linoleum, leaving two ugly black trails, jammed the table against the door and stood shivering and panting in the middle of the kitchen. Her back ached, she'd broken several finger-nails, and her teeth were chattering. She saw a bottle of Glenfiddich on the counter and took a swig out of it. The whisky burned its way down her throat, but she welcomed the heat. She took another swig before reluctantly putting the bottle down.

"All right, whoever you are, this game's gone on long enough," she shouted above the howling wind. "I'm searching this place from top to bottom. I've got a gun and a knife, and I'm ready to use both."

She found what looked like a pretty blunt carving knife from another drawer, took a brief tour of the living-room, then stepped cautiously into the hallway. Maybe the rolling pin didn't resemble a gun, but it would pack a punch if she had to use it. Past being frightened and fortified by two belts of whisky, Carissa welcomed her anger. She marched into the bathroom, pulled back the shower curtain and breathed a sigh of relief when no intruders were found standing in the claw-footed tub.

She looked inside the linen closet and then opened the door to her aunt's bedroom, which she felt sure she hadn't closed since her arrival. Taking a deep breath, she kicked back the comforter and searched under the bed, threw back the closet door and beat the clothes, releasing an odor of mothballs. She found an old set of golf clubs in a back corner and armed herself with a putter instead of the rolling pin. Finding nothing sinister in the guest room, she rattled the tower door, which was firmly locked, returned to the living room and kindled a fire.

Perhaps Aunt Jessica's ghost was playing tricks on her, but she strongly doubted even a ghostly form of her aunt would jeopardize her only niece's health by leaving doors open. It occurred to her, as she brewed tea, that a number of people might have keys to the lighthouse. Al Dyson and William Dansinger, her aunt's attorney, were two names that came to mind immediately. For all she knew, the Ulsters might also have a key. She could well imagine Blake Ulster laughing gleefully as he unbolted her doors and played childish games with the garage door-stop.

Leaving the tea to steep, she reluctantly headed back to the lighthouse door with her putter in hand. Despite her earlier bravado, Carissa was reluctant to step into the area where her aunt had died, but she had to stop putting off a search of the tower.

A fierce rapping on the front door sent the putter flying out of her hand. It landed with a clatter on the stone floor. Carissa leaned against the wall and fought for breath. She glanced at her watch. Two o'clock. Her heart rhythm slowed…Chuck Collins was a prompt man. Wonderfully so. With him in the house, she'd find the courage to tackle the tower.

"Ms. Yates," Chuck said when she opened the front door. His friendly smile turned into a frown. "You look pale; are you all right?"

"I'm fine." She stepped aside. "Please come in."

Chuck wiped his feet on the mat and stepped inside. He shivered. "You definitely need a new furnace. This place is freezing."

"It's not all because of the furnace. My back door was open when I came home."

"Forgot to latch it, did you?" Chuck shook his head. "Can't afford to do that around here. The wind's so strong, it'll tear things right off their hinges. Then you'll need a new door, too."

Carissa wanted to tell him she hadn't left the door unlatched, but thought better of it. No sense in frightening the man with tales of possible intruders. After she showed him to the furnace, she told him to go ahead with inspecting the radiators while she checked something in the lighthouse. She unlocked the door and pushed it back.

If the main house was cold, the lighthouse was glacial. A short foyer ended in a circular flight of metal stairs. Looking up made her slightly dizzy. At least the power company had been quick after she called; strong fluorescent lights illuminated the tower when she flipped the switch beside the door. No blood stains were visible either on the stairs or the floor. She felt profound relief.

Carissa wished she had her putter, but she didn't want Chuck to think she was out of her mind, wandering around with a golf club. She carefully mounted the stairs, her footsteps echoing. When she finally arrived at the top, she was completely out of breath. She walked around the lamp room until she faced the ocean. The view from downstairs was nothing compared to the one at the top of the tower. No wonder her aunt had been on those stairs. She must have loved to go up and look out at the scenery. What a feast for her senses!

Gray seas heaved all the way to the dim, shifting horizon. Breakers smashed against rocks far below Carissa's feet, spray rising to splash against the glass in front of her face. The majesty of sky and sea over-whelmed. The urge to become one with the elements out on the cat-walk almost overpowered her common-sense, but the wind was so strong, she knew opening the door would be an invitation to disaster. Visions came to her of what a fall onto those jagged rocks below would do to her body.

Restricting herself to walking around the circular floor inside, she examined the village nestling in the inlet, small craft rocking to and fro in the harbor, and the rhythmically surging ocean. So much power. So much unleashed energy. Like a wild, untamed animal, she thought, hands pressed against the glass like a small child.

"Ms. Yates, are you up there?" Chuck's voice floated up to her.

"Yes. I'll come down."

As she ran back down the stairs, it occurred to her that although they were fairly steep, they were well-graded and not at all dangerous. A sturdy rail ran all the way down one side. Why had Aunt Jessica fallen? The question nagged at Carissa. Perhaps she'd become dizzy for some reason and lost her footing?

"I'm going back to my store," Chuck said. "I've done some preliminary work, and I'll bring a couple of estimates over to you tomorrow. You definitely need a new furnace, and a hot water heater, too. I'd like to install vents instead of you keeping the old radiators your aunt's been using. Most of them leak, so your heat wastage is enormous. Quite frankly, you could do with a contractor, putting in decent insulation. You'd also do better with wall-to-wall carpeting and double-glazing."

"I appreciate the input, Mr. Collins," she said. "I trust your judgment after Steve's intro. I know you'll give me a fair deal. Let's go ahead with the heating system and the water heater as soon as possible. If you can recommend a contractor, too, I'll be eternally grateful. I want to live here comfortably, not like this. I can't even take my coat off."

"I'll get right on it," he promised, settling his hat firmly on his balding head. "I'll call you first thing with a starting date. It should be sometime within the next two or three days. I'll have to get the furnace delivered from Bangor, because I don't carry anything that large in stock. As you saw this morning, most of the homes are pretty small in the Cove."

"That'll be fine."

"Nice doing business with you." Chuck held out his hand.

Carissa shook it, feeling his firm, steady grip. As she watched him leave, she remembered the last sack of groceries still sat in her car. She went out to retrieve it and lock up the garage. The first thing she saw was a brick holding back the door. The paint can had disappeared.

CHAPTER SEVEN

AT FOUR O'CLOCK, Carissa made one more trip through the cottage, making sure all doors were locked and bolted, all windows firmly latched before placing her overnight bag into the Lexus. Staying there was out of the question until she had all the locks changed as well as a working furnace. She should probably invest in an alarm system, too. She'd lived in New York for years and never thought about security the way she was thinking about it after one night in Aunt Jessica's home. But she vowed she wasn't going to wake up in the middle of another night with the back door wide open.

Carissa was acutely aware that she lacked a support system. No friends left thanks to Matthew's isolation tactics and her own failure to resist. No siblings. No cousins. Her mother had made a career out of wedlock after Carissa's father left. Mom was now on her third marriage and living somewhere in Florida. Carissa couldn't even remember if it was Orlando or St. Petersburg, not that it really mattered—her mother seldom spent more than a couple of minutes on the phone when Carissa called. The only one who had really cared about her was Aunt Jessica.

Treacher's Cove beckoned in the late afternoon with winking lights reflecting off charcoal gray water. Even the wind had died down to a dull roar. Carissa forced herself away from her depressing thoughts by deciding to take a walk and look at the shops along the quay after checking into The Fisherman's Rest.

Maybe she could even work on her redecorating plans after registering at the inn. The drab living-room needed color to bring it to life. Even Aunt Jessica's exquisite needlepoint pillows weren't enough to brighten a color-scheme of white walls and brown furnishings with heavy maroon velvet drapes.

New rugs, Carissa thought as she passed the outskirts of the village. Maybe even wall-to-wall carpeting, as Chuck had suggested. She'd change the window treatments—something pretty but not overpoweringly feminine—patterned if her rugs weren't. She'd keep the living room furniture but get the couch and chairs reupholstered.

Her thoughts turned to the bathroom. Three words came to mind immediately: white, stark and cold. She'd paint the base of the claw-footed tub red for an instant pop and give it four black feet. A white mini blind for the window and rich red mats and towels. Pleased with her decisions, she thought of the two bedrooms. Sparsely furnished with old-fashioned iron bedsteads, mattresses of unknown age and rag rugs, everything needed to go into a dumpster...

She suddenly realized she had passed the inn, pulled into the first open parking space and walked back to the inviting lights of The Fisherman's Rest.

"Why, hello, Carissa." Steve Raymond came from behind the reception desk. "What's this? Moving out of the lighthouse already?" He took her bag.

"For a couple of nights. The furnace and water heater have to be replaced."

"Is your power on?"

"Yes, but I don't think I want to buy space heaters when I'll only need them for a few days."

He took her arm and steered her toward the desk, where a young woman stood. A very pretty young woman with hair like spun gold tumbling around her shoulders and touching her heart-shaped face.

Steve set Carissa's bag on the floor. The woman's blue-green eyes gave Carissa a frank once-over while she laughed at a joke tossed to her by one of three men walking into the bar.

"Sally," Steve said. "This is Carissa Yates. Carissa, meet my girlfriend, Sally Mainard."

"Pleased to meet you." Carissa offered her hand.

Sally took it in a very firm grip. "Steve said you had a wow factor," she said. "I don't think he was generous enough. No wonder you were in the fashion industry."

"Thank you." Carissa didn't know what else to say. She felt slightly uncomfortable.

"He told me your coloring was spectacular." Sally smiled. "I thought he was exaggerating, but no, he was not."

"It's the Irish heritage," Steve said, a lazy smile lighting his face.

He almost became handsome when he smiled, and the harshness left his features when he gazed at his girlfriend.

"Carissa's staying a few days," Steve said, handing her a pen and pointing to the registration book Sally slid across the desk. "The old heating system at the lighthouse went belly-up."

Carissa passed a credit card to Sally before signing the register.

"That oil furnace looked like something out of the Ark," Sally said. "I wouldn't have wanted to go down to that creepy basement to check its gauge, either." She passed the card back to Carissa.

"Chuck told me everything should get replaced and updated," Carissa said. "Leaky radiators, an old thermostat; it's a big job. The furnace has to be ordered and sent from Bangor. He assured me that shouldn't take more than a couple of days, but I'm not staying in the cottage again until I've got heat. He's also sending me a contractor. I might as well add insulation while everything's in an uproar. Then there's the kitchen, which looks like a time capsule from the nineteen-twenties. It could do with a new sink and cabinets. I may do some other remodeling, too. I'd really like a walk-in shower."

"You're really brave, wanting to live out there by yourself," Sally said. "It's really isolated. Kind of spooky, too." She glanced at Carissa and bit her lip. "Sorry, I shouldn't have said that. You've got to be a little jumpy already, knowing your aunt died there."

Carissa opened her mouth but nothing came out. How was she going to explain that she didn't believe in ghosts but couldn't face spending another night alone in the keeper's quarters? At thirty-one, she was a bit too old to be acting childishly.

Steve broke into the silence. "I think it's a lovely old place. I offered to buy it from Jessica once, but she turned me down flat. Told me to go find my own lighthouse and leave hers alone." He chuckled. "Feisty old broad." He started to laugh, and then looked at Carissa. "I'm sorry. That was disrespectful."

"No, realistic." Carissa felt grateful to him for lightening the mood of the discussion. "My aunt was definitely feisty. She clashed with the rest of the family on more than a few occasions."

Tears blurred her vision. Aunt Jessica had been her staunchest defender, even when Carissa had insisted on marrying Matthew Yates. Her mother had been against it. The one time she had actually been right. Aunt Jessica had only asked Carissa to wait six months, to make sure this was what she really wanted. Carissa knew she should have listened to both of them, but she'd been so flattered, so completely bowled over by Matthew's romantic proposal, his ring, and his plans for their future together.

Thankfully, Steve kept a box of tissues on the reception desk and slid them toward her. Carissa took one and wiped her eyes. Talking about her aunt had brought another wave of heart-wrenching grief. They had been so close until her marriage. After that, Matthew always managed to find some business trip overseas he needed her to make if she suggested going to Maine for a few days, and he refused to entertain Aunt Jessica. He said he didn't want anyone staying with them, invading their private space. Telling her aunt that she wasn't welcome in their home was one of the most difficult things Carissa had ever had to do in her life. Up until she had to tell Matthew she was leaving him, she reminded herself.

"You must miss Jessica very much," Steve said. He picked up Carissa's bag and took her arm. "I'll take you to your room."

"I can do that." Sally started to come from behind the desk.

"You look a lot prettier and way more inviting than I do when I stand there." He winked.

Sally gave a smile that looked a little forced. "Flatterer," she said, her voice low.

Carissa suddenly felt very tired and dispirited. The divorce had taken a lot out of her, the pending litigation even more. She had barely slept at all over the last three days. She placed one heavy foot after the other as she followed Steve through the lobby and up the curving wooden staircase. By the time they reached the second floor, she was clinging to the railing.

Steve glanced back. "You're exhausted," he said.

Before she could stop him, he'd swept her into his arms. He carried Carissa and her bag down the hallway.

"Please don't do this; I feel silly," she protested.

"Don't. It's all part of the Triple A service at The Fisherman's Rest. Don't worry—you'll be charged exorbitantly for it." His voice was jovial and laced with kindness.

Carissa stopped protesting and placed one arm around his neck for support. He was right—she *was* exhausted. Horribly so. Her legs felt heavy and shaky, her head even heavier. Whether her fatigue was from lack of sleep or the emotional toll, she couldn't say.

Steve put her back onto her feet outside a door at the end of the hallway. "This room's the quietest I have. It's as far from the bar as you can get, and the restaurant noise tends to soften by the time it filters through the rafters."

He unlocked the door and flipped a switch. Carissa followed him into a charming little room with a low, beamed ceiling. Dark, aged woodwork was brightened by a chintz bedspread and curtains. A small vanity with bowed legs and a chintz-covered stool urged her to sit and brush out her tangled hair. The bed beckoned even more with plump pillows and a down comforter. A thick mint green carpet cushioned her feet and made her want to kick off her shoes. For the first time since leaving New York, she felt safe and welcomed.

"It's lovely." She smiled at him without any effort.

He opened the closet and set her bag on the rack inside. "Get lots of sleep, Carissa. If you want dinner, we have room service."

"Thank you. Dinner's the last thing I want right now. I've had a ...a difficult time," she explained helplessly. He probably had enough to think about without listening to her problems, even if she gave him the abbreviated version.

As though he had read her thoughts, Steve leaned forward and squeezed her hand. "If you need a friend, I'm available," he told her, and then he left, closing the door quietly behind him.

Carissa stood motionless for a moment before placing the Do Not Disturb sign on the outside of the door knob, locking herself in and opening her overnight bag. She pulled off her clothes and got into her pajamas, ran a brush through her hair and decided those plans she had made to walk the harbor and go shopping were nothing but pipe dreams until she'd had a good night's sleep.

The wind had picked up, whistling through the trees outside and beating branches against the windows. Before getting into bed, she was going to make sure those windows were locked. No more night air for her. She crossed the room, pulled one of the curtains aside and checked the latch, which was firmly fastened. She looked through the window and paused. The wind had pushed away the clouds. The bay looked bathed by silver. Through waving tree branches, she caught glimpses of the lighthouse, dark and silent on the peninsula but haloed by pale moonlight.

"I'm not afraid of you," Carissa whispered, but her voice didn't sound convincing, even to her.

She crept into bed and pulled the covers over her head.

CHAPTER EIGHT

WHEN CARISSA WALKED downstairs the following morning, Hilly steered her into a parlor. The bright, sunny room was filled with comfortable couches and wingback chairs grouped around a fireplace. Game tables sat in front of two sets of bay windows. Hilly led Carissa over to the last set of windows, where a small dining table was set for one.

"Mr. Steve thought it would be nicer for you to sit here than in that big dining room all by yourself. Most of the other guests and regulars already ate." Hilly smiled. "Tea or coffee?"

"Coffee, please. Lots of it." Carissa glanced at her watch for the first time that morning and was taken-aback to see it was already five minutes past ten. "I'm so sorry—I overslept. Now I'm late for breakfast again."

"Not a problem, Miss." Hilly waved away excuses and pulled out a chair.

Carissa sat. In front of her was a neatly sectioned grapefruit. The china looked old, delicate and expensive, as did the utensils, gleaming with the texture of aging silver. She wondered if Steve treated all his guests to such luxury. "Is Steve here?" She asked.

"He went out for a while, but said to tell you he'll be back by eleven if you need help with anything."

"Thanks, Hilly."

"Of course, Miss." Hilly left, but returned quickly with a carafe of coffee, and not long after that, with a full Cottager's breakfast.

Carissa made short work of her meal and fortified herself with four cups of strong coffee. While she ate, she watched villagers chatting briefly with each other or fishermen unloading lobster pots, mending nets or working on their boats. The wind had steadied, continuing to flap coats but no longer threatening to tear everything away that wasn't tied down. The sign outside The Fisherman's Rest swung rhythmically with a comforting creak. Behind her, the ornate clock on the mantelpiece ticked with a dull, metallic constancy.

Turning in her chair, Carissa spotted a sign for Sally's Gift Emporium. She envied Sally and Steve their relationship, but knew she wasn't ready for one herself. She had a lot more healing to do, and she was still afraid that Matthew's burns might last a lifetime.

As she drank the last of her coffee, Carissa used her phone to look for fabric stores, finding several good options in Bangor, but none locally. She decided to check out of the inn and make the trip, but first, she needed to find out when Chuck's crew could start work.

"I was just about to call you," Chuck said when she called. "My crew's finishing up a small job. They can get to your place at noon. The drop box is on the way. Where are you?"

"I'm in town, but I wanted to drive up to Bangor today, if possible."

"You could still do that, if you don't mind leaving around five o'clock. The radiators need to come out as well as the old water heater. They'll install the new one and do some ductwork. After that, we need to wait on the furnace."

Carissa thanked Chuck profusely. Suddenly, things were definitely looking up. She noticed a black down coat in the front window of a small store across the street, walked over and bought one in bright turquoise because it was the only one left in her size. She also picked out two sweaters, one pink mohair, the other a nubby knit in shades of beige and brown. The owner of that store sent her to a shoe shop a few doors away. Carissa added a pair of sturdy boots, flat dress shoes and thick hiking socks to her purchases. Loaded with bags, on impulse she went into Sally's Gift Emporium. The tiny shop was packed with everything from driftwood sculptures in glass cabinets to cheap little souvenirs marked: 'I bought this at Treacher's Cove.'

A sallow-complexioned salesgirl named Verna eagerly explained that Sally, a talented sculptor with a workshop behind the Emporium, bought on consignment locally as well as from Bangor and Portland. She said Sally tried to avoid taking imported goods, believing that visitors who took the trouble to drive all the way to DownEast Maine should find a wide variety of crafts produced by local artists.

Carissa purchased a piece of scrimshaw, exquisitely carved into a replica of Treacher's Cove, a large ship in a bottle that was so detailed she could see tiny figures on the vessel's deck, and a set of coffee mugs decorated with winter scenes of Maine's largest towns.

"Would you please tell Sally I came to see her?" Carissa slid her business card across the counter when she paid. "I'd like to talk to her about taking some of my crafts on consignment as soon as I get settled. I specialize in needlepoint and embroidery."

Verna nodded and put the card next to the register. The bell above the door tinkled musically as Carissa left. The wind was picking up again. She checked her watch. She needed to get back to the lighthouse in a hurry. As long as Chuck's crew got done on time, she could still drive up to Bangor, spend the night and look for new carpeting and linoleum in the morning. Tile was out, or she'd need to cover both the kitchen and bathroom floors with rugs to cut down on the cold.

She decided to ask Chuck if she could give his foreman a key to the cottage. There wasn't much with any significant value in there, except, maybe Aunt Jessica's pattern books, which would have no interest to anyone but herself. From what her attorney had told her, waiting a few days before searching for them wouldn't make any difference to the pending case. Carissa also knew she'd ransack Aunt Jessica's cottage with a lot more enthusiasm if she wasn't doing it in frigid conditions. She pitied Chuck's workers and resolved to supply them with as much hot coffee as they could drink. Instant coffee, she reminded herself. Maybe that would be more of a punishment than an incentive.

As the Lexus bumped over potholes and rocked inside ruts on the track up to the lighthouse, Carissa's buoyant mood shifted into uneasiness. Would she find the back door open? Would the garage door be propped open? Would something else even creepier have occurred while she was gone?

With a sense of relief, she found the garage door closed and locked. The noise from a diesel engine announced the arrival of the drop box. Carissa quickly drove her car into the garage. The Lexus was looking more and more like a liability. Construction vehicles were going to worsen the condition of that rutted track between the road and the light-house. She needed to trade in her car for an SUV. Something with four wheel drive. She added visiting car dealerships in Bangor to her growing to-do list.

All doors and windows inside the keeper's quarters were secure. Carissa opened a can of tomato soup and made a tuna sandwich. While the soup finished heating, she unwrapped her scrimshaw and placed it on the fireplace mantle. The bottle with its ship inside found a home on an ancient oak chest beneath one of the living room windows.

The afternoon passed quickly. Chuck's men worked hard, installing a new water heater and removing all the old radiators. Debris piled up in the drop box. The men quit at 5:30 PM.

Chuck had called to tell her the new furnace should arrive in two days. He planned to have her heat running by the day after that at the latest, and agreed to supervise the crew himself. He assured Carissa it was not an inconvenience, as his wife frequently ran the appliance store. He made a recommendation for a hotel in Bangor and told her he'd pick up her spare key as soon as he closed his store for the day. She told him where to find it, dropped the key into an envelope and left it in the mailbox.

Chuck hadn't given her a line about the leaking radiators. Aunt Jessica's bedroom rug had a damp patch, and when the radiator in the living room was removed, a sizeable stain became visible behind the couch. The bathroom didn't even contain a radiator. An old space heater, coated with dust, sat outside in the passageway, an extension cord snaking from the guest bedroom. Aunt Jessica, so generous where others were concerned, was evidently a miser at home. Carissa made a late-arrival hotel reservation, locked up, double-checked everything, and set off for Bangor.

It was getting on for 9:00 P.M. by the time she arrived at the hotel.

The bar was open and still serving food, the receptionist told her. Carissa had the bellhop take her bag to her room and chose a table away from two men seated at the bar. A waitress took her order for a cup of vegetable soup and a small dinner salad. Carissa browsed local car dealerships on her smartphone over a cup of decaf coffee.

"Mind if I join you?"

The deep male voice startled her enough to knock over her water glass.

"Oops." The man tried to stop the rush of water with paper napkins. "I didn't mean to scare you."

"It's okay. I'm tired and a bit jumpy." Carissa hurriedly vacated her seat when the water flowed in her direction.

The waitress rushed over with a towel. "Why don't I move you both to another table?" She suggested, her smile thin.

Carissa hesitated. The stranger, tall, blond and handsome, didn't look like a deviant, but she wasn't about to let him think she was an easy pick-up.

"I promise I won't knock anything else over you if we share." The corners of his mouth twitched. "It'd be easier on Millie, and she wouldn't have to clean up two more tables."

Carissa abandoned plans for a solitary meal. "You've got a point," she said.

Millie scooped up Carissa's coffee and led them to another table. The two men at the bar said goodnight and left. The bartender brought out a mop and bucket.

"I never thought a glass of water could go that far," the stranger said.

"You'd be surprised," Millie said. She handed him a menu. "Would you like coffee, too?"

"I'll have whatever my dinner companion's having." He nodded toward Carissa. "I'm really hungry."

"I don't think what I'm having will fill you up, then," Carissa said.

"What are you having?"

She told him. He looked horrified.

"Forget the soup and salad," he told Millie. "We'll have two of your great cheese-steak hoagies." He turned to Carissa. "They're the best."

She thought about protesting she didn't want a sandwich, but her mutinous stomach growled loudly.

"Do you drink anything other than coffee?" he asked.

"Sometimes."

"Beer?"

"With hoagies?" She shrugged. "Okay."

"Good." He looked at Millie. "On my tab."

"Two beers on tap, two cheese-steak hoagies. Coming up." Millie left.

"Where did you travel from?" He asked Carissa.

She'd had time to check him out while he was talking to Millie. He wore a tweed sports jacket over a thick beige turtleneck sweater. His dark blond hair was cut short. Carissa wondered whether that was to keep an obvious waviness in check and lessen the impact of high cheekbones and a sculpted nose so perfectly shaped, it looked like it belonged on a statue instead of a man. He turned blue eyes to her and quirked one blond eyebrow.

"I came from Treacher's Cove, a little village at the mouth of…"

"…the Blended River," he finished, smiling. He extended his hand. "I'm Richard Ebberly, the architect and contractor Chuck Collins told you about. You must be Carissa Yates."

Dazed by the sudden turn of events, she mechanically shook hands. How could he make that connection? And what was he doing in Bangor, at the same hotel?

"You look a bit taken-aback," Richard said, grinning. "I've got a confession to make. I saw you briefly this morning, in the village. Al Dyson pointed you out to me. When I walked into the bar and saw you, I had to meet you."

"Oh."

Millie set two ice-cold beers in front of them, golden through the coating of frost on the glasses. Carissa took a sip. Once in a while she enjoyed a beer, and this one had the smooth taste of a good lager.

"When can you take a look at my home?" She asked Richard.

"As soon as you like. I've got nothing pressing—a couple of repair jobs and an extension on a cottage to complete. My work slows down at this time of year. The weather gets unpredictable and people don't want open doors during the winter. The work year this far up in Maine is shorter."

Carissa nodded. That all made sense. She felt a little less tense and told him about the tiny bathroom and outdated kitchen with the glacial mudroom and spider-infested basement laundry.

"That cottage could do with some updates," Richard agreed. "My dad was always trying to convince Jessica to remodel, especially the kitchen and bath, but I don't think she could be bothered."

"Did you know my aunt well?" Carissa was interested to find someone who talked about her aunt without mentioning her eccentricity in the same breath. Richard had also called her Jessica, which implied familiarity.

The hoagies arrived, interrupting their conversation. The sight and smell made Carissa very glad Richard had insisted on changing her order. He picked up the ketchup bottle and offered it to her. When she shook her head, he squirted a hefty serving onto his plate.

"I guess I knew Jessica as well as anyone else in the Cove did," he said. "She was a pretty private person. Not many visitors and few outings. She stopped coming to the village altogether about a year ago and got her groceries and newspapers delivered. The mailman picked up her bills and brought her stamps. She told William Dansinger, her attorney, that she didn't need anything else. He and my dad were friends and ate lunch together a couple of times a week, so I probably heard more about your aunt than a lot of other villagers did. "

"She hadn't been to New York in five years. Not since my marriage," Carissa said.

She stopped talking and took an enormous bite of her sandwich. She hadn't meant to mention her marriage or any other personal details. Richard had popped a couple of fries into his mouth. He chewed a couple of times and swallowed.

"I didn't realize you were married." He glanced at the door, a worried frown appearing between his brows. "Where's your husband. He didn't come up here with you, did he?"

Carissa shook her head. For some reason she didn't understand, she wanted to laugh. "There is no marriage anymore. I'm divorced."

Richard picked up his glass. "That's a relief. I thought I might have to explain myself to an irate husband." He took a big gulp of beer.

Carissa gave in to the bubbling laughter building inside her. "Somehow, I can't see you cowering in the corner, even if you had to deal with Matthew."

"Matthew Yates, the designer?"

Carissa nodded. Her mood, so positive before she said his name, took a hefty nose-dive. She put down the hoagie, which had suddenly become too big, too greasy, and too full of onions.

"I think I struck a nerve," Richard said, concern filling his voice. "Let's discuss your decorating plans, instead."

Carissa's impression of him improved considerably. Most men she had met since leaving Matthew wanted a blow-by-blow description of her failed marriage, then offered to help her forget her sorrows in bed.

"That sounds good to me," she said. "I was planning to do a lot of redecorating, but after one freezing cold night in the cottage, I'm leaning more toward reupholstering furniture, changing the drapes and spending more of my money on a walk-in shower and getting the washer and dryer out of the basement."

She tried another bite of her sandwich and sipped her beer. The choked-up feeling had passed. She drank deeply, relieved. Richard caught Millie's eye, tapped his glass and held up two fingers.

While they finished their meals and sipped their refills, Carissa filled him in on what she and Chuck had found.

Richard shook his head. "Your aunt had become more and more reclusive over recent years. The neglect you've told me about sounds like another symptom of that." He pointed to Carissa's empty glass. "Another?"

"No, thanks." She had a slight buzz, despite the big meal. "I want to be able to walk upstairs under my own power."

She thought of Steve carrying her to her room. That wasn't going to happen again with some other man, she told herself, hoping she wouldn't stagger when she stood up. Her life in Maine was definitely getting off to a strange start.

"So, why don't we do this?" Richard said. "I'll come by your home when I get back into town, which should be the day after tomorrow. I'll call you from the road and see if we can meet at say, three or three-thirty?

We can discuss what renovations you should really do first. Right now that sounds like it's going to involve a lot of plumbing. Careful planning will save you money in the long run. If you want to put new cabinets in the kitchen and maybe use the mudroom as more than an auxiliary freezer, it might be a good time to move the sink."

"But maybe I don't know what I want the design to be right now," Carissa hedged. "I may need to live with that kitchen for a while before deciding about the best flow and even the design and color for the cabinets."

"Okay. Fair enough. I'll look at the pipes and give you my opinion. Then when the plumber comes out, you'll already have a quote to work on."

"That would be much better. Thank you." Carissa wasn't ready to be pushed into a major renovation when she didn't even know if she wanted to stay buried in Treacher's Cove or sell the lighthouse and move on. Her original plan to live indefinitely in Aunt Jessica's home had shifted on its axis when she saw the potential cost, not to mention the strange events she'd experienced since her arrival.

Richard smiled. "When I show you my plans for your new kitchen and bath, you'll want to get started sooner than you think. If you don't like anything you see here tomorrow for the flooring and upholstery, give me a call. I'll see where else I can send you."

He pulled out his business card and handed it to her. Plain block letters announced: 'Ebberly Contracting and Architectural Design Services. Richard Ebberly, Licensed Contractor, Architect and CEO,' along with phone numbers, licensing information and a website link.

"Thanks, I'll be in touch." She tucked the card into one of her coat pockets, took her purse from the back of her chair and fished inside it for her wallet. "I have to get some sleep. I've got a busy day ahead of me." She noticed the bartender had turned off the lights behind the bar and was sitting with the waitress at a back table. They were chatting as they filled napkin holders and wiped down plastic condiment containers.

Richard waved away her attempt to pay. "I've got this. Call it a business supper." He glanced at the tab signed it and started to pull out some bills.

"Okay. Thanks." She smiled at him and got up. The waitress got up, too, and walked in their direction.

Carissa thought Richard Ebberly looked out of place in that little bar with the remains of a hoagie and an empty beer glass in front of him. He'd look more at home sculpted in marble and sitting in a museum. She could picture a wreath of Laurel leaves on his head, like one she'd seen on a bust of Julius Caesar.

"After we get through with the plans and my estimate on your plumbing, why don't I take you for an early dinner at The Fisherman's Rest?" Richard suggested. "I can't guarantee you won't be going home after dark, unfortunately, which will make it harder to avoid the potholes in that dirt track. You should get it paved before it takes out something vital on your car, like the muffler. I can put you in touch with a crew that'll give you a good price."

Carissa felt a little steamrollered. Was Richard taking kick-backs or did he really know everyone in Maine's construction and remodeling industry? She also felt uncomfortable for some reason at the thought of eating a meal at the inn with a man other than Steve.

"I'm not sure about dinner," she said. Trying to keep things on a lighter note, she added, "Maybe I won't like your estimate."

He laughed. "I'm not suggesting a date. You've got to eat, and by the sound of it, cooking any meal at the lighthouse right now is a challenge."

"Well, that's true," she admitted. "But I've already eaten a couple of meals at the inn, already. They were nice, but isn't there another restaurant in the village?"

"There are a couple of cafés and a tea room, but the other two restaurants are closed for the season. Why don't I take you somewhere else I think you'll like? It's called The Whitstead Tavern. Whitstead's a few miles south of Treacher's Cove and full of atmosphere."

Carissa hesitated a moment, but she would need to eat, and it would give her a chance to explore the surrounding area with someone who knew it very well. Discussing Richard's plans over dinner sounded a lot more appealing than doing it at the lighthouse. "Okay." She slung her purse strap over her shoulder. "It's a date."

"If you feel safe enough with me by then, I can drive you to and from dinner," Richard said. "Then we can take our time. I've got a four wheel drive that'll take that dirt track of yours in any weather."

Carissa's relaxed mood took a U-turn back toward the flashing yellow caution light. "How do you know *I* don't have a four wheel drive?"

"There are maybe a half-dozen vehicles in the lot outside. There's only one Lexus with New York plates."

"Oh." No wonder he had taken notice of her when he walked into the hotel. "I'll see you the day after tomorrow, then."

He nodded. "Like I said, I'll call you from the road and confirm the time. I have your aunt's landline number, unless you had it disconnected."

"I didn't, but let me give you my card. It's got my cell phone number on it." She took out her card and handed it to him. "There's one thing that still bothers me," she said.

"Oh?"

"Of all the hotels in Bangor, how did you end up here?"

"It's my favorite," he said. "Chuck knows that. Did he give you a recommendation?"

"He did. Was he aware you were coming up here, too?"

Richard shrugged. "I might have said something to him a few days ago. But I doubt he's got the imagination to play matchmaker, if that's what you're worried about."

"No, I doubt that, too," she said, thinking of her meetings with Chuck. Definitely not the matchmaker type.

"I wouldn't have minded if he had," Richard said. "I've enjoyed our supper."

"I enjoyed our supper, too, Richard. But let's get one thing straight right up front—I'm looking for a potential business relationship with you, nothing else."

"Yes, Ma'am." He saluted.

"And don't you forget it, Mr. Ebberly." She couldn't help smiling but she left the bar quickly, before he could walk her to the elevator.

When she glanced back, he was talking to the waitress, who was holding a small wad of bills in her hand and actually smiling. Carissa breathed a small sigh of relief and got into the elevator, her plans before bed including a good web search of everything to do with Ebberly Contracting and its CEO.

CHAPTER NINE

Steve Raymond closed the door of The Fisherman's Rest and headed for Sally's Gift Emporium. The air carried an early taste of winter, the harsh wind tinged with a bitterness that watered his eyes. He blinked and pulled up his coat collar.

His thoughts dwelled briefly on Carissa Yates. He hoped her heating system would get installed quickly or she'd be huddled up in front of a fireplace again with warmth on her face and ice at her back. He made a mental note to check on her later that day. He still had Jessica Malloy's landline number and thought a friendly call would make Carissa feel less of a stranger.

Maybe he could get Sally to invite Carissa to dinner and wangle himself an invitation, too, so he could eat more than his fair share of Sally's delicious chicken pie. His mouth watered at the thought. *Like one of Pavlov's dogs.* He smiled to himself. He was as conditioned to the smell of Sally's cooking as those dogs had been to the sound of a bell.

With that, he pushed open the shop's door and the bell tinkled overhead. He almost chuckled at the timing of the bell and the direction of his thoughts before turning his mirth into a smile for Verna, who had popped her head out of the stockroom.

"Hi, Verna. Where's your boss?"

"Sorting driftwood in the workshop." Verna smoothed wispy hair behind her ears as she sashayed toward the counter. What she probably thought passed as a coquettish smile broke up her usually bland expression. Crooked teeth peeked through thin lips and a slight dimple appeared at the right side of her mouth.

"I'll go check on her." Steve had to pass the sallow-complexioned salesgirl, who took the opportunity to press herself up against him. Sally had told him Verna was obsessed with him, and ever since, he'd done his best to avoid the girl whenever he could.

"Would you like a cup of coffee and a slice of my pumpkin pie? I baked it fresh early this morning." Verna pushed out her meager chest.

"That sounds wonderful, but I just had breakfast."

"Eating late, Mr. Steve, weren't you?" She smoothed the neckline of her blouse, her fingers lingering at the point where the top of her apron met the first button.

"I was too busy earlier." He backed quickly away. Usually, Verna's attempts at seduction amused him. That day, they only made him jumpy. "See you later," he said over his shoulder as he strode through the shop and opened the back door onto a breezeway.

He saw Sally through the glass in the workshop door. Her hair shone like liquid gold under the neon light over the workbench. He stopped to watch her sorting driftwood into two separate piles. Her slender, almost boyish figure was molded by denim jeans and a figure-hugging turtle-neck sweater, bright red in contrast to her whitewashed surroundings.

He wondered why he didn't ask her to move in with him. He was forty-two and had no roots other than the inn. Didn't he want a family before it was too late? If he died tomorrow, he'd be mourned for about a week by Cove residents and soon forgotten. A hollow feeling burned in the pit of his stomach that he hadn't felt in a long time.

As Sally placed an empty box on the floor and started to pull more wood out of another, he saw the center of the workbench held two large pieces of driftwood she must have selected to sculpt. A tree limb occupied a third of the bench while a smaller, delicately-shaped piece stood in front of it, branches bleached by salt water. He opened the door. Sally kept working, although she must have heard the door unlatch and felt the draft.

"Put the coffee on the stool, would you, Verna?" she asked, gesturing behind her with one hand as the other prepared to toss a gnarled and blackened chunk onto what must be the discarded pile.

Steve tiptoed over and kissed the nape of her neck. Sally's head snapped up, hitting him square on the nose. The gnarled wood flew across the room to land with a clatter next to a large window overlooking the bay. Stars exploded, blurring Steve's vision.

"Yow! Some greeting." He nursed his throbbing nose.

Sally turned, her face white and angry. "Never, ever do that to me again." One hand clutched her heaving chest.

"Scared you, huh?" He experimentally poked his nose. "I think it might be broken."

"Serves you right. I thought I was being attacked."

"You were." He gathered her in his arms despite protests and half-hearted swats.

"I want a boyfriend, not an assailant." She stopped struggling and looked hard at him. "Do you really think your nose is broken? I could give you a piece of ice to hold on it."

"A piece of ice. I guess that would be without the 'pack' part of it. You're a hard woman, Sally Mainard."

"I'm a jealous woman. You've spent more time with Carissa Yates during the last two days than you have with me. I heard you carried her up to bed while I was manning your reception desk. *Your* bed, Steve?"

He cursed silently. Who had seen them on the stairs and reported to Sally? "You should know better than that."

"No one really knows you. Not even me." Sally wriggled out of his arms and returned to her driftwood sorting, her actions rapid and mechanical. Dip in the box, select the appropriate pile; drop the wood. Return to the box; select another piece; drop it on a pile.

He watched her in silence while he gathered his thoughts. "Sometimes I don't even know myself," he said after three revolutions of box to piles had been completed. "Can you say you'll always know how you'll react to any given situation?"

"Ninety-nine percent of the time." She stopped sorting. "I can't say the same about you. I think I can read you maybe ten percent if I'm lucky. You shy away from any sharing that places your precious privacy in jeopardy."

He carefully placed his hands on her shoulders. Beneath his palms, he felt her quivering. "I used to be worse. I've made a lot of headway since I came to the Cove."

"Why can't you say you've made a lot of headway since you met *me*?" Her tone was plaintive, her voice small and breathless, unlike the usually self-assured Sally.

"I have." He wanted to comfort her, but he couldn't lie. He didn't relate well to emotional relationships. His admission, small as it was, would have to do.

Sally sighed deeply, her eyes closed. "You're going to break my heart."

"I hope not. I wouldn't have a clue how to glue it back together."

Her eyes flew open in consternation. Then she managed a laugh. "Rat. I don't know why I even bother."

"I don't know, either, but I'm glad you do." He kissed her lightly.

The door crashed against the wall and a scowling Verna bustled in with a tray. "Here's your coffee and pie."

Steve quickly released Sally and stepped back as Verna pushed between them to dump the tray on the stool beside the workbench. She poured coffee and added cream and sugar to Steve's, leaving Sally's black. Handing him his cup and a large slice of pie, which she almost dropped, Verna's cheeks flamed crimson. The coffee slopped onto the floor at Steve's feet.

"The pie looks delicious," he said.

The peace offering didn't sit well with her. "I'm going home," she announced. "Poppy should be here after lunch. The doctor's appointment was only for a checkup. We haven't had one customer since the shop opened, and now it's raining."

"Thank you for filling in," Sally said. She placed her coffee on one corner of the table.

Verna managed a nod, but her scowl remained. She left, the door crashing behind her.

"She's not a happy camper." Steve put the pie down. "What's her problem?"

"She's mad about seeing us kissing. Are you really so blind you can't tell she's in love with you?"

Sally picked up a knife and looked at him, her gaze accusing and angry. "A lot of women at the Cove have the hots for you. They think you're different from the rest of the men around here."

"Different in a good way, I hope." Steve looked at the knife. Long-handled and deadly sharp, it glittered under the neon light. "Thinking of using that on me?" He asked in an attempt to lighten the mood. "You'd have no reason; I'm always faithful to you."

Sally grabbed the larger piece of driftwood and began whittling. Her mouth, usually so soft and enticing, was held in a firm, stiff line. "Some-times I'd like to take something to you, whether it's a knife or a large piece of wood." She shook the piece of driftwood at him for emphasis. "I think you're playing with me, and I'm going to get hurt. It's my own fault for letting you do it." She laid down both the knife and the wood before facing him. "I want to be married, Steve." Her eyes locked with his. "I want to have a family before I'm too old to enjoy kids. I hoped they'd be your kids when I first started dating you, but that hope's fading."

Her glare was highly effective. Steve had to stop himself from taking a step away from her.

Sally turned her attention back to her driftwood. Wood chips flew. "You should leave."

"Sally…"

She refused to look at him.

"I guess I'll come back when you're in a better mood."

She continued working, transforming a branch into a delicate network of hills and valleys. Her silence accused Steve more than angry words ever could.

"I didn't take Carissa Yates to any bed, least of all mine," he told her, opening the workshop door.

The door flew out of his grasp and slammed against the weathered wood. Maybe Verna hadn't been using it to demonstrate her feelings after all. He glanced at Sally one more time before striding through the empty store. He paused long enough to flip the 'Open' sign to 'Closed' and pop the old-fashioned locking mechanism before carefully closing the front door of Sally's shop behind him.

CHAPTER TEN

CARISSA'S NOSE ITCHED. She rubbed it on one sleeve of her aunt's smock because she didn't want to take off her rubber gloves. The kitchen and bathroom had both been thoroughly scrubbed. Now she was working on the fireplace while the furnace was being installed. She ignored the chill and removed the last of the debris from the blaze she had kindled three days before. Her boxes were due to arrive within the hour, and Richard would be over at 4:00 P.M. He'd called to tell her he was running late from his meetings in Bangor.

A knock on the back door brought her head out of the fireplace. Chuck's men were going in and out of the house freely. Why would one of them start knocking? She heard it again. A soft but distinct knock. Carissa peeled off her gloves and shook her hair free from a scarf she had tied over her head. Her muscles ached from contorting herself under the claw-footed tub and then in the fireplace. She placed both hands at the small of her back and stretched. If she developed back pain, instead of sleeping she'd be lying in the dark listening for footsteps or anything else her active mind could conjure up in the middle of the night.

She opened the door to find Mai Ling Ulster.

Mai Ling smiled tentatively and held out a plastic container. "I thought I would bake you something to welcome you to the neighborhood."

"Come in." Carissa opened the screen and motioned her visitor inside. "I'm sorry it's so cold in here right now. The new furnace is being installed. Would you like some coffee?"

"Coffee? Yes. That would be nice." Mai Ling hovered inside the mudroom.

"I won't charge if you come all the way in and sit down." Carissa smiled. She turned on the one space heater she had decided she had to purchase and directed it at the table. "Please close the door behind you so it warms up in here."

"You charge?" Mai Ling looked perplexed.

"No." Carissa laughed outright. "I said I *don't* charge. It was a joke. Sit down; I'll get the coffee."

"A joke." Mai Ling blushed. "My English is not so good. My family came here from Vietnam ten years ago, but I lived at home, and we did not speak English."

"There's nothing wrong with your English. Jokes are always harder for people to grasp in a foreign language." Carissa had bought a coffeemaker, a grinder and several bags of coffee while in Bangor. She had kept coffee available all day for the workmen as well as herself. She filled two cups and placed them on a tray with cream and sugar, which she brought over to the table. When she opened Mai Ling's container, expecting some Vietnamese delicacy, she found instead a foil-wrapped loaf of what looked suspiciously like zucchini bread. When she removed the foil wrapping, it also looked undercooked and lumpy, but she was pleased her timid neighbor had made the effort.

Mail Ling looked around the kitchen. "You have been cleaning. It looks very nice."

"It does, but I've got a lot more to do. The furniture hasn't been moved in a while. There's a lot of dust in here."

"You and your aunt were…close?" Mai Ling took the coffee Carissa handed her. "I take it black," she said, waving away the offer of cream and sugar.

"We were very close. I loved my aunt. I miss her a lot." Carissa swallowed the lump that instantly rose into her throat.

The back door opened and one of Chuck's workmen traipsed in with a tool bag. "New thermostat," he said. "I'll put it in the hallway."

Carissa nodded. "Why don't we sit in the living room?" She suggested to Mai Ling. "I had just about finished cleaning out the fireplace. It won't take a few minutes to get the fire going again."

"I will help." Mai Ling pulled her thin cardigan across her chest. She looked like she was trying hard not to shiver.

Carissa wondered why her visitor had walked over without a coat. It wasn't as though she lived right next door. Mai Ling again wore a traditional dress made from thin silky material under the cardigan. Carissa stood and put the cups back on the tray.

Mai Ling seized the tray. "Please, you will go first."

Carissa unplugged the heater and brought it with them into the frigid living room. Mai Ling placed the tray on the coffee table, then sank to her knees in front of the hearth.

"Mai Ling, you're a guest," Carissa protested as the girl placed kindling into the grate.

"I can do this much faster than you. I light the fire every morning, and I'm sure you are used to having radiators." With deft motions she built a base of twigs and crumpled newspaper, which lit much faster than Carissa's effort had the first night she arrived at the lighthouse. She watched as Mai Ling carefully added larger twigs, then after the blaze caught, two logs, which sank into the fiery nest and readily ignited. Smoke billowed up the chimney and heat radiated.

"There." The young girl swept back her waist-length black hair. "All you have to do now is to keep adding logs. Never let it get too low or it will make smoke but no fire."

"Thank you. I'll do as you say. Now, come and have your coffee." Carissa held out the cup. Mai Ling took it but moved into a squatting position in front of the fire.

"Wouldn't you be more comfortable on a chair?"

"Sorry. For a moment I forgot my manners." Mai Ling quickly scrambled up, her eyes lowered.

Carissa wondered whether squatting was a custom for her visitor and felt an awkward silence begin between them. "I want you to be yourself," she said as she cut two slices of the very moist zucchini bread onto small plates and passed one to Mai Ling.

Carissa worked at chewing and swallowing the soggy and unappetizing gift while Mai Ling left hers untouched, but sipped coffee until her cup was empty.

"How did you and Blake meet?" Carissa asked, after rejecting several other more controversial conversation openers that included asking for Mai Ling's recipe, how she liked living in isolation with a surly husband, and whether she ever saw her parents.

"My father and a friend of Blake's had known each other for a long time. The friend was a sponsor for my family. One day he brought Blake with him when he came to dinner. My parents were very impressed that Blake had his own home and ran his family's business. They allowed him to court me. When he asked for my hand in marriage, they were very pleased."

Carissa's curiosity won out over caution. "Did you have any choice? Did you love him?" She blurted out, and then cringed over her audacity.

If Mai Ling told Blake everything, Carissa figured he'd be knocking at her door, telling her to mind her own damned business. She handed Mai Ling one of the afghans and tucked the other around her legs. Mai Ling draped hers around her shoulders. She remained silent and didn't make eye contact.

"I'm sorry," Carissa said. "That was rude of me. I should mind my own business."

Mai Ling's answer was to look directly at Carissa for the first time since arriving on her doorstep. "You are not rude," she said. "I do not love my husband. I never did."

"I'm so sorry, Mai Ling." Carissa's heart ached. "I'd like us to be friends."

"I would very much like a friend." Mai Ling spoke slowly, as though considering the idea. "My parents live in Boston. I have no one here. I do not drive, so I depend upon Blake to take me to the village to buy groceries. Often he takes my list and goes without me. He says I take too long and he is too busy to stand around waiting while I decide what to buy." She sighed and set her cup down very carefully, as though afraid she might lose control and throw it. "He does not want to drive to Boston so I can visit my family, although he had no trouble driving there when he was courting me."

Carissa heard the reproach in Mai Ling's voice, saw a barely-perceptible twitch at the side of her mouth and watched the girl's hands clench and unclench in her lap. Somewhere within her thin chest dwelled a deep rage.

The front door bell rang. Mai Ling looked terrified. "Blake," she whispered. "He was to be gone all day."

"No, I think it's my boxes. They're supposed to get delivered today from New York." Carissa threw off the afghan and got up. "If it *is* Blake, I'll stall him at the front door while you slip out the back. You can tell him you went for a walk on the cliffs."

"Thank you, my friend." Mai Ling fled into the kitchen.

Carissa opened the front door to find a burly man in a pair of overalls under a windbreaker. She caught sight of a moving company truck behind the other vehicles already in the driveway. "Burt?" She asked.

"That's me." He tapped his badge. "We're early. I hope that's okay."

"That's fine." Carissa breathed a sigh of relief. "I'm more than ready for you."

"Good. We'll unload as fast as we can." He looked back at the crowded forecourt.

"Heating problems," Carissa told him. "Do you need them to move their vehicles? They already unloaded the furnace."

"I can talk to them. Are they around back?"

Carissa nodded. "I'll leave this door unlocked. Let me know when you're ready. Everything will come straight down the hallway into the guest bedroom. I pushed the bed out of the way."

He looked up at the lighthouse. "This is a first, delivering to one of these."

"You'll only be delivering to the keeper's quarters, but it'll be a story to tell nevertheless."

Burt chuckled and stepped back off the porch. "Hold on," he told the man standing beside the truck with a dolly. "We can get closer. I'll get that other truck to switch places with us."

Carissa returned to the living room. It was appalling how little she had wanted to bring from New York. All her furniture and much of her designer clothing had gone to consignment stores. She wouldn't need any of it ever again, if Matthew won the court case. If he didn't, then she'd purchase new.

She found Mai Ling crouching on a kitchen chair. "It's safe," Carissa told her anxious guest. "It's only the movers."

"I would like to help, but I am now afraid Blake will come back. If he is gone tomorrow I could come for a short time."

"Tomorrow's Sunday. Does he work every day of the week?"

"Some weeks he does. He can also work until late in the evening, but I never know for sure. He will tell me he plans to be gone all day, then he comes back early."

Checking up on her, no doubt.

Carissa felt sadness for Mai Ling and anger at Blake. No wonder rage surged inside her new friend. She forced a smile as they said goodbye. The girl's sweater caught on the screen door spring and pulled off her shoulder, exposing a huge, yellowing bruise. Mai Ling ripped her sweater pulling it off the spring. Without looking back, she fled.

CHAPTER ELEVEN

RICHARD EBBERLY SMOOTHED his hair back with one hand and adjusted his tie with the other. He'd thought about wearing his suit jacket but rejected that idea in favor of a sweater. The temperature had dropped fifteen degrees since early morning, and he wasn't in to freezing, even to impress Carissa Yates.

Al Dyson had said he had a lot of information on her. Over the scotch whisky Richard bought him at The Fisherman's Rest, Al told him nothing that Richard couldn't have learned from internet research, but since the scotch was a double, Richard figured he might as well get his money's worth. Al's account was that Carissa had been hanging around the fringes of New York's fashion industry without much success until she met and married designer Matthew Yates. He'd made her career. Now divorced, she was trying to keep a slice of the pie by slapping him with a copyright infringement suit 'for some stupid design techniques' as Al put it.

Richard subsequently fact-checked Al's declarations and found most of them were actually true. He felt sorry for Carissa. She'd probably come out of that marriage with less than her fair share. He hoped she'd win her pending litigation. Jessica Malloy's creativity was well-known in the Cove. He thought it highly likely her niece had inherited that trait after hearing Carissa intended to remodel the lighthouse keeper's quarters.

Richard wanted to help her forget all about the past. Women usually found him witty and pleasant company, but Carissa had kept up a defensive wall the entire meal they'd shared. He sensed she might be willing to tolerate a superficial form of friendship, but he'd have an uphill climb if he wanted anything beyond that. He'd never shied away from a challenge, and he had a feeling Carissa Yates might be worth the extra effort.

He armed his state-of-the-art security system before leaving his farmhouse. Since inheriting the property from his father three years earlier, he had turned the house to a model home envied by local inhabitants and visitors alike. Sleek lines concealed high-tech, both in terms of insulation, solar power and appliances. Soaring ceilings now reached to the second floor, where he'd removed two tiny bedrooms. Contemporary had replaced rustic, with stainless steel and tile floors.

He strode over to a modern four-car garage. The old barn behind it had become an oversized protector for ATVs, a snow cat, 2 motor cycles and a 1965 Ford Mustang convertible he'd had restored.

The adjacent farmland had been parceled off and sold several years before he moved into the property, which still irked Richard from time to time. He would have liked to parcel it himself and build large, expensive vacation homes for the very rich. Instead, an estate of modest homes crouched along his property lines, hidden only by the addition of a stone wall and the services of a talented landscaper.

Even he couldn't stop progress, he thought, catching glimpses of lights through the trees as he drove out his front gate and glanced into his rearview mirror to see it swing closed behind his Jeep.

The trip to Carissa's home was accomplished over pitted backroads he knew well. The Jeep accomplished it without problems, despite jarring, pitching tracks demanding concentration and taxing even Richard's skills. He had driven the Cove's fire-truck during many of his college vacations and had a reputation in the village for being hands-down its best driver.

Arriving in front of the lighthouse, he jumped out and threw his black leather gloves onto the seat. He looked longingly at the buildings in front of him. His fingers itched to design a full remodel, but he doubted Carissa would be on-board with his ideas. The lighthouse and keeper's quarters would be a perfect showcase for his talents. He wanted to add more specialized and tasteful remodeling of existing properties to his already-impressive resume of renovated shopping centers and new home construction. Most of all, he wanted his reputation to be recognized not only outside the local area but the State of Maine. He wanted to leave the contracting business his father had built in the hands of a competent and trustworthy team while he expanded the architectural side.

Carissa came to the door in an emerald green woolen dress that hugged her curves like a devoted lover. Richard let out a low whistle of appreciation.

She blushed, so help him. He stepped inside a home that felt like it was warming after a long period of extreme cold. "You look great," he told her.

"Thanks, but you don't have to keep giving me compliments to get the job, Richard. I'd already decided to have you do the renovations for me, even before you give me the estimate."

"Never tell that to a contractor," he warned, returning her smile. "I may pad my bid."

"I don't think so. Your face shows integrity."

"That's what my mother always said."

"Was she right?"

"Sometimes. The rest of the time I was busy trying to look the part."

"Not building my trust, Richard, but come on into the living room, anyway."

She led the way, her hips swaying rhythmically in the narrow skirt. Richard found it hard to concentrate on mundane things like granite counter tops and porcelain bath fixtures.

"I could do with updates in the kitchen and bath," she said, turning to study him. "I'm not sure what else I want to change right now. The windows are drafty but they're original, I'm sure, and so pretty."

"Custom-built storm windows would protect them and keep you a lot warmer," Richard told her as he looked around. "I could give you some preliminary sketches in a few days, or you can get a digital version.

I'm really an architect. I inherited my dad's contracting business when he retired."

"Why don't you look around while I make us a couple of drinks?"

"Sounds good. Thanks."

"What would you like? Aunt Jessica was evidently a confirmed member of the cocktail generation. She has whisky, brandy, bourbon and rum. I don't drink gin, and apparently, neither did my aunt. There's no tequila, so she wasn't into mixing margaritas. I don't think wine or champagne are appropriate for these surroundings, even if I had them." She smiled a little wider, less tentatively. "Screeching winds and crashing waves conjure up visions of ancient mariners coming home to rustic taverns and hard liquor, not gilt drawing-rooms and flutes of champagne."

"You've got a point." He laughed. Any number of Cove inhabitants would fit that ancient mariner tag. He doubted any of them even knew what a gilt drawing-room looked like. "Bourbon's fine, on the rocks with a splash of soda if you have it."

"Done. Why don't you check out the kitchen while I fix our drinks? Or you can look around the rest of the quarters, if you prefer."

"I'll get a better feel for what you want if you give me the tour," Richard said. "Otherwise I might suggest changes you won't like."

He followed Carissa into the kitchen. She dropped ice cubes into their glasses. He hoped she would decide to become a permanent resident. He could make her unique home into a show-place she'd be thrilled to live in, as long as she didn't mind the isolation.

Carissa poured the bourbon and added soda. "You can prowl away," she said. "I'll sit in front of the fire and toast my feet until you get done." She held out his drink.

He took the glass from her, their fingers touching with a little maneuvering on his part. She didn't exactly pull away, but her hand didn't linger on the glass, either.

"Well." She waved an arm around at the kitchen. "It's a monstrosity, huh?"

His gaze wandered from the 1960's vintage stove to the chipped enamel sink and poorly painted white cabinets with doors askew. "It's a gut job, all right. The only thing worth keeping is the table. Nice, solid oak."

"I know. I'd like to relocate it to the living room and find better chairs to go with it. Maybe a bench on one side. There'd be plenty of space by the window, if I get the piano moved to the other side of the room. I'd rather eat my meals in there than out here." She glanced toward the mudroom door and shivered slightly.

"You should be a lot warmer now with the new heating system," Richard pointed toward the door. "Does this go straight outside?"

"No, there's a mudroom. That's still ductless and like a meat locker. I wondered if the wall could be taken out so I could utilize the space better. Maybe leave a small area tiled and some hooks to corral coats and boots, but I usually come in the front door, so that would still waste space."

"I'll check to make sure that's not a load-bearing wall. I could relocate your washer and dryer from the basement anyway, and Chuck could put in an extra register. You wouldn't hear the machines running with the door closed. I could add a window. Maybe move the pantry, or give you a broom closet. Make it part of the kitchen but still a little detached. I'll draw up the plans two ways and you can see which you'd prefer.

"While we're talking about walls, I could knock out the one between the kitchen and living room, make a breakfast bar and open up the space to give you a great, uninterrupted view of the water. There'll be plenty of room to put the table in front of the windows, and the piano won't get relegated to the darkest corner of the living room."

"Whoa, there. We've progressed from knocking out one wall to the complete rearrangement of three rooms. I don't think I'm ready for that, yet." Carissa leaned against the kitchen table. "My aunt would probably resent it. She might even come back to haunt me."

Her smiled looked a little strained. Richard took a swallow of his drink. The ticking of the grandfather clock was the only sound other than the wind, which moaned around the eaves, rattled casements and impolitely gusted down the chimney. If he lived there, he wondered how long it would take him to start hearing things go bump in the night.

Richard gave himself a mental reprimand. He'd never been superstitious or had any belief in ghosts. Either the bourbon was having an effect on him or it was the surroundings. The way Jessica had died bothered him. She must have had some sort of blackout spell to have fallen. She'd lived without incident at the Bennett Point Light for years. He wondered if there were blood stains on the tower steps and almost asked Carissa before restraining himself.

"Kind of lonely out here, isn't it?" He finished his drink.

"Not since *I* got here." Carissa put her own barely-touched drink on the counter. "I've had plenty of guests." She held out her hand. "I'll take your glass. Ready to look around the rest of the house?"

The wind gusted again and the old house creaked like a dowager with arthritis. "Not tonight," he decided aloud. "Let me draw up some plans for the kitchen, living room and mudroom first. If you like the direction I want to go, then I'll look at the rest of the house." He felt a desire to get out of Jessica Malloy's mausoleum of a home and take Carissa with him. The Whitstead Tavern sounded more and more inviting as the clock ticked on relentlessly.

The doorbell rang, startling them both.

Richard recovered first. "Expecting company?"

Carissa's face looked almost translucent under the stark lighting of the kitchen's fluorescents. "I guess I'd better see who it is." She headed for the front door.

Richard made himself another, stronger drink. He heard the front door creak open and a frigid blast of air blew around his feet. He needed to add a closed-in porch for her, he thought. No sense in letting all her heat escape.

"Steve!" Carissa said.

Richard heard the pleasure in her voice and felt frustration. He'd planned a leisurely evening with her. One free from unnecessary interruptions like the inn-keeper of The Fisherman's Rest.

"Richard, it's Steve Raymond," Carissa called.

"I came by to check on you." Steve's voice boomed. "It's still cold in here. Did Chuck's men finish installing the furnace?"

When Richard strolled in from the kitchen, Steve was rubbing his hands together in front of the fireplace. He glanced over his shoulder at Richard, his expression neutral but his gaze uncomfortably penetrating, like a reprimanding parent.

Richard clutched his drink tighter. The reaction annoyed him. Steve Raymond had a disconcerting, aggravating habit of staring people down, and he always succeeded, whether they had anything to hide or not. Richard found himself involuntarily checking out the blaze in the fireplace. He never could understand why The Fisherman's Rest and its owner were so popular with Cove residents. Richard thought Steve Raymond was a passive-aggressive bully, and the décor of his inn both boring and predictable.

"Nice of you to be so neighborly." Richard moved closer to Carissa.

Steve grinned. "Always happy to be neighborly to a lovely young woman." He winked at her.

Carissa laughed. "Oh, and if I was an old crone, I suppose you'd leave me alone."

Richard felt a pang of jealousy. Carissa was so comfortable with Steve already, and their light banter seemed closer to flirting than friendship. She was supposed to be spending the evening with her architect, not Steve Raymond. What the hell was the man doing out there instead of taking care of his business or having an evening with his hot girlfriend?

Richard hoped he wasn't looking as grouchy on the outside as he felt on the inside. He finished his second bourbon. "Even if you were ninety, I'd be out here checking on you," he told Carissa, trying for gallant.

"Thanks, Richard. I appreciate the thought." Carissa's smile was dishearteningly friendly, while her attention seemed to be more on Steve than her would-be date for the evening. "Let me get you a drink?" She offered Steve.

"What are you two having?" He glanced at the empty glass in Richard's hand.

"Bourbon with a splash of soda," she said. "What would you like, Steve?" She, too, looked at Richard's glass. "Another, Richard?"

"I don't drink alcohol," Steve said. "A glass of soda water with ice and a twist of lemon if you have it will do me fine."

"An innkeeper who's a teetotaler? That's an anomaly." Carissa took Richard's glass.

"I'll have a plain soda water, too," Richard told her. "I'm driving us to dinner. I've had enough booze."

Carissa left the room. Richard joined Steve in watching her. He wondered whether Steve was having the same fantasies he was about Carissa, and anger joined frustration and jealousy. He had always thought of Steve Raymond as an outsider, regardless of how long he had lived at Treacher's Cove. Prior to Steve's arrival, anyone who wasn't born and raised in the Cove was considered an outsider. How much they were integrated varied with their personalities and contributions to the community. Evidently, most of the Cove inhabitants thought Steve Raymond had contributed more than enough.

Steve surveyed Richard. "So, how did you two meet?"

"Through Chuck. Carissa needs an architect and contractor for some remodeling."

"I thought you were tied up with something else? Doesn't your business wind down in the winter, too?"

Frequently, the Cove was too small, Richard thought. Everyone learned everyone else's business. "That project'll be finished pretty quickly. Carissa's not looking to change the overall size of the house. Just modify the layout. No reason why we can't do most of the work through the winter, if we get the materials early enough."

"I can always spend a few more nights at the inn if things get too disruptive around here," Carissa said as she brought the drinks in from the kitchen. "You know, Richard, I think I should get rid of that piano. I don't play, and it's taking up a lot of space. I could have a wet bar in here, instead. Nothing big, but walking in and out of the kitchen like this isn't convenient. I missed everything you two said to each other while I was out there."

"You didn't miss much." Richard took his club soda from her. "Thanks."

"Of course." A slight frown had appeared between her brows.

"I was asking Richard how you two met," Steve said. "He told me through Chuck."

"Well, that's not entirely correct. We met in Bangor." Carissa looked from one man to the other. "Richard was staying at the same hotel. We met over a late supper in the bar."

Steve turned to stare at her. "What in the world were you doing in Bangor?"

"Looking for fabric and linoleum. I want to get furniture reupholstered and replace these heavy drapes. They've been here since I visited as a child. I don't even want to think about how much dust is in them."

Richard felt uneasy. If she'd already committed to fabric, she might reject a lot of his ideas. The only thing she'd seemed receptive to until Steve Raymond interrupted them was fixing up the mudroom. Hardly presentable to prospective clients as an example of his expertise. "Did you order anything?" He asked.

"I brought samples home with me. I was planning to make my choices, then call them." Her eyebrows rose slightly, followed by a disarming dimple at one corner of her mouth. "I suppose you want me to re-evaluate my selections based on all these walls you want to knock out."

"We've got an excellent fabric store right here in the Cove," Steve said. "If that's not big enough, the one in nearby Whitstead's got to have anything you could possibly want." Richard saw the glower on Steve's face. He seemed ready to take a very active role in welcoming Carissa Yates to the Cove and giving red or green lights to the companies involved with her projects.

"I'm very happy with the samples I got," Carissa said. "I appreciate your help no end with the furnace, Steve. Chuck's a wonderful resource. But fabrics are probably more in my wheelhouse than yours."

"Everything at the inn is right from sources at or close to the Cove," Steve said. "We really try to support our local economy. With the bad weather coming on, you won't want to be going to Bangor on a regular basis for anything."

"Probably not. Look, I'll try to buy accent fabrics and whatever else I can find locally, I promise, but this is my home and my choice." She sounded slightly angry.

Good, Richard thought. *She's got some spunk.*

"Why don't we go to dinner?" He suggested, glancing at his watch. "I made reservations for eight o'clock and it's already seven-fifteen."

"I'm sorry." Steve finished his tonic in two gulps and put the empty glass onto a coaster in the middle of the coffee table. "I spoke a bit out of turn, but the stores at the Cove and the families that own them really need the support from everyone in the community. I didn't mean to step on your toes and tell you where to buy if you couldn't find anything here that you liked."

Carissa nodded, but she didn't tell him she wasn't offended, or that what he'd said was okay.

"I'll walk you to the door," she said, instead.

"No need. I can see myself out. Enjoy your dinner." Steve paused. "I take it you're not dining at The Fisherman's Rest?"

"No. Richard's taking me to the Whitstead Tavern." Carissa looked from one man to the other, her eyes narrowing slightly. "I don't know if that's considered buying local or not."

"Nice place." Steve nodded. "I've eaten there myself. I recommend either the lobster or the Dover sole. The chowder's mediocre but they've got a good salad bar. Lots of selections and all fresh. I added a few more items to my own salad choices after eating there."

"Thanks. I'll remember your advice when I order." She smiled at Steve.

Richard seethed. Steve Raymond always managed to get into the middle of everything, including his semi-date-night with a prospective client. "We'd better get going ourselves," he told Carissa. "I'd like us to have time for a cocktail at the bar before we go in to dinner. It's a quaint place with lots of atmosphere. If we go late, though, it'll be too crowded in the bar to find a table."

"If you can get a window seat, you'll see the fishing boats coming back into the harbor," Steve said, his smile like a benevolent father.

Way to go, stealing my lines. Richard gritted his teeth and turned to Carissa. "I'll get your coat. Is it hanging by the door?"

"No, I'll get it. Thanks for stopping by, Steve." She smiled again at him before walking briskly toward the back of the house without glancing Richard's way.

"Take care of her." Steve strode down the front hallway.

"Of course I will." Richard bristled as he followed. Steve Raymond always managed to set him on edge. "I'm not planning to drink too much and drive us into a ditch on the way home."

Steve pulled on his sheepskin jacket and wound a scarf around his neck. "I wasn't implying you would." His shoulders squared after he pulled his knitted hat down around his ears. He looked even taller and more imposing than usual.

Richard held his ground. He had a feeling that flexing muscles had gotten Steve Raymond out of a lot of uncomfortable situations. "Let me get the door for you," he said, walking toward Steve at the end of the dark and narrow hallway. He needed to convince Carissa to put in a new door with glass inserts, paint the hallway a light color, and add some recessed lighting.

"Okay, I'm ready." Carissa swept down the hallway behind Richard. Her turquoise down coat off-set her Irish coloring to its best advantage. Richard almost let out a whistle of appreciation. "I'm going to be the envy of every man in the Tavern this evening."

Color warmed her pale cheeks. "Thank you, but compliments like that make me a bit uncomfortable."

"A modest woman. Wonderful." Steve slid her arm through his and tossed her keys to Richard. "I'll walk you out to the car. Lock up, Ebberly, would you?" He grinned at Richard over his shoulder. "You don't mind giving me a ride back to the Cove before you go to Whitstead, do you? You've still got forty minutes before your dinner reservation."

CHAPTER TWELVE

"THIS IS WONDERFUL, RICHARD." Carissa gazed through the window beside their table in the dining room of the Whitstead Tavern, glimpsing moonlight shining over dark water. "I'm so glad you suggested coming here."

"I knew you'd like it." Richard thought he'd never taken a more beautiful woman to dinner. He knew he was the luckiest man in the restaurant. "Have you decided what you want to eat?"

"What do you suggest?" She turned her attention back to her menu. "There are so many choices."

"Raymond already gave you a couple of recommendations."

"He did, but now I'd like to hear yours. After all, he's not here, and there are some specials."

"You've very diplomatic."

"No one survives eight years in *haute couture* without being discreet. One word in the wrong place, you find yourself blackballed."

It was the first time she had told him anything about her past. Richard thought she must have had a hard time. "Not an easy life, huh?"

He finished the highball he'd brought from the bar and pushed his glass aside. A small serving of wine and that was it for him. He didn't want her to think he was a lush. Last night he'd had two beers. Their next date needed to be lunch with soda or coffee.

"It had its moments." Carissa scanned the menu again. "So, what should I order?"

"Well, I have to admit Raymond's right about the chowder, but the seafood bisque is a lot better. I like the red snapper with dill sauce."

"Sounds wonderful. Add a baked potato with all the trimmings and a dinner salad for me. Why don't you order for both of us?"

"White wine?"

She nodded. He gave the waiter their order and they chatted about Richard's ideas for turning the front hallway from a dark cavern into a welcoming entryway. It wasn't until they were halfway through their soups that she decided to ask a question that almost made him choke.

"Did you and Steve have some sort of disagreement?"

Richard turned his attention to his wine, swirling the liquid around and taking a swallow before answering, "Why would you think that?"

"The atmosphere got colder than my barely-heated living room right after he arrived."

Richard tried a non-committal shrug. "I don't like his attitude. He's too cocksure, and it's his way or the highway. He's been like that since he arrived in the village two years ago."

Carissa finished her soup and laid down her spoon. "He's only been in business two years? I thought he'd inherited the inn from his family. It's so popular with the locals. He said he remodeled. Is that how you two met? Were you his architect or contractor?"

" No. He hired another architect and crew from Bar Harbor." Richard felt a familiar surge of anger at the thought of the brush-off Steve Raymond had given him. "So much for his great speeches about buying local."

Carissa's blue eyes turned thoughtful. "There's been bad blood between you two ever since."

Richard nodded. "You could say that, yes. We go out of our way to avoid each other."

"Sorry," she said. "I was just curious. I didn't mean to pry. I'm sure that felt like a bit of a slap."

"Let's talk about my plans for your kitchen," he suggested as the soup bowls were removed to make room for their main courses, steaming on large white plates. The red snapper looked so delicious, Richard's good humor returned.

"I don't think that's going to work well," Carissa said.

The good humor ebbed. *Damn it*, Richard thought, resigned to a miserable evening after all. And then he saw her smiling broadly at him, a wicked gleam in her eyes.

"I'm going to be *very* preoccupied with my dinner," she said. "I'm really hungry and this looks like it needs my full attention for the next few minutes at least. You can talk to me again, oh, in about five minutes."

She laughed, and Richard was happy to join her.

CHAPTER THIRTEEN

THE FOLLOWING THURSDAY, the fog rolled in. With an insidious relentless-
ness it slid across the water and drifted over the lighthouse and keeper's
quarters, covering everything in a damp white shroud.

Carissa had spent most of the past two days either sitting cross-legged in
front of the fire, fabric spread around her, or at her sewing machine on the
dining table, which had been moved into the living room and placed in front
of the window with help from the movers. Aunt Jessica's piano had found a
new home in a local church's rec room. The room looked larger and brighter.

The days had been busy, with Richard's crew putting in overtime to
insulate the attic. With new locks and latches on every door and window,
Carissa had decided she didn't need a security system. Richard had sent
over an electrician to update the fuse box. Floodlights replaced the
meager 60 watt bulb over the garage and lit the courtyard. The only
disappointment, and it was a big one, was that a careful, methodical
search of the quarters had been fruitless in locating pattern books, notebooks or sketches of Aunt Jessica's designs.

Steve had called the day before, asking how the work was progress-
ing. Carissa was happy to report real progress, although despite
Richard's determination to talk her into a kitchen and bath remodel

before the winter settled in, she couldn't face what seemed to be an endless disruption of the peace she had been seeking at the Cove.

The project she did agree to schedule was tearing down the wall of the mudroom, moving the washer and dryer into that space, building a broom closet and adding a register to heat it. Richard had convinced her it wouldn't affect the overall footprint of the house. The bonus would be never setting foot in that creepy basement again. The spiders could have all the abandoned canning jars, rusted cans and broken chairs. They could frolic and spin webs throughout the long-abandoned coal bunker. Carissa loved that idea more than anything else Richard had suggested, particularly when sometimes, late in the evening, she swore she heard things moving around down there.

That disruptive but necessary remodeling project was on her calendar for the last week of the month. She had unpacked all her boxes and with various pieces of rearranged or relocated, she felt much more at home. She had chosen paint colors and flooring, and had purchased accent fabrics and notions from the Cove's store, which she found surprisingly well-stocked.

Carissa rubbed her aching back. Her precious embroidery, beadwork and braiding were scattered over pillows and vests, belts and scarves. Ideas kept popping into her head with such regularity she felt exhilarated for the first time since her divorce.

Matthew had no business trying to take away her right to create, she told herself. What would he do now? Hire someone to reproduce her designs? Why couldn't he have settled for compensating her for continued use of the existing ones while paying her to create more?

She left her seat and walked into the kitchen, took a bottle of water from the refrigerator and drank away the bitter taste of animosity. Matthew never settled for anything that wasn't owned exclusively by the House of Yates, she reminded herself.

Carissa stretched stiff joints, knowing she needed exercise followed by food, a hot shower and sleep. She couldn't remember the last time she had eaten a full meal after her dinner with Richard. She'd had lots of toast, peanut butter and coffee—all 4 of the mugs she had bought at the Gift Emporium were lined up beside the sink with coffee dregs in the bottom of each. An open packet of oyster crackers sat on the kitchen table along with several string cheese wrappers.

Not good, she told herself, opening a can of chicken noodle soup and dumping it into a saucepan. She nibbled on stale oyster crackers as she waited for the soup to heat. If she hadn't had mice before, she deserved them after leaving food out for days.

The soup bubbled. She tipped it into one of her aunt's oversized soup bowls. Wiping steam off the kitchen window with a dish towel, she peered through. The landscape had disappeared except for a small patch of grass outside the window. She made out the ghostly outline of the fence, wisps of white floating like wraiths between the pickets. Carissa left her soup on the table and opened the back door. Fog drifted in, chilling and wet.

She closed the door quickly. She'd have to dress warmly and watch out for possible hazards. No walking on the rocks, but around the lighthouse shouldn't be dangerous if she was careful. Making quick work of the soup, she put on her outerwear. Pulling a scarf across her nose and mouth, she stepped out the front door. The fog enveloped her only steps from the cottage. Carissa paused and listened to the silence. The ground ahead cleared.

The fog wasn't *that* bad, she decided. Striking out for the pathway along the cliff, she walked less than twenty feet before a white blanket obscured everything. She decided she should march up and down the wall between her property and the Ulsters' instead of getting lost on the headland. She turned and walked in the other direction. Several feet later, she ran into a bush.

Well, that's strange.

She didn't remember a bush there. But where was 'there?' The fog shifted again, giving her a view of several bushes. She decided she was walking in the direction of the garage. Not bad. The wall lay slightly to the right. She skirted the bush and struck out for where she thought the garage was located. After walking for what seemed far too long, she heard gravel crunch under her feet. The forecourt or the edge of the driveway leading to the track? She wasn't sure.

She paused, slightly exasperated, then started off in another direction. *Right,* she thought, *walk to the right.* She felt wet grass under her feet.

Waves crashed appallingly close-by. She stopped again. In the muffled stillness, she couldn't tell where the sound was coming from. Alarm fluttered. She pushed it away. She wasn't lost or in danger, for goodness sake. She knew her property, and she should be near the garage, not the water. Walking outside had been a stupid idea after all. She needed to locate the lighthouse and head for it, but the lighthouse was whitewashed. So was the cottage. And the garage. They all needed to be bright, neon pink. She wished the lighthouse hadn't been decommissioned. She would have welcomed its rhythmic periodic flashing right at that moment.

"Damn it!" she said aloud.

"Carissa, is that you?"

The voice, muffled as it was, she knew belonged to Steve Raymond.

"Yes. I seem to have gotten turned around. I'm not sure where I am."

"Don't move. You're close to the cliff."

"I can't be." She took a few hesitant steps forward. "I should be close to the garage and the Ulsters' wall along their property line. But I don't remember grass growing under the trees." She peered up into the whiteness. "And I don't see any trees, either."

"I'm standing with my back against the garage, so you're not over here," Steve told her.

"There are four sides to the garage," she reminded him with more sharpness than she intended.

"I realize that, Carissa. I also realize your voice isn't anywhere near as close as the other side of the building."

"You stay there. I'll come to you." She took several tentative, sliding steps. The sound of the water increased. She was standing on wet rocks. "Steve, I'm sorry. I think you're right, and I just put myself even closer to the water."

"Stay where you are and keep talking. I'll find you."

He sounded worried, which made Carissa more concerned, too. She felt hot in her coat and pulled the scarf off her face. She took a deep gulp of icy air and coughed.

"Come on," Steve encouraged. "You can do better than that. Sing if you don't want to talk."

"You don't want to hear my singing voice, trust me. What would you like me to talk about?"

"Surely you can think of something. How about what you've been doing for the last few days?"

"Well, I suppose I could describe the unpacking of my personal effects in great detail, but that might bore you."

"It might." He laughed. "How did your dinner go with dear Richard?"

"Oh, no; I'm not falling into that trap. I found out you two have major issues to iron out. I'm not going to report one side's activities to the other."

Something brushed her arm. "My, you're fast. I thought you were further away..."

The shove sent her flying, hands splayed, arms beating the air in front of her. Rocks loomed up and the water sounded horribly close. Her hands struck the jagged aperture, stone slicing through her woolen gloves. "Steve!"

He couldn't have seen her, she thought as her hands groped desperately for a hold that would steady her. Her face was hanging over the cliff, her eyes fastened on a swirling, white open space.

The fog parted momentarily.

Sheer rock walls descended into the sea below. One false move and she'd be fish-bait. Frightened beyond the ability to scream, she braced herself against the sharpness of the rock, clinging despite the pain in her hands and knees.

"Carissa, what the hell's going on? Where are you? What are you doing? I told you to keep talking so I could find you." Boots rang against rock. "Jesus Holy Christ, what are you doing there?"

Strong hands seized her by her waist and lifted her up. She turned and buried her face against the haven of Steve's chest, her hands clutching his lambswool jacket, her breath searing her throat.

"I told you to stay still."

His voice sounded desperately angry, but fear colored the edges of its roughness. Carissa relaxed her grip and saw blood on the sheepskin. Hers, no doubt, she thought as the burning sensation in her palms increased.

"You could have been killed," he chided her. "The fog around here drifts in and out until people get totally confused and turned around, like you were just now. I've heard of people getting lost in their own front yards. One man was supposed to have about gone nuts before his family rescued him."

"That doesn't sound so far-fetched right now." Carissa took her hands off his coat and checked the rips in her gloves. The cold was probably numbing the pain. Her fingers could be shredded for all she knew.

The memory of the shove came back to her. "Did you push me?" she asked, looking up at him.

His coat collar partially obscured his angular face. A wool cap covered his head. His eyes looked back steadily at her. "What are you talking about? You must have slipped."

"No, I didn't. I was standing right where you told me to wait. Someone pushed me. It was a deliberate shove, not a bump. God, I'm tired of this. If you're the one playing stupid games, I want you to tell me right now."

"What stupid games? What are you talking about?" He looked genuinely confused. "I promise you it wasn't me who pushed you. If I was trying to send you over the cliff, why are we standing here talking about it? I picked you up off the edge, remember?"

The dampness had settled over Carissa like a suffocating blanket. She decided if Steve was a prankster with a bad sense of humor, she'd rather confront him in her warm house.

"I'm going inside to have coffee and a shot of brandy." She turned in the direction she thought the lighthouse should be. "You can come, too, if you want. I'm going to try to believe it wasn't you pushing me."

"You're going the wrong way, if you're going back to the cottage."

"And you know that how?"

"I've got sonar where fog's concerned. Ask anyone in town. I'm the only one who still walks around outside when it rolls in."

"I suppose you wouldn't let something like fog inconvenience you if you've got somewhere you have to be." She hesitated. He could be right. She thought the big rock to her left was closer to the road than the lighthouse.

"And I suppose the place you think I wanted to be was where I could push you off the cliff, like I knew you were out here trying to get yourself lost."

His voice sounded muffled. Carissa realized she couldn't see him anymore. Panic fluttered in her chest. "I didn't say push me *off* the cliff." She tried to walk in the direction she thought he was and found herself standing on the track leading to the road. "I only asked if you pushed me, period."

"You were hanging over the edge of a steep drop when I found you."

She couldn't tell where his voice was coming from. The track seemed to lead in both directions, and she'd lost sight of the rock. Carissa turned in a complete circle as the fog swirled around her, growing heavier either in her imagination or reality. The feeling of panic grew and her breathing came short and fast, the whiteness of it mingling with the fog. Her face felt wet. She realized droplets of water were dripping down from her hair.

"And you were the only one around," she said, and found she'd raised her voice.

"I was, at least the only one we both know about."

He was right beside her. Carissa felt him take her arm and propel her along. She didn't believe he'd pushed her, even though she had no idea how he had gotten to the lighthouse, a good two miles from town, on foot.

"Did you really walk all this way?" she asked.

"Absolutely. You think I'd drive in this fog?"

She thought about the narrow switchback road from the Cove. "Well, no."

The light faded as they trudged across the rocky headland. Thankfully, shortly afterward her feet touched grass and the picket fence appeared.

Steve guided her to the back door. "Got a key for this?"

"Of course." She pulled out her key ring and inserted her new key into the deadbolt.

They left their boots in the mudroom. Carissa flipped on the kitchen light and peeled off her gloves. Her palms were red and her fingers cut, but not deeply. She washed them, gritting her teeth when the soap stung, patted them dry on a tea towel and put water and grounds into the coffee-maker. She told herself she had nothing to whine over. A few scrapes were nothing next to what *could* have happened.

Steve hung his coat over the back of a chair. He threw his wet hat and gloves onto one end of the small table she had brought in from the guest room. Carissa saw him looking at the scrapes and gouges still visible on the floor from where she had dragged the dining table over to block the door while she searched the house for an intruder. He didn't say anything about it, but she saw him frown.

He rubbed his hands together. "It feels good in here. Your new furnace works great." He pulled the chair with his coat over closer to the register.

"Well worth the money. I can walk around without feeling like I need my coat on. I can't understand why Aunt Jessica put up with an old oil furnace."

"Your aunt was a stubborn woman." Steve rested his elbows on the table, his chin on his folded hands.

"Stubborn, yes, but she must have known what a difference a new heating system would make. She never spent a penny on new furniture, either. Everything's the same here as when I visited as a child."

"She wasn't into spending money on herself. She drove that old car of hers into the village once a week to stock up at the Market. She bought gas infrequently and had her car serviced twice a year like clockwork, Harry Donnelly at the local service station told me when he stopped in to have a beer one time after work. I figured she was living on a fixed income." He sat back. "She stopped driving a while back and got her groceries delivered, but William said she was doing okay. It was her arthritis that was limiting her."

"My aunt had a sizeable inheritance. She invested wisely and lived off the income, according to my mother. She told me Aunt Jessica was very frugal with her spending and was never hurting for money." Carissa worried her bottom lip as she mulled over why her aunt had never said she was having trouble with her mobility. "She used to come to New York twice a year and stay with me. That stopped after my marriage. She knew my life was very busy. She said she didn't want to interfere. I should have asked her more questions when I called. I shouldn't have been so self-centered. I never knew anything was wrong."

"You can't blame yourself, Carissa. Jessica was one tough, independent lady. She would never have asked you for help. She never even had a regular housekeeper."

"It wasn't dirty when I arrived."

"That's because William got a cleaning company in here. They got everything spruced up and put dust covers over the furniture."

"Oh, well that explains a lot."

Did they throw out all her patterns while tidying up? OMG.

"Exactly how bad *was* her arthritis?" She asked.

"You'll have to ask William. He should be back in a couple more days."

When she placed their coffee on the table, Steve opened the bourbon and held it over her mug.

"Tell me when." He tipped the bottle and a good amount landed in the coffee.

"That's enough." She dumped in two spoonfuls of sugar and stirred vigorously, her thoughts as turbulent as the mini whirlpool inside her mug.

Steve put the top back on the bottle without adding any liquor to his own coffee. He sipped and nodded appreciatively. "Good stuff. That'll take the edge off."

"How long were you out there before you said something to me?"

"Not long. I heard you walking around when I got here. I thought I'd better check on you since I hadn't seen you the last couple of days. The fog rolled in when I was halfway here. You might have fallen off the cliff if I'd turned back."

"Maybe you should call the inn and let them know you're here. They might be worried."

"That'd be handing the town gossips a juicy piece to chew on for weeks."

"Why?"

"Me, being trapped up here with an attractive young woman?" He burst out laughing.

"Trapped?" She didn't like the sound of the word. But when she glanced out the window, waning light barely illuminated the white blanket outside. She couldn't expect him to walk back to the village through that. What if he got lost, regardless of his 'sonar,' and fell over the cliff? Or, taking a less dramatic approach, what if he tripped and fell somewhere between the lighthouse and the road? He'd be in serious trouble.

"You're going to have to stay here." She tried not to sound as uneasy as she felt. "You've got to let someone know you're safe. It doesn't need to be the entire village. I don't want anyone gossiping about me, either."

She'd spent far too many hours trapped in her apartment while the paparazzi lurked on the sidewalk, hopeful they'd catch her with someone other than Matthew or her attorney.

She thought about the possible consequences to Steve, as well as herself, if Sally Mainard, for instance, heard her boyfriend had spent the night with Carissa Yates, regardless of whether it was in separate rooms. She finished her coffee and took the refill Steve offered her, laced with a more than generous splash of bourbon.

He leaned back in his chair, looking casually at home in his surroundings, like this was a familiar scenario for him—drinking laced coffee in Jessica Malloy's kitchen. Well, his wasn't laced, Carissa corrected herself, but still...

"Maybe I'll walk over to the Ulsters' and throw myself on their mercy" he said. "After all, you accused me of trying to throw you over a cliff."

"I didn't *accuse* you."

His eyebrows rose.

"Well, not really. Maybe it sounded like that at the time. But trying to stay with the Ulsters? I think not. You'd be lucky if Blake Ulster let you sleep in the wood shed. I think he's abusing Mai Ling, and he's a very jealous and suspicious man. He'd probably come out and hack you to death in the middle of the night. He can split a log like he's chopping through butter."

"Abusing how?" The playful look had gone from Steve's face.

"Physically. She looked frightened the first day I walked over to introduce myself. Then she came over here with a big bruise on her arm. And when she thought Blake was knocking on my door instead of the movers with my boxes, she bolted. She thought he'd come home early."

"So he checks on her to see what she's doing while he's gone. That's not cool. But hitting her? Blake's older and maybe jealous and insecure but I've never heard about him being violent, and I hear a lot at the inn. Maybe she fell and hit her arm on something."

Carissa's estimation of Steve Raymond's character slipped a notch. "I'm disappointed," she told him. "I thought you were more than just a typical man." She folded her arms and glared at him.

He shook his head. "I'm not trying to defend anyone, Carissa. I'm trying to be fair. You've got no proof Blake's abusing his wife. Mai Ling's shy. She likes to stay home and send Blake to do all the errands. He tries to get her to socialize more, but her English is poor and her culture's so different. Whenever she's come to any event at the Cove she keeps to herself and they leave early."

Carissa thumped her hand on the table. "What a crock. She's the ideal victim: isolated far from family and at her husband's mercy. She told me he takes her shopping list and leaves her behind. He won't take her to visit her family, and she doesn't drive. Could she take a bus into the village? Even if she could, it's a long walk to the road and she wears thin dresses and sandals. She came over here without a coat. I don't even know if she owns anything warmer. I bet she doesn't. He's got her right where he wants her."

"So, perhaps he was the one who pushed you? Since you've decided you're living next door to a monster, he'd be a much better candidate than me."

Carissa swept up the mugs. "You'd better get going if you want to avoid walking over to the Ulsters' home in the dark. Maybe Blake's got a gun and will shoot you by mistake, thinking you're an intruder." She put the mugs in the sink and turned off the coffeemaker before looking at him again.

"Sarcasm doesn't sit well on you." He got up. "You're really jumpy and short-tempered today. I think there's more going on here than getting lost on the clifftop and thinking a strong wind was a pair of hands. What else has happened to you?"

"Nothing." She vowed she wouldn't tell him if he was the last man on earth and Dracula was hanging upside down in her basement.

"Okay. If you change your mind, you know where to reach me. And try to think kinder thoughts about Blake Ulster. He's had a hard life. Mai Ling's been the only bright spark in it, and I've never seen him lay a hand on her, although I will admit I haven't seen much of her since he brought her to the Cove."

Carissa shrugged, unwilling to tell him what she really thought about his powers of observation. "So, you're going to spend the night with the Ulsters?"

He was already walking toward the front door. "Nah. I'm heading back to the Cove."

"Steve, it's two miles."

As she followed him, her anger dissipated. She knew she'd been uncharacteristically rude and shrewish. He flipped on the porch light and opened the front door. A swirl of fog entered the hallway. Outside, a thick layer of white obscured everything. He'd die out there, and she'd be responsible.

She laid her hand on his upper arm as he stepped outside. "Please stay here. Call the inn and tell them where you are. You can sleep in the guest room."

The fog already partially enveloped him. He towered over her when he came back into the hallway. He closed the door quietly and followed her into the living room, where he pulled out his cell and stared at the screen. "No service."

"You can use my landline." She pointed to Aunt Jessica's little desk, still stuffed with cards, envelopes and several colors and patterns of notepaper.

She left him in the living room and started washing dishes. As she rinsed the carafe, she heard the low murmur of his voice. It sounded so comforting, that male voice in the keeper's quarters. She realized she had begun to feel lonely again now the flurry of moving was over.

"Carissa?" Steve's voice held a note of disquiet. "I think you'd better come in here."

"Okay." Drying her hands on a towel, she walked into the living room.

Steve was standing beside the table under the window. "Come over here."

She walked around the back of the couch. On the floor was her beloved piece of scrimshaw, smashed to pieces. Steve pointed toward the fireplace. Smoldering on top of the logs were the results of two days and nights of work. All her needlework had been thrown onto the fire.

CHAPTER FOURTEEN

VIRGINIA GREELEY PUSHED OPEN the door to Burton's General Store. Familiar aromas of spices and fresh bread welcomed her. Nancy Burton bustled out from behind the grill fronting her little post office as the shop's bell tinkled. The bell was an unnecessary warning, Virginia thought. The only occupant of Treacher's Cove with better eyes and ears than Nancy was Virginia's beloved tabby cat, Hubert.

"'Morning, Virginia."

Nancy's horn-rimmed glasses caught the light from the door. Virginia knew behind those lenses Nancy was taking in every detail of her customer's clothing from Virginia's thick-soled Oxford shoes to her hand-knitted red scarf and matching hat.

"Good morning, Nancy." Her friend's scrutiny made Virginia's back stiffen.

"New accessories?" Nancy leaned against the narrow counter in front of her little postal center. "Never thought I'd see you in red. Trying to attract the attention of our newest congregation member?"

"Carissa Yates?" Virginia placed her shopping carrier beside a table prominently displaying locally-made jams and jellies. "Why would I do that?"

"Not the Yates girl." Nancy snorted. "Mr. Walter Barnes."

"That octogenarian?" Virginia laughed outright. Unfortunately, she thought she sounded a little breathless. Nancy would catch that slip.

She did.

"He's only seventy-eight and very spry." Nancy patted her tightly-permed chestnut hair.

Virginia noted the shade had darkened since she last saw Nancy less than a week ago.

"I wouldn't mind attracting his attention myself." Nancy lifted her chin.

"Nancy, you and I have stayed single all our lives. Why in the world would you want to take on a husband now? The man might have a heart attack and die, or end up an invalid. Then you'd be spending all your time and life-savings supporting him."

Nancy pouted, doing her best to look offended, but Virginia knew the Cove's postmistress was as careful about her family inheritance as Virginia was about her own. Longtime friends and sometime antago-nists, they had grown up on the same street, attended the same schools, nursed their parents through their last illnesses and buried them in the same cemetery. Despite their differences, they were from the same thrifty stock, Virginia reassured herself.

"Mr. Barnes took me to the Brickley House Tea Room yesterday. He was the quintessential gentleman." Nancy's long, pointed nose rose defiantly.

Virginia tried unsuccessfully to keep her expression neutral. Her eyebrows rose all by themselves, as though pulled by invisible strings. "We...ell," was all she could manage.

Nancy smiled, defiant and smug. "He's invited me out to lunch after church next Sunday. I asked him to sit in my pew, and he accepted."

Unable to think of anything charitable to say, Virginia felt a change of subject was in order. She opened her purse and searched for her shop-ping list. "Ah, here it is." She made a big production out of the discovery, waving the neatly folded list in the air. "I'd like three cans of that cat food Hubert adores, a five-pound bag of flour and some of those little imported cookies I bought last week."

"Baking?" Nancy bustled about, fetching the items.

"I was planning to make a cake for the church social."

Virginia placed her purchases in the shopping carrier while Nancy double-checked the scanner on a pad. She maintained her brain was more reliable than the new cash register she'd had to purchase when the till wouldn't open on the decrepit old one her father had purchased during Nancy's girlhood.

"The brain needs daily exercise," Nancy told anyone who dared to question her distrust. She refused to keep tape in the register and never gave receipts, despite complaints from the newer Cove residents. She'd taken proprietorship of the store over thirty years ago, and she wasn't changing her ways in the name of what she called 'doubtful progress.'

"So, what do you think of our other new neighbor?" Nancy asked.

"Who?" The zipper on Virginia's shopping carrier had caught on a stray thread hanging from one of her coat buttons. Virginia pulled a little too hard. The zipper's teeth loosened, and her button popped off, rolling under the display table.

"Carissa Yates, of course. I must say, I find it scandalous she didn't attend church last Sunday."

Virginia thought about getting down on her hands and knees to retrieve the button, but the display looked precarious, and her knees were beginning to complain whenever she knelt to scrub the inside of her bathtub. She'd sew on a replacement at home. She always kept the spare buttons when she bought a new coat. But when had that been? She took out her wallet. Years, she thought. She might very well have to settle for an odd button.

She turned her attention back to the zipper. If she loosened any more teeth, she would have to replace the whole thing, and she'd ordered it through a catalogue she had unfortunately thrown away. Like so many other businesses, the company had stopped sending out catalogues and gone online soon after Virginia's rash decision to recycle. Virginia didn't own a computer, thought the internet was the Devil's spawn, or close to it, and didn't plan to share her private information with the hackers she had heard were stealing everyone else's.

She'd have to take her stuck zipper to Percival Huddleston. He would know how to fix it, just as he fixed so many other problems in Treacher's Cove, she thought, pulling out $20. She had voted for him in the last election and helped bring him into his second term as

Mayor, so he'd better help her, or he couldn't count on her vote the next time.

"Look at you with a crisp new bill." Nancy took the money and made change with some dirty old notes that looked like she had used them to clean out a trash can.

"Perhaps you should call on Carissa Yates and invite her to join the congregation," Virginia snapped, annoyed with everything that had happened since she arrived in Nancy's store.

"I'm not walking two miles in this weather." Nancy looked outraged.

"You should have learned to drive a car."

"I've always had plenty of people willing to give me a ride anywhere I want to go."

"Then ask one of those people for a ride to the lighthouse. That poor girl needs to be welcomed into the community. It's isolated up at Bennett Point. Think of poor Jessica. She was lying at the bottom of those stairs an entire day before anyone found her."

"Yes, and you know who was the first person to find her, don't you?" Nancy's chin tipped up and the look she gave Virginia down her long nose was triumphant. She didn't wait for a response. "William Dansinger, that's who."

"I know that, Nancy. Everyone knows that. He was her attorney, after all."

"And a lot more, Virginia. Why the man was heartbroken. He still hasn't recovered, and his poor wife..."

"Patsy's always been resilient, even though she's an invalid. A pillar of strength through the whole horrible affair."

"Yes, that's what he was having. An affair. Forty years of it. Patsy *must* have known."

"Maybe she did." Virginia sometimes enjoyed gossip sessions with Nancy. Maybe more than sometimes, if she really admitted it. But not that day. Everything Nancy said was grating on her nerves. She reluctantly folded the dirty bills and put them into her wallet.

"Then why didn't she deliver an ultimatum to her husband to make him stop seeing Jessica?"

"Because she's a cripple, Nancy. William never forgave himself for backing his car over her in the driveway. Then there was the Multiple Sclerosis."

Nancy snorted in disgust. "He probably ran over her purposely. He hated her."

"He didn't. You made that part up. You and your morbid desire to find ulterior motives in everything. This isn't Cabot Cove, and you're not Jessica Fletcher." Virginia carefully placed dirty old coins in amongst the shiny new ones she had picked up at the bank. No debit cards for her. She'd heard way too much about the evils of online banking. She was a cash-only customer. "I'll see you at church," she told Nancy.

"You're in a rush."

"I need to get home. Hubert's waiting for breakfast, and I've got to start baking."

"Walter is quite fond of poppy-seed cake, so I hear. That's what *I'm* taking the church social." Nancy's smile turned into a wry smirk, but she winked.

Virginia wanted to stay in a huff, but failed. She laughed and waved goodbye as she dragged her carrier out the door. Nancy Burton might be annoying but she never failed to amuse.

The cold air felt refreshing, even with the persistent fog. Virginia pulled her red scarf across her nose and headed home, making a slight detour. She didn't want to be seen walking past Walter Barnes' cottage by Nancy or anyone else with whom Nancy shared her little tales of intrigue.

Virginia turned off the main street leading to the harbor and climbed the hill toward her cottage. The carrier hung heavy behind her and the wind blew at her back. She trudged along, watching the homes she passed to keep her mind off the strain on her arm. She knew she should have driven down to pick up the flour, but her clothes were beginning to feel tight, and she needed the exercise.

Mrs. Eldridge's bed and breakfast looked imposing with the faux Greek columns she'd added the previous spring to augment its elegant white façade and wide porch overlooking the village hub. The porch chairs sat vacant, facing the grayness of the harbor. Behind well-tended gardens lay the Benning house, its windows filled with cream lace curtains. Imported from France, Nancy had told her. Very expensive. Mrs. Benning had picked up the packages from the post office.

As Virginia passed by, she noted everyone seemed to be staying inside that morning. Mr. Chesney wasn't sweeping away dead leaves that had fallen from the maple overhanging the front walkway, Mrs. Thorndike's car still sat in the driveway, the garage door closed. Virginia passed no one and no cars came up the hill as she continued on, her breath becoming more labored. At the junction of Chestnut Street and Harbor View, she paused to rest. Her cottage stood close to the top of the hill. When she was young it had seemed the ideal location. Now she was 68, and the hill seemed to have become higher and steeper with each passing year.

A charcoal Lexus passed her. Virginia caught a glimpse of two people in the car. She saw a New York State plate on the back. Must be Carissa Yates, she decided. She turned to watch the vehicle. It stopped near the Benning house and the front passenger door opened.

Out stepped Steve Raymond. Virginia recognized his height, his broad-shouldered build and the old sheepskin jacket immediately. Now, there was something to ponder. What was Steve Raymond doing in Carissa Yates' car at nine o'clock in the morning? Virginia squinted, wishing her eyesight wasn't failing as well as her wind.

Steve looked angry. He thumped his fist on the roof of the car, then leaned down to speak through the open door. When he stopped to listen, he shook his head vehemently.

Brake lights at the back of the Lexus faded as he closed the door and moved away. He watched the car glide down the hill before shoving his hands into his pockets and striding off toward the harbor, head lowered and jacket collar pulled up. Whether that was because he was trying to shield himself from the wind or hide his angry expression, Virginia couldn't tell.

Her quarrel with Nancy temporarily forgotten, she summoned the last of her energy to tackle what remained of the hill. Thankful to be home, she opened her front gate and gulped in air, trying to gather the effort needed to drag the shopping carrier up the two steps into the cottage. Climbing roses no longer bloomed on the trellis above her head. Instead, dry and faded leaves rustled with the gusting wind. Virginia promised herself she'd cut them back later that afternoon, if she had the energy after her baking. She hurried along the walkway, bumped the carrier into the house and pulled off her hat, scarf and gloves. Leaving her Oxfords on the doormat, she headed for the phone to tell Nancy what she'd seen.

Then she remembered Nancy's remark about the poppy seed cake and the offer to seat Mr. Barnes in her pew. Virginia reversed her steps, dragging the carrier into the kitchen. She filled and plugged in her electric kettle. Let Nancy Burton find her own news. By the time she knew anything about Steve Raymond's argument with Carissa Yates, or about Carissa giving him a ride, that news would be old.

Virginia had no doubt she would find out something even better about them shortly. She thought Sally Mainard was probably going to be one angry woman very soon, and Sally's temper was legendary. She'd grown up in the Cove, left it right after high school to pursue a business degree, and suddenly and unexpectedly returned as a sculptor. Shortly after opening her gift shop, Sally had started her driftwood art, which had kept her living comfortably right through the winter, especially now she could continue working and shipping UPS, instead of waiting for the tourist season to bring customers.

Virginia unpacked the carrier and selected a can of chicken livers for Hubert. While he purred contentedly and nibbled his delicacy, she sipped a robust cup of Irish Breakfast and ate three of the special imported cookies she loved. There was trouble afoot in Treacher's Cove, she thought with more relish even than she had eaten the cookies. She allowed herself one more cookie, which she dunked in her tea to prolong the pleasure after her strenuous walk.

Maybe she should try a dose of her own advice and pay a neighborly visit to the lighthouse. It was about time someone other than the local innkeeper, himself an outsider, welcomed Carissa Yates to the Cove.

CHAPTER FIFTEEN

WARM SCENTS of apple and cinnamon welcomed William Dansinger home from his trip. Leaving his bags in the living room, he followed the aroma into the kitchen. Their housekeeper, Mrs. Dodds had left a loaf of Patsy's favorite apple twist bread cooling on a wire rack. He made coffee and got out a tray, onto which he placed a slice of the bread, pats of butter and two cups of coffee. Tucking the present he had bought Patsy under his arm, he carried the tray upstairs.

Patsy had resisted all attempts to move her bedroom downstairs into the formal living room that hadn't been used since she could no longer play hostess. Patsy and William had been occupying separate but adjacent bedrooms for thirty years, and she wanted to keep it that way. Whenever he tried broaching the subject, she would tell him in a quavering voice that sleeping a floor away would make her nervous, even if he put in an intercom.

William wondered whether his wife liked making him climb stairs every time she rang her little bell. She had nixed installing an elevator or a stair lift, breaking into tears and hyperventilating. William's task, if Patsy felt she was up to it, was to carry her down in the morning to sit on the terrace outside and carry her back up after she had her lunch. Patsy's schedule had remained unchanged as they grew older. Habits weren't to be broken, she said, even for William's convenience, which made him angry until she reminded him, as she so frequently did, that she wouldn't be in a wheelchair if he hadn't backed over her legs with his car.

William balanced the tray on one hip and cracked open Patsy's door. He didn't want to startle her, but he did want to surprise her. He peered inside. She appeared to be asleep, her pale strawberry-blonde hair spread out across the pillow. Her face had the translucency of marble in the whiteness of the fog-shrouded morning. William sighed deeply. So many years; so many regrets. He set the tray on a low table beside the bay window. Taking the present with him, he sat carefully on the edge of the bed.

"Patsy," he whispered, touching her arm tentatively. "Patsy, dear, wake up."

She stirred, murmured, and wrinkled her nose.

"Patsy, it's William."

Pale blue eyes opened. The ghost of a smile lifted the corners of her mouth. "William."

Her voice, sultry and filled with sleep, stirred a cord of remembrance deep inside him. Patsy, standing amidst the roses in her parents' garden, a basket of blooms in one hand. The ribbons of her straw hat had come loose and were tangled in her fiery red hair. His heart contracted. Those bittersweet memories became increasingly rare as Patsy's care and her growing demands erased them. Filled with sadness, he bent to kiss her cheek.

"Hello, dear."

"I must have drifted off." She looked over at the window. "The fog always makes me sleepy. Did you stay overnight in Bangor?"

"Ellsworth. The weather got too bad to continue driving. I called Mrs. Dodds. She didn't tell you?"

"She probably did. I took a sleeping pill last night, so I didn't wake for breakfast." She sniffed. "Do I smell apple twist?"

"You do. She baked you a treat to make up for the missed meal." He pointed to the tray. "I made coffee."

Patsy sat up. "Oh, good. I'm hungry."

William brought Patsy's coffee and bread over. "I thought several times while driving that I was all kinds of a fool for trying to come home early. It was a rough trip."

Patsy nodded, preoccupied with spreading butter on her bread. "Well, you made it." A shaft of sunlight struck the knife. "Look at that, William. The fog's clearing." She glanced at the window and squinted. "Can you tilt the blind? That's too bright."

He muted the light down to where Patsy declared she felt comfortable, which plunged the room into semi-darkness. It annoyed him that she wanted to live in what he termed a twilight zone.

"How about getting out of bed?" He forced enthusiasm into his voice. "You can bundle up and sit on the terrace. You always enjoy watching the water when the fog's drifting around. If you get too cold, I'll move you to the sunroom."

"I was alone last night," Patsy reproached.

"I know, and I'm sorry. I couldn't take an earlier flight. Mine was one of the last to land before they shut the airport. By the time I reached Ellsworth, I couldn't see anything beyond the hood of the car. Conditions were bad this morning, too. Why didn't you ask Mrs. Dodds to stay?"

"She offered, but she'd already told me she's hosting her grandson's birthday party later today. I insisted I would be fine, which I was. She thanked me when she came this morning. She'd been able to get her baking done. She's gone to do her marketing before putting up decorations at home. The party isn't until five o'clock, so she'll still come back here for a couple of hours this afternoon. Her daughter and son-in-law have a farm to take care of, so she always hosts the family celebrations."

"But they don't do any of the preparations? If I was Mrs. Dodds I'd ask them to come early and help her."

"She said they can't afford to hire help, so they have to take care of their animals. Cows, pigs, chickens. It sounds like a lot of work." Patsy shook her head. "I would never have married a farmer."

"I'm sure you wouldn't."

William tried to keep the sarcasm out of his voice. He wanted to add that she could never have gotten up early enough to cook breakfast before sun-up, let alone milk a cow. He decided he'd better change the subject before he said something Patsy would make him regret.

"Mrs. Dodds must have had a rough trip here this morning, the way the fog gathers in the bay."

"She came earlier than usual. Her husband brought her and picked her up. He's got that big truck. She knew I needed her." Patsy's tone was dismissive.

"I'll give her a bonus for doing that." William felt far more charitable toward their housekeeper than his wife that day. He drank his coffee standing up. "Patsy, I worry about a fire. I can't always be here overnight."

"I'm not moving downstairs. I won't have a nurse invading my privacy and having access to my home, and you know how anxious I get when you start talking about that elevator..."

She began panting. Her coffee spilled onto the comforter. William rushed over and took away the remains of her breakfast. He brought a towel from the bathroom and tried to soak up the coffee.

"It's ruined," Patsy complained. "My favorite comforter."

"I'll send it to the cleaners. You can use mine in the meantime."

"I don't want to use yours. I'll have to order a new one. I don't like stains." She pouted. Her breathing had normalized. She settled back onto the pillows and gazed at the window. "You couldn't give me a view like I have now anywhere downstairs."

William stifled a sigh. They'd had an extra set of windows installed beneath the original ones, giving Patsy a panoramic observation deck to the outside that she rarely used, since she kept the bottom set of blinds closed most of the time. But pointing that out had gotten him nowhere in the past. She had told him she wanted the option of seeing the outside world whenever she wanted to, instead of whenever he had the time and the inclination to take her downstairs, like he wasn't already doing that pretty much daily. He suddenly felt incredibly tired and defeated. He sat back down beside her.

"You'll just have to give up this silly plan to move me away from you and cater to my stubbornness." She smiled and touched cool fingers to his cheek. "I want to be right here, in the next room to yours; as I've been for the last thirty years, dear."

William tried not to let her see or feel his tension. He handed her the present. "Why don't you unwrap your gift?"

She smiled at him and tore off the wrapping paper. She looked at the label on the box. "Oh, how sweet of you—Bloomie's. I haven't been there in years."

"I know. You should come to New York with me next time. I'll stay a couple of extra days so you can shop at Bloomingdale's or anywhere else you'd like. We could take in a show."

Patsy shook her head. "I appreciate the offer, but I don't feel up to it. I'm finding even going downstairs a chore these days." She opened the box and took out a scarf and gloves. "They're lovely, William. Are you trying to suggest I get out more?"

"Yes. You need the air. You've spent more time in your bed these past couple of months than ever before. Lying in bed will make you weaker." He pushed her plate back toward her. "You should eat the bread Mrs. Dodds baked for you. It smells delicious."

"And where's *your* slice?" Patsy tore the bread in half. "You eat one piece, and I'll eat the other. Mrs. Dodds must be very worried about me to go to all this trouble. She's been taking on too much lately. She's not getting any younger. Sometimes I think taking care of me and this house and then cooking on top of that is too much for her."

"Don't tell *her* that. She expects to be taking care of you until she drops dead at the kitchen sink."

"William! What a morbid thing to say." Patsy shivered. "Would you get my blue bed jacket? It's in the top right hand drawer of the chest."

William opened the drawer, filled to the top with delicate nightwear. Three more drawers below held many more nightgowns, Peignoirs and bed jackets. Patsy rarely got dressed anymore. She usually wore a fleece robe and pajamas under her coat when she sat outside.

Suddenly, a yearning for Jessica's company almost overwhelmed him. His fingers unconsciously sank into lace and satin nightdresses and wispy wool bed jackets. He contrasted his life now with those times he had walked with Jessica on the headland near the lighthouse, their arms linked, their faces held defiantly toward the gusting wind.

Memories swept through him: Jessica, young and full of life and love, laughing as she skipped from rock to rock to search tide pools around the edges of the small beach beneath Penwithen, her family home. Visions of an older Jessica in the tiny garden beside her lighthouse, paintbrush in hand, telling him to keep still as she put the finishing touches to his portrait. Her eyes had been incredibly warm and bright as she scolded him for his impatience with sitting completely still for long periods.

"William? What's wrong, dear?"

Patsy's voice broke into his reverie. The memories receded, leaving pain that made him clutch his wife's bed jacket so hard, pain shot through his fingers. He took out the jacket and closed the drawer before turning to her with what he knew must be a bleak smile. "Nothing's wrong. You really should sit outside today. The fog's backing off, and you haven't been out while I was away."

Patsy looked at the weak sunshine trying to peek between the slats of the blinds. "Well," she said slowly. Her eyebrows drew toward each other, as though she was making a monumental decision. "Perhaps I'll go outside for an hour after lunch, when the dampness is gone."

"How about an hour *before* lunch, instead. The air may help whet your appetite." He pointed to the plate on her lap. "You've barely touched your half of the bread."

"I'll nibble again in a while. After my comforter got ruined, so did my appetite." She pouted again and looked down at the offending stain.

William's anger threatened to surge. Usually, he tolerated Patsy's complaints, but after the harrowing drive that morning, he had very little patience left.

"I need my jacket, dear." Patsy held out delicate white arms.

On the third finger of her left hand, the wedding band and diamond engagement ring reminded William of the folly he had committed so many years before. A folly he had learned to live with over almost four decades. He should have married Jessica.

He helped Patsy into the jacket. "I'm going to work in my office for a while. I'll be up to take you outside in an hour."

He took the cups and tray back to the kitchen. After pouring himself a second cup of coffee, he turned off the coffee maker and cleaned it meticulously. Patsy's little bell tinkled overhead. William wiped his hands and walked back upstairs. His back was bothering him, a reminder of the injury he had suffered during the Vietnam War. Patsy had been so vibrant in those days. He vividly remembered her laughter and spontaneity the day before he left. Two months later he was back in the States at Walter Reed Army Hospital. A chopper crash had resulted in six weeks of bedrest and pain that would most certainly remain with him for the rest of his life.

In his weakened state, it had been easy for Patsy to convince him Jessica had forgotten him. He didn't know she had joined the Peace Corps after he left. He only knew he hadn't heard from her. But there was Patsy, rushing to his side and waiting on him hand and foot when he arrived home. She had taken off her clothes and climbed into bed with him one afternoon, while his parents were at a wedding he didn't feel up to attending. He'd felt a lot better after a couple of hours with her, but not so well a month later, when Patsy announced she was pregnant. They'd married hastily, and he'd regretted it ever since.

He walked slowly down the long hallway back to Patsy's room. Telling Jessica on her return that he and Patsy were married had been the hardest thing he'd ever done. The anguish on her face had devastated him. In that moment, he realized he had thrown away the best and brightest part of himself.

He had paid for his mistake ever since. There was no child. Patsy had cried and told him she had miscarried. Their mutual sorrow had sustained them through their second year of marriage, when a chance remark to an inebriated company doctor at one of the law firm's cocktail parties resulted in him finding out Patsy was not only sterile, she always had been.

By then, she had been diagnosed with Multiple Sclerosis. He couldn't leave her—he was trapped. Her father had passed away shortly after their wedding, and her mother was riddled with arthritis. Despite Patsy's deception, and despite his realization that he had made a terrible mistake, he did the honorable thing and stayed with her.

Somehow, they had both learned to make the best of the situation. The charade of the perfect marriage was played so well, so many times, they came to believe it themselves. Many of their friends had far from satisfying relationships. A few had divorced. William refused to take the easy way out. Patsy depended on him and Jessica had fled to England after finding a job with the State Department. She remained overseas for ten years.

It took him a month to pluck up the courage to visit her after she finally returned to the Bennett Point Light and Treacher's Cove. When he did knock at her door, she invited him in, made them both a stiff drink and took him to bed. In her arms, he found the strength to go on. She understood both his anguish and his guilt over betraying Patsy, while comforting him with the knowledge that she had never wanted marriage. She liked her independence too much. When she tired of him, she sent him home. When she wanted him badly, she called him at his office and he'd stop by on his way home, sometimes to talk, sometimes to make love.

Once a week, they had a standing date. Patsy never called him at work, so he'd leave after a conspicuous lunch at The Fisherman's Rest, make a detour to pick up flowers in Whitstead and spend the rest of the afternoon with Jessica. She gave herself and her love freely, without question. She had no inhibitions, unlike Patsy, who once the ring was on her finger became colder than an arctic wind in January.

William pushed open Patsy's door. "What's wrong?"

He hoped his voice didn't betray his disturbed frame of mind. He had tried so hard to resign himself to Jessica's death. Finding her at the foot of the lighthouse steps had been the hardest thing he'd ever had to bear. Much harder than his experiences in the army or his marriage to Patsy.

"I wondered if you could help me bathe, since Mrs. Dodds had to leave so early."

William bit back his annoyance. He paid Mrs. Dodds handsomely for taking on additional responsibilities. That included Patsy's bath. He stifled a sigh and took off his jacket. "Very well, dear."

He turned on the water and carried her in to sit on the tub seat. She hated the wheelchair, only sitting in it for Mrs. Dodds to take her into the bathroom twice a week. Otherwise, she used a bedside commode William had the misfortune to empty. He had to bathe Patsy completely. Her assistance consisted of clinging to the rail on one side of the tub seat and bending forward slightly while he washed her back. When they finished, William's shirtsleeves were wet and so were his pants. He dried her and carried her back to bed. Wrapped in a voluminous white towel, she looked pale, fragile and old beyond her years.

"I'd like the pink flannel pajamas and matching fluffy pink bed jacket," she said, waving toward the chest of drawers. "If you're going to insist I sit outside, I need to be dressed for the weather."

"I didn't insist you sit out there when you've just had a bath," William said. He fetched her clothes and dressed her, bending on one knee as he slipped a pair of fluffy pink house shoes over her pink footies. His back ached, dull and wretched. She knew how bending and lifting aggravated it.

Patsy smiled and patted his cheek. "You made me *want* to sit out there." She placed an arm around his neck. "I'm ready."

William picked her up. Light and fragile as she looked, by the time he had walked down the hallway and the stairs, she felt as though she weighed at least two hundred pounds. He fetched her coat, scarf, gloves and hat from the hall closet and dressed her. He picked her up yet again and took her outside to her chaise, brought out two blankets, one to wrap her in and one to drape over her shoulders as she faced the ocean.

"That's wonderful, dear." She graced him with a delicate, lady-like smile. "It really is a little chilly, though." She shivered.

William wasn't moving her again. "Your body will adjust in a moment," he told her, straightening up and involuntarily clutching his back as a spasm rippled through him.

"Is your back troubling you again?" Patsy took a pair of sunglasses from her pocket and perched them on the end of her nose. Behind the lenses, pale eyes regarded him without a trace of sympathy.

"A little twinge." He forced himself to take his hand off the rippling spasm shooting from the base of his spine clear up to his neck. He turned away from her. "I'm going to work in my study."

"I need my bell," she told him. "I forgot it upstairs. You won't hear me from the other side of the house."

William reluctantly trudged back up the stairs. The bathroom was a mess. Mrs. Dodds would have to clean it up. She knew she needed to come back at 1:30 PM, party or no party. He took the bell to Patsy and found her dozing in watery sunlight. He placed the bell on the table beside her chair, taking care not to let the clapper touch any part of the inside.

There were several things he needed to do, including calling Carissa Yates and making an appointment to go over her inheritance. He crept inside and closed the door. He had barely reached the study when the bell tinkled.

Exasperated, he returned to the patio.

"My throat is quite parched, William. I really need something to drink." Patsy removed her glasses and smiled sweetly at him.

"Hot or cold?" He tried desperately to keep contempt out of his tone.

"Hot, I think." She shivered again, but it looked forced.

"I'll get you some coffee." He thought there was probably enough left in the carafe to be warmed in the microwave.

"I'd prefer hot chocolate." She smiled again, her eyes beguiling.

"Fine." He went inside and closed the door. The bell tinkled. He snapped the door back open. "What, Patsy?"

"I think I'd like another piece of my bread, too. Warmed."

"Very well."

He started the chocolate and sliced off a paper-thin piece of bread. The phone rang and the answering machine picked up: *"This is Mrs. Dodds. I can't make it back this afternoon. I slipped and fell in the Market. My ankle's all swollen. I got it checked by the doctor and an X-Ray. Nothing's broken, but he wants me to stay off it today and go back to see him tomorrow if it's no better. I may need several days off. I'm very sorry, Mr. Dansinger."*

The message ended. So did William's hope for an afternoon away from Patsy.

The bell tinkled again on the patio. William threw the bread knife into the sink and clenched his teeth. He was an unpaid servant for Patsy, who seemed to think he had nothing better to do than cater to her every whim.

"Who called, dear?" She asked when he brought her apple twist bread to the patio.

"Some salesman."

"Mrs. Dodds hasn't called to say when she's coming back."

"I expect she's still preparing for the party." William suddenly felt a sense of calm. "I'll make you a sandwich, in case she's delayed."

"How sweet." Patsy gathered the blanket closer around her and nibbled at her bread. "Perhaps I can take a little nap after I eat."

"That would be an excellent idea."

"I'm keeping you from your work, aren't I?" Again, she gave him a beguiling look.

"Not a problem. I'll get your chocolate. Do you want a ham and cheese sandwich? I know it's your favorite."

"That would be lovely, dear."

Back inside, he took two of his painkillers. When he placed the pill bottle back on the shelf, Patsy's sleeping pills fell down. William picked up the bottle and stared at it. She had said she wanted to take a little nap. He could make sure she took it, and he wouldn't have to listen to that damned bell anymore, either.

Crushing two pills, he added them to the chocolate and threw in two heaping spoonfuls of sugar to disguise the taste. He made her ham and cheese sandwich, placed everything on a tray and then hesitated. Patsy frequently took two sleeping pills. He crushed two more, stirred the chocolate vigorously, and added another teaspoon of sugar. Then he thought again. What if she didn't drink the whole cup? He crushed another one and added it with two more teaspoons of sugar. He took a small sip to test the flavor. He thought it tasted fine. She'd never know. He brought the meal onto the deck.

"Thank you, dear." Patsy took the cup and sipped. Her mouth wrinkled. "This is awfully sweet, William."

"It's a new brand Mrs. Dodds bought."

"New brand? I don't remember her mentioning anything about it. What's the name of it?"

"I don't remember. Patsy, I really have to get some work done."

"Oh, very well." She pouted, but let him get inside and shut the door. He leaned against the side of it and watched her sip the drink. He hoped she wouldn't set it aside like the bread. The wind picked up and pushed back the remaining fog. Patsy took several more sips.

William cleaned up the dishes and put up the pills. It began to spatter with rain. He cleaned up the bathroom. When the house looked spotless, he picked up his attaché case. He could see Patsy out on the patio, the wind blowing the ends of the blanket around her shoulders, her head on her chest.

The rain beat harder, spattering the windows on the north side of the house. William let himself out the front door, closed it carefully behind him and clicked the deadbolt into place. On the way to the village, he tossed his cell phone out the window.

CHAPTER SIXTEEN

STEVE WALKED BRISKLY into The Fisherman's Rest. In no mood for discussion, he tried to bypass Hilly, making for his office instead of checking in with her.

"Mr. Steve." Hilly's rosy cheeks looked faded, her mouth pinched, as though she had stood out in the cold too long.

"'Morning." Steve pulled off his hat and gloves, jamming them deep into the pockets of his jacket before hanging it on a peg outside the bar. "Business looks down today. Must be the weather."

"Miss Sally's been here," Hilly blurted. "She knows you weren't here yesterday evening. I—I told her you'd stepped out on an errand today. She didn't believe me. She wants you to go to the Emporium."

Wringing her apron between her fingers, Hilly shifted uncertainly from one foot to the other. Wisps of hair hung from her normally neat ponytail and there were coffee stains on her blouse. Hilly rarely spilled anything. Steve always told her she had the steadiest hands in the State of Maine. He swore under his breath, but Hilly evidently lip-read, because her eyes widened.

"Sorry." He wanted to go into his office and slam the door. Hilly wasn't paid to be an intermediary, and Sally had no right to keep tabs on him.

He'd tossed and turned all night on the lumpy bed in Carissa's guest room, then argued fruitlessly with her as she drove him to the village. He'd asked her who she was hiding from and why she couldn't go hide somewhere less potentially dangerous. She had told him to butt out of her business in no uncertain terms. He really didn't have the time or energy left to get into some meaningless fight with Sally.

The front door opened. Along with a blast of cold air, Al Dyson strolled toward the bar. Steve clenched his teeth. As though he hadn't got enough to cope with, here came the one inhabitant of Treacher's Cove he couldn't take in more than very small doses.

Al coughed, then sneezed explosively. Drawing out a dingy handkerchief he hawked, spat, and blew his nose like a trumpet. He stuffed the handkerchief back into one of his coat pockets and looked Hilly and Steve up and down. "Well, good morning. Looks like it's been a rough one around here."

Steve bit back a less than civil retort. Al looked disheveled. A yellow mark on his shirt collar might be dried mustard. Darker stains on his pants told of excesses in the bar. His rodent-bright eyes darted between Steve and Hilly, as though expecting some explanation for their own less-than-pristine appearances.

"What can we do for you, Mr. Dyson?" Hilly asked.

Al looked pointedly at the closed bar. "I guess I'll have coffee. Irish coffee to take the chill off. It's a bitch of a day."

Steve turned to go into his office.

"Join me." The remark was more of an order than a request. "We can sit in the parlor."

"I'll have to take a raincheck, Al. I've got paperwork and calls to make." Steve strode away. The door handle to his private sanctuary was actually in his hand when Dyson dropped his little bombshell.

"Pity the Yates girl is so set on staying at the lighthouse. I've had a nice offer for the place. Maybe with the bad weather and heating problems, she'll change her mind."

Regret filling him, Steve let go of the handle. "Someone's made an offer for the lighthouse? Who? This isn't someone planning to open an inn, is it? This area couldn't support another place like The Rest. The Whitstead Tavern's already eating into my business."

Al smiled like a benevolent monk. "Now, now, Steve. You know I can't divulge names of clients or their plans for a property."

"You could at least tell me if it's someone local or an outside party."

"Can't tell you a thing more than I already have." Al took the glass Hilly had brought him and headed for the parlor.

Steve reluctantly followed.

"I believe I'll have some breakfast, Hilly." Al took off his coat and tossed it over the back of a chair before sinking into one of the wingbacks beside the fireplace. A self-satisfied smirk hovered around the corners of his mouth.

Steve felt a real desire to wipe that smirk right off.

"We've stopped serving breakfast," Hilly said, her voice uncharacteristically curt. "I'm about to get the tables ready for lunch."

"Give him a menu, Hilly." Steve barely managed to keep the anger out of his own voice. "He can eat in here."

Hilly frowned, but she left without further comment.

"So, aren't you going to try to pump me for more information?" Al took out a pack of cigarettes, evidently thought better of it and shoved them back into a pocket. "Look, Steve, I know you're one of the residents who want to keep the Cove rustic, but progress has to come here before the younger generation moves away to the bigger cities. We don't have enough jobs here for them."

"You're wrong in thinking I don't support business growth," Steve said carefully. He didn't want Dyson to misinterpret his remarks and report them to the local Chamber of Commerce and Tourism, its only representative being the local postmistress and general store owner as well as chief gossip-monger, Nancy Burton. "But any growth has to be well thought out and demonstrate a benefit to the Cove. We get our fair share of tourists in the summer months. The Rest is usually booked solid July and August, and we get fall foliage leaf-peepers September and October."

"So turning a profit four months out of twelve is enough for your business?" Al's eyebrows rose. "I know you make enough out of the bar and restaurant to make payroll, but I doubt you're running in the black all year."

"I'm not about to give you figures for my profit margin."

"Didn't ask you to." Al leaned over, grabbed the poker and stabbed at the fire. "But I know most of the local businesses could do with a steadier income throughout the year, and those with families would like their children to stay in the Cove and raise their own families here. The fishing business isn't going to sustain us like it used to. The younger generation, well, they want cushier jobs in the tech or hospitality industries."

"That's not always true, Al. You're oversimplifying. I know of several families who have more than one generation tending their boats, and they're happy doing it."

"That lighthouse should be used for more than a place for visitors to take photos. It should become a resort. There's enough land up there to build a good one. I'm working on Blake Ulster to sell his property. Then I can really put a deal together for out-of-state investors. Maybe turn that tract of land into an amusement park. That would sure bring in the crowds."

"You and your deals." Steve shook his head. "You must have coined the term 'real estate speculator.'"

"I'm always working, Steve; you know that. Twenty-four-seven for the future of the Cove."

Steve had a far-from-suitable retort in mind, but held his comments since Hilly was back, armed with a breakfast menu.

"I don't need that." Al waved away the menu. "Scrambled eggs, hash browns and bacon with a side of biscuits and gravy will do."

"There are no biscuits left. I'll bring you toast to go with the rest of your meal." Without waiting for a response, Hilly turned on her heel and left.

"What's up with her?" Al poked at the fire again.

"She's tired, Al. She didn't sleep well."

With that, Steve made his escape. It was no secret Al Dyson's plans included being the next mayor. *Perish the thought.* Now Al had designs on turning Bennett Point into some no-doubt crass as well as commercial tourist trap.

Closing the office door behind him, Steve settled into his chair and tried unsuccessfully to relax. He took an unopened bottle of bourbon from the bottom drawer, opened it, poured a generous serving and sipped, remembering how when he first opened the inn, his customers had repeatedly tried to buy their host a drink. He had refused so many times, they finally stopped.

He gazed out the windows. The fog had receded all the way back to the mouth of the Cove. One corner window gave glimpses of the fishing fleet bobbing gently on a swell. A peaceful scene he always enjoyed, but if Al had his way, its days might be numbered. He idly wondered why lighthouses were so well-loved and romanticized. For him, the enduring solidity of Bennett Point Light was what appealed. Regardless of what happened around it, the lighthouse remained a sentinel on the rocks at the entrance to Treacher's Cove. At least, that had been true until Al Dyson revealed his newest get-rich scheme. Now Steve felt as though life as he knew it was about to take a nose-dive. He tossed back the rest of the bourbon in a single swallow.

Morosely, he thought back to the moment he noticed Virginia Greeley watching him get out of Carissa's car. Virginia had seen them arguing about Carissa remaining at the lighthouse, where Steve felt she wasn't safe after hearing about other, smaller but still disturbing incidents. Pranks, she had called them. Trouble, Steve had told her: Someone wanted her out of there. Carissa told him she wasn't leaving. End of discussion.

Virginia had probably rushed home to alert the rumor mill. One of those 'helpful' souls would no doubt enlighten Sally. It wouldn't take much of a leap for Sally to decide he hadn't spent last night at the inn after she confronted Hilly, who'd had to stay late and lock up. Fortunately there had been no guests to require on-site staffing. Steve knew he had done an uncharacteristically stupid thing, walking up to the lighthouse in thick fog to check on Carissa and then staying the night because he was too worried about her to leave.

But it seemed as though since Jessica Malloy's untimely death, things were changing rapidly at the Cove. Al Dyson's real estate deals; Carissa Yates becoming the brunt of someone's cruel pranks; his own relationship with Sally being jeopardized by his preoccupation with and growing attraction to Carissa. He opened the bottom drawer again and took out the bourbon. Everything was becoming too complicated, he told himself as he poured another drink. Way too complicated.

CHAPTER SEVENTEEN

Rain spattered the living-room windows of the lighthouse keeper's cottage. The murky landscape made the interior so dim, Carissa turned on all the lights in that room, the kitchen and the hallway. She hesitated in front of the bathroom, turned that light on, too, then muttered "Screw it" and turned on the lights in the bedrooms. She returned to the living room to watch a gunmetal gray sea churn in the bay. White crests formed as waves rushed to batter themselves against the rocks.

Even the ocean displayed self-destructive behavior, she decided, turning away to survey the meager remains of her sewing—one completed pillow cover and a half-finished vest. Both projects had escaped the burning by hanging over a kitchen chair. She still couldn't believe someone had destroyed everything else. Did Steve Raymond throw her work onto the fire yesterday evening? What possible motive would he have had? If it wasn't him, then someone else definitely had a key. Carissa wrapped her arms around herself and shivered. She looked around the room, seeing nothing else out of place.

Was Steve the one who had tried to push her off the cliff, or had another person hidden in the fog? Steve said he'd wanted to buy the lighthouse, but Aunt Jessica had told him to get his own. Perhaps he'd pushed Jessica down the stairs thinking he could buy the lighthouse as soon as it was put on the market.

But he'd said he wanted to keep an eye on her, Carissa reminded herself. He'd seemed genuinely concerned for her safety. Was it possible she'd imagined the shove at the edge of the cliff?

No.

If she'd learned anything from her disastrous marriage to Matthew, it was that people, even those who are loved, lie. Steve could have paid Blake Ulster to play the scary little tricks. Maybe Blake had gone one step further yesterday, when it seemed his much milder attempts at frightening her had failed.

Carissa didn't want to suspect Steve Raymond of anything heartless and cruel. But she had to admit he'd revealed a temper almost as frightening as Matthew's after showing her the smoldering remains of her crafting. When she refused to leave the lighthouse and move into the inn until a more suitable home could be found for her, he'd called her stupid and stubborn, like her aunt. She'd told him he was a controlling bastard. They'd slammed themselves into their respective bedrooms without supper, like two errant children.

Their impolite behavior had continued that morning, when she made coffee and he refused to drink it. Despite the fog, she'd driven him back to town after telling him he'd get killed on the road and she wasn't going to take the blame for his death, even if she didn't much care what happened to him at that moment.

After he refused to get out of the car in front of The Fisherman's Rest, telling her he wasn't going to accept responsibility for ruining her reputation with the nosy villagers, she had wanted to relent and fix their relationship, but Steve wasn't in the mood to reconcile anything, particularly after he informed her she'd stopped her car only feet from one of the worst gossip-mongers in town, retired school teacher, Virginia Greeley.

The phone rang, interrupting Carissa's whirling thoughts. Mai Ling's hesitant voice invited her to brunch. Blake was out of town again, this time on an overnight trip. Carissa happily accepted. No doubt, Mai Ling's brunch would be as inedible as her zucchini bread, but Carissa needed companionship. She had no fear of Mai Ling lifting the phone to spread gossip or telling Facebook friends that Carissa Yates was living next door to her at the Cove. Carissa was willing to bet that if there was a laptop, smartphone or tablet at the Ulsters' it was always kept away from Mai Ling.

She also wanted to find out what time Blake had left on his trip, even if it was to eliminate him as a suspect for both incidents the day before. She wondered whether someone was trying to frighten her into leaving or make her think she was losing her mind. But shoving her at the edge of a cliff went way beyond scare tactics.

She pulled on her boots and the rest of her outerwear before setting out for the Ulsters.' Lights twinkled in the distance, making it look more like 5:00 P.M. than 10:00 AM. Rain pelted her face with icy drops while the wind tried to tug her hair free from her coat's hood.

Mai Ling opened the back door before Carissa could knock, took her arm and guided her over the darkened threshold. "I am very glad you accepted my invitation. Please come in."

"Thanks for inviting me."

Carissa allowed the young girl to take her coat and hang it to dry in the mudroom. She pried off her boots and placed them at the end of a line of assorted footwear. The stone floor was frigid beneath her feet. Mai Ling was in house shoes. She offered another pair to Carissa, who gladly accepted before being ushered into a spotlessly clean kitchen that showed no signs of meal preparation. She wondered what she was going to be asked to eat and tried not to envision raw fish brought out of the refrigerator.

Mai Ling smiled shyly. "I hoped you would agree to come, but I saw your car leave early this morning, and I was not sure when you would return. I made a quiche. I thought if you could not come, I would freeze it. My husband likes me to warm a piece for him to eat before he leaves on a business trip."

"How did you prepare a meal and not make a mess?"

"I already cleaned up before I called you. I did not want you to think I am a bad housekeeper." Mai Ling gestured toward an arched doorway. "Shall we eat in the parlor? The fire makes it very pleasant."

"I'd love that. Can I help you? Carry in plates? Drinks?"

"No, thank you. You are my guest. I would like to serve you."

"Guest or not, I'd like to help. I would really prefer you think of me as a friend, Mai Ling."

"I would like that very much, too." Mai Ling brought two plates with slices of quiche out of the oven. She placed them on a tray and took two small dishes of carefully sliced and attractively arranged fresh fruit from the refrigerator. After handing Carissa another tray with a tea pot, small cups and glasses of water, she gave a little bow. "Please, follow me."

She led the way down a long hallway with open doors on either side. Carissa caught glimpses of a bathroom, a bedroom and a small sitting room with a big-screen T.V. The parlor held an oversized camelback sofa and two side chairs, pushed back to accommodate a small dining table set for two in front of a blazing fire.

Carissa sipped Jasmine tea and eyed the quiche. It didn't look watery, but if Mai Ling had trouble making zucchini bread, there was a good chance the quiche could taste like cardboard.

"The bread I brought you wasn't good," Mai Ling said. "I saw your face when you bit into it. Blake brought home frozen zucchini, and I tried to make it work. I want to assure you there is no such mistake today. I make this often. Blake calls it egg and bacon pie. I got the recipe from the back of an old can I found in the cellar. His mother must have left it there. I use ready-made pie crusts for baking and ordinary milk. It should be safe."

Carissa stuck her fork into the quiche and took a small piece. It was okay, she thought. Not great, but okay. She took a larger piece and chewed while Mai Ling watched, brow furrowed. Carissa smiled. Mai Ling's rigid shoulders relaxed.

"I am learning American cooking," she explained. "It is difficult to get all the foods I need to prepare traditional Vietnamese dishes in this small village."

"I'm sure it is." Carissa ate some fruit. "Can you order things online and get them sent through the mail?"

"I don't have access to a computer. Blake has one for work. He's very strict about me not using it and messing things up."

"Any time you want to get online, you can come over and use my laptop." Carissa would fix Blake's ability to isolate Mai Ling when he was away, even if she couldn't do anything when he was home. She and Mai Ling were going to become very good friends. To hell with worrying about Facebook contacts.

"Thank you." Mai Ling's expression had brightened considerably.

"And I'll pay for the order with a credit card and have UPS ship everything to me, if you're worried about Blake not liking that. You can at least prepare some of your own dishes for yourself when he's gone. It sounds like that happens frequently, from what you've told me."

Mai Ling nodded. "That is true. I could make Pho for you and our spring rolls, which have rice wrappers and are not fried."

"Sounds delicious. I've had some Vietnamese food before and loved it. We'll make a lunch date."

"Why did *you* move here?" Mai Ling asked. "Blake said you came from New York. Didn't you like it there?"

"I love New York. It's so different from here. People can be abrupt and they're always in a hurry. New Yorkers say what they think, and they don't care who knows it." She laughed at Mai Ling's consternation. "We complain about it and each other all the time, but there's little we'd change. We love the crowds, the fast pace, and being able to do anything and everything at any hour of the day or night."

"I would like some excitement for a change." Mai Ling sipped her tea and sighed. "Boston was a lot like New York in some ways—crowded, busy and full of life. Here it is so quiet. I take care of the chickens and we have a cow I learned to milk. I churn my own butter and bake my own bread. I felt very alone until you arrived. I did not see your aunt very often. She and Blake did not get along."

Carissa listened as wind intermittently rushed down the chimney, showering sparks against the fire-screen. "It's quiet here if you don't count the gale that's blowing constantly."

"So, why did you move here?"

Carissa had thought she could gloss right over her neighbor's original question, but Mai Ling hadn't forgotten. She shrugged. "I got divorced." Even saying that much made her palms moist. She wiped them on her jeans. "It's not completely over. I needed to get away and sort some things out for myself."

"I see." Mai Ling looked like she didn't see at all.

"I was married to a fashion designer. We're still fighting over my embroidery and braiding. They became such a part of his line. Kind of like Chanel..." Carissa saw Mai Ling's confusion. "...or Nike, putting the logo on so many of their products."

"Ah, yes. I understand, I think. Blake has a cap and tennis shoes with the Nike design on them."

"My husband's line wasn't considered *haute couture*, even though he'd been in the business for more than five years and had really tried to push his way into the shows. He needed something spectacular, and when he saw how my designs enhanced his garments, he knew he had found it."

Mai Ling nodded encouragingly and poured more tea for both of them.

"Aunt Jessica and I had spent summers together when I was a child. She taught me a lot of fancy stitchery. I made suggestions on simplifying the designs and depending on the embroidery, braiding and intricate stitchery to carry the simplicity."

"Like the jacket you are wearing?" Mai Ling pointed to Carissa's embroidered, quilted vest.

"Yes. One of my earlier efforts. My designs became more sophisticated later."

"It is very beautiful. I would love such a garment."

"I'll keep that in mind." Carissa smiled. She had several vests in her wardrobe that would suit Mai Ling after some alterations.

"Oh, I was not asking. I would not be so rude."

"I know you wouldn't. It would be my pleasure to make you a gift."

"Thank you." Mai Ling's smile lit her eyes. "So, your designs brought him success."

"A *lot* of success. Which he wanted to continue after the divorce. He wanted to keep the Yates name on the designs. They're mine, and he's not going to take the credit. I only agreed to the miserable monthly settlement because I thought I'd be getting an income from the designs for years to come."

"Ah, your husband is a...how would you say it?" Her brow furrowed while she searched for the right word.

"A smooth talker," Carissa offered.

"More than that." Mai Ling's brow cleared. "A swindler." She got up to collect their plates.

No one else had described Matthew in such bald and direct terms. "That's a pretty strong statement," Carissa said.

"Not from what you have said and the way you say it." Mai Ling regarded her with an unblinking stare.

Carissa shrugged. "I guess I'm not good at hiding my feelings."

"No." Mai Ling's smile was tight. "Hiding what you feel takes time and much effort." Without elaborating, she piled the dishes on one of the trays.

Carissa started to get up. "Here, I'll help you."

Mai Ling shook her head. "Please, sit. I will bring more quiche and hot tea."

"I don't know if I can manage anything else, Mai Ling," Carissa protested. "I'm really full."

"You eat like a tiny bird," Mai Ling observed. "You did not like the quiche, perhaps?"

"My appetite's been a bit off since the divorce and my aunt's death." The quiche had been edible, but Carissa definitely didn't want seconds.

"You must get out more. Exercise and take vitamins. Perhaps you could learn meditation. I get my exercise chasing the cow all over the pasture so I can get her into the barn to be milked. She doesn't like it. Blake said that's why she was cheap, and he threatens to have her butchered, but so far, I have been able to convince him I enjoy running after her. I told him it keeps my weight down. He likes me to be slim." She grimaced. "He likes it a lot."

Carissa fought off an image of what Blake thought liking anything a lot could mean for Mai Ling. "I've sat long enough. I need to take a walk. Would you like to come with me?"

"I think you will have to wait on walking." Mai Ling pointed to the window.

Carissa saw the rain had receded but the fog had started to roll back in. Her eyes were drawn to the lighthouse, standing strong and resilient against the elements. Through the bare branches of the trees on the property line, she spotted a black Cadillac sedan turning around in her driveway.

Carissa sprinted down the hallway, kicked off the house shoes and jammed her feet into her boots. She grabbed her coat. "I've got company, Mai Ling. I have to go. Thank you for brunch."

CHAPTER EIGHTEEN

ALTHOUGH CARISSA RAN, the car had left by the time she reached her driveway. A note hanging out of her mailbox told her William Dansinger had stopped by. She heard the landline ringing, stuffed the note into her pocket and peeled off her gloves as she hurried into the house.

She snatched up the receiver. "Hello?"

"Carissa! Where the hell have you been? I've been trying to reach you for an hour. I couldn't find your cell number."

"Steve?"

"Of course it's Steve. Who else would be concerned and yelling at you?"

"I can think of several people, including my ex-husband, who does it much better than you."

"Sorry." He took a deep breath. "Can I start over?"

"If you're more reasonable, yes."

"I'm always reasonable."

"You certainly are not. You were shouting at me earlier this morning with some woman standing right behind my car."

"That woman was Virginia Greeley. I didn't notice her at first."

"So now the whole village probably knows you spent the night at my home if she's got good ears." Carissa took a deep breath, fully aware her voice was rising to match his. "Is that why you're calling? To tell me we're the talk of the town?"

"No; I called to tell you Al Dyson may be involved in a scheme to frighten you away from the lighthouse and put it up for sale. He's got a buyer."

"I already know he wants me to sell. He told me that right up front, the evening he gave me the keys."

"Oh." Steve sounded really surprised. "That was news to me."

"Look, I could see Al having a second set of keys, but I had the locks changed on all the outer doors, and the windows all close tight now, too. He'd have no way of getting in. Not that I can see him shimmying through a window to burn my needlework."

"Someone sure did."

Was he telling the truth or trying to convince her he was? Carissa wasn't at all sure. "I'm still wondering whether you were the one who did it."

"Carissa, we already went through that last night and again this morning. I would have nothing to gain by doing that. I'm not out to frighten you. I'd like to keep you around."

"But maybe not out here at Bennett Point." She unzipped her coat and took it off, draping it over a chair. "Is that all you called about? I'm not going to be pushed out of here, so forget it."

"I called to tell you I stopped by the sheriff's office. Deputy Watkins is coming over to talk to you about filing a report on these incidents. He's probably been trying to call you to set up a time."

Carissa checked the answering machine. "I don't have any messages. I had brunch with Mai Ling Ulster. If you hadn't lost my cell number, you could have gotten hold of me. Now you're sending a cop? Why would you do that? I don't need a keeper, and I certainly didn't ask you to take on that role."

"Don't get snarky. I'm trying to help you."

"Not by sending the police. They'll think I'm imagining things."

"Look, not reporting the incidents you told me about would be, well, stupid. There's no way anyone would think you're imagining them. *I* believe you."

She tried to ignore the 'stupid' comment and focus on his belief in her. "Do you? Really?"

"I do, Carissa. Someone's trying to get you out of the lighthouse. I don't trust Al Dyson. Never have."

"So you really think he's the one doing all this?"

"Not the actual scaring part. I'm thinking more like Blake Ulster doing Al's dirty work for him."

"Could be," Carissa said. "Mai Ling said Blake's away a lot. I was about to ask her when he left on his latest trip when I saw a car in my driveway. I just missed William Dansinger. I'll go back and ask her. She can probably tell me if he was home when any of those other incidents happened."

"Why don't you let Deputy Watkins do that?"

"Great, then Mai Ling will know I'm accusing her husband of trying to scare me."

Steve hesitated a beat before answering. When he did, his voice was more measured. "Blake's scary at the best of times. I often think he could shoot all of us and be much happier alone. I'd like you to keep away from him."

"I came here to get away from New York, not my next door neighbors. I don't want to talk to the police or have that woman in town...what was her name...?"

"Virginia Greeley."

"Virginia," Carissa echoed. "I don't want Virginia to spread gossip about me. It could seriously hurt my court case if Matthew gets hold of anything he can use against me."

"I thought your divorce was over?"

"It is, but I'm fighting to retain my rights to my embroidery and braiding. It's a big suit. My ex would love to find something to hold over me."

"It's not the nineteenth century, Carissa. People won't really care if I slept over at your house, maybe with the exception of Sally. They'll all forget about it in a week or two."

"You really believe that? And what about Sally? She'll hate me."

Steve sighed. "I'll talk to her. Make her understand nothing went on between us."

"You'd better hope she believes you." Carissa heard the doorbell. "I have to go. Someone's at the door. It's probably that deputy."

"Be careful," Steve said. "I'll stay on the line until you tell me you're okay."

"I am *not* going to start being paranoid." She thought about hanging up, but he'd spooked her. She took the cordless with her. "Maybe Mr. Dansinger came back."

She opened the door and immediately regretted it.

"Matthew."

He looked older. His hair had turned silver at the temples—attractively silver, she thought grudgingly. Maybe the divorce and the ongoing legal issues had been more of a strain on him than she'd expected.

He gave her his best charming smile. "I come hundreds of miles and all you can say is 'Matthew?'"

Now she knew the hypocrisy behind that congenial mask, it left her unmoved. "What do you want?"

"It's cold out here. Aren't you going to invite me inside?"

He was shivering. Although loathe to do so, she stepped aside. "All right; come in. I suppose you expect coffee, too?"

"That'd be nice."

Belatedly, she remembered Steve was hearing every word. "Leave your shoes outside the door," she told Matthew. She left him unlacing his favorite pair of Pierre Cardin's and returned to the living room. "It's my ex-husband," she told Steve. "I'll call you back later."

"Do you want me to come over?"

"No, of course not; I can handle him."

"What's your cell phone number?"

She gave it to Steve and hung up, like she had everything under control.

What a liar I am.

She had never been able to successfully handle Matthew Yates. Carissa walked into the kitchen and opened the coffee canister. She wished she had the guts to lace the brew with rat poison. Aunt Jessica probably had some lying around in her creepy basement.

But Carissa had no time to look for anything that useful. Matthew's arms slid around her waist and his lips found the pulse point on her neck he knew was one of her primary erogenous zones.

"I've missed you," he whispered, and his voice was heavy with need.

CHAPTER NINETEEN

COMPLETELY REVOLTED and more than a little frightened, Carissa tried to get out of Matthew's embrace. She twisted away, the coffee canister catching him right in his groin. Her panic receded as he clutched himself and hobbled across the kitchen to sit slowly and carefully on a kitchen chair.

"Bitch," he managed.

"You'd better believe it."

Carissa filled the coffee maker and took a cup out of the cupboard. She heaped sugar into it, took away the carafe and held it under the coffee stream as she tried to wipe a smirk of relief off her face. She should have given him instant coffee, she thought. It might have resulted in an even faster departure. Matthew hated instant anything except sex.

She put the cup on the table beside him. "Here. Stop being a baby. I didn't hit you that hard. Drink up fast, tell me why you came here, and get out."

Matthew took his hand off his crotch. "Such a lack of hospitality for your reluctant ex-husband."

Carissa tried to ignore the impulse to knock the coffee into his lap. "I'm not a reluctant ex. I want you to stay out of my life. What are you doing here, and how did you find me?"

"I came because the divorce was a mistake. I intend to get you back."

"Because you know the designs are mine, and without them, your collections aren't worth zilch."

"You're mistaken. Those designs belong to me. They're part of the House of Yates, and they enhance my already stunning collections. You're going to lose your case, and it's going to cost you every penny of your settlement as well as any financial inheritance your aunt left you. Make it easy on yourself. Come back. We can compromise."

"Compromise? You abused me, and now you want to steal my designs."

Matthew's face had darkened dangerously, but Carissa was past caring. He was in her home, and she had the cordless right beside her on the kitchen counter. She picked it up and punched in 911.

"Take a hike. You're not getting me back or taking credit for my work."

"Dammit, Carissa, don't be stubborn." Matthew jumped up and seized her arm, his grip painful despite her thick clothing.

"Take your hand off me or I'll file assault charges. The sheriff's sending a deputy to check out my security system. He's on his way."

Matthew's hand dropped from her arm immediately. He glanced around. "I don't see any cameras."

"That's because they're hidden, but don't worry, they're recording everything."

He smiled. "You've always been resourceful, darling. I don't know what came over me. I'm desperate to have you back, and it's making me a little crazy. But I've changed—I've sworn off all the drugs and alcohol. I'm sober, and I love you."

"You only love two things, Matthew. Yourself and your clothing business. You're just as mean and cruel without the booze and coke. I don't want anything to do with you." She walked into the living room with him right behind her. "Put your shoes back on and get out of my house."

The doorbell rang. She hoped she'd find either the sheriff's deputy or Steve Raymond outside as she flung the door open. A man in a parka stood on the threshold, his badge clearly visible. Carissa felt profound relief. She would have preferred someone tall and muscular instead of short and slightly paunchy, but she'd take that badge anytime.

She smiled at him and beckoned. "Come in. Your timing couldn't be better. I was about to call nine-one-one to get this man out of my house."

The deputy looked past her, saw Matthew and put his hand on the butt of his gun.

Matthew's eyes widened. "I'm leaving." He snatched his coat from the rack. "We were having a little discussion, my wife and I."

"Ex-wife," Carissa corrected.

"Out," the deputy said, jerking his thumb toward the black Escalade with New York plates parked beside his green Explorer.

"I'll call later," Matthew promised. "I have the landline number. We'll talk."

"I've got caller ID." Carissa leaned against the wall to give him room to pass her in the narrow hallway. "I'm not picking up."

"Out." The deputy jerked his thumb toward the car.

"At least let me get my shoes on," Matthew protested, brushing unnecessarily against Carissa as he passed, his face only inches from hers. He was moving at a snail's pace, his smile mocking.

Carissa couldn't get away from him. She felt every inch of his body touch hers. He actually had the gall to rock back and forth to increase the effectiveness of the contact. Instinctively, she shoved him away.

"Bastard," she said.

"I'll be staying in Treacher's Cove for a while. It's a charming little village. I'm feeling very much at home." Matthew's smirk widened. "We should have dinner and try to resolve our differences without the lawyers. I'm sure I can convince you to be more reasonable, darling, given a little time."

"No, you won't," she assured him. "Anything you have to say to me goes through my attorney from now on. It's no good hanging out at the Cove. Go back where you belong and leave me alone."

"Are these yours?" The deputy picked up the shiny brown leather shoes from the doorstep.

"Yes. Thank you, officer." Matthew put out his hand.

The deputy turned and lobbed Matthew's shoes right toward the biggest mud puddle in the driveway. They landed with a splash and lay there on their sides.

"You..." Matthew's fists curled at his sides.

"What?" The deputy widened his stance.

"Nothing." Matthew stepped out of the house, grimaced as his socked feet touched the cold concrete, and walked stiffly past Treacher's Cove's finest. He turned toward Carissa. "I'll see you again, real soon," he promised before running through a mixture of rain and sleet toward the Escalade, stopping only to scoop up his shoes.

"I've got fresh coffee," Carissa told the deputy as he stepped into the hallway. "Would you like some?"

"If it's no trouble. It's gotten a lot colder out there over the past hour." He held out his hand. "I'm Deputy Watkins."

"Steve Raymond told me you wanted to get a report from me. Thank you for coming." She shook his hand gratefully. "Carissa Yates. I told Steve he needn't have called you, but now I'm very glad he did."

As she led Deputy Watkins into the kitchen, she made a mental note to buy a five-pound can of coffee next time she went shopping and to keep one of Aunt Jessica's golf clubs beside her bed.

CHAPTER TWENTY

WILLIAM FOLLOWED HILLY TO A TABLE. Ignoring his usual chair facing the window, he took one that gave him a view of both the restaurant and the front lobby.

"Coffee?" Hilly asked.

William desperately wanted a brandy, but he nodded. He never drank at lunch. Today would be the worst day to start. Hilly was too observant—she'd remember the sudden change. He quickly perused the menu and placed unsteady hands in his lap before she returned with the carafe. A trickle of sweat ran uncomfortably down his back.

"Weather's worsening again," she observed, pen poised over pad. "What'll you have?"

"Pot roast." His stomach was one big, churning pit. The thought of food nauseated him, but he had to appear normal, and he had to be highly visible.

Hilly scribbled and bustled off. Two other businessmen stood in the doorway. She seated them quickly before going back to the kitchen. Al Dyson's secretary, Millie Parsons appeared, smacking gum as she talked with her companion, the accounts clerk from Chuck's appliance store.

Millie saw William and waved one red-tipped hand. She spent hours every Saturday getting "the works" in Lindy's Beauty Parlor, he'd heard from Mrs. Dodds. He bet Al enjoyed those long red nails raking down his back. Rumors reported Millie and Al were in the middle of a sizzling affair completely out of proportion to Al's appearance. The skinny little real estate broker evidently had hidden talents.

The thought of Millie's nubile body writhing in Al's arms brought bile to William's throat. The man was as hairy as one of the apes in the San Diego Zoo William had visited on vacation with his parents as a child. He remembered Al going with him to the beach when they were in high school. Al always paraded around in a pair of bright red trunks, but takers were few and far between, even though Al told William the more hair on a man's body, the longer his ability to sustain an erection. *God,* William thought with disgust, *Al should be nicknamed Iron Man.*

Steve came out of his office. His gaze passed quickly over Millie as though willing her to be a figment of his imagination, then lingered momentarily on the businessmen before coming to rest on William. He came right over.

"Lunch, Mr. Steve?" Hilly placed soup in front of William.

"I didn't ask for soup, Hilly," William protested, knowing the way his hands were shaking, liquid would slop all over the table and end up in his lap. He wished Hilly hadn't filled his coffee cup all way to the brim.

"It's included in the lunch. No extra charge. I thought you liked homemade vegetable."

William shook his head. He knew a sheen of sweat sat over his upper lip and his breathing was too rapid. He felt slightly faint.

"I'll eat the soup, Hilly." Steve's voice made William jump.

I can't do this, he thought, panicked. *But if I leave, they'll know I was responsible. They'll know what I did to Patsy.*

Hilly took the unwanted soup and placed it in front of her employer. Steve calmly sipped, as though nothing was amiss. "Unusual to see you today, but I heard you've been out of town. Felt like a hot meal, huh? How was your trip?"

William forced himself to breathe slower. What was done was done. He couldn't go back and change things. It was already too late. He thought of his wife's demanding behavior, her selfishness. Her lies. "The trip went fine." His voice sounded calmer. He took a sip of water and wiped his mouth, blotting the perspiration from his upper lip. "I couldn't face a sandwich at my desk."

"How's Patsy?" Steve asked.

A normal question, but his hands shook harder. Hilly bustled back and set a full plate of food in front of him.

"Anything else for you, Mr. Steve?" she asked, her smile speaking volumes.

She absolutely worshipped the ground Steve Raymond walked on. William felt envious. He'd never had the opportunity to be the recipient of such devotion. But with that level of dedication came responsibility. Steve always had to ensure Hilly's happiness. Not that it was a hard task. Hilly seemed to want nothing more than to be the head waitress of The Fisherman's Rest. Steve treated her with respect and affection. Something Hilly had worked very hard for, William knew, after a checkered youth. Steve had been the only one in the village who had considered her hireable.

"Aren't you going to eat?" Steve asked.

William picked up his fork. "Of course. It looks wonderful, Hilly. Give my compliments to Eva. Her cooking's the best in the region." He tasted the pot roast. It probably *was* wonderful, but the piece of beef he tried chewing felt like a boulder when he swallowed. He took a gulp of water to help it down.

Hilly looked worried. "Is the meat tough?"

"No. Definitely not." He managed a half-smile. "I've got a bit of a sore throat. Must be the weather. New York wasn't this damp."

"How about a scotch or something to take the chill off?" Steve suggested.

"Well..." William stalled, although he wanted to accept immediately and ask for a double. "I don't usually drink at lunch, but I could do with something to chase the cold out of my bones. Scotch sounds really good."

"I'll get it, Hilly." Steve nodded toward the doorway, where three more people were standing in line. "You've got your hands full."

"Dora's late again." Hilly's voice sounded uncharacteristically sharp.

"I know. I'll give her my talk."

Although Steve's manner conveyed nothing, William thought he wouldn't like to be in Dora's shoes when the part-time waitress turned up for work.

While he tried to eat a little more of his meal and finished his drink, William watched the dining room fill steadily. Dora arrived and began serving, her cheeks crimson after Steve had pulled her aside for a few moments. Several people nodded at William, others smiled and waved. The volume of noise in the dining-room increased steadily, morphing into a babble of voices and clinking silverware over piped-in music. William wondered if anyone else had heard about Mrs. Dodds' fall. He wished someone would come over and tell him, so he could exhibit an appropriate level of shock that Patsy would have been left alone outside.

Would any of them even think it strange that Patsy was alone? Her solitary lifestyle meant her habits weren't generally known. No one but Mrs. Dodds and he knew Patsy liked to sit on the terrace until lunch. Maybe no one would say anything at all. Although the thought comforted him, he still had trouble eating. Steve brought him another scotch. William smiled gratefully and took a sip, careful not to gulp. He noticed Steve had brought himself a glass, too. William remarked on the unusual event.

Steve grimaced. "I've had a bad day. Hard liquor's the only thing that's taking the edge off."

William felt a bubble of hysterical laughter threatening to rise up his throat. He finished his scotch. Steve Raymond thought *he'd* had a trying morning?

Try murdering your wife, William thought.

For some reason, thinking about it didn't produce the same level of panic he'd felt before the scotch. Steve brought them both another refill. William forced himself to set the glass down after a few sips, worried he might get too relaxed and say something he'd regret later. If he told Steve too much, Patsy might be saved, and he'd be arrested for attempted murder. She'd sit in her wheelchair during his trial and when the time came for her to give her testimony, she'd accuse him of drugging her and leaving her outside to die. She'd look so pathetic and helpless; he'd never get out of prison. She'd wear that hideous pink bed jacket over pink silk pajamas and her fluffy slippers. The only satisfaction he'd have would be that someone else would have to carry her up a flight of stairs to that damned second floor bedroom every day instead of him.

Feeling another surge of anger, William caught Hilly's attention and pulled out his billfold. "I have to go. I've got things to do at the office," he said.

Steve waved away William's attempt to pay. "Lunch is on me. I see too little of you."

"Thanks. I appreciate the hospitality, but I'm going to pay my way. I'm planning to eat lunch here more often in the future. This hot meal really hit the spot." He carefully wiped his hand on his pant leg before offering it to Steve, who gave him a steady grip.

"How's Patsy these days?" Someone asked behind him.

The question came out of the blue, right when he was about to escape completely unscathed. He turned toward the speaker and damn, if it wasn't Percival Huddleston, their esteemed mayor.

"About as well as can be expected." William got up and took his overcoat from the back of the chair beside him.

"How's she managing with you gone and Mrs. Dodds suddenly laid up?"

Finally, someone had asked the question William had been waiting for, and it was delivered by the shrewd little rosy-cheeked man who knew everybody and everything in Treacher's Cove.

"What do you mean, Mrs. Dodds is laid up?" William tried to look confused. It was more difficult than he had imagined. He thought he achieved something closer to surprised.

"After her fall in the Market "

Everyone in Treacher's Cove referred to Everett's Grocery Store as the Market. William detested the familiarity of that term. "What fall?"

"She slipped and sprained her ankle this morning while picking up supplies for her grandson's birthday party later today. I thought everyone knew about it."

"*I* didn't. When was this?"

"Around nine o'clock. She fell in the fresh produce section. I bet you'll want to look into that with her. I'd say she's got a pretty good case of negligence. Something about wet spinach on the floor."

"I can advise her, if that's what she wants, but I doubt Mrs. Dodds would want to sue her own brother-in-law. Remember Fred owns the Market now. He bought it from the Everetts a year ago."

"Yes, yes." Percival nodded sagely, slipping his thumbs into the waistband of his pants. "I'd forgotten about that."

William clamped his lips together. What in the world was he doing, discussing Mrs. Dodds when he should be rushing off to save Patsy?

He stood up and pulled out his wallet. "I've got to go. I left Patsy on the back terrace, taking the air until Mrs. Dodds got back from the grocery store."

"Good Lord, man." Percival's fingers popped out of his pants. "Do you realize how cold it is out there? Freezing rain's been falling for the last hour, and it turned to snow about five minutes ago."

William turned and looked out the windows. A thin blanket of white covered everything beyond the glass. Snow flurries whirled. William tossed thirty dollars on the table and bolted, shrugging on his coat as he ran, hearing his rapid footsteps beating a tattoo on the sidewalk against the silent and steady onslaught of thickening snow.

God, those sleeping pills had better have worked well. His car was sitting outside Gus Morgan's Garage, its broken taillight replaced and the keys in the ignition. He waved to Gus, shouted thanks and tore the door open, jumping inside with more vigor than he knew he'd shown for anything in years. He might have come to resent Patsy strongly enough to have her slip into unconsciousness and die of exposure, but if he hadn't given her enough sedation, he would have subjected her to torment beyond anything she deserved, even after all those years she had made his life miserable.

He started the car, backed it out of the parking space and burned rubber as he pulled into the street. The back of the Cadillac fishtailed before he got it under control. Heart hammering and intense guilt threatening to overtake his determination to free himself of Patsy, he drove home, wiper blades working overtime to clear the swirling whiteness as he sped up the hill and left the Cove behind.

CHAPTER TWENTY-ONE

CARISSA FACED Deputy Watkins across her kitchen table. "I suppose you think I'm being hysterical and imagining things."

"If I thought that, I wouldn't be here." Watkins finished his coffee and pushed the cup aside.

"More?" Carissa reached for the carafe.

"No, thanks. I'd like to take a look around your house now." He got up.

"Of course. Where would you like to start?" Carissa picked up the carafe and cups. She noticed her hands were beginning to shake. She must have had at least five cups of coffee that day already. Watkins walked over to the mudroom door, turned the keys in both locks and opened it. An icy draft swept around the kitchen. "You got new locks everywhere, you said?" Watkins flipped on the light and walked into the mudroom. He opened the outer door, bringing a swirl of snow mixed with sleet into the kitchen. He hurriedly shut the door. "Sorry. I'll check outside after I get through in here."

"Brrr." Carissa shivered and wrapped her arms around herself. She'd already decided to ask Richard to send over a crew to tear down the mudroom wall and turn that unused space into a laundry room as soon as possible. "Snow, already? I thought it would hold off for a while."

"That's Maine for you. Fog one minute, snow the next." Watkins walked back into the kitchen. "Neither of these doors looks like they'd open by themselves."

"I'm the only one with keys now. No one else should be able to get inside, but someone must have yesterday."

"Did Steve have any ideas about who may be trying to frighten you?"

"He thinks Al Dyson may be paying someone else, possibly Blake Ulster."

Watkins grunted. He crossed the kitchen and pointed to the other two doors on that wall. "These lead to where?"

"The left one's the pantry; the right one's the basement."

"No lock on the pantry," he observed, opening the door and peering inside. "And no need. There's no space for anyone to hide in here."

"No. Definitely not."

Watkins opened the basement.

"I thought I locked that." Carissa frowned.

"Your washer and dryer are down here?" He flipped on the light and clattered down the first set of steep wooden stairs. "It's like Siberia in here."

Carissa walked over to the head of the stairs and peered down at him. A damp, musty smell drifted up from below. "I know. I hate going down there. Richard Ebberly wants to make the mudroom into my laundry room. I'm going ahead with that plan."

"Sounds like a winner to me." He continued down the second set of stairs. "Looks like a new furnace down here, and a new water heater, too."

Carissa wrapped her arms around herself and made her way down to the landing. The basement smelled even more stale and moldy from there. Cobwebs hung from the ceiling throughout the space below. She didn't want to go down the second set of stairs into that dingy space. She could see Watkins standing in front of the furnace.

He looked around. "Not much here," he observed. "I see a laundry chute."

"The door to that is in the bathroom," she told him. "That may be where the draft's coming from."

"There's a crack in one of the windows, too." He pointed.

Carissa forced herself to walk down the second set of stairs. The basement floor felt uneven when she stepped around on it. She looked to where Deputy Watkins pointed. The reinforced opaque glass on one of the two narrow windows indeed had a crack at one corner.

"There's another expense." She shook her head. "Everywhere I look, something needs fixing. I don't know why my aunt wasn't getting any maintenance done."

"Older people can't handle the upheaval," Watkins said. "They reckon they don't have a lot of time left, and they don't want to spend it or their money on things that don't particularly worry them day to day."

"I suppose." Carissa looked around the basement. With Deputy Watkins there, she felt less creeped-out. Slightly, she told herself as a cobweb became entangled in her hair. "I'm going back up," she told him. "It looks like Aunt Jessica kept her canning jars down here and a few cleaning supplies, but not much else."

"What's this wall here for?" He pointed.

Carissa had one foot on the staircase. "It's for an old coal bin, I think. It can't have been used in eons. The old furnace ran on oil."

"You're probably right." There was a creak. His voice sounded muffled. "I got the door open easily enough. The bin's empty. The inside's black and there's still a lot of coal dust. Some outside, too, probably from Chuck's crew installing the new system."

"I'm glad they didn't get any of that dirt upstairs," Carissa said.

They trudged back upstairs. Carissa locked it with the key hanging on a nail between the basement door and the pantry.

"You've heard noises in the basement sometimes?" Watkins asked.

"Yes, but I haven't seen any holes where varmints can get in. Chuck didn't say he or his crew had, either."

"There could be a hole somewhere in the foundation. Then you'd hear animals running between the floor joists."

"I suppose they could. That makes me feel more secure about the origin of the noises, but the thought of rats or something bigger running under my bedroom floor at night, well, *ee-eww.*"

Watkins laughed. "Let's go check the rest of the cottage."

The cold from the basement must have crept upstairs, Carissa thought, shivering. She checked the new thermostat. It was set to 55 degrees, although she'd programmed it for 72 degrees. She readjusted it. The heat clicked on only moments later, air fluttering the living room curtains.

"Have you had many visitors since you arrived?" Watkins had finished checking the window locks as he moved through the living room. He walked down the hallway to where Carissa stood. "If you leave your thermostat too low, your pipes will freeze."

Carissa wanted to tell him she hadn't left the thermostat too low, but she wasn't sure about anything anymore. Matthew couldn't have turned it down—she hadn't left him alone. Steve could have done it. Maybe he liked to sleep cold. But surely he wouldn't have left without readjusting it?

"I've had a lot of people through here," she said. "A work crew from Chuck's Appliances. The movers, but they were only here long enough to put boxes into the guest room. Steve's been here twice, Richard Ebberly for a consultation on renovating the kitchen, and Mai Ling Ulster, who's come in through the back door a couple of times."

Carissa thought about her keys, hanging behind the front door. They were in full view with the door closed, but she always escorted her guests when they left.

"Surely you don't think one of them is responsible? These incidents started before any of them came here except Al Dyson, who met me here and gave me the house keys." She thought about those keys. "I wonder if Al gave me copies? My aunt had a rabbit's foot on her key ring. The ones he gave me didn't."

"I'm just checking every angle. I don't want to make you even more uneasy." Watkins finished his short tour by rattling the lighthouse door. "Have you gone in here, yet?"

Carissa nodded. "All the way up to the light. I was a bit worried, but it's not scary in there. I have the only key. There's no other entrance, if that's what you're wondering. No one can get in from the outside."

"Maybe you should have some surveillance equipment installed," he said. "Then you'll find out who's prowling around."

"It sounds really paranoid, but you're probably right." It was a depressing thought. She'd come to Maine to escape that sort of scrutiny.

Watkins pulled out a card and handed it to her. "I talked to Jeremy

Thompkins. He owns a security business in Whitstead, so you won't be getting another Cove resident. He said he'd be happy to come out, give you some options and write up an estimate."

"Thank you." She glanced at the card. *More money. Yet another invasion of my privacy.*

"What's your ex doing here?" Watkins asked.

Carissa shrugged. "Checking up on me. Trying to get me to take him back. We're in a fight over my contribution to his business. If I win, he'll be in a real bind, especially with the shows next spring. He'd really like to put a stop to my court case."

"Maybe he hired someone to make your life here miserable. Make you want to go back to him. No telling what people will do."

"That's the truth." Carissa wondered if she would ever see a day when she didn't either think of Matthew or have to deal with him in some way.

"You'll be much better off if you get that surveillance equipment installed." Watkins pointed to the tower door. "I want to check the lighthouse."

"Okay. The key's in the lock."

Watkins opened the door and turned on the lights. The tower was even colder than the basement. He started up the stairs. Carissa pulled an afghan off the guest room bed, draped it around her shoulders and followed him. She knew by the time they reached the light, they'd both be a lot warmer and out of breath.

"Did my aunt have any enemies that you know of?" She asked.

"No." His breathing was already labored. "The coroner ruled her death an accident."

"Tough climb, huh?" Carissa stopped as Watkins paused to take a few deep breaths before continuing up the rest of the stairs. "I thought my aunt had arthritis, but she must have liked to come up here to look out."

"She walked with a cane," the deputy said. "I saw her with it whenever she came to the Cove. Then she stopped coming and turned into a hermit, so I have no idea how bad that arthritis got. The coroner said it was fairly advanced. We were all surprised she was found at the bottom of these steps."

"So you think that was odd, too?"

"Not my place to speculate, Ms. Yates." They reached the top of the tower and both stopped to rest. "We accepted the coroner's findings and closed the case."

"Her attorney found her?"

"Yes, he came to get her signature on some papers."

"He's very accommodating."

"Since it had gotten tougher for her to get to his office, he'd been coming here for at least a year. He arrived while the delivery boy was trying to bring in her groceries. The young man couldn't get Jessica to answer the doorbell. William had a key. He went inside and found her. The boy ended up making the call to us on Jessica's phone. William was so upset; he was the one who needed attention when the paramedics arrived."

"I see," Carissa said, because Watkins seemed to be waiting for a comment. She didn't see anything. It all seemed really suspicious, and William Dansinger sounded like a real lightweight. "Did anyone else come here on a regular basis? What about a housekeeper? The place was clean when I got here."

Watkins nodded. "Jessica had housekeeping services, but changed them frequently. She was never happy with any of them. Her mail was delivered right to the door. Her regular mailman rarely saw her unless she had to sign for something. We did check everything and talk to everyone who came here." Watkins sounded defensive. "Your aunt liked her privacy, Ms. Yates. She had all the services she wanted. She'd been complaining to William that she couldn't hold a needle anymore. That really bothered her. You probably know how much she loved to sew."

"I share that love."

"Do *you* have any enemies?" Watkins asked.

"Personally or professionally?"

"Either."

"Only Matthew, my ex. Thanks again for throwing his shoes in the puddle."

Watkins chuckled. "It was a pleasure. He looked like a scumbag to me."

"You have no idea."

Watkins walked slowly around the lens. "Do you want to take out a restraining order?"

"No. At least, not right now. I think he'll lose interest in a few days. He's trying to put a stop to my lawsuit. I'll call my attorney for advice. I guess I could talk to William Dansinger, too, since Matthew said he's going to stay at on at the Cove. If my aunt trusted Mr. Dansinger, then maybe I can, too."

"William's always had a good name here." Watkins looked up at the lens. "Amazing piece of machinery, isn't it? Pity it's not in use anymore. I miss its light."

"How long has it been decommissioned?"

"Twenty years. It was automated first. The keeper's quarters got boarded up. Next thing, we heard it wasn't needed at all. With the advances in navigation devices, the bay isn't the danger to shipping it once was. In the eighteen-eighties we had so many vessels flounder on the rocks, another cemetery had to be opened to accommodate all the lost sailors."

"That's horrible. Like a sick dinner-party anecdote." Carissa shivered. "Let's go down. It makes me think of my aunt falling to her death."

"You can go down, Miss. I need a few more minutes up here." Watkins took out his flashlight.

Carissa lingered as he made another circuit of the room. She watched him poke into corners and move various dusty objects leaning against the walls. She decided to help him by opening the doors of a cabinet. Inside she saw empty, dust-covered shelves.

"There's really nothing up here of interest to anyone, is there?"

"Not in there, that's for sure." Watkins dislodged a broom and dustpan. They fell to the floor with a clatter.

Carissa flinched and hated herself for it. She was being ridiculous. There was nothing at the top of the tower that would have lured Aunt Jessica, especially since walking the stairs had to have been painful. She opened the last cabinet. On the middle shelf sat an open box of flares and a flare gun.

"That's interesting." Watkins walked over and took out one of the flares, rolling it between his fingers. "It's still good," he said. "The expiration date's not until next year."

"Do you think these are what she was after?" Carissa asked.

"If she was, then she must have been desperate. I counted—we climbed one hundred and twenty-five steps to get up here."

"I did the same thing when I came up here a few days ago." Carissa took out the flare gun. "That's a lot of stairs to climb if Aunt Jessica wasn't even going outside anymore."

Watkins showed her how easy it was to load the flare gun. "You point it vertically and set off two if you're at sea to help pinpoint your location. You've got to be careful. It packs one hell of a punch." He put the gun carefully back in the cabinet and closed the door. "You're shivering. Let's go back."

They walked briskly downstairs. Watkins made sure the door was securely locked and bolted. He left the key in the lock.

"Maybe you should get a dog," he said.

"I'm not the Dobermann attack dog type," Carissa told him.

"You don't have to go that route, but a small dog would be great company and a good early-warning system. Dogs of any size tend to deter burglars."

"I've heard that."

"There's a shelter in Bangor. It's not that big of a drive, and they've got a website. You could look at available dogs before driving there. Shelter dogs make great pets."

"I'm sure they do. I'll think about it. I've never owned a pet. I don't know if I want the responsibility right now." She followed him to the front door.

"You've done everything else—changed the locks, given me a report. Get an alarm system, Ms. Yates. Or move. You could sell this place and find somewhere a whole lot more hospitable, not to mention warmer." He picked up his hat and set it firmly on his head before opening the door.

"I'm too much of a Malloy to give up and leave. Aunt Jessica left me this place in her will. She loved it, and if I wasn't getting all these scares, I think I would, too."

"You like the solitude." Watkins pulled up his collar against the wind.

"When I can get it." Carissa smiled at the thought of the constant stream of people who had invaded her privacy since she arrived.

"I'll call you when I've finished the report." Watkins stepped off the porch. "Give me a day or so. I'm a two-finger typist at best. I'll call you to come in and sign it."

"Thank you for coming out here and not laughing at me." Carissa watched as he waved and trudged off through a blanket of snow

She locked the door, pulled the afghan closer and stood in front of the fire to warm up. The temperature outside had dropped considerably. She was tempted to forgo a trip to the grocery store, but she had to stock up on food. Her stomach lurched at the thought of yet another round of chicken noodle or cream of tomato soup with sardines packed in oil or mustard set on stale crackers.

She should drop into William Dansinger's office before the grocery shopping. Checking her watch, she decided she should also treat herself to either an afternoon binge at the Brickley House Tea Room or an early supper at The Fisherman's Rest.

The idea appealed too strongly to ignore. Carissa quickly tidied up the kitchen and tamped down the fire. She caught sight of herself in the ornate mirror above the fireplace. Pale and drawn, without a trace of makeup. How Matthew must have loved that. He probably thought she was pining for him and unable to keep up appearances. She changed clothes, swapping green mohair for a mauve sweater and applied full makeup. Standing in front of the mirror, she took stock of her appearance again. Although she still felt tired and washed-out, she almost looked like herself.

CHAPTER TWENTY-TWO

CARISSA HEARD her next visitor's arrival long before the bell rang. Back-firing got closer and closer. Opening the door, she saw an old pale blue car as big as a tank in front of the house, foul black smoke belching from its tail pipe. The engine continued knocking even after the ignition had been turned off. Sputtering ended in a long drawn out wheeze and one last, spectacular backfire. Intrigued, Carissa watched as an older lady climbed out from behind the wheel. The door stuck open. The plump, stately matron kicked it, then butted it with her hip. The door crashed shut.

Satisfied, the woman straightened her hat, put a large clutch under one arm and stomped through the mud puddles in knee-high black go-go boots that belonged in the1960s. Over them, she wore a brown wool coat with a black lambswool collar. A good half-inch of black skirt showed below the coat's hem. Her fur hat sported a rumpled black veil that stuck out on one side.

"I've come to welcome you to the neighborhood, Miss Yates," the lady said.

"Thank you." Carissa watched as her visitor opened the gate and strode up to the porch.

"I'm Miss Virginia Greeley," the woman announced, as though that clarified any questions Clarissa might have.

Carissa played dumb, like she had no recollection of seeing Virginia that morning. "Hello," she said. She remembered her mother saying the first thing that happened when you moved into a small village was they asked you to give them money to rebuild the church steeple or something equally odd.

"Did you want me to donate to a local charity?" She asked, hoping to slow Virginia's momentum. "I'll be happy to do that. Let me get my purse."

Her visitor's expression registered disbelief. "Donate? Of course not. I *hate* charities. People need to get out and work for a living. I'm here as part of the welcoming committee. The rest of them wouldn't come out in this weather."

"Oh." Carissa felt relief that she wouldn't have to deal with a carload of matrons. "How nice of you. I heard about welcome wagons from my mother. She said they were all the rage in small towns back when she was young."

Miss Greeley harrumphed loudly. "I am a retired educator and the local historian, not some suburban housewife carrying around free mops and bags of candy." She drew up her shoulders and shifted her over-stuffed clutch to her hip. "I can tell you more about the origins of the Cove than anyone else in town, including Nancy Burton, who fancies she knows everything, or Percival Huddleston, who knows a lot more."

Carissa unsuccessfully ran over a short list of names in her head. "Percival Huddleston?"

"The mayor, dear. I thought everyone knew his name."

"I didn't."

"I can soon change that," Virginia assured her. "Tea would be nice," she added.

"It would have been so much better if you'd called ahead. I'm just about to drive into the village. I've got some errands to run, and I need to see my aunt's attorney. I missed him earlier."

"William won't mind if I monopolize your time for a little while." Miss Greeley energetically wiped her feet before placing one ugly boot onto the mat inside the door.

Carissa decided arguing would alienate Virginia and her good intentions. She could make a fast cup of tea and send her visitor off on her extremely noisy way. She stepped aside. "Come in, Ms. Greeley."

"I prefer Miss, but you may call me by my first name if you would like." Virginia sailed past like a battleship coming into port. She removed her gloves and hat, unbuttoned her coat and presented her back to Carissa. She began to shrug out of the coat. Carissa took the hint and the coat, which she hung on a peg. Incredibly heavy, it crouched on the hanger like a recently-slaughtered piece of game.

Virginia was already heading for the living room. She looked around. "You made some changes."

"A few," Carissa agreed. "There'll be a lot more once the renovations start."

Virginia looked offended. "Your aunt was too old-fashioned for your taste, I suppose."

"The kitchen's cold because of an unheated mudroom, and both the washer and dryer are down in the basement. I'd like new appliances and a much better flow to the kitchen." Carissa felt defensive. Who was Virginia Greeley to question what she was doing with the lighthouse keeper's quarters? "Have a seat." She gestured toward the couch. "I'm afraid I just put out the fire, but the new furnace is warming the cottage up nicely."

"No need to stand on ceremony." Virginia followed Carissa into the kitchen.

Carissa put on the kettle and pulled out a packet of chocolate chip cookies she had bought at a gas station convenience store on the way from New York, when she needed a quick sugar jolt to keep her awake. She put them on a plate and watched as Virginia made short work of eating three of them while the kettle came to a boil.

Virginia chatted about the history of the Cove then segued into her own history. After completing her undergraduate studies at Wellesley College, she found herself unexpectedly homesick and returned to fill a vacant position at the local elementary school, where she had taught fourth grade and library science until she retired. Despite her appearance and her initial introduction, Carissa found herself warming to Virginia, who felt she may have made a bad decision, giving in to the bout of homesickness instead of choosing a more adventurous life.

Virginia also did some thinly-disguised prying into Carissa's affairs. Carissa gave a shortened version of how she had come to Treacher's Cove. Virginia asked whether she would ever go back to New York. To visit, perhaps, Carissa said. But not to live. *Not with Matthew there.*

At the thought of Matthew, she felt herself breaking into a sweat. He was probably staying at The Fisherman's Rest, where he'd no doubt be spending time in the bar, buying rounds of drinks for the regulars and trying to find out everything and anything they knew about Jessica Malloy, the Bennett Point Light and its new owner. She needed to call Steve and warn him about Matthew, but not with Virginia Greeley within earshot.

She studied her watch, stood up and loaded the dirty dishes onto a tray. "I'd love to continue chatting, but I really need to see William Dansinger."

"He'll be home for sure. Their housekeeper fell in the Market this morning."

"Oh, that's awful." Carissa watched warily as Virginia's ample bosom expanded to where the buttons on her floral print blouse looked in imminent danger of popping off.

"She has a very bad sprain and won't be back at work for days." Virginia leaned forward conspiratorially. "Mildred Prentice said Mrs. Dodds' foot was so black and swollen it was hard to get her boot off."

"Ouch." Carissa winced at the thought, remembering how she sprained one of her own ankles during a tennis lesson when she was first married to Matthew. By the time the coach had carried her to the locker room and put an ice pack on her ankle, they had trouble removing her shoe, even unlaced. She'd hated tennis ever since. Matthew had only pushed her into taking lessons to keep her body slim and trim for him. He liked the feel of her bone structure beneath his hands, he'd told her— her ribs, her hips...

"Carissa, dear, I don't think you heard a word I just said." Virginia stood up. "I think it's time for me to go home."

"Sorry," Carissa said. "I've got a lot on my mind and no groceries."

"Then we'd both better get moving, hadn't we?" Virginia sailed back down to the coat rack. "It would be nice if you helped me." She presented her back.

Carissa wondered how her visitor managed to wrestle herself into that coat at home as she waved Virginia away, her backfiring car leaving a trail of black smoke.

CHAPTER TWENTY-THREE

Relieved to be alone again, Carissa called the primary number on William Dansinger's business card, expecting a receptionist to pick up. The phone buzzed several times before sending her to an answering machine. She didn't leave a message.

Why wouldn't an attorney be available to his clients during the day? She asked herself. Perhaps because he was semi-retired if he was around the same age as Virginia. He probably had limited office hours. Carissa tried the second number. Another answering machine clicked on, telling her neither William nor Patsy could come to the phone. Since he hadn't left her any other options, she asked him to call her and hung up. Belatedly, she realized she hadn't left her cell number.

Carissa hated playing phone tag. She wasn't going to call back and leave yet another message. Flipping through Aunt Jessica's address book, she found an address for the Dansingers. She'd drive by their home while she was out and leave her card if no one answered the door. Her stomach growled, the piece of quiche long digested. An early supper at the Brickley House Tea Room would hopefully stop her from filling her grocery cart with junk food. When she'd driven past, the quaint little shop had looked very inviting with its bubbled windows and Dickensian décor.

She gave the Dansingers' address to her navigation system before bumping over even deeper ruts on her way to the road. Carissa kept seeing dollar signs with every pot hole. Chuck's vehicles and the moving van had left their marks. Paving the track was going to have to come before her remodeling plans or it might become impassable for her car. She saw herself traipsing in and out of the basement with her dirty laundry for weeks unless she hired a housekeeper.

She almost missed the Dansingers' driveway. Obscured by an over-grown hedge, it was barely visible. Carissa applied the brakes too heavily and slid to a stop on a thin film of ice. Promising herself she would trade in the car for an SUV with 4 wheel drive ASAP, she turned into a narrow driveway lined with a thick layer of privet. Snow flurries drifted past the windshield. The trees thinned out rapidly, giving her a view of a house perched on a hill overlooking the Cove.

A sprawling two-story, its architecture placed it somewhere around the nineteen-thirties. Awnings draped a wrap-around porch that no doubt embraced not only the sides but the back of the house. Stained glass graced tops of windows and a transom above the front door. The garage doors were closed. No lights showed in the windows despite the darkening sky.

She parked and got out. Snow tingled against her skin, flakes catching on her lashes. She blinked and hesitated. It seemed no one was home, but if Patsy Dansinger was an invalid, surely someone had to be there. Carissa walked up three concrete steps onto the front porch and pressed the doorbell. She didn't hear any answering ring or buzz.

She stood uncertainly on the front porch while snow flurries thick-ened. William had wanted to see her. Their housekeeper had injured herself that morning. He *had* to be home. She pressed the bell again but heard nothing except rustling, ice-encrusted bushes. She knocked loudly three times in rapid succession. Nothing. She should leave, pick up a few things for supper at the Market and go home before the weather wors-ened any further.

But before giving up, Carissa decided to take a quick look at the back of the house. Maybe the Dansingers couldn't hear her knocking. She stepped onto a weed-clogged path at the side of the house. Missing one of the flagstones, her boot broke through an ice-covered puddle. The sound rang out like the crack of a pistol. She stopped. What was she doing, snooping around some stranger's property in the middle of a snow storm?

Looking for answers, she told herself.

She jogged the rest of the way. If there were no lights around back, she'd leave. The Dansingers might be upstairs, taking a nap. She'd look pretty silly if they woke up and saw her snooping around. They might even call 911.

The rear of the house faced the ocean. She saw two Adirondack chairs on the extensive terrace, one piled high with blankets. A small table beside that chair held a plate containing a soggy mess; a cup balanced on top of the blankets. She moved in for a closer look. Soaked blankets swaddled a thin human form. Carissa reached out to take the cup away. Her hand touched fingers, ice cold and blue.

A soft moan came from the blanket-draped head. Carissa pulled back the cover. A woman's face, white as the snow falling around them except for blue patches beneath glazed and vacantly staring eyes, scared Carissa more than she wanted to admit.

"Mrs. Dansinger?"

The eyes focused on her briefly before closing.

"We've got to get you inside. Whatever are you doing out here?"

Carissa tried to open the patio door, but it wouldn't budge. She looked around and thought fast. If Patsy Dansinger was an invalid, chances were good she'd never make it to the Lexus even with help. Carissa knew she couldn't carry the woman that far, and a low wall between the side and the back of the house would stop her bringing the car closer. If she left to get help, Patsy could die.

A shed stood at the back of the garages. When she tried that door, it was unlocked. Overstocked with all kinds of tools, she found plenty of choices to break glass.

"Sorry," she muttered as she smashed a hoe against a window. It shattered with a sound as cold and brittle as the surrounding air.

Careful to keep her sleeve over her arm, Carissa reached through and opened the window. Dragging the other Adirondack chair over, she used it to stand on while she climbed inside the house. If alarms were ringing, they must be the silent variety, and she could only hope they'd bring help. She unlocked the patio door and slid it open. The interior of the house felt overly warm, especially against the frigid temperature outside. Carissa pulled off the sodden blankets and shook Patsy, who opened her eyes and blinked myopically.

"Can you walk?"

Patsy shook her head.

"Do you have a wheelchair, then?"

Another shake. "No. William ca-ca-carries m-me."

"I can't do that. I'll have to get you onto the ground and drag you inside."

Patsy's eyes opened wide that time and focused really well. She looked incredulous.

"I'll be careful, I promise. I want you to help me as much as you can." Carissa peeled away the final blanket to expose a thick coat buttoned over a pale pink housecoat, pink flannel pajamas and pink, fuzzy slippers. Patsy didn't look *that* heavy.

A door slammed somewhere in the house.

"Patsy?" A male voice shouted. "Patsy? Dear God, Patsy!"

Lights blazed inside the house and a man came running through the living room, tall, stylishly dressed and with a mane of silver hair.

"William," the woman whispered.

"My darling." He looked pitiful with his white face and wild eyes. He stopped right in front of Patsy's chair and looked at Carissa. "Who are you? What are you doing here?"

"I'm Carissa Yates. Not that it matters right now. We need to get your wife inside as quickly as possible."

"Of course, of course." He picked Patsy up like a rag doll. "I thought Mrs. Dodds, our housekeeper was coming shortly after I left."

He paused to look at the hoe and the broken window before carrying his wife into the house. Carissa followed.

"I stopped by your home earlier," William said. "Didn't you see my note?"

"I did. I tried calling the numbers on your card, but I couldn't get any response. I came here to either see you or leave you my cell phone number."

William dumped Patsy on the couch and grimaced as he straightened up. "I went into town to do some work after I stopped by your home. I had lunch at The Fisherman's Rest, where I found out Mrs. Dodds fell in the Market and sprained her ankle. Imagine my shock."

Carissa wondered how big and strong Mrs. Dodds was, if she was supposed to carry Patsy in from the terrace. "I heard about her fall."

William gathered his wife back into his arms. As he lifted her, he grimaced with pain.

Carissa stepped forward to help him.

"I'm fine." He shook his head. "It's an old back injury." He grunted.

"Where's the bedroom?" Carissa asked. "I'll help you get these wet clothes off her. We should get her into a hot bath to warm up." She expected him to tell her somewhere down the hallway from the living room. Instead, he headed for the stairs.

"I'll do it," he said over his shoulder. "How did you find out about Mrs. Dodds' accident?"

"Virginia Greeley told me while she was giving me her version of a welcome visit. She said since the housekeeper fell, you would be home taking care of your wife."

"You broke my window." William was halfway up the stairs. "It's frigid in here."

"I'm sorry. I'll take care of it and get Mrs. Dansinger a hot drink." Carissa refused to be put on the defensive. She felt very unsettled about his behavior. She found a panel of switches on the wall beside the stair-case and flooded the downstairs with light. The kitchen was close to the front door. She ran out to her car, took Richard Ebberly's card out of her purse and called him while she filled an electric kettle and looked for tea.

"I'll get someone over there right away," Richard told her. "No charge. Sounds like it was an emergency. I can get the window boarded today and see what needs to be done to get a replacement. It may or may not be stock size. You never know with these old houses."

Carissa heard water running overhead and the low murmur of William's voice, indistinguishable words echoing from what must be an upstairs bathroom. The kettle rumbled, steam erupting from the spout. "I should go," Carissa said. "Thank you, Richard."

"If you need anything else, let me know. William can be a bit difficult sometimes. He should ask the doc to visit. He makes house calls to Patsy."

Carissa thanked him again and said goodbye. She found a teapot and matching cups in one of the cabinets. A sugar bowl sat next to the coffee maker. She had no idea whether Patsy liked milk in her tea, but decided cooler tea would get into Patsy faster. She took a half gallon from the refrigerator and tipped some into a small jug. The only thing she lacked was the tea.

She opened a cabinet over what looked like the message center. A blinking red light on the answering machine distracted her. A cascade of packets, canisters and coffee filters dropped from overhead. Carissa tried to deflect them. Her elbow hit the answering machine. A mechanical voice announced there were four messages. Carissa saved an open canister of coffee from upending onto the floor.

William's voice came from the machine, saying he'd be home shortly, followed by one from Mrs. Dodds, explaining about her accident. Carissa saw a package of English Breakfast, took out three teabags and dropped them into the pot. She thought about trying to stop the machine, but she had such a mess on the counter, she didn't want William to see it and think all she did was wreak havoc. The kettle boiled. She listened idly to the answering machine while she poured water into the teapot. A third message, from an auto repair shop, told William they had time to fix his broken tail-light. Carissa remembered seeing the light was broken as the Cadillac drove away from her house.

She looked out the kitchen window. William's car was parked beside hers. He had taken the time to turn it around, but it was parked at an angle. Both tail-lights were intact. Her heart skipped a beat. William must have gone into town to get his light fixed. But if he'd picked up the message from the auto shop, why hadn't he heard the one from Mrs. Dodds?

She heard her own voice asking William to call her before the machine announced there were no more incoming messages and clicked off. Her thoughts jumbled and alarm bells ringing in her head, Carissa poured a cup of steeped tea, adding milk and a spoonful of sugar. Passing a wet bar on the way to the stairs, she saw a bottle of brandy and grabbed it.

William was dressing Patsy in flannel pajamas as she complained weakly about not being put into her "prettier nylon nightie." Carissa glanced into the ensuite bathroom as she passed it. The floor was covered with water and wet towels. William looked up and saw her.

"I made tea," Carissa said. "I didn't know if Patsy drinks alcohol or not, but a shot of brandy in it might be a good idea."

"Thank you." William took the cup from her and added brandy. He avoided eye contact. "I'm sorry I shouted at you. I was horrified when I saw Patsy."

"Do you want me to call the doctor?" Carissa asked. "I already have someone coming over to board up the window until the glass can be replaced. Of course, I'll pay for the repair."

"I haven't had time to think about calling the doctor." William rolled back wet shirt sleeves. His jacket lay on the floor outside the bathroom. "I'll do it now." He picked up an address book from Patsy's nightstand, flipped pages and then punched numbers into her cordless phone.

Carissa wondered why he didn't pull out a cell phone and use that. She laid her hand against Patsy's face. It felt surprisingly cold. She wondered why the bath hadn't been more effective. As William spoke with the doctor and gave him a report of Patsy's condition, Carissa supported Patsy's head and tried to get some brandy-laced tea into her mouth. Patsy's eyes stayed closed, but she was taking little sips. Tea dribbled down her chin onto the pajama top.

William finished his call. He looked at the soiled pajama top and went over to the chest of drawers. "I'll have to change everything," he said as he pulled out a violet nylon nightdress, a whisper-thin crocheted bed jacket and footies.

"Those won't be warm enough," Carissa protested.

"Patsy can't bear to be soiled. The doctor's coming right over, and she doesn't have any other flannel that's clean."

"We can put one of those thicker woolen bed jackets over the pajama top."

"Everything has to match." William looked rebellious.

"Oh, for goodness sake, Mr. Dansinger." Carissa wanted to let go of Patsy so she could shake him. "If you insist on undressing your wife again, you could kill her. She's still really cold, even with all these bedclothes and the flannel."

"She'd never forgive me if she died in a mismatched outfit," he said.

Patsy opened one eye, then the other. She looked up at Carissa. "That's true," she said. "More tea, please."

Carissa hoped William felt the same degree of relief as she did. "Yes, Ma'am." She brought the cup back to Patsy's lips and watched as a touch of pink crept across the woman's chalk-white cheeks.

William threw the clean nightwear back into the drawer and slammed it shut. He went into the bathroom. Carissa heard him cleaning up.

He had to keep up appearances no matter what, she thought with a stab of anger. *He's probably more worried about how the broken window looks than about the draught from it.*

She tried to put herself in his shoes, finding his wife outside in a snowstorm with a broken window and a stranger, and wondered how she would have reacted.

Not like William Dansinger, she decided. Never like him.

CHAPTER TWENTY-FOUR

MATTHEW FINISHED his second dry martini and popped the olive into his mouth. After taking a hot shower and changing clothes, he felt more himself. He'd tried to forget his visit to Carissa, but his mind kept replaying the scene from the moment she hit him with the canister to when he had to run across the driveway in his socks after that pissing excuse for a deputy sheriff threw his shoes into a puddle. He should never have married Carissa, he told himself. He'd let his dick do the talking.

"Another drink?" The bartender stared insolently.

Matthew was tempted to knock back a couple more martinis, but he didn't like getting out of control, especially in unfamiliar surroundings. He might say something he'd regret later. "Nope. I've had my limit. Put the tab on my room charge."

He slid off the bar stool and reached into his pocket to search for small change to tip the bartender. The guy might be a surly type, but Matthew couldn't see the sense of making an enemy where he planned to stay at for a while. He pulled out a nickel, two dimes and a quarter and laid them on the bar.

"I'm Steve Raymond, the owner. I don't need to be tipped." The man pushed the coins back toward Matthew, stowed the empty glass under the bar and wiped the counter energetically, like he was trying to erase all evidence of his guest's visit.

"You sound like you don't want my business." Matthew put the coins back into his pocket.

"Let's say I wouldn't be crushed if you took yourself and your business elsewhere." The man's already-harsh features morphed into granite.

"That's one helluva way to treat a guest. What the fuck have I done to you?" Matthew clenched and unclenched his fists as he wondered if the big guy was physically as well as verbally aggressive. One of those oversized fists could do a lot of damage to his face.

"Nothing yet, but you've done a whole lot to a friend of mine."

"I see." Matthew relaxed his fists. "Carissa's been tattling. She convinced everyone we knew in New York that I was a son-of-a-bitch out to rip her off."

"She came here wanting to start a new life. Now *you* turn up. Has to be a reason for that. She said the divorce was final."

"It is, but now she wants a bigger slice of the pie. What a way to repay me after everything I did. I took her from sewing samples to embellishing *haute couture.*" He looked at the inn's owner and wondered if the guy even knew what that meant, let alone understood what an honor it was for Carissa.Steve Raymond shook his head. "From what Carissa told me, her aunt taught her to sew, and she has something unique you're trying to steal from her."

"She tells that story to anyone who listens. She gate-crashed a private party to meet me, she manipulated me into marrying her, and then after she got everything she could ever wish for, she dumped me and tried to take credit for my signature designs. But I'm here to resolve this fight. She'll see it my way after she listens to reason."

A florid-faced man at the other end of the bar tapped the bottom of his glass against the wooden surface. "Another draft, Steve? A man could die of thirst in this watering hole today. Isn't that right, stranger? Give the man a drink on me, Raymond. Maybe we'll both get some service that way."

"Keep your shirt on, Al." Steve Raymond walked over and grabbed the man's glass.

Matthew's mind filled with memories of those years with Carissa.

Becoming aware of her talent, he quickly moved her from the cutting room into the design process. She was pinning those embroidery pieces onto his gowns while he was trying to get her into bed. Although she'd accepted kisses and a limited amount of groping, he couldn't get to home base. He'd finally realized that if he wanted anything more, he was going to have to marry her. By then, the first show with her braiding was over, and they had more orders than the House of Yates had ever seen. He took her to dinner, they rode up to the top of the Empire State and he proposed.

She'd accepted. That was the real beginning of his problems. She'd modified the wedding dress he designed for her, adding seed pearls in intricate patterns across the lace bodice and down the sleeves. Steve Raymond pushed another martini across the bar. Matthew forced himself out of his reverie long enough to nod his thanks and lift his glass to the stranger who had paid for it. His mind wouldn't leave his wedding day alone. He felt a pang of remorse about the way things had gone after they left the reception.

Carissa had worn a short organza number, a white cloud with undertones of the traditional 'something blue' for the reception. Again, she'd embellished it, that time with lace embroidery. Guests were already clamoring to order copies of both gowns. Matthew had tried to show enthusiasm, but his only goal was for the two of them to put in a token appearance before going upstairs to the bridal suite, where he could finally get what she'd refused him before.

He'd taken her standing up against a wall as soon as he'd closed and locked the suite's door. The one-of-a-kind gown had ripped with every thrust of his hips. He remembered the tears on Carissa's cheeks and the small drop of blood on her lower lip where she'd bitten it when he rammed into her without even kissing her first.

A painful back blow brought him back to the present.

"Hey, bud...wake up!"

Matthew's elbows slammed onto the bar. "What the fuck?"

"Sorry about that."

His shoulders were massaged with all the gentleness of a pair of backhoes.

"Relax. Lighten up."

A raucous laugh echoed in his ears. The owner of those hands swung one short leg over a barstool and hoisted himself onto the seat next to Matthew.

"Al Dyson," the guy said, grabbing Matthew's hand and pumping until Matthew thought his shoulder was about to dislocate. "Steve, bring a bottle of whisky and a couple of shot glasses. No more cocktails. Let's have a *real* drink."

Matthew glared.

Dyson threw back his head and guffawed. "The designer's got spirit. You look like a whisky man to me."

Matthew thought back to his youth in the Bronx. Ripple and cheap beer had once been his drinks of choice. He'd developed a taste for martinis when he moved into the realm of the rich and famous.

"If you're buying, I can stomach whisky," he said.

Al Dyson belched loudly and farted. Steve Raymond dumped a half-empty bottle of Four Roses and two shot glasses in front of them before stalking off to serve two new arrivals.

"Planning on staying long?" Al unscrewed the top from the bottle and filled the glasses. He took one and held it up. "Cheers. Here's to new acquaintances."

Matthew clinked glasses and watched Al knock the whisky back. He followed suit, feeling a less-than-smooth liquid burn its way down his throat. He managed to avoid coughing and watched Al refill their glasses.

After the fifth shot, Matthew began to feel lightheaded and queasy. Mixing drinks was always a mistake, especially on an empty stomach. He pushed the shot glass away. "That's enough for me, man. I need dinner."

He stood up unsteadily and pulled out his billfold. The leather felt slick and hard to hold. It fell to the floor.

"I told you I'm buying." Al half-fell off his stool and stood reeling back and forth.

Watching him made Matthew feel even more nauseated. He had to pick up his billfold. He bent over. So did Al. They smacked heads. The next thing Matthew knew, he was on the floor with Al lying on top of him. The man reeked of stale sweat, whisky and beer. His jacket felt damp against Matthew's cheek.

Laughter erupted. Al was pulled off him and another set of rough hands pulled him to his feet. Matthew looked up to see Steve Raymond's disapproval. *Christ, the guy's a big son of a bitch.*

"You'd both better eat." Raymond grabbed one of Matthew's arms, then after some hesitation, one of Al's. He propelled them into the dining room, sat them at a back table with low lighting and called out "Hilly?"

A waitress came running over. "Yes, Mr. Steve?"

"Coffee. Lots of it. Leave a carafe on the table and make sure their cups stay full. Bring them roast beef, steamed vegetables and rolls. Nothing greasy. I don't want vomit anywhere in my place. The meal's on me. Yates is already registered. Get Al a room, too. It's snowing, and I'm not having him trying to get home when he's been drinking." Steve Raymond left.

Hilly ran for the kitchen. She returned with coffee, which Matthew only had time to sip twice before a steaming plate of vegetable soup was set in front of him. On the other side of the table, Al Dyson picked up his spoon and began slurping like some medieval beast in a bad B-movie.

After they had eaten the roast beef and the room stopped spinning, Matthew began to take more notice of his surroundings. He liked what he saw. The old inn oozed atmosphere. If its host had been capable of oozing even a fraction of the congeniality Matthew sensed in the conversations going on between the diners and the staff in the restaurant, he decided the place would be filled to capacity year round, blizzards or not. He finished his third cup of coffee.

Hilly tried to give him a refill. Matthew pushed his cup away. "Enough. That's the last time I skip lunch and drink with Al."

Dyson gave another grating, raucous laugh. Matthew braced for more back pounding, but instead, Al gave Hilly his credit card and sat back in his chair. "The meal's on me. I caused the ruckus; I should pay for the clean-up, not Steve." He grinned at Hilly before turning back to Matthew. "After a full meal, I really miss smoking." He folded his hands across his middle and sighed. "I got rid of fifty pounds to get healthy, but I can't stop losing my hair. Doesn't seem fair, and it still hasn't brought me the fulfilling sex life I was hoping for. I guess it's true you can't have everything, but I sure keep trying."

"We all do." Matthew was ready to get up and leave, but he saw Steve Raymond standing in the lobby, talking to a very pretty woman. He would rather not get too close to the inn's owner so soon after making a drunken fool of himself, and he wanted to see what sort of relationship the man had with that woman.

"So Matt, tell me about yourself and your lovely ex-wife," Al said.

"Not much to tell." Matthew shrugged. "The divorce was her idea, not mine."

"Want her back, huh?"

Matthew nodded, his gaze still on the couple having an intense conversation in the front lobby. "That's why I'm here—taking another shot at reconciliation."

"Hmm."

Hilly dropped off a leather folder. Al checked the bill, scribbled in a tip and signed off on it. He turned to see what was taking Matthew's attention from him.

"Maybe you'll get lucky, if someone else doesn't interfere." Al slid his credit card back into his billfold and tucked it into his back pocket, leaning across the table in a conspiratorial manner. "I think he's got the hots for your ex, although I'm not sure he's fully aware of it himself, yet. The whole town's beginning to talk about his interest in the Cove's new resident."

A stab of jealousy ripped through Matthew. He glared at Steve Raymond, now leaning casually against one of the hewn beams supporting the reception desk as he rubbed one hand up and down the slender blonde woman's arm. She had a pert little rack Matthew would like to feel up, and a boyish butt he wanted to cup in his palm. He swore she wasn't wearing a bra, which meant to Matthew that she was probably wearing very little in the way of panties, either. A portly man with cropped gray hair left his coat on a peg near the front door and joined them.

"Who's Raymond talking with?" Matthew asked Al.

"Sally Mainard, his sculptor girlfriend, and Percival Huddleston, our long-time mayor."

"She's a looker. What's he hanging around Carissa for?" He was muttering to himself more than Al, but his companion answered anyway.

"A man likes variety. I'm sure *you* do. Sally's outgoing and knows who and what she likes. She makes no bones about it." He grinned and shook his head. "She sure sent me packing real fast. I sold her the shop and the apartment above it. Great view of the water front, excellent location for her gift shop and workroom. Gets tons of tourist traffic in the season. But she sent me packing when I tried to kiss her after she got moved in and was showing me how she'd arranged her furniture in the apartment. Right in her bedroom, in front of that queen-sized bed, too. I thought it'd be a great chance for her to show her gratitude, but she didn't. *Women.*" He snorted.

The thought of Al Dyson trying to get into Sally Mainard's pants made Matthew want to laugh. He reckoned she'd want a lot more than a referral to a piece of good property to get up close and personal with the likes of that man. "How long have she and Raymond been going together?"

"About two years. They started keeping company right after she rejected me and he bought the inn. Not a deal I made." Al grimaced. "Damn place was about to fall down. He put Christ knows how much into it, but he sure does make a good living out of it."

"He's only lived here two years? He acts like he's in charge of the whole town. How often do you guys elect a mayor? Huddleston should be real worried about keeping his job next time."

"Huddleston's a hard man to beat. He's serving his second term and getting the voters ready for his third. I ran against him last year and the bastard won. Ran his campaign on his previous record of cleaning up pollution in the harbor and orchestrating a big bump in the tourist industry."

"What was your angle?" Matthew watched Al's eyes narrow to slits.

"I wanted to turn the goddamned lighthouse into a resort and pump some money into this shit-assed little backwater. I lost that deal when Jessica Malloy refused to play ball and sell the place. Now I've got another big fish on the line and here comes your ex-wife, refusing to sell the fucking place again. That Malloy family sure knows how to hold up progress and screw with my life."

"Can you find me a winter rental?" Matthew asked. "Like yesterday?"

"You bet." Al grinned. "It'll be my pleasure."

CHAPTER TWENTY-FIVE

HUBERT ARCHED his back and slid his rotund body around Virginia Gree-ley's ankles. She stopped scrutinizing her playing cards and smiled down at him. "Does my precious little Hubikins want his dinner?"

Hubert purred like a riding mower at full throttle.

"Let's finish this hand, Virginia." Nancy pushed her glasses up the bridge of her nose and shifted impatiently. It had been far too long since she beat Virginia at anything, including Hearts.

Virginia gave one last glance at the upturned card on the table in front of her and collected the rest of the deck. "Hubert needs his food. He's elderly, and it's not good for him to be hungry." She stood, still holding the cards. "Tea, Nancy?"

Nancy slapped her own cards onto the table face-up. "A perfect hand and Hubert needs his food." She glared at Virginia. "I'd like to know what you were holding. Hubikins was a timely interruption, I'd say."

Virginia sniffed disdainfully and set the cards on the buffet. "I baked a poppy-seed cake," she offered.

Nancy's favorite. She gave one last glance at her cards before gathering them into a stack and placing them in the middle of the table. "I'll help."

Virginia's nose was in the air. She picked up Nancy's cards, shuffled them into the deck and put the cards away in the top drawer of the buffet. "Very well."

They followed Hubert's swinging hips and raised tail into the kitchen.

Nancy got out plates and forks, a knife to cut the cake and two napkins. Virginia opened a small can of cat food and emptied the contents onto a Spode china tea plate. When she bent over to put the plate onto Hubert's plastic tray, she grimaced slightly. Hubert, his purring reaching a crescendo, eagerly gulped down the food.

"Is your knee bothering you again?" Nancy asked as her friend filled an electric kettle.

"A little," Virginia conceded.

She never liked to discuss her 'little aches and pains' as she called her arthritis. She had confided in Nancy only when her right knee became so swollen, she'd had to take a cab to the doctor and stopped by Nancy's store afterward to pick up a small bag of groceries. That was over a year ago. They hadn't discussed the arthritis since, but Virginia had taken to using a cane sometimes, particularly for longer distances and when the cold, rainy weather set in.

Virginia limped over to the refrigerator and took out a carton of milk. Nancy felt contrite about her behavior with the cards. "Why don't you sit in front of the fire and let me bring in the tea?"

Virginia drew herself upright. "I'm quite capable..."

"I know, Ginny. Let me do it, please. I'll feel more of a friend than a guest." Nancy put her hand on Virginia's arm.

"Oh, very well. If it means that much to you, Nance." Virginia took her cane from the back of a kitchen chair and walked back to the living room.

Nancy smiled to herself as she got out a tray. It had been far too long since they were Ginny and Nance. Lately, since the arrival of Walter Barnes, they had barely been on speaking terms. She sighed. Life had become complicated since Mr. Barnes had come to town, but she enjoyed his attention too much to give him up. She felt like a teenager when he sent flowers or candy. If only Virginia didn't think him good-looking, too, life would be better than it had been for a long time.

Nancy regretted goading Virginia about the church social. Her own poppy-seed cake was vastly inferior to Virginia's. But Walter had sung its praises when he tasted it. He had bought the whole cake at the church fundraiser that week, and they had been keeping company ever since. She wanted to tell Virginia he had proposed marriage, but she knew how her friend would react. Nancy didn't enjoy being called a fool by Virginia, however many years they'd been friends.

"Isn't that tea ready yet, Nancy?" Virginia's voice carried loudly from the living room.

She definitely had retained a teacher's ability to project her voice, Nancy thought. "Just letting it brew," she called, hurriedly unplugging the steaming kettle and pouring boiling water into the teapot, which already contained several Earl Gray teabags. She loaded everything onto a tray and stirred the tea liberally, hoping it would have steeped enough for Virginia's taste by the time she got it into the parlor.

Virginia had heaped more logs onto the fire. A formidable blaze shot sparks up the chimney behind a massive fire screen. The warmth was almost overpowering after the relatively chilly kitchen.

"You should keep all your rooms at an even temperature," Nancy warned, carefully placing the loaded tray onto the coffee table and settling into a chair opposite Virginia. "I'll play mother," she said.

She poured the tea, added milk and used tongs to drop two cubes of sugar into Virginia's cup before passing it to her.

"I like a roaring fire." Virginia jerked the saucer out of Nancy's hand, tea slopping over the rim of the cup. "You filled this too full," she complained, snatching the linen napkin Nancy offered her.

Nancy watched Virginia drape the napkin over her lap and pour the spilled tea from the saucer back into her cup. She decided not to argue the point that Virginia was responsible for spilling her own tea. "I like a good blaze, too, Ginny," she remarked instead. "But your arthritis is going to be affected by the lower temperature when you leave this room."

"Nonsense." Virginia stirred her milky tea with audible clinking, as though she was planning to put the spoon right through the bottom of the cup. "Let's change the subject."

"Let's." Nancy took a sip of her tea. Passable. It could have brewed at least two more minutes. Virginia would probably remark on that, too, unless they found a safer topic to discuss. She cut the cake and passed Virginia a piece.

Virginia set her cup carefully on the end table beside her chair before taking the plate. "I visited Carissa Yates yesterday." She stabbed her cake with a pastry fork and broke off a small piece, which she popped into her mouth.

"You did?" Nancy forgot everything else, astonished at the thought of Virginia doing a welcome visit to any new Cove resident. "Has the Yates girl made a lot of changes? I heard she had a new furnace installed and asked Richard Ebberly to completely gut the kitchen." Nancy watched all the redecorating shows on TV. She liked the word 'gut.' It implied destruction. Any remodeling at the lighthouse would be 'gutting' in Nancy's view.

"She hasn't changed much as yet." Virginia took another sip of her tea. "Jessica's things have been moved around. The kitchen table's now in the window where the piano used to be and the little Formica table Jessica had used for sewing was in the kitchen. I thought the living room looked a bit crowded but quite homey." Virginia speared another piece of cake and stopped speaking to chew.

"How does she like living out there? It was always so cold and drafty in the winter. I would hate the way the waves pound at the cliffs all the time. I don't know how a young woman could stay out there alone." Nancy suddenly felt cold. She pulled her chair closer to the fire.

"In my opinion, she's not doing at all well. She had dark circles under her eyes and she was so pale, Nance. I almost asked if she'd like to spend a couple of nights in my guest room. I heard she stayed at the inn while the furnace was installed."

Nancy had finished her cake. She put her plate back on the tray. "I don't know why Jessica was so attached to that place. I think it's creepy." She shuddered.

"Your imagination is much too vivid." Virginia finished her own cake. "Have another slice," she offered, wielding the knife.

"No, thank you. I had a big lunch." Nancy pushed back indignation at Virginia's bald statement. Her imagination was *not* vivid. "I'll take more tea." She held out her cup.

Virginia poured for both of them and nodded in silent approval as she saw the tea was stronger.

"I'll give Carissa Yates another month, at most," she predicted. "When winter really hits, she'll run back to New York."

"I doubt it." Nancy thought Virginia had given her too much milk. The tea was lukewarm when she tried it. "Her ex-husband's in town, you know. He came into the store to tell me he might be getting mail during the next few days. He said he'd rather pick it up from the post office than have it delivered to The Fisherman's Rest."

"You met Matthew Yates?" Virginia's eyes widened. "What does he look like?"

"Handsome. Tall. Well, tall to me. I suppose he's really medium height, if compared to say, Steve Raymond."

"Handsome how? Describe him. Dark, fair, clean-shaven, bearded?"

"My, you're inquisitive. He's dark-haired and has a moustache. Not a big one. Very well-groomed, as a designer should be. He's got brown eyes, a tan, and an arresting smile." Nancy paused, remembering Matthew Yates' even and very white teeth. "I think he's had a lot of dental work," she said. "And maybe Botox." She felt very current, talking about the treatment she'd read about in one of the magazines at the shop during a slow period.

"He doesn't sound like much of a designer to me." Virginia finished her tea. Hubert jumped onto her lap and made a big production of settling down, his paws kneading Virginia's thick woolen skirt until she soothed him with a rub behind his ears. Her hand traveled down his orange striped back. His purring rose to the pitch of an outboard motor.

"And what does a designer look like?" Nancy watched Virginia's rhythmic stroking send Hubert into kitty ecstasy.

"Well, not as *you've* described. I've seen some photos of Ralph Lauren, and he doesn't look anything like that."

"He had a navy, roll-necked sweater under a heavy black cashmere coat when he came into the store, along with black loafers." Nancy remembered how impressed she'd been with his assured manner.

"He sounds quite dashing." Virginia's eyes had a far-away look. I wonder why Carissa left him?"

"The press said she claimed he'd been abusive."

"Are you still reading the tabloids, Nancy?" Virginia clucked her tongue. "Shame on you. You know as well as I do that nothing in those miserable rags is true."

Nancy felt like one of her friend's former students. "There's no smoke without fire," she snapped before she could stop herself. *Honestly, Virginia Greeley is the most annoying, self-righteous, bothersome, tiresome...*

"You might be right."

Nancy stopped in the middle of her self-indulgent and satisfying internal tirade to stare.

"Stop looking bug-eyed, Nancy. What in the world is wrong with you?"

"I've never heard you admit you might be at fault."

"That's because I so seldom am."

Nancy watched Virginia's mouth twitch. They both burst out laughing at the same time.

CHAPTER TWENTY-SIX

MATTHEW ROLLED OVER, opened his eyes and groaned. He pulled a pillow from the other side of the bed and flung it over his face. The last thing he needed was a hangover, but a hangover was definitely what he had. He groped for the phone, squinted and punched the code for room service.

"Coffee. Lots of it," he croaked into the receiver. "And Tylenol, if you have it. Otherwise, whatever you've got."

No noise, he thought, carefully putting the receiver back on its cradle. No sudden moves, either. His head pounded as he half-crawled to the shower, where he stood under the water for a long time. When he returned to the bedroom, a pot of coffee stood on the vanity. Matthew drank three cups in rapid succession before taking his smartphone back to bed with him. He got a fast update on the state of his business, called his attorney and found the trial date on Carissa's case had been moved yet again. Swearing profusely, he got the name and number of a private detective agency.

The phone was answered on the first ring: "Halstead and Willis. This is Halstead."

The voice was hard, sharp and powerful. Matthew liked the businesslike tone. He explained his needs quickly and concisely. Halstead promised a preliminary report in twenty-four hours. They discussed terms and came to an agreement. Halstead and Willis had come highly recommended; Matthew had no reason to doubt he would have Steve Raymond's background report in his in-box by the following day.

He drank another cup of coffee. His headache felt better already.

CHAPTER TWENTY-SEVEN

NOVEMBER.

Richard Ebberly waited impatiently as the phone rang on and on. He decided Carissa wasn't home and started to hang up.

"Hello?" Her voice sounded breathless.

"It's Richard Ebberly. Are you okay?"

"I'm out of breath. I was in the tower."

"Without your phone?"

"Yes. I've never been someone to keep my phone close. That's why we all have voicemail."

Richard felt alarmed. "What if you had an accident or got locked out of your house for some reason? The low temperatures and the wind chill factors here can turn something minor into life-threatening in a very short amount of time."

"Richard, I'm not outside." She sounded like she was almost laughing at him.

"Fair enough, but you could fall down the stairs." The minute he said it, he wished he hadn't.

"I'm not in my seventies and arthritic," she said after a long minute.

"I know. That was insensitive of me. I'm sorry."

"You should be." She sighed heavily. "Are you calling to check up on me?"

"No. I'm calling to tell you I'm sorry you're having a rough time with this move."

"That's a good description for it." Now she sounded angry. "I moved up here for some peace. Almost from the moment I arrived, it's been one thing after another. The broken furnace, a faulty thermostat and outer doors that won't stay closed. Then Steve Raymond sent Deputy Watkins over to take a statement from me because someone may be playing stupid tricks to scare me into selling the lighthouse."

"I heard about all that," he said.

"The rumor mill?"

"Pretty much, yes. It's a small town; word gets around."

"Last night, I really thought about selling and leaving. I swore I heard someone walking around again. I kept my bedroom door locked and didn't get out of bed to investigate. Today, standing up in the tower and looking at the incredible view, I decided either I'm hearing noises made by the wind or I've got a ghost. Whatever. I've made up my mind to dig in my heels and stay. I've never believed in ghosts. I think someone flesh and bone is trying to get me out of here. I want the police to find out who that is and send that person or persons to jail."

"Another stubborn Malloy." He wanted to tell her to give up on the lighthouse and let him find her a rental cottage in the village, but he knew she'd refuse.

"And proud of it," she said. "Now, what did you call about? I hope it wasn't just to chat, or you brought me out of the tower for nothing. I'm not in the mood."

"I didn't. Can you come into town today?"

"I could. Do I have a good reason to do that?"

"You do. I've got preliminary sketches to show you of the changes I'd like to make to the cottage. I redesigned the kitchen, incorporating the mudroom space. I also took out the wall between the living room, dining room and kitchen to give you an open concept. I think you'll like it. No expensive additions or relocations of doors and windows."

"So now you want to tap my bank account, too, huh?"

Richard wasn't sure how to respond to that, but suddenly, Carissa laughed.

"I've watched your bottom line, I promise," he said, encouraged. "If you don't like my designs or you think they're too much, we can discuss priorities in more depth. It won't be as big an investment as you think, being used to New York prices. Labor's cheaper up here and so are some of the materials."

"Okay, Richard. I'll look at your plans, and we'll see if we can work things out. What time?"

"How about eleven and I take you to lunch?"

"This afternoon would be better. I've wasted too much time already this morning. I'm skipping lunch."

"You'll waste away."

"I doubt that. I ate a good breakfast, and I've planned a healthy dinner. No more tomato soup and stale crackers. Aunt Jessica's bare pantry has been fully stocked. So has her old refrigerator, which will be another appliance to replace somewhere down the line."

"Okay, if you won't stay for lunch, how about eleven o'clock, and I'll have you out of my office before noon? I've got another client arriving in fifteen minutes to go over plans for a loft conversion."

"It's ten o'clock, so that should work." Carissa sounded all business.

"It's a date," Richard told her. "You still have my card? The office address is on there."

"Your card's right beside the phone."

"The office is a block north of The Fisherman's Rest."

"Okay. Easy to find. If you're still tied up with the client, I'll walk over to the inn and get coffee to go," she said. "It'll give me an opportunity to show Steve I'm fine and he shouldn't worry about me."

The last thing Richard wanted was Carissa spending more time with Steve Raymond. "I won't be tied up," he promised. "When I make an appointment, I keep it."

"Me, too. See you in an hour. And by the way, no dating for me. 'Bye, Richard." She hung up.

Richard felt he'd been firmly rejected for anything except possibly his skills as an architect.

CHAPTER TWENTY-EIGHT

CARISSA CHOSE a pair of wool pants and a bulky, hand-knitted sweater for her meeting with Richard. The outside temperature had actually dropped since she got up at 7:00 A.M., with banks of clouds hinted strongly of snow. She pulled on thick socks and boots, her down coat, and one of Aunt Jessica's knitted hats. Her gloves, left in one of her pockets, were slightly damp. That was a rookie mistake, she thought. She hunted around and found a pair of Aunt Jessica's woolen mittens that smelled of mothballs. At least they wouldn't have holes, she told herself as she tried to ignore the pungent odor.

Steve Raymond would approve of her coat. No more lectures about inappropriate outerwear. She'd tried to keep away from him since the last time she'd taken merchandise to Sally's Gift Emporium and gotten a chilly reception. Sally had thawed sufficiently to take two boxes on consignment, one containing six embroidered vests and eight pillows Carissa had trimmed with her own braiding, the other filled with many of the crocheted afghans and hand-hemmed blankets Aunt Jessica had left stacked in the guest room wardrobe. Carissa had kept the most beautiful for herself, but she didn't need ten more afghans and five extra blankets, all brand new and wearing hand-embroidered tags from the

Bennett Point Workshop. She wished that along with those tags, they would have sported Aunt Jessica's unique patterns, but none did.

Sally hadn't asked whether Carissa had anything else to sell, or even whether she was feeling more settled. Their transaction was completed in less than 5 minutes, after which Sally went into her workroom, leaving Carissa with a distinct impression Sally was never going to forget or forgive. Steve must have made good on his promise to tell his girlfriend about spending the night at the keeper's quarters, Carissa decided as she trudged away from the Emporium. Sally had to have a very fertile imagination and a lot of trust issues to go with her creativity. Carissa resolved to find another outlet for her crafts, perhaps in Whitstead.

One of her errands today was to go back to the Emporium and see how many of her consignment items had actually sold. She had been unable to find any of them listed online when she checked Sally's website. She closed and locked the cottage's front door, rattling the door knob and pushing against the door before walking over to the garage, her head lowered against the screaming wind. She backed her Lexus out of the garage and reluctantly climbed out to close the garage door. Chuck Collins had warned her with good reason that it could be torn right off its hinges. She bolted it and drove away, blasting the heat as soon as the engine warmed.

She made a mental note to stop by the florist and pick up a bouquet for Patsy. She could drop it off before returning home. William probably wouldn't be too pleased, but Carissa didn't care. William shouldn't have left his wife outside even if the housekeeper was expected.

The Dansingers were a strange couple, Carissa thought. William seemed obsessively tidy, while Patsy was equally obsessed with color-coordinated nightwear, no matter how unsuitable for someone suffering from hypothermia. Carissa hoped she wouldn't become as set in her ways as she grew older. Aunt Jessica appeared to have developed a few quirks herself. Carissa felt another wave of sadness sweep over her.

One thing she did feel sure about was that Aunt Jessica didn't color-coordinate *her* nightwear. Carissa smiled at the thought of what she had found in her aunt's bedroom: A vivid red and black tartan flannel night-dress at the foot of the bed and the bright pink furry slippers she had been using since she arrived. She did wonder why she hadn't found a bathrobe, since the keeper's quarters were incredibly cold, but the thought ran through her mind that Aunt Jessica might have been wearing it over her clothes when she fell.

Carissa wondered again whether her aunt was trying to get to something important in the tower, or to hide from someone. But what, or who? She'd take another look in all the cupboards and dark corners when she returned to the cottage. Perhaps there really was something of value up there, hidden amongst the dust and rusted tools. She doubted she'd find her aunt's pattern books up there, but she had run out of other options, other than the basement, which she had forced herself to search fruitlessly while doing her washing one day.

As she drove by the harbor, she saw the fishing fleet being tossed about like plastic toys in a child's bathtub. Waves crashed against the piers, spray showering over clusters of stacked lobster pots. Milk-white caps rode toward the shore in relentless processions. Against the Lexus's windshield, snow flurries danced; crazed ballerinas in a fast-moving chorus line.

She glanced at the time: 10:45 A.M. She could run one of her errands before meeting Richard. She pulled into a parking space between his office and the tiny police station.

"Deputy Watkins is out on a call," the dispatcher, Dot Ellis told Carissa, her gum clicking loudly. "The sheriff's on leave."

Carissa left a message, asking the deputy to call her, then stopped by the florist. A bouquet of fragrant pink carnations and baby's breath made a good gift for Patsy and were carefully stowed on the passenger's seat. Carissa still had time to get her coffee at The Fisherman's Rest. But instead, she decided to find out if her pillows and vests were selling. When she walked into the Emporium, Sally came out of the stockroom.

"Oh, it's you." Sally sounded downright disappointed.

Carissa forced a smile. "I wondered if you were ready for more consignment items from me."

"Nothing sold yet." Sally stayed at the back of the shop.

Carissa glanced around. She didn't see any of her goods. "Where did you display them?"

Sally sniffed and pushed her hair back from her shoulders. "I asked Verna to put them out. They should be here somewhere."

"I'll look around." Carissa laid her keys and purse on the counter so she could pick up a delicate shell night-light. The one on display glowed pink and peach. "How much is this?"

"Ten dollars." Sally had moved over to the counter. She drummed her fingers on the glass covering a display of scrimshaw.

Carissa strolled around the crowded store without seeing even one of her items. "I think Verna forgot to put my goods out."

"I'll speak to her." Sally's manner oozed animosity.

Carissa wanted to reassure Sally she could feel secure about her relationship with Steve, but figuring out a way to broach the subject was even more difficult than she had imagined before walking into the Emporium. She felt sure anything she said about Steve that morning would provoke a confrontation.

Sally emptied a box of souvenir spoons onto the counter and started polishing them.

"I could take my items to Whitstead if you're not really interested in selling them," Carissa said. "I'm fairly sure there'll be another gift shop that'll take them."

Sally stopped polishing, tipped the spoons back into the box and began rearranging trays of cheap rings and pens beside the cash register. "Please yourself."

"What have I done to offend you?" Carissa asked.

Sally's eyes widened. "Smooth piece of New York trash, aren't you?"

Carissa forgot all about controlling herself. "Look here, Sally Mainard," she said, striding over to the counter. "Something's eating you. I'm not after Steve, if that's what you think." She put one hand on top of her purse and laid the other over her keys.

Sally crashed her fist down inches from Carissa's fingers. "You've been trying to steal Steve Raymond from right under my nose."

"If I'd tried, I'd have succeeded."

"Is that right?" Sally leaned across the counter, her face inches from Carissa's, her eyes spitting fire. "Full of yourself, aren't you?"

"Not as much as you are." Carissa slowly took her purse off the counter without breaking eye contact. "I'm warning you—don't start a fight with me. I'm fresh out of goodwill right now."

Sally's lips curled into a sneer. "Me, too."

"So give me back my consignment items right now." Inside, Carissa wanted to quake. Outside, she tried to exhibit the same level of control Roland Finch, her attorney had schooled her to use with Matthew.

Sally stomped off into the stockroom, blonde hair streaming behind her. She returned quickly with Carissa's boxes, still sealed with packing tape. "Here, take your miserable stuff." She threw the boxes onto the floor, turned her back and left, crashing doors between the store and her studio.

Carissa had trouble getting her boxes out of the Emporium. After struggling through the doorway, she tried to power-walk away, just in case Sally was watching, but the boxes were too heavy. Sally had managed to carry both boxes out of the stockroom without any visible straining while Carissa felt her muscles begging for relief before she'd even crossed the street. She still had to go up the hill from the harbor to where she'd parked her car. Large wet snowflakes made the cardboard slick. Her fingers slipped and both boxes tumbled onto the sidewalk. Carissa felt like kicking them all the way to her car.

"You look perturbed." Steve's voice held a note of laughter. He scooped up the boxes.

"Perturbed? You have no idea."

"Where are you going with these? I saw you stomping out of the Emporium. Is something wrong?"

"Wrong is an understatement." She headed up the hill, Steve falling into step with her.

"You want to talk about it? Anything I can do to smooth things over?"

"You? Ha! That's funny."

"I don't see you laughing."

"Sally thinks I'm a threat."

"I'm sure she does."

The softness in his voice shocked Carissa. She stopped and faced him. "Don't go weird on me, Steve. I don't need any more complications in my life right now."

"I guess you know your ex-husband's in town. He's staying at the inn."

"I do know. You let that slime-ball stay at your hotel?" She felt betrayed.

"Hilly checked him in while I was gone. I was tempted to throw him out, but I figured I'm an inn-keeper, not a moralizer."

"You'd better ask for your money up front. Matthew Yates is likely to leave without paying his bill."

"Is that what he did to you?"

"That's really rude." She walked the rest of the way back to her car with Steve a few steps behind. She popped the trunk without looking at him.

"Sorry; I apologize." He put the boxes inside and closed the trunk before looking at her. "What I said was completely uncalled for." He shook his head. "I keep treating you like a close friend. I feel protective of you, and yet I get into arguments with you at the drop of a hat. I don't understand myself."

"I don't understand you, either. Or myself. I know what you mean about the close friendship. But you keep overstepping your bounds. I told you I don't need a keeper."

Steve stuck his hands in his coat pockets. "A reporter came into the inn this morning. He tried to reserve a room but I told him I was fully booked and sent him to Whitstead. I'm thinking he either followed your ex or was told where to find him."

Carissa tried to tamp down a surge of panic.

"Maybe I can convince Matthew to leave town," Steve said. "I'll tell him I've got his room booked all the way through Thanksgiving."

"No one's going to get Matthew out of town unless he wants to go," Carissa said. "Telling him you're booked will only make him find some-where else to stay. I'll have to talk to him myself. That's the only way to get rid of him."

"I hope you have more success with him than you did with Sally."

"She refused to display my consignment items. That's what's in these boxes. I'm going to look for another store in Whitstead."

"She'd heard about me carrying you up to bed at the inn. No one saw me come down the back staircase into the kitchen to chat with Eva, the cook. That made Sally angry. After I told her I'd spent the night at your cottage, she really tore into me."

"I bet she did." Carissa stared at the boats rocking in the harbor. The sight made her queasy. "If you hadn't insisted on arguing with me loudly with the car door wide open, maybe Virginia would have thought I'd only given you a ride."

"I doubt that."

When Carissa looked up at him, she knew what he was going to say even before he opened his mouth.

"I can't say I blame Sally for believing I've got feelings for you," Steve said. "I've wanted to take you to bed ever since we met."

"Interesting things you learn when you take a stroll," said a voice behind them.

Matthew Yates stood a couple of feet away, snowflakes gently drifting onto his bare head.

CHAPTER TWENTY-NINE

WHERE MATTHEW YATES WAS CONCERNED, Carissa had frequently found the coward's way out was the right way. She figured this was one of those situations.

She fled, jogging up Harbor View Road to leave Matthew, Steve, Sally, and even her appointment with Richard far behind. She didn't stop until her breath ran out in front of a picket fence with an arbor over the gate. The mailbox read "Greeley." Without pausing to wonder what Virginia would think about finding a panting, sweaty and distressed woman on her doorstep, Carissa opened the front gate and walked through. To her surprise, as she latched the gate behind her, she heard a voice.

"Come on in, dear," Virginia said as though she'd been expecting her guest. "I've made a pot of herbal tea. It's excellent for calming the nerves."

Carissa stepped inside the house and took off her hat. "Thank you."

"No problem at all, dear. Hang your things on the hallstand and follow me." Virginia smiled.

Carissa did as she was told. Photographs in heavy frames lined a narrow hallway. Faces stared down at her as she passed, their poses stiff and formal, their clothing vintage. Virginia led the way into a parlor with a cross-beamed ceiling and burgundy flocked wallpaper.

"Have a seat. I'll get the tea." She pointed to a table in a bay window overlooking the garden.

Carissa saw bare-branched trees bending in the wind on the other side of the glass. Heavy ticking from a grandfather clock and crackling logs made the room cozy and companionable. Wingback chairs flanked the fireplace. Lap blankets beckoned visitors to settle down and pull the warmth of wool around them. A coffee table held books and a sewing basket. She heard her hostess setting out cups in the kitchen. Tension eased from her shoulders and she sat.

A crystal bowl filled with ripening pears graced the middle of the oak table. A bookcase in one corner overflowed with tomes ranging from Shakespeare to Henry James and Agatha Christie. Apart from the scent of the pears, the room smelled of furniture polish, wood smoke and the faintly musty smell of old books and antiques. Carissa loved it.

Virginia bustled in with a tray. She poured tea and handed Carissa a delicate china cup and saucer graced with violets. She moved the pears to make room for a plate of finger sandwiches and plates.

"I don't think..." Carissa began.

"Nonsense. You need something to tide you over until lunch."

Carissa took a white-bread finger sandwich and bit into it. Home-made pimiento cheese. It tasted heavenly. She eyed wafer-thin turkey on rye and took one of those, too. A third sandwich held cream cheese and cucumber. She wondered how Virginia had made so much in such a short amount of time. White frosting drizzled down the sides of a cake.

"Cranberry nut," Virginia said. "My mother's recipe."

"Cranberries fresh from some bog, no doubt."

"Of course. Three miles away. My mother took us on the bus to gather them when I was a child."

"You had siblings?"

"Two sisters, one brother. I'm the youngest. Roger, my only surviving brother, lives in Boston." Virginia smiled. "He's a retired violinist. He used to play with the Pops."

Carissa returned the smile. "I love to hear about families. I don't have much of my own. My dad left many years ago and hasn't kept in touch. When my mother divorced for the second time I lost interest in stepfathers. I'm an only child."

"I know. Jessica told me a lot about you. She loved you like a daughter."

Tears welled up in Carissa's eyes. "I loved her dearly. She really pushed me to go to design school. I had no self-confidence but really good grades. She convinced me I could do it. When I graduated with honors, I really thanked her. Now, I'm not so sure." She used a tissue from her pocket to wipe the tears away.

Virginia selected a couple of sandwiches. "So, what are you doing at the Cove? Burying yourself here won't stop your horrible designer ex-husband from hounding you. I read all about the divorce and your legal issues in the scandal rags." She pointed to a pile of magazines on the floor beside one of the chairs. "Nancy Burton at the post office called me a few minutes before you arrived, telling me she'd seen you fleeing up the hill toward my house after having an intense discussion with Matthew Yates and Steve Raymond."

"No wonder you were looking out for me." Carissa felt she'd walked into some sort of trap.

"Have another sandwich." Virginia pushed the plate toward her.

Carissa shook her head. She drank the rest of the tea. Virginia poured her another cup, and without asking, cut her a slice of cake.

"What were you arguing about?" Virginia asked.

Carissa debated telling Virginia to mind her own business, but what could Virginia possibly tell anyone else that hadn't been said twenty…a hundred times over by the press and social media? Over two more cups of tea, she gave her hostess an abbreviated account.

"Hmm." Virginia poured more tea and stirred a spoonful of honey into her cup. "Matthew is going to be a real nuisance. He'd just come out of Nancy's shop when he saw you and Steve. He'd already rented a mailbox for a month the day he arrived. He told Nancy he'd be extending that rental through the New Year at least. He said Al Dyson found him a rental cottage for the winter."

Carissa's worst fear had come to fruition. She dropped her cup. It broke. "I'm so sorry." She burst into a real crying jag that time. No fooling around with a few tears. She took tissues from the box Virginia slid across the table and shoved them against her mouth.

"Oh, dear." Virginia got up and hurried out of the room. She returned with a tea towel, a bottle of port and two glasses. "I think we can be forgiven for drinking before noon." She glanced at the grandfather clock. "It's not that far off."

While Carissa calmed down and mopped up spilled tea, Virginia poured port almost to the brim of two oversized wine glasses. "Drink it right down," she urged, whisking away the broken china and replacing it with the port. "This will bring the color back into your cheeks."

Carissa swallowed half the port without stopping to take a breath. Her brain continued to swirl around as though someone had pulled a plug and all rational thought was escaping down an open drain. She struggled to come to terms with the reality of Matthew living at the Cove and spying on her all winter. Her hands began to shake.

He couldn't. He wouldn't.

But she knew, even while she tried to deny it, that Matthew was capable of anything. He wanted her back, and if he got what he wanted, the legal problems would go away. The House of Yates would be safe from litigation, and so would Matthew.

CHAPTER THIRTY

"I won't be bullied by him anymore. He can spend eternity here if he wants, that egotistical…" Carissa managed to stop herself before launching into a tirade of swearing. Across the room on a display stand sat a large Bible, open to a passage that had undoubtedly been read that morning. A small box on one side of the table was marked "Promises."

"Have another port." Virginia filled both their glasses and held hers up. "Let's toast to your resolution not to have that man dictate your life."

Carissa was definitely willing to drink to that resolution and more. She raised her glass while silently attaching an addendum: Matthew falling off the dock and being swept out to sea. Then she saw the Bible again and retracted the bit about being swept away. But she wanted him to flounder around for a while in cold water that hopefully reeked of fish.

"You and Jessica are very much alike," Virginia said when she'd consumed her second glass of port.

"Oh? How's that?"

"The same basic grit and determination. Your aunt and William were leaders of the younger set here. Patsy was a wannabee."

"Didn't my aunt grow up in Bangor?" Carissa frowned, trying to remember whether her aunt had ever mentioned being at the Cove before she purchased the lighthouse.

"In its heyday, the Cove was far from a sleepy fishing village. But times do change." Virginia finished her drink. "Both Jessica and William's families built summer homes here. William lives in his year round."

"Where did my family stay?"

"Penwithen. Three miles north of the Cove. It has been boarded up for years."

"Why?"

"I believe mostly because of the accident, dear."

"What accident?"

Virginia's eyes widened. "Why, the one where Patsy got hit by William's car. You didn't know about that?"

"Aunt Jessica never talked much about her younger years."

"Well, I suppose she wouldn't. She never forgave Patsy. Jessica was convinced it was no accident—Patsy wanted William at any cost."

"Aunt Jessica and Patsy were rivals?"

Virginia got up. "I've got something to show you." She hurried out of the room.

Aunt Jessica and another woman had fought over William Dansinger? Carissa wondered what else her aunt had kept to herself.

Virginia returned with a bulging photo album. Sitting beside Carissa, she carefully turned pages filled not only with photographs but old newspaper clippings and postcards, fragile pressed flowers and locks of hair. Virginia gave a condensed history of Jessica and her older brother Edgar, Carissa's father. Tales of them not getting along had evidently not been blown out of proportion.

Virginia stopped turning pages when she came to a photo of three young people and an old-fashioned car. "There's Jessica with William and Patsy in front of his Oldsmobile. He was so proud of it."

Carissa leaned forward. She was astonished to see how much she resembled her aunt. No wonder William Dansinger had looked shocked when he saw her for the first time. Jessica's smile radiated joy. Her firm hold on William's arm looked proprietary. Standing at the other side of

William, Patsy held a hat in both hands. Her smile looked uncertain, her pose stiff.

"He taught Jessica to drive," Virginia said. "She would travel at high speed between here and Machias or Bucksport. People tattled about her. She got an undeserved reputation for being loose."

"But this was what? The early sixties? That sounds like a generation earlier, when Amelia Earhart and others were breaking barriers."

Virginia smiled. "You don't know enough about the years of bra burning and marching for equality." She poured more port. "Women were expected to wait for men to marry them so they could find their identities. Jessica found hers by going to nursing school and taking a position at Maine Medical Center in Portland instead of studying art at Boston College, as she had originally planned. People were shocked."

Carissa had never realized that Aunt Jessica was such a rebel. A bit eccentric, maybe. Her aunt must have kept her revolutionary ways in check when her niece visited. "She loved William very much, didn't she?" She asked Virginia. "I see it on her face."

Virginia nodded. "After Patsy's accident, everyone thought the love affair was over. Only we know differently." She sighed. "Forty years of stolen moments. I don't know how William made it through Jessica's funeral. He broke down afterward and wasn't seen for days."

"Forty years?" Carissa knew she couldn't have heard correctly. "Virginia, let me get this straight; my aunt and William carried on an affair for forty years?"

Virginia stopped turning album pages and looked up. "Dear Lord, you didn't know? I presumed she'd taken you into her confidence. I'm so sorry!"

Her hand squeezed Carissa's wrist gently. Carissa drank more port. She began to feel a little lightheaded. "Why did William marry Patsy instead of Jessica?"

"He backed his car over Patsy's legs at Penwithen. She was in a wheelchair for months. He felt dreadful. Myself, I've always wondered whether Patsy stepped behind the car on purpose. She'd be capable of doing that." Virginia nodded emphatically and drained her glass.

"Why isn't Patsy walking now?" Carissa asked.

"Multiple Sclerosis."

Carissa thought about William carrying Patsy up and down stairs. He'd grimaced when he lifted her. "Does William have back trouble?"

"Since Vietnam. A helicopter crash. He was in bed for months. Patsy nursed him, despite a slow recovery from her own injuries. She was still limping at the wedding. Soon after they married, she was diagnosed with the M.S."

Carissa put her hand over her glass when Virginia offered her another drink. Her head was already spinning. "Where was my aunt?"

"Overseas. In time she came back to the Cove and took up residence at the lighthouse after it was decommissioned. That's when you started to visit. We'd see you and be so thankful Jessica had someone else to love and be loved by." Virginia stopped speaking and dabbed her eyes with her napkin.

Carissa thought back to the days when she'd take the train to Bangor, where Aunt Jessica would pick her up and bring her to the Cove in an old Jeep. Jessica would chat all about everything but Carissa's home life. A rolling kaleidoscope passed through her mind of day trips with picnics, beachcombing, and learning Aunt Jessica's embroidery and braiding techniques.

"Patsy resorted to the oldest trick in the book to get him to marry her. She climbed into bed with him and told him she was pregnant," Virginia said.

Carissa ran both hands through her hair and tugged hard, relishing the pain that diverted her thoughts from the way her heart was contracting. She couldn't even imagine how her aunt must have felt.

"Even though the war itself wasn't popular, the Cove embraced William's service to his country. Their wedding was the event of the year. Patsy wore white and was completely radiant."

Virginia turned a couple more pages in the album until she came to a wedding photo. She tapped one finger against the image. "There they are; the unhappy couple, or at least, William was already; Patsy soon after."

Her finger trailed across to the opposite page. There stood Aunt Jessica as Carissa remembered her, leaning against the Jeep with the lighthouse in the background. Her aunt, arms folded, her smile failing to light up her features.

"That was the day she took ownership of the Bennett Point Light," Virginia said. "She asked me to celebrate with her. We drank champagne and then she slammed the bottle against the tower and threw the broken glass over the cliff. 'There,' she said. 'Now it's official. I'm home to stay.'"

"So sad." Carissa thought she understood why her aunt hadn't shared that chapter of her life. The grief must have been almost overwhelming.

They sat in silence while the fire crackled and the grandfather clock ticked.

"Do you know why my aunt got involved again with William?" Carissa asked after the lump in her throat dissolved.

"She told me they met on the cliffs one afternoon. He'd become a successful small town lawyer and inherited the family home, but his marriage was empty."

"Why didn't he divorce Patsy? Surely he couldn't have felt continuing guilt over that accident."

"Her illness stopped him. At first, he thought she was malingering. He threw all her belongings out the front door and changed all the locks, but her specialist told William his wife wasn't malingering at all. She'd been hospitalized in Bangor."

"So again, he felt guilty."

"Yes, and patched things up. A lot of water had gone under the bridge for both of William and Jessica when they met later on the cliffs. William had become cynical about love, and Jessica wasn't ready to take on any more heartache. I think they felt more comfortable snatching a few stolen moments. He'd visit her to discuss some legal issues, and stay the rest of the afternoon. Or he'd say he was going to take his walk, and she'd pick him up. Jessica confided in me one day when I begged her to get out and socialize more. I swore I wouldn't tell anyone, and I never have. Not until right now, when it won't make any difference. Jessica said all her needs were being met, and she didn't lack for anything." Virginia eyed the port but didn't touch the bottle. "Who was I to counsel her? I'm one of the village's old maids."

"Did Patsy ever find out?"

"If she did, I never heard about it. But she was already so difficult to live with; I can't imagine William would have seen any difference in her attitude."

"I should have called and visited more." Carissa shook her head when Virginia offered her more tea or another glass of port. "I was so involved with my own problems. Too involved. I feel so guilty. But why didn't she contact me? I would have come."

"So you didn't get her letters?" Virginia sounded surprised.

"Letters? No."

"She wrote at least two. I mailed one of them myself after I visited her. Nancy Burton told me Jessica had come to the post office in a cab shortly before her death and mailed you a one of those big padded envelopes."

Carissa knew instantly that Matthew had to be involved somehow. But how could he have intercepted her mail? She frowned, trying to remember just how long it had been since Aunt Jessica had written. "It must have been at least six months since I received a letter from my aunt. Maybe longer. Do you remember when you mailed the letter for her?"

"Let me think." Virginia drummed her fingers on the table. "I remember meeting Walter Barnes while I was in the post office talking to Nancy. He moved to the Cove at the end of August. That would put the letter I mailed going out either late that month or very early in September. The big envelope left maybe a week later."

Carissa wanted to confront Matthew and shake him by the lapels of whatever designer jacket he happened to be wearing. How *dare* he triage her mail and keep her out of contact with the one person she could always count on to be on her side and give her sound counsel. It *had* to be him. One letter going astray, okay, she'd buy that, but two? He must have paid off the concierge or the mail carrier to divert them. Or he'd tampered with the lock on her mailbox. Then she wondered whether he had even bothered to read them, or he'd tossed them in the trash like he had tossed away his marriage.

"Why do you think Aunt Jessica was in the lighthouse tower?" Carissa asked Virginia. "It doesn't make sense. Why would she climb those steps if she was in pain? My God, how was she getting into the basement to do her laundry?"

"She had a housekeeping service, so she didn't have to go to the basement, but I've been asking myself about the tower stairs ever since she was found. I thought perhaps she'd heard a strange noise and fell while investigating." Virginia poured them both more port without asking Carissa. "I'm not much of a believer in ghosts, but I had called Jessica to check on her a couple of weeks before, and she told me she was experiencing some strange phenomena. I wondered if she'd been over-medicating or having one too many hot toddies, which she was very fond of. Scotch, honey and lemon with boiled water, if I remember rightly. I thought perhaps she was skipping the water part. Anyway, she told me she had heard whispering from different parts of the house, and she kept finding her doors open. Especially to the mudroom and the back door."

Ice climbed Carissa's back. She took a big gulp of port. "I've had trouble with those doors, too. I had the locks changed and it stopped. But my new thermostat was turned down low yesterday."

Virginia took a hefty gulp of port, too. "Oh, my. There were reports of the lighthouse being haunted, but until recently, Jessica had said that was a bunch of nonsense."

"What sort of tales?" Carissa finished her drink. Suddenly, she was too hot. The heat from the fireplace, her heavy clothing, the port...she felt like she needed air.

Virginia must have had the opposite reaction. She got up and put two more logs onto the fire. "Let's sit over here," she suggested, plopping onto one of the wingbacks and drawing a blanket across her lap. "Speaking about ghosts, noises and whispering sent cold chills right through me."

"I'm so sorry." Carissa tried to ignore the heat building inside her and sat in the other chair. "I shouldn't have brought all this up."

"I don't remember if you did, dear, or whether I actually started it with that photograph album. But you needed to know the history." Virginia smiled. "It's not all doom and gloom around here, you know, although like every other village, we have had our share of scandal, and we New Englanders do love our ghost stories. They make the long, dark winter months a bit less arduous and boring."

"I don't know about that. I'd welcome some mundanity in my life right now." Carissa managed to return Virginia's smile. "I wondered how many people had keys to the keeper's quarters when I first arrived. So I had the locks changed, but with all the people who've been in there since, I'm wondering if someone managed to make a copy of my new keys, too. I should get the locks changed again." She sighed. "Deputy Watkins gave me the number of a security company. I've got to stop procrastinating and make the call to get an estimate for an alarm system."

"An alarm system would work as long as your intruders have substance." Virginia pulled the blanket up a little higher. "I know one of the lighthouse keepers passed away in the tower. He was a little too fond of drink, from what I heard. He fell down the stairs and broke his neck. Jessica always said she didn't believe in spirits, but that last call I had with her, she sounded like she was changing her mind." Virginia yawned. "I'm getting sleepy. I'm sorry."

Carissa got up slowly. She still felt a slight buzz. Not enough to affect her balance, but definitely enough not to drive. "I'll do the dishes before I go," she told Virginia. "Then I'm going to walk down to the police station and see if Deputy Watkins came back."

"It would be a good idea for you to look at the police report on Jessica's death." Virginia's eyes had closed. Her feet were propped up on an embroidered footstool. A huge orange cat had settled onto her lap, his purring audible across the room.

"Thank you so much for all the information," she told Virginia.

"Just lock the door on your way out, dear," Virginia said. The cat watched Carissa with unblinking eyes.

She loaded the tray, put the depleted bottle of port back with its neighbors on a wheeled serving cart and located the kitchen. As she washed dishes, she thought about all the revelations of the last hour. Her aunt's accident didn't sound like an accident anymore. She was determined to get to the bottom of what had caused Aunt Jessica's fall.

William Dansinger instantly became one of her primary suspects, until she thought about how much he had loved Jessica. Much more than his wife, who he may purposely have left outside in freezing cold weather. If William wanted to kill anyone involved with Jessica's death, then he should have jumped off the cliff, she thought as she closed Virginia's front door and headed down the steep street toward the harbor, a biting wind stinging her face and watering her eyes.

CHAPTER THIRTY-ONE

CARISSA DUG around in her purse as she walked, found breath mints and gum and used both before pushing open the door to the tiny police station. An attractive forty-something woman greeted her from behind the counter and introduced herself. Mavis Watkins was not only one of two dispatchers, she was also the secretary and married to Deputy Watkins, who was still out on patrol.

Disappointed, Carissa told Mavis what she wanted.

"You can submit a request to view that report." Mavis printed up a form and handed it across the counter. "I'll give it to him as soon as he gets back. The sheriff's on leave, taking care of his wife."

"I heard she's very ill." Carissa said.

"Yes, unfortunately, she is." Mavis didn't elaborate. Evidently she wasn't a member of the gossip mill. She placed a pen on the counter. "You can fill out the form right over there." She pointed toward a small desk beside the window.

It was 12:30 P.M, and Carissa still hadn't called Richard to apologize for missing their appointment. After completing the form, she sat and stared distractedly out the window, barely noticing anything while she tried to think of a reasonable explanation to give him. She wasn't going to launch into an account that included her running away from an uncomfortable situation.

The best option was to walk over to Richard's office, tell him she had been unavoidably detained, and offer to reschedule. But she didn't want to talk to another man wanting to convince her to do something she might regret later, like tearing down a wall or even worse, going on a date. She had a feeling she could easily get much too involved with Richard Ebberly if she wasn't careful.

Still feeling the effects of the port and hoping Mavis hadn't detected the odor on her breath, Carissa walked over to the Brickley House Tea Room, bought a cup of their Royal Wedding blend and lingered over it with a copy of the local newspaper as the wind whipped everything around in the harbor. Forty-five minutes later she headed for Penwithen.

It was easy to find, the name on a worn plaque set into a crumbling stone wall. Although the gates were locked, the wall presented no challenge. Carissa left her car parked on an easement and climbed over at a place where the stones had tumbled to the ground sometime in the past, grass growing up between them. The driveway was filled with debris from fallen tree branches and pitted with iced-over potholes. In places, she had to step off the path to dodge overgrown bushes rustling hollowly, their frozen leaves moved by the gusting wind.

Penwithen faced the ocean. Boarded and bleak, it stood bravely against the elements despite its ramshackle appearance. Carissa walked around to the back of the house. One of the boards covering a ground floor window had rotted. She pushed it aside. Broken glass showered her boots. She turned on her smartphone's flashlight and peered inside. A horrible stench of decay wafted up her nose.

She almost gagged, wrapped her scarf over her nose and mouth, then looked inside again. The thin beam of light revealed ghostly forms of covered furniture. Carissa wondered whether any of it was salvageable. It seemed a crime to let it all rot in the shell of a house that had once been her family's home. She wondered why her mother had never mentioned Penwithen. It hadn't been included in her aunt's will, either.

Carissa cautiously moved back, the broken glass crunching under her feet, and walked across a spacious concrete terrace marred by long, jagged cracks. An intricately filigreed but badly rusted wrought iron fence with traces of green paint ran around the perimeter. Tall columns similar to those on the front porch reached up to a second floor balcony.

Her father was older than Aunt Jessica by a couple of years. He was the one who must have inherited Penwithen. But where he was, no one knew. Or no one was willing to say. Although she could understand her mother's resistance to discussing her ex-husband, Carissa wondered why Aunt Jessica had never volunteered any information about her own brother. Even Virginia, so chatty about everyone and everything else at the Cove hadn't spoken about him or shown her any photographs. Carissa wondered what she could do to establish her right to ownership of the house. She felt an affinity with its loneliness and appreciated its refusal to surrender to its fate.

William Dansinger would be the ideal person to advise her. He probably knew more about her family than anyone else. Leaving the terrace behind, she took a narrow path that soon merged with another running close to the edge of the cliff. She spotted a stone staircase with an iron rail that must lead down to a beach far below. She braved a look down the numerous steps. The wind gusted again, and she retreated quickly. *Not for all the money in the world.*

Before returning to her car, she stood in the middle of the spacious forecourt and tried to envision William backing over Patsy on a clear and sunny mid-summer day. What was Patsy doing standing behind his car? It wasn't as though she couldn't have stood plenty of other places. Carissa hurried back to her Lexus, glanced over at the flowers still lying on the passenger's seat and drove to the Dansingers.'

She parked next to William's Cadillac, took the bouquet with her and walked up the steps onto the front porch. She rang the doorbell, counted to sixty and rang it again.

The door flew open.

"What the devil do you want now?" William Dansinger asked.

CHAPTER THIRTY-TWO

CARISSA HELD OUT THE FLOWERS. "For Patsy."

"I'm *so* sorry." William ran a hand over his face. "I've been plagued by a bunch of kids who want to see the sick lady who sits on the porch in all weathers. I thought it was them again." He stood aside and beckoned. "Please come in." He took the flowers. "Why don't I make some hot tea and put these into a vase?"

"Thank you." She smiled at him, but he didn't smile back.

He took her coat and hung it on a hall stand. "Have a seat in the living-room. I'll bring in the tea." He gestured toward the back of the house, illuminated only by one table lamp.

Carissa added her hat and scarf to the stand. She watched William plug in an electric kettle and fill a vase with water before she walked down the hallway into the living room. She noted the broken window was still covered with plywood and wasn't sure she wanted to ask when the replacement would arrive. Perhaps it was better to let William lead the conversation with an update on Patsy's health and see where things went from there. She turned on a couple more lamps and took a tour of the room, noting paintings of beautiful landscapes and seascapes gracing the walls. A cabinet held trophies William had received for tennis in his younger days.

While she contemplated an oil painting of the Bennett Point Light at sunrise, he brought in a tray containing all the elements of a formal tea—a china pot and cups, a sugar bowl with silver tongs sticking out of cubed sugar and a small jug of milk.

"It'll take a couple more minutes to steep," William said. "Your aunt gave us the set and taught us how to make real English tea. The water's not the same, so she said it never tastes quite as good, but it's close. I thought you'd like it. An olive branch from me. I should have thanked you for saving Patsy instead of shouting at you. I'd like to take this opportunity to apologize. I'm not really a surly man." He actually smiled.

Carissa wasn't sure if he was manipulating her by tugging at her heartstrings, or he was genuinely extending that olive branch. "I'd like to accept your apology," she said slowly. "I've got to tell you, however, I still have reservations about what you did, leaving your wife out on that patio with a storm brewing."

"She always insists on sitting out there." William put the tray onto the coffee table and poured a small portion of tea through a strainer into a bowl. "Ah, it looks ready." He poured more tea through the strainer into one of the cups. "Sugar? Milk?"

"A little milk. I learned about tea parties from going to the Ritz Carlton and Lady Mendl's in New York."

"What, no Russian Tea Room?" William's eyebrows rose and a sound like dry, crackling leaves appeared to be his version of a laugh.

Carissa thought he probably hadn't laughed at all since her aunt died and something in his throat had rusted. "Oh, I went there a couple of times, but honestly, I never really got into the whole tea experience."

William handed her a delicate china cup and saucer with a rosebud pattern. She brought the cup to her lips. Aromatic steam slid up her nose. She sipped. The tea was delicious. "Mmm. Far superior to the Brickley House."

William nodded. "See. The ritual and steeping make the best cup of tea."

"So, how's Patsy doing?"

"Still sick." William settled back in his chair. "The doctor wanted to have her admitted, but he thought she was too ill to make the long trip to the regional hospital. We have private duty nursing around the clock instead. That's working out much better. Patsy doesn't like hospitals and doesn't do well in them. She's far happier here, where she can keep an eye on me." His dry chuckle was grating. "That's what she likes to do best."

Carissa thought William looked disheveled. His suit was rumpled, his shirt collar soiled with coffee. Yet he had brewed her a delicate cup of tea and presented it like a true host, serving Jessica's niece with a treat he thought she would appreciate. Carissa suddenly felt very sorry for him. He'd not only lost the love of his life, he'd been the one to find her dead. And he was tied to the demanding invalid upstairs who 'liked to keep an eye' on him.

"Have you had lunch?" Carissa asked.

William looked startled. "What time is it?"

She glanced at her watch. "Two-thirty. I haven't eaten, either. Would you like a sandwich? I can make some for both of us."

"I'd like that. But you're a guest…"

"No, I'm a visitor who wants to help. Jessica's niece."

"You look a lot like she did when she was younger," he said. "Beautiful, but in your own way."

Carissa had expected to go on not liking William, but he was beginning to touch her heart. She got up and placed her empty cup on the tray. "Sit tight. I'm good at finding my way around a kitchen."

William ran a hand over his chin. "I forgot to shave. If you don't mind, I'll go upstairs and make myself more presentable while you're preparing those sandwiches."

"Take your time."

She made short work of putting together peanut butter and jelly sandwiches. Not wanting their meal to be formal, she set two places in the breakfast nook overlooking the driveway and garage.

Everything in the kitchen was meticulously arranged and labeled. Even the cleaning materials under the sink were alphabetized. But looking inside the refrigerator, she realized no one had gone shopping recently. There was enough milk left to fill two glasses. A small packet of potato chips divided equally helped fill the plates. Only a quarter loaf of white bread remained after she finished making one sandwich for herself and two for William. The freezer held a couple of individually frozen meals.

William returned to the kitchen in a pair of jeans and a thick Fair Isle sweater, his silver mane combed but still damp, his chin and cheeks minus the inch of white stubble. "This is very kind of you, especially after the way I acted the other day." He sat down and started drinking the milk.

"I know about your affair with my aunt," Carissa said.

William choked.

Carissa jumped up to pound him on the back but he waved her away.

"I guess that was a little brutal," she admitted. "Sorry."

"It certainly was direct." He wiped his eyes. "Who told you?"

"Virginia."

He grimaced. "She would. I never understood why Jessica confided in that blabber mouth."

"Virginia said she never told anyone else. She thought I already knew."

William sighed heavily. "Secrets have a way of being found out sooner or later."

"Does Patsy know?"

"Lord, no. You're not planning on telling her, are you?" He looked across the table with widened eyes. "Is that why you really came here today?"

"No, of course not."

"Then why *did* you come. To bring flowers? Really? Or to find out if I deliberately left Patsy outside?"

"You're pretty direct, too."

"When needed."

His stare was of the piercing variety. Carissa refused to be intimidated. Those tactics might work in a courtroom, but not on her.

"You said it yourself—the truth will out," she told him, staring right back. "What you did the other day, that's between you, Patsy, and maybe the police if anything else happens to her and I find out about it. I've been wondering why Penwithen wasn't included in Aunt Jessica's will. Is it because my father's still alive? If he is, then where is he?"

William's eyebrows rose. "Virginia told you about that place as well? Hasn't she been the chatty one?"

"She filled me in on a lot, but I think you know even more. I drove out to the house. It's rotting away. The real Malloy heritage. Not the drafty old lighthouse and keeper's quarters."

William drank the rest of his milk.

Carissa waited.

"I don't think Penwithen can be saved," he said.

"I'd like a second opinion on that. Richard Ebberly could probably make that decision for me. If it *is* salvageable, and I have the right to it, then it would give me a lot more room. The lighthouse may be quaint, but it's turning out to be a real money-pit, and it's only got two tiny bedrooms and one bathroom. Not really what I'd like to invite guests."

"Is that the real truth, or are you getting spooked about living where Jessica died?"

Carissa shrugged. "Maybe a bit of both." She paused before dropping her potential bombshell: "Especially since I think it's possible she might have been murdered."

"Murdered!" William went as white as the snow flurries that had started drifting around outside the windows.

"I've been told she had limited mobility and a lot of pain from arthritis. So what was she doing on those stairs?"

The color started seeping back into William's cheeks. "I've spent a lot of sleepless nights wondering the same thing."

"I tried to see the report at the police station, but I had to put in a request. You were the one who found Aunt Jessica. Can you tell me what you saw?"

"Like what?" He sounded wary. "Her body was at the bottom of the stairs. The delivery boy was with me when I found her. We went in after she didn't answer the door. She didn't answer when I called out, either, so we started searching for her. Then I saw the tower door was open. She never went in there. The other people you talked with were correct. Her arthritis was too bad for her to climb those stairs, or so I thought until I saw her."

"She was on the floor or the stairs?"

"She was face-down toward the bottom of the stairs, like she was on her way down." William shifted in his chair. "Do we really have to discuss this right now? Rehashing Jessica's death is asking a lot of me, and I'm sure you'll get the full report from Deputy Watkins soon." He swallowed hard and looked at his lap.

"I really do need to know. If someone pushed Aunt Jessica or otherwise caused her death, I want that person charged. Everyone I've talked to at the Cove says they're wondering what she was doing in the lighthouse tower. No one thinks it was normal for her to be there, including Deputy Watkins. But no one's doing more than talking about their doubts. You loved my aunt. Why aren't you pushing to get those questions answered?"

"Because my relationship with her was never known, except by Virginia Greeley. We kept it secret out of respect for Patsy and her illness. Not loving Patsy was my cross to bear. Jessica refused to allow me to hurt Patsy in any way after she came back from overseas. She made me take an oath. I've kept my word all these years..." He trailed off.

Carissa could imagine the jumbled thoughts whirling in his head. His love for Jessica, the complicated relationship he had with his wife.

"You owe me one for the other day," she told him. "I could have told Deputy Watkins what I thought after finding Patsy locked out of the house. And I listened to the messages on your answering machine. I didn't mean to...my elbow hit the machine by accident when something was falling out of a cabinet. I heard Mrs. Dodds calling to tell you she had fallen in the Market. That message was before the one I heard about your car being ready for pick-up after the taillight was fixed.

"If you were in town the whole time, you could have waited there to pick up your car. I also wondered why you'd have them call you at home instead of on your cell? I know you have one. It's printed on the card you left for me. And with your wife sick, you wouldn't risk being out of contact."

William looked like he couldn't believe what he was hearing. "God, you know how to hit below the belt," he said after a long minute. He pushed his chair back and got up. "I lost my cell phone somewhere on the road from Bangor. I stopped several times because of the bad weather, so it could be anywhere. I haven't had time to pick up a replacement." He got up and walked out of the kitchen.

Carissa followed him into the living room, where he stopped in front of the bank of windows. Snow continued to fall outside, blanketing everything. She wondered if William was reliving the scene with Patsy or the one where he found Jessica's body.

"Jessica was lying so still, her legs stretched out on the stairs," William said, his voice quivering. "I remember she was wearing the gray skirt and a plum-colored sweater she called her best outfit. "

Carissa felt a stir of self-loathing at what she was putting him through, but she reminded herself he'd probably tried to kill his wife. "No coat?"

He shook his head.

She thought about those fluffy pink slippers she had been wearing. "What did Aunt Jessica have on her feet?"

William turned and frowned. "Shoes, I think. Yes, black brogues."

"Did she normally wear those in the house?"

"No. Her feet hurt when she wore shoes. She was usually in pink slippers. Furry things."

"The slippers were at the side of her bed when I arrived," Carissa said. "If she was wearing shoes and her best outfit then she must have been going somewhere or she'd just come home."

"She hadn't been past her picket fence for a while." William gazed out the window again, his brow furrowed. "I wonder where she could possibly have been, or where she was planning to go?" He ran a thumb over his newly-shaven chin. "That's definitely strange. I hadn't thought about the shoes until now. Did you find her coat in the closet? Alpaca. She'd had it for years."

Carissa shook her head. "I remember that coat. I didn't see it when I bagged up her clothes for donation. She had a moth-eaten fur stole hanging in one of those zip-up garment bags and an equally chewed-up fur coat in the guest room wardrobe that was mink or something similar. Definitely not Alpaca. I'll ask Deputy Watkins whether they took the coat."

William nodded. "Good idea."

"Does Patsy know you were the first one to find Aunt Jessica?" Carissa asked.

"Yes; I was too shocked and distraught to hide it."

"Didn't she wonder how you got in?"

William's color drained again. "I never thought about that. But the grocery delivery boy knew where Jessica had a key hidden. So if Patsy had asked, that would have been a reasonable explanation. She wouldn't want a blow by blow description of the scene."

"No, I suppose not." Carissa couldn't stop herself. She had to know. "Why didn't you leave Patsy and marry my aunt?"

"Shh." William glared and pointed to the ceiling.

"This is a big house, and I'm not shouting. Do you really think she can hear us?"

"I wouldn't put it past her. Patsy's capable of a great many things. I've found that out to my cost over the years."

"Is that why you left her outside the other day?"

"No, of course not. I thought the housekeeper was coming. Her husband often drove her when it snowed. He would have lifted Patsy inside. He did that frequently. When he didn't come, Mrs. Dodds was able to wheel the chaise inside herself, and Patsy would stay in it until I came home." He looked at Carissa, his gaze direct and unflinching. "You didn't know it had wheels, did you? You didn't look."

Carissa colored up. "I didn't," she said. "But I bet if I talked to the guy at the garage, or Deputy Watkins did, there would be a discrepancy between the calls and when you were in town."

William's eyes narrowed. "Jessica told me you were smart. But you need to be careful, Carissa. You may be too smart for your own good."

"Are you threatening me?"

"No, giving you a friendly warning. I've got no intention of hurting Jessica's favorite niece." He gave her a half-smile. "It's not me you need to look out for around here. It's the likes of Al Dyson and those gossip-mongers, Virginia and Nancy."

Carissa wondered who she should believe. William was obviously used to controlling his feelings after years of living with Patsy while loving Jessica. However, despite his outwardly-calm demeanor, she sensed he was a man unraveling at the seams.

"I'd like us to get along," she said. "I need your help with Penwithen. My aunt trusted your judgment, and I'd like to do that, too."

He nodded. "I'd like that, myself. I'd rather be on your good side."

He collected up their few dishes, carefully stowing them into already regimental lines of plates, cups and glasses in the dishwasher. He took a couple of unused bowls back to the cabinet and paused to straighten two cups that were slightly out of alignment.

"Are you always so compulsive?" Carissa asked as he readjusted the mats on the table.

"Probably." He took the dishtowel she had thrown onto the back of a chair and tucked it over the handle on the oven door.

Carissa remembered the mess he had tidied up in the bathroom after bathing Patsy, and how he had wanted his wife in coordinated night-wear. But the outside of the house, where Patsy never went, had over-grown flowerbeds and paint chipping off window frames. Maybe William wasn't the only obsessively tidy one in that marriage.

"I've picked up some good habits from Patsy," he told her, echoing her thoughts. "But since she became too ill to oversee the garden, and I've felt too overwhelmed trying to take care of my clients as well as my wife's needs, some things have gotten out of hand."

"I'm sure they have. I've felt overwhelmed myself, lately." The thought of battling Matthew again in court depressed her. "Can you work on Penwithen for me?"

"I already *have* been working on it, as a matter of fact," William said. "Jessica had asked me to. She didn't want any loose ends when the time came, she said. She asked me to find her brother...your father."

"And did you?"

Carissa's mother had given her a very short history of their marriage, which included her father drinking heavily and being unfaithful on a regular basis. Her mother had finally reached her breaking point and divorced him when Carissa was in kindergarten. They'd had no communication with him since, and as far as Carissa knew, neither had anyone else in their family.

William nodded. "I received a report yesterday from the private investigator I hired. I was going to call you today and ask to come over to see you. Instead, you turned up on my doorstep. Life can be quite surprising sometimes."

"It can," she said, unable to think of anything else to say at that moment. After all the years of not knowing, she was going to find out where her father was living.

"Why don't we go to my office?" William suggested. "It's more private there. I don't like discussing legal matters where Patsy's nurse could overhear us."

"Okay." Carissa followed him into a large room at the far north corner of the house. It held a large desk and a row of bookcases lined with leather-bound books. She took a seat in front of the desk while William opened his attaché case and brought out several folders.

"This might not be an easy conversation," he warned her. "I'm not sure how close you were to your father. What memories you have of him."

"Not much. Over the years, he's become a shadowy figure."

"Memories do fade." William sat in the oversized black leather chair behind his desk. "Sometimes for the best." He opened a folder and slid some papers across the desk toward her. "I'm sorry to tell you that your father is deceased. He passed away in a nursing home several months ago from cirrhosis of the liver."

"That's not a shocker, judging by my mother's tales of him arriving home drunk or hung-over on a frequent basis," Carissa said, although inside, she felt like she was experiencing an earthquake.

"Perhaps not, but don't we all wish our problematic family members would straighten up and mend their ways?" William gave a gentle half-smile, his eyes kind.

Carissa's opinion of him moved up several notches. "Yes, I suppose we do."

"He had apparently mended his own ways a little too late in life for his health," William continued. "He had been in a committed relation-ship with a woman for the past five years, but they had never married and they maintained separate residences. He passed away peacefully in Corpus Christi, Texas." He pointed to a copy of a death certificate. "He did leave a will, which makes everything a lot easier."

"He left everything to his companion," Carissa said with a sinking feeling. She didn't care about money, but she doubted a woman living in Texas would want to saddle herself with the responsibility of renovating a dilapidated house up in Maine. If she did anything, it would probably be to sell the property for whatever she could get for it.

"Your father did the right thing, Carissa," William said. "He did leave what little money was left after the final expenses to his significant other, but he left you Penwithen. There's a letter for you, too." He took out an envelope and slid it across the desk. "I'm going to get us both a glass of water while you have a few moments of privacy to read this." He got up and left.

Carissa sat looking at the envelope. It must have come expedited, she thought, if it had traveled from Texas. Either that or William had been holding it. She took a deep breath. No sense in getting upset. Her father had been found, and he had written her a letter. She picked up the envelope, which was sealed, and used a letter opener lying on the desk to carefully slit open the last communication she would ever have with her father.

His penmanship probably reflected his illness. She had trouble reading some of the writing, which was spidery, faint in places, and uneven in size. However, the gist of it was clear—he told her he had always loved her, had never forgotten her, and was sorry for being a complete failure as a father. He knew he could never make up for his absence, but she should be glad he hadn't been there for the majority of her life. He told her he had severed all ties with his family and tried to make a new life for himself in C.C., which she guessed had to mean Corpus Christi.

She couldn't stop tears from running down her face, dug a tissue out of her pocket and wiped her face before tackling the second page of scrawled handwriting. Her father said he had finally stopped drinking, worked and found happiness with someone he called 'Flo.' He explained he wanted to leave this woman some token of his gratitude for her devotion, but he owed it to Carissa to give her the opportunity to decide what to do with the family home, which had been left to him by his own parents. He ended the letter there, his handwriting trailing off into barely legible gibberish. He had managed to sign it 'Dad.'

A gentle knock at the door startled Carissa. "Come in," she said.

William carried two glasses of water, one of which he placed in front of Carissa. Grateful, she downed the entire glass while he sat and shuffled through papers in the other two folders.

"Thank you," she said.

"You need to thank Jessica, really. She didn't like loose ends, and she said at our age, anything could happen. Unfortunately, that was all too true."

"So what happens now?"

"I'll try to make the entire process as easy as possible for you. You can move forward with making decisions about Penwithen. I'd recommend you call Richard Ebberly as soon as possible. He's an excellent architect, and he learned the construction business from the best—his father, who has been my friend since we were in grade school together." William smiled a gentle smile. "Families and friendships here at the Cove go back generations."

"They do." Carissa felt a sense of closure. "I need to keep thanking you, William. You've been looking out for my family since before I was born."

"Always a pleasure."

"Maybe not always with me."

"We've had our differences. We may have more in the days ahead, but I'm sure we'll work our way through them."

"I know you don't have a lot of love for Penwithen. My aunt didn't, either. But if can be saved, I'd like to do it. Move into it myself and try to bring more jobs to the Cove, perhaps. I know Sally Mainard takes consignments from local women, but I'd like to expand on that. Maybe bring back more crafts and create a hub here. I haven't formed anything definite in my mind, but I'm trying to move past renovating the keeper's quarters into finding a more permanent home that's mine alone. The lighthouse isn't that, but Penwithen is."

"I'm sure whatever you choose to do, it'll benefit the local economy. Jessica believed you to be highly gifted and talented. She told me she knew you would have a bright future, although she was very worried about you when you were married to Mr. Yates."

"With good reason. And now Mr. Yates is planning to spend the winter here." Carissa sighed.

"He's an outsider. You are not. You're one of us, and we will be looking out for you. Any time he becomes a threat, however small, you have resources here, whether it's me taking legal action or the police department dealing with him."

"You have no idea how relieved I feel, hearing that." Carissa stood up. "I've taken enough of your time. I'm going to repay your kindness by going grocery shopping for you this afternoon."

"There's no need..."

"Yes, there definitely is, because I saw the contents of your refrigerator and your pantry. Both are really depleted. I could do with the exercise, and I've got to apologize to Richard for not keeping an appointment I had with him this morning. You have no idea how relieved I feel right now. My day, which started out so badly, has radically improved."

"I did make out a shopping list," William conceded. "And you're right, we do need food. I had thought about calling to get a delivery. Can I give my list to you, instead? I'll reimburse you with a check as soon as you come back."

He brought her a lengthy list from the kitchen while Carissa put on her coat.

"Why don't we agree to make the cost of the groceries a retainer for your services?" She suggested, opening the front door.

"You don't even know how much my retainer is," he said, following her onto to the porch.

"It can't possibly be more than I paid my divorce attorney." She walked quickly down the snow-covered path to her car.

CHAPTER THIRTY-THREE

STEVE STRODE into The Fisherman's Rest. A flurry of snow followed him inside before he got the door closed. He pulled off his parka and flung it onto a hook, peeled off his gloves as he marched into the bar and tossed them behind the counter. They landed inches from where Hilly stood.

"We have another new guest," she said, her eyes darting between Steve and a man seated on a stool halfway down the bar. "This is Mr. Halstead."

Steve forced himself to normalize his breathing as he strode over to the dark-haired man. "Steve Raymond." He held out his hand. "I'm the proprietor."

The man had a firm grip. "Dean Halstead."

"What brings you to Treacher's Cove on a day like this?" Steve tried to look more welcoming. He even managed to plaster a smile on his face, although it was difficult. "It's too cold for anyone to make the Cove into a vacation spot."

"I've got business here." Halstead looked at Hilly. "A drink for the landlord, please."

Steve shook his head. "Thanks, but I'll have to take a raincheck." He turned to Hilly. "I'll stay here. You can help Eva in the kitchen."

"There's nothing to be done in the kitchen," Hilly said. "Lunch is over."

"Then start dinner."

"It's too early. Eva doesn't like to start dinner until four o'clock." Hilly looked at him as though he'd lost his mind.

"Then go home for a couple of hours if you can't find anything else to do."

"Mr. Steve, in the two years I've worked here, you've never told me to go home." She drew herself up, a small hen with all its feathers ruffled. "Are you unhappy with my work?"

"No, of course not. Just go home, Hilly. Rest up until the dinner rush. Spend some time with your grandmother."

She opened her mouth to protest again, looked at him and closed it. With pursed lips she walked into the lobby, changed from shoes to boots, slowly drew on her coat, took gloves out of her pocket and put them on even more slowly, one finger at a time, making a big production out of the whole process.

Steve waited, counting to ten so many times, he became even more aggravated. The last thing he wanted was to snap at Hilly, but by God, if she didn't get her butt out the door within the next ten-count, he'd grab her by the cheap, fake-fur collar on her coat and help her on her way.

"I'll be back at four." Her hand was on the door.

"Fine."

Steve leaned both forearms on the bar. He needed time to cool off before the inn filled late afternoon. The last thing he needed was Hilly's well-intentioned attempts to calm him down. He was too pissed at Matthew Yates and liked it that way.

"Four," Hilly repeated, as though she expected him to break down and call her back.

Steve refused to look at her. He energetically cleaned up all the wet spots on the bar with a towel and felt an icy draft circulate around him as Hilly left. He should have listened to the architect and had a vestibule built into the reception area to keep the place warmer. Dean Halstead said nothing, although he must have felt the blast of cold air.

Steve washed the few dirty glasses and stowed empty beer bottles inside cases under the sink. While he worked, he wondered where

Matthew Yates had gone after their little argument outside Burton's Grocery Store. He took the empties into the frigid storeroom. He preferred beer on tap. It was less messy and time-consuming, and it stayed cold without having to sit in a cooler. But a lot of his regulars wanted to nurse their beers in bottles, so he had to accommodate them.

He couldn't seem to rid his mind of an image: Carissa flying up the hill, leaving him to face her ex. His hands clenched as he thought how close he had come to punching the smirk right off Yates' face.

"Lusting after my wife, Raymond?" Matthew had asked. "Gets under your skin, doesn't she?"

Hoping to regain control with routine work, Steve brought two full cases of bottled beer back into the bar, popped open the drain on the large ice chest beneath the counter and heard water gurgling. He started restocking the chest and figured he'd add more ice while he had it open. He looked up to find Matthew Yates standing on the opposite side of the counter.

"You need to get out of my place," Steve said. "We've got nothing left to discuss. Carissa's not your wife anymore, so you've no right interfering."

"Is that so?"

Matthew already had a drink in his hand. Hilly must have served him in the parlor. His half-full highball glass tipped, emptying itself all over the counter. Steve grabbed a dry towel and mopped up the spill while he fought a desire to throw Yates out the front door. He glared at Carissa's ex.

"She was mine for five years; she'll be mine again." Matthew didn't look at all intimidated. "Keep your hands off her, or you'll live to regret it."

"Don't try to threaten me." Steve glanced over to see Halstead's reaction, but his new guest had moved to the back of the bar, where he sat shrouded in shadow.

"I never threaten." Matthew tossed a ten dollar bill onto the counter, turned and sauntered into the front lobby.

Halstead tossed a $5 bill onto the bar and left, too, giving Steve no more than a passing look, his face expressionless as he glided out behind Yates. His charcoal gray suit blended with his surroundings, so did his dark hair, flecked lightly with white at the temples. Steve wondered what business Halstead could have in town. The population of the Cove kept growing, despite the winter weather. Matthew took his hat from a peg beside the door while Halstead went upstairs. They didn't acknowledge one another.

The front door opened. Accompanied by a flurry of snow and frigid air, Sally walked inside. She smiled at Matthew, who smiled right back.

Without removing her coat, Sally continued into the bar. "I need to talk to you," she told Steve. She glanced back at Yates, still standing in the lobby and taking his time about pulling on gloves. "Privately."

"I can't leave the bar untended. I sent Hilly home for a couple of hours."

"That was pretty stupid of you. We're having a snowstorm. She'll have trouble making it back to wait tables this evening." Sally's eyes gleamed with open hostility. "I guess you've been too preoccupied to notice."

Steve weighed his options. If a couple of regulars came in, they could serve themselves. They'd done that in the past. If Matthew Yates decided he wanted another drink, he could go fuck himself. If Halstead came back downstairs, he'd think the bar was closed and wait for it to reopen.

Steve dried his hands and came out from behind the bar. "We can talk in my office." He tried laying a hand on Sally's arm, but she brushed him off. He followed her into his inner sanctum, closed the door and leaned his back against it.

Sally went to stand by the window, her silhouette framed against a blanket of white outside. "Everything's changed between us since Carissa Yates came to town," she said, her voice brittle.

"Nothing's changed. You're imagining things." He tried to sound reassuring, but his statement sounded like a lie, even to him.

"How can you possibly say that?" Tears glistened on Sally's cheeks. "I love you, Steve, and you're treating me like I mean nothing to you."

He needed to choose his words carefully. "Look, Sally, I care a lot for you. But I'm not the marrying type. We've talked about this already. Several times."

"So you expect me to stand by while you chase Carissa? Have an affair with her?" Sally dashed away tears with shaking hands.

"Hey, hold on; you're jumping to conclusions. I feel sorry for Carissa. She's alone in a strange place and her ex turned up uninvited. He's a complete bastard who's trying to get her to go back to him. He wants to steal her designs."

"Why can't you let her fight her own battles?" Sally's pale features looked ashen in the stark light. "You've never stood up for me like you are for her."

"You've never needed anyone to stand up for you. You're a strong woman. Carissa's had a rough time in the past, and she's in mourning for her aunt."

"All men are alike—you're attracted to weak women who play the victim."

"Carissa's not a victim. She just needs some neighborly help. I don't see why I can't offer that. You've got no grounds to get upset. I've never been unfaithful to you, and I've never made you false promises."

"Sometimes, I need emotional support, too, even though you seem to think I can do without it." Sally's voice had turned soft and plaintive.

Steve felt ashamed of himself. It wasn't Sally's fault his day had gone like shit. He took her in his arms. She balled up her fists at first, but didn't push him away.

"You're a bastard," she said.

She didn't sound angry. He rested his head on top of hers before burying his nose under the neckline of her sweater. His nostrils filled with familiar scents of Sally—musk perfume and peach-scented body wash. He felt a stir of desire as he pressed closer, her body aligning with his. Her lips met his, her mouth opened, her tongue met his. Steve cupped her breasts and began stroking. Sally murmured her approval, but as he moved his mouth to her ear, he noticed snow swirling harder and faster outside the window. Sally was right—they were having a really heavy snowstorm.

He knew he should stop what he'd started. He didn't have the time for it, and his office wasn't the place for anything but a quick, stand-up fuck. He was going to have to get Hilly back ASAP. Hilly and Eva both needed to stay overnight. Otherwise, he'd be making sandwiches for his guests that evening and cooking breakfast in the morning. He could do it, but not with the speed or finesse of his staff.

Even as his hands slid up under Sally's sweater, he hoped Carissa had gone home. He'd better walk Sally back to the Emporium to give himself a few Brownie points after starting to arouse her and not finishing the job. His thumbs circled her rock-hard nipples. Maybe they could have make-up sex in her apartment...

He realized Sally's hands were busy unbuckling his belt. One finger slipped under his waistband to stroke his belly-button. He felt himself harden in response.

"I closed down the Emporium," she said. "No one's going to shop for gifts in this weather. I can stay and help you here." She unbuttoned and unzipped his jeans, snuggled close and nipped his neck. "We could *really* make up," she purred.

She was unusually docile, he thought as her hand slid down inside his shorts. The tips of her long fingernails raked lightly. Steve suddenly felt uneasy. Sally's idea of making up after arguments frequently involved spontaneous, primitive and even savage sex. His back tingled at the memory of those same fingernails gouging his flesh the last time they'd fought. This time, her hand was in a much more vulnerable area. He started to pull away.

"Don't you *want* to make up?" Her blue-green eyes turned wary.

"Of course I do."

She started stroking, insistent and focused. No fingernails. Steve's wariness floated away somewhere as his arousal increased. He thrust one hand between her thighs. She bit his lip.

He tried to pull away, but she held him prisoner, her fingers, including those nails, right where she wanted them.

"That bite's for thinking about cheating on me," she said, smiling sweetly. She pulled her hand out of his pants and stepped back.

He watched her shrug out of her jacket while he blotted the blood off his lip with a napkin from his desk. With one quick movement, she pulled her sweater over her head. Sally never wore a bra. She ran her hands over her breasts, closing her eyes and sucking in her breath as she tweaked her own nipples.

"Make love to me, Steve." Her tongue slid slowly back and forth over her lower lip, keeping rhythm with her hand movements.

"Dammit, Sally. Why do you do this to me?"

"Because you've been bad to me, and I don't know why. I give you the best sex you've ever had in your life. You've told me that. But your full attention isn't on me, anymore. It's on Carissa Yates, and I don't like it."

He watched her lower the zipper on her tight jeans and roll them slowly down her legs. She unzipped her boots and stepped out of them, then kicked off her jeans, leaving her only in a skimpy white nylon thong that hid nothing.

He was fast losing all control, although a part of his mind was trying to draw his attention back to the possible consequences if any residents of Treacher's Cove passed by the office window. Maybe most of his office did face an alleyway, but one window had a full view of the harbor, the lights were all on, and the blinds were open. He locked the door and snapped off the lights.

"Come over here," she commanded, rotating her hips provocatively. "Show me how much you care about me, then I'll think about forgiving you."

She lowered the blind behind her. He jerked the other cord right before he picked her up, pushed his chair out of the way and put her on his desk, where the leather pad would make her more comfortable. He balanced her buttocks on the edge while he cleared the desk top with one hand, everything crashing to the floor. Sally giggled and thrust her breasts at him.

"Not yet," he told her. He hooked his arm under her thigh and pulled her leg out to the side. "I've got something else in mind first."

"Oh, yes." She lay back, touching herself.

No one could see them, Steve told himself as he watched her arousing herself. His fingers took over for hers.

Sally began to moan. "More," she gasped.

"I'm going to give you a lot more," he promised. But as he lowered his mouth to deliver on that promise, a sudden shadow caused him to glance up at the window.

The blind had jammed on one side. He locked gazes with Matthew Yates, nose pressed against the glass, grinning at him.

CHAPTER THIRTY-FOUR

Carissa knocked snow off her boots before traipsing into Everett's Market. She pushed a grocery cart up one aisle and down the other as she filled it with canned and frozen foods William could easily heat. She added a selection of fresh fruit and a bagged salad, milk and butter, deli sliced ham and two loaves of bread. When she arrived at the checkout she noticed Matthew behind her, pushing a cart with groceries, toiletries and snacks.

Rather than look at him, and unwilling to match stares with a gaggle of kids hanging all over the cart in front of her, she took inventory of Matthew's provisions. A quart of milk, a pound of coffee, a dozen eggs. Peanut butter, mayonnaise, deli meat and sliced cheese, and a loaf of whole wheat bread. His favorite Lindt chocolate. Macadamia nuts and Pretzels. Two six-packs of cheap beer. Large sizes of mouthwash, toothpaste, anti-perspirant, shampoo and body wash. She involuntarily glanced up as his cart bumped her hip. His mouth twisted into a grin of amusement at her startled expression.

The grin really annoyed her. She rationalized his presence in the store —it was the only supermarket in town. His only other choice was Nancy Burton's very limited selection of local goods and specialty items. The one thing that puzzled her was Matthew shopping at all. During their marriage, she'd never even caught him making coffee. Now he looked like he had enough staples to last him for a week, maybe more. And he'd bought industrial-sized toiletries, too.

"What are you doing with all that?" She hoped she sounded bored.

An elderly woman in front of the cart full of children had loaded the belt with soups, cat litter, canned and bagged cat food and gossip magazines for the long winter evenings. She brought a fifth of Jim Beam from the bottom of the cart and placed a divider. The woman with the kids only had 2 gallons of milk and a family-sized packet of cereal. Carissa breathed a sigh of relief. She'd have William and Patsy's groceries paid for and bagged before Matthew had a chance to make her life really miserable.

"I want to look and smell good while I'm staying at the Cove." Matthew leaned his forearms on the cart's handle. "And since I've signed a lease to stay here all winter I'll need to keep food at home, in case I get snowed in." He pointed to a selection of movies at the back of his cart. "I've gotta have snacks to go with these, too."

"You poor thing. Forced to watch movies while snacking alone." Carissa couldn't keep the sarcasm out of her voice. Despite all efforts, a ball of anxiety formed in the pit of her stomach. "You won't like it here," she told him. "This place is too small. Everyone knows each other's secrets."

"Does everyone know ours, then?" His eyes were dark and accusing.

Carissa maintained eye contact with maximum effort. He loved intimidation tactics, and she wasn't going to give him the satisfaction. "They will if you insist on staying here. I'll tell them all about the real you."

The line moved forward. The gaggle of kids left with their mother. Matthew leaned companionably against the back of her cart as Carissa unloaded the contents onto the belt.

"I like the Cove," he said. "It makes a nice change from New York."

An undercurrent surged between them, as it had so often in the past. Carissa felt the tug. Matthew's smile warned of hidden meanings and twisted schemes.

"I've already met so many interesting people." His voice was sweet as nectar. A gleam in his eyes hinted at amusement. Slowly, he looked down to study his manicured fingernails.

I bet you have. "They won't talk to you when they find out what you're really like."

"Carissa, darling, you're trying to ruin my reputation."

He was enjoying the banter, damn him. *"Your* reputation precedes you, wherever you happen to go," she told him.

He threw back his head and laughed.

The line behind Matthew had lengthened. All chatter in the vicinity of that cash register had ceased. Carissa tried to appear interested in the tabloids on one side of the check-out. Unfortunately, she saw her own face side by side with Matthew's under a blazing headline that announced: NO MORE, SAYS DESIGNER'S EX-WIFE. SEX SCANDAL REVELATIONS!

The checker began running Carissa's purchases through. She breathed a sigh of relief. The checker was moving fast.

"Seen Steve in the last couple of hours?" Matthew asked.

The knot in Carissa's stomach doubled in size. She was right—he was definitely up to something. He wasn't just hanging around the grocery store to annoy her. "No, of course not. I've been busy."

"Me, too." Matthew stood watching the progression of her purchases down the belt. "What's that?"

"What's what?" Carissa looked at the assorted cans and boxes.

"The big one in the middle."

"Cereal, Matthew. Haven't you ever seen it out of the bowl?"

"Price check!" Yelled the cashier, waving a small packet in the air. "Trojans. Packet of twelve."

Carissa protested. "Those aren't mine."

"They were in with your other items, ma'am." The cashier, a pimply girl who looked to be in her early twenties smirked, the rubbers held between her fingers. She twirled them at shoulder level.

A sacker walked over, long hair falling in his eyes and a red nose. He sniffed loudly. "Price check?"

"You sure you don't want them?" The girl waved the Trojan packet at Carissa.

"I'm very sure."

The checker placed them in full view on top of her cash register. "You can re-stock them after you bag her groceries, Bert," she told the sacker. He sniffed loudly, shook open a paper grocery sack and started to load Carissa's groceries into it as quickly as the checker sent them to him. He transferred the filled sack to the grocery cart and started filling another.

Carissa turned to Matthew. "You put them there while you were distracting me," she accused.

He was wearing one of his most angelic expressions. "I thought you might need them."

"I've got no use for condoms right now. When I do, it's no business of yours." Carissa shoved her credit card into the reader and tried to avoid making further eye contact with any of them.

The pimply-faced girl eyed Carissa, Matthew and the tabloid, which he had taken out of the rack and opened, the photos and banner headline fully visible. "Oooh," she exclaimed. "It's both of you." She pointed at the paper and motioned the sacker to look, too. "Right here in the Market."

Matthew smirked. "Both of us," he said, waving the paper.

"I've always wanted to be a model." The girl struck a pose.

"I'm sure you have." Matthew coughed and jammed the paper back into its rack.

Carissa pushed her cart further forward and the sacker dropped the last two bags into it.

"Sure you don't want the rubbers?" Matthew asked from close behind her.

Carissa decided to ignore him.

"I can take your bags to the car," the sacker offered, stepping forward to effectively block a smooth retreat.

"A certain inn-keeper should've been using one a while ago."

Matthew's voice had dropped, but not low enough to exclude the two Market employees. They stood staring, the checker's mouth wide open.

What is Matthew talking about?

He leaned in close to Carissa and whispered, "I saw him with Sally in his office." He gave her several lurid details, setting her cheeks aflame.

"I'll take the groceries out to your car, Ms. Yates," the sacker said, pushing hair out his eyes. "I'm one of Mrs. Dodds' grandsons. She works for Mr. and Mrs. Dansinger."

Carissa nodded and let him take the cart. She followed him as he set off at a jog through the store and out into the parking lot, where the snow was growing steadily thicker. He loaded the bags neatly into her trunk in a matter of moments. She tried to tip him, but he refused.

"The Market takes care of our customers," he said. "I'm Howie." He smiled. "The other sacker's named Bert."

"Thank you." She shook hands with him before jumping into the Lexus and gunning the motor. Her tires barely made traction with the icy surface of the lot but she kept up her pace until she had left the Cove behind and was negotiating the twists and turns up the road to the Dansingers.' She wasn't in the mood for a detour, but she wouldn't need to chitchat with William. She'd drop the groceries and hurry home.

Carissa realized she was going too fast when she almost missed the turn into the Dansingers' almost completely obscured driveway. She hit the brakes hard, fishtailed, over-corrected and then really lost control of the car, which took out the mailbox. Evidently the privet hedge had grown over a wall. The Lexis crashed into it and stopped.

CHAPTER THIRTY-FIVE

CARISSA FELT REALLY STUPID. Large snowflakes joined privet leaves already covering her windshield. She laid her head against the steering wheel and cried. She wasn't even sure why. Perhaps it was the accident, although she didn't feel hurt. She was going to lay the blame for her melt-down on Matthew. She'd held everything together until the moment he told her he'd seen Steve and Sally engaging in sex right in front of a window at The Fisherman's Rest.

William wrenched open her door. "I heard the crash. Are you okay?"

"Yes, I think I'm fine. Sorry about your mailbox."

He helped her out, his hands icy. He had no coat on.

"You'll freeze," she warned him, but she needed the support. Standing, she felt shaky, her legs unsteady. She looked at her car and groaned. One front wheel leaned at a crazy angle.

"Looks like you broke the axle," William said. "Come on, let's get you inside. Did you hit your head?"

"No." She started crying again. "I'm okay. Really."

"That's what counts. Everything else will work out," he assured her as he coaxed her up the driveway. The private duty nurse came rushing out and took her other arm.

"I was going too fast, and I was driving distracted. I acted like an idiot."

Carissa allowed them to steer her into a recliner in the living room and elevate her legs but although she allowed the nurse to take her pulse and blood pressure, she adamantly refused to let the woman call an ambulance. The nurse wasn't happy, but returned to Mrs. Dansinger after instructing William how to watch for a concussion, which included not allowing Carissa to fall asleep. She also told him he was not to allow Carissa to borrow his car.

"I left my keys and purse out there as well as your groceries," Carissa told William after the nurse finally returned to her first patient. "I've got to call a wrecker."

"I'll bring you the cordless and the phone number for Gus Morgan's Garage. He'll take care of your car." William left but quickly returned with the phone and a card with the garage's information on it. "Only show in town," he said. "Tell Gus I told you to call."

"I will. Thank you." Carissa tried to ignore a pounding headache and sore neck. She wondered whether the nurse would approve of her taking a couple of Tylenol.

"I'll get your things and the groceries." William went out the door and closed it quietly behind him.

Carissa made the call. Gus sounded doubtful about sending out a wrecker. He told her if the hill had become too icy, the car would have to stay where it was, since it was pretty much off the road. He told her she wouldn't be able to ride back to town in the wrecker, even if it made it up to her car. William brought her purse, then made a couple of trips to get the groceries into the kitchen.

Carissa called her insurance agent, who asked about the damage. She wanted to be specific and insisted on going back outside to take a closer look. William went with her. Thick snow had made short work of burying the landscape under a thick, suffocating blanket. Even the constant crash of the waves below the cliffs had become muffled. Drifting snow had transformed the Lexus into a white sculpture.

William rubbed one hand over his chin. "I think you'll have to take my word about the damage, unless you're planning on dusting all this off. Trust me; you did a good job of denting it and scraping up the paint as well as damaging the axle. It's not driveable. I'm glad you were just shaken up."

"I'll have to call a cab," she said. "Gus said I can't get a ride with the wrecker, which may not even make it here."

"You're welcome to stay here overnight."

"That's a generous offer, but I'd rather sleep in my own bed tonight. I know I'm going to be really stiff and painful tomorrow, and I'd rather be home." She didn't tell him she was already feeling the effects of the crash.

"All right."

He drew her arm through his as they walked slowly back to the house and poured her a glass of brandy, which she drank in the kitchen as he put away the groceries. She didn't offer to help him, since she knew already how precisely he would want to place everything on the shelves.

"You remind me so much of Jessica," he said. "Looking at you brings so much pleasure, but pain, too." He stopped speaking, and his eyes filled with tears.

Carissa didn't know what to say. A lump formed in her throat. William put on a good front, but in private, he really wasn't the cold fish she had first thought.

"I went half-crazy when she died," he said, speaking softly. "I guess that's why I did what I did the other day." He walked over to the window and stared out at the whiteness beyond. "I was completely lost. It was as though everything I had been was taken away from me. And yet, while I was grieving inside, Patsy was still here, demanding things day and night." He stopped and took a deep breath.

The silence lengthened between them as Carissa tried to decide how to respond. "I'm so sorry," she said finally. It probably wasn't enough, but she couldn't possibly know how he'd felt.

William shuddered, as though wrenched from his memories. "Patsy was worse after Jessica died." He sounded really angry. "It was as though she was punishing me for being bereaved. I almost threw myself over the cliff the day I found Jessica, but I knew she'd call it the coward's way out. I couldn't disappoint her again."

Carissa was puzzled. "Why do you think you disappointed her?"

"I should have waited for her to come home from Europe. Instead, I sought the comfort Patsy offered. I felt guilty about what I'd done to Patsy, too." He cupped his face in both hands and shook his head. "I was so stupid, so self-centered. So *weak.*" He turned to face Carissa, and suddenly, the grief and anger were gone. "I was so startled when I saw you on the patio the other day. For one glorious, foolish moment, I thought Jessica had come back to take me with her."

"Oh, William."

"Patsy was terrible the day Jessica died. Worse than she'd ever been. You know why she makes me carry her up and down those stairs? It's a punishment. She thinks I caused her illness."

"Why on earth would she think that?"

He shrugged. "Because she's Patsy." He glanced at his watch. "It's four o'clock. Patsy always has tea at four." He filled the electric kettle and plugged it in. "Patsy always got what she wanted. For some reason, I couldn't see that before I married her. She had been writing to Jessica all the time she'd been away, but hadn't told her about me being wounded and unable to write."

"No one else told Jessica?"

He shook his head. "You have to understand…war does that. People get so wrapped-up in their own lives—worrying about family members —protesting—they don't get involved with others as much. Jessica's parents were long dead, and her brother—your father—had gone off to New York after he got a medical discharge from the army on account of his war wound."

Carissa couldn't help smiling. "Some war wound," she remarked dryly. "He got shot in the butt."

William nodded. "Probably running away from the enemy."

"Probably. You knew my father all right."

"Always shirking responsibility." William shook his head. "He and Jessica were so different."

"Where did Jessica go when she left here? Virginia said it was over-seas, but wasn't specific."

"England. I've wondered over the years why Virginia didn't tell Jessica about my injury while they were corresponding." He shrugged. "But Virginia and Nancy were always so preoccupied with themselves; they didn't have much time for other people's problems."

"Preoccupied with what?" Carissa couldn't imagine anything more important than telling a friend that her boyfriend had married someone else.

He managed a quick smile. "Usually, fighting over some man. Ironically, all the bickering drove suitors away. Neither Virginia nor Nancy has ever married. Now they're both setting their sights on that retiree who came into town right before you moved here, by the name of Walter Barnes."

"Who were they fighting over at the time?"

"Percival Huddleston. He had the sense to marry a fine woman from Whitstead."

Carissa thought how well the lives of inhabitants in small communities became intertwined, often, it appeared, with disastrous results. "I thought I was coming to a peaceful, even boring little village. Instead of that, I've landed in a soap opera."

"We're not all bad or dysfunctional." William's smile finally reached his eyes. "We do help each other out."

"I'm glad to hear that."

Her smartphone rang. She hurried back into the living room and felt a twinge in her back as she picked up the phone. The wrecker was on its way. At least she would be able to leave the Dansingers. She heard footsteps on creaking stairs.

The nurse walked into the kitchen. "Mr. Dansinger, your wife's asking for you," she told him. "She's a lot more alert."

William nodded. "Tell her I'll be right up."

The nurse nodded and turned on her heel. White shoes made no noise until she hit the creaky stairs again. The kettle whistled loudly. William turned off the stove, dropped teabags into the tea pot and poured water over them.

"I told you Patsy's tough." He put a cozy over the pot and placed it on a tray already holding cups, a sugar bowl and a small plate He opened a packet of shortbread and shook a couple of cookies onto the plate while Carissa poured milk into a jug. "She'll be her usual bossy self in no time." He held out his hand. "If you're gone before I get back downstairs, just close the door behind you."

Carissa wondered whether a cab would be willing to take her home in a snowstorm. She really didn't want to take William up on his offer to stay, but a quick check of the weather forecast showed a projection of at least a foot of snow.

Feeling trapped and completely without options, she decided she should stop procrastinating and call Richard Ebberly to apologize for standing him up. When he answered the phone, instead of being angry, he asked if she was safe. Carissa felt overwhelmed by his kindness. She gave him an abbreviated account of the altercation with Steve and Matthew, then about her accident.

"I'm coming to get you," he said.

"The roads are really bad. Even though Gus said I can't hitch a ride back to the village with the wrecker, I'm going to try."

"Uh-uh. You're not coming down that steep hill in a wrecker. I pass the Dansingers and the lighthouse on my way home. I won't be going out of my way. Remember, I told you my Jeep can make it anywhere in any weather."

"All right. You've convinced me. Thank you—you're a life-saver."

A few minutes later, flashing lights told her the wrecker had arrived. The driver was grumpy. The roads were becoming impassable he told her when she walked out to meet him. He plodded off to hook up her car and did it really quickly. Her Lexus left, red lights on the roof and flashing hazard lights at the rear contrasting vividly with the blanket of white before they disappeared into the gloom. Carissa plugged the electric kettle back in, made herself a cup of herbal tea and sat at the kitchen table to wait for Richard. A grandfather clock in the hallway ticked monotonously. She almost nodded off before the doorbell rang.

"I'll get it," she called up the stairs. "It'll be Richard Ebberly. He's taking me home."

Silence answered her. She wondered if all three people upstairs had fallen asleep.

Richard was dancing from one foot to the other when she opened the door. His hands were deep in the pockets of his thick down jacket, his nose reddened by a viciously icy wind. He waited inside the hallway while she pulled on her outerwear.

"I've got to thank you again and apologize for this morning," she said as she tugged on her last glove. She heard the stairs creaking again in the background.

"Forget about it; I already have." Richard put his hand on the door knob.

William came into the hallway. "Nice to see you again, Ebberly." He shook hands with Richard. "Be careful," he told both of them. "I've been watching the weather forecast while Patsy and the nurse have been napping. This storm's a bad one."

Carissa impulsively reached up and kissed his cheek. "Be careful yourself," she whispered.

"I will."

His wintery smile sent a pang through her. Richard put his arm around her waist and held her against his side all the way to his Jeep. The snow was already deep enough to go inside the tops of her boots. Carissa felt the coldness as it melted into her socks.

Richard tucked a rug around her after he got her settled into the passenger's seat. Carissa smelled pizza. The pleasant odor of tomatoes, basil and cheese reminded her she hadn't eaten all day.

Richard's driving skills were awesome. He stayed on the road despite drifts that obscured everything, including ditches and downed tree branches.

"You've got five minutes to throw some clothes into a bag," he told her when they drew up in front of the keeper's quarters. "I'm kidnapping you for pizza and beer, and then you're spending the night at my house."

"Richard, I don't think…"

"I'm not planning to make any moves on you, if that's what you're thinking. I couldn't go home and sleep tonight knowing you were marooned out here without a car. I heard you've had some problems."

"Who told you that?" Her voice was sharper than she'd intended.

"People are wondering if Jessica's ghost is walking. I'm more pragmatic. I think whoever's trying to scare you off is made of flesh and blood."

"If I get into any trouble, the Ulsters are right next door," she offered, doubtful herself about the quality of Blake Ulster's help.

"Don't even try to convince me Blake's going to help anyone but himself. He keeps his wife away from everyone and makes it his mission to be as rude as he possibly can."

"Maybe, but I'm not going to run away from home. I had new locks put on by an out-of-town locksmith. I'm working on an alarm system."

"'Working on' isn't installed, Carissa."

She shook her head, adamant.

"I can't eat an extra-large pizza all by myself."

"You could give me a couple of slices before you leave." She couldn't help smiling. He looked too appealing. His golden hair had been tousled by the wind and was curling up around his wool cap.

"You're a stubborn woman," he grumbled.

"It runs in my family." She opened the Jeep's door.

"Yeah, right." Richard sighed heavily and grabbed the pizza from behind her seat. "Fine, let's go."

He followed her to the front door. She felt some anxiety about him even being able to leave when she found herself trekking through snow that was now up to her knees. She unlocked the front door and walked into the hallway. Everything was quiet, but for some reason, the hairs at the base of her neck bristled.

Stupid, she thought. *You're listening to these silly stories and believing them.* She flipped on the light and kept going.

"It's cold in here," Richard said from close behind, his voice startling her. "See," he said. "You're jittery. Don't tell me you're not."

"I am *not* jittery. But I don't like people sneaking up behind me. I like boundaries."

"Fair enough. I'll remember that. But why is it so cold in here?"

"I don't know. I think the new thermostat's faulty." She tossed her outerwear onto a chair and gestured toward the couch. "Have a seat. I'll check and see if it's reset itself to fifty-five again."

She couldn't help sneaking another look at him before going into the hallway. He put the box on the coffee table, peeled off his coat and draped it across the back of a dining chair. He wore a pale gray turtleneck that molded his incredible physique.

As the ex-wife of a world-class designer, Carissa could appreciate physical perfection. Richard's face should be adorning every major magazine in the country, his body gracing runways world-wide. What in the world was he doing in a small and remote fishing village?

Finding the thermostat set at 50 degrees that time, she turned it back up and told Richard he could make a fortune as a male model. She quickly quantified that observation by reminding him her own career had made her an astute judge of physical attributes.

Richard laughed. "So not my bag. I love what I do. To me, there's nothing more satisfying than turning an old, ramshackle building into a functional showcase of modern living."

"This house included?"

"Maybe."

He had removed the pizza from a zippered warming case. He flipped back the lid and the aroma intensified. Somehow, though, it didn't smell as appetizing as it had in the car. Something underlying vied with the pizza, and it wasn't pleasant. She thought she'd taken her garbage out before leaving. What else could be wrong in that cottage? The plumbing?

"I hope you like mushrooms and green peppers. I wasn't sure what toppings to get. I knew you weren't a vegetarian after you ate that steak hoagie in Bangor, but I still waffled about pepperoni."

Watching his long fingers, Carissa's mind left any preoccupation with the possibility of stopped-up drainage pipes. Her mind conjured a graphic fantasy of what Richard's fingers could do to her body. She tried to ignore the inner heat and told herself she'd either been alone too long or wasn't as immune to good-looking men as she'd hoped.

"I'll get plates," she muttered, bumping into a chair as she turned away. Instead of letting him watch the swing of her hips as she moved unhurriedly out of the room, she charged into the kitchen in an undignified and ungainly rush, imagining Richard's amused reaction.

She turned on the light and froze. Blood spattered walls, windows, counters and floor. In the middle of the sink was what appeared to be a butchered cat, its pathetic orange striped tail dangling over the edge.

CHAPTER THIRTY-SIX

CARISSA'S horrified scream brought Richard bounding into the kitchen, where he found a bloodbath.

"It must be a stray," she said. "But oh God, it looks like Virginia's fat orange cat. I think I'm going to throw up."

Richard fought nausea, too, as he took in the extent of the carnage. A broken window pane above the sink was probably the point of entry. The cat could never have cut itself so badly on the glass. He stifled his revulsion long enough to peer into the porcelain sink, where he spotted a cleaver and a pair of rubber gloves.

"Come out of here." He tugged at her. "I'll call the police."

"They're not going to drive out here in the middle of a blizzard to look at a cat's remains." She shook him off. "God, what a dreadful thing for someone to do to an animal. I've got to call Virginia and ask if Hubert's there. He was fine when I saw her today; he was sitting on her lap when I left."

"I doubt it's Hubert," Richard said, searching hastily for the right words. "He's a real housecat. That's why he's so big, although he *is* part Maine Coon." Going against the queasiness in his stomach, Richard tried taking a closer look at the cat. It was definitely oversized, but the extent of the butchering had rendered it a mangled mess. Richard balked at putting his bare hands onto the remains in search of a collar and tag. "Thankfully, if there's anything to be thankful for, it wasn't you who got cut up with a cleaver."

He dragged her out of the kitchen and sat her on the couch while he called the sheriff's office. The phone rang and rang before Ray Watkins finally picked up. The deputy listened to Richard's story.

"Listen," he interrupted, when Richard paused for breath. "Why don't you take Carissa to your house? I'm not driving up from the Cove in this weather, and I've got to contact Animal Control and probably the Humane Society in Bangor for advice. Laws are different for animal cruelty."

Richard felt exasperated. "You mean Virginia's pet isn't worth your time to investigate?"

"I'm not taking the chance of getting stranded or having an accident to investigate a cat's death in the middle of a blizzard, even if it does turn out to be Hubert. I'll call Virginia. When she assures me Hubert's toasting his girth by the hearth, I'll call you back and set both your minds at ease."

"It's not just the extent of the butchering that cat suffered, Ray. It's the thought that someone deliberately broke into Carissa's home to do this."

Watkins sighed. "It could be teens, trying to scare her. Maybe someone even paid them to do it. We've all heard the rumors about some corporation wanting to turn the lighthouse into a resort."

"They'd have to be deranged to cook up something like this." Richard couldn't believe Ray Watkins was that detached and disinterested. He wished Sheriff Crosby was back on duty. The sheriff would *make* his deputy get out to the lighthouse. "Any corporation that set out to frighten a woman like this to cut a real estate deal without even making her an offer first has got to be run by a maniac."

"Why don't you let me talk to Carissa?" Watkins sounded a lot calmer than Richard felt he should. "I'll convince her to go home with you tonight. That is, if you can still get there in this storm."

"I can make it."

"I thought you'd say that. I used to want to issue you more speeding tickets than the sheriff allowed me to." He gave a slight chuckle. "He said you had a future as a race car driver if you decided not to go into the family business. Now I kind of admire your expertise."

Richard knew when to accept defeat. "I hope you'll come out here tomorrow. And you'll let us know Hubert's safe as soon as you call Virginia?"

"I will. Now, let me talk to Carissa."

Richard watched as she had a short conversation with Watkins, verifying Richard's account and reiterating how important it was that Watkins notify them if Hubert wasn't the victim. She finally said, "All right; I'll go," and handed Richard his phone.

"It won't take me long to pack a bag." She set off down the hallway, turning on lights as she went.

Richard took a moment to put the lid back on the pizza, the sight and smell of it aggravating his nausea. He doubted either of them had any appetite left for food. He'd fix them both a stiff drink as soon as they were inside his home. Carissa was true to her word. In less than 5 minutes she'd changed clothes and packed an overnight bag. They left without another word.

The drive to his house was completed at a crawl. Despite his best efforts, the Jeep slid and sideswiped a tree. He told Carissa it wasn't worth the delay to get out and inspect the damage. Richard got the Jeep moving again after a couple of tense minutes when the wheels couldn't grab traction. He swore under his breath.

Carissa sat silently beside him, hands clenched together in her lap. He admired her courage. She'd handled herself well in several tense and horrible situations that afternoon. Hopefully her strength didn't come from a lot of practice sparring with her ex. He wanted to get to know her a whole lot better without having to work through misconceptions that put a blanket umbrella over all men.

Eventually, after a trip that lasted twice as long as it would have in clear weather, lights winked out of the darkness. Richard hit the remote and pulled into the garage. The door closed behind them, shutting out howling wind and swirling snow.

"You're a very good driver," Carissa said. "I was terrified the whole way, but we didn't get stuck."

"It was close, especially when I hit that tree." He watched her climb out without waiting for his help. He took a quick look at the damage to the left side of the Jeep, decided a good body shop could repair it and grabbed her bag from the back seat. They trudged through snow drifts to the kitchen door. Richard flipped on the lights and ushered Carissa inside.

"No cats," she said with a nervous giggle, pointing to the stainless steel sink, and then she burst into tears and leaned heavily against the counter. "I'm sorry, I don't feel so well."

Richard thought she looked close to fainting. He steered her into the living room. "What we both need is a drink." He took off her coat and left her on the couch, shook off his own outerwear and draped both coats over the backs of dining chairs before going to the wet bar. "Brandy? Scotch?"

She fished a tissue out of her pocket. "Anything will do. I haven't eaten since sandwiches with Virginia at lunchtime, so don't give me too much unless you plan on carrying me up to bed." She shook her head, groaned and held it in both hands. "You're probably planning to do that, anyway. God, I'm dizzy."

While he put ice into two glasses, he kept an eye on her. She managed to kick off her boots. Her gloves, hat and scarf joined them on the floor. Seeing Richard watching her she looked back, her eyes sparkling brightly in the muted light.

Richard wasn't sure if she was going to start crying again. He wouldn't have blamed her if she had. "All I've got in mind right now is getting you warmed up and calmed down," he told her. "Not fainting would be an additional plus." He decided brandy would work better than scotch. He threw the ice into the sink, took out two snifters and poured generous servings of St. Remy.

"You had the same scare I did," she said. "How come I'm the only one feeling faint?" Her brow furrowed.

He picked up the glasses. "Living in rural Maine all these years, I've seen a lot of dead animals."

"I suppose that's true." She got up and walked over to take her drink from him. "While you were driving here, I had this crazy thought that maybe you had wanted to take me home because you were the one who did that dreadful thing, and you wanted to make sure I saw it. If you got me to sell to you in a hurry, after you remodeled you could flip the light-house and cottage for a huge profit."

"Carissa, I would never...."

"No," she interrupted. "That was a stupid, random thought. Paranoia on my part. You were as shocked and revolted as I was." She peered at him. "You still look pale. I'm sure I do, too." Suddenly, she placed her hand on his forearm and rubbed her thumb slowly across the wool. "Maybe sex isn't the best way to comfort after a shock like we both had, but if you made love to me, I wouldn't object."

He gazed into her blue eyes. Their clarity sucked him right in. He took a swallow of brandy. "Drink," he ordered. "I'm desperately trying to be a gentleman. Don't make it so hard for me. I don't want you waking up tomorrow morning and telling me I took advantage of a really bad situation."

She took several sips of her St. Remy. "I let Matthew Yates take advantage of me for five years. I know what that's like. This isn't the same thing." She took his snifter and set both glasses down. Unsteady fingers crept up under his sweater, pulled the t-shirt out of his pants and found his skin.

Richard inhaled sharply. She was offering herself and he was about to refuse the gift. He didn't know who'd be more surprised. He pulled away, his pulse racing like a Kentucky Derby contender in the last stretch.

"Don't," he said.

"You don't want me?" Her eyes widened.

"I'm not saying that. I told you—I'm not taking advantage of this situation."

"And what if I want to be the one to take advantage?" She peeled off her sweater and the turtleneck underneath it, leaving herself wearing only a delicate black lace bra. She put her arms around his neck, her lips moist, full, and invitingly close.

Too close. Richard couldn't help himself. He kissed her, lightly at first, then deeper and hungrier. He got rid of the bra and his own clothes shortly afterward. In a matter of moments, they were completely naked and stretched out on the rug in front of the empty fireplace. She was a supple partner who seemed to anticipate all his moves. When he drove into her, she opened herself to him, her hips twisting in such a way that he exploded into her, his breath coming in gasps.

Although Carissa had made little mewing noises, he strongly suspected she'd faked an orgasm. Whether that was to please and fool him or herself, he had no idea. The act saddened him. She'd willingly instigated their love-making, but she hadn't received the pleasure he'd wanted to give her. Richard knew he'd had trouble controlling himself. He cursed himself for rushing and gathered her in his arms.

Carissa shivered. "Can you light a fire? Now we're done, I'm getting cold really fast."

Done, he thought. Just *done?* Like it was her way of thanking him, and now the transaction had been completed, there would be no intimacy between them?

He fought against the disappointment; against the feeling that she had belittled the act. "We could go upstairs to bed," he suggested, tracing the outline of her lips with his finger. Encouraged when her lips quivered, he ran his finger all the way down the center of her body, between her pink-tipped breasts, across her quivering stomach and into the dark thatch between her legs. When she sighed, he slipped his finger further into the warmth there.

"I...I don't think that's necessary, do you?" Crimson tinted Carissa's cheeks. She wriggled away. "I should get dressed." She got up and gathered her clothes together. "That was...umm...nice. Thank you." She stepped into her panties and quickly pulled them up her legs.

Richard ignited the gas fireplace. "I wish you wouldn't get dressed so quickly. You make me feel used." He put on his underwear, still felt exposed and added his sweater.

Carissa was also wearing her sweater, but her pants and bra lay beside her as she sat on the couch. She had difficulty meeting his gaze.

"I'm going to get us something to eat." He handed her a soft throw from the recliner. "This'll keep you warm for a few minutes. The fire puts out a lot of heat." He stopped at the wet bar and brought her brandy. She was sitting as he'd left her. At least she hadn't gotten completely dressed again, he thought with a spark of hope.

"I'd really love a cup of hot tea." She tucked her knees up to her chin. She seemed perched for flight but with nowhere to go.

Richard brewed tea before heating split pea soup and making thick sandwiches of roast beef, all leftovers from dinner the night before. His housekeeper cooked three times a week and he ate left-overs on nights he didn't eat out. He took the loaded tray into the living room and placed it on the coffee table.

"Thank you," she said again.

"For dinner or sex?"

"I'm sorry, Richard. You're right—I used you. I was angry at someone else, and I took revenge the only way I knew how."

Richard laid down his sandwich after one bite. "I see." Now he thought he knew how women felt when men left right after sex.

"Oh, Richard."

Carissa moved closer. They sat side by side, barely an inch between them, yet Richard felt she was miles away emotionally.

"I don't want to hurt your feelings, but I don't want to lie, either."

He felt her hand stroking his bare thigh. "Don't do that unless you mean it," he said sharply, jerking his leg away.

"You wanted to use me the other day." Her voice was quiet.

He took a deep breath. "I did, yes. I won't deny it. But now, I want more. I want to see passion on your face. I want to give you pleasure and hear you whisper my name. We shared nothing during sex. You even faked an orgasm."

She turned away, tears on her cheeks. "I've never had one. I've been told I'm either frigid or I'm unlucky enough to be a woman who doesn't have them. Matthew got tired of trying to arouse me, so he taught me how to give him the maximum pleasure in the fastest amount of time."

Richard thought he could easily hate Matthew Yates. "Was it him you were mad at today?"

"Not only him." She sighed deeply. "Life's so complicated sometimes."

Richard leaned back and gathered her against him. "Tell me," he urged, gently kissing her cheek, her eyelids, and her mouth. He drew the throw over them both and felt her body warm and relax.

Carissa finally spoke, and when she did, she talked for over an hour about Steve and Matthew and Sally. She talked about the pending court case and the worry of losing it. She spoke about the hounding paparazzi and the lawyers and her aunt. She talked about the need for isolation and her fears about the lighthouse.

When she finally finished, Richard got up. "I don't know that I've got any useful advice for you right now, but I can do one thing, and that's take you up to my bed, where I'm going to start teaching you all about having an orgasm."

She didn't resist when he took her hand and led her up to his bedroom, turned the lights down low and played soft music. He took his time as he had never done before. When she rose up, arching her back, he knew she was enjoying sensations she'd never felt before. But when she started twisting her hips, his hands stilled them.

"Don't move, 'Rissa. Let me do it for you," he whispered against her neck before he took her lips again. He thrust into her, rotated his hips and thrust again. She gasped. He placed his fingers between them.

"Oooh." Her expelled breath was a sigh filled with awe.

"Did you?" He whispered.

"Yes, oh yes." Her voice held exultation, her face radiated pleasure. "Oh, Richard." Tears matted her lashes.

He kissed them away. "No time for that. You're a woman now, you know, in every sense of the word."

"I know. Oh, I know." She pulled him down to her. "Now I can really thank you. Give me a few minutes to recover, and we can repeat that wonderful experience all over again."

"I don't know if I can that quickly." He laughed softly against her skin. "You may have worn me out."

"Really? I thought architects were invincible." She giggled.

The sound of pure joy sent a thrill through Richard. He'd held himself back long enough to give before taking. The effort had been worth it—a hundred times worth it. Lethargy started to overcome his body. He snapped off the lights and used the remote to turn off the music.

"Can you leave the music on low?" She asked. "It's really beautiful."

"It is." He turned it back on. "New Age. You can't beat it." He felt incredibly content. "Mind if we catch a couple of hours sleep?" He couldn't keep his eyes open.

"You sleep. I'll lie here and hold you while I recreate every second of our lovemaking in my mind." She nuzzled his neck, kissed his cheek.

"Fair enough." With Carissa's unmistakable scent filling his nostrils along with the smell of hot, sweaty and completely satisfying sex, Richard drifted off to sleep.

CHAPTER THIRTY-SEVEN

STEVE GAVE up trying to reach Carissa on her landline. He tried her smartphone again, only to get sent into her voicemail. She had to be ignoring his calls. Matthew Yates had probably told her what he'd seen through the office window. Steve berated himself for being an idiot. If it wasn't Matthew, it could have been someone else. He'd wanted to run outside and grab Yate's throat, but what reason would he have given for attacking the designer? Protecting his girlfriend or his own right to privacy?

He gritted his teeth. Sally had pulled her clothes back on and left, but not before coolly appraising Matthew. Yates had returned that look with interest, and then sauntered away before Steve had gathered his wits enough to pull the blind down the rest of the way.

He knew he should throw Yates out of The Fisherman's Rest, but he couldn't face the guy. Sally's exhibitionism had been escalating over the past few months, and like a damned fool, he'd allowed the situation to continue. No, he corrected himself; he'd been an active participant.

One morning they'd had sex in the tiny kitchenette beside the storeroom, Verna ringing up purchases only feet from the closed door. Sally had been the instigator, but he'd been a willing partner. If her goal was to prove that where she was concerned, he couldn't control himself, then she'd met it.

He ran a hand over his face. What if they'd been spotted by Veronica Greeley or Percival Huddleston instead of Matthew Yates that morning? Even worse...Carissa. Maybe Sally was hoping shame and embarrassment would force him to finally commit to her. People might be more apt to look the other way if they were watching a married couple. Maybe not.

Steve couldn't sit still any longer. "I'm leaving," he told Hilly as he put on his parka. "I don't know when I'll be back."

She stopped polishing glasses and stared at him like he'd lost his mind. Steve anticipated there would be few dinner guests with snow piling up outside.

"Could you stay the night?" He zipped up the parka, pulled his hat down over his ears and calculated how long it would take to complete the long walk ahead of him. "I may need you to close up."

"If you need me to, yes." Her voice held a hint of disapproval.

"I'll be gone at least three hours. Probably longer." He wrenched open the door. Snow flew in, its stinging cold hitting him squarely in the face.

"Be careful," Hilly said. "You're not going far, Mr. Steve, are you?"

"No, not far," he assured her before stepping outside. He closed the door quickly, before Hilly asked any more questions.

Wind tossed snow around as he trod resolutely away from the harbor. Slick as wet glass, ice clung to trees and power lines. Snow drifts blanketed everything. The conditions hampered even Steve's long legs. His rasping breaths contrasted with stillness broken only by distantly pounding waves. By the time he reached the track leading up to the lighthouse, he was sweating beneath his heavy clothing.

Steve attempted to speed up, but his legs were too tired. Arriving at the keeper's quarters, he rang the doorbell, got no response, and followed that up by pounding the door. Worried, he felt around for the step, buried beneath several inches of snow, and thrashed his way to the back of the cottage through snow drifts up to his thighs. Carissa had complained about the mudroom door repeatedly coming unlatched, but it was firmly locked when he tried turning the knob and pushing on it.

Frustrated, he stepped back and noticed something dangling out the kitchen window. He pushed through a drift almost as high as the sill to see a red gingham curtain, stiff with ice, hanging through a broken pane.

Thoroughly alarmed, Steve slid his hand through the jagged hole and popped open the window. He wondered whether Carissa had carried through with her plan to alarm place. If so, then she needed to ask for a refund. He eased the window open and shouted out to Carissa before climbing over the sill and bracing himself on the edge of the sink. The kitchen was in darkness. Muted light in the living room must be coming from a table lamp. Its glow sent a shaft of light that traveled only as far as the kitchen doorway.

As he eased himself down, his right hand touched something slick, yet sticky. Revolted, he let go of the sink, slipped and crashed to the floor. He got up and ran into the living room. The cold, untouched pizza in the middle of the coffee table worried him more than he wanted to admit. He strode through the house, calling Carissa's name and flipping on lights as he went. The bedroom closet door stood open. Carissa's bed was rumpled with clothes scattered across it and the floor. Three dresser drawers were partially open. He didn't see her big suitcase, nor, when he looked in the bathroom, any toiletries. Her cape hung on a peg by the door, but he thought he remembered her wearing a turquoise coat when they were arguing earlier in the day. He hurried back into the living room and called the police station.

Watkins seemed remarkably calm. "She's spending the night with Richard."

"Who the hell suggested that? I've got plenty of open rooms at the inn. She could've stayed at no charge. That guy's a lying, manipulating sack of shit."

"She'll be fine." Watkins' sounded surprised at Steve's agitation. "Maybe you've got a beef with Ebberly, but I don't. He would never hurt Carissa." The deputy's voice suddenly changed to a lower pitch when he added: "Unless you know of a reason he would."

Steve wanted to tell Watkins exactly what he thought of Richard Ebberly, but he'd only be speaking from jealousy. "No," he admitted. "I don't."

He'd walked all that way in the snow for nothing. Now he'd have to walk all the way back, after he'd had visions of taking care of Carissa himself. He saw the bottle of Glenfiddich and walked over to Carissa's little bar to pour himself a drink. He debated... did he want ice? *Maybe*. Watkins was still talking. Steve forced himself to listen.

"People are saying you've been acting irrationally since Carissa arrived," Watkins said.

Irrationally? Steve wanted to laugh. He'd told Carissa he wanted to take her to bed; he'd almost had sex with Sally within full view of anyone passing by; and now he'd tramped two miles through a blizzard and broken into Carissa's home. Her very *cold* home. He downed the whisky and poured himself another.

"I'm not acting irrationally; I'm acting like I'm certifiable, Ray," he said, walking into the hallway to check the thermostat. 50 degrees. *Was Carissa trying to conserve heat by freezing her pipes?* "Forget it. I'm going home so we can all get some sleep."

Watkins said goodbye and hung up.

Steve turned the heat up to 65 degrees and turned off all the lights except the table lamp Carissa had left burning in the living room. About to leave, he decided to tear the lid off the pizza box and shove it between the window latch and the broken pane. He didn't bother turning on the kitchen light. A bad odor filled the kitchen, but he was too tired and mad to investigate further. Let Richard Ebberly take care of it. He was probably taking care of all Carissa's needs right at that moment. Steve allowed his imagination to run free as a punishment for the whole insanity of the day. The more he fantasized, the angrier he got, especially when he imagined Carissa and Richard entwined together in some stupid Karma Sutra position.

He turned to leave and paused, listening to the wind whipping around the cottage. Its isolation had no appeal for him. If Carissa would consider selling it to him at some time in the near future, he'd try to get local backers and turn it into a tasteful hotel complex, not the tacky resort he expected from Al Dyson's client.

The house groaned in response to the latest wind gust and something scurried around inside the roof. Rodents, Steve decided. Carissa needed an exterminator. He swore footsteps were coming down the tower stairs.

He shook his head. *Five minutes alone in this place and already my imagination's working overtime.*

Nevertheless, he beat a hasty retreat, leaving the new deadbolt open, but managing to secure the door using the old lock below it. Steve decided that would be enough of a deterrent until Carissa arrived back home. No one in their right mind would come up the almost-impassable track to burglarize the keeper's quarters during a near-blizzard. How the back window had gotten broken, he had no idea. Maybe Carissa had done it herself, or she'd locked herself out and Richard Ebberly had smashed his way in through the kitchen window while carrying a large pizza. Steve started to pull on his gloves and saw something dark on his right hand.

Carissa had mentioned she was feeding a stray cat that had appeared at the door right after she moved in. Maybe that's what had broken the window, trying to get at food Carissa might have left on the counter, or even that pizza in the living-room. He shuddered. Maybe the cat, or even a squirrel or possum had cut itself and that's what his hand had slid on —animal blood. He jammed his hand into the snow, wiping it around thoroughly before drying it against his pants. He reluctantly pulled his glove back on. Maybe the animal had also urinated in the kitchen, which could be the origin of the stench.

He continued to torture himself with more images of Carissa in Richard's arms as he made his way back to the road and started the long walk down the hill into the Cove.

CHAPTER THIRTY-EIGHT

RICHARD LEANED his elbows on the kitchen counter and watched the coffee pot fill. He still couldn't believe he'd left Carissa sleeping in his bed. When he'd awakened at 7:30 A.M. to find her next to him, he'd known he was incredibly lucky. An extended television news broadcast showed truckers, commuters and farmers dealing with the blizzard. Richard felt all of them. He was willing to bet they'd all rather be home than dealing with white-out conditions.

Carissa wandered into the kitchen, her hair tousled. He smiled when he saw his bathrobe wrapped around her, the sash trailing behind.

"'Morning." She smiled at him in a sleepy, sensuous way,

"Good morning, sleepyhead. Want some coffee?" He bent his head and kissed her lightly, forcing back an instant need to take her in his arms and plunge his tongue into her mouth to taste her sweetness.

"Mmm; yes. It smells wonderful."

"Mug or cup?"

"Mug." She looked beyond him to the windows and shivered. "Definitely a mug. I want to wrap my hands around it. Brrr, it looks cold out there."

Richard nodded toward the TV set. Images of motorists digging frantically around their cars with snow shovels flashed across the screen. "It's definitely a Nor'easter. You want cream and sugar?"

"Cream. I'll get it." She padded over to the refrigerator, hips swaying.

Richard slopped coffee onto the counter as well as into two mugs and took a gulp of his black coffee, burning the roof of his mouth. Hurriedly, he filled a glass with water and drank it right down.

Carissa returned with the heavy cream he kept on hand for guests. Concern filled her eyes. "Richard, are you all right?"

"Fine." He coughed.

One elbow on the counter and her gaze fixed on the images provided by WLBZ in Bangor, she stirred cream into her coffee.

Richard watched her, his burning mouth momentarily forgotten. "Do you know what you're doing to me right now?"

She turned to face him. "I have a strong hunch after last night." She glanced down at his pajama pants. "Maybe it's more than a hunch." She put down the spoon and sighed. "I think we should talk."

"I think we should do more than talk." He took her in his arms and kissed her. Her lips didn't open as they had the night before, but he persisted, probing with his tongue while his hands opened the robe.

She tore her mouth from his. "Richard..."

He pulled her closer.

She placed her hands against his chest. "Richard, please don't. Things have become too complicated as it is. Don't take advantage of me. You know I can't go anywhere."

"You tried to use me last night," he said, attempting to control his rapid breathing. "Now I'm taking advantage of you?"

"I want to talk."

"Fine, but can't we make love first?"

"No."

Her spine felt like a steel cable. Richard closed the robe and cinched the belt around her waist. "There, is that better?"

"A little," she conceded.

"Let's sit on the couch." He propelled her into the living room, sat and pulled her onto his lap.

She tried to squirm off.

He stopped her. "This is fine."

"No, it's not. I can't concentrate on what I want to say."

"Yes, you can. It's all relative. Think of me as a friend."

"How can I do that when your erection's pushing against me?"

"Forget it; I'm trying to." He forced a smile.

She gave him a half-smile back.

"I'm sorry; I'm really confused right now." She looked anguished. "I'm sure I'm undersexed. Matthew let me know that in no uncertain terms. I had such a good time last night; I don't know why I'm not lying down right now, begging you to do even more exciting things to me than you did last night."

"Why are you trying to analyze your feelings instead of just enjoying them?"

She wouldn't make eye-contact. "Am I?"

"You know you are."

"See, it's part of my failure to please, and my aversion to sex."

"I didn't think you had an aversion to anything last night, and as far as pleasing, you were nothing less than terrific, once we got over your initial hang-ups."

"Then why is it the thought of making love with you this morning makes me want to run and hide?"

"Probably guilt about enjoying yourself. That's a hang-up we haven't tackled yet. Did you see a counselor after your marriage broke up?"

"No; I was too busy trying to run away from everything."

"And you're still running." He stroked her face. "You have to stop."

"I know." She laid her head on his shoulder. "I didn't think I'd have to cope with this sort of problem at Treacher's Cove. I thought I'd have time to heal."

"It's hard to heal when you're trying to do it alone." He settled her more comfortably on his lap and began caressing her shoulders. She stiffened again, but he ignored it, massaging the tension with gentle fingers.

"But if I reach out to others, I'll have to learn to trust again. That's too difficult."

"Difficult, yes. Too difficult, no. People weren't made to live alone. You can't expect to be any different or you'll end up like your aunt, isolated on a damned clifftop with only the gulls and wind for company. There's too much passion in you for that."

"Passion?" She contemplated the word, her fingers drawing circles on his chest as his hands drew larger circles on her back. "I've never associated that word with myself."

"Who in the world did you get involved with besides Matthew?" Richard couldn't believe a woman like Carissa could have had a succession of bad relationships.

"You don't even want to hear about all that." She pushed away and sat up.

"Shhh." He pulled her back down. "Relax. Nothing's going to happen that you don't want."

She sighed. "Are you ever going to give up trying to get me back into bed?"

"Probably not." He kissed her forehead and brushed the hair back from her face. "Why is that so hard to take?"

"I need friends, not a lover."

"Why can't I be both? I won't push you into anything you don't really want, I promise. Cross my heart. But if you're only looking for friendship, why did you initiate sex last night?"

"Because I was mad with Steve Raymond."

Richard's spine went rigid after that remark.

"I know you don't like him. He doesn't like you much, either."

Richard shrugged his shoulders in an effort to show Steve Raymond's disapproval didn't matter to him. "Old news. Why are *you* mad at him?"

"Matthew told me he saw Steve and Sally making out." She looked away. "They were right in front of a window. He took great delight in giving me lurid details. Earlier yesterday he'd overheard Steve telling me he wanted to take me to bed."

Carissa's cheeks turned crimson, but they weren't the only item in the room associated with the color red. Richard's vision clouded with it.

"Matthew could have lied," she said.

"He does that?"

She shook her head. "He's got a lot of faults, but that's not one of them, that is until we started fighting over my embroidery and braiding. Then he was lying left and right." She stopped. Bit her lip. "No. He usually takes great delight in exposing the truth and seeing the results.

One of the biggest reasons I'm having trouble proving he stole those designs."

"So you used me for revenge sex. That's one hell of a turn-off."

He left her on the couch. She huddled there, looking like she was the one to be pitied. He trudged upstairs and took a long shower. When he walked out of the bathroom she was sitting fully dressed at the end of his neatly-made bed.

"I called the weather service," she said. "The storm's expected to pass sometime this afternoon. They're not recommending any travel. I wanted to leave before you got out of the shower, but I couldn't find any service that would pick me up."

"I'll check things out in a few minutes." He paused, aware of his nakedness beneath the towel. "If you don't mind, I'd like to get dressed."

"I don't mind," she said in a small voice.

Richard glared at her, but she remained sitting demurely, her legs crossed at the ankles like some prissy schoolmarm.

"This isn't a peep show," he snapped.

Her face turned pink, but she held her ground.

He took out clean clothes and headed for the bathroom. Then he changed his mind. This was *his* house. He turned around to face Carissa, whipped off the towel and stepped into his underwear.

She sat like a statue, her eyes fastened on his face, her hands clenched in her lap. He pulled up the briefs and put on his t-shirt, quickly followed by a flannel shirt, pants and a cable knit sweater. He paused. "Is that enough of a show, or do you want me to take them back off?"

"Only when you're able to forgive me for being such an idiot." Her hands shook. "I took advantage of you. I used you to get back at Steve."

"Damned right, and don't you ever forget it."

Turning his back, he took a pair of hiking socks out of a drawer and went back downstairs. His coat was damp. He'd been in such a hurry to get Carissa into bed, he hadn't taken the time to hang up his wet outerwear. He laced his feet into Sorel boots, put on the coat and shivered as dampness touched his neck. He took a dry hat, scarf and gloves from the coat closet before trying to open the front door, which wouldn't budge. He pushed it with his shoulder. No effect. It had to be blocked by a snow drift. Richard swore under his breath and strode through the house to wrench open the back door.

Drifts confronted him, covering the bushes on either side of the pathway from the kitchen door to the garage. Tracks made by the Jeep the night before were completely obliterated. What in the hell was he going to do? Even the Jeep wouldn't go through that deep snow. He had to get Carissa home somehow or she would drive him crazy. He made his way through snow up to his knees as he passed the three-car garage and headed for the utility shed, which held a used snowcat he had purchased on sale at the end of the last winter. He could take her home on that as long as it started.

The problem with dumping Carissa at the lighthouse was the broken window and the dead cat. Regardless of how angry he was, he couldn't leave her with the horror of cleaning up the mutilated remains. He'd have to do it for her, regardless of the revulsion he felt at that moment. Ray Watkins should be calling soon to give them an update on Hubert's whereabouts and what he'd learned from Animal Control and the Humane Society, Richard thought as he battled his way down the path in front of him. Maybe Ray or a worker from one of the agencies would want to take those remains for evidence.

The shed doors opened outward. He shook his head. His dad hadn't wanted to spend the money on a new door with an electronic opener after finding out how much the upgrade to the garage had cost. Richard had remodeled the house after his father's death, but he hadn't touched the shed doors, either. Like father, like son. And now he'd have to clear a path for the wooden doors to open before he could even see whether the snowcat was an option. It had come with a plow attachment, which had convinced him it would useful to clear his driveway. Now he hoped the snowcat would be able to do a lot more than that.

CHAPTER THIRTY-NINE

MATTHEW OPENED the door and stood aside for Halstead to take off his boots. The snow had finally stopped right before Halstead's call. Matthew's mood was steadily improving every day he spent at Treacher's Cove.

If the P.I. had interesting news to share about Steve Raymond, there had to be something in Raymond's past to use against him as well as the sexual episode Matthew had observed yesterday and detailed for Carissa with excellent results. Matthew's goal was to make the man totally disgusting to his ex-wife, and he was on the way to achieving that.

He rubbed his hands together, more from anticipation than cold. He'd jacked up the thermostat to 75 degrees and brewed a pot of coffee before Halstead's arrival. His next door neighbor had volunteered to act as his housekeeper during his stay, and they'd struck what Matthew felt was a bargain for her services, which included shopping and cooking for him as well as cleaning. He liked having other options to meals and drinks at The Fisherman's Rest, where he doubted he'd find a warm reception.

Halstead hung up his coat and started to offer his hand. "Good to meet you, Mr. Yates."

Matthew didn't believe in shaking hands with hired help. He turned his back. "Come into the living room. Coffee?"

"Thanks. Black."

Halstead followed Matthew into the living room. He sat at the small dining table and drew both a file and a lap top from his attaché case as Matthew poured coffee.

"I've got what you wanted." Halstead flipped open the file. "He's not using his full name. I had to come down here and lift his fingerprints before I could ID him. He's wanted for manslaughter in Newark, New Jersey, where he owned a bar."

"Excellent." Matthew tried to control the grin that threatened to split his face from ear to ear. He gave Halstead his coffee. The referral to the P.I. service had paid off and then some.

Halstead continued. "His full name's Steven Raymond Tanner. Apparently the guy he killed was his business partner, Kurt Lipton. Tanner and his partner owned a bar in Newark. Apparently, the partner signed the papers, but Tanner put up the money. I'm still digging into why they had that agreement. Anyway, the partner was addicted to gambling and lost a considerable amount of money, which he needed to pay back in a hurry. He went behind Tanner's back and sold the bar, causing an argument that escalated into a brawl, during which Tanner hit Lipton over the head with a bar-stool. Lipton died."

"I'm not surprised, seeing the size of that son of a bitch."

"I could take care of Tanner without getting close enough for him to touch me." Halstead patted his jacket, where a bulge indicated he was packing.

Matthew shrugged. Any good P.I. would make sure he had a license to carry, and given the size of Steven Raymond Tanner, Halstead wouldn't even need to be a very good shot. "So he ran."

"As soon as he made bail. He liquidated as many of his assets as he could. He sold his house to one of those shady 'we pay cash for houses' outfits. Then he disappeared. That was two years ago. You want me to blow the whistle on him?"

"Not yet."

Getting Steve Raymond arrested might not be enough. Matthew liked neatness and order in his life, and he already had a couple of very disorderly items on his hands...his divorce and Carissa's designs. He was two strikes away from the pennant already. He had no intention of increasing that number to three by allowing his emotions to sway his judgment.

"Do you need anything else?" Halstead drew the file back toward his attaché case.

He was a nondescript man in a dark gray suit. Even his tie was made up of indistinct gray stripes. Matthew wasn't sure he'd be able to pick out his P.I. in a lineup. Halstead's face was flat, his eyes brown, his hair butchered more than styled. He'd melt into any crowd and be forgotten the moment he passed out of sight.

"I don't need anything right now," Matthew said. "But why don't you stay on at the inn for a while? Scope things out. Let the locals believe you're a potential investor in a resort scheme. They'll buy it. Al Dyson, the local real estate guy is trying to get some sort of deal going. Make friends. Maybe they'll trust you enough to tell you something useful. No one'll tell me anything. They've already bonded with my ex-wife." He rolled his eyes, unable to completely control his frustration.

Halstead nodded. He handed over an invoice. "This is for the preliminary leg work. If you want me to stay on this case, the same terms are applicable."

"Fair enough." Matthew pulled over his checkbook and wrote, signing his name with a flourish. He liked his name—the flowing M and Y made it a work of art. He handed Halstead the check. "Do I get to keep that file?" He pointed to it, resting on Halstead's attaché case.

Halstead nodded. "It's a copy." He tapped his laptop. "Everything's in here." He pocketed the check without looking at it, slid the laptop back into his attaché case and stood up. "I'll see myself out."

Matthew waited to hear the front door close behind his P.I. before taking more coffee into the living-room. He settled on the couch with Steve Raymond's file. He knew one person in the village he could get tell him anything he wanted to know. He smiled with anticipation at the thought of how he was going to get her to open up.

A discreet knock at the back door announced his new housekeeper's arrival. Mrs. Beachum planned to spend the next couple of hours baking and making casseroles. She had brought two bags of groceries with her. Matthew picked up the file and left; his destination, the Emporium. He'd bought unflattering snow-gear the day before. Nothing he'd ever wear in

Manhattan, but definitely a lot warmer than his black wool coat and Pierre Cardin shoes, and a good investment if he wanted to avoid frostbite.

Repulsive Al Dyson had done well with the rental cottage. It was a little far out for a comfortable stroll through the village, but secluded. Matthew whistled under his breath as he closed in on a little tête-a-tête with Sally Mainard.

CHAPTER FORTY

SALLY FINISHED UNPACKING the last consignment crate and stood upright. Her back ached. She arched it to relieve the spasm. As she did so, the bell above the shop door tinkled. She turned to find Matthew Yates framed in the open doorway.

She looked him over. His down coat didn't mold his body as well as his overcoat had done, but his tanned skin contrasted against very pearly whites as he smiled at her. Sally wondered why Carissa had divorced her handsome husband. "Been to Bermuda lately?" She asked.

"I went a couple of months back." His grin widened as he closed the door behind him and walked toward her.

Caps, Sally decided. No one's natural teeth were that straight or even; at least no one she had ever known. "You hang out at a tanning salon between trips?"

"Of course. Keeps my mood optimistic and looks good for publicity shots."

He wasn't a tall man, but the word 'imposing' pretty well summed him up. His dark hair and eyes and that neat mustache completed the look, especially when he shrugged off the bulky jacket to reveal a black cashmere sweater over black jeans, both of them hugging his compact body. *Definitely sexy,* Sally thought, feeling a stir of desire.

"Can I help you with something?" She watched him peruse a display of plastic blueberries in tiny baskets. "Or would you rather browse?"

"I think I've already seen what I want."

His direct gaze felt a little unsettling as well as exciting. "Is that so, Mr. Yates?" She walked around to the back of the counter, her fingers trailing across its glass surface.

It had been too long since she'd openly flirted with an attractive man and it felt *really* good. First that shit, Richard Ebberly had dumped her. Then Steve Raymond came along. He helped her forget about the humiliation of that rejection, but he'd refused to marry her. The Cove was becoming dull and her life even more unfulfilling...until Matthew Yates showed up.

"Can I take you to lunch?" Matthew placed his hands only inches from hers on the counter.

"I don't think so. I don't want to be fuel for the local gossip-mill. They all think I'm with Steve exclusively."

"Who's a part of that gossip-mill? You need to share that sort of information." He leaned against the counter.

"Oh, well, Nancy Burton at the General Store and Veronica Greeley, a retired school-teacher are the worst." Sally grimaced as she thought about the trouble those two old hens had caused since she'd returned to the Cove. "They're two dried-up old virgins with nothing better to do than cause trouble with their snooping."

She watched Matthew run the tip of his tongue over his lips. The gesture was deliberate. It wasn't a sign of nervousness or discomfort. She felt duped. Her temper flared. "I guess you don't fall into that category, do you?" She snapped.

"I guess not." He grinned a slow, lazy, knowing grin that said far more than any words. "Let's say I'm more the appreciative audience member type."

"Is that right?" She looked down at their fingers, now almost touching, and withdrew her hands. "So what exactly do you want at the Emporium?"

For one moment, she thought she saw the bantering facade shift, and something else became visible. A band of steel behind a thin veneer, she thought. Matthew Yates was definitely not a weak man.

"What I want and what I get depends entirely on you." Matthew leaned his forearms on the counter. His face became level with her breasts, and he didn't raise his eyes.

Despite the fact that he was blatantly playing with her, Sally's nipples hardened in response. She felt them thrust against her sweater.

"Nice," Matthew said. "Very nice. Did you knit the sweater yourself?"

Not what Sally was expecting. She found herself scrambling to react appropriately. "No. No, I didn't, but it was hand-made by someone in the village. Would you like to see more of her work?"

Belatedly, she remembered the other sweaters, hats and mittens were in the stockroom. She had no intention of going in there and having Matthew Yates follow.

"Do they all have flowers like this one?" His finger almost touching her breast, he indicated a prominently up-thrust poinsettia.

Sally gasped and stepped away, bumping the shelves in the crowded little area. Fragile glass figurines and shell sculptures cascaded to the floor. She tried to save the rest of the display. Matthew rushed to help her.

"Get away." She admitted defeat as the last sculpture slid past her hand and crashed amongst the others. "I think you've done enough damage for one day."

Matthew grabbed her. Before she could even think about resisting, he kissed her with a savageness stronger than anything she'd ever wished from Steve. She gasped and opened her mouth. His tongue plunged in as his hands caressed every inch of her. Sally surrendered completely, powerless to stop him. When he released her, his mouth curving into a smile as he looked down at her flushed face, all she heard was her own ragged breathing. All she wanted was for him to finish what he had started.

"We're two of a kind, Sally," he told her. "When you're ready for great sex, give me a call...or come over and visit."

He laid his business card on the counter and added something to the back of it, his manner completely unhurried even as she struggled to regain her poise. She found herself following him as he shrugged back into his coat and walked unhurriedly toward the door.

"I'll pay for the damage," he said. "Send me the bill."

Suddenly he stopped, and she almost ran into him. He looked down at her, and his index finger drifted down the length of her arm, making her flesh prickle with anticipation. She stared mutely at him, for once bereft of words. She should be swearing at him and kicking him out of her store, she thought. She wondered what was wrong with her.

"You could also bring that invoice over yourself." He gave her a light peck on the lips. "I left the inn. My new address is on the back of my card. Text before you come, so I make sure I'm there."

She watched as he left the store and crossed the street, strolling toward the post office. As she stooped to pick up the remains of her display, she decided Matthew Yates would pay very dearly for the damage.

Anticipation surged through her. *Very dearly, indeed,* she promised herself.

CHAPTER FORTY-ONE

CARISSA WATCHED Richard from the kitchen window as he plodded toward the garage through snow up to his knees. She had no idea what to do. She couldn't stay with him any longer after what had happened between them the previous night. Now her hurtful behavior had driven him out of the house. Looking at the difficulty Richard was having even getting to the garage, she couldn't imagine how he planned to get her out of there. Even the Jeep couldn't make it through that deep snow.

Until the roads were cleared or the snow melted enough, she was trapped, and Richard was stuck with her. Looking up at leaden skies, she wasn't even sure the snow was taking more than a short break. As if on cue, a low murmur of voices on the TV drew her attention. She watched local reporters struggling through waist-deep snow and cars buried halfway to their roofs. A weatherman scrolled through maps and spoke about a concentrated low bringing more precipitation into New England. She decided to check on Virginia.

Breathless and anxious when she answered the phone, Virginia only said: "Hubert's still missing," before breaking down.

Carissa's heavy heart sank even further as she listened to Virginia's sobs. The likelihood that Virginia's fat old companion would ever return home was fading fast.

"I'm so sorry," she said, trying not to sound too dismal. How could she offer hope when her mind instantly conjured up an image of that orange striped tail hanging out of the sink?

Distractedly, she returned to spying on Richard, who was working his way around the side of the garage. He disappeared from view.

"He's fourteen years old," Virginia hiccupped through her sobs. "He's really an indoor cat, but he likes to prowl around the garden some-times. I wanted to give him an outing before the storm came. It's all my...my...fault."

"I'm sure he'll turn back up." Carissa said, unable to think of anything more encouraging. Virginia wailed.

"I wish I could help you look for him, but I'm snowed in."

Carissa managed to stop herself from adding she was at Richard's home. She didn't think Virginia would approve. She fervently hoped Hubert had spent the night with some neighbor. The other options were far less appealing—either he had frozen to death or he was in her sink—in pieces.

Afraid she was going to retch up her coffee, she headed for the powder room beside the front door.

"When the roads get plowed, could you stay and help me look for Hubert?" Virginia asked. "I could really use the company."

"Don't you have someone else who lives closer?" Carissa hedged.

If Hubert really was in her sink and Virginia found out Carissa had known about the death before the storm hit, she would probably be furious.

Why would anyone be so vicious? There had to be a reason for such a heinous act...either it was done out of spite, or it was a warning. *Next time it could be me, or someone I know.*

The retching feeling had subsided. She stopped rushing for the powder room and looked out the living-room window. Richard hadn't reappeared after walking out of sight around the side of the garage. Panic threatened to set it. She had to get Virginia off the phone and go investigate. Maybe Richard had fallen, or something had fallen on him. A branch heavy with snow, or a weapon held by a murderer...

Virginia was still babbling as Carissa shoved her feet into her boots and grabbed her coat.

"Your company was so welcome when you were here the other day, dear. Surely you don't want to stay at the lighthouse while Richard's having the kitchen torn out, do you?"

Carissa didn't want to lie to Virginia, but she had to get off that phone. "My ex-husband is staying at the inn. I don't want to bump into him. Your home's too close. I was thinking of taking a trip during the renovations."

"I heard your ex-husband moved to a rental cottage on the edge of town." Virginia blew her nose.

"Oh."

Matthew had moved to more permanent digs?

Carissa held the phone between her ear and her shoulder as she pulled on her coat. "He won't be cooking for himself, so he'll still be going to the inn for meals, and then he'll want to hang out in the bar."

Virginia sighed. "I won't press you. You've got better things to do than stay with an old woman who has lost her...her...beloved cat." She started crying again.

Carissa heard a door opening. As long as it was Richard doing the opening, she'd feel a little less stressed. She ran back into the living-room and saw him walk into the garage.

"Virginia, that's not true. You've made me a lovely offer that's going to be difficult for me to accept because of Matthew staying in the village. As soon as I can get over to your house, I'll help you look for Hubert. He probably spent the night with one of your neighbors."

"Surely they would have called me if he had," Virginia said.

Carissa watched Richard re-emerge with a snow shovel and go back around the side of the garage. Her hope of getting back to the lighthouse rose, but nausea returned when she thought about having to clean up the kitchen.

"I'll get the guest room ready for you just in case," Virginia said. "The bed is always made up, but I'll give you a couple more blankets and open the heating vent."

"Okay." Carissa felt bulldozed.

She needed to be outside helping Richard instead of tiptoeing around Virginia's feelings. She wished she'd never called her new friend in the first place.

"I'm going to make some calls," Virginia said. "Perhaps my neighbors all slept in because of the storm."

"That's a good idea, Virginia." Carissa saw a tactful opportunity to end their conversation. "I'll call again as soon as I know when I can get to town. Please call me if Hubert comes home." She cringed. That was a stupid thing to say. *"When* he comes home," she amended.

"Goodbye, dear. I'm going to speak to Deputy Watkins and make him aware Hubert is missing." Virginia hung up.

Carissa put down the phone and stared at it. So much for being discreet and caring. That was going to backfire on her PDQ when Virginia spoke to the deputy.

She tugged on her hat and gloves before going outside. She needed something constructive to do and shoveling fit the bill. She followed in Richard's footsteps as much as possible, but since his legs were longer than hers, so were his stride lengths. Carissa found herself sinking thigh-deep. By the time she reached the garage, she had built up a sweat.

She looked inside. .The Jeep stood on one side of the garage, various other pieces of equipment sat behind it, a heavy-duty red Dodge Ram pickup truck occupied the middle, and another black truck, older and with various dings and dents sat at the end. She spotted another snow shovel hanging on a hook and took it with her to where Richard was busy shoveling snow away from the doors of a large shed.

He glanced at her as she joined him. "Decided to help me get you out of here faster, huh?"

"I think it's best for both of us." She tossed snow onto the top of a drift. "I talked to Virginia. Hubert still hasn't come home. I don't think he ever will, and that makes me very, very worried about your safety as well as Virginia's and Steve's. I don't think Sally likes me, so I'm a little less concerned about anyone going after her, and I doubt my contact with the Dansingers would send up any red flags. Al Dyson could talk his way out of anything, and since I haven't really had contact with anyone else, I'm not going to worry about their safety. But I do think someone at the Cove has a grudge. Matthew's a good suspect, but he wouldn't do the dirty work himself, and I honestly can't see him condoning violence, even if it's directed at an animal."

Richard stopped shoveling. "Why in the world would you think you've got an enemy here?"

Carissa reminded him about all the small incidents at the lighthouse before opening up about being shoved in the fog on the clifftop.

Richard's brow furrowed deeper with each incident. At first, she suspected he thought she was being ridiculous as she described finding open doors and garage doorstops that came and went. Even the lowered thermostat could be explained as faulty, but he agreed the replacement shouldn't be malfunctioning as well, unless the wiring in the wall was the cause. He also agreed the incidents were escalating.

"If Matthew hired someone, they went way too far last night. If Al Dyson's responsible, I couldn't see him condoning Hubert's murder. In any case, I hope whoever paid someone to scare me away didn't knowingly hire a psycho."

"We've got to get you somewhere safe." Richard continued shoveling, but at a faster rate.

"There's no 'we' in this. You could be in danger now. If you can get me to Whitstead, I'll hide out there until the roads are passable enough for me to get further away. Do you think Deputy Watkins is reliable? I'm not sure I should even be confiding in him. Maybe he's being paid to look the other way, and that's why he wouldn't come over to the lighthouse last night."

"Ray Watkins is a straight arrow." Richard stopped shoveling. "So are the other Cove residents. You're pointing fingers at people I've known my whole life."

"That's what makes it so difficult for me to be taken seriously. Richard, I want to know the truth...do you think I'm hysterical? Even crazy?"

"I don't think you're anywhere close to crazy," Richard said slowly, as though measuring his words, "but apart from your ex, the only person I can think of who could be at the bottom of any of those earlier stunts, like opening your doors and moving bricks and paint cans in your garage is Al Dyson. If he's been paying someone else, like Blake Ulster, who lives next to you and is weird to start out with, the question is why? Wouldn't it have been easier to ask you to sell the lighthouse and make you one hell of an offer?"

"He broached the subject the afternoon I arrived, but I told him I wouldn't sell. If he tries to make an offer again after what we found in the kitchen yesterday, then I'll put my money on him being responsible."

"That would definitely tip the scales in his favor," Richard agreed. He started shoveling again.

"I'm going back to New York as soon as the weather clears. Coming here was a stupid mistake. I'm not going to have any peace. Virginia told me Matthew rented a cottage, so he's going to make my life miserable while he's trying his best to get what he wants—me back with him and no more dispute over who owns the embroidery and braiding designs."

Richard shook his head but didn't comment further. They worked side by side, yet she felt like they were miles apart. After close to an hour, he finally managed to pry open the shed doors. Inside sat a snowcat.

"It hasn't been run since I bought it used at the end of last winter," Richard told her. "Let's hope it starts." He got into the cab. "Can you make coffee and maybe a sandwich for us? I don't know how long it'll take to get you down to the Cove. I've got to check fluids and see if this will keep running before we go anywhere on it."

"Okay."

She knew nothing about snowcats and it wasn't the right time to learn. She went back inside the house, brewed coffee and made sandwiches from luncheon meat and sliced cheese. In the background, she heard an engine rumbling, dying, rumbling and dying. She found an insulated cup and took hot coffee out to Richard.

The engine stalled again as she walked into the shed. Richard had the housing off. He looked up. "If you think telling me to hurry is going to have any effect on this thing, you're sorely mistaken."

"I didn't come out here to harass you." She held out the insulated cup. "I brought coffee."

"Thanks." He took the cup and sipped. "You make good coffee."

"Yes, I'm not completely useless." She tried smiling at him, but he didn't respond. "If you want, I can bring you a sandwich. But I'd really like it if you took a break and ate the sandwich with me in the kitchen."

"I can eat once we get underway. If it takes much longer to get this going, we'll be riding in the dark. I know these roads well, but even I could make a mistake in these weather conditions."

"Okay. I'll bring you more coffee if you haven't come to get me in thirty minutes." She started to walk out of the shed, but felt she needed to do more for his kindness than offer him coffee and a sandwich. "I'm really sorry about this morning," she said.

"You're telling me this now? Why? Are you feeling guilty? You want to unload in case some guy on skis comes here and whacks me? Forget it." He went back to cleaning parts.

"Don't be difficult, Richard. I'm offering an apology because you've taken care of me when you're not trying to push me into having sex with you."

"Difficult? Christ!" He closed the housing. "*I'm* being difficult? I'm not the one who's blowing hot and cold. I don't like having my emotions milked." He settled into the driver's seat and turned the key in the ignition. The engine roared to life and stayed that way without sputtering.

"I'm not doing anything of the sort," she shouted.

She watched as he maneuvered the vehicle slowly out of the shed. The plow at the front pushed snow away, clearing a path. She closed both the shed doors before following in the snowcat's wake, feeling the vibration and wondering if her eardrums were about to pop.

Richard stopped beside the front door and got out, leaving the snowcat running. "I still can't see why you're so anxious to leave. I thought you liked me a lot yesterday, but I guess I was just a convenience."

"Oh, Richard." Carissa put her hand on his arm. "Would you stop complaining about my behavior and listen to reason? You may not be safe with me here."

"I've got a security system and my father's shotguns. You'll be perfectly safe. Who's going to try to drive out here through all this snow, anyway?"

"I don't know, but I'm not taking chances with your life."

"Fine. You're not going to stop agitating, regardless what I say. Go on into the house. I'll close up while you're getting your things together. I can bed down in my office tonight and hope the roads improve tomorrow. I always keep a packed bag at the office, so I don't need to do anything except lock up when you're done."

Carissa quickly repacked and joined him outside. Richard stowed her bag under a tarp at the back of the cab. She climbed into the passenger's seat and placed the cooler between her feet. No seat belt, she noted. She'd better hope she didn't fall out somewhere along the route. Richard might trundle off, leaving her behind.

He locked up and climbed back inside the cab. He looked tired and slightly disheveled, with hair curling up around his woolen hat and golden stubble covering his chin. His scowl stopped her from trying to make conversation. He was really upset with her, and rightly so. She sat quietly, hoping he might become more receptive to talking after a while. They rattled slowly along. Carissa watched Richard manipulate the steering controls and the gears, trying to learn how to operate the snowcat in case she needed to take over for any reason.

After an hour of silence, she tried breaking it. "Can we talk about what happened between us now?"

"I haven't had enough sleep, coffee or emotional warmth to discuss anything with you. Let's just get this drive over with."

"Can I get you more coffee?"

"Not until we get to the lighthouse. We'll take a short break there."

It was going to be a very long and difficult drive in every way, she decided, settling down in her seat and staring at the white landscape slowly slipping by. It was 11:00 AM, and a watery sun wasn't doing much to penetrate the snow.

CHAPTER FORTY-TWO

THEY STOPPED off at the lighthouse long enough for Richard to find the cat had a tag on its collar, which he removed and put in a plastic bag while Carissa waited in the front hallway. She told him she couldn't face seeing her kitchen in daylight, but he did convince her to warm up inside while he took photos with his phone and emailed them to Deputy Watkins. The thermostat had to be cranked up again.

They both stayed silent during the trip down to the Cove, but Carissa kept her hand on Richard's leg, and he didn't object. She needed human contact, and his leg felt very reassuring. They went straight to the police station. Deputy Watkins had already contacted both Animal Control and the Bangor Humane Society. He got Hubert identified by the tag. Gus Morgan had a contract to plow the main streets of the cove and his snow plough had done its work. Richard and Carissa went with the deputy in his Explorer to break the news to Virginia.

Afterward, Nancy Burton came over to be with her best friend. Carissa agreed to take the pine box Virginia had brought from her bedroom closet. Virginia had prepared for Hubert's passing in a way she thought would bring her some measure of comfort, but she had expected him to die from old age, not a savage attack.

Both Carissa and Richard spared Virginia the exact details of Hubert's death, telling her only that he had been found deceased on Carissa's property, and that Virginia should not try to reopen the box once Deputy Watkins had sealed it. Virginia agreed, although she did ask why the deputy was going to the lighthouse as well, and if either of them had any idea how Hubert had managed to trek two miles out of town in a blizzard. Richard told her cats were known to climb inside the engines of warm vehicles. He didn't elaborate. Eyes widened by horror, Virginia stopped asking questions.

The storm had passed and the main road had been cleared, but the track to the lighthouse proved a challenge for Ray Watkins, who asked Richard to take the wheel. Even for him, the icy drive proved to be a challenge. Sliding on ice, they almost wiped out on a tree before narrowly avoiding ploughing into a snow drift as high as the Explorer's hood. When they finally arrived at the keeper's quarters, Carissa found her front door partially open.

"I thought you closed it," she said to Richard.

"I did. And I locked both bolts with the keys you gave me. I know you were upset, but didn't you see?"

"No."

Carissa had been glad to run out of the house, tossing her keys to Richard on the way. She hadn't stopped running until she was in the snowcat.

"Get back." Deputy Watkins had his gun out.

He pushed them aside and cautiously entered the cottage. Richard's arm slid around Carissa's waist. He held her tightly as he retreated to the Explorer. They waited in the vehicle until Watkins reappeared and gestured for them to go inside.

"I want you to tell me if anything looks different," the deputy told Carissa. "I know the kitchen's a mess, but take a good look around."

"I can't." She shuddered.

"Sorry, but you need to do it."

Richard's hand squeezed her shoulder. "It'll be okay," he said into her ear. "I'll be right behind you."

Carissa leaned her cheek against Richard's hand. It felt so warm and strong and comforting, she believed he more than had her back. While she followed Deputy Watkins down the hallway toward the living-room, she heard Richard closing and locking the front door behind them.

She fought a wave of nausea when they entered the living room. Weak sunlight lit the interior of the house. "Where's the top of the pizza box?" She asked

"Out here," Richard said. He was standing in the doorway to the kitchen. "It's jammed against the broken window. Someone else was here after we left."

"Jessica's bedroom looks like it was trashed," Watkins said.

"That was probably my fault," Carissa said. "I was really panicked and Richard was rushing me. I made a mess of the bathroom, too, while I was packing."

Watkins took a look in the kitchen sink. His face registered revulsion. "Looks like the size and coloring for Hubert. The collar confirms it, but I forgot to ask Virginia if he's chipped."

Carissa stayed in the living room. Richard's back provided an effective screen from the carnage in her kitchen. "Do you think it's wise for me to stay with Virginia for the next couple of days?" She asked Watkins. "She wants me to, but it may not be safe for her. She'll probably try to pump me for more details about Hubert's death, too."

Watkins came back into the living room. He unzipped the bag he had brought with him and pulled out a camera. "Honestly, Carissa, I can't give you an answer to that right now." He looked unsure how to operate the equipment he had brought with him. "Bangor's be called in to take charge of this case as soon as they can get here. This is too much for our little department. They told me since the weather's so bad and this is an animal, to take photos and clean the cat out of the sink. They'll dust for prints as soon as they get here." He walked back into the kitchen, still fumbling with the camera. "Animal Control, the Humane Society—you name it, they want to be involved."

Richard followed Watkins. "Let me do that for you, Ray." He took the camera. "I've got one similar to this." He began taking photos from a variety of angles, first of the sink, then the blood-spatter on the walls, table, floor and window.

While both men worked, Carissa made herself busy, too. She got the pine box out of the Explorer and placed it on the coffee table.

She had to move the open pizza box to make room for it. The sight and smell of rancid pepperoni and congealed tomato sauce made her desperately afraid she was going to vomit into Hubert's casket if she stayed in the cottage much longer. She sat on the couch, where she could see the two men in the kitchen without being in there herself.

"The blood wasn't smeared when we were here," Richard said. He pointed to the edge of the sink. "Is that a boot print, Ray?"

Watkins peered at the mark. "Looks like it. You'd better get a shot of that."

Richard took several shots from different areas before lowering the camera and walking over to the mudroom door, which he found was locked. "Do you think whoever was here after us came in through the broken window but went out through the front door?"

Watkins nodded. "Looks like it." He indicated a line of pale but visible crimson boot prints going through the kitchen. "They stop when they come to the living-room rug." He glanced at Carissa. "The rug absorbed the blood. By the time he got to the hallway, there were no more prints."

Richard took photos of the prints, the rug and the hallway.

"Had to be a male," Watkins said. "Look at the size of them."

Carissa knew she had to move somewhere other than the lighthouse. Her misgivings about staying with Virginia grew. She had a stalker who had turned violent. She fervently hoped Richard wasn't in danger, too. "I bet my ex-husband's responsible for all this," she said.

"You really think he'd chop up Virginia's cat?" Richard laid the camera carefully back inside its bag.

"Not him personally; he wouldn't soil his hands. He must have paid someone else to do it. There's no one else around here who could have any possible reason for killing Hubert."

"But why would he have Virginia's cat butchered?" Watkins stopped scribbling in his notebook. "How would that affect you, apart from the obvious revulsion when you found it?"

"He wants me move back to New York. If he made it impossible for me to remain in my home and made it too dangerous for people to befriend me, then he'd leave me no choice."

Richard's eyes mirrored the concern on his face. "You don't have to let him win."

Carissa hid her face in her hands. Darkness was preferable to seeing the look on Richard's face.

"Virginia won't blame you for Hubert's death," Richard said. "She's not like that. She'll take you in. I'll willingly stop by as many times during the day as you girls want me to. My office is right down the bottom of the hill. Ray will keep an eye on both of you, too."

"How can you possibly believe she won't blame me?" Carissa found hiding behind her hands wasn't as comforting as she'd thought. She looked right at Richard. "How would *you* feel if the pet you loved was found butchered in some acquaintance's sink?"

"Furious, but not at my acquaintance, who's just as much a victim. I'd want a piece of the person who did it."

"You're a man, not a sixty-eight-year-old woman. That's you talking."

"I guess it is." He sighed. "You want to sit in the car?"

"After I take a look around to see if anything else has been disturbed." She forced herself onto her feet.

"I won't be much longer," Watkins said. He used the tip of his pen to look under a towel at the edge of the sink.

Richard hustled Carissa down the hallway to her bedroom. He brought her large suitcase in from under the bed in the guest room, moved clothes out of the way and opened it on Jessica's bed. "Take whatever you need for the next few days. If you find you've forgotten anything, I'll come back here and get it. If Virginia has changed her mind, you can sleep in my office. There's a comfortable couch, a small kitchenette and a full bathroom. It's got an alarm system, too."

She was about to tell him she wasn't going to spend another night with him in the same building.

"I can stay at the police station tonight if the weather doesn't clear up enough for my trip back on the snowcat," he added. "They keep a cot in one of the back rooms."

"Okay." She figured she was out of other options.

Richard went back to join Watkins. She heard them talking in undertones as she started packing methodically, as Aunt Jessica had once taught her. Neatly folded sweaters went into the case with rolled turtlenecks, silk thermals, underwear, and socks. She suddenly remembered how Matthew wanted his drawers arranged at their apartment: Underwear on the left, t-shirts on the right, top drawer. Socks in the second drawer, casual shirts folded into the third...

"Hey, daydreamer." Richard's voice startled her. She dropped her jeans on the floor.

They both bent over to pick them up, knocking heads.

"Ouch!" She saw stars for a moment.

Richard sat her on the bed and took her cold hands. His concern brought tears to her eyes.

"Are you really going to admit defeat and move back to New York with Matthew?" He asked.

"I don't know. I've made such a mess of things here. I've got involved with too many people, and now you're all fighting amongst yourselves."

"The fighting was going on way before you came. You can't take credit for that." He smiled.

"Oh, Richard, you seem to have a knack for making things sound less dire than they really are." She got up and he handed her the jeans. "I'd thought about asking you to renovate Penwithen for me if I stayed. I'm not comfortable here at the lighthouse. It feels like Aunt Jessica never really left."

"You're serious? You want to open Penwithen back up? What a challenge. I don't even know if the place can be saved."

"That's what William Dansinger said."

"Do you have the keys? You didn't go in there, did you?"

"No." Carissa closed up the suitcase. "I tried shining a flashlight through one window, but I couldn't see much. It smelled really bad in there. Moldy. I'm sure the roof's leaking." Her stomach churned at the memory of the stench that had come out of the house when she pulled the board loose. It brought back the metallic smell in the lighthouse kitchen. She pushed Richard aside and ran into the bathroom, retching until her throat was sore and her stomach muscles painful.

When she returned to the bedroom, Richard was putting a pair of tennis shoes and extra boots into her case. He crammed Jessica's pink fuzzy slippers into a pocket at the front. Carissa didn't interfere. She felt too depleted to argue over anything so inconsequential.

"Feeling better?" He asked.

"A little."

"Anything else you can think of?"

"No. All my toiletries and hairdryer are in the other bag, along with nightwear and another change of clothes." Her head swam. She had to grab the edge of the dresser for support.

Richard sat her down. He brought a cold cloth from the bathroom and dabbed her face. "You need to rest," he told her. "We've got to get you somewhere you can do that."

Watkins walked into the bedroom. "Ready, Carissa?"

She nodded. "I think I should stay at the Whitstead Tavern instead of Virginia's or Richard's office, but how am I going to get there?"

"The road's ploughed," Watkins said. "I got updates. The storm ended and the main roads are getting some attention, but it'll still be a slow process."

"I can get you to Whitstead, if that's what you really want," Richard said. "I can use one of my construction trucks."

"I don't want anyone else but you two to know where I am," she said.

"Whatever you want." Richard had her suitcase in hand. "Let's go. At least you're showing you trust me as well as Ray."

"If anything happens to me, Deputy Watkins will know who to go after, won't he?"

"That's a real comfort." Richard grimaced. "Ready, Ray?"

"Ready as I'll ever be, I reckon." Watkins had the camera bag over his shoulder. He hefted the casket containing the cat's remains and several evidence bags. "Damn, this box is heavy."

Richard left the suitcase and took the casket from Watkins. "Can you handle Carissa's case instead? It's on wheels, although I guess you'll have to carry it through the snow to the Explorer. Carissa, can you grab his evidence bags?"

They all trooped out and Deputy Watkins locked the front door. He placed yellow crime scene tape across it. "No excuses for anyone who tries to go inside."

"You'd better call the Whitstead Tavern and make sure they're not fully booked," Richard told Carissa after they were all settled in the

Explorer. "Are you sure you want me to drive this back to the Cove?" He asked Ray.

"Better you than me. I've had enough driving over icy roads today." Watkins had elected to sit in the back seat with Hubert's casket and his equipment. Carissa passed him the evidence bags, noting the lid of the pizza box inside one of them.

"Did you leave the broken window open?" She asked.

"Nope. I broke up a cardboard box I found in the mudroom."

"Thank you, Deputy," She said.

"Please call me Ray."

As they left the lighthouse behind, Carissa wondered how much Al Dyson's potential buyer would be willing to pay for Aunt Jessica's home, and whether that buyer was willing to overlook things like bloodstains in the kitchen. The last thing she saw in the side mirror before Richard guided the Explorer onto the icy track was the porch light on the keeper's quarters, winking at her through the bare branches of the trees.

CHAPTER FORTY-THREE

CARISSA AWOKE with a headache in her room at the Whitstead Tavern. She looked at the bedside clock: 8:30 P.M. She checked her smartphone. No new messages. She took an Advil, turned on the TV with the volume lowered and listened to a weather update as she took her nightclothes out of the suitcase. No more snow and a slight warming trend sounded promising. She turned on the shower. Steam rose in billows and she shivered with pleasure as she stepped beneath the water. Although she had crawled into bed fully dressed, she felt really cold.

She stayed in the shower a long time, washing her hair twice and conditioning it thoroughly before stepping out and wrapping herself in an oversized, fluffy white bath towel. Her decision to stay at the hotel had been a good one, she assured herself. Her throat felt scratchy, and she wondered if she was coming down with a cold. Assorted teabags in a little plastic holder beside the coffee maker looked promising. She heated water and chose herbal peach, feeling caffeine was probably the last thing she needed. A knock at the door startled her. No one except Richard and Deputy Watkins knew where she was staying. She hadn't asked for any room service, and she'd placed the Do Not Disturb sign on the outside of her door.

"Who's there?" She asked. Even her voice sounded scratchy. She cleared her throat.

A muffled male voice answered. It sounded like Richard. Carissa felt a mixture of irritation at him invading her privacy and pleasure that he'd ignored her by either bringing take-out or offering to take her down to dinner, although she was far from hungry. In fact, she still felt slightly queasy. She looked down at the towel and shrugged. Richard had seen her in far less. She made sure the chain was secure before cautiously opening the door enough to peek out into the corridor.

Steve Raymond came into view.

Carissa gasped and clutched the towel closer. "What are you doing here?"

"I was so frantic, Ray Watkins told me where to find you. Let me in, Carissa. I've got something important to tell you."

"You can tell me from out there. I don't know how you managed to get past the desk, but I'm going to call them and complain about the lack of security." Shaking inside and out, she hid her body behind the door. Anyone could have come up to her room. Richard's offer for her to stay at his office with a security system sounded a whole lot better than the Whitstead Tavern at that moment.

"I can't stand out here and tell you. Ray made me promise to sit you down before I gave you the news."

Panic surged. "You're frightening me, Steve."

"Then let me in. I'm not going to hurt you, for goodness sake."

"Wait a minute." She started to close the door.

He stuck his foot in the gap.

"I want my privacy." She slammed the door against his foot.

"If I didn't have a boot on, that would have really hurt. Stop playing games and let me in before other guests get curious."

"I might want them to see you."

He took his foot out of the opening. "Please," he said.

"All right. Give me a minute. I just got out of the shower."

Her nightclothes were on the end of the bed. She thought about pulling clothes out of her suitcase, but that would take longer, and she wanted to get rid of him as quickly as possible. She dressed in pajamas, a bathrobe and Aunt Jessica's fuzzy slippers, which made her think of

Richard and smile at his thoughtfulness. The throbbing in her head intensified when she bent over, and she took a moment to drink half the water from a bottle sitting beside the coffee maker and marked 'Compliments of the Management." She double-knotted the belt on her bathrobe, slid off the chain and stood aside. "Come in."

Steve seemed larger every time she saw him. He filled the doorway and dwarfed the room. He stood looking around, as though unsure of where to sit.

"Take the desk chair," she told him.

He sat and flipped on a lamp. "You look awful."

Carissa sat on the end of the bed. "I don't feel good. I think I'm getting a cold. Okay, tell me the news. I'm sitting. Did Matthew do something? I already know about the cat."

"Nothing to do with either Matthew or Virginia's cat. Richard Ebberly had an accident. He ran off the road and hit a tree. Some neighbor's kid was out walking the dog and saw Richard's headlights. If he hadn't been passing by, or if the car's battery had run down, Richard probably would still be out there."

The room started spinning. Carissa fought her way to her feet and swayed. She started retching. Steve grabbed the wet towel she'd left on the bed, held it under her chin and half-dragged her into the bathroom. He held her head while she vomited until only dry heaves remained, then carried her to her bed and dumped her on it.

He wasn't being very sympathetic, Carissa thought. She'd gone to bed with a headache, gotten up with one and now, after the heaving, her head was pounding and her teeth were chattering. She realized that she wasn't just tired, cold or shocked; she was ill.

"Richard's going to be okay, isn't he?" She tried to sit up, felt worse and sank back against the pillows.

"I don't know." Steve sat beside her. "He's very badly hurt. He's got a concussion and several broken bones. Watkins said they only had a rough idea of how long he'd been lying out there. Maybe an hour; maybe more."

"Where did they take him?"

"He got airlifted to Bangor."

Carissa groaned. After the vomiting, she felt too weak to move. Tears coursed down her cheeks as chills set in. "Was he in his car? He'd been driving his snowcat."

"Which he took home. Neighbors saw him. He stopped to chat with them for a couple of minutes. They'd been plowing their driveway. He told them the roads were improving, so he was going to get cleaned up, drive his Jeep over to Whitstead and take his new girlfriend out to dinner." Steve glowered at her when he said "new girlfriend."

"So you're placing the blame for Richard's accident on me?"

"No, of course not. His Jeep was totaled. How he got out alive is anyone's guess. Funny, I'd always heard he's a really good driver."

"He is." Carissa struggled up onto her elbow. "He drove me to his house from the Cove in the middle of that blizzard. Deputy Watkins was joking with Richard about being the best driver in this area. He had Richard drive his Explorer to and from the lighthouse this afternoon."

"It only takes one little mistake on ice," Steve said. "It could have happened to any of us."

"I want to go to Bangor." She tried to get up, became really dizzy and nauseated, and sank back. "I'm sick. I can't believe it. Not now."

Steve placed a cool hand on her forehead. "You're burning up. I'd better get you to urgent care. There's a clinic a few blocks from here."

"No." She shook her head. Bad idea—her headache intensified. "I'm sure it's the flu. I hope I didn't give it to Richard."

"Look, Carissa, I'm sorry about everything. I know about you and Richard."

"How?" She grabbed one of the complimentary tissues in a box beside the bed and wiped her runny nose.

"I went over to your place yesterday evening. I was worried about you."

"You're the one who put the box top over the broken window and left the door open."

"The answer is 'yes' to going over there, but 'no' to leaving your door open." He took her hand. "I went there to apologize for what Matthew told you about and try to explain my behavior."

"I don't need explanations, especially if they're about what Matthew saw."

"Matthew Yates is a total bastard. He spied on Sally and me through a window."

"I don't want to hear any more about that, Steve. I heard enough already, believe me." She pulled her hand away.

"Don't shut me out, please." His voice had lost its hard edge and taken on a note of pleading.

"What you do with Sally is between you two. The fact that you chose to do it in public is a little shocking, but it's really none of my business."

"Can you forgive me?"

"Why in the world would you want my forgiveness?"

"You should know that better than anyone else." His voice lowered. "You know the way I feel about you. Do you need me to tell you again?"

"No, I don't. I can't take anything more right now. I need to get over this illness so I can go to Bangor and be with Richard."

"Richard Ebberly can take care of his own damned self!"

The harshness of Steve's outburst and the anger on his face shocked her. "What in the world do you have against Richard?"

"He got Sally pregnant, told her to get an abortion and abandoned her."

CHAPTER FORTY-FOUR

Matthew heard the doorbell, told his publicist he'd call her back later and hung up the phone.

Halstead, he thought as the bell rang again, but when he opened the door, Sally Mainard stood on his doorstep.

Dressed in a hooded, lambswool-lined suede jacket and black leather boots over black skin-tight jeans, she radiated sex.

"Hi." She smiled.

"Hi." He waited.

"I came to compare notes on the nosy neighbors at the Cove."

"Then you'd better come in before any of those nosy neighbors sees you at my door."

He felt her brush against him and took a deep breath of a musky perfume as she glided over the threshold into the hallway. It would be an interesting visit, he thought, smiling to himself.

"I'd better take off my boots." She bent over and pulled down zippers, stepped out gracefully and wriggled sock-covered feet.

"Let me help you with your coat." Matthew took it off her shoulders and hung in on the hallstand. "I wondered if you'd take me up on my invitation."

"I had a sudden impulse this morning, after deciding it wasn't worth opening the shop."

"Too much snow, huh?"

"Yes, which means no out-of-town visitors. My gift shop doesn't make a living off local traffic. I do most of my business online during the winter."

"What sells best, your sculptures?"

She nodded. "Online. Locals aren't into my driftwood creations. I sell a lot of hand-knitted and crotched items during the winter, online and even from the shop. I do all right. I'm never short of cash." She smiled, lips pink and moist as bubblegum.

"I'd like to buy something," Matthew said. "I wasn't in the shop long enough to see everything you have to offer."

"You weren't," she agreed. "I've got a lot of sculptures in my wood-working shop. I'll take you in there, and you can see if there's anything you want. I should be open tomorrow."

"Good. You can help me decide."

She walked down the hallway into the living room.

"Pretty generic, don't you think?" He gestured around.

"You could do with a decorator."

"Are you good at decorating as well as creating?" He stepped closer. Her hair looked pale and fragile, like spun gold.

"You're taking too much for granted, Matt." Sally tapped his nose lightly with one pink nail. "I'm much harder to get than you think."

"Is that so?" He grinned and walked into the kitchen. "Coffee?"

"How about lunch, instead? It's noon."

"Is it?" He looked up at the kitchen clock, a smiling black cat, eyes and tail moving rhythmically. Both hands were on midday, but there was no chime; maybe because it was broken. Matthew was glad for the silence, although the clock itself ticked loudly. "I spent the morning on my business."

"I suppose you're working up deals for your spring collection."

She ran one finger along the edge of the butcher block counter and watched him dig around in the refrigerator until he came up with sandwich meat and processed cheese squares.

"I'm working a year ahead," Matthew told her. "But I'm making final arrangements for Fashion Week. It's coming up fast."

"Bologna and cheese? How original. I thought you'd offer me caviar and canapes," Sally said.

Matthew threw the bologna and cheese packets onto the counter, tossed a loaf of white bread over next to them, took mayonnaise and two beers out of the refrigerator door and closed it with his hip. "I hate caviar." He took plates from a cabinet. "Have a seat." He gestured toward the bar stools on the other side of the counter.

Sally opened the bologna and cheese while Matthew spread mayonnaise on the bread slices.

"You want mustard?" he asked, sliding a plate and knife over to her.

"No, this is fine." She made her sandwich. He popped the tops off the beer bottles.

She watched him bite into his sandwich and take a swig of beer. He guessed his behavior surprised her. Matthew never dressed casually, even when alone. Today he'd chosen a beige cashmere sweater over knife-pleated woolen slacks.

In contrast, Sally's jeans were faded to a pale ice-blue. Her sweater was an oversized popcorn stitch number that came almost to her knees.

"I thought you were hungry." He gestured toward her untouched food.

"I am. I was studying you. You're an enigma, Matt."

"No one calls me Matt."

"Carissa even calls you Matthew when you're alone with her?"

"She does."

Sally shrugged. "I'm an informal sort of person. My real name's Sophia. Can you imagine?" She laughed. "I've been Sally all my life, except where my mother and grandmother are concerned. To them, I'll always be Sophia." She stretched, raising her arms above her head, her body moving like a contented cat, hair sliding from her shoulders to flow down her back. "It feels good to be somewhere warm. My apartment's drafty. Bad insulation."

Matthew told himself that Steve Raymond was a lucky man. Why he wanted to mess around with Carissa was beyond Matthew, even though he had to admit she was beautiful in her own way. There was something untouched and naive about Carissa. Matthew had never succeeded in taking that away from her. He thought there would be no naivety with Sally. She oozed sensuality with every move, every nuance.

Sally bit into her sandwich and dabbed her lips on her napkin as she chewed. Matthew imagined those lips doing imaginative things to his body; those even white teeth nipping at his skin. He had no doubt she'd come over for a specific reason, but if she wanted to play a few teasing little games as foreplay, he had no objection. Anticipation was definitely something to be savored.

———

"So, tell me a little about yourself," he urged, finishing his beer and settling back to watch her. They had moved to the dining table. Sally had her feet up on another chair as she sipped her beer after finishing her sandwich.

She shrugged. "Not much to tell. I grew up the middle child of a conservative New England family that proudly traces its lineage back to the Mayflower." Her voice had taken on the tones of an upper-class New Englander. "My mother and grandmother were instrumental in raising me to perform the many refined tasks of a young woman expected to marry well and become the bored wife of a Boston banker."

Matthew brought two more beers from the refrigerator. "I take it you rebelled against such a fate." He offered her a bottle.

"You could say that." She took the beer and put it beside her half-finished one. "My father lost his shirt on the stock market and committed suicide. My mother was pregnant. She had to move in with my grandmother, whose husband had moved them here when he retired, and then died on her. Both my mother and my grandmother were like fish out of water in the Cove. By the time I was thirteen, all I wanted was to escape this hole."

"And did you?"

She nodded. "In high school, I screwed half the senior class, decided none of them was worth a second night in the sack and applied to art school in New York. I'd always had a talent, so I wasn't particularly surprised when I got accepted. Mom and Grammy were appalled at my career choice until they heard gossip about my extra-curricular activities here. Then they got behind me accepting the full scholarship and getting out of the Cove."

"Out of sight, out of mind, huh?"

"Something like that. They got out of here themselves, moving to Florida. They send Christmas cards and email infrequently, but they don't visit, they don't do Facebook, and they don't expect me to show up to family functions. I sold several sculptures and did some shows, but I couldn't seem to love New York's art scene. I liked working with drift-wood and for some damned reason, I missed Maine. I was surfing the internet one evening and I saw the studio and gift shop advertised. The price was right; I remembered the scenery around the Cove and all the availability of raw materials for my sculptures. When I made a trip here to check things out, the local men didn't look too bad, either."

"Meaning Steve Raymond?"

"Meaning Richard Ebberly. Steve came later." She finished the rest of her first beer.

Matthew sensed discord, one of his favorites. "Something went wrong in paradise?"

"Yeah." She took a swig from her second beer. "It was a long time ago. Water under the bridge. How about some background on you?"

"Born and bred in the Bronx." He laughed at her consternation. "Hard to imagine, right? That's where I learned to love bologna and cheese, cheap wine and beer. Some of those habits are still with me."

"I thought you'd grown up in a similar background to mine."

"Nah, opposites attract, you know."

"But you said that you and I were one of a kind."

"We are. We know what we want, and we go after it. We don't waste time on bullshit when we know what the outcome's going to be. Just like your visit—you and I both know we're going to end up in bed—that's a given. The one thing I want to know is if you're trying to use me for some sort of revenge against Steve Raymond. If you are, then get out. You screw me, you don't screw elsewhere. That's the cardinal rule. I give it to you as rough as you want it, and I bet you want it pretty rough." He leaned forward and caressed her cheek before clasping her chin in a tight grip. "Don't you?" He squeezed harder.

Sally gasped, but she didn't try to pull away. She stared back without blinking. "Steve Raymond and I are finished. I want marriage; he doesn't."

"If you want marriage, then you're not going to get it here, either. Carissa and I have unfinished business."

"So what do you want to mess around with me for?"

He shrugged, continuing to hold her chin, which was turning white. "The same thing you want from me. Information exchange, followed by excitement and down and dirty sex."

Sally finally struggled out of his grip. "You've got me wrong. I don't want to be slapped around and tied up." She got up. "I'm leaving. I don't know why I came here in the first place."

"Impulse, you said." Matthew stayed seated. If he pushed too hard, she'd run. He thought she'd come to a definite decision when she arrived, but evidently this was only a fishing expedition. He smiled reassuringly. "I don't think you were misled."

"Maybe not, but I'm feeling confused." She ran one hand through her silky hair.

Matthew fought the urge to grab her and take her right there on the floor. He didn't mind a little force, but Sally would be much more fun as a willing partner. "Sit back down and finish your beer. I promise I'll behave. Besides, you were going to fill me in on some of the local inhabitants, and I really want that information."

Sally hesitated a moment longer before sighing and dropping back into her chair. "Okay, Matt. Who do you want to know about?"

Matthew felt smug and satisfied. He'd have to troll a little longer, but the little fish in front of him was reeling in slowly without putting up an exhausting fight.

"Tell me about Richard Ebberly," he said.

"I told you he's off-limits."

"How can he be when I don't even know him? The only information I've got is that he's the local architect and contractor, so he probably gives people a lot more than they want and rips them off at the same time."

"Unfortunately, you're wrong on both counts. He was born and bred in the Cove, went away to get his degree and returned when his father retired, left him the business and moved to Cabo San Lucas. Richard Senior said he'd had enough of Maine winters, and he'd been in a long-distance relationship with some rich widow he'd met when he was vacationing in Cabo the year before. Richard remodeled his father's house and his office here in town."

"So, is he any good?"

She looked sharply at him.

Matthew laughed outright. "I mean as an architect."

"No wonder I'm confused." Sally finished her beer. "He's definitely talented. He wanted to remodel the keeper's quarters for Ms. Malloy, but she wouldn't have any of it. I heard she told him to get lost. I do remember Richard was quite upset, so that's probably more than hearsay. He's a big fish in a small pond. He updated and upgraded the Whitstead Tavern. It used to be some ramshackle affair that was a regular hangout for fishermen straight off the boats and employees of a boat repair place located right next door." She wrinkled her nose. "It stank of turpentine, varnish and fish. I went with him when he was doing preliminary measurements and sketches. I thought I might get some ideas for my sculptures." Her grimace spoke volumes.

"What else has he done?"

"A shopping center with restaurants and hotels for Broyling Harbor. The place was a floundering little community close to the border with Nova Scotia. Since it was at the end of some dead end road, no one ever passed through. Anyone who went there turned around and left right away. By the time Richard finished, it had been made into a resort. I heard it's making millions. The town's mayor had a vision and Richard Ebberly's a hero over there."

"Did he take a financial interest in it?"

"Not that he told me. He was apparently very convincing with his bid and his ideas, because the project got bankrolled. Can we talk about someone else?"

Matthew was reluctant to leave the subject of Richard Ebberly. He sensed a deep history between the architect and Sally Mainard, but she was about to clam up, which didn't suit Matthew's purpose.

"What about Steve Raymond?"

Sally's brow knitted and the corners of her mouth turned down.

"What do you want to do—discuss all my male friends? I thought you'd want to hear about people like Percival Huddleston."

"The mayor?"

'You've met him?"

"Briefly. That's about all I needed." Matthew fetched two more beers. He took the empties and stashed them in the trash. No sense in reminding Sally how many she'd had. She took a long swig from the bottle in her hand, then ran one finger under her nose. "Mmm, I'm getting a bit of a buzz."

"Have another sandwich," he urged. "The beer isn't strong. Remember, I only like the cheap stuff."

She joined him when he laughed. She refused anything more to eat, but agreed to get comfortable in the living-room, where she described each prominent village member from chief gossipmongers, Virginia Greeley and Nancy Burton to Al Dyson, who Sally dubbed "the crookedest real estate broker in the state of Maine." Matthew filed names away. His recall was excellent, and he planned to give Halstead plenty to check into after Sally left.

It was close to 3:00 P.M. when Sally placed her nearly-empty 4th beer bottle onto the coffee table and yawned. "Time for me to go," she said, peering at her watch. "I've got a sculpture waiting on me. I usually sculpt from four until nine or so at night."

"I'm the opposite." Matthew stood up with her. "I like to get up at dawn and work until noon, then give myself the rest of the day off unless I'm in the middle of a collection, when I can work fifteen to twenty hours at a stretch for weeks."

"Sounds like way too much work for me." She walked into the hallway and put on her boots.

When she straightened up, he wrapped his arms around her and covered her breasts with his hands, very gratified to find she wasn't wearing a bra. He kneaded gently.

"Matt, I told you no." She started to struggle.

"Relax. This is only a parting gift."

He worked one ear with his lips and tongue while he continued caressing her. She gasped and leaned back against him. He felt the urge to laugh, but confined himself to whispering graphic descriptions of what he really wanted to do to her. It would have been easy to go further at that moment; the tempo of her breathing had increased and while one of her hands closed over his, the other clutched his thigh. He released her, feeling her sag momentarily before recovering.

When he dropped her coat over her shoulders, she turned around, her eyes glazed, her cheeks flushed.

"Thank you for an interesting visit." She held her face up to him, her lips puckering.

"You're welcome." He grinned at her, guided her to the door and opened it. "Come again."

Her face registered both disappointment and anger. "When?"

The fish had been hooked and was ready to land in the boat. Matthew allowed himself a victory smile as he lightly kissed those down-turned pouty bubblegum-pink lips, sealed tightly against him for only a moment before opening. He gave her what she wanted, holding her tightly, caressing her back before grabbing her buttocks and thrusting himself against her. He had to admit he was as turned on by their encounter as she was, but he forced himself to draw away, to leave her wanting so much more. He'd go online and check out a couple of his favorite porn sites after she left. Pleasuring himself that afternoon while thinking of her would provide him with a great deal of satisfaction.

Her expression, filled with disappointment, said it all.

"Tomorrow," he told her. "Plan to spend the day."

"And night?" Her voice was a soft purr of anticipation.

"Not yet. Let's try each other out first."

She yanked up her sweater and quickly flashed him her breasts before closing her coat. "Until tomorrow, then," she said. "Are you working until noon?"

"Come for lunch again," he told her as he started to close the door.

"Bologna and cheese?" She asked.

"Of course. And cheap beer."

CHAPTER FORTY-FIVE

CARISSA STAYED in bed for two days, with Hilly as her nurse. Steve had told her he trusted Hilly more than anyone else, and Carissa felt too ill to argue. Hilly had also convinced her mother's doctor to make a call to the hotel. He prescribed Tamiflu, lots of fluids and rest.

On the third day, against Hilly and Steve's protests, Carissa borrowed a car from Deputy Watkins and set out for Bangor. She had to pull over several times to rest. Her head throbbed and her stomach knotted. She drank 4 bottles of water and all the broth Hilly had put into a flask. When she tried nibbling crackers, dry heaves threatened.

When she pulled into the hospital's parking lot and staggered into the front lobby, a worried receptionist lifted the phone. "You're at the wrong entrance for the ER," she told Carissa. "I'm calling for one of our volunteers to take you there in a wheelchair. Please sit down and wait."

"I'm not a patient." Carissa leaned against the desk for support. "I'm here to see one."

Given directions to Richard's floor, she tried not to sway as she walked over to the elevators, but by the time she got to the nurses' station, she was afraid her legs were going to give out. She checked in with the ward clerk, who brought the treatment nurse out of the medication room. That resulted in summoning the charge nurse, who told Carissa she needed to be in bed, not visiting an acutely-ill patient.

Carissa broke down into a flood of tears and told them how far she had driven to see Richard. His doctor was consulted, and a compromise reached. Carissa's temperature had to be taken. If the thermometer registered 98.4, she could gown and mask before spending five minutes with Richard. Much to her relief and the surprise of the staff, she earned those precious minutes.

Pushing open the door to Richard's room, she heard medical equipment beeping, whirring, clicking and monitoring. Lines ran from IVs inserted into his chest up to bags hanging around a pole like clusters of misshapen, overgrown grapes. She crept forward. Richard's head was bandaged, both eyes closed and blackened. A long, jagged gash led from his chin to his left ear. Covered with steri-strips, it looked raw, ugly and painful. His left arm was immobilized in a cast from shoulder to hand, the other bandaged from wrist to elbow. Both his legs were in casts, the right one below the knee, the left one above it. A sheet lay across his midsection. His toes were exposed.

Carissa stifled a gasp. If he heard her, he would know how terrible he looked. She sat beside the bed and gently touched his right hand. Richard murmured and grimaced. She moved her fingers to his upper arm, where the bruising wasn't as severe.

"Richard, it's Carissa," she whispered.

His eyes flickered and partially opened. His cut and swollen lips moved, but no sound came out.

"Can you hear me?" She asked. "If you can, please show me somehow."

The thumb of his right hand moved.

"I had the flu. That's why I didn't come right away. I don't understand what happened; you're such a good driver."

His mouth moved again. A gurgling sound came out.

Carissa fought back more tears. "I'm so sorry; that was stupid of me. You shouldn't waste your energy trying to speak. I'll ask you questions it'll be easier for you to answer, but not today. The nurse is going to throw me out of here in a few minutes." She tried to put brightness into her voice. "I'll come again as soon as she lets me back in."

His whole hand moved on that. Bruised and swollen fingers attempted to hold her wrist.

"I'll stay as long as I possibly can," she promised, sliding her fingers into his palm.

He gurgled again. What had to be a heart-rate monitor beeped faster.

"You've got to calm down or they'll make me leave," she warned.

The door opened and two nurses walked in on silent feet. "You'll have to go. You're upsetting him," the charge nurse said.

Richard's gurgling cry startled them all. He flailed, IV lines swinging like strands of spaghetti.

"Richard, please." Carissa sat back down. "I'm not going anywhere." She looked at the nurses.

"I'm not," she said. "He wants me here."

The younger nurse checked the IV ports. "Everything's fine, but you mustn't move around like that." She patted Richard's shoulder.

"So you're not a family member." The charge said. She looked accusingly at Carissa, as though her mind had already been made up.

"No, a very close friend."

"Only family members should be visiting right now."

"Richard's father lives in Florida. I'm his girlfriend. We've been talking about getting engaged."

Richard actually turned his head and stared at her. The monitor beeped even faster.

Carissa tried to ignore both Richard and his monitor, which wasn't easy. "I insist on talking to the doctor."

"And I insist you leave. We gave you five minutes, and they're up. If you don't go voluntarily, I'll call security." The charge nurse placed her hands on her hips. "I'm following doctor's orders. Mr. Ebberly needs rest and quiet."

The door opened and a man in a white coat entered, a stethoscope hanging around his neck. "What's going on?"

"Mr. Ebberly has been unnecessarily upset by this visitor, who now refuses to leave."

"Are you Richard's doctor?" Carissa asked. "I'm Carissa Yates, Richard's girlfriend. Almost fiancée." She felt her cheeks flaming and hoped her fever wasn't rising again. "I drove for hours to see Richard as soon as I felt well enough to travel. He wants me here. Please don't make me leave."

"Fully recovered now, I hope?" Dr. Lister peered at her intently over the tops of his wire-rimmed glasses. "Have you eaten today?"

"No. I tried eating crackers but they made me nauseated. I've had plenty of fluids, though."

He turned to the nurses. "Please order Ms. Yates a tray. Better make it a light diet; I doubt her stomach's up to a full meal."

"That's highly irregular, Dr. Lister," The charge nurse said.

"Perhaps, but if we don't get some food into her, we're going to have another patient on our hands. And make sure she has one of those pull-out beds, a blanket and a pillow, so she can rest." He looked back at Carissa. "All right?"

She nodded. "Thank you. How long can I stay?"

"If you don't make Mr. Ebberly agitated again, at least an hour." He looked at Richard, who gave a thumbs-up.

"Do you have any allergies?" He asked Carissa.

She shook her head. He took out a pad and scribbled, tore out two pieces of paper and gave them to the charge nurse. "Please have these filled at the pharmacy and brought to her." He turned back to Carissa. "I've prescribed something to calm your stomach and a mild sedative."

"Thank you. Knowing Richard's doing better has eased my mind already."

Dr. Lister smiled at Richard. "If you behave yourself, your friend can stay."

Richard didn't attempt to respond verbally that time, but his eyes shifted from the doctor to Carissa and stayed on her.

"Both of you should get some rest." Dr. Lister smiled at Richard and Carissa before turning on his heel to leave the room. He paused at in the doorway. "If you need anything else, Ms. Yates, please have the nurses call me."

"I'll be right back," she reassured Richard before following the doctor into the corridor. "Dr. Lister, I do have a couple of questions."

He stopped. "Fire away. I figured you didn't want to talk in front of him."

"Is he really going to be all right?"

He stood, hands clasped behind him, and studied his shoes for a moment before answering. "Patient privacy is something I respect, but you've driven up here when you probably should still be in bed recovering, so I believe you deserve a few answers, especially since you two are almost engaged." The doctor gave Carissa wry smile. She had the grace to blush again, but she held his gaze. Who was to say Richard wasn't her fiancé?

"He's doing a lot better today," Dr. Lister said. "It was touch and go there for a while, but he's pulling out of it very well. Exposure's a nasty thing. His head injuries look more severe than they actually are. He had a concussion and extensive cuts and bruising. They shaved off half his hair in the ER to suture the worst lacerations. He's not going to be too pleased when he sees the result."

"His hair will grow back. That's the least of his worries." Carissa grimaced at the thought of what Richard might actually think about his new hairstyle. "What about his arms and legs?"

"Multiple fractures. He also broke a couple of ribs and badly bruised his jaw. He's pretty sore, and that makes it hard for him to get up the energy to talk. Add the swelling around his mouth and chin, and that's a real deterrent. That's why he's got a nasal-gastric tube right now, delivering nutrition. As soon as the swelling goes down, I'll take that out and give him a soft diet. No injury to his spine. He could do with some plastic surgery to his face, but we deferred that for now."

"Can you tell me how long before he'll be able to talk?"

"His speech is going to be pretty difficult to understand for a week or so. People hate having tubes up their noses, but it's preferable to having a surgically-inserted tube into the stomach. We don't like to do that unless someone can't eat on a long-term basis."

Carissa wrinkled her nose at the thought of all those tubes. "When will he be able to go home?"

"He'll stay here a couple more weeks until he gets more mobile, then I'll ship him over to the rehabilitation unit to gain more independence, even with those casts. It's amazing what those therapists can accomplish. They'll teach him to get around in a wheelchair and take care of most of his own dressing and bathing. His right wrist is only sprained. He's got a good-sized laceration from broken glass on his forearm. Once that heals, he'll be able to function a lot better."

To Carissa, Dr. Lister's optimism sounded far-fetched. How Richard could learn to take care of himself, even in a wheelchair, was beyond her understanding. She'd thrown some clothes into an overnight bag and stashed it in the trunk of Deputy Watkins' car. She'd be okay for a couple of days at least before she needed more clothes or a laundromat, she decided. Short-term, all she wanted to do was rest and be with Richard.

After she'd taken the medication to calm her stomach, she managed to eat most of the meal sent up to her. The pull-out bed had been brought in. At first she dozed fitfully, the whirring and clicking of the IV pump disturbing her, but she really felt she could sleep without taking the sedative. Eventually, exhaustion did take over and she fell into a heavy sleep, from which she was awakened by noises on the other side of Richard's bed.

"What are you doing?" Sitting up, she felt slightly dizzy. "Is that one of the nurses? Why don't you have the light on?"

A dark figure stood over Richard's bed. Carissa reached for the hand control that had been attached to the bedrail, but it was gone. Alarmed, she got up and started to feel her way around the bed, only to be shoved back by a pair of strong hands. She lost her balance and grabbed the foot-board for support. The door to the corridor opened partially and Carissa saw a figure slip out. She glimpsed someone in a dark, hooded coat before the door closed and plunged the room back into darkness.

She fumbled her way over to the door and snapped on the overhead light. Richard was pulling weakly at a pillow covering his face.

Carissa took the pillow away. "Are you okay?"

He gave her a thumbs-up.

She located the hand control dangling over the left side of the bed and used it to call the nurses station, but no one responded. Afraid to leave Richard alone, she opened the door and shouted for help. A nurse came running. Carissa realized the nurse must think Richard had taken a turn for the worst.

"He's all right," she said.

The nurse slowed her pace to a fast walk. "What's wrong? Are you ill?"

"No, but someone came into the room and put a pillow over his face."

The nurse hurried to Richard's bedside. She checked his central line. "Thank goodness that didn't get pulled out." She turned to Carissa. "How do you know someone put a pillow over his face? He might have done it himself. He's been a little restless these past few nights." She looked at her watch. "We've been doing two hour checks on him, but he's not due one for another hour."

"Noises woke me up. It was really dark in here, but I'm positive I saw someone leaning over him on the other side of the bed."

"No staff member would come into this room without turning on the light."

"That's what I thought."

The nurse walked rapidly to the door. "Stay with him," she told Carissa. "I'm going to alert security, the charge nurse and the administrator on duty."

CHAPTER FORTY-SIX

THE ROOM and the corridor outside became congested as Richard was thoroughly examined and Carissa's statement was taken. She insisted the police were called and even more people arrived. She denied having a vivid dream.

None of the evening shift staff reported seeing a stranger, and Carissa couldn't give more than a vague description of the intruder. Security cameras didn't catch anything or anyone out of place. Whoever had planned to murder Richard hadn't known Carissa was in the room.

Dawn broke while she sat in the small visitors' lounge. A nursing assistant brought her coffee and a small bag of toiletries. She cleaned herself up in the visitors' restroom and actually feeling hungry for the first time in days, walked down to eat breakfast in the hospital cafeteria while Richard was getting bathed. At 8:00 AM, it was crowded with staff and visitors of all ages and ethnicities. Carissa nibbled on toast and scrambled eggs, drank a glass of orange juice and a cup of tea.

Virginia called with the news that Hubert's remains had been taken away by Animal Control. Virginia had decided not to ask for the remains to be returned. Instead, she planned to make a little memorial in her garden once spring arrived. She broke down a couple of times during the call, but was more worried about Richard and Carissa than herself. How terrible it must have been to see Richard so badly injured, Virginia wailed. How had the best driver in the county run off the road and landed up against a tree?

Carissa had no reasonable answer for that question, other than a somewhat stock "accidents happen, even to the best drivers." She did reinforce Deputy Watkins' instructions for Virginia not to accept any gifts or open the door to anyone she didn't know well. It was a sad time for the Cove, Virginia said, when the peace and calm of the village had been so violently disturbed.

Carissa contacted Deputy Watkins, who told her to keep the car until she had made other arrangements. He was happy to hear Richard was slowly recovering. The Jeep had been towed and an investigation launched to discover the accident's cause. Weather conditions or driver error were the usual suspects, Watkins said, but he still wanted Richard to make a statement as soon as he was able to do so. The deputy ended the call by telling Carissa her requested report on Jessica Malloy's death was ready.

Carissa felt she needed to be in two different places, several hours apart. She wanted to read that report on her aunt's death, but Richard needed her vigilance and support. After what had happened the previous night, she wasn't leaving him unprotected between the regular staff checks.

Dr. Lister asked her to stay with Richard until the following day at least. Carissa was the only one who had seen the intruder. Richard remembered nothing, making that clear with hand gestures and head shakes. The nursing staff, hospital security and local police appeared to be doubtful that an intruder had even existed. Carissa adamantly denied having a nightmare over and over.

More tests had been ordered for Richard and he was taken away to Radiology. Carissa was encouraged to take a break and eat again. What she desperately wanted instead was a shower and a change of clothes. She booked herself into a nearby motel and spent three hours away from the hospital to take a lengthy shower followed by a two hour nap. Returning to the cafeteria at noon, she ate a club sandwich and drank a soda. Feeling stronger, she tackled a call to Steve.

"I don't like Richard, but I certainly don't wish him any harm," Steve said. "If you're asking whether I had anything to do with his accident, I did not. I've heard he's an excellent driver. He's taken people home from work and ferried others to be with elderly family members isolated outside the village when most others wouldn't even venture out on the roads."

"He got us out of a really bad skid the night of the blizzard," Carissa said.

Steve grunted. "Not his finest moment. I saw a gash on one of the trees at the edge of your driveway."

"He pulled us right out of it. I didn't even have time to be frightened."

"Ray Watkins said there's an investigation into his accident. I hope they check the brakes."

"I'm sure they'll do that and a lot more."

A momentary silence developed. Steve broke it first. "So, how's Ebberly doing, anyway?"

"Better physically, but..." She hesitated to tell Steve what had happened.

"But what? His concussion was actually a head injury that'll impair him in the future?"

"No, although you might like that."

"You're reading me wrong. I don't mean harm to anyone, even him. But I don't like what he did. He took advantage of you."

"He did not. I was the one who took advantage, or tried to." She loosened her grip on her phone when her hand started cramping.

"I find that very hard to believe," Steve said.

"I had a really bad fright when we found that cat. I needed comforting."

"Comforting. There's a word for it."

Carissa cringed. Steve wasn't helping her get through their difficult conversation one bit. "Why did you go to the lighthouse?"

"Because I was worried about you."

"You could have called to check on me. You didn't need to walk through a blizzard and break into my home."

"The window was already broken, so technically, I didn't break in."

"Semantics." She was done cringing. Steve had no business being difficult.

"I went back and cleaned up the kitchen," he said. "I brought Hilly and her mother. They changed your sheets and tidied up while I was doing that. I re-stocked the refrigerator and the pantry, so you'll have plenty of food. I know you won't come back to the inn, but I don't want you staying in Whitstead; it's too far from the Cove. I don't drive, so it's one hell of a walk."

"I don't know what to say."

"Thanks?"

"Of course, thank you. I'll pay you for the groceries. But I don't think I can stay at the lighthouse again."

"You won't see anything out of place, I promise. You wouldn't even know anything happened."

"But I *do* know. My aunt, Virginia's cat, Richard...Steve, that's too much violence for any small village. I really wonder if I'm to blame for everything that's happened since I arrived. Maybe I've gotten someone really angry at me."

"What are you talking about? That's nonsense."

"Is it?"

She thought about Matthew and the copyright infringement case. He was angry, but surely not *that* angry. He knew nothing about cars, either, as far as she knew. Certainly not enough to tamper with one. And he'd never get his hands dirty, let alone murder a cat. Was he vindictive enough to get someone else to do that for him, instead? If so, then who?

Steve's voice broke into her rambling thoughts. "It's definitely a bit far-fetched, Carissa. But if you're right, then you should be here with me instead of babysitting Ebberly in Bangor. I can protect you if you agree to stay at The Rest, at least until the cops finish their investigation."

"Richard's doctor asked me to stay until tomorrow. Richard's agitated if I'm not with him."

"I know where he's coming from. I'm agitated when you're not around."

"Don't joke; it's serious," she said, but she wondered if she really *was* being overly-dramatic.

"I think you're putting too much emphasis on yourself. That thing with the cat was definitely bizarre, but Jessica's death was ruled an accident, and as for Richard's accident, well, I had no business making him sound like he was some legendary driver."

"What if the investigation finds a mechanical failure that couldn't have happened by accident?"

"Then I'd think Ebberly pissed off someone he'd done business with."

"I suppose that's a possibility. It's difficult to communicate with Richard right now to find out what happened. His face is so bruised, he can't talk. I feel so sorry for him."

"Yeah, well, don't feel *too* sorry."

"I'd feel sorry for you if you were in a hospital bed."

"Don't fall for Ebberly's helpless act."

"He *is* helpless. He can't even hold a cup right now."

"Good, then he can't make a grab for you. Listen, I'll get Sally to drive us to Bangor tomorrow and we'll pick you up."

"You don't need to do that. I borrowed a car from Deputy Watkins. He's in no hurry to get it back."

"Fine. Suit yourself." Steve sounded put out. "I was trying to do you a favor. I heard about your car."

"I know you're trying to help me, but I've got to help myself. I was planning to trade in my car for a four wheel drive SUV. I'll see what I can do about renting one while I'm up here. My car can go to a junk yard as far as I'm concerned. I'll let my insurance deal with it. I'll have to figure out how to get Deputy Watkins' car back to him, but I'm not dealing with that problem today. "

"Okay, that all makes sense." Steve sounded less defensive. He took a deep breath. "You're not still mad at Sally, are you? She says she's gotten over being mad at you. She was jealous of your friendship with me and she said she over-reacted, refusing to put your consignment out for sale at the Emporium."

"She was childish about the consignment, but I can't blame her for being jealous. You've made no bones about your intentions, Steve."

"I know. And you put me in my place. I told Sally, and we patched things up. Mostly."

"What do you mean...mostly?"

"We're still not sleeping together."

"I wasn't asking about your love-life."

"You'd rather hang out with that bastard, Ebberly, than me, wouldn't you?" Steve drew in a very loud deep breath. "I'm a true friend, Carissa. Ebberly's only out for one thing, so you'd better be well-protected."

"He's not a bastard, and it's none of your damned business what I do or who I do it with, as well as what method of protection I use."

"Carissa, I'm sorry. Don't hang up on me. But I'm warning you, Ebberly's no good."

"What makes you so sure Sally's telling the truth about their relationship?"

"Because she was a basket case after they broke up. That son-of-a-bitch dropped her like a rock after he found out about her pregnancy. He told her to get an abortion because he had no intention of marrying her or giving her child support. If you weren't well-protected the other night, and you get pregnant, he'll do the same thing to you; I guarantee it."

Carissa had no words for Steve and his accusations. She hung up.

Since parting from Matthew, she'd seen no reason to renew her birth control prescription. She hadn't raised the subject of protection; neither had Richard. She'd better find a gynecologist while she was in Bangor. No more slip-ups for her. She'd already found out she wasn't pregnant that morning, but she was going to have to be way more careful going forward, not that a repeat performance with Richard was even a pipe-dream for the near future.

She still couldn't bring herself to believe Sally's story. The Richard she was getting to know was far from cold-hearted and ruthless. But if Sally *wasn't* lying, then Carissa knew she had made a huge mistake trusting him.

Second only to trusting Matthew Yates.

CHAPTER FORTY-SEVEN

DECEMBER.

Instead of remaining at The Fisherman's Rest, Dean Halstead had rented a small apartment over a gift shop that had closed for the season. The apartment suited his needs and was well-heated by old steam radiators that hissed away companionably. He rented enough furniture to make it look like he was using it as a home as well as for business and hung a plate by the door, identifying him as a marketing analyst. He figured the Cove's winter inhabitants wouldn't have any reason to consult his services, but they'd be more willing to accept him and answer his questions if he joined the community. He didn't feel knowledgeable enough to follow through with Matthew Yates' suggestion about representing a real estate conglomerate, but he cozied up to Al Dyson, who was only too happy to gain a new friend and potential ally for the resort development.

Halstead convinced Matthew to go with the revised plan and presented him with invoices for the apartment, furniture and utilities. Although Matthew paid promptly, he made it clear he expected progress, and he expected it expeditiously...like yesterday.

Dean felt he could learn to like the slow pace of Cove life. From his living room windows, he looked out on white, snowy roofs touched by sparkling frost. The cramped office space he shared with his partner in New York and his cupboard-sized walk-up studio apartment seemed a world away from his new life of rented comfort.

He sauntered over to The Fisherman's Rest for a beer and sandwich before the walk to Matthew's cottage. He had juicy information to give Matthew Yates, hoping his mercurial client would be pleased for a change. Maybe Yates would even stop pressing him to move faster.

"Hi Dean." Steve Raymond raised his hand in greeting. "The usual?"

Halstead nodded. "Yep." He sat at his favorite table, where he could watch the bar and reception area without appearing nosy.

Steve brought him a frosted mug filled with Halstead's favorite beer on tap and walked off in the direction of the kitchen. The rest of the bar was empty except for Percival Huddleston, who nodded a greeting. Dean raised his mug in response.

Huddleston was a harmless, insipid sort of man, Dean thought idly. The mayor dabbled at fixing things for the many older inhabitants, especially the two old spinsters, Virginia Greeley and Nancy Burton. A widower, Huddleston should be searching for a new wife. He should chase Virginia Greeley, Dean thought as he sipped his beer. It looked like Nancy Burton was about to tie the knot with that newcomer, Walter Barnes, who was probably a con man.

Halstead had thought about running a trace on Barnes, but if he had turned up something, he wouldn't have been able to tell Nancy without blowing his cover. He'd also thought about threatening Barnes, but decided it wasn't worth the trouble. Virginia Greeley might be more of a match than Barnes had bargained for. Nancy Burton was her best friend, and Virginia wasn't about to let him take Nancy for a ride. Virginia was a sharp old bird. Halstead had a healthy respect for her.

She'd visited him the day after he moved into his apartment, wanting to know what sort of business a marketing analyst did. Virginia was the only one in the Cove who really kept him on his toes. She told him she was the local historian, and as such, was expected to keep tabs on everyone.

He'd concocted a story about being tired of paying New York prices and hearing about the Cove from his client, Matthew Yates. He told Virginia he could work remotely. When he explained what a market analyst did, Virginia looked suitably impressed. Her sharp eyes checked the apartment as she walked around, and then she asked him where he kept all the tools of his trade. Halstead explained he was using his laptop while the rest of his home office was being shipped. The next day he told Matthew he had to install enough equipment to make him look legitimate. Matthew, who said he had already spent what he thought was far too much on furnishings and the rental apartment, became livid. Why had Halstead let that old hag into his apartment in the first place?

Dean asked if Matthew wanted the villagers to accept him as a new member of the business community. He'd been invited to the next meeting of the local chamber of commerce. Yates swore in terms more fitting a sailor than a world-class designer before agreeing to provide whatever Dean needed. Halstead almost *felt* like a market analyst with everything set up. He kept CNN running continuously, subscribed to and consulted the New York Times, Bloomberg and any other number of newspapers and magazines to keep himself informed and provide him with a superficial knowledge of his supposed business in case Virginia or anyone else questioned him again.

"How's business?" Steve Raymond had brought in a plate of corned beef on rye.

Dean's mouth watered at the sight of the food, served with potato chips, a small bowl of cole slaw and a dill pickle. "Pretty good. I'm still having to convince some clients I can manage their accounts from here, but most of them have realized technology can easily replace face-to-face meetings. Then they like the convenience."

Steve chuckled. "Cutting anyone's commute time in New York these days must be a big bonus."

"Yep." Dean bit into his sandwich.

"Good?" Steve pointed to the plate.

Dean nodded, his mouth full. He decided if Steve Raymond was feeling chatty, he might as well see how much the man was willing to divulge about his past. He swallowed and wiped his mouth with a napkin. "You talk like you've got some experience with New York traffic,"

"Oh, I've been around," Steve said, his manner off-hand. "I tried a few places on for size before coming here. This is home now. I finally settled down, and I like my life a lot."

Dean Halstead thought the inn-keeper must have nerves of steel. No doubt he'd learned over the years to keep his composure while remaining vague about his background.

"Have you always been in the hospitality industry?" Dean asked, taking another bite of his sandwich.

"One way or another, I guess." Steve shrugged. "I'm more at home behind the bar than any place else, but I've learned how to operate a hotel. Hilly keeps the restaurant going. She sits with the cook and plans the weekly meals. They take care of supplies, so all I have to do is review everything and pay the bills."

Dean felt a little uncomfortable. Steve Raymond was becoming a friend. Halstead liked his easy manner and direct gaze. The big guy had made one bad mistake that was going to follow him around for the rest of his life. Dean regretted giving Matthew Yates the report he'd compiled. He wanted to tell Steve to go back and face the music. Maybe he'd get a reduced sentence if he turned himself in. Hilly had a giant crush on Steve, was highly competent, and would be able to keep Steve's business running until he returned.

"I've been around a lot, too," Halstead said. "Traveling gets old sometimes."

Steve nodded, his face guarded. "So, what are you up to today?"

"I worked all morning. Now I feel like playing hooky. I thought I'd drive north and check out the scenery on the other side of the village. I need an outing. I'm going stir-crazy in that apartment. That's the down-side of working from home—I see that laptop from the moment I get up to the time I go to bed."

"I can relate," Steve said. "Your best plan would be driving out to Penwithen. It's a deserted house on the edge of the cliffs, and it's close to the village. Easy to get onto the property even with the gate closed. There's a small beach good for swimming in the summer. Don't try to get into the house—it's falling apart. I'd avoid the beach right now, too—the steps are probably slick, and the railing hasn't been repaired in years."

"Thanks, I'll keep that in mind. Sounds like a good place for a walk. I like to do photography, too. I'll take my camera."

Steve looked a little startled. "You take photos professionally?"

Halstead cursed himself. "Nah. It's a hobby. I'm good at getting garbage cans and the backs of people's heads into my shots, but I like to do it."

A couple more people walked into the bar.

"I'll leave you to finish your sandwich," Steve said as he moved toward them.

Halstead recognized one of the men as the owner of the local hardware store. The other two he'd seen around town infrequently.

Sally Mainard walked in. Dressed in a short fur jacket and tight pants inside hip-length boots, she was a feast for any man's eyes. Halstead knew Matthew had been playing games with her. He wondered if Sally knew what she was getting herself into, involving herself with Yates. To Dean, though, she looked like a girl who could take care of herself. Her blue-green eyes coasted briefly over him before settling on Steve, who left the group at the bar.

"Hi," Steve said to her, his smile filled with genuine pleasure.

The group at the bar laughed raucously.

Sally looked at them with a little frown between her eyes. She peeled off red leather gloves.

Steve drew her closer to Halstead's table. Dean made a production out of opening The New York Times and hid behind it.

"Can we go somewhere private and talk?" She asked.

"It's lunchtime," Steve said. "It'll be difficult; I'll have to close the bar. Can't it wait a while?"

"No, it's important," she said.

Percival Huddleston must have had enough of being within earshot of the guffawing. Dean peeked around the edge of his newspaper and saw the mayor standing close to Steve and Sally.

"I can watch the bar for you, Steve," Huddleston said. "As long as no one gets too fancy with me and asks for a Cuba Libri or something. I can't even spell the names of those fancy drinks, let alone make one."

Steve laughed. "A Cuba Libra is only a rum and coke, Mr. Mayor."

"Oh." Huddleston grinned, not looking at all embarrassed. "I thought that was some foreign, exotic drink you had to light on fire or something." He winked at Sally.

Halstead lowered his paper. He decided the mayor might be more than an odd-job man after all. His manner seemed more relaxed than insipid.

Steve looked over. "You can pay Percival or Hilly for your lunch, Dean. The ticket's behind the bar."

"I'm the newly-hired bartender." Huddleston rubbed his hands together. "I suppose there's no pay?"

"Free beer?" Steve smiled.

"Better than cold, hard cash any day of the week." Huddleston took his empty mug behind the bar and filled it as Steve walked with Sally toward his office.

Halstead would have liked to be a fly on the wall in that office. He thought about ordering another beer and lingering, but he usually only drank one with his meal. He didn't want to deviate from habit and draw attention to himself. He got up and paid his check in cash, leaving a good but not overly-generous tip.

Percival Huddleston was polishing glasses. "What are you up to, today? More work?"

"No, sightseeing. I told Steve I've felt stir-crazy lately."

Halstead leaned against the bar and watched Steve and Sally, who had stopped in front of the reception desk to speak with a couple going into the restaurant. Hilly appeared with menus and the two couples split apart. Steve placed his hand on Sally's back as he guided her through the doorway into his office. Halstead noted she flinched slightly.

He turned his full attention back to Percival Huddleston. "Steve recommended I try walking around Penwithen."

"Nice area," Percival said.

The door to Steve's office closed. Halstead put on his coat.

"You need directions, or you know where you're going? Huddleston asked.

"Guess I could do with directions. All I know is it's north of town."

"It's a straight shot. Take the highway about three miles and look to the right. There's a plaque in a stone wall and a big iron gate that's rusting. If it's locked, park right in front of the gate and climb over the part of the wall that's crumbled. Vandals keep messing around. They frequently pick the lock on the gate to go in and see what they can steal. They find out there's nothing worth taking, but then they spray paint the house."

"Thanks."

Halstead walked out of the inn and hesitated a moment on the curb, debating whether he should see Matthew before or after his excursion. He wondered if Sally had come from Matthew's cottage. Feeling unsure of his reception, he got into his car and called to see how the land lay.

Matthew's greeting was decidedly frosty.

"I'll be over later to give you a full report," Dean told him. "I found out some very interesting information about a couple of people."

"You could give me that information over the phone," Matthew snapped.

It must have been a very bad day, Halstead thought. "How does Sally Mainard aborting Richard Ebberly's baby strike you?"

There was a short pause. "Damned interesting," Matthew said. "Why can't you get over here right now?"

"I've got more checking to do first." Halstead refused to face Matthew Yates right then. The man needed to chill out for a while.

"Fucking inconvenient for me. I'm only paying to keep you in luxury." Matthew's voice grated like sandpaper on concrete.

Dean's usually unflappable mood developed a kink. Yates made it sound like he was speaking to a servant, not a highly-trained professional. Matthew Yates could go fuck himself.

"I can't rearrange my schedule on that short notice," Dean snapped back.

"Fine. I'll see you at four o'clock, then. That'll give you two hours to take care of whatever's more important than bringing me the information I've already paid you for."

The silence produced when Matthew hung up was more profound than anything else he could have said. Damn, the man was in a foul mood. "Fine," Halstead told his phone before putting it in his coat pocket.

He looked at his watch: 1:15 P.M. He stopped home long enough to brew coffee to fill his flask, pull on hiking boots and exchange his wool coat for a parka before getting behind the wheel of his black Toyota 4-Runner and following the narrow road as it wound up the hill out of town. Halstead drove carefully, watching the landscape slide by. Homes dwindled down quickly from numerous to few, and then to none. Trees gave way to bare rock; he saw the boarded-up house.

The gate was unlocked. The vandals must have been busy again, Halstead thought as he turned his 4-Runner into the driveway. He wasn't worried about them still hanging around...he could take care of himself in any situation.

He drew up close to the front entrance and opened his door. The wind blew strong and fresh. He got out, inhaled deeply and looked around. Beyond the house, he saw the ocean heaving. Spray from the breakers washed the cliffs, and he could see for miles in both directions. A few scraggly trees broke the monotony of the headland, their bare branches reaching for the sky like emaciated arms. Penwithen was a bleak, lonely place. Dean wondered who had built it. He thought he knew why they had left. He couldn't even imagine being inside while storms raged.

His boots crunched over frozen snow as he walked around the house. Leaving the leeward side, he continued windward and fully understood the difference as the gusting wind almost took his breath away. He saw a board hanging off one shuttered window and trudged over to look inside. A moldy smell came from the interior. Dean retreated, taking a trampled path through the snow toward the cliffs.

As he trudged along, warming up inside his coat with the exertion, he noticed the stairs to the beach that Steve had mentioned. Testing the railing, he found it loose. No way was he going to take the chance of walking down to the beach, even though he could see the tide was out as he carefully peered over the cliff.

Suddenly, he thought he heard the crunch of snow behind him. As he turned, something heavy hit him above his left ear. The blow was so strong, his vision blurred. He staggered and grabbed the only thing available—the loose railing, which became looser. A second blow hit him on the back of the neck. The railing came away in his hand and he pitched forward, unable to stop himself.

He shouted as he fell, the wind screaming into his open mouth as rocks rose up to embrace him. He felt searing pain as granite crushed his nose and dug into his face. His mouth filled with blood. Stunned and unable to protect himself, he felt hands pushing the rest of his body and his legs over the cliff-edge. He tumbled out into space and heard gulls screeching as he flew with them all the way down to oblivion on the boulders waiting below.

CHAPTER FORTY-EIGHT

CARISSA LOOKED hard at Richard as she paced back and forth at the end of his bed. She stopped and faced him. "I have to know the truth. Did you get Sally pregnant and then desert her?"

Richard shook his head and grimaced.

"So tell me what really happened."

She'd bought a legal pad, clipboard and an assortment of pens. He was using the black marker. He scribbled, turned it and pushed it toward Carissa.

Not my fault. Steve won't believe me.

"Why?"

He started scribbling again, paused, shook his wrist and continued Carissa refused to wait any longer to get to the bottom of the bad blood between the two men. She sat while Richard labored his way to the end of one page and tried to start a second. The first page kept falling onto his hand.

Carissa tore off the page "Keep going. I'll read while you write." She might not be able to decipher every word he'd scrawled, but she figured she could fill in the spaces.

Sally wanted to be with Richard from the moment she arrived at the Cove. Their sexual encounters became rougher and more frequent.

He became increasingly uncomfortable with their relationship and told her he wanted to end it. She was agreeable to the split. She had decided Steve Raymond was a better candidate for a long-term relationship.

There was one glitch—she was pregnant with Richard's baby and needed to get rid of it. She had no interest in continuing the pregnancy or marrying him. She asked him to pay for the abortion. He wasn't comfortable, but she was insistent, going to his office as well as his home, screaming at him and even hitting him. She told him if he didn't give her the money, she'd harm herself and tell Deputy Watkins that Richard was responsible.

Carissa tore the next page off. He started scribbling again without looking at her.

When he gave Sally more money than she had asked for, he hoped that was the end of his nightmare, but he'd reckoned without Sally giving Steve her own version of their affair, followed by the local rumor-mill putting its own spin on everything.

He decided to ride out the storm without defending himself, believing things would blow over, which they mostly had. He threw himself into his career and Sally appeared to have established a good relationship with Steve, minus all the drama she'd had with Richard, who had made a pact with himself to avoid becoming romantically-involved with anyone else at the Cove. A promise that hadn't been difficult to keep until he met Carissa.

He had stopped writing. She looked at him. He put down the marker and held up the pad. He had written 'I LOVE YOU' in big letters. When she said nothing, he put down the pad and tried to take her hand.

She kept both hands out of his reach. "I'm not ready."

Richard was writing again: *Why so terrible to love you?*

"I can't even get Matthew out of my life, and you want me to get into a serious relationship with you? Too complicated, and I'm not even sure I believe what you wrote, either."

That time, after he finished writing, he tapped the pad. *Not lying about anything.*

"I'm too mixed up for this, Richard." Carissa got up. "I'll hire a private duty nurse for you and go home to the lighthouse. Steve said he got everything cleaned up and put back the way it was. I'm not sure I can handle staying there again, but I'm going to try."

Richard was scribbling again. He thumped the pad. *I want home, too.*

"No. You're too ill. They won't let you take a long ride in a car."

Private ambulance. No nurse. Signing self out.

"That's ridiculous, and you know it. You've got to stay here and get therapy."

Richard threw the pen and pad across the room.

Carissa decided staying and arguing would only make things worse. "I'll call the nurses' station later and check on you."

"Call," Richard rasped, low and hoarse. He pointed to his smart-phone, lying on the bedside table.

"Okay." She kissed his forehead before grabbing her coat and purse. When she stepped into the corridor, she glanced back. His eyes were closed.

"I'll call later," she promised.

He ignored her.

By the time she got into her borrowed car it was 2:00 PM. She drove over to the nearest car dealership and bought a 2 year old silver all-wheel drive Ford Edge. Her biggest problem was how to get the car to the Cove, but she was able to make arrangements for a salesperson with family in Whitstead to deliver the Edge to her the coming weekend. He assured Carissa he'd have no trouble getting a ride back.

She picked up a burger and fries and returned to the motel at 7:30 P.M. As she ate, she flipped from one TV program to another, unable to concentrate on any of the images flickering across the screen.

CHAPTER FORTY-NINE

Matthew, unaccustomed to waiting for anyone, refused to continue waiting for Dean Halstead. The detective was 15 minutes late. Matthew's call to Halstead's smartphone went straight to voicemail.

Weighing the possibility of inviting gossip against his fury at being stood up, Matthew tried locating Halstead at The Fisherman's Rest. Hilly answered the phone. No, she said, they hadn't seen Mr. Halstead since he had lunch there at noon. She told him Steve Raymond had returned from an errand and she would ask if he knew anything. She put down the phone while Matthew stood tapping his foot and distractedly watching the sun sink closer to the horizon.

"Mr. Halstead went sightseeing at Penwithen," Hilly said.

"Where the hell is that?" Matthew looked at the snow. Halstead may have gotten his car stuck somewhere.

Hilly gave directions. Matthew cursorily thanked her before hanging up. He pulled on his outerwear and warmed up his car, the only motivation for the drive being an opportunity to vent his seething rage when he rescued his P.I.

Matthew prided himself on his winter driving skills but drove slowly, mindful of the twists and turns the road took as it climbed out of the village. He kept in the tracks made by other vehicles and watched for

Halstead's car. Hilly had said the boarded-up house could be seen from the road, but with dusk fast approaching, Matthew wasn't so sure.

Hilly's directions proved sound. He found the house and saw Halstead's rental Jeep Cherokee parked in the driveway. A strong wind tugged at him as he got out of his Escalade. What a godforsaken place to build a house, he thought as he surveyed a barren landscape covered in snow. No wonder the house was boarded up—whoever owned it must have consigned the crumbling mausoleum to its fate.

Taking a flashlight from his glove compartment he checked the Jeep, finding it locked and empty. Matthew followed tracks in the snow from the Jeep to the back of the house, then alongside the cliff, where they were joined and even partially obliterated by a second set of larger prints. Both sets converged in an area of disturbed snow. The larger impressions left the scene via the north side of the house. The wind roared, threatening to knock Matthew off his feet. He looked around. Halstead was nowhere to be seen. Matthew shouted, but no one answered.

He wondered if there was beach-access. Maybe Halstead had met someone and they'd gone down to the beach, or he'd gone down alone, since the other prints led away from the cliff. If Halstead was walking around below, he wouldn't hear anyone shouting on the cliff. Matthew hesitated. He'd have to move closer to the cliff-edge to find out whether there were stairs. Reluctantly, he took two steps forward. The top of a railing came into sight. It didn't look at all stable as it rocked back and forth in the wind gusts.

If Halstead had used that for support while he walked down a flight of stairs in that weather, the man must be a gymnast. Matthew took a couple more steps, mindful of the gusting wind. Something that looked like blood streaked the railing, which he now realized was leaning at a crazy angle into space. He reluctantly leaned further out in an attempt to see if Halstead was clinging to the railing or was sprawled out on the steps. The wind almost carried him over the cliff. He tried to jump back, lost his footing and slipped, sprawling backwards in the snow.

Matthew swore as he struggled back to his feet and dusted himself off. Something was desperately wrong, and since he had already told Hilly he was looking for Halstead, he couldn't follow his first instinct, which was to get into his car and drive without stopping to New York, where he could leave any unpleasantness to his attorney. Reluctantly, he called the sheriff's office instead. Watkins answered immediately and promised he'd get the emergency response team activated.

As ordered, Matthew stayed on-scene, first in his car, then after Watkins's arrival, inside the deputy's Explorer. Emergency vehicles soon filled the forecourt, illuminating Penwithen with flashing lights that made it seem even emptier and more foreboding. They set up arc lights and used ropes to rappel down to where Halstead's battered body lay. They reported his fall had taken him onto rocks jutting up like rows of broken, jagged teeth. His face had been crushed. His limbs were twisted into puppet-like positions, and his smashed skull had been picked at by gulls. Matthew watched his top-notch P.I. being loaded into the coroner's vehicle inside a body bag.

"Someone will have to be notified," Watkins told Matthew. "Family?"

Matthew wondered why Watkins thought Dean Halstead was his best friend.

But instead of sarcastically asking the deputy why he thought anyone in Matthew's position would have their employees' families on speed dial, he managed to control himself. His attorney would counsel him to appear helpful but slightly distant. He pulled Halstead's business card out of his billfold.

"I suppose his partner, Willis, would have that information," Matthew said.

His palms began to sweat. If this wasn't handled correctly, his reasons for knowing Dean Halstead would be common knowledge in the Cove. When Carissa found out he was paying someone to spy on her, she'd be furious.

Watkins poured black coffee from a flask and handed Matthew a cup. "Was Mr. Halstead working for you in this capacity?" He pointed to the business card, prominently displayed on the dashboard. "I see he had another occupation, other than the one he set up here at the Cove. Private Investigator. That's interesting."

Matthew managed a non-committal grunt as he sipped the coffee, which was surprisingly good.

"I'll take that as a 'yes.'" Watkins took a sip of his own coffee, held in a stainless steel container. "Who are you having investigated in the village? I suppose my first thought would be your ex-wife."

"Carissa, yes. Discreetly." Matthew conceded.

"I don't much care for snoops," Watkins said. "I'll be informing Carissa about your relationship with Mr. Halstead."

Matthew groaned inwardly. But if Carissa was the only one with her nose out of joint, he could handle her. It was the rest of Halstead's 'snooping' that he didn't want to become general knowledge. He had enough dirt on the principle players in that village to cause a lot of damage, and he was going to take full advantage. He hoped he could get into Halstead's apartment and find the hard copies of the updates the P.I. had planned to give him before anyone else did, including Deputy Watkins, who might be a little more shrewd and insightful than Matthew had expected, judging by those opening questions.

"Now, Mr. Yates, tell me how you knew Mr. Halstead was out here in the first place."

That question Matthew could easily answer. "We'd arranged to meet at my house. We were going to play cards. When he didn't show up, I got worried and called the inn. I knew he ate lunch there most days. Hilly told me where he'd gone. I thought I should check on him, since he was close to an hour late."

"You and Mr. Halstead were friends before he came to the Cove, then?"

"No." Matthew shook his head. "We were both single men new to a small village. We bonded."

"Quickly," Watkins commented.

"I'm staying in a rental cottage. He was sharing living space with his office. We were both bored."

"Is that right?" Watkins jotted notes onto a small pad he had taken out of a coat pocket. "I'm wondering why both of you decided to spend the winter here in the first place. As you said, it's boring."

"Maybe we both needed a time-out from our busy lives."

Matthew tried to sound mildly surprised at the deputy's probing, when inside he was beginning to feel a stir of real alarm. He hadn't thought about the repercussions of calling Watkins. He should have gotten back in his car, driven right past Penwithen and gone to whatever village lay to the north, spent time there, been visible, and said he hadn't found Penwithen if anyone asked later. He could be sitting in his cottage right then with a whisky and soda in hand instead of drinking coffee in a cop's car while trying his best not to sound evasive.

"Maybe." Watkins ran a hand over a low growth of stubble on his chin. "But I find it hard to believe two complete strangers from New York arrive at the Cove within a week of each other and both decide to spend the winter. That's a big coincidence. And you just happen to have Mr. Halstead and Mr. Willis's business card on you. Isn't that something?"

Matthew avoided responding to that question. "I thought I'd enjoy some down-time away from New York before gearing up for the spring fashion shows. Try to convince Carissa to come back with me. Mend our partnership, if not our marriage."

"I'd better get your statement in writing," Watkins said. "Why don't you get in your car and follow me back to the station? That way, we can get everything we need while it's fresh in your mind."

"Don't you have to stay at the scene?"

"No, the sheriff's on his way. He should be here in a few minutes. He'll be taking over. He asked me to interview the witness. That's you."

"I didn't witness anything."

"We'll need to check out all those footprints to really assess that, won't we? The I.D. bureau's coming from Bangor."

"Holy crap. Sounds like you've activated the entire emergency system for someone who probably made a spur-of-the moment stupid decision to take those stairs to the beach and lost his footing when the rail came away from the cliff."

"That's one very plausible scenario, Mr. Yates, but there are others. For instance, there are three sets of fairly large footprints. Two of those sets go around the house and onto the cliff-side path, the other set leads away from the cliff, avoids the forecourt and ends at the far north end of the property. Whoever belongs to those footprints had a vehicle parked there. He or she scaled a four foot wall to get in and out of Penwithen instead of driving in and out of an open gate. There are two sets of tire tracks coming in and none going out. Those bigger footprints converge with the other two sets leading around the house only at the edge of the cliff. What size shoe do you take, Mr. Yates?"

"A ten. You'll see my footprints are one of those two sets going around the house. I was wondering about that larger set of prints, myself."

"They're bigger than a size ten." Watkins looked pointedly at Matthew's stylish half-boots. "And they look more appropriate for the weather, which means they're probably from one of the locals."

"You can check my car if you like. You won't find any other shoes or boots in there."

"You could have thrown them away after you pushed Mr. Halstead."

"You can tell from the high shine on my shoes that I haven't been walking all over out here, and if I had thrown shoes over the cliff, I would think they'd have been found right near Halstead's body."

"They could have gone out to sea or been carried by the wind to a different part of the beach."

"What about the tide?"

Watkins looked at his watch. "Not a factor. The water's not going to get any higher for a while." He opened his door. "Enjoy the coffee. I'll be back."

Matthew swore extensively once the deputy was trekking back toward the group at the edge of the cliff. His decision to do the right thing was about to backfire on him. He took out his phone and called his corporate attorney for advice. Matthew soon learned he was going to need a local lawyer. He sat sipping coffee and wishing he had done any number of things other than checking on Halstead as he waited for word from the corporate attorney on who he could count on to represent him in Treacher's Cove.

CHAPTER FIFTY

CARISSA WALKED into the sheriff's office to review the records of her aunt's death.

"The deputy's out," the dispatcher, Dot Ellis announced around her gum. "That new businessman in town, Dean Halstead was found dead." She smacked her gum loudly, perhaps to add a note of drama to her announcement. "Bottom of a cliff. A big investigation's going on right now." Her cheeks fairly glowed and her chest puffed out. "All this activity in the Cove; it's so exciting. We're getting detectives and the I.D. bureau sent from Bangor. Imagine. The sheriff's back on duty, too."

Carissa thought back to the one time she had seen Dean Halstead in Nancy Burton's store, when she had picked up a large package of fabric samples. Non-descript. A Conservative dresser. He'd nodded but avoided eye contact when Nancy introduced them, then quickly left. Carissa had thought him stand-offish until she admitted she hadn't exactly been busting down doors to make friends since her arrival at the Cove.

Dot was still smacking her gum and holding a note pad, which had very little scribbled under Dean Halstead's name. Carissa could read Dot's notes easily. She'd always had a knack for reading things upside down. Matthew still had no idea how she had learned some of the things she knew about him and his business.

"How did Mr. Halstead die?" She asked. "Do they know, yet?"

"Fell off a walkway, *right off the cliff* onto the rocks below." Dot shivered, but with a decided gleam in her eyes. "His face is all smashed in. The coroner's on-scene. It was the beach-access from Penwithen. That house has been closed up for years. You wouldn't catch *me* trying to walk down a rickety set of stairs in this weather."

"Me, neither," Carissa said. Dean Halstead must have been short on common sense and eyesight, unless those stairs were in way better shape than the house, which she doubted. "I guess I'll have to come back."

"That'd probably be best. If the detective's coming, the deputy'll probably be busy for the rest of his shift. He may even have to work *overtime* on this."

"Can I leave him a message?"

"Sure." The gum cracked like a pistol shot. Dot pushed a pad and pen across the counter.

Carissa wrote quickly, letting Watkins know she didn't mind if he called late in the evening or even the following day. She folded the paper in half and slid it back to Dot, who speared it onto a vicious-looking spike already containing a sizeable stack of papers.

"He'll be in touch," Dot promised, her voice nasal and high-pitched.

Carissa wondered how Deputy Watkins could understand his dispatcher over a police band radio. "I'll call tomorrow morning if I haven't heard from him."

Dot nodded and returned to her work, nails clattering on the keyboard, gum clicking.

Carissa sighed, frustrated. Now what? She could go to Virginia's or she could go back to the lighthouse. The thought of returning to where Hubert had perished brought a ripple of disgust. Consoling Virginia when Carissa felt like she was somehow at least partially responsible was almost as off-putting.

Steve Raymond strolled into the little office, dwarfing both the furnishings and Carissa. "I saw you driving through town," he said. "Are you staying at the Cove or going back to babysit our famous architect?"

"Staying." Carissa curbed a snappy retort about Steve's snide behavior toward Richard.

"At the lighthouse?"

"Maybe. Even though you cleaned up the mess, I don't know if I can face that kitchen, at least until it's been renovated, and with Richard far from well, that's not happening in the near future."

"I cleaned everything up. Even the glass got replaced."

"Is that how you got in, by breaking the window, I mean?"

"It was already broken, but yes, that's how I got in the first time—through the window. When I went back with Ray the front door was open, which was weird, because I swore I'd locked it behind me. I felt cleaning up the kitchen was the least I could do after leaving your door open overnight. Your heating bill's going to be through the roof. I'm really sorry."

"A big utility bill is the least of my problems right now." Carissa felt the beginning of a pounding stress headache. Changing the locks hadn't done anything to stop the doors from opening by themselves. Maybe the thermostat had moved itself back down to 50 degrees and saved her some money. That would be a plus within all the minuses. She wondered why Watkins had allowed Steve to clean up before the I.D. bureau arrived from Bangor. And now detectives were being sent to the Cove as well. Bangor Police Department must be half-empty.

Steve took her arm and began guiding her outside. "'Bye, Dot," he said cheerfully.

"'Bye, Steve." Dot's gum cracked impressively as the door closed.

"Why don't you stay at the inn tonight?" He asked. "It'll be a lot more pleasant than anywhere else you can think of."

Carissa wanted to disagree, but arguing felt like too much trouble.

"Carissa Yates. What a pleasure." Ray Watkins stopped right in front of them. "What can I do for you? We've had a little trouble. Mr. Yates is helping us out." He stepped aside as Matthew arrived, his brow furrowed and his mouth tight.

Carissa didn't like the sound of 'helping us out.' "I heard our newest resident fell from the cliff outside Penwithen," she said.

"Halstead?" Steve sounded incredulous.

"That's right." Watkins stamped his feet, knocking off snow. "There'll be an investigation. It looked like a railing gave way on the beach-access when we first arrived, but that railing's been tampered with. That's about all I can tell both of you. That might even be sharing too much, but there'd be no reason to suspect either of you of being responsible for his death. You'd have no reason."

"Are you going to head that investigation?" Steve asked.

"Me? Nah. Above my pay scale." Watkins walked around Carissa and opened the door to the police station, motioning Matthew inside. "They're sending a couple of detectives from Bangor. The sheriff feels we've got too much to handle locally, and with this death, he's right."

Carissa heard Steve's swift intake of breath at the mention of the Bangor detectives and wondered at his reaction.

"The deputy wants me to make a statement," Matthew said. "I went looking for Halstead after he missed our card game. I was worried when he hadn't called and was a half-hour late. I didn't even see the man's body. All I saw were footprints and blood on the broken railing." He glowered at Deputy Watkins.

Watkins blandly ignored Matthew's comments. "It's a lot warmer inside," he said, still holding the door open.

"What do you think this is, Ray, a barn?" Dot's nasal voice carried a lot of volume.

Watkins let the door close.

"I'm sorry to hear about Mr. Halstead," Carissa offered. "Do you know if he has any family?"

"I have no idea," Watkins said. "Mr. Yates gave me a business card, so I can contact Mr. Halstead's partner. Mr. Yates evidently doesn't know anything about his friend."

Carissa saw Matthew's face darken and hoped Watkins was ready for the blast she knew was coming.

"I make it a point never to pry into other people's business," Matthew said.

Well, there's a lie, Carissa thought. *We started out as business associates; then friends. He wooed me, wed me and took advantage of me.* She glared at Matthew, who ignored her.

Watkins' sharp little eyes darted from Carissa to Matthew and back. "Was there something you needed, Ms. Yates?"

"Oh, yes." Carissa dragged her gaze away from Matthew. "I came to ask if I could see the written report of my aunt's death."

"Come back inside," Watkins said. "Mr. Yates?"

Matthew reluctantly walked into the lobby, quickly followed by Watkins and Carissa. Steve lingered on the sidewalk. "I'll talk to you later," he told Carissa. "Please stay at the inn tonight."

"I'll see how I feel," she told him before the door swung shut behind her.

"Dot, would you get the records of Ms. Malloy's death for Ms. Yates?" Deputy Watkins took the mound of papers off the spike Dot had placed on the desk. He thumbed quickly through them and dumped them all in the trash can she held up. He sighed. "This used to be such a quiet little backwater. Now it's a three ring circus. A dead resident, a dead cat, and now a dead visitor..." His voice trailed off. He shook his head.

Carissa felt her aunt's death had acted as some kind of catalyst. She wondered whether Halstead had been acquainted with her aunt in some way, but she thought not. A marketing analyst would have no reason to consort with a reclusive resident in a Maine fishing village. Carissa looked askance at Matthew. Maybe Halstead wasn't what he seemed. Since when had Matthew taken up card playing with strangers?

"What do you want with your aunt's death report?" Steve asked from behind her.

Carissa jumped. "What happened to you seeing me later?"

"I thought better of it. Sorry, I didn't mean to shake you up." He placed one hand on her arm. She felt it, even through the thickness of her down coat sleeve. She thought of him with Sally naked in his office and stiffened.

"I've got a confession to make." He shoved his hands into the pockets of his parka and shifted his feet. "I moved some of your things into your old room at the inn."

"You had no business doing that. I'll pick them up after I get done here."

"You said yourself you didn't know where to go. The inn's the best option."

"Here's the report." Dot slid the file across the counter. "You can use the little desk over there in the corner. It's got good lighting if you turn on that banker's lamp."

"Thanks." Ignoring Steve, Carissa made herself comfortable at the desk and opened the file.

He followed. "What do you want to look at that for?"

"My own peace of mind."

"If you're really going to stay alone at the lighthouse tonight, you'd better find lighter reading material than that."

"I'll read whatever I want."

She scanned through the details of how, when and where, trying to detach herself from her emotions as she saw everything laid out in crisp, formal language. She also ignored Steve, who continued to stand watching her. Finally, after a strained and lengthy silence, he rested his forearms on the desk and tried to catch her eye. His hands almost touched hers.

"Why are you snapping my head off and avoiding me?" He asked. "It wasn't my fault Richard got run off the road. I don't drive. I don't even own a car."

"You could have borrowed one from someone else." She tried to keep her voice down. Dot was typing, but she kept looking across the room at them.

"And returned it with a big dent?" Steve's deep baritone rumbled with the effort of keeping his voice lowered. "I was behind the bar at the time the accident probably happened. I stayed there all evening. You can ask anyone."

"You hate Richard. You don't like me being friendly with him."

"I'm not trying to tell you who you should or shouldn't have as a friend. But I did tell you to be careful of him."

Carissa wished Steve had stayed on the sidewalk. "Didn't you ever think about asking Richard to tell you his side of the story Sally gave you?"

Steve sighed heavily. "Richard looks after Richard. All he cares about is getting what's good for him." He managed to make eye contact with her. "He got you into bed, didn't he?"

Carissa's cheeks flamed. The typing had stopped. "That's none of your damned business," she told Steve through clenched teeth.

"It's the truth, though, isn't it?"

Dot's chair scraped. She grabbed her coat and knocked on the office door behind her desk before opening it a crack. "I'm going on break, Ray," she piped. She was still trying to get her arm into her coat sleeve when she ran out the front door.

"Thanks for spreading gossip," Carissa told Steve. "Now everyone in the Cove will know about my sex life. Get out of here and make sure you have my things waiting for me at the reception desk when I come to pick them up."

He looked like he wanted to argue with her, but he saw how angry she was and must have thought better of it. The door slammed behind him. Carissa took a deep breath and tried to focus on the report, but tears kept welling up and making the print swim. *So much for making friends at the Cove.*

She was fast becoming as entangled in village life as the rest of the residents, and she didn't like it one bit.

CHAPTER FIFTY-ONE

CARISSA'S ARRIVAL at the lighthouse proved uneventful, a blessing after the stress of the previous week. No pizza on the table. No mutilated cat in the sink. A vase of red roses on the table, a card sticking out of it that said: 'Welcome Home, Carissa. From Steve and the Staff of The Fisherman's Rest.'

She checked all the other rooms and found everything neat and orderly. Steve and his impromptu cleaning crew must have done a forensic-style cleanup, for which she was very thankful.

She called the hospital and talked with Richard's private duty nurse, who reported he was asleep. He hadn't spoken since she arrived, but he'd eaten all his supper, which Carissa agreed was a very good sign. The nurse also said he had insisted on keeping his smartphone right beside him. Carissa felt raging guilt after hearing that report. Richard had asked her to call *him*, not the staff. She left her phone number with the nurse and said she would call him after his breakfast the following morning.

For once, the wind had died down. The silence felt deafening. Carissa made a fire and watched TV with a cup of herbal tea. A depressing review of plunging stocks, never-ending overseas conflicts and bills that hadn't made it through Congress summed up the national news. Local news wasn't much better. She surfed channels for something lighter, settled on the rerun of an old sit-com and drew the blue blanket covered with wandering moose over her shoulders.

The doorbell rang, startling her. Tea splattered the blanket. Carissa put down her cup and headed for the door. If Steve Raymond was on her doorstep, she'd tell him thanks for the cleanup and send him on his way. If Matthew was outside, she'd slam the door in his face. Turning on the outside light, she made sure the security chain was in its place before cracking the door open. Mai Ling stood on the porch, coatless as usual, shivering with her arms wrapped around herself.

Carissa took off the chain and threw the door open. "What are you doing out there in the dark? Come on in. Don't you ever wear a coat?"

Mai Ling's eyes filled with tears. "I had to see you. My friend, I have missed you. I did not think it was so cold outside."

Carissa spotted a livid bruise on Mai Ling's right cheek. "My God, what happened to you?" She put her arm around her neighbor's shoulders and gently walked her into the living room. "Here. Sit by the fire and warm up."

Mai Ling settled onto the couch and Carissa tucked an afghan around her young friend. Tears flowed down the girl's cheeks.

"Do you want to stay the night?" Carissa asked.

"Yes, please." Mai Ling took a tissue from the box Carissa offered her. "I want to leave my husband. Blake hit me. He said he could kill me if he wanted to. Can I use your phone to call my parents?"

"Of course." Carissa gave Mai Ling the cordless phone. "I'll make us something to eat and drink."

Wondering where Blake Ulster was at that moment, she brought her smartphone into the kitchen. He must have left on one of his frequent out-of-town trips, she decided, otherwise Mai Ling would never have had the courage to leave the house. As she made chicken noodle soup and smoked turkey sandwiches, she overheard Mai Ling speaking rapidly in Vietnamese, her voice choking at times. Carissa brought the food into the living room and set it on the coffee table. Mai Ling wiped tears from her face and blew her nose.

"Do you take anything in your tea?" Carissa asked.

Mai Ling shook her head. "Blake did not hit me today. It was two days ago. Some of my teeth are loose."

Carissa tried not to look as appalled as she felt. "What did your parents say? Are they coming to get you, or do you need money to take a train?"

"My brother will come. He should be here sometime tomorrow. He is very angry. My father and mother are very sad. They thought Blake would be a good husband." Mai Ling looked at her lap. "My father asked if I had given Blake a reason for his violence."

"It sounds like your parents don't have a good understanding of abusive relationships," Carissa said, trying not to sound judgmental, or as angry as she felt toward Mai Ling's parents. "Once domestic violence starts, it never stops. I know. My husband verbally abused me. He destroyed my self-confidence. I rarely spoke when he was around, and even when he wasn't. I never went out alone."

"You?" Mai Ling looked up, her eyes wide. "You seem so strong."

"Now, maybe." Carissa was able to give a thin smile. "Once I got away from him, I was able to regain my self-confidence. Hopefully, you'll be able to do the same."

The doorbell rang, followed by thunderous pounding on the door.

"Blake!" Mai Ling jumped to her feet, one hand fisted over her mouth. "I must hide. He will kill me."

Carissa's heart soared right into her throat. So much for assuming Blake Ulster was miles away. Mai Ling must have slipped out while he was asleep.

"The door's locked. He can't get in." Carissa grabbed the cordless. "I'm calling the police."

The phone at the sheriff's office rang and rang before Dot finally picked up. Meanwhile the pounding on the door continued, interspersed with what sounded like kicking.

"The deputy's eating supper at the inn," Dot said. "I'll call him."

Carissa didn't want to waste any more time. "I'll do that myself."

The pounding stopped.

Mai Ling cowered beside Carissa, who wished she had closed all the drapes and blinds. She called The Fisherman's Rest and Steve picked up.

"Blake Ulster's outside the lighthouse," she told him. "He's pounding on the door and trying to kick it down. I'm sure he'll stop doing that soon and put something through a window. Dot told me Deputy Watkins is eating dinner in your restaurant. Can you tell him I need him here right away?"

The sound of shattering glass brought a scream from Mai Ling.

"What the hell's going on?" Steve asked. "Who was that?"

"Mai Ling. Blake's doing what I said he would...breaking in."

Something in the hallway crashed to the ground. He'd broken the glass in the tiny powder room next to the front door and must be climbing through. Carissa's stomach hollowed out. She pushed Mai Ling behind her.

"Hurry!" She whispered into the receiver.

Steve's shout made Carissa take the phone from her ear, but she quickly put it back. She heard him yelling for Hilly to get the deputy.

"Carissa, are you still there?" Steve asked.

"Yes, and so is Blake," she told him as Blake Ulster's figure filled the entrance to the living room.

"You tell Blake I'll kill him if he harms you or Mai Ling. I'm coming with Ray Watkins. I'll put Hilly on the line. Stay with her."

"Ms. Yates." Hilly's voice sounded high-pitched, semi-hysterical.

"We're okay, Hilly." Carissa kept Mai Ling behind her as she edged away from Blake, trying to put the couch between them. "The deputy's on his way with Steve Raymond," she told Blake.

Blake's answer was to curl his lip into a snarl.

Carissa hurriedly backed up a couple more steps and tripped over Mai Ling's feet. "You should leave, Blake," she said. "Mai Ling's not going home with you tonight. She's staying here."

Blake growled like a rabid dog, his face mottled. "Get over here, wife. Stop making us look like fools." He held out his hand. "Let's go home."

Mai Ling's response was an unintelligible gurgle. Clinging to Carissa, her ragged breathing conveyed her terror more than any amount of crying or pleading would have done.

"She's afraid of your temper," Carissa told him. *There's an understatement.* She tried not to cower, even as she stepped back again, pushing Mai Ling along behind her.

"You're interfering where you've got no right. Like your aunt." Blake advanced, his long strides making short work of the distance.

Carissa tried to swallow her fear. Surely he wouldn't try to harm either of them with help on the way? It wouldn't take long for Steve and Deputy Watkins to get there. She remembered how much satisfaction Matthew had gotten out of intimidating her. Blake Ulster was just another bully.

Drawing herself up, she returned his glare. "Mai Ling came to me for help, and I'm going to give it to her."

Blake laughed, sharp and ugly. "*You're* going to help her? The woman who ran away from New York is going to be courageous and fight for someone else when she can't even stand up for herself?"

"I will," Carissa promised, finding Mai Ling's cold hand and squeezing it reassuringly.

Blake came even closer. Mai Ling ran for the kitchen. Carissa backed up again, collided with the dining table and dropped the phone. She heard Hilly frantically calling her name.

Blake's boot crushed the phone as he lunged. Carissa managed to jump aside, but the flower vase toppled over when Blake crashed against the table. The vase rolled across the polished mahogany before hitting the floor. Water, roses and broken glass flew everywhere. Mai Ling screamed from the kitchen.

Carissa looked at the remains of her welcome home bouquet and the water soaking into her aunt's prized Chinese carpet. "Damn you. Get out of my house."

If she hoped her bravado would jolt him to his senses, she was sorely mistaken. Blake's breath whistled between clenched teeth. He pushed his soiled windbreaker to one side and drew a hunting knife from a sheath on his belt. Carissa asked herself why she hadn't tried stalling him first instead of going straight for provocation. Maybe because pleading had never worked with Matthew. Neither had tears. She moved slowly toward the kitchen while she tried unsuccessfully to remember if she had left a key in the mudroom door. Panic threatened to take over, but she fought it. *Concentrate,* she told herself.

She'd never make it to the back door before he caught up with her. And even if she did, how was she going to grab Mai Ling and take her, too? If they were able to make it into the mudroom, locking the door would only delay Blake moments. He'd make short work of the mudroom door while they were running around the outside of the cottage in the snow without boots or coats. Or he'd simply go out the same way he'd come in and confront them as they ran for the garage. They'd never outdistance him. If they hit him with the only available weapons in the mudroom, brooms and mops, what would happen after that? Certain death, she thought, unless Steve and Watkins arrived on wings. The garage itself was in need of repair, its door a flimsy barrier at best. Her borrowed vehicle was locked. Its keys were in her purse, on the settle right next to the front door.

Carissa felt her courage slipping away along with what was left of rational thought.

She mustered up the calmest tone she could under the circumstances and addressed him. "Be reasonable, Blake. Is Mai Ling really worth thirty years in the slammer?"

"Maybe. I intend to find that out."

He continued to move closer. Carissa could now see every line etched on his weather-beaten face, the spittle at the right corner of his mouth and a nick at the bottom of his left ear lobe. He held the knife poised in front of him like a dagger.

"Maybe you're worth it, too."

His eyes held hers. She saw hate and madness in them.

He had stopped when he spoke. Now he started moving again. If she could keep him talking, maybe they had a chance of prolonging their lives. She felt Mai Ling touch her back.

"What have you got against me?" Carissa asked.

"You've caused trouble from the minute you got here. It's time for you to go. I tried scaring you off, but you're like your aunt—you don't scare easily."

"You! You're the one who's been messing with me?" She saw Aunt Jessica's copper bed warmer sitting on the table. *Who had moved that from its usual position on a hook beside the fireplace? Maybe Steve had knocked it down and hadn't put it back?*

She gave herself a mental shake. *Keep your thoughts straight,* she told herself. She grabbed the bed warmer. It was an unwieldy weapon, but it might keep Blake a little further away. "You want a piece of this?" She asked, wondering what was wrong with her. She sounded like someone from a bad B movie. But she swung the bed warmer in a wide arc. "Come on, try your luck," she told him as he laughed at her.

"Carissa, please." Mai Ling's voice sounded as high-pitched and hysterical as Hilly's had been.

"He's going to get what he deserves," Carissa said. "He's made me into a nervous wreck. Half the Cove thinks I'm a basket case."

Blake laughed again, his vicious cackle prickling the hairs on the back of her neck.

"You think you can take me on? *You?*"

He sprang, his feet landing on Aunt Jessica's soft couch and sinking in. He lost his balance, pitching sideways. He grabbed the back of the couch with the hand that was holding the knife and lost his grip. The knife clattered to the floor right as Carissa delivered a glancing blow with the bed warmer between his ear and his shoulder.

He roared with pain. "Stupid bitch!"

Her momentum had carried her too close. His fingers sank into her neck, gripping like a vise.

Carissa opened her mouth to scream, but no sound came out. She tried to suck in air, but nothing happened. Blake's fingers dug deeper. Stars exploded like a firework display. She tried to gouge his eyes, as she'd been taught in a long-ago self-defense class, but she couldn't reach him. Her strength ebbing fast, she tried sticking her fingernails into his hands, but he held on firmly.

Her legs began to give way. Out the corner of her eye, she saw Mai Ling drop down, then come back up with something glittering in her hand. Blake's victorious roar turned into a yelp. The grip on her neck loosened, and then fell away. Her strength gone, Carissa gulped in air, sank to her knees, then sat coughing and gasping for breath. The pain in her throat pulsated, but the stars receded and her vision cleared.

"You've killed me." Blake's words were the faintest whisper.

Carissa turned to look. Mai Ling's hands slid off the hilt of the hunting knife buried deeply into Blake's back. He was lying over the back of the couch, his face turned toward his wife, standing over him.

Carissa needed to stand up. Her legs quivered, but she managed to use the arm of the couch for leverage. She pointed to the kitchen. "Call nine-one-one," she told Mai Ling. "My phone. Kitchen table. Get ambulance." Her throat was so dry, she couldn't continue.

Mai Ling stood motionless, staring at Blake. "You deserved it," she told him. "It's all your fault."

Blake moaned. Carissa saw blood seeping from his mouth.

Shouting and pounding feet announced Watkins and Steve's arrival. Pandemonium ensued. Carissa was unceremoniously picked up by Steve and placed on a chair by the hearth. She heard them working on Blake, but it was too late.

Ray Watkins put Mai Ling onto the chair opposite Carissa's.

"He was choking her," Mai Ling explained. "I had to do something. He was going to kill both of us. He brought the knife with him."

"What started this?" Watkins sounded all business.

"I came to ask Carissa for the use of her phone. I wanted my parents to take me away from Blake. He was beating me. Then he threatened to kill me."

Watkins looked at Carissa's neck. "That's got to hurt."

She nodded.

"You want me to call who first?" Steve had his phone out.

"I'll notify the sheriff myself." Watkins rubbed one hand over his chin. "He's not going to like it. Two deaths in one day and both of them possible homicides."

"Mai Ling stopped Blake from murdering me," Carissa croaked. "That's not homicide."

She started coughing and couldn't stop, despite the pain. Steve gave her a bottle of cold water he must have gotten out of the refrigerator. Swallowing hurt her throat, but at least the water stopped the coughing.

"That's for the court to decide," Watkins said, his voice sharp. "You'll have to make a statement, Mai Ling, so it's best you keep quiet until I start asking you questions. You'll both have to come down to the station so I can get your statements." He took off his hat and rubbed his head. "The Cove's never had this much trouble. Not until Jessica's death and your arrival." He looked pointedly at Carissa.

"Don't go blaming her," Steve said. "The only thing she did was help Mai Ling."

"I'm not taking sides or placing blame on anyone," Watkins said. "I've got to call Doc Hale, the coroner, and tell him his services are needed again. I'm going to step into the kitchen. Don't any of you move, and don't touch anything."

He looked from one to the other for affirmation. No one spoke, but they all nodded. Carissa looked across at Mai Ling, sitting bolt upright in the wing-back chair. With Blake's danger removed, she appeared completely calm.

"I want to call my parents again," Mai Ling said.

Steve glanced at the kitchen, where a background rhetoric could be heard from Ray Watkins, presumably giving his report to the sheriff. "I can't let you do that. Ray said to sit tight, and that's what we're all going to do." He pulled over a dining chair and sat beside Carissa. "How are you feeling?"

"I'm okay. My throat's sore, but then, I was choked."

"I couldn't take the abuse anymore," Mai Ling said. "I didn't think he saw me leave."

"You need to save your statement for when Ray talks to you," Steve cautioned.

"I'm calling my family." Mai Ling started to get up. "If I can't do it here, then I'm going home."

"No, you're not." Ray Watkins came back into the room. "The sheriff'll be here in a few minutes. The coroner was on his way to Bangor. He's turning around. Neither of them is a happy camper."

The smell of fresh blood was beginning to make Carissa nauseated. "I'm going to call William," she said. "Mai Ling has the right to an attorney, and I probably should get some advice, too."

CHAPTER FIFTY-TWO

THE FOLLOWING HOURS were a blur for Carissa. Feeling too exhausted to go anywhere else after giving her statement, she agreed to stay at The Fisherman's Rest. Mai Ling had to spend the night in jail, but William was determined to get her out on bail the following morning.

Carissa breathed the crisp, clean air, heavily loaded with the tang of salt as she left the police station, Steve beside her. She looked up at the stars, visible between scudding clouds that ghosted across the face of the moon.

"Feeling better?" Steve asked. He linked arms with her in a friendly way. "How's your throat?"

"I'm okay. My throat's bruised, but it'll heal in a few days. I'm worried about Mai Ling. She doesn't deserve to spend even one night behind bars. I'm not sorry Blake Ulster's dead—he was a complete brute. I just wish she hadn't been forced to stab him. But if she hadn't, I wouldn't be here."

"I don't think anyone in the Cove's going to miss Blake." Steve shortened his steps to match hers as they strolled toward the well-lit inn. "I've had my suspicions about his relationship with Mai Ling since I arrived at the Cove. Trouble is, she never confided in anyone. Hell, she never even came to town. He did all the marketing."

"That's a classic isolation tactic. Matthew tried to do the same with me. Succeeded, where Aunt Jessica was concerned."

"He was abusive toward you?"

Carissa shook her head. "Not physically. He was more subtle than Blake Ulster, believe me." She stopped talking. She had vowed not to discuss her issues with Matthew after their divorce. She wanted to move on, restricting any disagreements to the current court case, which she hoped to win. That would hit Matthew where it really counted for him —financially.

Steve trudged through the snow at the edge of the sidewalk, his head bowed. "Your ex is a hard man to figure," he said after they had walked another block. "I can't get a handle on him."

"Neither can anyone else." Carissa felt really uncomfortable discussing Matthew with Steve. "Let's talk about something else."

"We're running out of safe subjects," he said. When Carissa looked at him, he chuckled softly.

"We are," she agreed. "But it's no laughing matter."

"Are you going to give up on the lighthouse and move back to New York?"

"Probably. Richard could practically demolish the cottage and I think I'd still get creeped out in there. Besides, I can't seem to escape Matthew wherever I go. In a city as big as New York, I can at least put more distance between us."

"How did he know you were here?"

"He must have found out my aunt left me the lighthouse. I don't know how that could have happened—it certainly wasn't publicized anywhere." She frowned. "I wonder how he *did* find out."

"Why did you want to look at the report of your aunt's death?"

"Because I wanted to check a couple of things that bothered me."

"Are you going back there tomorrow?"

"Hopefully. Depending on what happens with Mai Ling and her brother." A sudden gust of frigid air made her shiver. "Steve, why doesn't the sheriff resign? Deputy Watkins is doing everything. He looks really tired and stressed out."

"Sheriff Crosby offered to resign, but the county wants him to finish out his term. Not much usually happens around these parts, so it didn't seem much of an issue at the time."

"I bet everyone's feeling differently now. Three deaths, two in the same day?"

"That's a lot," Steve agreed. "For the Cove, that's unprecedented, but change comes slowly and sometimes painfully around here. No one wants to take off the old and put on the new, whether it's clothing, businesses or anything else. Percival Huddleston's in his second term as mayor and looks like a shoo-in for a third. Ray Watkins will get promoted when Sheriff Crosby resigns, so why not let Ray get his feet wet while he can still get advice whenever he needs it? All he has to do is pick up the phone. The sheriff's always at home with his sick wife."

"If Deputy Watkins was investigating petty crime, like parking violations or vandalism, that would be a solid plan, but if Matthew's telling the truth, Dean Halstead was probably murdered. I believe my aunt was, too. This isn't the time for on-the-job training."

"Which is why I heard Bangor's sending a couple of detectives to help out. We'll just have to wait and see what shakes out. At least Blake's death seems pretty straight-forward, if I can even say that about a man's passing."

Carissa sighed. "I'll be glad to get into bed tonight. I hope I can sleep, that's all."

"I put your things in the same room."

"You didn't take them out this afternoon, after I told you to, did you?"

"No. I had a feeling you'd change your mind later."

"I should be angry with you, but if there's somewhere I can even think about sleeping tonight, it's that room. The bed was so comfortable."

"I'm glad to hear that. But it's missing one thing," he said.

"What's that?"

"Me."

He swung her around to face him and his lips found hers in the darkness. Carissa thought she should be pushing him away, but ever since she'd met him, she'd wondered if what she felt for him was more than friendship. His kiss was soft, gentle, and exploratory.

Suddenly and unexpectedly, she thought of Richard. Despite the initial awkwardness of their encounter; despite their arguments; he'd ignited a fire in her she had never expected or experienced before. She felt nothing of that surging passion with Steve.

He stepped back. "That didn't light any sparks, did it?" He brushed a thumb across her lips. "Is it that damned Richard?"

"Probably." She had trouble looking at Steve, knowing the sadness in his eyes wouldn't be reflected in hers. Instead, she fixed her gaze on a button right in the middle of his chest. "Maybe it wouldn't have happened for us, anyway. Some things are better left as dreams."

"I guess they are, but I'm very disappointed. Are you really hung up on that guy?"

She jammed her hands in her pockets and kicked at a pile of frozen snow. "I don't know what I feel for Richard. He got hurt before there was much time to...analyze feelings." She was lying. Her feelings for Richard were growing deeper than she wanted to admit.

"He'll be okay. Richard's as strong as...well...an ox," Steve said.

"I know. He'll fight staying up in Bangor and getting therapy in their rehab unit. He wants to come back to the Cove as soon as possible. Earlier than he should. But even if he does, I can't see how he can cope with his both his recovery and his business."

"Winters are usually slow for his contracting business. Richard always plans ahead financially. Even I have to admit he's got a good head for business. He'll be okay. I don't doubt he's made contingency plans for finishing whatever projects he has going right now. Richard would do that. His father was that way, from what Percival and Al have told me. They said he trained his son right."

"Sounds like there was a lot of respect in the Cove for Richard's father."

"He was a strong and good man, according to everyone I've talked to. Pity his son's not the same way."

They started walking again. The air felt like an icy blanket on Carissa's shoulders. At a street corner, they stepped away from the shadow of the buildings into a pool of light from a street lamp.

"I swear I didn't tamper with Richard's brakes or anything else on his Jeep," Steve said.

Carissa felt really uncomfortable. "I never implied you did."

"Tell me the idea never crossed your mind."

She wanted to give him reassurance, but she wasn't going to lie. "I can't."

"I see." He sounded infinitely sad. "Come on. It's freezing out here and you need rest. It's going to be one hell of a day tomorrow."

"It's that way every day, it seems, here at the Cove," she said.

CHAPTER FIFTY-THREE

Matthew carefully wriggled away from Sally's clinging arms. His back smarted. *Damn, her nails are sharp.*

He swung his legs off the bed and sat up. The cottage felt cold now they weren't writhing around together and sweating profusely. He reached for his bathrobe on the floor. Sally stirred and murmured in her sleep. Matthew dispassionately looked at her beguiling face, so young and innocent in repose. How those blue-green eyes changed with her moods—dark emerald with anger, bright green with passion and frenzy, bluer with need. A chill ran through him.

"Matt."

She rubbed one hand under her nose and brushed hair from her eyes. Completely naked, she sprawled without any self-consciousness as she stretched both arms over her head. "Where are you going?"

"To turn up the heat." He leaned over to get his bathrobe and felt her hand on his back. Her thumb slid down into the cleft of his buttocks as he started to get up.

"I didn't make you hot enough?" She giggled.

He vividly remembered pleasure followed almost instantaneously by sharp pain. "Uh, uh." He stepped out of her reach.

"Oh, come on, Matt. Look at me."

He couldn't help turning. He still wanted her, but not as badly as he had before they'd had sex. Sally arched her back and wriggled provocatively. "We could experiment with ice cubes."

"The hell we could. I'm freezing already."

He walked out of the room. Her adolescent provocativeness was beginning to annoy him. He refused to follow Steve Raymond's path, where Sally appeared to be the leader, demanding sex wherever and whenever she wanted it. She was well-used goods, he thought, remembering her affair with Richard Ebberly. He didn't mind the thought of having sex with her in some public place, but it would be at his initiation, not hers. He turned up the thermostat and made himself a whisky and soda, which he downed in three gulps. The half-light of late morning filtered into the living-room. He decided it was time for Sally to go home. He had work to do at Dean Halstead's apartment.

Although he'd overslept due to unexpected but highly pleasurable nocturnal sex, he doubted the local law-enforcement, such as it was, could organize sufficiently to cope with all the mayhem breaking loose in the Cove, even if reinforcements were sent down from Bangor. Somewhere, either in Halstead's apartment or with the man's partner sat the information Matthew had paid for but not received. He was determined to retrieve it as soon as he got rid of Sally.

"How about one for me?" Sally sounded sulky. "Are you always so rude after you get what you want?" She sidled up to him, the comforter draped around her.

"I'm not much for lying around in bed all morning hugging and kissing. We satisfied each other, and I've got business to take care of." He poured two drinks and gave her one.

She rolled the glass around before taking a sip. "I could have been better satisfied if you were more capable...and bigger."

Rage bubbled up inside him. He knew his inadequacies and didn't need any reminders. He'd given her as much gratification as she could possibly want. So what if he'd been a bit early? He'd managed to hold on long enough the second time, even if she'd had to work a while to get him ready.

Carissa hadn't complained. She wouldn't have dared. He wished, not for the first time, that she hadn't found the strength to leave him. Life was simpler when he had her at home. If he had performance trouble with extra-marital partners, he blamed the issue on his deep love for his wife and his sudden inability to cheat on her.

"It's time for you to go home." He wrenched the glass out of Sally's hand.

Her eyes darkened to a deeper green than he had noticed before. "No one tells me to get out before I've been satisfied." She tossed aside the comforter and stood with hands on hips and legs spread apart. "Get on your knees and deliver."

"Who the fuck do you think you are?"

He threw the contents of his glass at her. Whisky and ice cubes splashed over her and trickled down her flat, smooth belly. She gasped.

"You're only a whore I gave a good time. Now, get out."

A flush rose up Sally's neck and blossomed across her cheeks. "What did you call me?"

"You heard, slut."

She grabbed his arms and her fingernails sunk into his flesh. "How dare you!"

"Get your hands off me." He tried to shake her off, but she clung. "Get your fucking hands off!" He managed to free one arm and slapped her across the face. "Bitch."

"Cheap bastard," she countered, ripping at his bathrobe belt like a frenzied dog. Her slapped cheek flamed crimson.

"Tart. Filth." He yanked her hair.

"Jack-off," she said, bruising him with both hands.

It was Matthew's turn to gasp. The force of his erection left him breathless. He knocked her to the floor and fell on her, harder and more ready than anyone had ever made him. She met him thrust for thrust, blow for blow, torment for torment. When they finally collapsed, sweaty and spent, side by side on the cold linoleum, he grabbed her and held on.

"I told you we were alike," he grunted into her hair.

"I made a man out of you today, Matt," she panted. She rolled over and straddled him. "Now it's time for you to make a woman out of me."

"You're gonna kill me," he gasped.

Sally laughed and slid down his body. "You'll never die a better death."

CHAPTER FIFTY-FOUR

CARISSA AWOKE TO RINGING. Opening one eye, she grabbed her smartphone. "Hello?"

Richard's voice was muffled and indistinct. "You're okay. Good. I was worried about you when you didn't pick up your landline."

"Why didn't you call my cell first?" She glanced at the bedside clock: 10:30 A.M. He should be in the middle of physical therapy. "Where are you?"

"Home."

She was no longer half-awake. "What are you doing there? You weren't supposed to leave the hospital. Doctor Lister told you, I told you..."

"Didn't listen to any of you," Richard said.

"Is someone with you?"

"Nurse Fields."

"Thank God. I'm coming over."

"Good." He hung up.

Fuming, Carissa brewed coffee, took a quick shower and got dressed. Steve was behind the bar when she passed by on her way out of the inn. He threw down the cloth he'd been using to polish glasses and caught up with her before she reached the front door.

"Where are you off to?" He grabbed her arm.

"Out." She shrugged off his hand.

"Can I ask where?"

"No. I don't need a keeper."

He looked hurt.

Carissa decided she owed him a short explanation. Very short. "I'm going to visit a friend."

His eyes narrowed. "You're not going to get into any more trouble, are you?"

"I never get into trouble; it follows me around."

Steve caressed her cheek with the briefest of touches. "Be careful."

"Always."

His concern made her pulse quicken, but it also annoyed her. Carissa had no intention of becoming anybody's possession again, and she felt Steve could become controlling very quickly. She said goodbye and made sure not to look back while she walked to her car.

The trip to Richard's home went smoothly on cleared roads under a sunny sky. She parked and walked up to the front door, which was opened promptly by Nurse Fields.

"Come in, Ms. Yates." The private duty nurse looked relieved. "I'm very glad to see you. Mr. Ebberly signed himself out AMA—against medical advice. He had no objection to me accompanying him, thank goodness."

"I'm so glad you came. Thank you." Carissa stepped inside the house. It couldn't have been easy to convince Richard he needed help.

"He's in the living-room." Nurse Fields took Carissa's coat.

Richard sat in his wheelchair beside the gas fireplace, flickering cheerfully with gentle warmth.

"Are you trying to kill yourself?" She asked.

He managed a half-smile despite the yellowing bruise on the lower half of his face. Someone had shaved the rest of his hair off. "That's not much of a greeting. ' Welcome home' might be more appropriate."

"I think I liked it better when you couldn't speak."

"You would." He picked up a legal pad from the end table beside him and flipped back a few pages. He held up the one that said 'I LOVE YOU.'

"Unfair." Carissa walked over to him.

"Do I get a kiss at least?" He raised his face. The lines around his eyes deepened.

"When was the last time you took your pain medication?" She gave him a gentle peck on the lips before dropping to her knees beside his wheelchair. "Richard, why did you have to come home? It's too dangerous. Two people have died at the Cove since your accident, and the police are investigating at least one of those deaths. You're in no fit state to fight back if anyone comes after you."

"And you think the hospital's safer after I had a pillow held over my face?"

Carissa had no answer for that. Either he remembered the incident now, or he believed she had witnessed it.

"I've got an alarm system and surveillance equipment," Richard said. "What measures have you taken?"

"None yet, but I'm calling in that expert from Whitstead." She avoided his accusing glare. "I *am*, Richard. I haven't slept at the lighthouse since I came back from the hospital. Mai Ling Ulster stabbed her husband there yesterday."

Richard nodded. "I saw that on the news. I couldn't stay at the hospital any longer, leaving you alone. You've got to move in with me."

"I can stay with Mai Ling if she makes bail. Her brother's on the way. She wants him to take her back to Boston, but I don't think that'll be possible."

"Is William her attorney?"

"Yes. He thinks if she pleads self-defense he can get her acquitted. Blake would have killed both of us if she hadn't stopped him." Carissa shuddered when she thought how close she'd come to being choked, but she didn't want to tell that to Richard. "I think he attacked me first because I'm bigger and stronger than Mai Ling, and he knew she was terrified of him."

"Not terrified enough if she stabbed him." Richard didn't sound at all convinced.

"She was trying to save me. I'm so grateful she came through for me like that."

Richard tried shaking his head and grimaced. "Damn, my neck's sore. Whiplash is a bitch." He shifted in the wheelchair. "I wonder why Mai Ling stayed with him. Couldn't she have gone back to her family?"

"She said her parents thought the sun rose and set on Blake. They wouldn't believe her when she told them she was being abused."

"Not the sort of family I'd want on *my* side."

"Tell me about it." Carissa turned up the heat on the fireplace. "If anything good will come out of this, and believe me, there won't be much, it's that with Blake dead, the weird stuff going on at the lighthouse is over. He told me he was the one trying to scare me away."

"Did he confess to mutilating the cat, too? The other things you told me about weren't really harmful—doors left open, your thermostat being messed with, that sort of thing."

"What about the noises I heard in the basement? Things being moved around? He'd have had to spend a lot of time and effort setting those up. He'd have been creeping around inside the keeper's quarters at night, too." A shudder swept through her at the thought of Blake invading her space while she slept. She turned up the heat again. The fireplace roared. "Yikes! Even thinking he might have been creeping around my home at all hours gives me chills."

"You're going to roast me if you keep talking about it."

"Oh, sorry." She felt the heat blasting and adjusted the dial. "I spent last night at the inn."

"You could go back home now, since the danger from Blake's over."

"With blood all over the place again? No thanks. Besides, the danger from Blake may be over, but what about the other two deaths?"

"That's true. My brain's still not operating on all four burners. Sorry. I saw the news reports about those deaths. Reporters will be heading this way. Steve's going to have a full house at the inn."

"I hadn't thought about that. I don't want to be anywhere close to reporters. They'll recognize me and start asking questions. Either that, or Matthew will make sure to point me out and make up some tale about me. Then they'll be knocking on your door, too. What fodder for them, my affair with you while Matthew's trying to reconcile with me and people are dying left and right." She put her face in her hands. "Oh my god, what a mess."

"How about tabling all this and having something to eat and drink?"

Richard suggested. "I can only take so much doom and gloom right now. Otherwise, I start having flashbacks to the moments before my accident." He held up both arms, one casted, the other in a splint. "I can't wear a watch, but the way my stomach's rolling, it must be lunchtime."

Carissa took his hand. "I'm going to call Dr. Lister tomorrow and ask if he'll continue seeing you as an outpatient, even if you did sign yourself out of the hospital. You need on-going care, Richard, and I'm willing to bet there aren't any orthopedic specialists locally."

"There aren't. But I couldn't stay in that hospital any longer. Why don't you and Mai Ling move in here? I've got plenty of guest rooms. You could even sleep in my master suite. It's got a big TV and a fireplace...well, you've seen it." He stopped when Carissa ducked her head.

"That's really generous," she said, "but where are you sleeping? Not the couch..." She looked at it. "...too soft and not long enough, either."

Richard grimaced. "That would kill my back, for sure. No, there's a pull-out bed in the study. My father bought it. He said if he was going to stay here, he might get to the point when he couldn't make the stairs. He didn't want to add an elevator or a stair lift. I kind of wish he had right now. He did put in a full bath downstairs. I can get grab bars installed and order a bench when the casts come off and I get the okay to shower."

"Good. You're not so ill-prepared here as I thought." Carissa gently ran her thumb over the uninjured parts of his hand. "No live-ins for you while you're recuperating. I think Mai Ling would be happier in her own home with her brother for company if she gets out on bail. As for me, I want to be able to come and go as I please, so it's The Fisherman's Rest for me unless those reporters actually materialize. Steve Raymond promised he'll keep an eye on me. I'll make sure it's just that."

"Okay. For now." Richard sighed. "I know I don't have any choice as far as telling you where to stay, but at least if you're in the middle of town, you'll have plenty of eyes on you."

"Exactly." She gave him a light kiss. "I'm going to see about a hospital bed for you. An electric one. A pull-out isn't going to give you enough support, and you can't adjust it. As long as you promise you won't fire Nurse Fields, I won't worry about you when I'm not here."

He ran his fingers through her hair. "I'll fire Fields immediately. Then you'll have to stay."

"I hired her, so you can't."

"You're splitting hairs."

Richard had more difficulty getting his words out. He was visibly tiring, and he'd already told her he needed to eat. She brushed his tousled hair and smoothed the creases around his eyes. "How about taking a short nap while Nurse Fields and I make lunch?"

"Only if you promise to stay for lunch." The look in his eyes made her heart skip.

"I promise. Now." She turned his wheelchair in the direction of his office. "Let's get you into bed for a rest."

"Nurse Ratched'll be outraged if you put me to bed," he said with a chuckle.

"Maybe I should let her do it, then."

"I said she'd be outraged. I didn't say I cared if she was."

"Richard Ebberly, you're incorrigible."

"I hope so. Makes me more interesting."

She pushed him into the study. The bed looked as though it had been made up for a military inspection. She pulled back the covers, took off the wheelchair footrest closest to the bed and lined his wheelchair up with the bed as she had been instructed at the hospital. Then she removed the armrest, which gave her more trouble than she thought it should. Finally, the little button at the front popped out.

"So much for renting in a hurry," Richard said. "It's probably bent or something. We'll try WD-40 on it first, then if it still sticks, I'm calling the company to exchange the wheelchair. The last thing I need is something that's difficult for me to manage myself."

"The last thing you need is trying to do everything yourself," Carissa cautioned. "If you're looking to get Nurse Fields out of here any time soon, forget it."

"Killjoy."

"You'd better believe it."

"At least I know you care."

"Oh, Richard. Just get on the bed. Now's not the time to get into a discussion about our relationship."

"Then give me a time when it will be."

"We'll talk in two weeks."

"That's a long time off."

"Probably not long enough for me, but if giving you a deadline will get you out of this wheelchair any faster, then I've given you what you asked for."

"Fine."

He sighed heavily before sliding from the wheelchair to the bed with very little help from her, which eased her mind about his returning strength. After she helped him swing his legs onto the bed, Richard managed to grasp her around the shoulders and pull her into bed with him.

"That's better," he said.

He sounded out of breath. Carissa wondered if he was exhausted or excited, and wasn't sure which was preferable. "If you don't behave, I'm going to break something else," she warned. "You're too frail to be playing games like this."

"I'm stronger than I look." His lips were in her hair, on her face. "God, I feel alive for the first time since my accident."

"A little *too* alive for this stage of your recovery." She tried to pull away.

"Please don't—I only want to hold you close." He took her with him as he rolled onto his side, her back resting against the wall. "Will you stay, at least for a while? There's no reason for you to go back to the Cove, is there? Mai Ling won't be released until tomorrow morning at the earliest."

"I'll stay as long as you rest. If you don't behave I'll leave, and I won't come back until you're well."

"At which time, I'll be able to chase you. You're safer with me right now."

"That may be only too true." She settled her head onto the pillow beside his. "You've remembered more about the accident?"

"Some." His brow furrowed. "The weather had turned bad. I had the defroster on max and the wipers slapping at snow that kept coming faster and thicker. Ice started forming outside the windshield while it was fogging up inside. I played around, lowering the heat, cracking my window. But the ice on the windshield kept building. I thought about getting out and scraping, but I was worried about getting hit by another driver, and I figured I still had enough visibility to get home safely. I know the road so well, I could navigate it without the lights on my car, so I was sure I'd be okay." He stopped.

Carissa shifted onto one elbow and looked down at his troubled face. "What is it?"

"I'd passed the lighthouse. I wanted to call to check on you, but I didn't want to take my attention off the road for any reason. Talking to you would definitely have done that." He gave her a brief smile.

"I wish you'd come to the lighthouse instead of trying to get home," she said.

"Yeah, me too. Anyway, I remember right after that, I started to make the turn onto my usual short-cut, but I realized the snow was already too deep even for the Jeep to make it down that road. That decision may have saved my life, because I had to use the longer but wider and more traveled route with homes on both sides. I took it slower than usual, and I was going uphill, which must have masked the issue with my brakes.

"After I crested the hill, the Jeep started to pick up speed. I pumped the brakes. Nothing happened. I thought I was driving on a sheet of ice. I couldn't slow down, and I completely lost traction. Since I was heading for the snow bank at the side of the road, I thought I'd use it for resistance, but all that happened after impact was a huge arc of snow totally obscuring what little view I had through the windshield. Damn stupid, but I was beginning to panic even before that happened."

"I'd have panicked long before that, Richard," Carissa said. "Anyone would."

He grunted, sounding unconvinced. He probably felt his reputation as a legendary winter driver had been tarnished, she thought, like that mattered more than surviving a really bad wreck.

"At that point, my memory begins to fade in and out," Richard continued. "I stomped on my brakes like sheer willpower would force them to work. I was half-standing and trying to see through a windshield that was so packed with snow and ice...." He shook his head. "Hopeless. I called myself a few names I'd rather forget. I knew I was going to crash, and I hoped if I did it right then, the snow bank would hold and I'd just get stuck and really jarred up. Fat chance. The last thing I remember was trying to aim for a clump of smaller trees instead of the old-growth timber. Then something rushed up and everything went black." He closed his eyes.

"Oh, Richard." Carissa felt guilty for making him relive the horror of that accident, but she didn't want to take the chance that his mind would decide it was too much for him and throw a dark shadow over the event. "Your brake lines *must* have been cut."

"Maybe." He opened his eyes and stared at the ceiling. "I always prided myself with being the best driver in the Cove. Either I was too cock-sure, or someone wants me dead." He shook his head slowly side to side. "Who in the hell would do that? I know Steve Raymond wouldn't miss me, and probably Sally wouldn't, either, but why would they do anything to me this late in the game? Sally and I haven't been an item since Steve arrived."

"Could it be one of your clients? Did you do something that cost someone a lot of money?"

"No way. I know my business, and I can produce a list of references as long as you like."

He sounded genuinely offended, and very fatigued. He'd done more talking since she arrived than the entire time he'd been in the hospital.

"You need rest," she said. "I'll help Nurse Fields with the meal and wake you when it's ready."

"Don't let me sleep more than an hour. Otherwise I'll have a restless night."

"Okay. I promise."

"I'd like to have you promise a lot more."

"I know." She placed her fingers against his lips. "But not now. We're both too emotional."

His sigh barely warmed her fingers. "Okay. But I warn you; I'm going to bring this up again."

She tried to figure out the best way of getting out of the bed without bumping him too much and started wriggling toward the end of the bed.

"Don't do that. You're jostling my ribs. Give me a minute, then sit up and slide off."

"Oh, I'm so sorry." She stopped squirming and stayed where she was until his breathing became deeper, his chest rising and falling softly beneath her head.

That quickly, he'd fallen asleep. Carissa stayed where she was. She realized how nurtured and protected she felt, which was ridiculous, since Richard needed help getting anywhere or doing anything.

She decided she was beginning to lean on him altogether too much, and she had to change that as soon as he was well enough for her to leave town without worrying about him.

Nurse Fields' silhouette appeared in the doorway.

"He's asleep," Carissa whispered.

"Why didn't you call me? I could have helped you get him into bed."

"He did most of the work. I was only here to make sure he didn't lose his balance."

With a little help from Nurse Fields, Carissa managed to get off the bed without disturbing Richard. The nurse placed pillows under Richard's arms. Carissa pulled the covers over him. Her hand reached out of its own accord to smooth his hair from his forehead. Her heart contracted. He looked so helpless.

"He'll be fine," Nurse Fields said from behind her. "He's very tough."

"I know."

Carissa thought she was going to start crying, but that wouldn't help Richard. She wondered whether the same person who had tried to push her off the cliff was also responsible for tampering with Richard's brakes and pushing Dean Halstead to his death. But why?

They tiptoed out of the study and Nurse Fields closed the door. Who or what was the common denominator for everything? Carissa thought as she followed the nurse into the kitchen. Al Dyson and the shadowy developer for the lighthouse? Steve? Matthew? She shook her head. She couldn't see Matthew as a murderer. And why would Al Dyson pay Blake Ulster to do more than try to scare her out of the lighthouse?

"Would you like some coffee before I start lunch?" Nurse Fields asked.

Carissa broke away from the thoughts swirling around her head. *Accusations without merit,* she thought, plastering a smile on her face for the nurse's benefit. "Sounds really good. I'd like to help with lunch."

The brightness in the open-plan living areas cheered her. Even though Richard trusted his security system, she wondered whether it could be disabled as easily as his vehicle. She wouldn't discount anything at that point.

"Why don't you relax by the fire while I make the coffee?" Nurse Fields suggested.

Carissa looked at the leaping flames and the couch, full of soft cushions and comfort. "I will in a minute. I want to freshen up a little first."

"There's a bathroom right next to the study," Nurse Fields said.

"I don't want to risk waking Richard up by running water." Carissa grabbed her purse and made for the stairs. "I know my way around. I'll use one upstairs."

She closed Richard's bedroom door before calling Deputy Watkins on his cell and giving him an account of what Richard had told her.

"Don't worry, Carissa," he said. "Those Bangor detectives are checking everything. I expect they'll want to count the fillings in my teeth next." He chuckled.

"I don't see anything funny in all this." Carissa felt his flippancy was completely out of line.

"I know you're upset, but don't worry so much. You need to relax and let those of us in law enforcement do our jobs. You've been through a lot. Maybe you should get an appointment with Doc Kingston so he can prescribe something to calm you down. I can give you his number. He's been looking after all of us at the Cove for the past fifteen years."

Carissa felt like telling Watkins' what she thought about him giving her unsolicited advice, but she managed to control herself.

"I'm not over-reacting, Deputy Watkins. Richard's remembering more about his so-called accident. Right now he's taking a nap, but if you call in a couple of hours, he can verify everything I just told you." She heard muffled voices in the background before someone else started speaking.

"Ms. Yates...Carissa...this is Sheriff Crosby. I heard about your hysterics at the hospital."

Deputy Watkins might well believe some of her concerns, but by the tone of Sheriff Crosby's voice, it sounded like he definitely did not. Carissa made sure to inhale deeply before answering. The last thing she needed was to sound angry, defensive or 'hysterical' at that moment.

"The police in Bangor are investigating that incident at the hospital," she said, grateful to hear the calm quality of her voice. "I talked to Richard a few minutes ago. He said he had no brakes right before his accident."

"Richard had a bad concussion. He's confused. What possible motive would anyone have to kill him?"

"I don't know. Isn't that your job to find out?" Carissa cringed right after that thought flew out of her mouth. So much for keeping her temper and not being defensive.

Silence answered her. She knew Sheriff Crosby had entirely too much on his plate at that moment and probably didn't want to add to his load by giving her concerns any credence.

Tough. If he can't do the job, then let him resign.

She refused to stay silent while all those men ran rough-shod over her concerns. She'd stayed silent far too long during her marriage. That period of her life was over.

I am not hysterical, she told herself firmly. *I don't imagine things.*

"So tell me, Sheriff," she said in as controlled a tone as she could. "Even if you won't listen to me when I tell you someone's trying to kill Richard Ebberly." She ignored what sounded like a derisive snort. "If my aunt was riddled with arthritis to such an extent that she had stopped going out of her cottage, why did she put on street shoes and try to climb the lighthouse tower? The report says she had dirt on her shoes. Where would she have gotten that?"

Silence answered her. Carissa knew she had his interest.

"Her slippers were at the side of her bed when I arrived, where she must have left them to put on her shoes. Her purse has never turned up, neither have her keys. I'm pretty sure Al Dyson gave me a spare set. My aunt always had a rabbit's foot on her key ring.

"If she went out, did she leave the front door unlocked? And what happened to her coat? According to the report, she wasn't wearing one, and I haven't found a coat anywhere in her home. William told me she had the same old black alpaca she'd worn for years. She was also wearing what appeared to be her best dress and a fur hat held on firmly with three hat pins, which must have been to stop it blowing off outside. Explain that to me, Sheriff. I read the report of her death. There's a lot about it that needs investigating. I think she was murdered, and I want to know why. I want to know why you and Deputy Watkins haven't done anything about finding out what happened at the lighthouse before she fell."

After a palpable silence, he cleared his throat. "You're very thorough, Ms. Yates, and very convincing."

"Yes, and not hysterical, either. I can't have imagined any of those details, since they were in the report Deputy Watkins made." She slammed down the phone.

She paced, arms folded, up and down Richard's bedroom while she tried to calm down. What was the matter with all these people at the Cove? They seemed unwilling or incapable of seeing anything that wasn't right in their little world.

The phone rang. She picked it up.

"Ms. Yates."

"Sheriff."

"I'm sorry. I'm very tired and hungry, and in a bad mood. I shouldn't have taken my frustrations out on you. But there's so much happening at the Cove, and it all seems to have started with Jessica's death and your arrival."

Carissa felt slightly vindicated, but she didn't like the sound of 'and your arrival,' like he was placing the blame for all the mayhem at her door.

"I just spoke to the Bangor detective who was sent to help us with the investigation into Mr. Halstead's death, which looks very suspicious. A lot of people are asking questions, not only you. Some of them have made me very uncomfortable, and, I admit, defensive about my abilities as well as those in my small department."

"I'm sorry to hear that, but I'm very willing to talk to any of you about Aunt Jessica, the incidents that have happened to me since I arrived at the Cove, and what I saw in Richard's hospital room."

"Good, because the Bangor detective's on his way over there."

"Now?"

"Yes."

"Richard's sleeping. He's very weak, and he's got to eat lunch. His nurse is making us all something right now."

"Detective Giddings wants to interview *you*, Ms. Yates."

"Oh? About my aunt or the hospital, or both?"

"We're both very disturbed about some aspects of your relationship with Steve Raymond."

"You are?" She felt completely taken-aback. "Why?"

"We want to know why he would take it on himself to clean up your kitchen after the dead cat was found there. We also want to know how he could visit your home more than once without leaving any fingerprints."

"I can't answer those questions. Why don't you ask Steve?"

"We intend to do that, Ms. Yates. But we also need you to tell us everything you know."

"Of course. But surely you're not suspecting Steve of being the one to put the cat my sink?"

"Right now, we're looking at everyone, Ms. Yates."

Carissa didn't find that at all comforting.

CHAPTER FIFTY-FIVE

DETECTIVE GIDDINGS HUNG his coat on the rack beside Richard's front door. Tall and lanky, he looked like he needed a good meal. And a better tailor, Carissa thought, noticing too-short sleeves and sagging lapels. The detective had also chosen a weird shade of iridescent blue-black for his suit, giving it the appearance of a discarded fish-skin. His own coloring was dark and swarthy, his brown eyes small and accentuated by excessively long brows.

"This way," she said, leading the way into the living-room.

Detective Giddings openly surveyed his surroundings. "Very nice."

"Mr. Ebberly told me he inherited the home from his father. He did some updating, but the basic footprint stayed the same." Giddings' open appraisal annoyed Carissa—was he there to interview her or snoop?

Giddings nodded. "I heard he's a good architect."

With that, the detective continued roaming around, leaving Carissa standing beside the fireplace. He ambled past the large island separating the kitchen from the dining area, his fingers running across the backs of four bar stools. He stopped beside Nurse Fields, busily chopping tomatoes. She paused, knife in hand, and looked at him with raised eyebrows.

"Detective Giddings, Bangor Police Department," he told her. "I need to speak privately with Ms. Yates."

Nurse Fields gave him a look of open disgust. "Mr. Ebberly needs to eat."

"And the faster I conduct my interview, the faster that'll happen." Giddings locked gazes with her.

Carissa thought of a pissing match and wasn't sure who'd win. Nurse Fields was a forceful woman. Giddings didn't look like much of a cream puff, either. After a staring contest that lasted at least 30 seconds, Nurse Fields upended the chopping board over a large salad bowl and tipped the tomatoes in with the lettuce. She took her time securing plastic wrap over the bowl before sliding it into the refrigerator and turning down the heat under a large pot on the stove.

"I'll be watching over Mr. Ebberly," she told Carissa, ignoring the detective completely. Her starched white uniform rustled as she walked down the hallway. A door closed quietly.

Giddings lifted the lid off the pot and sniffed. "Beef stew. Very aromatic."

Carissa wondered whether he would have the gall to pick up the spoon resting on the counter and take a taste, but he replaced the lid and moved away.

"This looks like it used to be a farmhouse," he said, and then he stopped at the end of the counter, where a cordless phone sat charging. He started leafing through what looked like an organizer he found beside it.

"Apparently, the original house was smaller." Carissa snatched the book from him and jammed it into the nearest drawer. "It could have started out as a farmhouse. Please sit down in the living room, Detective. Would you like coffee or water?"

He smiled as he walked past her, pausing on the way to the fireplace to look through several pieces of mail on a side table. "Coffee would be good. Cream and sugar?"

Carissa wished she had herded him into one of the chairs beside the fireplace as soon as he had taken off his coat. She snatched up the mail and jammed it into the same drawer as the organizer. "Coffee; coming right up."

Nurse Fields had made a full pot. Carissa wanted the detective to drink up, ask his questions and leave, so she poured only enough to fill two small cups. After a short search through cupboards filled with sparkling glassware and tasteful white dinnerware she found a small pitcher, half-filled it with milk and tipped sugar into a bowl. She put everything onto a tray and brought it to the coffee table. Determined not to let Detective Giddings get too comfortable, she turned the heat up on the gas fireplace and felt an instant blast of warmth.

Giddings had taken a seat on one side of the fireplace. Carissa gave him a cup of coffee before perching on the edge of a leather chair facing him. He picked up the milk jug and offered it to her. She shook her head. He poured a generous serving to his cup and offered her the sugar. She shook her head again. He added two heaping spoonfuls to his own cup and sat back, stirring slowly while his eyes darted between her and various points of the room.

Carissa watched as his gaze came to rest on a closed door at the far end, which she now knew went into the study. Any minute now, she thought, Giddings would ask to see what was behind it. She wondered if she could tell him he needed a search warrant and send him packing. She already disliked him with his nosy behavior, his open snooping.

"Please try to relax, Ms. Yates," Giddings said. "I'm not here to interrogate you."

"Well, isn't that a relief?" It came out with a sarcastic bite she didn't regret, although she knew it would raise her open-hostility level from thinly-veiled to visible.

Giddings' eyes flickered momentarily but he sat silently drinking coffee until she leaned back and took a sip from her own cup.

"So you think someone tampered with Mr. Ebberly's brakes," he said.

"Yes."

"I reviewed your report about the alleged attack in the hospital."

Carissa wanted to dispute the 'alleged' comment, but decided the detective might be purposely trying to bait her, perhaps to see if he could trigger the hysterics Sheriff Crosby had accused her of having.

"He left the hospital against medical advice," Giddings said. "Did you know that?"

"Not until he called to tell me he was home."

"Do you have any facts to back up your accusations?"

"They're not accusations, they're facts. I'm not given to making things up, and I don't get hysterical. Far from it." She thought of the jousting bouts with Matthew and his attorneys.

"We're having the Jeep thoroughly checked for mechanical flaws, including the brakes."

"I heard that."

"I'll need to speak with Mr. Ebberly. See if he has any additional information or insight."

"He may not remember much about what happened in the hospital. He was pretty doped up at the time. He's beginning to remember more about what went on before the accident, though. He told me..."

Giddings held up his hand. "I want to hear the details from Mr. Ebberly. I spoke with Dr. Lister, the ward clerk and all the nursing staff on duty that evening. No one saw or heard anything except you screaming about someone trying to suffocate Mr. Ebberly with a pillow. They thought you'd had a nightmare."

Carissa felt betrayed. "How could they say that? What reason would I have for trying to suffocate Richard? I was so worried about him, I slept on a pull-out in his room."

"They never suggested you tried to harm him. They thought you might have dreamed he was having trouble breathing and you were trying to readjust his pillow."

"That's stupid."

"Not as stupid as the incidents Deputy Watkins reported you telling him about: paint cans moving in and out of the garage; the back door opening by itself in the middle of the night; your sewing being burned in the fireplace."

Carissa couldn't stay silent. "What about me nearly being pushed off a cliff? What about Dean Halstead falling to his death at Penwithen? What about Richard's accident, and how he now remembers he had no brakes?" She stopped to take a breath. Giddings didn't interrupt, which caused her to plunge on. "Then there was the mutilated cat and Blake Ulster. He confessed, right in front of his wife, that he'd been trying to scare me out of the lighthouse."

Giddings didn't respond. His gaze stayed fixed on the contents of his coffee cup.

"Well?" Carissa asked. "What do you have to say about all that?"

"Those are certainly troubling incidents." He sounded like he was choosing his words very carefully. "Mr. Ulster could have been taunting you, not confessing. According to your own report as well as Mrs. Ulster's, he seems to have been a very volatile man."

"Volatile's an understatement," Carissa said. "But I think he was too angry to waste time taunting me. He *knew* about the incidents. I never said anything about them to him or Mai Ling. He must have had keys. Either my aunt gave Blake a key at some point or Al Dyson made a copy somehow. Al met me with keys when I first arrived. I think they were copies, because my aunt always had her lucky rabbit's foot attached to her key ring."

"Even if Dyson had paid Ulster to scare you away, or Ulster had decided to scare you, how was he able to continue the pranks after you got all the locks changed?" Giddings was frowning.

"I don't know."

She wondered who or what was still monkeying with the new thermostat at the cottage and making those strange noises in the basement. Someone flesh and bone; or did Aunt Jessica want her niece out of the keeper's quarters? A chill came over Carissa, and she turned the heat up again.

"Your ex-husband is spending winter at the Cove," Giddings said. He unfastened all three buttons on his jacket.

"Matthew's a constant thorn in my side," Carissa said. "We're in a contentious court case over my designs right now, and he wants me to give up all rights. I won't do it."

Giddings started writing in a notebook he had placed on the table. "I heard about that case." He paused and looked at her. "I read the scandal rags while I'm in line at the grocery store, just like everybody else. I also spoke with Mr. Yates, who seems a bit slippery, but don't quote me on that."

"He's more than a *bit* slippery," Carissa said. "I wish he would go away and leave me alone. He thinks he can get me to reconcile with him and go back to New York."

The detective grunted. "Talking to you, I'd say he has a very slim chance of succeeding. Did you know Dean Halstead was a private investigator your ex-husband hired to dig up dirt on you here at the Cove?"

"*What?*"

"I confronted Mr. Yates about after I spoke with Halstead's partner in New York. Your ex-husband admitted he'd hired Halstead to get information about your relationships with Steve Raymond and Richard Ebberly."

"Ooh, that bastard. I want to..." She stopped, reminding herself she was with a detective. "I'd like to give him a piece of my mind," she finished. It sounded really lame, but telling Giddings she wanted to kill Matthew by whatever means she had access to wouldn't benefit her.

"I'm sure you do." Giddings' eyes were a disconcerting shade of brownish-black in the flickering light cast by the fire.

"I want to know if you believe I was involved in Mr. Halstead's death," Carissa said.

"Not at this point. However, it seems unlikely that a man with Halstead's background—he was apparently an exceptionally good private investigator—would chance walking down a steep set of stairs on a cliff-side using an unstable rail for support during gale-force winds. He'd already been warned about those steps, too, when he was at The Fisherman's Rest."

"You think he was murdered," Carissa said.

"I think it's highly likely." Giddings looked toward the kitchen. "Is there any more of this coffee? It really hit the spot."

Carissa relented and brought in the pot. While they both drank two more cups, Giddings asked more questions. Had she ever seen or heard of Halstead in New York? Did she remember Matthew mentioning the man during their marriage? Did she ever see any paperwork or business cards from Willis and Halstead? She shook her head to everything.

"How well do you know Steve Raymond?" Giddings asked.

"Not all that well, but I think of him as a friend. I'm sure Matthew knows a lot more if he hired Mr. Halstead to investigate Steve and Richard."

Giddings gave another half-smile. "Probably. But Mr. Yates consulted a local attorney and is being very uncooperative. Fortunately for law-enforcement, Mr. Halstead kept very good records and submitted them promptly and regularly not only to Mr. Yates, but to Mr. Willis. We'll get them, but it'll take time. Would *you* be able to convince Mr. Yates to speak with us?"

"Me? I'd be the last one." She felt like laughing.

"I think the sheriff's giving you less credit than you deserve. Deputy Watkins has had far more interaction with you. He doesn't think you're hysterical or that you're an unreliable witness. He said if you can handle living at the Bennett Point Light and being married to Matthew Yates, you can handle a lot."

Carissa felt less defensive and more charitable toward Ray Watkins, but what was Giddings really expecting her to tell him about Steve or Richard that he couldn't find out from anyone else in the village, including Ray or Sheriff Crosby? Only Sally's abortion, she thought, and Richard supposedly acting very badly.

"All I can tell you about Steve Raymond is he's warm, caring and understanding," she said. "He doesn't make a lot of demands. He's a bit over-protective sometimes, and too controlling for my taste. I already had that in my marriage. I'll never go down that path again."

She stopped and mentally backed up. *I'm not here to talk about my issues with Matthew.*

"Go on." Giddings leaned forward.

Carissa found she'd jammed her hands under her thighs. She drew them out, pulled a knitted throw from the arm of the chair and wrapped it around herself. "For instance, when Steve couldn't reach me by phone, he walked all the way out to the lighthouse to check on me in the middle of a really bad snowstorm," she said.

"And then he broke in."

"He said the window was already broken. I didn't notice that while I was there with Richard. I was too busy looking at that awful mess in the sink." She shuddered.

"You don't need to elaborate," Giddings told her. "Just give me the facts."

"Just the facts, Ma'am." She couldn't even manage a smile, her mind choked with images of the carnage in her kitchen. "I wouldn't have expected any less of Steve. He thought I might be lying injured some- where inside the cottage."

"But he didn't stop to notice what he was climbing over when he crawled through your window?"

"I only left one light on in the living room before Richard took me out of there. It was probably too dark for Steve to see anything at all in the kitchen."

"That wasn't a cat in your sink, by the way," Giddings told her. "It was a possum. Road kill probably."

"What?" Carissa didn't believe him. "But I saw orange fur, and a possum tail, isn't it well, hairless?"

"A taxidermist in Whitstead reported a break-in two weeks ago. He was robbed of an orange tabby cat displayed in his window."

"*What?*"

Carissa didn't know whether to laugh, cry or scream. She grabbed a handful of tissues from a box on the coffee table and shoved them against her mouth.

"No animals were killed in your kitchen, Ms. Yates. The blood all over the walls and floor? Fake. Halloween variety. The guts? Chicken. As for the tag on the collar, it would be easy to get one made up at the pet store in Whitstead. They've got a machine."

Carissa leaned back in the chair, her mind reeling. "I...I don't understand. I'm so relieved those weren't Hubert's remains, but he's still missing, and who would go to such elaborate lengths?"

"The possum had been kept in a freezer, probably for some time, since it had evidence of freezer burn. Someone planned this. It wasn't done spur of the moment."

"But how did you...? What made you...?"

"The so-called pranks you've been experiencing led us to believe that although they've escalated the longer you've remained at the Bennett Point Light, none of them involved actual bodily harm."

"But the destruction of my sewing, that was malicious..."

"I agree, but you've never been physically harmed. Whoever is doing this wants you to leave the lighthouse. We're investigating Al Dyson's part in all this and hoping to extract a confession."

"What about me being pushed? That was an attempt at actual physical harm."

"You weren't pushed over the cliff. We believe that was Blake Ulster.

He'd lived next to the lighthouse his entire life, so he'd have easily been able to find you and then go home without you seeing him because of the fog. We're not going to look any further for bogeymen coming out of the woodwork. That part of the investigation has been closed by Sheriff Crosby. You can go back to the lighthouse and stop worrying about anything else happening there."

Carissa wanted to disagree, but common sense told her to replace the faulty thermostat and get an exterminator to check for rodents in the basement before insisting something more sinister was lurking in the keeper's quarters.

"No prints were found in the kitchen," Giddings said. "Steve Raymond told us he used gloves to clean up. He did a really thorough job. More than thorough. There were very few prints anywhere. I suspect what we did find are yours, but I want you fingerprinted to verify that. I'd also like to get Mr. Ebberly's prints since you said he was with you when you both found the...ah...supposed cat."

"Richard and Steve have both been in every room. Richard did a walk-through while we were discussing renovations to the cottage. Steve stayed overnight in the guest room one time when the weather got really bad."

"Overnight?" Giddings' eyebrows drew toward each other.

"Nothing happened between us. I told you, he's a friend." She felt really resentful.

"Noted." Giddings poured his 4th cup of coffee, adding cream and sugar. "I've heard there was rivalry between Ebberly and Raymond even before you arrived."

There it was. The elephant in the room. Carissa's attempt to regain her composure flew up the chimney.

She shrugged, hoping it didn't look as forced as it felt. "They both dated Sally Mainard in the past." She tried to keep still, but found herself fidgeting. "Steve doesn't like Richard because of something that happened between him and Sally."

Carissa decided turning up the heat in the fireplace had been a very, very bad idea. Instead of sending the detective away faster, she was the one beginning to sweat and wish she was outside in the snow. She lowered the heat.

"You're talking about Sally Mainard's purported pregnancy," Giddings said. "Nancy Burton told me about that."

"Nancy's one of the village's primary gossipmongers." Animosity toward Nancy surged. Carissa tried to tamp it down before returning to her seat. "Why did you say 'purported?'"

He stopped jotting in his notebook. "We only have Ms. Mainard's word, with back-up from the gossip-network. It'll be very difficult for us to verify her pregnancy unless she allows us to access her medical records, which she hasn't."

"Why are you interested in that procedure, anyway?"

"We're working all background details, and we deemed this relevant, given the reported animosity between Raymond and Ebberly." He tapped his pen against the notebook. "I'm going to ask you, Ms. Yates: Were you or are you having an affair with either or both of these men?"

Carissa's cheeks flamed. "We're friends, nothing more." She wanted to cross her fingers.

"I see," Giddings said, looking like he didn't believe her. "Do you have any idea why Steve Raymond took it upon himself to clean up your kitchen? He told Watkins he didn't want you seeing the mess, and he was in a hurry. He was definitely wearing rubber gloves, and he's refused to allow us to fingerprint him."

Alarm bells went off in her head. She had thought Steve had done an amazing clean-up of the kitchen. Now it appeared he had also wiped down the rest of the cottage. Why would he do that, unless he wanted to try to erase any evidence of his visits, or someone else's?

"He told me the same thing, about not wanting me to go home to that mess. He even had his waitress, Hilly, and her mother drive over to houseclean and change the sheets on my bed."

"Why does he walk everywhere? He doesn't have a driver's license."

"You'll have to ask him. I know it's unusual for a man not to drive, but what business is it of mine?"

"Watkins said while he was taking additional photos, gathering evidence and talking to the Humane Society, Raymond left him and went into the back of the cottage. Did you or Mr. Ebberly go back there for any reason the evening you found the animal in your sink?"

"We both did. Richard made me pack an overnight bag before he brought me here. Steve told me he'd looked in my bedroom and thought it had been ransacked. Until he talked to me, he thought there'd been a burglary, and I might have been abducted."

"I believe while he was there with Watkins, he went around trying to wipe his prints off everything. When he was unsuccessful, he came back with his staff member and her mother so he could finish the job."

CHAPTER FIFTY-SIX

"HI," Richard said from the other side of the room. "I'm Richard Ebberly."

Carissa felt overwhelming relief. She wouldn't have to answer any more questions without someone to back her up. Nurse Fields pushed Richard's wheelchair over to where Detective Giddings sat. She gave Giddings a sweet smile. *The smile on the face of the tiger,* Carissa thought, gratefully.

"I'd shake hands, Detective, but as you can see, that'd be difficult." Richard held up both arms.

"That was quite an accident," Giddings said. "You could easily have been killed."

Nurse Fields left Richard's wheelchair in front of the coffee table, applied the brakes and brought him a large plastic container with a long straw, which she placed into a cup holder hanging off the armrest.

"You need to finish all that water before dinner," she told him before going toward the stairs. "I'll be in my room if you need me."

Detective Giddings ignored the glower Nurse Fields gave him and turned to Richard. "Ms. Yates believes your brakes were tampered with."

"Yes." Richard told Giddings the same story he had given Carissa. "My memory's coming back," he said. "That was no accident."

Giddings flipped his notepad back a few pages and tapped it with his pen. "There was a lot of black ice that night."

"My Jeep has four wheel drive. I wasn't speeding, and I'm a very good driver. Ask anyone around here."

"I did. They all agree with you. Let me ask you another question, Mr. Ebberly: Do you really believe someone attempted to smother you with a pillow while you were in the hospital? Do you remember that incident more clearly now as well, after discussing it at length with Ms. Yates?"

Richard glanced sharply at Carissa. "Are you suggesting she coached me? I might have been knocked unconscious, but I don't have brain damage. Everything was hazy for a while, but after I started talking about the accident, I remembered pumping my brakes without any results. That's when it became clear to me that something had happened to them. As for the hospital incident as you call it, when I woke up, Carissa was shouting and I had a pillow over my face. When I tried to push it off, I felt someone's arm. Whoever was pushing that pillow down was on the side of the bed closest to the door, not on the window side, where Carissa was. I tried to grab the arm. My hand went almost all the way around a wrist, but I couldn't hold on. It was too painful."

"Did you feel any jewelry—a bracelet, a wristwatch?"

"No."

"How about hair on the arm? Or was that person wearing long sleeves?"

Richard's brow furrowed. "I think there was a sleeve. Maybe a coat sleeve."

"Perhaps you're mistaken, and it was a uniform sleeve; a hospital employee trying to rearrange your pillow. Ms. Yates shouting probably frightened that person away."

"Why would a nurse or a nursing assistant run off?" Richard asked. "And why was the room dark? Night staff always turned on a light when they came in. It's a real sleep-buster, but you know who's there."

"Maybe they didn't want to disturb either of you. But the pillow may have been something they didn't want to leave too close to your face. They must have known it was against hospital policy to leave the light off, so whoever it was left quickly before getting caught and reprimanded."

"That's possible," Carissa conceded. "Were there any new employees on shift at the time?"

"No, and we've interviewed everyone, right down to the janitor. They all deny going into Mr. Ebberly's room except the staff assigned to him. Both those employees reported doing their regular checks and said everything was in order both times. They had documented in his chart. Both said they turned on lights but neither of you awakened. Dr. Lister told me he had prescribed a sleeping aid for you, Ms. Yates."

Carissa refused to back down. "I didn't take it. I *know* what I saw."

"Did you see that person leave the room, Ms. Yates? Anything that would give us some idea of height and build?"

"No. I only got an impression of a figure bending over Richard's bed. Then running footsteps. Pretty loud ones."

"Hospital employees all wear rubber soles, like the private duty nurse you have, Mr. Ebberly." Giddings wrote more in his notebook. "I doubt you'd say they had loud footsteps."

"That's true." Carissa felt her vague description gain a little traction.

"Why didn't you take the sleeping pill?" Giddings asked.

"I was afraid I wouldn't hear Richard if he needed something. I knew the nurses were checking on him regularly, but that wasn't enough for me."

"You're a bit of a control freak," Giddings said, a twitch at one corner of his mouth.

"I am. Working in the fashion industry made me that way."

Giddings turned to Richard. "Is there anyone other than Steve Raymond who might wish you harm? I heard about the reason for the bad blood between you."

Richard looked at Carissa, who shook her head.

"Who did you hear that from?" He asked Giddings. "Steve Raymond?"

"A number of people."

"The rumor-mill," Carissa said. "Nancy Burton, for one."

Giddings shot her a warning look. She closed her mouth, but she wondered whether his investigation was beginning to center on Steve rather than Matthew's meddling or Blake Ulster carrying out scare tactics for Al Dyson.

"I don't have any professional rivals," Richard said. "As for Sally Mainard's abortion, that's old news. For me, it's water under the bridge, but Steve still thinks I'm pond scum. We don't talk. End of story."

"Let's talk about something else," Giddings said. "I spoke at length with Mai Ling Ulster. If she's telling the truth, Blake was out of town when the animal was left in your sink. We're checking to see where he went and who he met. We suspect that as well as being paid by Al Dyson to scare you out of the lighthouse, Ms. Yates, he was involved in one of those fringe groups attempting to change some of the local land development laws to suit themselves."

"To allow rezoning of his property and the lighthouse?" Richard asked.

"Yes. There's a lot of money involved. It's a big case that would take a lot of time to explain."

"Not to me. I'm pretty familiar with what that conglomerate's been trying to do. I'm one of the naysayers. It'd make changes to the Cove the villagers might very well regret in the long-run."

Carissa thought about all the people she had met and how tourism and an influx of seasonal workers could impact the tranquility of life at Treacher's Cove. But it would also bring new jobs to keep the younger population at home. Those who weren't interested in the fishing industry had little else in the way of job prospects.

"So if I could be scared into selling the lighthouse, Blake Ulster would have benefitted, too," she said. "His property has more useable land-space for developing a resort."

Giddings nodded. "The Cove would become a major tourist destination with all the pros and cons."

"I wouldn't be one to vote for that," Richard said. "I made my own views known at the last town meeting. People thought I was trying to manipulate the local real estate market for my own good. No such thing. I've got plenty of work with the project I'm working on now. After that's completed, I may be working on something out of state. I've had a couple of really lucrative offers."

"You're not a suspect, Mr. Ebberly," Giddings told him.

"I would hope not." Richard licked his lips. "I know Nurse Ratched left me water, but how about a glass of juice, Carissa?"

"Sure." She got up. "Is this going to take much longer, Detective? Richard mustn't take his pills on an empty stomach." She stopped beside Richard's wheelchair and put her hand on his forehead. He felt slightly clammy.

"I'm okay." He gave her a half-smile. "Just thirsty."

"A few more minutes," Giddings said. "How about giving Mr. Ebberly a snack?"

Carissa knew they weren't going to get the detective out of the house until he decided he was ready to leave. She sighed heavily to add weight to her disapproval before going into the kitchen and opening the refrigerator, where she took out cheese sticks, and the pantry, which yielded crackers and a large jar of peanut butter. As she made up a small plate for Richard and poured juice, she heard the detective giving details about Blake Ulster's background.

"He marketed small machine parts," Giddings said. "It's a family business, with Blake taking care of Maine and Massachusetts. His two brothers service the rest of New England. They're headquartered in Bangor. His father's in his late-seventies and still at the helm. I got the impression they're all pretty forceful in personality and ruthless with any competition."

Carissa brought in Richard's juice and snack. "I bet they are, if they're anything like Blake." She could well imagine what sort of household Blake Ulster had grown up in.

"Mrs. Ulster said her husband was jealous of her friendship with you."

"He should have been more afraid of me reporting him for abusing her. Mai Ling had bruises. I was going to try to get her to leave him, but she was so terrified of him, I don't know if I'd have been successful."

"He'd already had trouble with your aunt, Mrs. Ulster said. Jessica Malloy went over there at least once and told him she was going to call the cops if he touched his wife again."

"My aunt saw bruises or heard him yelling at Mai Ling?"

"Mrs. Ulster said your aunt went over to ask Blake to do a small repair job for her. The Ulsters were in the middle of one of their frequent exchanges, which apparently consisted of Blake accusing Mrs. Ulster of being a bad wife, poor housekeeper, bad cook or whatever. Ms. Malone heard him hit his wife. She intervened."

"My aunt was awesome." Carissa smiled. "But I think it got her into real trouble. I don't believe that fatal fall was an accident."

"Deputy Watkins told me about you going off at the sheriff." Giddings again looked like he was about to crack a smile, but didn't. "You sure know how to stir things up, don't you?"

"I told the sheriff his report had inconsistencies, and then I told him what those were. My aunt couldn't have climbed those stairs..."

Giddings put up his hand. "Let's leave that for now. I've been called in to investigate Dean Halstead's death and get some answers as to why Mrs. Ulster killed her husband. Whether it'll end up as a case of self-defense or she orchestrated it to look that way by involving you, is what I'm here to determine."

"I see," Carissa said, for want of a better comment.

She wondered why anyone would think Mai Ling was capable of such deviousness, but was anyone at the Cove who they projected themselves to be? Maybe Mai Ling was actually a conniving murderess instead of a cowering victim. And if Steve Raymond had taken the time and trouble to wipe down every surface in her house, he had to be hiding something. Could she really safely return to the keeper's quarters?

"I'm getting really tired and hungry," Richard said.

Carissa looked at him. He was slumped down in his wheelchair.

"A couple more questions, and then I'm done for now." Giddings had come to his feet along with Carissa. "Ms. Yates, are you romantically involved with anyone locally?"

So he wasn't going to accept that 'friends only' off-handed explanation she'd given him earlier. "I wouldn't class my relationship with either Richard or Steve as romantic," she said, hoping that would satisfy him.

"Have you had intimate relations with either of them?"

Carissa blinked, almost dumbfounded. "What business is that of yours?"

"Detective Giddings..." Richard started.

"I didn't ask you; I asked her." Giddings' voice was as sharp as his expression.

"My private life is that," Carissa warned.

"Is this really necessary?" Richard asked in a quiet voice.

"If it wasn't, I wouldn't be asking."

Giddings folded his arms across his chest and gave Carissa an uncomfortable stare. Until that moment, she'd thought her confrontations with Matthew had been the worst moments of her life.

"Richard and I have been intimate." She avoided looking at either of the men. "I only kissed Steve Raymond." Despite her desire not to make eye contact with Richard, she couldn't avoid it.

He stared right back, his face ashen.

"When did you kiss Steve Raymond?" Giddings asked.

"A couple of days ago."

"Did Mr. Raymond know you had been intimate with Mr. Ebberly?"

"Yes." A flush worked its way up her neck to her face.

"And what was his reaction at the time?"

"He was...upset."

"How upset?"

"Very." She clamped her mouth shut. Giddings was forcing her to paint Steve into a corner.

"Do you think he was the one who tampered with Mr. Ebberly's brakes?" Giddings asked.

"No. Well...I...I don't know." Carissa felt she was stumbling all over herself. "You're asking my opinion. That's unfair."

The detective turned to Richard. "I understand he hadn't spoken to you at any length from the day he found out about Ms. Mainard's abortion until a couple of days before your accident. Is that true?"

"You could say that, I guess." Richard shrugged. "We've exchanged a few words over the last couple of years if we happened to end up in the same place, like Everett's Market. It's hard to avoid people when you live in a small village."

Giddings nodded.

"I don't think Steve would wait two years to kill me, do you?"

"He might have more reason now, knowing about your relationship with Ms. Yates, who he seems to want for himself."

Carissa knew why people cracked during interrogations. That interview had taken a really nasty turn. "I'm not a commodity to be fought over," she snapped.

"Men have murdered for a lot less," Giddings said.

CHAPTER FIFTY-SEVEN

RAY WATKINS MADE sure Dot was on break and the station house empty before sliding open his top desk drawer and taking out a manila envelope. He opened the report and read it for the 4th time, but it didn't read any differently than it had the 1st time he read it. Ray sighed heavily. Unless there was a glitch in the IAFIS system, there was a real problem, and he was going to have to make a decision over what to do about it.

The fingerprints from the lid of the pizza box had come back. One set identified as belonging to Richard Ebberly, the other set with a match in the IAFIS system. The full name for the owner of those prints was Steven Raymond Tanner, and he was wanted in New Jersey for the manslaughter of his business partner. Watkins had quickly printed a copy of the information and deleted it before researching Steve's case thoroughly and discretely at the library. Epergine Willsley, the librarian had no objections to him getting some reading done while the library was closed at lunchtime. She turned off most of the lights on her way out, leaving one over the centrally-located reading table.

The only public computer terminal at Treacher's Cove hummed on, unaffected by the power-saving measures. Ray quickly selected the three books he had decided to use for his cover: "Breathing New Life into Your Already-Satisfying Marriage," "Exotic Plants for Indoor Gardening," and

"Exciting New England Destinations for A Summer Vacation." That should give Epergine enough material for her next gossip-cum-coffee-klatch, Ray thought, opening all three on the table before turning to his research at the computer. He pecked around on a couple of flower-delivery and hotel-finding sites before honing in on his actual quest, which was to find out everything he could about Steven Raymond Tanner.

Ray scanned the details, finding out about Steve's argument with his partner, and the partner's death. He found out Steve was a fugitive. All attempts to locate him had failed.

Until now, Ray thought, leaning back in the uncomfortable chair. He looked at the grainy photo of a slightly younger and thinner Steve Raymond before returning to another search, this time for 20th anniversary gifts—Bahama cruises and suggestions for hotels and activities for a long weekend in Boston. He really did need to give his wife, Hilda a reward for putting up with him for 20 years, he thought as he surfed what looked to him like total-waste-of-time packages to see ballet or opera performances while spending exorbitant amounts of money on food and accommodations. She would like those. He would find them excruciatingly boring.

Then he thought of New York. He could get input from Carissa. As both a woman and a New Yorker, she'd have better suggestions for what Hilda would like to do and see. He'd treat his wife to a long weekend in The Big Apple. It would be expensive, but if they took the train from Bangor instead of flying and they didn't stay right in the city center, maybe he could afford it.

The lights flickered back on. He realized he had been in the library for an hour, and he'd left both his phone and his radio at the station. Hilda would be wondering why he hadn't gone home for lunch as usual. He knew she'd planned to make cottage pie, one of his favorites.

"Did you get what you needed, Deputy?" Epergine asked as she took off her coat.

"I did." He stood up and gave her a good view of the travel site before closing it. "I want to surprise Hilda for our anniversary next year."

"How nice!" Epergine took off her hat. "Where are you thinking about?"

"Ah, if I said, then it wouldn't be a surprise, would it?"

Ray walked past her as he shot that little rebuke. Epergine paused in the middle of putting her purse away in one of the cupboards behind the desk. She blinked. He smiled, put on his hat and strolled unhurriedly out of the library, but once he was on the sidewalk, he picked up his pace. He pulled down the brim of his hat and avoided making eye contact with the people he passed. He had made one decision during that period of quiet reflection, but not about any weekend get-aways.

He wasn't going to mention the IAFIS report to the Bangor detectives. If he let things ride, maybe quiet would return to the Cove again. The squabbling Yates couple might mend their differences and go back to New York. Detective Giddings and his disturbingly quiet associate, Detective Johannsen might also leave, returning to Bangor and more interesting cases to pursue after they decided Dean Halstead had made a bad decision at the top of those stairs and fallen as a consequence.

Yes, and pigs might fly over the Cove at any minute, Ray told himself. He had already wondered whether Jessica Malloy's death was an accident, and now Treacher's Cove had two more bodies with the coroner.

He glanced up at the leaden skies. No self-respecting pigs would fly under those circumstances, he told himself, even if the weather held for the rest of the winter.

CHAPTER FIFTY-EIGHT

DESPITE RICHARD'S protests and her own misgivings, Carissa left for the lighthouse soon after Detective Giddings drove away. She called Steve right after she took off her coat and turned the thermostat at the cottage back up from its habitual 55 degrees.

"I'm calling to warn you that the lead detective from Bangor is very interested in you," she told him.

"I heard." He sounded angry. "Where are you?"

"Home."

"That damned lighthouse?"

"Yes."

"You think that's wise, under the circumstances?"

"What circumstances? Another death here? At least this time I know who and why."

"You're becoming obsessed with that place, like your aunt."

"I am not."

Silence ticked on for what seemed a long time, but Carissa refused to break it.

She thought about Penwithen while she waited for Steve to make the next move. After Richard got stronger she'd take him over there so he could give her an honest opinion about whether the house could be saved. If not, then she'd have it demolished. Richard could design and build her a new home on the property. Something with big windows overlooking the water and a craft room with a southern exposure, where she'd have more light to work in. She could develop her own designs instead of using Aunt Jessica's and have a workshop added later so Cove residents would have a better place to work than a large resort that would ruin the Cove's tranquility. She could still make the Cove her home, but not the keeper's quarters at the lighthouse. She was beginning to think Aunt Jessica didn't want her there. All the problems she'd had couldn't be explained by Blake Ulster sneaking around the basement, opening doors and turning down the thermostat.

"I didn't have anything to do with Dean Halstead's death," Steve said in her ear.

Carissa jerked back to reality. "I never thought you did. But that detective asked a lot of questions about where you were and what you were doing. I felt like he was making you into his prime suspect. He believes unidentified fingerprints they found in my house may be yours. I told him if they were, it was because you'd cleaned up the kitchen mess and stayed overnight one time when the weather was bad."

There was another silence. "I wore gloves when I was cleaning up," Steve said. "I wiped down everything, because I was worried I had left blood behind after I came through the window and touched the sink. Damn...I wonder if I messed up when I first went into your bedroom."

"Well, you obviously didn't get *all* your prints off, unless the other ones are from one of Chuck's workers when they installed the vents and ductwork for my new heating system. What were you doing touching things in my bedroom, anyway? You can get into the bathroom from the hallway."

"Your bedroom was a wreck. I checked for more dead animals and tidied up at the same time."

"Putting your hands all over everything."

He sighed heavily. "I really screwed up. I like my privacy, and I don't want anyone invading it. You should know how that feels, to have people poking around where you don't want them to be."

"I do, but I'm caught up on the fringes of that celebrity garbage because of Matthew's business. And I didn't make that much mess in my bedroom," Carissa said. "You were prying. You knew Richard was with me when I packed the overnight bag. You were looking to see what I might have taken and if he'd left anything, like what, clothing?"

"I didn't mean to pry. It just happened when I got in there."

"I wish I could believe that. I really do."

No answer.

"What are you hiding?" She asked. "Why are you so worried about leaving your fingerprints?"

"I've got to go," he said. "More customers came in, and I'm the bartender tonight."

"You'd better make sure you have your ducks in a row when that detective interviews you. He's pretty intimidating."

"I will. Thanks, Carissa." Steve hung up before she even had a chance to say goodbye.

So much for trying to help Steve Raymond. Either she wasn't very good at it, or he hiding something really big in his past. *He'd arrived two years ago in the Cove and set up his business with what? Cash?*

A tiny sound startled her. It sounded like something scraping on the back door. Carissa's heart shot into high gear, thudding in her ears like primitive jungle drums. Grabbing the poker, she tiptoed through the living room into the kitchen. The mudroom door stood open. She wondered whether the police had left it like that or someone else had been inside her home. The door was an analogy for what she felt about the lighthouse: one big swinging, open door for anyone who wanted to come inside.

Then she heard the noise again, but much closer and clearer. Mewing and scraping on the outer door.

Her heart skipped a beat, making her lightheaded.

Dear God, the ghost of Hubert wants inside.

She lost her grip on the poker, which clattered onto the floor.

Maybe Blake Ulster isn't the only one trying to scare me, or Al Dyson has already replaced him. She picked up the poker.

Cowering in the kitchen isn't going to solve anything.

She slid back the bolts, unlatched the deadbolt and pulled the door open.

A gust of wind hit her full in the face. With a tiny meow, an emaciated grey and black striped cat slinked over the doorstep and wiped itself across her legs before gliding into the kitchen.

Carissa closed and locked the door before leaned back against it while her heart rate slowed. The cat took a tour of the kitchen before basking in front of hot air blasting through the heating vent. It blinked at her and meowed.

"You scared the living daylights out of me," she said, unsure whether to laugh or cry. "I thought you were fat Hubert's ghost." When she walked over, the cat looked up at her and meowed again.

Carissa bent to pet him. Purring, he raised his back against her palm. Beneath his fur, she felt every bone in his back.

"You haven't had much to eat in quite a while," she told him as she took an old chipped saucer from a cupboard and opened one of Aunt Jessica's stockpiled cans of sardines.

The cat looked up and meowed again, piteously that time. Carissa found herself smiling; something impossible only minutes before.

"All right, already," she told the cat, now weaving between her legs. "I don't have cat food, but I bet these will be a really good substitute."

She placed the dish on the floor and watched the cat take great gulps of sardine, barely pausing to chew before swallowing.

"You're one starving little animal. I wonder where you came from? Aunt Jessica doesn't have any cat food or cat dishes in here, so I doubt you're hers. I can't see the Ulsters having a cat. I could use some company. Tomorrow I'll buy a litter box and see if we can make an indoor cat out of you. It's too cold for you to be prowling around in the snow. If we get along, then I'll have to get a carrier and take you to the vet for shots. That's if we don't find your owner. Nancy Burton's got a bulletin board in her shop. I'll call her in the morning and see if she's got a posting for a missing cat that isn't Hubert."

Carissa placed a dish of water next to the saucer and the cat lapped greedily before sashaying into the living room and jumping onto the couch.

"*Do* make yourself at home. I suppose you'll want me to start a fire for you, too."

The cat energetically kneaded an afghan before settling down on top of it.

"Well, I know where you're sleeping. I may very well join you. I'd enjoy some company."

Carissa pushed back thoughts of Blake Ulster climbing onto the couch and losing his balance right before Mai Ling stabbed him. She looked involuntarily at the floor and realized for the first time that the rug was gone. It had been heavily stained with blood the last time she saw it.

Thankfully, the couch was clean when she looked at it. Then she realized it was a different couch. Everything was in order, like nothing had ever happened. There was even fresh kindling ready to light a fire. She wondered how many times Steve had been to the cottage after Blake's death. So much had happened since she arrived at the Cove, events were all becoming jumbled together in one big revolving cyclone that kept spinning faster. She pulled the fire screen aside, lit the paper beneath the kindling and waited until the flames had ignited everything before cautiously adding more fuel.

A car door slammed outside. Hurriedly pulling the fire screen back into place she went to the front door, turned on the porch light and slid the chain into place before cracking the door open.

Steve stood on the step. "You won't need that." He pointed to the poker in her hand.

She shook it at him. "Don't give me a hard time. I've had more than enough of that, lately."

"Fair enough."

She took off the chain and opened the door. He stepped inside, took off his boots and hung up his coat before following her into the living room. She returned her would-be weapon to its rack.

"What are you doing here?" She asked as Steve warmed himself in front of the fire. "I thought you had customers to take care of?"

"I did. Business slowed down. Hilly's closing for me."

"Whose car did you borrow?"

"Virginia's. She didn't even ask me any questions. Strange days at the Cove."

"Tell me about it."

"The Bangor detectives must be staying in Whitstead. No one offered them rooms at the Cove. Virginia told me that. They're certainly not staying at The Rest." Steve looked at the cat on the couch. "Where did he come from?"

"No idea. He scared the life out of me, scraping at the back door a few minutes ago."

"Do you have anything to drink in this place? It's cold in here, even with the heat pumping."

"The thermostat was turned down again when I got home. It has to be faulty." She walked over to Aunt Jessica's little bar. "I've got scotch and brandy."

"Scotch sounds like a winner."

"You want ice? Soda?"

"No thanks. Straight will do fine."

She poured his drink and a small brandy for herself.

Steve knocked back the scotch in one gulp. "Do you know why the sheriff sent for reinforcements from Bangor? They don't think they can handle investigating Dean Halstead's death without help?"

He was trying to sound casual, but one look at his tightly clenched jaw made Carissa wonder why he was so uptight. "They didn't give me any information. All I can tell you is I got grilled. Detective Giddings didn't go easy on Richard, either."

"Richard got interviewed at the hospital?"

"No, he's home."

Steve looked incredulous. "That soon? I thought he was at death's door."

"Richard's tough and stubborn. He came home with a private duty nurse."

"You'd better look out if she's pretty."

"Harsh and uncalled for, Steve."

"Sorry." He went over to the bar and poured himself another scotch. "I don't know why there's an investigation. Penwithen's crumbling. Those steps can't be in any better shape."

"Detective Giddings doesn't think Dean Halstead would be that stupid. Someone at your inn told him the steps were unsafe before he went there."

"He could have tested them and slipped or the wind could have knocked him over. It gusts really badly around that point." Steve knocked back the scotch and looked at the bottle.

Carissa eyed him uneasily. "That's true," she said. "One of those gusts nearly knocked me over when I was out there, but then, I'm not a man. Dean must have weighed about one-eighty."

"You checked him out that closely?" Steve half-smiled.

"I worked in the fashion industry. It's my business to know things like that. I bet you weigh two-thirty."

"Two-twenty-nine." He shook his glass at her. "Another drink?"

"This is the first time I've seen you drink anything except coffee or club soda."

"It's been a while," he agreed. "Club soda won't do it for me tonight. Sally dumped me for Matthew Yates this afternoon. Now I find I'm about to get investigated by some Bangor detective."

"Sally did *what?*"

"You heard me." He walked past her and poured himself another, much larger drink, which he downed in two gulps.

"I can't believe she'd be so stupid."

"Thanks for the vote of confidence, but I can't compete with a rich designer from New York." Steve shook his head. "Life's sure got a sense of humor. I wanted to be with you, but Sally stood between us. Now, she's not, but Richard Ebberly is."

He put down the glass, strode over and put his arms around Carissa. She smelled the whisky on his breath and felt the sheer size of him pressing against her. The heat of the fire was at her back, making her feel trapped and slightly panicked. Steve was overwhelmingly large when he was sober, and he'd already let her know how much he wanted her. Would he be reasonable after a couple of drinks?

"I'm free for you," he said. "I want you to be free and ready for me. You've got no future with Richard Ebberly." And then he kissed her, not gently, but roughly.

She struggled and tried to pull back, but he held her tight.

"Let me go." She put her hands against his chest and pushed hard. The kiss had been wet and whisky-laced. Not at all romantic, and not at all fulfilling. She realized Steve Raymond was someone she wanted at a comfortable length away.

"Why?" He tried to kiss her again.

Carissa averted her face and his lips landed close to her ear. "This isn't the time to start another relationship. You're confused and hurt." Her heart was pounding; she had trouble breathing.

"What are you, a psychiatrist?" He stared at her. "You really don't want me, do you?" His brow furrowed. "You'd already had sex with Richard Ebberly before his accident. You didn't tell me. You led me on. Christ, you're stupid, if you think he's good for more than a quick fuck."

Carissa was shocked by his crass language. What had happened to the friendly and gentle giant she'd grown to like so much?

Steve's hold on her tightened to the point of pain, his fingers digging into her back. Carissa tried again to push him away.

He called me stupid for making my own decisions.

The panicked feeling flew away, replaced by anger and determination.

I've had enough of being called names; of being thought of as insignificant, easily manipulated and yes, stupid.

"Whoever I choose to make love with is none of your damned business," she said, and then she balled up her fist and hit Steve in the chin so hard, the pain in her knuckles took her breath away.

He took his hands off her, but the slap he gave her sent her reeling. She stumbled against the couch, lost her balance and hit her forehead on decorative wood trim at the front of an armrest. Steve walked away without even asking if she was okay. The front door slammed and Virginia's car left, tires squealing. Carissa made her way down the front hallway. She fastened the deadbolt and shot both bolts home before sinking onto the settle.

The Steve Raymond she had just encountered was an angry stranger who had frightened and repulsed her. What a contrast from Richard, who was always so gentle and protective, even when she made him angry. She didn't feel as concerned for Steve's welfare or as committed to his innocence as she had less than thirty minutes before. She wondered whether he had been drinking before he even arrived.

She sprawled on the couch with an ice pack and the cat for a while before checking the damage to her face. The imprint of Steve's hand showed in shades of dusky red overlaid with midnight blue. Her forehead sported an egg-shaped lump. Unless she wanted to press charges against him, she'd need to stay home for the next few days. What if Detective Giddings wanted to ask her more questions? Did she even care enough about Steve to hide her injuries or the reason for them?

Carissa felt Steve was on some collision course with fate, and she had trouble finding any empathy for him.

CHAPTER FIFTY-NINE

CARISSA GOT a bottle of water from the refrigerator and swallowed two Tylenol. The landline rang. She wanted to let it ring, but then she wondered whether Nurse Fields might be trying to get hold of her, or worse, Sheriff Crosby or Detective Giddings. She hurried back to the living-room and picked up.

"I made bail." Mai Ling said. "My brother brought me home. I saw lights in the cottage. Would you like to come to dinner?"

Carissa heard the happiness in her neighbor's voice and felt relief that one person in the village was actually having a good day.

"I've come down with a bad cold." She hoped she'd sounded nasal enough and coughed loudly.

"I am so sorry, my friend. I will bring you soup."

"You're so kind, but no, I don't want you or your brother walking over here in the snow. I've got plenty of food. I'm so happy you're home, Mai Ling."

"Me, too. Mr. Dansinger and my brother both believe there will be no charges," Mai Ling said. "They say I will be able to go back to Boston very soon."

"That's wonderful news." Carissa sniffed.

"Did you know that your husband has been calling all over town for you?" Mai Ling's tone sounded conspiratorial. "Mrs. Greeley brought me lunch before I was released. She told me he has been worried about you."

Carissa realized she had left her smartphone on vibrate after leaving Richard. She looked at her answering machine, which showed no incoming calls. Matthew mustn't have tried very hard, she thought, wondering what was so urgent. Maybe he had news about the pending case. If so, it must be something in his favor. Her stomach started churning. She looked at the kitchen clock: 8:00 PM. Too late to reach her New York attorney unless she called him at home. After she said goodbye to Mai Ling, Carissa called Roland Finch at his office, planning leave a message, but he picked up.

"Carissa." He sounded excited, something rare for him. "I've been trying to reach you."

It must be about settling the copyright infringement case. "I'm calling from my aunt's home. I've been moving around a lot over the last week or so. Did you try my cell?"

"Yes. I left two messages earlier today. Why have you been moving around? What's wrong with your aunt's lighthouse? Too drafty or too haunted?" He chuckled.

"Some of both, probably. I've had to make a lot of changes I hadn't planned on, and then a couple of people had..." she searched for the right wording "... accidents."

"I'm sorry to hear that. I hope your friends are all right. I've watched the news reports on the blizzard. We've counted ourselves lucky back here to miss that storm."

Carissa didn't feel like getting into a long discussion about her disastrous move. She needed some good news from Roland.

"Are *you* all right?" He sounded concerned. "The case is coming to court in less than two weeks. I need you to be at your best."

"I'll be fine, Roland. I promise." *So much for Matthew settling out of court.*

"You sound tired, and I have a feeling you've got more to tell me, but you're not ready. Try to rest up before your trip back here. Matthew's secretary, Priscilla Baldwin called me today. She'd called you several times today, but like mine, they went to voicemail. She told me

Matthew's spending the winter at Treacher's Cove. That must be a strain on you. I can't think why he'd do that, but as we both know, Matthew's unpredictable at the best of times. Priscilla doesn't want Matthew to know she's trying to reach you, and I promised to pass that on. She asked you to call her at home. If you have a pen and paper handy, I'll give you her number."

Carissa jotted Priscilla's number onto the notepad Aunt Jessica had left beside the cordless phone's base. After receiving a quick update about the case and a reassurance that Roland thought they stood a good chance of winning despite the lack of evidence, which she thought was polite window-dressing for 'there's really not a snowball's chance in hell of you coming out ahead,' she chatted with him about the remodeling project and tried not to sound too stressed out before saying goodbye.

While changing into sweat pants and an oversized sweater, she listened to three calls from Matthew, two from Monica asking her to call without notifying Matthew, and one from Richard telling her he still wished she'd spend the night. She wondered why Steve thought tidying up a bedroom meant putting absolutely everything away. She opened the top drawer of the highboy and found her black leather organizer hidden under a pile of Aunt Jessica's utilitarian woolen drawers.

"Either he thinks I'm a mind reader or he must wonder about my choice of underwear," she muttered before taking the organizer to the living room and adding Priscilla's home number before calling.

Priscilla must have been hovering over the phone. She picked up immediately. "Mrs. Yates," she said. "I'm so pleased. Oh, dear, I meant to say Ms. Yates." She sounded flustered.

"It's okay," Carissa reassured her. "My phone was on vibrate and I've been really busy today. My attorney called and gave me your message."

"You might think what I'm about to tell you is really awkward, coming from me, but Mr. Yates pays my salary, that's all. You know I've never had much use for him."

"Not very loyal, Priscilla, but I won't tell him." Suddenly, she wanted to smile. It felt good after the day she'd gone through.

"If you ever need an administrative assistant, I'll leave him without giving notice," Priscilla said.

Carissa remembered Matthew's administrative assistant resembled a puffer fish when she got riled, which could happen when she was fending off reporters trying to get any information they could pry out of her about trends for each new season. She also remembered Priscilla being efficient and trustworthy.

"Anyway," Priscilla said. "That's not why I tried to reach you. You got a package from Ms. Malloy. I didn't know where to send it. I need your new address."

"A package from my Aunt Jessica?" Carissa's bad day took a totally unexpected upswing. Could that package possibly contain the evidence she had asked her aunt to send?

"Yes. It was mailed from Maine on October 1st. It looks like it was sent first to your old address, then to the business address. Someone in the mailroom was efficient enough to spot that and gave it to me to send on to you."

Carissa had to sit down. The package was mailed three days before her aunt was found dead.

"I don't know why she mailed it," Priscilla said. "She could have just brought it with her when she visited Mr. Yates. I'd have been glad to make sure you got it."

"Wait a second. Back up. Did you say my aunt visited Mr. Yates?"

"Yes. She called several times before she came, but I don't know what was said, because I'm not in the habit of eavesdropping on Mr. Yates' private calls."

"I'm sure you're not. What day and time did she go to see him?"

"Late in the afternoon on November 2nd. He'd told me to leave early, but I was still finishing up a few things when she arrived around four forty-five. I took the letters down to the mailroom myself because Mr. Yates wanted them to go out that day. When I came back upstairs to pick up my purse and coat, Mr. Yates and your aunt were having a fierce argument. I could hear their voices right through the door. I don't know what they were saying, but Ms. Malloy was shouting at the top of her lungs. I left quickly, because Mr. Yates would probably have fired me if he'd found me there after telling me to go home."

Bile churned in Carissa's throat. "Can you overnight that package to me? I'll reimburse you for whatever it costs." She thought about where to have it sent. Not to the lighthouse and certainly not to Nancy Burton's store. The only person she trusted right then at the Cove was Richard. She gave Priscilla his address and hung up.

The phone rang again instantly. Carissa snatched up the receiver. "Hello?"

"Carissa," Matthew said. I've been looking all over for you. Where have you been?"

CHAPTER SIXTY

CARISSA'S first thought was to tell Matthew to go take a hike, but he sounded more upset than angry. Thinking about Aunt Jessica visiting him only two days before her death and Priscilla saying they had argued, Carissa skipped goading him.

"What do you want, Matthew?" She leaned her aching cheek against the ice pack.

"I have to see you. I tried your smartphone, but my messages all went to voicemail."

"I've been busy. What's so important? I'm tired."

"I need to see you. This is something I can't tell you on the phone. Are you at the lighthouse? I'll come right over."

"To tell me what? That you had my mail forwarded to you? That my aunt was in your office two days before she was found dead?"

"Carissa..."

"Don't try to find excuses, Matthew. I want the truth, and I want it now."

"Fine. You want the truth; here it is...it wasn't my fault. It was an accident; I swear. We were arguing and Jessica fell. She hit her head on my desk and died, right there in my office. What was I going to do? I carried her out to the car and drove her back to the lighthouse. It was after hours. No one saw me."

Carissa had to sit. She landed half-on and half-off the couch. *He hadn't tried to get help for Aunt Jessica. He'd bundled her into his car and driven her all the way to Maine?* She needed both hands to hold the phone when she realized what he must have done when he reached Bennett Point Light.

"You carried her into the lighthouse and threw her body down the stairs to make it look like the accident happened here, didn't you?" Tears blurred her vision. "You didn't even try to help her. My God, what sort of monster *are* you?"

"She was beyond help, believe me. I panicked."

"You're trying to tell me you stayed panicked all the way from New York to Treacher's Cove?" She wanted to rip his heart out. Hers was breaking into little pieces.

"I couldn't take a chance the police would think I'd caused her death. I'd have been ruined. The House of Yates would never survive a scandal like that."

"If you'd treated her with respect, she wouldn't have had to make the trip to your office in the first place, and she certainly wouldn't have been shouting at you."

"How do you know she was shouting? Who told you?"

"Do you really think I'm going to give you that information? Really?" Angrier than she had ever been in her life, Carissa stood up and began pacing.

"It would be better if you told me and one person got fired instead of everyone who was left in the building when Jessica got there."

"You wouldn't..."

"Of course I would. I told you, this was *not* my fault. Your aunt lunged at me with her cane. I sidestepped. She lost her balance and fell. I couldn't risk any misinterpretations. You've *got* to understand." He sounded desperate.

"I'm going to hang up on you and call the police."

"Let me explain a couple of things before you do that. You'll ruin your own future. Knowing you might react like this, I called my attorney and sent him a notarized letter. I've relinquished my claims to those disputed designs. You're to retain the copyrights. All of them. The embroidery, the braiding, the beading, the lot. I'm also giving you half the business."

"*Now* you decide to do all that? You *coward!* That's not going to stop me from getting you arrested. I don't believe the story you concocted about my aunt having an accident. I think you killed her because you were afraid she was going to tell you she could produce proof the designs were hers and mine."

"Jessica told me she'd left everything to you so you wouldn't need any of my damned money. She said she'd mailed you the original designs. I admit I had your mail intercepted. But no package came. I thought she must have been lying, but I couldn't be sure."

"So you moved to the Cove to keep an eye on me and see if any mail from my aunt turned up here. What were you planning to do then, Matthew? Kill me, too? Kill Nancy Burton if the package got delivered to her post office?"

"Of course not. I want you to come back to me. I've changed, Carissa. I'll be a good husband. The House of Yates is poised to turn the fashion industry on its head. The fall line is waiting for your final touches."

"I'm sure you're sincere about everything you've just told me. It all comes down to me giving you permission to use those designs. The ones you killed my aunt for. You're not getting them, and that's the end of it."

"Don't make that decision now. I can see you need to sleep on it. Get some distance from your emotions, then you'll see reason. You can't stay in this backwater. You need to come home with me. I'll spend the rest of my life making up for my mistakes, darling. I swear I will."

"You? Swearing anything that's not a profanity? Spare me. You promised to love and honor me. Instead, you made me feel like a piece of dirt under your shoe. You kept me away from my aunt, stole our designs..."

"I wasn't thinking clearly."

"There's another lie. You never do anything without it benefitting you while screwing everyone else. That Bangor detective told me you hired Dean Halstead to spy on me. You really think I'm going to believe you're giving me half your business? That I'd come back to New York and work alongside you?" She wanted to throw something. Anything.

Instead, she paced around the living-room while the cat stared wide-eyed from his roost on the afghan.

Matthew sighed heavily. "You're not being open-minded about this."

"Open-minded? About my aunt's death and you not telling me what happened?"

"I just told you everything."

"And I'm going to tell all of it to the police."

"They won't believe you. I'll deny everything and tell them you're being vengeful. The divorce was contentious and there's the ongoing litigation. I was already interviewed by Detective Johannsen and told him my intention in moving here was to win you back and prove to you I can be a good husband."

"What you are is an unmitigated bastard."

"Who wants you back. Call me what you want. I'm telling you there'll be no more secrets between us. We'll start with a clean slate. Me being a dutiful and loving husband. You getting what you want."

"I'm not listening to any more of this bullshit, Matthew."

"We can start afresh. You'll have the legal contract that gives you half the business. What more could you want?"

"I want Aunt Jessica back."

She slammed down the phone.

CHAPTER SIXTY-ONE

CARISSA COULDN'T DECIDE what she wanted to do first—drive right through Matthew's front door or call the police and tell them about his confession. It was a toss-up, but she felt she had to review their conversation before she did anything else.

He'd drawn up a contract to give her half the business. He'd stopped the copyright suit in its tracks. Had he done all that in an attempt to implicate her in her aunt's death? Like they'd planned her aunt's death together, and they'd decided Matthew would bring Aunt Jessica's body back to the Cove and throw it down the stairs to give Carissa sole rights to the designs?

She couldn't discuss her concerns with Roland Finch. He wasn't a criminal attorney, and he'd probably tell her to call the police even though Matthew had said he'd deny everything.

Matthew was right when he'd said the House of Yates wouldn't survive the scandal. It had been difficult enough for him to keep the business on track during their divorce. Then the copyright infringement case impacted the willingness of clients to order merchandise. Matthew had been trying to convince them he would be able to continue producing those unique and sought-after designs while that was by no means certain.

Carissa tried to detach herself from her anger and put herself in Matthew's shoes. Was he telling the truth about Aunt Jessica's death? Had he panicked? Perhaps. But solving a huge problem by making it go away in such a callous and thoughtless manner? *She* would never have decided to do that, but then, she wasn't Matthew Yates.

She looked at the time. Too late to go over to Richard and dump on him. She wasn't the best winter driver, either. Carissa sat down again and petted the cat. She nixed calling Sheriff Crosby. Telling him Matthew had confessed to driving her dead aunt across several States and flinging her down the lighthouse stairs to save himself and his business from bad publicity sounded like a half-baked fairytale. Talking to Deputy Watkins would be senseless, since he reported to the sheriff.

She decided to call Detective Giddings and see how he reacted. When he answered, she could hear him chewing. Carissa briefly explained the reason for her call.

"So he's guilty of covering up an accident and moving a body," Giddings said. "Hard to prove any of it unless he's willing to make that a formal confession. I doubt evidence was collected, but I'll talk to the locals tomorrow morning."

"What about talking to them tonight?"

"Is Mr. Yates going to run away?"

"Well, no, probably not. He told me he'd deny everything and there's no proof it happened."

"He must have covered his tracks well."

"I don't doubt that, knowing Matthew as well as I do."

"Then I suggest we both call it a night. I'll get a statement from you tomorrow morning and then I'll talk to your ex-husband. Goodnight, Ms. Yates."

The detective had too much on his plate, too, she thought. He was more interested in solving Dean Halstead's murder than refereeing a 'he-said, she-said' domestic dispute, which was how she figured Giddings was looking at her story. Maybe the local police would be more inter-ested in solving Jessica Malloy's death, but maybe not, since it had already been ruled accidental.

Matthew would have had his office forensically scrubbed by a cleaning crew. He might also have had it painted, had new carpeting installed and changed the furniture. *He'll get away with it,* she thought, brewing tea while she tried to turn her frustration into something more useful.

Then it hit her: What if Matthew had second thoughts about his confession and came over to take care of the only loose end? He had no way of knowing she'd talked to Giddings. She had trouble swallowing her tea. The cottage creaked as the wind whipped around it and gusted down the chimney. A wave of smoke blew out of the fireplace. The cat joined Carissa in the kitchen.

Should she stay at the lighthouse or leave? If she left, where could she go? She certainly wasn't going to slide down that treacherous hill on solid ice to reach The Fisherman's Rest, and she had no desire to see Steve Raymond that evening. She could place Virginia in danger by asking to stay with her. The thought of driving to Whitstead was much too daunting.

Carissa decided she'd have to stay right where she was. She double-checked that all windows and doors were locked before settling onto the opposite end of the couch from the cat, who had returned to the warmth of the fire after the smoke dissipated. He rose, stretched, and curled up next to her feet.

She wanted to avenge her aunt's death. Matthew Yates should pay for what he'd done. But how could she get justice for Aunt Jessica when, as Detective Giddings had told her, there was probably no evidence of Matthew's crime other than the confession he'd made to her? What was the punishment for transporting a dead body from the scene of an accident? Her head ached and the bruise on her cheek throbbed.

Carissa watched the flames die in the fireplace. The furnace clicked on and warmed the house. She imagined Matthew being taken away in shackles to a prison with high walls topped by barbed wire. That image finally lulled her to sleep.

CHAPTER SIXTY-TWO

CARISSA AWOKE to knocking on her front door. Her limbs felt leaden, her mouth dry. The cat jumped off the couch when she moved. She looked at her watch. 9:00 A.M. The knocking stopped, only to be replaced moments later by someone tapping a living room window. When she pulled a drape aside, she saw Mai Ling Ulster standing outside, wearing what looked like a man's hunting jacket. She hurried to open the back door. Mai Ling rushed inside.

"You haven't been answering your phone," she complained. "Your ex-husband is dead. He was found on his kitchen floor. He must have slipped and hit his head."

"What?" Carissa couldn't believe her ears. "How did you find out?"

"Miss Greeley. A friend called her after seeing the police car and asking Deputy Watkins what had happened."

As though on cue, the doorbell rang. Mai Ling and Carissa looked at each other.

"Your face," Mai Ling said. "What happened to your face?"

"A misunderstanding." Carissa opened the front door to Ray Watkins.

"Ms. Yates," he said. "May I come in?"

So formal. So somber. Carissa knew why he was there. She stood aside. "Yes, of course. But you're a little late if you're here to tell me my ex-husband's dead. Mai Ling got here ahead of you. The gossip-mill's in full-swing this morning." She watched him knock snow off his boots before stepping inside.

Deputy Watkins closed the door. "I'm here to bring you to the station. Detective Giddings gave us an update on Mr. Yates' confession." He stopped when he saw Mai Ling hovering in the living room. "Good morning, Mrs. Ulster. I understand you told Carissa about Mr. Yates?"

Mai Ling nodded. "Virginia Greeley called me. Was that wrong?"

"It would have been better if it had come from the police," he gently chided her. "Perhaps you could make us coffee?"

Mai Ling crept off into the kitchen like a dog that had been kicked.

Deputy Watkins turned to Carissa. "Go ahead and sit down, Ms. Yates. You look pretty shaken up." He peered at her now they were out of the darkened hallway. "What happened to your face?"

She hadn't made a decision on what to say about the slap. Now it looked like she was going to have to decide in a hurry.

"Did Mr. Yates do that?" The deputy asked.

"No, Steve Raymond did."

His eyes widened in surprise. "With what? And why?"

"His hand. We had a disagreement...a misunderstanding. He slapped me and I lost my balance. I hit my forehead on the new couch." She pointed. "That wood trim."

"You should have called to report that. He assaulted you." Ray Watkins had drawn himself up. His right hand rested next to his gun.

"I don't think I want to press any charges. Steve was very upset, and he'd been drinking."

"He never drinks." Ray Watkins looked bewildered. "He's got no history of violence here at the Cove. Even when he's had to deal with rude and abusive guests or drunks in the bar. I don't understand."

"Tell me about it. That's why I didn't do anything about it last night. Mai Ling just woke me up. And now I find out Matthew's dead?" She slumped down onto the couch. "This is all too much. I feel like I'm in the middle of a really bad nightmare. I'd really like to wake up and find none of this happened."

Watkins picked up an ice pack from the floor. "This is barely cold. Do you have another one?"

"No, but I've got Tylenol. I should take some." She got back up. "It's in the kitchen."

"Do you want me to ask Mai Ling to go home while we talk?"

"No. I've got nothing to hide from her." Carissa hoped Mai Ling hadn't used the instant coffee.

"When did you last see Mr. Yates?" Ray Watkins asked.

"Not for the last two days at least. I was with Richard at his house yesterday. I left after Detective Giddings finished interviewing me and arrived home around eight last night. That's when Matthew called and told me Aunt Jessica had slipped and hit her head while they were arguing in his office."

There was a scream from the kitchen.

They both jumped.

"What the hell?" Watkins strode into the kitchen ahead of Carissa.

"What is this animal doing in here?" Mai Ling sounded hysterical.

"Oh, my God, the stray cat." Carissa rushed in behind Watkins. Mai Ling had the back door open by that time. Carissa saw a blur of grey as the cat fled outside.

Mai Ling was shaking from head to foot. "Blake killed that cat," she said.

"Obviously, he didn't." Deputy Watkins closed and locked both doors. "Could we have a little less drama around here? Would that be asking too much?"

Carissa wasn't sure whether Mai Ling was any calmer than she was at that moment. "I'll make the coffee," she decided. "Have a seat, both of you." She gestured toward the kitchen table.

Mai Ling had poured water into the coffee maker. Carissa added a filter and spooned in the coffee. She still felt like she must be dreaming. Her mind couldn't seem to grasp the fact that Matthew was gone. How could the man who had plagued her life be dead before his 45th birthday?

"Matthew fell?" She asked, pushing the button to start the brewing cycle.

"Looks like it," Deputy Watkins said. "Where do you keep the cups?"

"Bottom shelf, middle cabinet, right next to the stove."

While she stared at coffee filling the carafe, she heard a cabinet open with a shrill squeak and cups clinking. Carissa carefully wiped a single tear that had trickled down her bruised cheek before turning around. She watched Mai Ling open the refrigerator and take out coffee creamer.

They all stayed silent as they went through the motions of getting coffee into the cups and those cups onto the kitchen table. Carissa took a bag of cookies out of the pantry and shook them onto a plate. Sugar cookies. The ones Aunt Jessica had always bought. How ironic. She hadn't even noticed she had chosen them while at the supermarket. Matthew had been behind her at the checkout that day. Trying to embarrass her by putting Trojans in with her purchases.

He loved stupid little games like that, Carissa thought with a sudden pang of regret. Perhaps she had been too judgmental. Too ready to find fault with everything Matthew did. The outwardly suave and sophisticated designer had enjoyed playing boyish pranks. That should have been endearing. Had she thought him more malicious than he actually was? Had she only seen the bad side of him because that was all she wanted to see? For the first time since her divorce, Carissa actually felt a sense of loss.

"So," Deputy Watkins said after they had all sipped coffee and he had eaten three cookies. "You had a misunderstanding with Steve? About what?"

Carissa was too tired and saddened to find excuses. "He said Sally dumped him for Matthew. He wanted to tell me he was free to have a relationship with me. I told him I wasn't interested."

"And that made him hit you? Even if he'd been drinking, I don't understand why that would make Steve Raymond furious."

"I told him I was with Richard."

"That would do it." Ray nodded. "Are you?"

"Am I what?" Carissa downed two Tylenol with a glass of water. She refused to look at Mai Ling, who had made little noises over first Steve, then Richard. Carissa felt like she was being judged and found guilty of loose behavior.

"With Richard." Ray Watkins slurped coffee.

"That has nothing to do with your investigation," she said, chagrined as well as embarrassed.

"It might, but since you're getting defensive, I'll leave it up to the detectives to decide whether to pursue that line of questioning any further." Ray put down his cup. "Let's get back to Steve and what time he left here."

"Right before Matthew called, so I guess around nine o'clock."

"I should leave." Mai Ling stood up. "My brother will be wondering where I am. We are deciding what I should take back to Boston and what should be sold."

Carissa knew she'd made a bad decision, believing she had no secrets to hide from Mai Ling. She didn't want her neighbor leaving on a possibly sour note. "Please take some coffee with you," she said. "Your brother would probably like a cup. There's a flask in the pantry you can use."

"Thank you." Mai Ling shrugged into the big jacket. "I will come back later to see how you are doing."

While Deputy Watkins chatted inconsequentially about the weather and the state of the roads, Mai Ling filled the flask. She pocketed two cookies wrapped in a paper towel, then paused with the mudroom door open. "Blake did kill that stray cat. I saw him throw it into the furnace."

Ray Watkins watched the door close behind her before commenting. "She probably saw him with one cat out of a whole pack," he told Carissa. "I bet there's a feral colony out in the woods."

"This cat didn't seem feral," Carissa said. "It was yowling and scraping at the back door yesterday evening. Did Aunt Jessica have a cat? I didn't see any bowls or food around here."

Watkins shrugged. "I never set foot in this place until the morning I answered William Dansinger's call about finding your aunt, so I have no idea." He stopped, cleared his throat and took another sip of coffee. "Let's talk about why you won't press charges against Steve."

"He wasn't acting normally yesterday," Carissa paused. Did she really want to dig in her heels and not have Ray or the sheriff at least warn Steve about his behavior? What if he did the same thing again?

"Because of him being drunk?"

"I don't know if he'd been drinking before he got here, but he looked like he had. Acted like it, too. I had told him I didn't want visitors, but he borrowed Virginia's car and came anyway. He wanted to be more than a friend to me." She bit her lip. "He had a couple of scotches and then tried to kiss me. I told him to leave. That's when he got upset, asking me whether I was with Richard, which I told Steve was none of his business. That made him angry. I know there's been bad blood between Richard and Steve for a while, but I didn't realize how bad until he slapped me."

"Sally Mainard had told Steve she was dumping him for your ex-husband?"

Carissa nodded. "I found that hard to believe, too. Sally and Steve seemed so happy together."

Deputy Watkins drained his cup. "Detective Giddings asked me to give you a ride to the station after I broke the news about Mr. Yates. Would you like to change clothes first?"

"Yes, please. Shower, too. Can I have thirty minutes?"

"Take your time." He put the cups onto the tray. "I'll wash up."

The thermostat had sunk to 55 degrees again. Carissa readjusted it before putting warmth back into her body with a hot shower. After drying her hair and getting dressed, she stopped shivering. A generous layer of concealer couldn't hide the bruise on her cheek, but she decided adding more would make her look like she was auditioning for a role in kabuki theatre. She pulled on black leather boots and checked herself in the mirror. A pale gray cashmere sweater with a cowl neckline under a black woolen jacket and black jeans. Not widow's weeds, but subdued enough.

She told herself she had been a fool, thinking Matthew ever loved her. In the past she had tried to make allowances for his behavior, telling herself he'd had to be tough to make it in the fashion industry. A man who'd grown up in the Bronx. A man who had beaten the odds to bring his designs to the runways of New York, Paris and Rome. But he'd done all of it over the backs of everyone who had helped him, including her. She definitely wouldn't be mourning him, and she wasn't going to wax sentimental for someone who had tried so hard to leave her with nothing but regret.

Ray Watkins concentrated on his driving during the trip to the police station. Carissa took the opportunity to work on keeping her story short and to the point. No rambling off-subject, she told herself. No sharing information that didn't need to be shared, like Steve kissing her once before and her rebuffing him.

Detective Giddings escorted her into Sheriff Crosby's small back office. The sheriff himself was nowhere to be seen, but William was sitting in front of the desk, his attaché case open. Carissa felt both surprise and trepidation. Had Roland Finch contacted William or had the local police?

"I'll need a few minutes with my client," William said.

The corners of Giddings' mouth turned down. "I'm sure you will." He left, the door closing quietly behind him.

"Your New York attorney called early this morning, and Ray Watkins called right after that," William said. "Both of them thought you should have an attorney present when you gave your statement. I have to know one thing: Did you do it?"

"Do what? Kill Matthew?" Carissa sat, panic setting in. "I wanted to at times, but of course not."

William smiled briefly. "I appreciate your honesty about wanting to do the deed; don't be that forthcoming when you're giving your statement to Detective Giddings."

"I won't. How did Matthew die? Mai Ling Ulster said he fell in the kitchen. Had he been drinking?"

"The amount of alcohol in his system wouldn't have made him that unsteady. He was found face-down on the kitchen floor. You probably heard he slipped and hit his head. I believe the police have allowed that story to float around, but the facts may be different."

"There's been a lot of slipping and falling going on around here, lately," Carissa said.

William nodded. "Too much to ignore any longer. Detective Giddings and his partner are focusing on Dean Halstead's fall as well as your ex-husband's."

"Someone pushed me when I was out walking in front of the lighthouse," Carissa said.

"I heard about that. You're going to have to answer a lot of questions, Carissa, not just about your own activities, but your interactions with Halstead and your ex-husband. Were you aware Halstead was a private investigator hired by Matthew?"

"Not until Giddings told me. It made me very, very angry. Am I really a suspect?"

"Your alibi's being checked. Detective Giddings' prime suspect right now is Steve Raymond, but it looks bad for both of you. Steve for being furious over Sally's rejection and you for a host of reasons, including anger over Mr. Yates moving here. Then there's that contentious pending court case. I believe Giddings thinks you and Steve may even have acted together. What happened to your face?"

The panic ramped up. Carissa told William about everything that had happened to her since she arrived at Treacher's Cove. She omitted nothing, including the noises in the cottage basement, the faulty thermostat, her anger at finding Matthew had paid a P.I. to spy on her, and finally, her interactions with Steve and her fledgling relationship with Richard. It was a lot, but William nodded, took notes and remained calm and non-judgmental throughout.

"Steve hasn't been acting like himself for the last couple of days," Carissa finished up. "He had to be hurt and angry over Sally's rejection. Maybe even jealous. But taking that out on Matthew, or even worse, working out a plan with me to go over and murder a rival, just because he's my ex?" She paused, her mind racing through the probabilities. "No," she said, when William remained quiet. "No way."

William took a moment. Carissa waited and wished she had a glass of water. Her mouth had dried up while she was talking. William was probably worried about getting her out of the station without charges being filed. She had no alibi for the time period when Matthew was murdered except Steve's drunken visit.

"Richard's interest in all this is being investigated," William said finally. "Al Dyson has a buyer for both the lighthouse and the Ulsters' property. Al admitted to paying Blake to harass you, but denied any contact with Richard about the resort project."

"Richard would never get involved with a scheme to frighten me out of the lighthouse."

William tapped his pen against his notepad. "I don't believe he would, either. Giddings can dig around and insinuate all he wants. Richard Ebberly and his father have always been above reproach in their business dealings. Richard's personal life, however, that's had some low points, and I'd caution you not to put full trust in him."

"Sally Mainard's accusation?"

"That's probably the biggest black spot. Richard's been a bit of a tomcat in the past."

"Many men are, if they're handsome, rich and personable."

"Your opinion of men isn't very high, is it?" William looked rueful. "I know what you think of me personally, but I assure you I'm a good attorney. I can represent you as well, if not better, than anyone from Whitstead or Bangor."

Carissa took her time answering. She didn't want to offend the man Roland Finch had singled out for her, but she wasn't going to place her freedom on the line by keeping her reservations to herself.

"I'm going to listen to Roland Finch's advice for now and retain you. You know far more about this village and its inhabitants than I do." She took a deep breath. "This is what I think: I doubt anyone from outside the Cove drove here yesterday expressly to murder Matthew. For one thing, the weather was too bad. For another, he wouldn't let a stranger into his home. Matthew knows...knew better than that."

"You had multiple good reasons to be angry with him," William said. "The pending case, his move here, his meddling and attempts to spy on you and dig up dirt about your affairs..."

Carissa held up her hand. "Enough said. It looks bad for me, doesn't it?"

"Let's say it doesn't look good. But I've had worse cases." He patted her hand. "Giddings will be recording your statement. Dot set up the equipment in their really cramped interrogation room. I asked to speak to you in here before that happened. You must only answer questions, not volunteer information unless you clear it with me. Be brief. Don't give your opinion, and try not to get defensive or angry. I'll be present to guide and advise you."

Carissa started to shake. This was what Mai Ling must have felt like. She wondered how she could possibly survive in a room even smaller than the one she was sitting in, especially when it would be occupied by William, Giddings and recording equipment.

William opened the door. "We're ready."

CHAPTER SIXTY-THREE

"You despised your ex-husband." Giddings leaned forward across the table in the stiflingly-hot interrogation room. "You moved to the light-house after your aunt's death, leaving behind a pending court case you had initiated."

Carissa nodded, following William's directions. *Keep your answers short. Don't embellish.*

"Yes."

"Mr. Yates followed you here."

"Yes. He told me he wanted to reconcile."

"Did you believe him?"

She looked at William, who nodded.

"No, but I'm sure he thought reconciliation would stop the court case."'

"Did you know he had recently made legal changes that gave you half the business?"

William's eyebrows rose.

Carissa nodded. "He told me during a phone call, after I refused to let him come to see me."

"This phone conversation was when?"

"Yesterday evening. Before Steve Raymond came over."

"A moment," William said.

Giddings didn't look happy, but he nodded.

"Why didn't you tell me this?" William whispered in Carissa's ear.

"I thought he was lying."

"Be very careful how you answer any more questions about this."

She nodded and turned back to Giddings.

"Apparently, Mr. Yates was feeling guilty about his treatment of you, Ms. Yates. Isn't that right?"

"I can't answer that question. I have no idea how Matthew felt."

"Yet you were married to him for five years?" Giddings looked incredulous.

Carissa carefully considered her answer. "He sounded remorseful, but that's meant nothing in the past. He'd say anything to get what he wanted. Not just to me. He'd use that trick on anyone he did business with. He was a very good, very ruthless CEO."

"So that's how you'd describe his relationship with you? Ruthless? That's pretty cold."

"Living with Matthew was like living in Siberia when he was unhappy with me. But after he moved here, something was different. I'd say he only sparred with me."

"In what way?"

She told Giddings about her encounter with Matthew at the supermarket. About his calls. "Our relationship here at the Cove was strained but civil," she finished.

"He left you everything in his will," Giddings said. "He had the papers drawn up and filed a week ago. It looks like he planned to end the copyright infringement case with a settlement. I already spoke with his attorney this morning. I expect you'll be getting a call from yours after this interview is over."

"You have no reason to doubt Ms. Yates' statement. She's been more than forthcoming." William sounded sharp and authoritative. "Unless you're planning to charge my client with anything, we're leaving. She's very tired and needs rest."

Giddings' dark eyes turned to William. Cold. Impersonal. "I'm not quite finished, Mr. Dansinger." He turned his attention back to Carissa. "Were you and Steve Raymond conspiring to murder your ex-husband?"

She'd been expecting that question. She didn't flinch, and following William's instructions, she forced herself not to speak defensively. "I don't even know Steve well enough to share anything about my life. Certainly not well enough to hatch a plot to murder my ex-husband. As for Matthew leaving me everything in his will, I'm sure that was a calculated move. He never did anything that wouldn't benefit him in some way."

Carissa recounted her conversation with Matthew's secretary and how Matthew had been waiting to intercept her aunt's package.

"If what you're telling me is true, Mr. Yates was on the brink of disaster," Giddings said.

"It's all true, and there's a lot more." Carissa leaned back and folded her arms. "You can ask any of his employees, but especially Priscilla Baldwin, who had no illusions about her boss."

"Why are you refusing to press assault charges against Steve Raymond?" Giddings asked.

Carissa felt exhausted, mentally and physically. The interview had taken a lot out of her, and her face was really hurting. "I won't say I ever want to be alone in a room with him after what he did to me, but he was angry and hurt by Sally's rejection."

"You said he'd been drinking. That's out of character for him too, from what I've heard."

It was William's turn to agree. "I've never seen him drink any kind of liquor."

"Maybe he's hiding a drinking problem," Giddings said. "I'm bringing him in for an interview."

"Can I go home now?" Carissa asked.

"I'd like you to stay at my home instead of the lighthouse," William said. "That place has given you nothing but trouble."

"That's kind of you, but I'll be more comfortable at home," she said. "A stray cat moved in with me. I'd like to get supplies for him while I'm in the village."

William stood. "Is my client free to go, Detective?"

"For now." Giddings rubbed the stubble on his chin. "But I reserve the right to re-interview her."

"Fair enough." William gave a very thin smile. "Carissa?"

She gladly left, breathing in crisp, cold air as she and William paused on the sidewalk outside the police station.

"Where's your car?" He asked, looking around the parking lot, which only contained a couple of police vehicles and a Toyota 4 Runner as well as William's Cadillac.

"Deputy Watkins brought me here. I'll call a cab after I pick up the cat supplies."

William swung his attaché case from one hand to the other. "I'm still thinking about that package Jessica mailed. She was agitated the entire week before her death. She told me she thought Matthew was keeping you prisoner, which I said was nonsense. Little did I know Mr. Yates was diverting your mail even if he couldn't keep *you* in check." He looked at the ground. "I should have accompanied Jessica to New York, but I was too much of a coward. I was afraid it would anger Patsy as well as feed the rumor-mill."

"You can't take the blame for what happened, William. We both know how willful and independent Aunt Jessica was." *That's the truth,* Carissa thought, remembering how her mother had spoken with frustration about her sister.

"She never allowed anyone to help her if she thought she could do it herself. Evidently, that included confronting Matthew. I'm willing to believe what he told me—that her death was an accident, and he panicked."

William grimaced. "She couldn't have climbed those stairs. You were the only one who realized that. All of us here at the Cove ignored the obvious."

"Matthew always said I had a good eye for detail. I would catch mistakes—one or two bad stitches in my patterns—and get them corrected, even if it meant hours of work. Matthew always griped about the delay, but then he'd nod his approval after the problem was fixed and tell me I was a pain in the ass, but a very dedicated and astute one."

She tried to smile, but her vision blurred. She wasn't sure whether the tears filling her eyes were for Aunt Jessica or Matthew. He'd been so ruthless, yet he had left her everything in his will, and he'd stopped the litigation over the designs. Had Matthew really been trying to mend his ways? She would never know. Perhaps that was the saddest part of their entire complex relationship.

"Are you going to be all right?" William asked. "Is there someone I can call for you? Richard? Your mother?"

"No, I'll be fine." She squeezed his arm. "Thank you for representing me so well. After the way I've treated you, that came as a very welcome surprise. I need to clear my head. Doing something completely mundane like shopping for cat supplies may help. Is there are pet store in the village? I don't want to go to Whitstead. I know there's a bus, but it'll take too long."

"No pet store, but the Market's got to have pet supplies." William started to walk away, then turned and came back. "I don't know if the cab service in Whitstead is running. You may have to take the bus home. If you feel you can't do that, please call me. I'll come back and pick you up."

"Thanks again for everything."

"You're very welcome." He trudged off toward his car.

Ray Watkins came out of the police station. "You should have let me know you were done. I was in the break room. I'll take you home."

"I've got shopping to do," she told him. "I can take a cab or the bus."

"No cabs are running today because of the weather. Buses are on chains. I'm not leaving you to walk from the nearest bus stop down that long track to the lighthouse."

"Fair enough. Thank you; I know I wouldn't love carrying cat supplies from the bus stop home."

"I'll take you to the store." He pulled out his keys.

"You're in the middle of a work day. I can walk to the Market. I'd like to; it'll give me a chance to decompress after that interview."

"Okay." Ray nodded. "Call me when you're done and I'll pick you up from there." He walked back inside the station.

Carissa took an exhausting walk to Everett's Market. While she sweated inside her down coat, she asked herself why Matthew had made her the beneficiary of his will. He wasn't expecting to die, so it *must* have been a ploy on his part. Maybe he'd hoped to distract her from wondering how Aunt Jessica had really died or wondering who Dean

Halstead really was as he sneaked around the Cove. Maybe the House of Yates was in financial trouble.

Pausing before climbing over a pile of snow at the intersection between the harbor road and the street leading to Everett's Market, Carissa took several deep, cleansing breaths and told herself she should stop speculating. As she clambered over the top of the snow pile she slipped, sliding down the hard-packed dirty snow on her back. Her feet hit the ploughed street. She rolled onto her side, picked herself up and dusted off before looking for traffic and crossing to the other side.

Despite her resolve, Matthew continued to fill her thoughts. He had badly needed her designs. Unless they'd been able to resolve their professional differences, he wouldn't have had the time to get the designs back onto his spring collection. Panting from exertion, Carissa stopped on the other side of the street while she decided whether to climb another snow pile or continue walking in the street until she came to the parking lot's entrance. She opted for staying on the street, which felt slippery as glass. Few cars dotted the parking lot ahead, but lights streamed from the store, and she spotted a bag boy loading groceries into the back of a large SUV.

She walked carefully through the parking lot, appreciating some stability from gravel crunching under her boots instead of ice. She was willing to bet Matthew's generosity toward her would have ended if she had agreed to return with him to New York. The supermarket's door opened and warm air encircled her.

I'm going to inherit the House of Yates and screw up. Fear balled in Carissa's stomach. Could she get the spring collection to the all-important fashion shows and continue Matthew's legacy, even with her designs back in play? If she hadn't learned enough from her husband about running his business, she could send both the company and her own assets spiraling down to an ignominious end in bankruptcy court.

The enormity of the responsibility Matthew had given her suddenly weighed her down, like an anchor girding her waist. Carissa grabbed a grocery cart and pushed it toward the pet food aisle of Everett's Market while failing miserably to envision herself as an effective CEO.

CHAPTER SIXTY-FOUR

MAI LING'S BROTHER, Quang was trying to convince Detective Giddings his sister wasn't a flight risk if she returned to Boston.

Carissa heard part of the exchange as she waited for Ray Watkins, who had been told to finish his reports before taking her home. Dot and Mavis were both in the office. Dot's nasal tones assured several concerned callers that the buses were still running and the Market was open. Carissa wondered why people thought the local sheriff's office should be the information hub. Hearing Quang saying he didn't want his sister living alone in an isolated farmhouse for the rest of the winter, Carissa pondered how much longer it would take before Al Dyson made a large-enough offer make that developer happy. She also wondered whether Richard was involved in the plans, regardless of how vehemently he had denied it. If he was, she had no doubt Detective Giddings would ferret that out. She finished the coffee she had brought back with her, and tossed the cup into a garbage can.

Watkins finally came out from behind the front desk. "Ready?"

"You bet."

After he dropped her off, and she assured him she didn't need him to do a walk-through of the cottage, Carissa turned up the thermostat and called Chuck to arrange for a replacement. She got a recommendation from him for an exterminator and set up that appointment as well. The thermostat had to be reset three times over the next hour, and she swore she heard footsteps in the tower that couldn't have been made by a rodent, unless it was wearing combat boots.

She turned on the TV to keep her mind off everything else, pulled a cable knit cardigan over her sweater, added hiking socks to her ensemble and settled down in front of a roaring fire with a cup of herbal tea and Aunt Jessica's well-worn copy of "Pride and Prejudice." The murder mystery she had brought with her from New York remained untouched on an end table.

CHAPTER SIXTY-FIVE

THE FOLLOWING MORNING, Mai Ling brought over a pot of soup. The pho tasted as good as it looked, filled with thinly sliced beef and rice noodles in a flavorful broth. Mai Ling had brought a bag filled with bean sprouts, basil and a quartered lime.

"My brother asked me to make soup for all of us this morning," she said. "We already ate at six o'clock. He is chopping wood and taking care of the cow. He said she needs to be sold and I must move into a hotel or rent a room from someone in the village. Do you think it would be possible for me to rent a room from you? I promise I will not be a problem, but I cannot take any money from Blake's account or benefit from the will until after the investigation has been closed. Blake's family is very angry and suing me. I could cook and clean for you. I do not know what else to do. My family is very worried about me causing them so much difficulty."

"They should have thought about the possible consequences before they married you off to Blake," Carissa said. "I'm sorry if I'm being rude, but I'm really angry with them. I'm glad your brother came, but now he finds he can't take you back to Boston, his focus is on trying to get you stashed somewhere until you're free to leave, and they're not even going to help you pay for a room."

Mai Ling's eyes filled with tears. "They cannot afford to help me, but they are very worried now I have been told I cannot leave after all. As soon as I am allowed to go, they will take me in. It will be a big sacrifice. I will never marry again, and I do not know how to do anything except clean. I will have to find a job doing that, but it does not pay well, and my English is not good. My brother speaks excellent English."

"Of course you can stay with me. If you want to earn your keep, cleaning this place will help to keep you busy but it won't bring in enough to pay legal fees. Do you drive?"

Mai Ling shook her head.

"Then I'll teach you. Once you get your license, you can start driving Blake's car and that'll give you more options. I'm sure you can go clean other people's homes, too." She thought of how she had researched agencies for someone to help Aunt Jessica in the past, but her aunt had refused to let anyone into the cottage. "You could also become a live-in caregiver. I'll help you look online for suitable jobs."

"Thank you, my friend."

Mai Ling brushed tears away and took Carissa's empty bowl to the sink. Carissa left her friend washing dishes and took a shower.

The doorbell rang soon after she had dried her hair and added a small amount of makeup. William, Detective Giddings and Deputy Watkins stood outside.

"They asked me to meet them here," William explained as he stepped inside. "They want you to have legal counsel whenever you speak with them."

Carissa looked at Giddings with a sinking feeling. "Are you getting ready to read me my rights?"

"Not yet, but it may come to that." He barely made eye contact as he followed William inside.

Deputy Watkins paused on the threshold. He sniffed the air. "What are you making?"

"Mai Ling brought over Vietnamese soup."

"It smells really good. I didn't get a chance to eat yet."

With dark circles under his eyes, a good inch of stubble and a wrinkled uniform, Ray Watkins looked as though he hadn't slept. Carissa followed the three men into the living room.

"I've got more questions." Giddings sat at the dining table and pointed to the chair opposite. "Have a seat."

She did, with William next to her. He opened his attaché case and brought out his notepad and pen. Deputy Watkins wandered off into the kitchen. Carissa heard the murmur of voices as he talked with Mai Ling.

"How's Mr. Ebberly doing?" Giddings asked.

The question surprised Carissa. "I haven't seen him since you and I were both there."

"I've been mulling over these supposed accidents. I believe there's a pattern to them and a link. That link is you, Ms. Yates."

"Me?"

"That lead me to ask myself whether someone in the village has a grudge against you, or you're orchestrating these accidents because of something you're trying to hide."

"I've got nothing to hide, and I haven't lived in the Cove long enough for anyone to develop a grudge."

William was looking intently at her. She shifted uncomfortably in her chair, which felt like it had turned to concrete while she sat on it.

"I see Mai Ling Ulster is visiting again," Giddings said. "Or has she moved in?"

"She brought me breakfast, then she started cleaning up while I took a shower. She asked if she could stay with me and clean my home to repay me. Her brother's worried about her safety, living alone out here."

"Perhaps he should be more worried about his sister staying here with you than anywhere else, although it looks like you two get along very well."

"We do get along. I like Mai Ling." Carissa didn't say anything else. She noticed William's grip on his pen had tightened.

"She probably worships the ground you walk on. You helped her get out of an abusive situation with a domineering older man."

"I didn't tell her to stab Blake Ulster, if that's what you're implying."

"Careful, Carissa. I'd caution you to think before you speak," William said.

"I don't need to. That's the truth. I gave my statement, already."

The phone rang. Carissa tried to ignore it, but after hearing low voices in the kitchen, the ringing stopped and Mai Ling hesitantly came into the living room.

"You have a call from Mr. Ebberly," she told Carissa.

"I'll have to call him back," Carissa said.

Giddings was staring hard. William looked worried.

"Please tell him I'm talking with Detective Giddings right now," Carissa added.

Mai Ling nodded and scurried back into the kitchen. Carissa took the opportunity to draw in some deep breaths.

Mai Ling came back. "He said you should have William with you. I told him Mr. Dansinger came with Detective Giddings and Deputy Watkins."

"This village is a real hotbed for gossip," Giddings said. "I suppose Ebberly knew we were coming here, although I don't know how, unless..." He called out to Watkins. "What's the name of that dispatcher in your office, Deputy?"

Watkins came to the doorway, a large wedge of cheese in his hand. "Dot," he said. "Dot Ellis." He saw Giddings looking at the cheese and hurriedly put both hands behind his back. "Do you need me to call and ask her to do something?"

"I think she's done enough already." Giddings gritted his teeth. "Even the damned dispatcher's a cog in the rumor mill."

He changed his line of questioning to ask Carissa more about her conversation with him the previous evening.

"Priscilla told me she heard Matthew and my aunt arguing loudly before she left the office," Carissa said.

"Your aunt went to New York?" Watkins sounded incredulous.

"Yes, and if all of you had looked more closely at the report, you'd have realized she must have been out somewhere before she died. I've been telling everyone who will listen that there was mud on her shoes. And how could she have climbed the lighthouse stairs when her arthritis was so bad she hadn't even left her home for the past year?"

"Well?" Giddings looked accusingly at Watkins. "What have you and your office got to say about that?"

Watkins colored up. "It got overlooked," he muttered. "We'll have to look back into the case, but it was already ruled accidental."

Giddings rolled his eyes.

"I'm sure we can find records to verify that trip," Watkins said. "Cab, plane, train, or whatever, unless a friend took her and brought her back." His gaze darted to William.

"You'd better find that out, hadn't you?" Two spots of color had appeared on Giddings' cheeks. "Christ, these local law-enforcement agencies."

"I'm sorry," Watkins said, although he looked far from contrite. "I've been trying to take care of everything that's happened around here while the sheriff has been on leave. Let me tell you, I've about had it up to here." He put his hand under his chin.

Giddings turned to face Watkins. "Add that search to your other assignments and you'll be putting in a full day for the first time since you got sworn in."

Without a word, Watkins stalked across the room and turned toward the front door. Carissa heard the door open and close, none too gently.

Giddings swung back around to face her. "Did you confront your ex-husband about your aunt's visit? Is that why he confessed?"

"Yes, during the call he made the night he died. I accused him of killing her. It was pure conjecture at the time, but he sounded really shaken up after I said that."

"How did he manage to get your aunt out of the building? He would have had to carry her."

"Priscilla said it was late. The offices had all closed for the day. Matthew had private access to the garage from an elevator in his office."

"But aren't there cameras in the elevator and the garage?"

"Maybe not in Matthew's elevator, but the garage, yes, I would think so."

"How long would they keep the tapes?"

"I have no idea. Why would you ask that?"

"Because a lot of companies re-use them. Sometimes within twenty-four hours."

"So we may never know how he got my aunt out of his office."

"Perhaps he offered to drive her back and then killed her on the way," Giddings said. "You told me he often lied to you and others."

"I'm not going to even think about that. I can't even wrap my head around him not calling for help when she fell in his office."

"How awful for you!" Mai Ling stood in the doorway. She held a tray with three cups.

Carissa smelled coffee. Giddings must have, too. He jumped up and took the tray from her. "Thanks," he said. "Wouldn't you like to go home?"

"No," she said. "I am preparing a meal for us to eat tonight. My brother can take his dish back to my house and eat there."

Giddings brought the tray over to the table. "I'd prefer you to go home, but if you won't then please stay in the kitchen, Mrs. Ulster."

. Carissa tried to give her friend a reassuring smile, but her mouth wouldn't cooperate. Mai Ling retreated to the kitchen.

"Why are you still living here after all that's happened?" Giddings helped himself to sugar before pushing the bowl toward Carissa.

"I don't really have any other place to go."

"What about the local inn? If you're not pressing charges against Mr. Raymond, you've got no real reason to avoid him, do you?" Giddings added milk to his coffee.

I should have seen that coming.

Giddings gave her one of his dark stares. "Well?"

The doorbell rang. Mai Ling ran through from the kitchen. "I will get that," she said.

While Carissa considered her answer to Giddings' question, she heard a male voice. A familiar one. Her heart dropped.

"What's going on?" Steve said as he strode into the room, his boots leaving wet footprints.

CHAPTER SIXTY-SIX

STEVE HAD WONDERED why William Dansinger's car was parked in Carissa's driveway. Now he wondered even more why Detective Giddings had hitched a ride to Carissa's home with the Cove's only attorney.

Giddings didn't look at all friendly. "Mr. Raymond. What a surprise. You can answer a few questions for me."

Steve had to take a seat opposite Carissa, which forced him to look at the result of his angry slap. Her face looked terrible—bruised and swollen not only on her cheek, but her forehead. He'd struck her far harder than he'd thought, and she must have hit her head when she fell.

She'll never forgive me. She must have called the police.

"What questions? He asked Giddings, trying to keep the anxiety out of his voice.

"Let's start with the time you got here yesterday, and the time you left."

"Well, let me think...I guess I came around seven. I didn't stay more than thirty minutes."

"What was the argument about?"

"Sally had broken off our relationship, and I was free to be with Carissa. I've wanted to be with Carissa since the moment we met, but she told me she's not interested. She's involved with Richard Ebberly. I told her what I think about that." Steve wanted to kick himself. His explanation sounded self-serving and rambling, even to him, and then there were those bruises on Carissa's face.

"Interesting." Giddings said. "Life in Treacher's Cove sounds like a soap opera."

The unmarred side of Carissa's face colored up. "I'm not involved in that side of village life. I don't reciprocate Steve's feelings, and I've never gave him any encouragement."

She looked only at the detective. Steve felt completely shut out.

"I was merely making a remark." Giddings had a supercilious half-smile.

Steve thought the detective was trying to look as though he was above rooting around in people's lives. He wanted to pick Giddings up by the scruff of the neck and throw him out of Carissa's cottage. Kick him to the curb. Tell him to go back where he belonged and leave the Cove to take care of its own.

"Living in Bangor, I always thought coastal fishing villages were quiet little places where nothing ever happened." Giddings chuckled mirthlessly, the sound reminiscent of dry leaves skidding over hard-packed dirt. "This particular village makes a lie out of that thought. Isn't that right, Mr. Raymond?"

Steve shrugged. "The Cove wasn't sleepy when I arrived, but it was a whole lot less chaotic."

"That was two years ago, if I remember rightly." Giddings' half-smile had turned into a smirk.

Steve had an uneasy feeling he had just stepped into quicksand. He nodded.

The detective regarded him for a long minute before shifting his attention back to Carissa.

"But the real trouble didn't start until your aunt's death and your arrival at the village, did it?" Giddings asked her.

Steve couldn't stop himself from jumping in to defend her. "That's unfair, blaming Carissa."

She glared at him. Steve ignored the warning. Someone had to stand up for her rights. William Dansinger wasn't saying a word. Steve tried staring at him instead of Carissa, but annoyingly, William was busy writing on a notepad.

"I'm merely making an observation." Giddings' attention had shifted back to Steve. "You seem defensive, Mr. Raymond. Why is that?"

"I don't like outsiders making reckless judgments."

"Ms. Yates is an outsider." Giddings left that remark hanging.

"She's never been that," Steve protested. "She used to visit her aunt on a regular basis back when she was younger. William told me that, didn't you?"

William glanced up. "She did, but Ms. Malloy kept Carissa very busy. We didn't see much of her." He smiled at Carissa.

"Ah, yes. Mr. Dansinger. Another very deep well." Giddings transferred his attention to William.

Dansinger stared right back at the detective without flinching, but Steve thought the attorney appeared paler than usual. Then he saw color had drained from Carissa's face. Steve wondered what she knew about William that she might or might not have shared with the Bangor detective. He told himself he had to chill. Giddings was attempting to goad any or all of them into sharing information he thought they were trying to hide.

"So where do you think your relationship with Ms. Mainard will stand now Mr. Yates is dead and is no longer a rival, Mr. Raymond? After all, Ms. Yates has made it abundantly clear she's not interested in you, romantically speaking." Giddings wasn't even looking in Steve's direction.

"Sally made it clear we were finished." Steve refused to elaborate.

"You don't like being told no by anyone, do you?" Giddings' voice sounded like syrup, cloying and sticky. "Are you really expecting me to believe you won't try to console Ms. Mainard?"

Steve felt like he was sitting under a heat-lamp. A voice inside him was gaining momentum, and it was telling him to leave; to run long and hard. But Steve refused to listen. If Giddings knew about New Jersey he'd have had the cuffs out way before now. Maybe even his gun, although Steve thought that might not be Giddings' style.

"No all relationships can be easily repaired by talking things out." Steve shot a quick look at Carissa, who was staring at the table.

Giddings was now scribbling on a pad. Steve wondered what he'd just said that either needed to be recorded for posterity or used against him later.

"You seem to have trouble maintaining relationships, Mr. Raymond. Richard Ebberly stole Ms. Yates right out from under your nose."

"Carissa has a bad taste in men," Steve said. "Richard Ebberly's a no-good piece of shit."

Giddings looked like he wanted to snicker. "Now we're getting to the meat."

Steve tried to tamp down the anger building inside him. "There's no meat." His jaw felt tight and he was speaking from between clenched teeth. "My opinion of Ebberly's no secret. I told Carissa about him deserting Sally when he knew she was pregnant. Sally had to pay for her own abortion."

Giddings scribbled on his pad again. "And you got into a fist fight with Mr. Ebberly over Ms. Mainard, didn't you?"

"I did." Steve refused to say anything more about that fight. He'd broken a couple of Richard's bones, but not his damned nose. The pretty boy had remained intact, ready to charm yet another woman into falling for him. A woman Steve wanted for himself.

"That's enough, Detective Giddings." Carissa was on her feet. "My relationships with any of the Cove's residents have nothing whatsoever to do with my ex-husband's death."

"Oh, but I think they do, Ms. Yates; I really think they do." Giddings' narrow features took on hawk-like intensity.

"Can he keep asking these insulting questions?" Carissa looked at William. "Can't you stop him?"

"Your attorney." Giddings shook his head slowly. "Your attorney is no doubt Mr. Raymond's attorney, Mr. Ebberly's, and a host of other inhabitants of Treacher's Cove."

"I wouldn't know that." Carissa folded her arms across her chest.

"Sit down, Ms. Yates. We're almost finished." Giddings looked toward the kitchen. "Ms. Ulster?"

Mai Ling appeared in the doorway, a knife in her hand. "Detective Giddings?"

Giddings looked at the knife but made no comment. Instead, he

asked if she would bring in more coffee, including a cup for Steve. Steve wanted to refuse, but thought he'd been churlish enough for one day. He took the cup from Mai Ling and took a few sips.

"I only have a couple more questions," Giddings said after Carissa sat back down. "Have you any reason to believe Matthew Yates knew about your relationships with Mr. Raymond and Mr. Ebberly?"

"Matthew makes...made...it his business to know everything about me." Carissa sounded both tired and resigned.

"Didn't you throw Mr. Yates out of your hotel, Mr. Raymond?"

"Not bodily, but yes, I did."

"Was that after an argument?"

"No. He knew I wanted him out of my place, and he was ready to move on, anyway."

"So he rented a cottage and planned to spend the winter."

"That's what I heard. He didn't confide in me."

"When was the last time you saw him?"

Steve had to think. "Over a week ago. He was going into Nancy Burton's store. She told me he picked up his mail there."

"You haven't seen or spoken to him since?"

"No. He wasn't a regular diner, and I didn't run into him outside the inn."

"How did you find out about his death?"

"It's all over town. News travels fast in the Cove. Hilly, my head waitress got the news from Nancy Burton."

"I see."

Giddings put away his notebook and pen as he stood. Steve realized the detective hadn't even removed his coat.

"At this point, I have no evidence that Matthew Yates' death was anything but an unfortunate accident. However, in view of the fact that Dean Halstead, who was working for Mr. Yates at the time of his death, also slipped and fell from a cliff, I'm not making any judgment calls while I wait for the results of the forensic evidence collected and the coroner's report."

"I can show the detective out." Mai Ling walked into the living room.

"How did you get here, Mr. Raymond?" Giddings asked. "Did you drive? I'd appreciate a ride back. Watkins left me stranded."

"I walked. I don't drive," Steve said.

"And yet you borrowed Virginia Greeley's car for your trip up here yesterday, when you slapped Ms. Yates around before driving back to the Cove," Giddings said.

Steve had walked right into that trap. He could have kicked himself.

"My brother will drive both of you," Mai Ling said. She picked up the phone without asking for permission, said a few words in what Steve supposed was Vietnamese, and hung up. "He will be over with the car in a moment," she said. "If everyone has finished their coffee, I will take the cups to the kitchen."

"Let me help you with that." Giddings rushed over to take the tray from her.

Steve thought he'd better be helpful and took his cup over to Giddings. "I prefer to walk," he said, pulling on his coat and cramming his knit hat on his head. "Take care, Carissa." He mouthed 'I'm sorry' to her on the way out of the living-room. Under no circumstances was he going to ride back to the Cove with Detective Giddings.

"That's a long way in the cold," Giddings warned as he walked into the kitchen.

"I enjoy the exercise."

Steve said goodbye to Mai Ling and Carissa as he strode toward the front door. He wanted to get away from Giddings as fast as possible. When he stepped onto the porch he saw lights coming up the track. Mai Ling's brother, he figured. He decided to take the cliff walk back to the road.

CHAPTER SIXTY-SEVEN

"That coffee was delicious," Detective Giddings told Mai Ling as he took the tray into the kitchen.

Carissa heard the front door close loudly. Not a slam, she decided, but Steve was going to make sure her door was firmly secured before he left.

The interview with Giddings had exhausted her. She wanted to take a nap on the couch with Aunt Jessica's afghan wrapped tightly around her. She thought Steve had looked really tense the entire time. She hoped he hadn't gone over to warn Matthew to leave her alone the day before and lost his temper It was also possible they could have argued over Matthew's relationship with Sally.

The doorbell rang. Giddings came ploughing through the living-room, Mai Ling in his wake. "That's got to be your brother, Ms. Ulster," he said over his shoulder. "I don't want to keep him waiting." He charged down the hallway. Mai Ling followed. She came back into the living room with a puzzled expression.

"I do not understand," she told Carissa and William.

"What don't you understand?" Carissa saw the plate of chocolate chip cookies no one had touched. She took one and broke it in half before popping a piece into her mouth.

"It appears the detective felt the need to take one of your coffee cups," Mai Ling said. "But he didn't put any coffee in it. He just placed it inside a plastic bag from that box you left out on the counter."

Carissa had a sinking feeling. "Do you know whose cup?"

"Steve Raymond's."

CHAPTER SIXTY-EIGHT

SALLY WAS HANGING delicate wind chimes when Steve walked into the Emporium the following morning. She wore a pale lilac cashmere sweater over black skinny jeans, the outfit stunning against her wheat-gold hair.

She gave him a sideways glance and finished hanging the wind-chime in her hand. "What do you think? I bought them from an artist in Portsmouth. He didn't want to do consignment, so I purchased them outright."

"They're beautiful," Steve said.

Pastels of green, pink, blue and yellow shimmered. Triangles and squares, prisms and hexagons. Glass vied with pottery. Sally ran her hand through the forest of colors, setting up the sounds of a hundred tinkling streams; the chorus of a thousand song birds; the promise of a fresh new day. Steve could imagine the heavenly sounds produced when a warm breeze stirred them.

"I fell in love with all of them, so I bought a crateful." Sally gazed around at the gently swinging chimes. "I hope I can sell them all; they cost me a fortune. I'll have to take photos and put them online."

"I'll take one right now," Steve said. "The one with all the iridescent blues. It's so delicate; it looks like it'd break in a breeze."

433

Sally firmly batted the one he'd pointed out. It swung against its neighbors, clattering forcefully. She laughed at Steve's audible gasp. "They're very resilient."

Her eyes sparkled and a wicked smile formed on her lips as she grabbed the chime, pulled it back and released it. The tinkling grew in volume until it became a cacophony louder than dueling church bells on a Sunday morning. The prisms collided as though bent on destruction, but the jostling did no damage.

"What are they—plastic?" Steve walked around beneath the display and peered up at them.

"Almost. They're made out of some new compound the guy put together. I forget what's in them, but they all come with a little explanation sheet. He threw one of the chimes on the floor and stomped on it to prove it wouldn't shatter. I was impressed." She detached the blue wind chime from its hook and climbed down.

"No wonder you bought a crateful. When people see mine, you'll sell one to each and every Cove resident. Those online shoppers had better get in line." He took the chime from her and carried it over to the counter.

Sally followed him. She picked out a box and tore a length of blue tissue paper from one of the rolls behind the counter. Steve watched her graceful, unhurried movements.

"Did you hear about Matthew?" He asked, carefully watching for any signs of distress.

Sally paused in the middle of pulling a length of white tissue. Her eyes regarded him with the same degree of interest he thought she might have exhibited if he had told her Virginia Greeley was going to have tea with Nancy Burton.

"Yes." She finished pulling off the paper, added it to the blue tissue and used both to line the box.

"Are you okay?" He wanted to see emotion. After all, she had left him for Matthew Yates. Surely she should be exhibiting some signs of grief?

"I'm fine." She tore off a length of gold paper and began wrapping the wind chime.

"Is that all you've got to say after you shook the dust of our relationship off your feet to start one with him?"

Sally finished wrapping and sealed the package with a two pieces of tape, her moves deft. "What more do you want to hear? I'm not giving you a blow-by-blow or making comparisons. Men always think it's about size and staying power."

Steve threw up his hands. "That's not what I was asking and you know it. I'm not going to start a stupid argument with you over who was better in bed."

"What Matthew and I had going is my business. I told those interfering, judgmental Bangor detectives the same thing."

"I'm sorry." Steve thought he knew how she felt. One round with Giddings, and he'd come close to punching the guy.

"You should be." She slid the box across the counter toward him. "Do you want me to send the invoice over to the inn?" A small dimple appeared at the corner of her mouth. "You haven't even asked how much your little purchase is going to cost you."

Steve pulled out his billfold. "Let me see." He peered inside. "I have two twenties and a ten...fifty dollars. How much change do I get?"

"You get layaway for that," she said, smiling outright. "The chimes are a hundred and twenty apiece."

"A hundred and *what?*" He turned to look at his chime's brothers and sisters.

"I told you they were expensive," Sally admonished, sounding like a teacher rebuking a student.

"What did you pay for them in the first place?" Steve turned back to face her.

"Sixty each."

He couldn't help himself. "Sally, that's crazy. You'll take a bath on these things."

Her bantering tone vanished. A quirk replaced the dimple at the corner of her mouth. "I can handle my own business, thanks, without any financial advice from you." She took the box off the counter and tossed it onto a shelf beneath.

"Hey, I said they were expensive. I didn't say I didn't want mine."

Steve leaned over the counter in an attempt to grab the box. To his total surprise, Sally struck his arm.

"Get off my counter," she said, her voice high and brittle.

"Sally, I want the damned chime. I'll bring you the rest of the cash this afternoon, after the lunch rush is over."

"Get out of my shop." Her eyes were full of tears.

He started to walk around the counter to hold and console her.

"Get out!" She backed up.

"Sally..."

"I mean it. Get out of here, now. Before I call Watkins." She grabbed her smartphone.

"You're upset about Matthew and you're projecting your grief and anger onto me," he told her.

He stayed at the other end of the counter. Sally had a quick temper. He wouldn't put it past her to throw the chime, her phone, or whatever else she had within reach. And he couldn't blame her. She had been happy when he walked in. Now he'd evidently gotten what he now knew he had secretly wanted—her complete breakdown.

"Of course I'm upset." Tears flowed down Sally's cheeks. "What do you think I'm made of...wood?"

"No." Steve took two small steps forward.

Sally wiped her nose on her sleeve. "I need to keep tissues in here," she complained. "Look at me, Steve. I hope you're satisfied. I was doing fine until you walked in here."

"I know. I'm sorry. I was a pig." He closed the distance between them and felt relief when she laid her head against his chest. "Come on." He put one arm around her and drew her from behind the counter.

"Where are we going? I can't leave the shop."

"Yes, you can. For a few minutes. I'll turn the sign around. People will know you're taking a break." He took her with him to the door, which he locked. He turned the 'Open' sign to 'Closed' and set the little clock on it to read 'We'll be back at 11:00 A.M.' Keeping his arm around Sally, he guided her into the stairwell and up to her tiny kitchen in the apartment above the shop.

"Tea or coffee?"

"Nothing, thanks." She found a box of tissues and loudly blew her nose.

"Water, then?"

"Okay." She wiped her eyes and blew again, then threw the balled-up tissue into a large open garbage can next to the back door. "You really are a bastard, Steve."

"Why? Because I made you cry? Keeping your emotions locked up inside isn't healthy."

He gave her the water and watched her sip slowly, her eyes downcast, like she was trying to decide whether to tell him something important, or not.

"I loved Matthew," she said quietly.

Steve couldn't stop his eyebrows from rising.

"Big surprise, huh?" She put down the glass.

"That was really quick."

"We were the perfect match sexually. Not like you and me."

She looked up at him and he squirmed as unwanted images of Sally naked and entwined with Matthew Yates flew into his mind. He felt like a voyeur who had gotten more than he bargained for by his peeping.

"He understood what it takes to please me." Her red fingernails raked a path across the table.

"How about I make us both a sandwich?" Steve asked, completely uncomfortable with her revelations. He opened the refrigerator without waiting for a response and took out sandwich meat, cheese and a loaf of bread. He balanced a jar of mayonnaise on top of everything and dumped them onto the counter while keeping his back turned.

"I'm not hungry," she protested. "It's the middle of the morning."

"It's close enough to lunch." He set out plates and started putting the sandwiches together.

"Matthew liked his women model-slim. He loved my body."

Steve realized Sally was beside him, smoothing her hands over herself in the slow, sensual way he had seen so often before. It had turned him on when they were together, and he was somewhat ashamed to say it was doing the same thing to him as he placed the top slices of bread onto the sandwiches.

"You haven't gotten anywhere with Carissa, have you?" Sally asked.

"Now look who's poking her nose where she shouldn't." He handed her a plate.

Sally looked at the sandwich and put it on the table. "I love it when men pull the old double standard. It's okay to ask me questions about my sex life, but it's not okay for me to ask you."

"I didn't ask you anything about your sex life. You volunteered. Sit down and eat your sandwich." He pointed toward the little Formica table with its two wooden mismatched chairs. "Look, can we stop arguing and go back to being friends?"

"I don't like male friends." Sally pouted. "If you want to go back to being my lover, that would be okay."

"I thought you were in love with Matthew and grieving over him?"

"You must have gotten all the grief out of me." She sat down and took the top off her sandwich, wrinkling her nose at the ham and cheese. "Matthew wasn't going to marry me. He told me that. You never wanted to marry me, either."

"I never said that, Sally. I said I wasn't *ready* for that sort of commitment."

"Richard Ebberly wasn't, either. Men are all alike. They want women to do everything for them, then they won't step up when it matters most."

"Don't even talk about me in the same breath as Ebberly," he warned.

Sally jumped up and left the room without another word. Steve heard footsteps running down the stairs and through the shop. Presently, he heard a door slam and then something being thoroughly beaten in her workroom. He wrapped both sandwiches in foil and put everything back into the refrigerator. No point in following her. She needed to work off her anger for a while. He wondered where Erna was that morning. Sally usually had the girl working in the shop until after lunch and later than that sometimes, when it was busy. But he also knew that during the winter most of Sally's sales were online. He wondered again why she would spend so much money on wind chimes out of season. Their brilliance and beauty wouldn't show as well in photographs, and he was sure she'd had to set their price too high. She should have haggled more over that crate filled with them, he thought as he washed up the few dishes and left them to drain.

He gave himself a mental shake. Sally's problems weren't his business anymore. She had told him in no uncertain terms that she didn't want him as a friend, and he couldn't give her the type of commitment she wanted. For him there would be neither marriage nor children.

He paused downstairs in front of the counter while he contemplated taking his wind chime and leaving the fifty dollars. He decided against it. Right as he opened the door, he felt something behind him. The hairs at the back of his neck prickled to attention and a cool breeze blew across his skin. He shivered and turned his head to look. He swore something moved at the periphery of his vision, but then it was gone.

The wind chimes swayed, tinkling softly. The velocity of their swinging increased when he opened the front door and a fresh breeze blew through the shop. Steve stepped out into the street and closed the door against the chiming. He shoved his hands into his pockets and headed across the street, waving to Percival Huddleston, who was closing the little visitors' center for lunch.

CHAPTER SIXTY-NINE

January.

"I think it is a shame." Mai Ling stuck her fork into the sweet and sour pork that had been delivered from the China Palace in Whitstead and popped a large piece of green pepper into her mouth.

"You don't like the food?" Richard was slowly working his way through a bowl of won ton soup.

"Oh, no, it is very good, Richard. Thank you." Mai Ling put down her fork.

"I'm sorry I forget to ask for chop-sticks," Richard said. "I wasn't thinking." His brow furrowed. "I might have some in one of the kitchen drawers."

"I do not need them; I am an American." Mai Ling pushed out her thin chest. "I use a fork."

Carissa was amused by her friend's proud tone. "That custom doesn't apply when eating Chinese."

"So what were you referring to, if not the food?" Richard pushed the remains of his soup aside. Nurse Fields replaced it with the Kung Pao shrimp he had ordered and a small bowl of sticky rice.

His progress was nothing less than phenomenal, Dr. Lister had said at the follow-up appointment. All casts had been removed, but he still had to wear a brace on his left wrist. His left foot was encased in a boot, the ankle heavily wrapped. Richard could now transfer in and out of his wheelchair independently, but needed help to push himself around the house. Removing all the rugs hadn't made that any easier, much to his disappointment.

"I meant it was a shame the police believe Carissa could have hurt Mr. Yates."

"That's a nice way to put it," Carissa said. "I know Detective Giddings still thinks I was involved, even though Matthew's death was ruled an accident. Matthew had been drinking, slopped whisky on the floor and slipped. End of story. " She looked at Richard, who hadn't touched the shrimp. "Sorry, we shouldn't be talking about this over dinner."

"I don't see why," he said. "We don't have much else to talk about except all these accidents. Halstead's death was another one. He was blamed for displaying a monumental lack of judgment. I never met him, but he doesn't sound like a stupid man. Only a fool would try to walk down those icy steps to take a walk on a rocky beach in winter."

"I think the coroner is as tired of all this as Detective Giddings and Sheriff Crosby." Carissa took a second small serving of fried rice. "They want all this to blow over. I'm not so sure that's possible."

"Me, neither." Richard sat back in his wheelchair, shifted his weight around and grimaced.

"But you had no reason to kill Mr. Yates, my friend." Mai Ling vehemently shook her fork.

Carissa smiled ruefully. "That's far from true. I had five years of reasons."

"The official line is that Matthew and Dean's deaths were accidental, but I know Ray Watkins doesn't agree," Richard said. "My advice to both of you is to stop talking about who did what and why. Neither of you wants to find yourselves investigated by that creep from Bangor and his sidekick, who seems to be completely silent and halfway invisible."

"You've got that right about the sidekick," Carissa speared a piece of broccoli. "I've never even met him. Johannsen. Giddings apparently sends him out to do all the dirty work, like trudging around for hours in the snow, but he can't have found anything useful. I still wonder why they didn't pursue that second set of footprints at Penwithen."

"Because they think Halstead met someone else who was checking the place out and that person left before his accident and went on to Whitstead or somewhere else further up the coast." Richard started eating again.

"And they didn't try to find him or her, I guess," Carissa said.

Richard chewed and swallowed. "They did, but the search came to a dead end. Dot's been very liberal with giving out details to Nurse Fields, who meets her for coffee a couple of times a week, and Ray's come over here a couple of times to chat."

"What hasn't been closed is the speculation in the Cove about you, me and Steve." Carissa decided her eyes had been bigger than her stomach as far as that extra serving of fried rice was concerned. "People stare at me and whisper to each other. I feel like I need a big scarlet letter A glued to my coat."

"That's crazy. This is the twenty-first century." Richard thumped his right fist against the wheelchair armrest.

"That's enough." Nurse Fields stood up. "I'm clearing away these dishes. There's Bavarian Cherry ice cream for dessert and decaffeinated coffee. Perhaps Ms. Ulster would be kind enough to help me?"

"Of course." Mai Ling sprang to her feet.

The two women made short work of taking all dishes, glassware and cutlery into the kitchen. Carissa heard the refrigerator open and close. Companionable chatter assured her Mai Ling felt comfortable in her new role as Richard's temporary live-in housekeeper.

"Let's go into the den and neck," Richard stage-whispered. He leered at her.

Carissa couldn't help herself. She burst out laughing. "You're too much, Richard. I'm supposed to be in mourning, you know."

"Why? You're not a bereaved widow; you're a divorcee."

"Still..."

"Still, nothing."

The ice cream and coffee arrived, interrupting any further discussion.

"You should take a nap, Mr. Ebberly," Nurse Fields said after Richard had eaten two servings of ice cream and refused the coffee.

"I'm not tired," he protested.

Nurse Fields wheeled him out of the living room, anyway. Carissa heard him telling the private duty nurse she was a tyrant.

"Let's do the dishes before I go home," she said to Mai Ling.

They made short work of cleaning up the kitchen. As she added soap to the dishwasher, Carissa thought about her looming return to New York. Everything was in place for her to take the helm at the House of Yates in a week's time.

She needed to stop procrastinating and sell both Penwithen and the lighthouse. All she had to do was call a realtor. One in Whitstead. Not Al Dyson. As she wiped down the counters while Mai Ling took out the garbage, she told herself that decision was the easy one.

The problem she didn't want to face was what to do about Richard. She was falling in love with him, and there was no way they were going to be able to continue growing closer with so many miles between them. Her life was in New York. His was in Maine. She should do them both a favor and leave before her heart got broken for the second time.

CHAPTER SEVENTY

"I'm GETTING MARRIED, GINNY," Nancy Burton announced, her face glowing.

Nancy had barely touched the high tea Virginia had spent half the morning preparing.

Virginia knew her lifelong friend was about to make a complete fool of herself unless she was stopped.

"Is that right?" Virginia forced herself to continue crocheting.

"I'd like you to be my maid of honor," Nancy said.

Virginia barely managed to contain a derisive snort, but noticed her crocheting had sped up when she had to draw more yarn out of the bag at her feet.

"Well, Ginny? Will you do it?" Nancy leaned forward.

"You shouldn't have accepted his proposal," Virginia said. The crochet thread snapped. She fussed under her breath.

Nancy's joyful expression collapsed into a frown. "What do you mean, Virginia? I suppose you're going to tell me what a fool I'll make, wearing white and getting married in church, like I'm a young woman. But I've waited my whole life for this. I'm not getting cheated out of it because I'm older than the average bride."

"That's not what I was going to tell you, Nancy." Virginia threw the crocheting into the middle of the table. "What do you know about this man? Have you even seen any photos of his family? Did he tell you where he came from? What work he used to do? Whether he has a pension that could support both of you if you gave up the shop?"

Nancy rolled her eyes. "We're back to all that again?"

"Of course we are. Why haven't you had a background check run on him by a reputable private detective? You know of one—Mr. Halstead's partner in New York. Matthew Yates employed that company, and as much as I disrespect him for having Carissa's activities at the Cove investigated, I think his judgment in choosing Mr. Halstead for that position was sound. Ray Watkins can give you the partner's name and phone number."

"Virginia, I do believe you're jealous."

Virginia couldn't stop herself. "You're getting old and senile, Nancy Burton."

"You *are* jealous!" Triumph rang in Nancy's voice. "You have nobody, while I have a man who loves me. Why, you don't even have a pet anymore. You have no one."

Tears welled up in Virginia's eyes. "What a cruel thing to say."

Nancy clapped her hands. "I'm right; I'm right. You're old, alone and jealous."

"And that makes you happy?" Virginia forgot about her arthritic hip and jumped up. "You've changed, Nancy. You're not the person I knew." Her hip throbbing, she limped over to her Queen Ann secretary and opened the middle drawer. "I shouldn't even give you this after the way you've acted today, but I'm a true friend. Read it." She threw an envelope onto Nancy's lap.

Nancy looked at the return address printed at the top left corner. "New York? Willis Detective Agency? I don't need to spend money on hiring anyone. You already did that behind my back!" She threw the envelope onto the floor.

"Read it, if you've got an ounce of sense left in you," Virginia said.

Nancy looked down at the envelope. Her complexion paled. "I don't want to."

Virginia looked at Nancy's silver hair. Twenty years ago, Nancy would have been more reasonable. Now she must be desperate to find love without stopping to question who was offering it.

"Do you want me to tell you what it contains, then?"

"No." Nancy got to her feet. "I'm not going to listen to any more of your venom. I know I've asked for some of your barbs over the years, even delivered some of my own, but this is over the top."

Virginia tried her best to speak gently, instead of responding with more sniping. "I agree it's time to stop all this back-biting and bad-mouthing. But my instincts were right when I decided I should ask Mr. Willis to investigate this man. You must *not* marry Walter Barnes, Nancy."

With daylight fading, Nancy's outline began to blend with her surroundings. Virginia reached for the lamp.

"Don't," Nancy pleaded, but it was too late.

As light flooded the area around the table, Virginia saw tears on her friend's wrinkled cheeks.

"Oh, Nance," she said. "I would have given anything to be wrong about this man." She pulled a chair over next to Nancy and placed an arm around her friend's shoulders. "I swear to you—I only thought of you when I did this. I wanted you to be happy. But Walter Barnes is not who he says he is. His criminal record goes back years. He's a swindler and a forger. He's done time on two separate occasions. He married two other elderly women, outlived them and claimed their estates. He spent all their money on extravagances and gambling. He specializes in moving to small towns and finding his marks, as Mr. Willis called them, from within church congregations."

Nancy sobbed. Virginia grabbed her unfinished project—a table runner to which she was attaching a crocheted border—and handed it to Nancy, who dabbed her cheeks and blew her nose on it before she saw the still-attached crochet hook.

"Ginny!" Nancy held up the hook. "I'm not the only one who's growing senile."

Virginia took back the table runner. "I suppose not."

"I'm sorry for calling you terrible names and doubting your friend-ship." Nancy fished in her skirt pocket and came up with a crumpled tissue. She dabbed her eyes.

"Well, I'm sorry Walter Barnes isn't who he says he is."

They both sighed, almost in unison. Virginia reflected how alike she and Nancy really were.

"I'm so sorry about Hubert, too," Nancy said. "I should never have said what I did."

"I knew you didn't really mean what you said, Nance. " Virginia squeezed her friend's hand. "I cherish the time I had with him. Would you help me build my little memorial in the back garden when spring comes?"'

"Of course. It would be an honor." Nancy managed a watery smile.

Virginia decided they needed a pick-me-up. "Why don't I put the kettle on and we'll have more tea? With brandy, this time."

"That would be lovely," Nancy said.

CHAPTER SEVENTY-ONE

"So, what are you going to do?" Virginia asked, watching Nancy tip a liberal serving of brandy into her Earl Grey tea.

"I'm going to give Walter 'The Swindler' Barnes the boot and take a vacation. The first one I've had in twenty years." Nancy took a sip of her spiked tea. "Somewhere warm. Florida? The Bahamas?" She smiled. "Want to come with me?"

"I'd love that." A vacation sounded totally exciting to Virginia. "When would you leave?"

Nancy didn't even pause to think about it. "Monday."

"That's a week away!"

"Don't you think you can be ready that quickly?"

"I certainly can." Virginia drew herself up and put down her empty cup. "Let's call that travel agent in Whitstead; the one in the ugly strip shopping mall."

"Better than that, let's take your car and drive over there tomorrow morning. We could make a day of it—our travel arrangements, followed by lunch at the Whitstead Tavern."

"Sounds wonderful." Virginia felt giddy with delight at the thought of leaving the winter behind. But then her mood sobered. Nancy still had to face Walter Barnes. "Do you want me to come with you when you tell the groom the wedding's off?"

"No. That's a chore I can take care of myself. I'm even looking forward to it, the more I think about him trying to take my life-savings." Nancy looked at her watch. "Seven o'clock. I'm supposed to be cooking supper for us this evening. He said he loves my cooking. I suppose what he really loves is the fact that I'm a cheap, obliging date." She got up. "I'll be here at ten o'clock sharp tomorrow morning, ready for our adventure."

"I'll be waiting with bells on," Virginia promised.

CHAPTER SEVENTY-TWO

MARCH.

Banks of charcoal gray clouds loomed ominously on the horizon. Gunmetal grey water seethed beneath a leaden sky. Carissa stood at the top of the cliff and marveled at the raw ferocity of nature. The sea boiled against the rocks below, surf pounding and spray flying up to be caught by the wind and tossed against her skin. She touched her tongue to her lips and tasted salt, raised her face to the elements and breathed deeply. Her return to New York had been a triumph. She hoped this last trip back to Maine would bring closure.

She turned away from the cliff. Matthew would have smiled with pleasure at the slew of orders pouring in. She wished she could retain that image of him, but it always became superimposed by the one of him at the funeral home. She still wasn't sure why she had asked to view his body. Some deep-rooted desire had urged her to bid a final farewell to him. Dressed in a superbly-tailored suit of charcoal wool over a pale grey shirt and silver tie, his black hair and moustache trimmed to match his favorite publicity photo, he had looked the epitome of what he had striven for in life, but nothing like the husband she had loved.

He had fought so hard for an equal footing with other more famous designers, Carissa thought as she walked slowly back toward the lighthouse. Even after he achieved success he had continued refining his own image. He knew his working-class roots showed at times, although Carissa had done her best to help him smooth out the rough edges. At least in that endeavor, they had been a team. She stopped to look up at the whitewashed lighthouse with mixed feelings. Part of her felt attached to it, the other part still felt apprehensive about being inside the cottage. Since her arrival, the newly-replaced thermostat had lowered itself three times. Either wiring was faulty somewhere in the house, or Aunt Jessica didn't appreciate her niece's return.

She returned to thoughts of Matthew. So many condolence cards and messages had arrived at the offices, they had filled box after box. Matthew's influence on the fashion industry had been touted in all manner of media outlets. Pundits spoke of how his revolutionary designs had transcended the national scene before being embraced internationally. Carissa wondered whether Matthew would have been shocked to learn how much he would be missed.

His family, kept at a respectable distance during Matthew's lifetime, had clamored for his body and contested his will. Carissa did the only thing she could to repay him for finally giving her his respect—she had him interred at a small upstate cemetery, where the elite went to their final rest.

Having satisfied her conscience, she ordered an ornate tombstone that reflected Matthew's lowly beginnings and lack of class. Two chubby cherubs with fat cheeks and even fatter backsides blew trumpets toward heaven at the feet of a barely-covered angel. The inscription read: MATTHEW YATES, DESIGNER AND ENTREPRENEUR, followed by his age: 45.

William Dansinger and Roland Finch had their hands full after what Carissa belatedly-recognized was a self-indulgent, spiteful jab at her ex-husband. Matthew's mother made sure to get a photo taken of her clutching flowers and weeping in front of Matthew's grave with the offensive tombstone prominently displayed. It was eagerly picked up by social media as well as being plastered onto the front pages of tabloids. SHOCKED AND APPALLED read the headline of one magazine she read while passing a news stand. COLD-HEARTED AND DISRE-SPECTFUL blasted another in a convenience store. Her photo had been strategically placed beside Matthew's.

Roland's recommendation, backed up by William, was to appease the family financially. They were able to come to terms by agreeing to accept Matthew's cash reserves, which were sizeable but still relatively modest since Matthew had only kept six months of expenses readily available.

Carissa didn't need the money. She had funds from Aunt Jessica's estate as well as ownership of Matthew's business. She made sure she retained legal and exclusive rights to the Yates imprint as well as the fashion house itself. Standing in the building after hours, she had realized she was in familiar territory and would be able to pick up where Matthew had left off. Her artistry may have embellished Matthew's basic concepts, but the cut of his gowns and his use of textures had complimented the intricate and delicate embroidery and braiding. Looking at his designs and fabric choices, her only doubt was whether she would be able to duplicate his unique sense of style. Would buyers accept her as a substitute, even if she had the support of Matthew's staff?

You can do this, she told herself. *You trained for this day the entire five years you were married to Matthew. Put the advice of your psychologist into practice: compartmentalize the abuse; remember the teaching moments.* She avoided listening to the clamoring of naysayers forecasting doom for the House of Yates and listened to her instincts. The collections went onto the runways. The orders rolled in. And most satisfying of all, the business forged forward with its new CEO.

Priscilla Baldwin had remained at her post along with the majority of the staff. Matthew's secretary was indeed a gem. From Carissa, she received the recognition she should have had from her previous employer, which included a sizeable salary increase and the title of personal assistant to Ms. Carissa Yates.

Frigid air brought Carissa back from her daydream. Shivering, she hurried back to the cottage, which had been readied for her by anonymous 'friends of the village' as a small note propped against the coffee maker had told her when she arrived back at the Bennett Point Light. Not completely anonymous, Carissa thought, knowing William Dansinger was the only one with a set of keys. Fresh flowers graced the middle of Aunt Jessica's dining table, the refrigerator and the pantry were stocked with staples, and a bag of her favorite coffee sat behind the welcome note.

Her worries were over, Carissa told herself. Matthew's condo had sold the day it hit the market, and she had rented an apartment in the Garment District. It was an expensive rental, but she had wanted to make sure the business was on an even keel before she invested in any more real estate. Her return to Maine was to be brief.

She was seriously leaning toward a wrecking ball making short work of Penwithen, but she felt a sense of responsibility toward the crumbling family mansion. If it could be saved, or part of it salvaged for a rebuild, then that's what should be done. She'd make a final decision that week while sorting through the contents of the lighthouse. She would have some of Aunt Jessica's belongings shipped to New York. What remained would be donated to charity before the property went on the market.

Since her departure, Treacher's Cove had claimed one more victim in what sounded like a strange twist of fate. While making his return trip to Bangor a few days before Christmas, Detective Giddings had stopped at a gas station and interrupted a robbery in progress. He was shot and killed. Another detective was supposedly taking over his cases. Carissa felt sure any lingering doubts about the 'accidents' at Treacher's Cove would be shelved and life at the Cove would return to normal.

She welcomed the savage wind thrusting rude fingers through her hair as she walked up to the gate in the picket fence. The crisp, clean quality of the coastal air invigorated her. She looked at the flower beds that would fill with daffodils, narcissi and tulips in the spring. Carissa's plans to sell the lighthouse blew away with the wind gusts. Selling Bennett Point Light to an unknown buyer would consign it to an uncertain fate, possibly with detrimental results to the community.

Instead, she had a much better solution. She knew who would enjoy tending her aunt's bulbs and who would find peace at the lighthouse, surrounded by her aunt's treasured, rustic possessions: William Dansinger. He had finally left Patsy to the care of her private duty nurses and moved into a small apartment above his office in the Cove. William had a lot of healing to do, and Carissa felt the lighthouse could help him. She unlocked the back door, walked through the mudroom into the kitchen and tossed her coat over the back of a chair. After her walk, a fresh pot of coffee sounded wonderful.

Mai Ling's brother had also returned to Treacher's Cove. Carissa had seen a U-Haul truck and a van in the Ulsters' driveway when she arrived two days ago. He and a couple of others, either brothers or friends, had been loading boxes and furniture into it from the Ulsters' home. Mai Ling must be moving out and moving on. Carissa hadn't heard anything from her friend, but William had told her the investigation over Blake Ulster's death had also ended when Giddings' died. With a ruling of involuntary manslaughter, William told her Mai Ling had left her temporary position as Richard's housekeeper and returned to her family in Boston.

Carissa took her coffee up to the lantern room, sipping while she watched waves rolling in regimental lines toward the shore; a relentless, pounding army ageless as time. Despite the thrill she'd experienced when she returned to New York and the world of *haute couture*, the wild beauty of Maine continued to attract her.

She wanted to help the villagers of Treacher's Cove keep their families intact and provide more opportunities for them to earn a living wage in their own community. She had once thought about establishing a place where crafters could work and artists could create. Why would she abandon that idea when Penwithen was available?

She watched the play of light and shadows on the water. Living in an apartment year round suddenly didn't seem so appealing. Carissa decided to call Richard and arrange for him to give her his opinion about what could be done to make Penwithen into a retreat for her and a workshop for the community. Would that even be feasible?

As she walked back down the circular staircase, she held the banister in one hand and her empty coffee cup in the other. She still didn't like the stairwell, even though Aunt Jessica hadn't fallen there. She took out her phone when she returned the kitchen, poured more coffee, told herself to stop procrastinating and scrolled down to Richard's number. She hadn't called him since arriving back at the Cove, and she felt very guilty.

"Hello, love." He sounded so cheerful. His voice was much stronger and deeper. "How are you?"

"Doing well, Richard." She tried to sound bright and friendly, but even with her best effort, her voice developed a slightly breathless quality.

"I heard you were back." He didn't say anything else. He didn't have to. She'd been in town for 48 hours and had been seen by just about everyone except him.

"I'm sorry," she said. "It was rude of me not to call. I felt...feel somewhat awkward."

"No need to be. You rebuffed me. We're still friends. There's no need to avoid me."

She let out her breath in a long stream of relief. "Thanks."

"What can I do for you?" He laughed. "I'm still stuck in the wheelchair, thanks to an infection Dr. Lister told me would end in an amputation if I didn't stay off my left foot. I've been on IV antibiotics for weeks. I managed to strain my left wrist again, too, so the brace is back on that. Never, *ever* break as many bones as I did."

"I'll try not to break anything, and that's a promise." She smiled. He did sound better, despite the obvious set-backs. "I called to ask if you'd be up for a drive over to Penwithen today, but I guess not."

"I finished the antibiotics a couple of days ago. I've got another follow-up appointment on Monday. I'm hoping for a clean slate, so I can get back on both feet. Dr. Lister doesn't even want me crutching around my house on one leg in case I fall, like that's going to happen. I would *love* an outing. What are we going to do at Penwithen? Deliver a eulogy for it?"

"Don't make rash decisions until you actually see it again. I'd really like to save it, but I'm ready for the worst news if that's what you have to give me. Maybe some pieces could be incorporated into new construction. I feel I've got to make a decision. I inherited it, and I'm afraid it's unsafe. I could be held liable if someone got injured trying to get inside it, even if I post 'No Trespassing' signs everywhere on the property."

"So you'll pick me up. Say one o'clock? We could have an early dinner afterward in Whitstead."

"You're not stir-crazy are you?" She laughed.

"I'm ready to go nuts. I haven't been out of this house in weeks."

CHAPTER SEVENTY-THREE

OMINOUS WHITE CLOUDS were gathering on the horizon by the time Carissa and Richard arrived at Penwithen. She parked the rental Jeep Cherokee in the forecourt.

"That early dinner may have to wait for another day," Richard said, looking up at the sky after he transferred from the SUV into his wheelchair. "It looks like another storm's blowing up."

"We won't be that long." Carissa tucked a blanket around his legs. They felt lighter and thinner than they had right after his accident. She realized he'd lost muscle bulk as well as strength. A pang of regret shot through her. She should have made time to check on him while she was in New York, regardless of how busy she had been. He'd gone through weeks of hell after she left. Nurse Fields hadn't spared any details while Carissa waited for Richard to finish getting ready for his outing.

The wind held the tang of salt spray. Richard shivered. Carissa started to push the wheelchair. One of the front casters ran off the side of the concrete path. The wheelchair rocked. Terrified it would tip over, she grabbed his shoulder.

"I'm okay." He leaned to the opposite side and grabbed the wheels. "Here, let me help you. I've gotten pretty good at this, even with the brace on my wrist."

Between them, they got the wheelchair back onto the path and over to the front steps of Penwithen. "I love those columns," she said. "Do you think the porch can be salvaged?"

"Debatable." Richard carefully wheeled himself from one side of the porch to the other. "Dry rot, termites, and there's a hole big enough for some fairly large rodent family to live underneath."

"How big of a rodent?" Carissa started to pull his wheelchair back.

"Oh, probably a skunk."

"Great. We're going to get sprayed as well as snowed on."

"No spraying as long as we leave him or them alone. Let's look around the sides and the back. Things at the front look pretty bad enough, and it's not even facing the ocean."

"You're not sounding very encouraging," she said.

"Have you talked to Mai Ling?" He asked as she pushed him over a flagstone path at the side of the house.

"No, but William told me she got to keep the contents of the house. Blake's family kept the house itself. There wasn't much in Blake's bank account, but Mai Ling refused to fight his family over the property. She moved in with her brother and his family. Got away from her parents, but that brother seemed a bit controlling to me. One good thing is that Blake collected antiques and stored them in the basement. Apparently she'll get a good price for most of the pieces at auction. That'll help get her on her feet."

Carissa watched Richard survey the disintegrating clapboard on the south side of the house. He'd developed fine lines around his eyes and a pinched look to his mouth since his accident. Nurse Fields had said plastic surgery was on hold until the infection in his leg had been resolved. With the long scar running between his chin and left ear, he wasn't the same flawlessly handsome man she'd met in the hotel restaurant the past fall. To Carissa, he looked even more appealing. She reminded herself this was a business meeting, not a chance to renew their on and off love affair.

"I do love it here," she said, panting as she helped push the wheelchair onto the extensive back patio with its incredible view. Pounding surf crashed onto rocks along the coast. "It's so beautiful. If I was one of my ancestors, I'd want to build here, too."

"I'm very glad you're thinking of living at the Cove part of the year," Richard said. The wind caught his scarf and threatened to tear it from his neck.

Carissa bent over him to pull it back into place. He wrapped his arms around her and kissed her. His lips felt cold and tasted of salt. "We should keep moving or you'll freeze to death," she told him, her fingers running down his cold, scarred cheek before she gently pulled away. "I was selfish, asking you to come out here with me."

"I'm fine," he said. "A little cold won't hurt a native Mainer."

"Maybe not, but if you do catch pneumonia, I won't hear the last of it from Nurse Fields or Dr. Lister."

"Okay, let me take a good look at the back of this building." He turned his wheelchair to gaze up at the house.

"Is it about to collapse?" She asked. A gutter had fallen since she was last there.

"Not while we're here, but since the roof's rotting out, pretty soon." He pointed to where the gutter had come down. "There's one result. More will follow as the damage spreads. The columns back here don't look in as bad shape as I would expect, and there are really nice tile floors at both entrances that could be salvaged, if removed carefully. I can't see the window frames under the boards. That may or may not be a good thing—moisture can sit between the plywood and the frame, setting up a moldy environment that turns wood into sawdust. The siding would all need to be replaced. I'm hoping the doors are intact. I remember wrought iron and beveled glass at the front. I heard there were a pair of French doors back here."

"Did you ever go inside?"

"No. I don't even remember who was living here when I was a child. It's been abandoned for years. I do remember looking out the car window when we came here to drop something off one time. That's when I saw the front door. I was only maybe nine years old, but it made an impression on me, even then. I can recall sunlight hitting the beveled glass. My dad gave me a lesson in architectural styles on that trip and used Penwithen as one of the examples. I think he was dropping off wallpaper samples, but I never remember him actually doing any work here."

When they reached the north side of the house, he shook his head. "Looking grim, 'Rissa. Lots of rot."

Despite the strong wind, Carissa caught the smell of decay seeping out from beneath the boarded windows.

"If you want my frank opinion, and I believe that's why you brought me out here, this house needs bulldozing." Richard poked at the siding. "Damage is so extensive, it's hard to figure out how the place is still standing. Without seeing the inside, I can't tell you which parts could be used in a new home. I can make sketches of different styles I think you might like, including another colonial. Once I'm back on my feet and the boards come off, I can give you the diagnostic and cost breakdowns."

"That sounds like a terminal prediction, all right." She couldn't keep the disappointment out of her voice.

"My mother said there's a spectacular circular staircase with wrought iron banisters inside. She also talked about a wide reception hall with another tile floor. They all may be salvageable, but with probable holes in the roof, no promises."

The wind screamed around the side of the building and almost knocked Carissa over. She grabbed a rail edging the back patio, but it came away in her hand. She dropped it and leaned against the building.

"Careful." Richard's hands went to his wheels as an ominous creaking came from the overhang. "Maybe we should get back to the car."

"Okay."

Richard and his wheelchair were heavy and the rocky terrain wasn't being at all helpful. The velocity of the wind gusts had increased, bringing those billowing storm clouds a lot closer.

"Keep a firm grip on my chair," Richard said. "I don't want you getting blown over the edge like Dean Halstead."

"I'm not going anywhere but back to the car with you."

She started pushing him again and grunted as her calves protested. She tried using her hip to force the wheelchair forward. Sweat trickled down her back.

Richard took his hands off the wheels to shake them. "I'm wearing out, and my left wrist is really complaining. We should have gone back the way we came. This path's in worse condition."

"Too much effort to turn your wheelchair around now."

She used every bit of her strength to push the wheelchair the last few feet onto the smoother concrete at the edge of the forecourt. Getting back to the shelter of the car would be a real relief.

But when she looked at the driveway she saw it was empty. With a feeling of visceral panic, Carissa realized her rental Jeep Cherokee was gone.

CHAPTER SEVENTY-FOUR

"It can't be gone," Richard said. "It didn't drive off by itself."

He knew he was shouting at Carissa, but couldn't help himself. Coming to Penwithen had been a big mistake. Storm clouds billowed like a pyroclastic event, racing low and white. The wind had increased to gale-force, and he was tiring at a frightening pace.

"Well," Carissa shouted back, arms thrown wide. "*You* tell me where it's hiding."

"You don't just lose a car," he said, teeth chattering. "Someone must have stolen it. Did you leave the keys inside?"

"Yes, I left my keys in the unlocked car. My purse and cell phone, too."

"Why would you do something that stupid?"

"I thought they'd be perfectly safe. Who else would come up here in the dead of winter?"

"The person who stole the damned car, that's who!"

Carissa's arms slammed against her sides. She stalked off to the other side of the house and peered around it, as though she expected the Jeep to be hiding there.

"I'm sorry I shouted," he called.

Carissa came back. "Where's your phone? Can't you call someone to come and get us?"

"My phone's at home, charging in the kitchen. Since Nurse Fields took off while we're out, she won't wonder where we are for a while, either."

"So I'm not the only space cadet here, am I?" She looked rightfully angry. "Where do you get off telling me I'm stupid?"

"I didn't exactly *call* you stupid. I implied it." He glared at her, and she glared back, hands on her hips. Richard decided he was not in a position to be antagonistic. "Look, arguing isn't going to bring back the car. I'm sorry. I did something stupid, too."

"Maybe neither of us was thinking about self-preservation when we came here. I know I wasn't. Being this close to you made...makes me nervous. But I honestly didn't think anyone else would be roaming around up here in this weather."

"They shouldn't," he agreed. He decided he wouldn't address her remark about being nervous around him at that time. It was a conversation better left for a less stressful moment. "We're lucky it's not snowing, but I think that's going to change pretty rapidly." He gestured toward the incoming cloudbank. "We'll have to take shelter, but not in this house, even if we figure out a way to get inside. I wouldn't set foot in it if I was back on my feet and wearing a hard hat."

"Are there any other houses around here?" Carissa was looking at the other side of the road, where stands of trees dotted a steep hillside.

"Not for a couple of miles and no guarantees anyone's home. If I remember rightly, the owners are seasonal residents."

"Then I'll have to push you back to the Cove."

"I don't think either of us could handle you taking me down that steep road. It's filled with potholes, and remember, it's a good three miles of switchback turns. You'll have to leave me and go for help."

"You want me to leave you out here by yourself? That's crazy, Richard." She looked stricken.

"No, it's the only sensible solution."

Carissa stared at him, then looked at Penwithen. "Okay, I'm wasting time. If I'm going to do this, I'd better get on with it. Let's get you into a more sheltered place. Which porch is in the worst shape?"

"The front for the overhang, the back for the exposure. The service porch on the north side is the best bet. I wish it was on the south side, but God forbid anyone visiting would have to pass by it if they were walking around to the back of the house." He pointed to the still-decorative flagstone path leading from the forecourt around the south side of the house, and then to the cracked concrete walkway to the north.

"The wind's blowing a lot harder on that north side," she said.

"Yes, but it's still the safest place. The overhang's wider and reinforced. You can help me position my wheelchair so most of me gets covered. I'll hunker down while you go."

"I don't like this," she said, but she started pushing him.

Richard hung onto the armrests as the wheelchair rocked and bucked over the uneven concrete. "I'll take full responsibility. I refuse to be pushed down that hill. The wheelchair would gain momentum and you wouldn't be able to stop it. Then I'd get tossed out and probably break another bone or two. Does that make you feel any better?"

"No, but I'll go with it." She positioned his wheelchair under the meager shelter and locked it. "Richard..."

"Don't stand around gushing about how bad you feel for bringing me up here. I'm an adult. I wanted to get out of the house, and I really want to get this project started as soon as possible. Now, will you please get going before I freeze my butt off?"

She planted a quick kiss on his cheek. "I'll be back as quick as I can," she promised.

"You'd better."

Her footsteps faded rapidly. He thought she must be running and hoped she'd pace herself. Otherwise she'd become exhausted and still be out in the open when those clouds brought snow and freezing temperatures.

Scraggly bushes behind him rustled angrily, keeping time with wind gusts as the first bands of sleet made landfall. Richard scrunched down inside his jacket. His knitted cap protected his head, the blanket provided some protection for his legs, and his insulated gloves were keeping his hands warm, but his face was getting colder by the minute. He took off one glove, made sure his down coat was zipped up as high as it would go and adjusted his scarf to cover his nose and mouth. After shoving his cold hand back into the glove, he flapped his arms to restore circulation and tried not to think about how Carissa would soon be wet and cold, too. He tried not to glance at his watch, but couldn't help himself. Five minutes passed, then ten. He started to squirm around. Fifteen...fifteen long goddamned minutes...

Christ, his back and butt ached. He tried to shift himself from side to side to relieve the pressure but the doorway was narrow and his left leg was elevated. He knew if he leaned over too far, the wheelchair could tip over and get wedged in the narrow entranceway. Richard felt wretchedly helpless and berated himself for being completely unprepared. Carissa may have left her purse and keys in the car, but he had done something equally bad by leaving his phone behind. He took some comfort in knowing it may not have gotten any service up at Penwithen. A very small comfort.

At the twenty-minute mark since Carissa had gone for help, Richard asked himself why he had fallen so far into the invalid roll that he was depending on everyone else to think, act and do everything for him. At twenty-three minutes, he got another reminder of how utterly dependent he had become—he hadn't taken the time to use the bathroom before leaving home, and now he wished he had.

Try to ignore it, he instructed his brain. He sneaked another look at his watch. Thirty minutes. It felt more like an hour.

The sleet had turned to snow, flurries blowing into the porch and landing on the blanket. The overhang wasn't going to provide much protection if the snow worsened. Richard released his brakes and cautiously backed up his wheelchair while leaning his trunk forward, as he'd been instructed during his training sessions with the physical therapist. He felt a bump as the back wheels left the small threshold between the path and the porch. One move in the wrong direction and at least one of his wheels could run off the edge of the path. Then he'd be really in trouble. He needed to lower the elevated left leg rest to improve his balance and maneuverability. He took the blanket off his lap and hung it carefully over one armrest before lifting his leg and struggling with the mechanism to lower the leg rest. Although he'd practiced on the hospital's wheelchair until it had become relatively easy, he hadn't practiced enough with the rental, and he wasn't having an easy time of it.

He'd become all too dependent on Nurse Fields. All too lazy. That wasn't going to continue any longer. He had another appointment in Bangor coming up in a few days and hoped for good news. As soon as he got cleared to use his crutches, he was going to thank Nurse Fields for her excellent work and send her off to her next case.

The leg rest lowered with a jerk. Relieved, Richard got his booted foot back onto it, flipped up the right footplate and got the calf pad out of his way. With that foot on the ground, he had leverage. Using heel and fore-foot alternately, he was able to turn his wheelchair around without falling backwards into the bushes.

Suddenly, above the roar of the wind, he heard the crunch of tires on gravel. *Carissa must have stopped a car on its way out of the village.* His adrenaline surging, Richard wheeled himself to the corner of Penwithen and saw a charcoal gray Jeep Cherokee rolling into the forecourt. A feeling of alarm washed over him. Why was Carissa playing stupid games? Or had she found her car somewhere down the hill and driven it back up?

The figure getting out of the vehicle wore Carissa's long, turquoise down coat. Why had she changed from the shorter beige coat she'd been wearing when she picked him up? And she'd also worn a red hat with matching gloves and black knee-length boots with beige pants tucked inside them. This person was wearing brown boots. He couldn't see her pants, but her gloves were brown. He couldn't see a hat under the hood she had pulled down over her face.

Richard had a very bad feeling about the figure coming toward him. He was sure that was Carissa's rental car. It had California plates. They'd joked about the car probably not liking the change from sun to snow.

Without a word, the person walked around him, turned the wheel-chair toward the back of the house and started pushing. The power of the wind took his breath away. Snowflakes stung his cheeks and flew into his mouth when he opened it to protest. Richard saw the cliff edge looming closer and thought of Dean Halstead.

He applied the wheelchair brakes hard and fast. His attacker's momentum brought him or her into contact with the back of the wheel-chair. Richard heard a swift intake of breath and figured at least one of the push handles had made an impact. Desperate, he reached out, grabbed a handful of coat with his right hand and pulled.

Flailing arms and kicking feet encouraged him to grab more coat with his left hand and hang on grimly, despite pain shooting through his wrist. His attacker's head came over his right shoulder. Richard felt hair against his face. The wheelchair toppled sideways, taking Richard and his assailant with it.

He heard grunting as the person struggled to escape. Richard swung his arm and connected. A muffled scream assured him he'd been successful in striking something vital or painful. Frantic thrashing rocked the wheelchair. Richard felt himself sliding out of the seat. As he landed on the hard, cold and snowy ground, he heard his attacker leave. Rapid footsteps fled across the concrete, leaving him bruised and breathless but exultantly alive.

He lay on his back and gulped in air as snow fell onto his upturned face and dropped onto his tongue. Somehow, he didn't care whether he was wet, cold and exhausted.

For the moment, that was more than enough.

CHAPTER SEVENTY-FIVE

"I THINK the price of commodities has risen too high over the last year," Percival Huddleston said, tipping his glass back to drain the last few drops.

"The unemployment rate certainly hasn't helped *my* business," Al Dyson remarked from his seat at the other end of the bar.

Steve grinned and continued polishing glasses. He found the repetitive activity soothing, his patrons' banter restful. The morning had gone really well. Sally had agreed to have a late lunch with him, and he was planning to call Carissa afterward.

She'd made it clear she didn't want to be seen with him at the Cove, and he didn't want Sally knowing he was talking to Carissa, either. His plan was to talk her into having a quiet dinner at the Whitstead Tavern and then giving him a ride back to the outskirts of Treacher's Cove. He'd catch the bus to Whitstead from the edge of town, instead of at the stop right in front of Sally's Gift Emporium.

Start this relationship back up slowly, he told himself. *Carissa will come around. If she doesn't, then put all your effort into mending your relationship with Sally.*

"What do *you* think, Steve?" Percival asked.

Steve brought his wandering thoughts back to his customers. "I don't think anything's worse than it was last year, Mr. Mayor. I agree the unemployment rate's affecting sales and folks here at the Cove are having a hard time making ends meet, but as far as my own business is concerned, everything's about the same as usual, and I'm fine with that."

"I'd be happy with a nice little moneymaker like this place." Al moved closer to the bowl of nuts on the bar and took a handful, popping them into his mouth. His cheeks swelled like a chipmunk storing food.

"You could have had the inn," Percival reminded Al. "It was falling apart when Steve bought it. As I remember, and I do have a fine memory, you turned your nose up at bidding on it, saying it was a piece of —ahem—crap."

Al swallowed a couple of times to clear the nuts and held up his empty glass. Steve gave him another beer on tap. Al took a large gulp and wiped froth from his upper lip with the back of his hand before belching loudly. "I thought the dump had termites. And it *was* a dump," he said to Steve.

"It certainly was," Steve agreed as he wiped condensation rings from the bar and placed a coaster under Al's glass.

"You're always talking about making a quick buck and putting life back into the Cove by opening this business or that." Percival drummed his fingers. "Seems to me you could do a lot more if you talked a whole lot less."

"You've got no room to talk, Perce," Al said, his face mottling.

"Slow it down, guys," Steve begged, refilling Percival's glass with sherry. "If you'd start pulling together instead of against each other, the Cove might turn around financially this coming tourist season."

They both looked at him with suspicion clearly etched on their faces. "What do you mean?" Percival asked.

"Al has the know-how to sell empty houses and shops. Percival, you've got the gift of the gab. You could attract new blood to the Cove."

"You think Carissa's finally ready to sell that damned lighthouse?" Al asked. "I could get her a really good deal. We all know what a great amusement park it'd make."

"It'd make an even better resort if the Ulster place was included in the deal," Steve said. "Maybe the Ulster family would listen if you both talked to them about the benefits of selling that place."

"Hmm," Al said.

Steve knew a shrewd mind motivated by greed was grinding away behind Al's bovine face.

Al took another sip of his beer. "That's food for thought."

"You still have that conglomerate interested in turning the lighthouse into an attraction?" Percival asked.

Al slammed his half-empty glass down on the bar. "I *did*, but the last time I approached Carissa, I thought she was going to throw me off her property."

"That was a while back, though," Steve said. "Carissa's not going stay here permanently now she's got that fashion business to take care of. I heard she's been talking about restoring Penwithen. She won't want two homes here."

"She wants to restore that junkyard reject? Jeez. Does she have a death-wish?" Al stopped. "Not a good choice of words, considering what's been happening around here lately." He took another sip of his beer and smacked his lips. "What about giving me something else to drink, Steve? This doesn't taste good."

"Let me switch you to a bottle of Allagash." Steve wasn't going to argue over the fact that he'd served Al the same beer on tap for the last three and a half glasses. He reckoned the deaths at the Cove had soured Al's taste buds.

"You should talk to her while she's here, Al." Percival sipped his sherry.

"Yeah, I should. Hold that other drink, Steve." Al dug around in his pockets and came up with the exact amount for his beers, plus a nickel tip.

Percival, who had watched Al count out the change, snorted. "Sure you won't go broke leaving that sort of a gratuity?"

Al made a noise impressively close to a horse whinnying. "I'm going over to talk to Carissa right now." He took his hat from the top of another bar stool, carefully set it on his head and nodded to both Steve and Percival before waddling out the door with a "See ya later," shot over his shoulder.

"Damn that man; he makes me madder than a wet hen." Percival finished his own drink and checked his watch. "Two-thirty. I'd better pass by Virginia's house and then get over to the grocery store to make sure that girl Nancy hired is doing her work."

Steve nodded as he cleared away the glasses. "Have you heard anything from Virginia or Nancy?"

"Not yet, but I expect a postcard any day now. What a pair of jet-setters—a Caribbean cruise followed by an extended stay in Florida. Nancy hasn't had a vacation in at least twenty years, and Virginia never got one because she was caring for her parents when she wasn't teaching school. I reckon that cruise idea was the best one Virginia's had in years. They both needed to get away for a while after the winter we've all had."

"Hard to believe it's already pretty much over." Steve leaned his elbows on the bar.

The deaths in and around the Cove seemed to have taken all the revelry out of all the holidays, including New Year celebrations. Despite his denials, nothing was the same as it had been before, even at the inn. Steve's evening business had dwindled to Percival, Al and a half-dozen other staunch regulars. He'd had to lay off his part-time waitress. Hilly stayed busy enough, but he knew she wasn't earning the tips she had prior to all the mayhem. Cove residents just weren't going out in the evenings unless, like his regulars, they didn't cook for themselves.

"Not my favorite time of year." Percival pulled on his coat. "I wonder why I don't go to Florida myself. Give up the mayoral responsibilities. Hell, maybe I should pack up and retire there."

"You'd never do that. You love the Cove too much."

"I'm loving it less with every passing season."

Sally sauntered into the bar. Steve hadn't even noticed her come in the front door.

"Hi," he said, for want of anything better in the way of a greeting.

He hoped she wouldn't foul up his plans to meet Carissa for dinner. He doubted it. Sally had laid off her own part-time helpers, and monitored the shop herself while she worked on her sculptures in the afternoons.

Sally pulled off her hat, her pale hair flowing over her shoulders and down her back. It had grown considerably longer that winter. Steve thought she looked damned good. She unzipped the coat slowly, her cardigan-covered breasts thrusting through the opening like two overripe fruits being released from a tight peel. She tossed the coat onto a bar stool, leaving her in the figure-hugging purple cardigan over the tightest black pants he'd ever seen. Her hips swayed provocatively as she walked over to the bar. Steve couldn't take his eyes off her, and he was willing to bet the mayor of Treacher's Cove couldn't, either.

"Nothing was going on at the Emporium, so I closed and worked in the back for a couple of hours. Then I got bored, so I've come here to have coffee before our lunch date." She smiled at Steve.

"A good decision." Percival nodded approvingly, his breathing rapid and shallow. He picked up a napkin from the bar and blotted his forehead. "It's hot in here."

"It is." Sally unbuttoned the cardigan, revealing an even tighter-fitting turtleneck of pale lavender. As usual, she was not wearing a bra and it was patently obvious.

"You know," Percival said, his gaze fixed on her breasts, "you should try mail order. I bet you'd get a lot of customers."

Sally shrugged off the cardigan and hung it over a bar stool. Her breasts bounced. "I do get a lot of orders through the internet," she said.

"I bet you do." Percival sounded like he could barely breathe.

Sally rolled her pink, glistening tongue over her top lip, then back and forth over the bottom lip, before nibbling it lightly with her teeth.

"Well..." Percival backed up into the two bar stools behind him. One of them almost fell over. He steadied it before tipping his hat toward Sally. "I'd better be getting along." He almost ran out. A gust of raw wind sailed into the bar as the front door opened and closed.

"What were you trying to do, give that poor man a heart attack?" Steve walked around to the front of the bar.

"Of course not." Sally giggled. "Percival's so much fun to tease. He gets completely flustered when I'm around."

"If you always give him a performance like that, he will be."

Sally shrugged. "Harmless fun. You should know me well enough by now to realize."

"Do you really want coffee?" He asked.

"I do." She peeled off her gloves and took them with her as she walked to a secluded and darkened table at the back of the room.

Steve paused to watch more than her backside in the tight pants. She had a high level of salt-stains on her boots. She'd been in deep snow, which was unusual for someone who usually stayed in the heart of the village. Her coat was really wet, too, water dripping from it onto the floor. The only weather event from the last three days had been a strong wind. He hung up Sally's coat and went in search of Hilly. As he passed through the front entrance, he noticed snow on the mat. He hoped Sally hadn't fallen in it on the way from the Emporium. So much for seeing the back of winter.

When he returned, Sally had gotten herself a glass of water. She had made several areas of the table wet and was drawing designs in the moisture. He walked over, sat down, and grabbed all the napkins from the adjacent table when he saw what she had been drawing.

"What's up with you this morning?" He erased graphic outlines of male anatomy.

Sally laughed. "Have you suddenly turned into a prude?"

She'd taken off her boots. Her toes started caressing the front of his pants.

"Our coffee'll be here in a minute," he protested, even as his body responded to the stimulation.

"Then we'll be alone, again." Sally smiled. She raised her turtleneck and giggled.

"Good God, Sally. Put that sweater down." Even while he was protesting, Steve was wishing he hadn't been so quick to ask Hilly for that coffee. "The lunch-time crowd will be here in less than an hour," he added as Hilly's footsteps approached. Sally lowered her sweater but her foot stayed where it was. In fact, it started rubbing harder. He had two choices—try to play it cool until Hilly had put the coffee in front of them and left or slide his chair back and look really awkward.

"Nice to see you, Miss Sally." Hilly smiled as she set the tray down and placed the cups in front of them.

"You, too."

Sally beamed up at Hilly while her toes did things to Steve that made him want to gasp.

Mercifully, Hilly must have sensed they wanted to be alone. "I'll put the closed sign outside the door," she said as she left.

Steve let out a sigh of relief. Sally got to her feet and pulled him up, too. Her mouth opened readily when he took her in his arms and kissed her.

"I've missed you like crazy." He pushed the turtleneck out of his way.

"You have, haven't you?" She moaned and thrust herself against him, grinding her hips.

They moved across the floor while they kissed and groped each other. Steve heard the murmur of voices as patrons came into the inn for lunch, but he couldn't seem to care what was going on outside the darkened bar. With surprising strength, Sally pushed him back against the bar. The wood bit into his spine as she rammed herself against him.

Someone knocked on the bar door. "Hey, I thought the bar was supposed to be open," a man complained.

Steve recognized the voice. It belonged to one of his regulars, Dick Floresheim from the phone store. "We're closed for maintenance," he shouted. "There's a leak under the sink." He tried to push Sally away, but her nails bit into his wrists like sharp little daggers. "Stop it," he told her. "Right now. This is crazy; my customers will hear."

"They won't. I'll be quieter, I promise."

She pulled down the zipper on her pants, grabbed his hand and tried to shove it inside. The zipper's teeth were worse than her nails. Steve stopped holding back. He tore his hand away and shoved her.

She staggered a little as she came into contact with the bar stools, but she laughed. "Are you too chicken to finish?"

"Are you out of your mind?" He felt blood trickling into the palm of his hand. He was willing to bet his back was bleeding, too.

Suddenly, the door flew open, bringing a frigid gust of air with it. Over Sally's head, he recognized the first man striding into the bar as the Bangor detective who had been Giddings' shadow. Right behind him, Ray Watkins struggled to keep up. Incredibly, both had their guns drawn.

"What the hell is going on here?" Detective Johannsen came to an abrupt halt. Ray almost ran into his back. The detective scowled. "Are you all right, Ms. Mainard?"

Sally pulled down her turtleneck and zipped up her pants. "I'm fine."

"What *is* this?" Steve felt a frisson of fear.

"I think you know what this is," the detective said. "Remember me?

Detective Johannsen? I inherited the Cove cases after Detective Giddings got killed. They were a mess. So, apparently, was his car. But when his wife finally got around to cleaning it out, an interesting thing turned up: an evidence bag containing a coffee cup. It was from Carissa Yates' home. I had the prints run. Steven Raymond Tanner, I'm placing you under arrest. You might have run from prosecution in New Jersey, but you're not running from me. I'm working on tying you to the other deaths at Treacher's Cove." He glanced at Sally. "You've had a very lucky escape, Ms. Mainard. I hope you'll be willing to make a statement."

"Of...of course." Sally looked bewildered as she turned her head toward Steve. "This has to be a mistake."

"You want me to tell her or you want to do it yourself?" Detective Johannsen asked, his voice as cold and penetrating as a blast of frigid air from a Nor'easter.

Steve tried not to react, but inside he felt the shock spreading throughout his body. He kept his mouth shut and shook his head.

"Nothing to say in your defense, Mr. Tanner?" The detective waved Ray Watkins forward. "Cuff him and read him his rights, Watkins. We'll get him booked at the station."

Deputy Watkins started to edge forward warily, as though Steve had suddenly turned from a friendly inn-keeper into a ten foot tall werewolf.

Sally screamed, so loud and long all three men recoiled. She staggered and fell wildly against the heavy wooden bar stools. They toppled, taking Sally with them. They all slammed right into Johannsen. With Ray Watkins right behind him, the detective couldn't jump back fast enough nor keep his balance. He fell, his weapon discharging into the ceiling and bringing down a large chunk of plaster.

Steve took the opportunity to scramble over the bar, grab his old coat off a peg and sprint out through the delivery door into the alleyway behind the inn.

CHAPTER SEVENTY-SIX

CARISSA RAN, slipped, slid and recovered as a mixture of wet snow and sleet peppered her and the rutted road in front of her. Head down, she almost collided with a car laboring up the steep hill. At the last possible moment, she heard an engine above the constant howl of the wind and threw herself onto a snowbank at the side of the road. A familiar old blue Chevrolet screeched to a stop.

Carissa stayed where she was and tasted blood from her bottom lip. Her left elbow smarted and her left hip ached. The driver's door opened and legs swung out. Definitely not Virginia's legs, Carissa thought. Long and very muscular male legs were encased in heavy denim. She looked up to find Steve Raymond glaring down at her.

"What the hell are you doing out here; trying to get yourself killed?" He dragged Carissa to her feet.

"Of course not. I was running to get help for Richard. I'm so glad to see you. Someone stole my car."

"That's ridiculous." Steve brushed her off with as much gentleness as he might have given a piece of cheap furniture. "Are you hurt?"

"Just bruised I think. I had to leave Richard behind at Penwithen in this terrible weather. We have to go there immediately."

Steve pulled a tissue from a box on the passenger's seat of Virginia's car and thrust it at Carissa. "Your lip's bleeding."

Carissa touched the tissue to her lip, saw a larger amount of blood than she was expecting and applied pressure. "Did you hear what I said about Richard?" She mumbled around the tissue.

"I did. And about your car, too. It's all ridiculous, and I can't help you."

"What?"

"I can't go back to the Cove." He glanced over his shoulder.

"Why not? Did someone report you for taking Virginia's car? She wouldn't care. She let you borrow it before, when you drove out to the lighthouse."

"No. Nothing like that. But I'm not going to stand here explaining myself. Keep on jogging. You'll probably have plenty of company in a few minutes."

"You're not leaving without me. Richard could freeze to death." She grabbed Steve's arm.

"I don't give a goddamn about Richard Ebberly. I've got to go, right now." Steve shook her off and ran back to the driver's side. The car was belching black smoke and backfiring.

"Well, I don't give a damn whether you like Richard or not." Carissa flung herself in front of the car. "You've got to help us or he'll die. You'll have his death on your conscience."

Steve laughed mirthlessly. "He won't be alone. Get the hell out of the way."

"No."

The snow had turned back to sleet, which beat a steady tattoo on the car's hood. Steve gunned the engine, which started smoking in response.

"Please, Steve," she begged. "Please forget how much you hate Richard and think of him as a human being who's going to die if you don't help." She wondered whether Steve would actually run her over. He looked frustrated enough to do it. Carissa refused to think he was capable of it. She stayed where she was and tried to make eye contact.

Steve sat staring through the windshield for the longest minute, his hands gripping the wheel. At last he looked directly at her. "Get in."

Carissa didn't give him a chance to change his mind and drive off without her. She raced over to the passenger's side and jumped in.

"I'm getting punished," Steve told her as he shifted into first gear. The old car, its momentum destroyed by the unscheduled stop, made clinking noises and stayed where it was. Steve pressed his foot down harder on the accelerator. The clinking increased. He swore, allowed the car to roll back in neutral, shot it back into first gear and hit the gas. The Chevy Caprice bucked. Its wheels squealed in response, rumbled, gained traction and catapulted the car forward as though released from a slingshot.

Carissa braced her hands against the dashboard and hoped Steve wasn't going to strip the transmission. "Punished for what? This vendetta with Richard?"

"No, for being responsible for my partner's death two years ago."

They careened around a hair-pin turn. Carissa smelled burning rubber. "You killed somebody? Is that why you said Richard wouldn't be the only one on your conscience?"

"Yes. It was an accident. After all this time, the cops finally caught up with me." He coaxed a few more miles an hour out of the complaining vehicle. "This is a poor excuse for a getaway car. I hope Virginia's insurance replaces it with something newer."

Carissa ignored the aside about Virginia's choice of transportation. "How did the cops find you?"

"Those deaths in the Cove. I guess I was collateral damage."

He told her about Kurt's accident. How they'd argued and he'd panicked. How he'd stopped running when he arrived at the Cove and had thought he was safe until Giddings arrived and started poking into everything and everyone's business.

"Oh, my God." She couldn't think of anything more relevant to say.

"I've got to get over the border and hide in Canada," he said as they crested the last hill and Penwithen came into sight.

"You'll need a passport," she said.

"I'll ditch this car and find a way over that doesn't include a checkpoint. They can't watch every inch of the border day and night."

"Give me your cell phone. I'll call and get help sent up to Richard. That way you can leave."

"I left my phone on the counter under the bar. I had to escape through the back door. I was lucky I keep this old coat there. I use it when I take out the trash. Think that's symbolic?" He forced out a hollow-sounding laugh.

Carissa was again unable to come up with a suitable answer. She watched the windshield wipers slapping ineffectively at the sleet. Virginia Greeley definitely didn't do regular maintenance, she thought as a half-detached wiper blade swing through the air in front of her face.

"Stop the car," she decided. "I'll run back to the village."

"Richard won't survive that length of time. Sit tight. When you got me to stop and pick you up, you made me into Richard Ebberly's last hope. It must be karma, or something. Maybe I'm meant to save his life to atone for Kurt. Who knows?" He sighed heavily. "What I *do* know is I'm going to load Richard into the backseat of this car and we're all going to the Canadian border. I'll leave the car with you. All I'm going to ask is that you do whatever you feel is right after you give me two hours head-start. I can't go to prison. I already ran once—they'll throw the book at me. I'll do thirty years. More, looking at Johannsen. He's fierce now he's not trailing behind Giddings."

"Do you even have any money?"

"Only a few bucks in my billfold. How much do you have?"

"My purse was stolen along with the car. Sorry."

Steve's fingers whitened on the wheel. "I've got no luck at all. Not even bad luck."

As he swung the Caprice into Penwithen's driveway, Carissa saw her rental had returned.

CHAPTER SEVENTY-SEVEN

DETECTIVE JOHANNSEN SLAMMED down the phone. "I should have seen this coming."

"I can't believe he ran like that." Ray Watkins looked bewildered. "What was he thinking?"

"I don't know what *he* was thinking, but you'd better put on your own thinking cap and figure out where he's hiding. You're telling me we've looked everywhere and talked to everyone. But one of these villagers has to know something. Someone's covering for him, or he's stolen a vehicle nobody's missed yet."

Watkins wrung his hands. "I'll call William Dansinger. Maybe Steve contacted him."

"Okay. That's plausible, since Dansinger is the Cove's only attorney."

"I'm never going to get used to calling Steve Raymond by another name." Watkins shook his head as Johannsen slid the phone across the desk. "Steve Tanner doesn't sound right."

Watkins punched in a number, muttered under his breath and redialed. Johannsen wanted to rip the phone out of the deputy's hands and dial the number himself.

"Make it short and to the point," he instructed his subordinate.

Watkins spoke briefly with Dansinger while Johannsen scoured a map of the local roads to figure out a plausible escape route for someone on foot. Nothing seemed feasible, even for Steve Raymond, noted to walk for miles in all weather. Unless he was still hiding in the village, he had to have stolen someone's car. But no one had reported a missing vehicle. He refused to admit they were coming back to the drawing-board. Someone had to have seen a running man fitting Tanner's description. It wasn't like he was hard to spot.

Watkins put down the phone. "William says he hasn't seen or talked to Steve since yesterday."

Johannsen felt the weight of responsibility lower itself onto his shoulders. It had been a whole lot easier when he only had to listen to Giddings barking orders instead of thinking for himself, but he'd been working toward this promotion to lead investigator for over a year, and he wasn't going to fail on his first case.

"Who would lend him a car on short notice and refuse to tell us?"

Watkins shrugged. "Maybe he took Sally Mainard's, but I doubt it. He ran out the back of the inn. His cell phone was still under the bar. Hilly said he used to keep an old coat by the back door to use for deliveries and trash runs. That's gone. He probably had a pair of gloves and a hat in the pockets. He'll keep warm enough to walk around town, but not to hike out of here in this weather." Watkins looked at the map in front of Johannsen. "He'd have to be some kind of magician to get his hands on Sally's car key, too."

"He might have broken into the car or into her shop. Take her keys and go check. Tell her to sit tight with Dot. She wants to go home, but Tanner may try to contact her. I don't want her talking to him without one of us listening in."

Watkins nodded and bustled out. Johannsen sighed and stretched. He wanted to do something more constructive than manning the phone at the station house while listening to Dot pecking at reports and Sally Mainard bitching about being bored. He downed the rest of Dot's insipid coffee and took another mental run-through of possible places for Steve Tanner to hide. None of them offered more than a temporary shelter. He had to leave town, and since he didn't own a car, he had to use someone else's. But whose if not Mainard's?

Johannsen blamed both himself and Deputy Watkins for allowing Tanner to escape. He'd counted too heavily on the shock-value of their arrival. What had resulted was a complete fiasco. Sally Mainard had panicked and he'd done something he thought he would never do—accidentally discharged his piece in a stressful situation. He could only hope Watkins didn't mention that little detail to Sheriff Crosby. If he did, Bangor would no doubt follow up, and he'd kiss his promotion goodbye.

Johannsen's throat dried at the thought. He reviewed the bar scene yet again, cringing while he did so. While he was getting out from under Sally Mainard and at least three bar stools, Watkins had stumbled over the step into the bar area and knocked over two big empty metal barrels standing next to the back door of the storeroom. The only blessing had been Watkins' refusal to disturb Sheriff Crosby, who was reportedly sitting beside his wife's deathbed in a nursing home somewhere close to Whitstead. Maybe Watkins had facilitated Steve Tanner's escape, or perhaps he hadn't wanted to report his own disgraceful performance when he tried to apprehend a felon. Whatever the reason, Johannsen knew it was no good rehashing their mistakes. The only way was forward, and he swore he was going to redeem himself by putting Steve Tanner in cuffs before the sun came up on another day.

He refocused and scanned through the listings of Tanner's possible hiding places again. That waitress, Hilly Franks would hide him, Johannsen felt sure, but he doubted that had happened. No, Tanner had run, just as he had from New Jersey, when he jumped bail two years ago. Johannsen felt he needed more help, but if he called Bangor for reinforcements, he'd be doing traffic duty for years. He used a red pen he had found on the desk to score through one location after another. He' already reviewed them with Watkins, but he wanted to satisfy himself they couldn't have missed anything.

Watkins had put out a BOLO. Unless Steven Tanner was some kind of mutant greyhound, he had to be driving. The Canadian border wasn't that far away. Johannsen notified them himself. No fooling around while Watkins and Dot took extra time that might mean the difference between apprehension and the need to ask for cooperation from a widening circle of authorities.

The pen ran out of ink three listings from the bottom. He could leave the list as it was, but ever obsessive-compulsive, he opened the middle drawer of Watkins' desk and rummaged around for another red pen. He tried 3 ballpoint pens on the back of a grubby manila envelope before finding one that worked. But before returning the envelope to the drawer, he thought he'd better make sure he hadn't damaged whatever was inside. He pulled out a report on Steven Raymond Tanner's finger-prints, dated several weeks back.

Johannsen swore profusely. Either Sheriff Crosby, his deputy or maybe both of them had known about Steve Tanner's real identity and hidden it. Since it sounded like Sheriff Crosby hadn't spent more than short periods behind his desk in months, Johannsen put his money on Ray Watkins. Johannsen wasn't sure whether he felt enraged or hopeless. This investigation could have come to a conclusion the day that report arrived. He walked into an empty front office. Propped against Dot's keyboard, a note said she and Sally had gone to The Fisherman's Rest for dinner. So much for keeping Sally Mainard isolated and under surveillance. The front door flew back and hit the wall. A gust of frigid air hit Johannsen full in the face.

"Sally's car was parked opposite the Emporium." Watkins' voice trailed off as he saw Johannsen holding both the paper and the manila envelope. He cleared his throat nervously.

"Well?" Johannsen waved the paper.

Watkins slumped into a chair at a small desk on the other side of the counter. "I've got nothing to say except I chose to ignore the report. Steve Raymond...Tanner...is no murderer."

"This report doesn't say he is. But he did skip bail before his trial on a manslaughter charge. You should have told us. Now look what's happened. He's on the loose and the sheriff and the coroner were so anxious to close the cases on Halstead and Yates that both deaths were ruled accidental. Something smells really bad around here, and the first step in unraveling everything is getting Steven Tanner back into custody and questioning him."

"Steve's been a real asset to this community." Watkins' mouth set into a stubborn line.

"Spare me the character-witness crap. You've put the economic benefits of keeping Tanner here ahead of the safety of everyone in Treacher's Cove. This is a violent man who killed his partner with his bare hands."

Watkins dug a peppermint candy out of one pocket, unwrapped it, popped it into his mouth and sucked noisily.

Johannsen refused to admit defeat. "Get out of here and go door to door again I want you to make sure everyone's cars, SUVs, pickup trucks, vans, delivery vans..."

"Okay, I get it. Make sure no one's let him take a vehicle or he hasn't done it behind their backs. But let me tell you, since you came back inside, the weather's gotten a whole lot worse. It's cold as hell out there. Sleet alternating with snow and a high wind blowing everything around. We need more help. We should ask Whitstead."

"You let me worry about what we need. Get out there and start searching."

Watkins left, but didn't close the door properly. It blew back open. A frigid gust of wind brought a mixture of snow and sleet onto the wide rubber mat covering the threshold.

"*Ray!*" Dot's nasal tones rang out as she trotted over the mat. "None of us were born in a barn around here, dadgummit." She had to lean her shoulder against the door to get it closed. "What is *wrong* with everyone around here, lately? Can't we all just *get along?*" She looked at Johannsen for some sort of comment.

He felt really tired suddenly. "What did you do with Sally Mainard?"

"I left her sitting in front of the fireplace in the parlor at The Fisherman's Rest with a big glass of brandy." Dot tossed her gloves, hat and scarf to dry on a metal tray covering the top of an old-fashioned steam radiator behind the counter. "She said if you want to talk to her again, you can go over there and do it. She's not moving, except to go upstairs to bed. Hilly already gave her a room key."

"I suppose I've pissed off Sally Mainard enough for one day," Johannsen admitted.

Dot nodded. "That's no lie. But why are you riding Ray? He's a good man and a dedicated lawman."

"Ray's been hiding evidence." He threw the fingerprint report down in front of her. "Look at the date."

She scanned the report. "Oh, crap."

"Exactly. Steve Tanner could be in Canada by the time we get through searching the village for him."

"He'd have to use someone's car or he'd freeze to death before he could hitch a ride. No one's out driving around in this weather." Her forehead puckered. "He'd have to use a vehicle that wouldn't be missed."

"Who would own that?" Johannsen felt he'd been under-utilizing Dot. Maybe she did smack gum and peck at reports, but she was also a busy-body who probably knew everyone's business.

She tapped one long red fingernail against her front teeth. "We've got some stay-at-homes, but they don't have cars. Then there are those who have several, some which run, some which don't. Then there are the farmers..."

"Let's take the farmers out of the equation along with the stay-at-homes. Who else? What about the seasonal visitors. Do they bring cars with them or leave vehicles behind in garages for the winter?"

"OMG." She stopped tapping her teeth. "Nancy Burton doesn't own a car or drive, but Virginia Greeley does. They're on vacation together. Virginia never locks her garage..."

Johannsen felt like slapping himself. Here they were, trying to figure out how Tanner had left so quickly...or at least *he* was, as a stranger in that tight-knit community. He remembered Steve Tanner had borrowed Virginia's car on a previous occasion—the night he got into an argument with Carissa Yates out at the lighthouse and slapped her.

He must have done it again.

Virginia Greeley wasn't around to notice her car was gone. But how had Tanner managed to get the car out of the garage and drive it off without any of those nosey neighbors seeing anything? Johannsen thought about the steep hill up from the harbor. "Where does Virginia live?"

"Close to the top of Harbor View. You think he pushed the car out of the garage and then coasted down the hill? But he'd have had to start it almost in front of this building, in full view of anyone passing by."

"Is there another way out of the Cove without coming all the way down to the harbor?"

"Well, I suppose he could have taken a left onto Chestnut Street. There's a partially-paved road that leads off from there to go past some homes on the point. It meanders around and several roads split off from it. A couple eventually go down to the coastal highway." She grimaced. "Not much of a highway, but it eventually runs into others he could take to the border. He'd know about all those side roads around here. He walks all over in all kinds of weather."

He'll ditch Greeley's car at the border and walk until he finds some place to cross.

Johannsen knew he had to stop Tanner before he had to put in a request for deportation. He ran back to Crosby's office, holstered his Glock and shrugged into his coat. He heard the phone ring in the outer office and Dot's nasal tones as she answered.

"Ray's on the line," she called. "He found the garage door open and Virginia's car gone."

Johannsen heard her telling him they weren't born in a barn as he ran out into the parking lot, leaving the station's front door swinging behind him. By the time he had warmed up his car and scraped the windshield, Watkins was running into the parking lot.

"He couldn't have come through town, or we'd have seen him," Watkins said as he jumped into the passenger's seat of Johannsen's Explorer. "He took a real rough road that winds around the top of the hill and then rejoins the highway."

"Dot helped me figure that out, too." Johannsen buckled his seat belt. "I know where he's heading."

"Canada," Watkins said.

Johannsen nodded as he pulled out of the lot. "Which road should we take?"

"That back road'll take more time. He'd have to keep his speed down unless he planned to leave his transmission behind. But he's probably reached the coastal road by now. He'll have to stay on that for at least ten miles before he can get to a secondary road that's passable in this weather."

"Lucky for us. What's Virginia Greeley driving?"

"A 1988 Chevrolet Caprice. Sedan. Big as a house. Hard to miss."

"It must suck gas like a leech."

"Just about." Ray was able to update the BOLO with details of Virginia's car. Johannsen felt marginally better about everything, including his fellow-officer, as they began the steep climb up the road he hoped would lead them to their fugitive.

CHAPTER SEVENTY-EIGHT

"I DON'T KNOW how the car got back here." Carissa didn't like the look on Steve's face.

The keys were on the driver's seat, right where she had left them. Her purse lay untouched on the back seat. All doors were unlocked.

She took off, running toward the north side of Penwithen. "I'm going to get Richard," she called over her shoulder. "We can argue about this later."

"You can argue with yourself," Steve shouted back. "I'm leaving."

Carissa heard Virginia's car door opening with a screech of protest. She stopped and turned to face him. "Don't you dare. Richard's going to be really cold and stiff from sitting too long; I'll need help putting him inside the car."

"Goddammit, Carissa," she heard, but the sound of footsteps crunching over gravel reassured her Steve had a conscience.

She raced around the corner of the building and stopped. Richard and his wheelchair were nowhere to be seen. She felt a hand on her arm.

"Get back," Steve whispered. "I'm having visions of Halstead going over the cliff. If anything happens, you're to leave. Get in your car and drive down to the Cove before you even call for help. Promise me."

"I promise."

Steve pushed her behind him and cautiously sidestepped toward the back of the house. Carissa followed tentatively. He stopped at the corner. She tried to peer around his arm.

"Didn't I tell you to stay back?"

"Sorry."

"I mean it."

"Okay."

When he moved forward again, she inched along behind him. Suddenly he took off, leaving her completely unprotected at the corner of the house. The wind was so strong, it almost took her off her feet. Through whirling snow and stinging sleet she saw them: Richard on the ground; Steve flinging the wheelchair aside, checking Richard for injuries and talking to him before picking Richard up like he weighed nothing.

"I'm okay," Richard reassured her when she ran up beside them. "I'm bruised and colder than I've been in my life, but that's all."

Carissa righted the wheelchair and Steve sat Richard on the seat.

"What happened?" Carissa saw cuts and bruises on Richard's face. "We've got to get you into the car."

"I'm all right, except I could do with a good shot of brandy."

Although his voice sounded weak, Carissa saw Richard smile.

Steve gave a short laugh. "You're in luck. Virginia's got a flask in her glove compartment." He pushed Richard's wheelchair slowly but steadily over the uneven ground toward the flagstone path leading back to the forecourt.

Carissa walked alongside the wheelchair, Richard's gloved hand in hers.

"Why don't you run ahead and get the cars warmed up?" Steve said. He tossed her Virginia's keys.

"Of course." Carissa wondered whether Steve was more concerned with getting her away from Richard than warming him up, but she obeyed, anyway.

Steve lined Richard's wheelchair up with the passenger's side of the Jeep.

"Do you think I can really trust this car hasn't been tampered with?" Carissa asked. "What if the brake lines are cut?"

Steve looked at her across the roof. "That's a good question." He turned the wheelchair around and pushed it over to Virginia's car. "You two had better go back in this one. I'll take my chances in the Jeep. It'll be a lot faster and easier to drive."

"If the brake lines are cut, a whole lot faster," Richard said as Steve helped him into the front passenger's seat of the Chevy.

"Wait," Carissa protested. "I can't drive this thing; it's like a tank. Let me get my purse. I'll use my smartphone to call for help." She ran over to the Jeep and grabbed her purse.

"I doubt you've got a signal," Richard said when she came back. "Drive the Caprice, 'Rissa. I'm already in it."

Steve stowed the wheelchair inside the trunk and slammed the lid. "It's kind of like driving a boat; what's not to love about that?" He patted Carissa's shoulder companionably, then gave it a quick squeeze.

She watched him walk over to the Jeep and open the door.

"Allow yourself extra space and you'll be fine," he told her. "I'll leave your rental this side of the border."

"Take care of yourself," was all she could say before he closed the door. Although her heart ached for him, she felt he was making a very poor decision.

She watched him turn the Jeep around. But as the SUV started to roll away, flashing lights glowed through the gloom. Snow swirled around headlights as the police vehicle ground to a halt, blocking the end of the driveway and ending Steve's would-be escape.

A loud voice told him to turn off the engine and get out. Steve got out slowly, hands raised in the air, keys clearly visible between his fingers. Carissa heard "Face the car. Put your hands on the roof. Spread-eagle your legs."

Steve glanced back at her. She mouthed 'sorry' before Detective Johannsen reached him. She continued to watch as he was cuffed by Deputy Watkins and placed into the Explorer's back seat.

"Damn," Richard said quietly.

"Yes, damn," Carissa echoed.

Steve had saved Richard's life at the expense of his own freedom.

CHAPTER SEVENTY-NINE

"I'VE ALREADY ADDED RESISTING arrest to the list of charges," Johannsen said, his face ruddy with cold and ill-humor. "I'm not giving Steven Tanner any more chances to run."

"He panicked," Carissa said. "But he stopped to help us, which proves he wasn't planning to run any further." She crossed her fingers inside her pockets. Would Steve contradict her, and she'd get caught in a lie?

Steve looked like he couldn't have cared less who tried to intervene, or what he was being charged with as Deputy Watkins marched him inside the station, dropped a bag containing the contents of Steve's pockets, his belt, his phone and his wristwatch and his coat onto the counter in front of Dot and pushed Steve into a cell. As the lock ground into place, squeaking no doubt from long disuse, Carissa felt like a part of her had been locked up with him. He had been the first Cove resident to extend her a friendly, helping hand.

Detective Johannsen turned to her. "I want you to take Mr. Ebberly home and stay there with him. As soon as we're finished here, I'll be out to take statements from both of you. It's more important now the fugitive's in custody that Mr. Ebberly gets taken care of. He could have frostbite."

"He's dressed in very heavy clothing," Carissa said. "But I'm going to get him checked out at the urgent care clinic in Whitstead before I take him home. We can both give statements after that. I'll stay at Richard's home tonight to make it easier for you."

"I figured that's where you were going, anyway." Johannsen looked aside at her as he scribbled a signature on the form Dot handed him. Dot's expression stayed neutral, but her hand was trembling as she slid Steve's belongings into a large envelope with his name on the front.

"You figured wrong." Carissa glared at Johannsen, her cheeks reddening. "I'm staying at my own home...the lighthouse...while I'm in town for a short visit. I'll be returning to New York in a few days. Steve needs to call William Dansinger right now."

"Don't worry; he'll get his phone call," Ray Watkins said as he took off his wet coat. "He already asked for it."

Detective Johannsen took off his own coat. "You can talk to Tanner tomorrow," he told Carissa. "Call around noon. We should know more by then."

"That's far too late in the day for Steve to make arrangements for the inn," Carissa protested.

"Hilly and Sally can take care of things," Steve shouted from the cell. "Call Sally, Carissa."

"So much for 'no outside communication.'" Johannsen rolled his eyes. "What's this place made of—plywood?"

"We don't get crime at the Cove," Watkins protested. "On odd occasions, we've had to contend with a drunk or a shoplifter. Those are usually visitors, and they're not much of a risk."

"Oh, right, the precious Cove wouldn't harbor any rowdy inhabitants." Johannsen rolled his eyes again. "I'm calling Bangor and New Jersey, Ray. You can take a phone in to Tanner so he gets his one call. Ms. Yates, I want you to report your location as soon as you're finished at the clinic."

Carissa brought Richard up to speed as she drove the Jeep to Whitstead. Pushed along by strong winds, the storm had passed quickly, leaving the late afternoon crisp, clear and blanketed with a brand new layer of white.

"So, you feel up to talking with Sally or you want me to do it?" Richard asked.

"If she gets difficult, I'm not above reminding her she spent two weeks screwing my ex-husband's brains out," Carissa said. "I think that makes us even. Matthew had originally moved up here to reconcile with me."

"Did he really stand a chance of that?"

"No."

"Good."

"How much time do you think Steve will have to do?" She asked.

"You're asking the wrong person." Richard laid his head back against the seat. "I'm great with building permits. That's my forte. Crime and punishment, not so much, but I doubt Steve'll get off with a slap on the wrist."

Carissa felt a lump form in the pit of her stomach.

Once Richard was in an examination room she called William but the call went straight to voicemail. Carissa figured he was either on his way to Steve or at least talking with him by phone. Finding no other excuse to put off the call, she took Sally's card out of her purse and dialed.

"Hello." Sally conveyed her annoyance very effectively with that word.

"This is Carissa Yates."

"I know. I have caller ID."

"Sally, please don't be belligerent."

"If you called to insult me, you're being effective."

"I didn't. I'm not. Please don't hang up."

"Why not? I don't think you and I have much left to discuss."

"Did you know Steve was arrested?"

"I was in the bar when they came for him. Thanks to me, he escaped. I pushed the bar stools onto that Bangor detective. He fell and made a complete fool of himself by firing his gun into the ceiling. While all that was going on, Steve ran out the back door."

"He got caught after that."

"I know, and I heard you're to blame," Sally said.

Dot must have activated the telephone tree again, Carissa thought.

She decided to circumvent what could be a long, heated discussion. "Sally, Steve asked me to call you."

"Why would he do that?"

"He wanted me to ask you to help Hilly take care of the inn."

"I'll get right over there." Sally hung up.

Carissa leaned her head on the wall. If she ever had to face Sally Mainard again, it would be too soon. But she had to admit Sally did have a legitimate reason for being angry. Steve was the decent human being she knew him to be. He'd put Richard's needs before his own. If he hadn't, Richard could easily have died.

She checked the time. Only 10 minutes had passed since Richard was wheeled into a room. She drove over to a discount store in a strip shopping mall across from the clinic and bought him an outfit to replace his wet clothes. The receptionist had taken his down jacket and hung it next to a radiator in the clinic's office.

When Carissa returned with her bags, she was taken into a room where Richard sat smiling on a gurney. His follow-up appointment with Dr. Lister had been moved up to the following day. The X-Rays taken at the clinic had shown complete healing, and he had no signs of frostbite.

"This doesn't mean you get to run all over the place," the clinic doctor warned.

"But I can stand up on two feet and walk short distances," Richard said. "That's so much more than I could do before this afternoon." He looked at the bags. "You went shopping, Carissa? I hope those are for me."

"They are." Warmth spread through her. After all the trauma, something good had finally happened.

"I'll send in an assistant to help you," the doctor said as he headed for the door.

"I won't need help." Richard slid off the gurney. His legs shook. He sat right back down. "I'm too excited."

"You're too weak," Carissa said. "I'll help you." She took packaged underwear out of the bag.

"Let us know when you're ready.

They're bringing you a walker, but you're getting back into that wheelchair to leave this clinic," the doctor warned as he left.

"I'm fine with that." Richard grabbed the underwear and untied his hospital gown.

"I didn't bring shoes. I didn't think you'd need them," Carissa said. She busied herself getting the rest of the clothes out of the bag.

"Thanks, Carissa," he said after a lot of rustling.

She took a quick look. He was wearing the t-shirt and briefs she had bought him. They fit—very well. Her heart skipped a beat, and she chided herself for noticing. She handed him the pants, then helped him pull the sweater over his head, because by then he was getting tired and had difficulty lifting both his arms up high enough.

He took the opportunity to slip those arms around her and pull her against him. "You have no idea how great it feels to be able to stand on two feet again," he said.

"I can imagine." She gave him a squeeze. "You'll be able to chase all the girls again now."

"The only girl I want to chase is you, and you're still too fast for me." He kissed her.

Desire swept through her. With Richard, she always had trouble maintaining her distance. "Maybe you should stop chasing so hard," she said.

"You're staying the night at my place?" His eyes held naked longing. "It's been too long since we were together."

With that he kissed her again, and the power of that kiss took her breath away. The door flew open, the wheelchair banging against it.

Carissa gently pulled away. "Your ride's here."

A male nursing assistant helped Richard into his coat, then into the wheelchair.

"Almost dry," Richard said, running his hands over the coat. "I feel a whole lot better than I did when I got here."

"Ready to go?" The CNA handed a folded walker to Carissa before unlocking the wheelchair.

"More than ready," Richard said.

CHAPTER EIGHTY

DETECTIVE JOHANNSEN, so bland and silent during his last trip to Treacher's Cove, had come into his own without Giddings holding the reins, Carissa thought as she faced him across Richard's dining table.

"How would you describe your relationship with Steven Tanner and Sally Mainard?" He asked.

She chose her words carefully. "Sometimes friendly, sometimes strained. Sally has a jealous streak."

"You've filed a couple of reports about threatening behavior from an unknown person or persons while living at the lighthouse," Johannsen said, flipping through his notes. Richard lay in a recliner close to the fireplace, feet elevated under a blanket, his gaze shifting between Carissa and Johannsen as the interview progressed.

"I have." Carissa nodded. "But since Blake Ulster's death, I've only heard a few noises coming from the basement, which are probably mice. I've got a cat now. I'm hoping he'll take care of those for me while I'm here."

"Al Dyson confessed to hiring Ulster to frighten you into selling the lighthouse," Johannsen said.

"Which almost got me killed as well as Mai Ling. Can't Al be punished for that?"

"He's already in danger of losing his real estate license. The conglomerate attempting to purchase your property denied any knowledge of the scare tactics. Their corporate attorney said the understanding with Mr. Dyson was that he would act as an intermediary in negotiations with you as the beneficiary of Jessica Malloy's will. Negotiations with Ms. Malloy had already failed. Charges may very well be brought by the district attorney's office. Neither Dyson nor that corporation are out of the woods yet."

"I'm very glad to hear that. Getting terrorized isn't something anyone should go through. Neither is getting abused. Poor Mai Ling..."

"We're getting off-track," Johannsen broke in.

He continued, giving information only to clarify the direction of his questioning. Carissa wished in retrospect that she had insisted on waiting until William wasn't preoccupied with Steve's complicated issues, but she had no wish to lengthen the time she had to make herself available to the police, especially the Bangor detective. She felt Detective Johannsen doubted her guileless participation in the events at Treacher's Cove and the Bennett Point Light. Eventually, after prying into every corner of her life, he turned his attention to Richard, who seemed not to be holding anything back in talking about his relationships with Steve and Sally as well as his business dealings.

Finally, Detective Johannsen seemed satisfied. He tucked his notebook and pen into a jacket pocket, stood and looked from Richard to Carissa. "Although I can't reveal any details about Ms. Mainard's medical records," he said, pausing to pull on his coat, "I'm going to tell you something, Ms. Yates, for the sake of your relationship with Mr. Ebberly." He looked squarely at Carissa without the laser-sharp stare she had come to expect from him. "Mr. Ebberly's version of the abortion story has merit."

Carissa didn't know how to respond to that remark. She kept her mouth shut and nodded.

"You both need to make yourselves available for further questioning if needed." Johannsen walked over to the front door, Carissa following behind.

"Steve's really in trouble, isn't he?" She asked as Johannsen stepped outside the house.

"He is. And you have some tough decisions to make, I think." Johannsen walked over to his car.

Carissa started to close the door.

"Sometimes, you have to take chances when you're offered something special out of the blue," he said. He climbed into his car and left.

Carissa lingered on the front door mat, watching the taillights of Johannsen's car fade into the darkness. Snow swirled around the outdoor security lights over the garage. The wind, so angry earlier in the day, had turned into a breeze that stirred the tops of the trees. Peace reigned, and she inhaled the serenity along with cold, bracing air.

"That's quite a draft you're letting into the house," Richard called. "Can we eat supper? I really need to get into bed and stretch out."

CHAPTER EIGHTY-ONE

"THANK YOU," Carissa said as she lay in Richard's arms in the study, where he'd exchanged the hospital bed for a queen-sized pillow-top. "I'd reached the point where I thought I'd never be happy and have a normal relationship again."

"You were in a very sad place." He kissed her lightly and brushed the damp hair from her forehead.

Carissa had never felt such tenderness from a man. Richard's underlying strength was back when she ran her hand over his upper arm, feeling power beneath the skin.

"You're determined to go back to New York next week, aren't you?"

"I must." Carissa propped herself on one elbow and looked down at him. "Hundreds of employees are depending on me. The next show in Paris comes up in July. Matthew prepared me for this. I didn't realize it at the time, because I was too preoccupied with his cruelty, his multiple affairs, the backstabbing..."

She stopped, drew a deep breath that brought with it not only Richard's unique scent but somehow, his Zen. The tension building inside her floated away.

"Shhh..." His fingers rhythmically stroked her arm.

"You're right; that's enough of the negatives." She snuggled against him. "Matthew had enough confidence in me to leave his crowning achievement in my hands, despite what had happened between us. I'm determined to make this the most successful year for our business. I've got so many ideas, Richard. Aunt Jessica continued to create. That package she sent, it had enough new patterns to last through at least five more seasons, as long as the embroidery and braiding remain as popular as they are right now. And I want to expand the prêt-à-porter—ready-to-wear. Matthew wanted the House of Yates to be known only for *haute couture.* I want every woman to be able to wear something with our label."

"I'm very happy for you, and very sad for me."

Richard's voice sounded shaky around the edges. Carissa tried to tell herself it was from fatigue. She shouldn't have let him talk her into getting into bed with him. She should have slept on the couch. But she hadn't, because she needed to say goodbye to him in the most intimate way.

"I can't stay at the Cove," she told him. "Coming to the lighthouse...that was a hiding place. A temporary one. Even now, after the threat from Blake Ulster's horrible pranks is gone, I still hear things, experience things." She stopped. He'd probably laugh at her, scoff at her interpretation of things that went bump in the night.

"You think the place is haunted."

She looked at him. He wasn't laughing at her. He wasn't scoffing.

"I do," she said, finally able to give voice to her misgivings. "And even if they're just remnants of Aunt Jessica, they frighten me."

"I did research on the lighthouse," Richard said. "Some years back, when Steve and I were both thinking about what could be done with it once your aunt was no longer there. A keeper died in the cottage...from natural causes, before you start freaking out. He loved that assignment, his wife told the author of an article on Maine lighthouses and their automation. She believed his spirit was still there, unlocking the tower door, walking down the lighthouse steps."

"I've heard that," Carissa whispered. "Mostly when the wind's really strong and a storm's blowing in."

"That's when he would check the light more frequently," Richard said.

"I hear whispering, too." She shuddered. "I haven't heard it this trip. Maybe it stopped, or maybe I've been too tired to lie awake listening for it."

"Then I'd better make sure you get enough exercise tonight." Richard ran his hand beneath the covers.

"Stop that, Richard Ebberly. We need to get some rest; especially you."

"I need to make the most of having you here." He rolled her onto her back.

"I think I read somewhere that people who've been through severe emotional trauma have incredible sexual appetites afterward," she said as his lips trailed down her neck.

"I think what you read is true."

Carissa found it difficult to concentrate on saying anything else after that.

CHAPTER EIGHTY-TWO

"I DON'T KNOW where anybody is. Call Dot at the police station. This isn't the local branch of Missing Persons." Sally Mainard slammed the receiver back onto its cradle.

Al Dyson popped his head around Steve's office door. "Trouble in Paradise?"

"It's nothing."

Sally disliked Al as much as she knew Steve did; maybe more. She wanted to slam the door in his face. But alienating even one of Steve's regular customers while William Dansinger was working on getting Steve bailed out could prove harmful to Steve's business.

She forced a smile. "Is there something I can do for you, Al?"

"I want a meal." Al walked into the office. "I can't find Hilly anywhere. I took my life in my hands and went to the kitchen door to ask Eva who was waitressing today. She threw a pot at me. I think it was cast iron. Sounded like it when it hit the floor right in front of my feet. Eva told me Hilly was the only waitress assigned to the dining room and she was supposed to be there. Eva said you're in charge, and you're making a mess of it."

He looked pretty self-satisfied for a man who had almost gotten hit by a flying chunk of iron, Sally thought, but she frowned. She hadn't checked the schedule. If she had, she'd have seen there were no other waitresses scheduled. She'd have to get into that dining-room and wait tables herself. At least she had the bar covered by Percival that evening. If Steve remained behind bars, she'd have to find a permanent replacement.

Steve hadn't been keeping proper tabs on his employees lately, she thought. She remembered him giving Hilly an entire afternoon off a few days ago. Sally didn't like or trust Hilly, and she didn't like it that Steve did. That waitress had designs on Steve, but it wasn't going to happen. The girl was plain, overweight, and too much of a Mainer. Way too much of a hick for someone from, as it turned out, New Jersey.

"I'll take care of things," she told Al. "Go sit in the dining room. I'll bring you a scotch. On the rocks and on the house."

"I brought Millie with me. She'll take a scotch as well. I want the liver. She'll have crab salad and a cup of chowder." Without thanking Sally, he left.

Sally controlled herself before shouting he should avoid organ meats. She had no idea why Steve continued to offer liver as one of the Thursday choices. As for Millie Parsons...well, she was half her boss's age and not unattractive in a countrified, bumpkinish kind of way. Sally couldn't understand what the woman saw in the crude, hairy little real estate broker.

As she headed for the kitchen, she watched Al waddle through the dining-room with that distinctive rolling gait of his and join Millie, already seated at his usual table. He gave his assistant a big, sloppy kiss on the neck. She giggled but didn't pull away as he sat down. Sally saw one of his hands start to massage Millie's thigh.

Sickened, and thankful the dining-room was completely empty, Sally pushed open the kitchen door. "Eva, have you seen Hilly?" She asked.

The cook looked up from cutting left-over cold roast beef into thin slices for the evening's sandwich special. "No. I haven't seen her since right after the breakfast rush. She didn't say she was going anywhere, but with everything so topsy-turvy around here today, she might have forgotten to tell me."

Sally nodded. "Can you plate liver for Mr. Dyson and a crab salad and chowder for his assistant? I'll take their meals out to them."

"I'll do that, Miss Sally. You've got better things to do than wait tables, unless it gets busy. Can you call Hilly's grandmother and see what's keeping her?"

Sally thanked Eva and left by the service stairs; happy she didn't have to walk back through the dining-room for another look at whatever the nauseating couple was getting up to now. She took the stairs to the second floor, strode along the corridor and descended the main staircase. When she walked into the bar, Percival Huddleston was mixing a drink for Nancy Burton's ex-fiancé, Walter Barnes.

"Make sure it's extra dirty," Walter said over the sound of the shaker.

"Duly noted, Walter." Percival took the lid off the shaker and carefully upended it over Walter's martini glass.

Walter wore his thinning hair greased and carefully combed in an attempt to disguise the pink skin beneath. Sally thought it wasn't very successful.

"Hello, gents." She managed to smile at Walter as well as Percival, despite her contempt for Mr. Barnes, pegged as the worst type of opportunist. Luckily, Nancy had seen through him and taken off on a long vacation with her best friend and ally, Virginia. Sally hoped they'd stay gone all winter. She could do with a lot less prying eyes and tattling for a while.

"Have you seen Hilly?" She asked Percival. "Eva hasn't. There's no waitress for the lunchtime meal."

"I haven't." Percival started washing out the shaker in the sink behind the bar. "You think she stopped by the police station to see Steve?"

"I'm sure she'd have called if she was running late." Sally drummed her fingers on the bar. "If this keeps up, Steve won't have a business to come back to after he gets out."

"Maybe he'll only be in there overnight," Percival said. "Let's all think on the positive side. William's an excellent attorney."

"For local issues. I'm not so sure he can handle Steve's problems. I should intervene and call someone in from Bangor."

"Why don't you wait a little longer before you do that; give William a chance to review Steve's case? His business isn't limited only to the Cove."

Sally allowed her frustration to show by sighing loud and long. "This isn't just Cove business, Percival. It's Steve's entire future."

Percival turned off the water and started drying the shaker. "William Dansinger graduated with honors from Harvard Law School. He may not have had to deal with any big issues here at the Cove since, well, since Roman Schlosski ran his neighbor down with a tractor back in the late nineties, but that doesn't mean he can't handle this. I'm sure he's retained all his considerable abilities."

"Oh, Percival, you're too loyal to the natives." Sally shook her head.

"Go call Hilly's grandmother. She's sure to know if Hilly planned to stop off somewhere before work."

"That's what Eva suggested. Fine; I'll do that. Would you please take Al and his assistant a couple of freebie scotches? On the rocks. It'll keep them busy while Eva gets their lunches plated. According to Al, she threw a pot at him when he poked his head into the kitchen."

Sally left Percival laughing and Walter snickering over his extra-dirty martini. She returned to Steve's office. Hilly's grandmother, Carrie Deavers was hard of hearing, but once Sally had succeeded in getting her concerns across, Carrie said she thought Hilly was at the inn. She'd left the house at her usual time that morning, starting out for work thirty minutes after her mother drove herself to Whitstead in the family car.

"I'm sure she'll turn up," Sally tried to reassure the now-frantic old woman. She wished she hadn't made that call, but it was necessary. "Hilly probably had a couple of errands to run and Steve forgot to tell me."

"Where's Mr. Steve? Why isn't he calling?" Carrie's voice cracked.

"He had to help the police with some...um...inquiries." Sally heard Carrie sobbing. "I'll call as soon as Hilly arrives at the inn. You do the same if she comes home, or have her call me, okay?"

"Of course."

Sally told Percival what she'd found out, or rather, what she hadn't.

"I'm going to close the bar," Percival said. "I doubt we'll have a lot of customers in this weather. I'll try to find Hilly. If it suddenly gets busy here, call my cell and I'll come back."

"That's a great plan. Thanks, Percival. You always know what to do."

"Third term as mayor coming up, Sally." He patted his chest. "I must be doing something right. I believe it's because I put the Cove before myself."

"Your selflessness is one of your greatest assets, Mr. Mayor."

Sally gave him her best beaming smile. It never hurt to stroke Percival Huddleston's ego. Her business would benefit from any referrals he made, and with his current push to get Treacher's Cove into all major Maine guidebooks, both the Emporium and her sculptures would gain more recognition.

She strolled into the parlor and looked out the window. The snow had stopped, and the sun was struggling to peek through the clouds. Maybe the weather was about to clear up, which could mean more customers for the restaurant and the bar. She hoped most of the locals had brought lunch with them that day. She didn't want to deal with packed tables and piles of dirty dishes.

"I'll stop by the police station to let them know our concerns," Percival said from behind her. He handed her the bar's key. "Walter's going to finish his martini in here."

"I don't think you should involve the police, yet. Hilly probably went to the dentist or had a doctor's appointment she forgot to tell Steve about. I can call in Abbey, if necessary; she's not working anywhere else since she got laid-off from the inn." Sally watched Percival zip up his coat. "If you go to the police, Steve's sure to overhear what you're saying and start worrying," she added.

"I'll call if I have news. You let me know if Hilly turns up." Percival left.

A flurry of snow landed on the mat as the door closed behind him. Sally noted he hadn't agreed with her about not visiting the police station. She went back into Steve's office and made a few calls that yielded no results about Hilly's whereabouts but spread the word around about her being a no-call, no-show at work. There were only three guests, and they all readily agreed to eat lunch together at one table after hearing the waitress hadn't come to work, which made Eva's job a whole lot easier and kept Sally out of the dining room.

Neither of the two housekeepers had been trained to wait tables, which Sally thought was an oversight. She called the afternoon house-keeper and told her to stay home, much to the woman's disgust over her shortened hours, and therefore, shortened paycheck. Sally wasn't worried—if the woman quit, she'd have to get on a bus and work in Whitstead, which would take a larger cut out of any paycheck.

The sun gave up the fight and the snow returned. Percival called with an update. No one had seen Hilly since she left home for work. Ray Watkins had added a missing person to his already-overloaded to-do list. Dot had used the phone tree to mobilize volunteers for a search party organized by Percival.

Sally felt far better informed about Hilly than Steve. Percival told her Carissa Yates was with Richard Ebberly, which made Sally even more disgruntled.

Why wasn't Steve released? She was willing to put up bail money. He wasn't a flight risk with the weather the way it was that day—snow, snow, and more snow. The inches mounted as Sally's frustration grew over Detective Johannsen's stubbornness. Even if New Jersey authorities were working on extradition, Steve didn't need to be sitting in a cell while they completed the process. He could be back at his business and back in her arms. She needed some comforting, herself.

While she waited for further news, Sally wandered around the quiet inn. How many hours had she spent there? Countless, and for what? To take care of it while Steve served time? To be his girlfriend but nothing more? Sally's anger ignited and she returned to the office.

No man had ever been faithful to her. Even Steve had confessed he wanted Carissa Yates. As for Matthew Yates; he had lied. He'd told her they were two of a kind, but all he had really wanted was to make Carissa jealous. Sally thought that given time and Matthew's insistence, he'd have worn Carissa down, and she'd have willingly given him the rights to all those stupid patterns she kept harping about. Then they'd have gone away and life at the Cove *might* have returned to normal. Steve would have gotten over Carissa and begged his faithful girlfriend to take him back. Sally skated quickly past the part where she had told Steve she was leaving him for Matthew.

Sally told herself she'd been dumped by three lovers for Carissa Yates, an insipid woman with questionable talents and a proclivity for looking and acting like she needed the assistance and protection of every big, strong man with whom she came into contact. Sally felt alone and used. Discarded.

She wanted marriage and children. She was more than ready, and at 36, she had to move forward. She'd go over to the police station and talk to Steve. He would have to make a commitment to her if she was going to manage his business until his legal troubles were resolved. He'd have to cut her in for a percentage of the inn. Fifty percent, she thought, leaning back in his leather chair. She'd look for someone to help her; manage the inn when she couldn't be there herself. She'd open the shop until noon, continue sculpting at her regular hours, then work at the inn late afternoons and evenings, when she'd greet the guests and mingle.

She sifted through eligible Cove residents for the assistant manager position and settled on Richard's admin. assistant, April Travers. Two birds with one stone, Sally thought, smiling to herself. She'd dangle a salary increase and maybe a 10% share of the profits. That might be enough to get that girl away from Richard, whose business would be screwed without her, especially while he was recovering from his car wreck.

Making lemonade out of lemons had always been her specialty. Sally smiled as she rocked gently in Steve's chair. His incarceration could end up being very profitable for her, if handled the right way. And he'd be so indebted to her, and so thankful that he even had a business to come back to after he got out of prison, he'd give her the one thing she wanted most: a stable future.

She pushed the chair back and put her feet up on the desk, wiggling her toes inside the fashionable boots she had purchased in Whitstead. She pulled over the guest register she had brought with her from the reception desk and looked over the information provided by the three guests. One of them looked especially interesting. She'd check in with them while they ate lunch. He'd be bored, she was bored. They might just get to amuse each other for a while that afternoon.

She needed a distraction from the graphic pictures floating around in her mind of what Carissa and Richard had been up to last night. She vowed she wasn't going to lie alone in bed while Steve languished behind bars. She looked again at the register and tried to remember which name belonged with which guest. She'd prefer the younger one with the tight body over the other two, older and with slight paunches. But if she wanted no-strings-attached sex, one of those older men might be a better lover and a better bet to keep his mouth shut and move on after she was through with him.

CHAPTER EIGHTY-THREE

STEVE STARED up at the dark ceiling from his bunk in one of two small jail cells at the back of the police station. In a couple of days he'd be extradited to New Jersey. Manslaughter charges with a couple of extras tacked on, such as evading arrest in New Jersey, evading arrest in Maine, and whatever else Johannsen and the District Attorneys from both states racked up. He knew Johannsen wanted to reopen Dean Halstead's case and probably look closer at Matthew Yates's fatal slip in his kitchen, too. And then, of course, there was Richard Ebberly's wreck, which was no longer classed as an accident.

Steve tossed and turned on the narrow and too-short bunk. Jealousy and anger were excellent motives for tampering with the Jeep's brakes, Johannsen had said. A sweat broke out on Steve's brow. He kicked off the army surplus blanket. He really needed to talk to William ASAP, but it was the middle of the night, and Steve thought a panic attack probably wasn't a good enough reason to get anyone else out of bed. He swung his legs off the bunk and sat up, placing both feet on the cold floor. *Think,* he told himself. *Advocate for yourself.*

Someone had left impressions from size 11 boots on the cliff where Dean Halstead had fallen. Uneven tread lengths and depths were noticeable leading away from the scene of what had looked to be a scuffle at the edge of the cliff. Those footprints had continued through the property and over the fence to where a vehicle had left its own impressions of studded tires belonging either to a truck or an SUV. Damn little to go on, Steve thought. But he didn't own or have access to any such vehicle and his size 14 foot wouldn't squeeze into a size 11 boot under any circumstances.

He had no alibi for the time Matthew died, but there had been no evidence Yates had been murdered, either. *Unless Johannsen and the coroner were withholding evidence.* Steve broke out into a fresh sweat, despite the cold creeping up his legs.

Why he had gotten so angry with his partner, Kurt, over their business in New Jersey? Maybe Kurt *had* signed away everything they'd worked for together, but did that deserve getting hit with a metal bar stool?

He still remembered his fists connecting with Kurt's face, his stomach, his chest. The last thing Steve remembered was picking up the stool. After that, everything got fuzzy. He wasn't sure whether the crash he heard had been the stool hitting Kurt or Kurt's head striking the brass foot rail that surrounded the bar, something that ironically, Steve had argued against as too expensive and a trip hazard for patrons.

The memories were too raw, even at a distance of two years and hundreds of miles. He'd pushed them into some dark place in his mind. Bringing them back made him realize he hadn't deserved the quiet, peaceful life he'd enjoyed at Treacher's Cove.

He thought about the people he knew, and how much their opinions mattered to him: Percival, Hilly, William, and Ray. He'd lied to all of them. He'd messed up his relationship with Sally by not telling her he could never marry while he was hiding under an assumed identity. And then there was Carissa. He'd overplayed his hand, alienating her and sending her into Richard Ebberly's arms.

Steve rubbed both hands over his face. He'd been fooling himself about everything. He was a real, bonafide jackass. He deserved everything that was coming to him.

He lay back down and stared up at the ceiling again. Everything and anything, he thought. And it would all be arriving very, very soon.

CHAPTER EIGHTY-FOUR

CARISSA BROUGHT Detective Johannsen into the dining-room. A cheerful blaze flickered in the fireplace. She turned off the sitcom they'd been using as a distraction from the day's events.

"There are holes in your statements," Johannsen said. He took a digital voice recorder and laptop out of his attaché case as well as a notebook and pen from a pocket in his jacket.

Carissa added a log to the fire and brought three bottles of water in from the kitchen.

"I want you to tell me everything that happened today," Johannsen told Richard. "And I do mean everything. Don't leave anything out, even if you think it's unimportant."

Richard shrugged. "Okay. After Carissa pushed me around the outside of Penwithen, I told her it should be demolished. I thought some of the woodwork could be salvaged, like the porch columns out front, maybe the tile floors, and maybe some of the doors, but I couldn't tell about those until the boards covering them got pried off."

"That's enough of the architectural information," Johannsen said. "I get the picture. I could see the place was a ruin, and I'm no building contractor."

"My father inherited the property, but my mother and I never knew," Carissa said.

Johannsen nodded. "I'm sure Mr. Ebberly couldn't go into the house, but did you, Ms. Yates?"

"No. It was boarded up except for the bottom of one window at the back of the house. A board had come off. I tried looking inside, but the smell was too awful. Decay, mold..." She shuddered.

"Did you see the board lying around anywhere?"

"No, but with all the snow on the ground, it could have been covered over."

"We decided to go home after I saw how bad the north side was," Richard said. "Carissa wheeled me around to the front of the house. That's when we realized her car was gone."

"You didn't hear it leave?"

"Too much wind," Richard said.

"Too much noise from the surf crashing against the rocks, too," Carissa added. She thought about Dean Halstead falling over the cliff and pulled a blanket over her knees.

"Didn't you lock the car, Ms. Yates?"

"No. This is coastal Maine. People don't usually steal cars from private property."

"Except, according to both of you, someone did." Johannsen's tone was accusing.

"I know, and I feel really stupid." Carissa didn't need a lecture. She'd already beaten herself up mentally for placing Richard at risk.

"Tell me again what happened after that," Johannsen said.

Carissa was more than relieved to move on. She praised Steve for coming to Richard's rescue, omitting the part where Steve had refused to help Richard and had tried to leave her on the road. Johannsen then wanted more details about the mystery person who had attempted to push Richard and his wheelchair off the cliff. Carissa felt really uneasy hearing Richard's attacker had worn a turquoise coat similar to hers.

"There's a malicious pattern to all this," Johannsen said. "Mr. Ebberly, I want you to think really hard and give me a better description of the person who got out of Ms. Yates' car. You recounted all the flaws in the building, so you've got good recall. Surely you can remember more about the person who tried to kill you?"

"I couldn't see any features. He or she had pulled the coat's hood down low and had a scarf covering the lower half of his or her face. The coat fit really well. Height, about five-six or five-seven, so that doesn't help—could have been a smaller man or a tallish woman. Knee-length beige boots. I couldn't do much except watch him or her walk up the driveway. I'd backed my wheelchair out from under the side porch and got one of my wheels stuck off the side of the path. I was pretty much trapped there, waiting to see what would happen. One thing that might help is I knew it wasn't Carissa by the way she or he walked."

"How's that?"

"Carissa walks very distinctively." He smiled at her. "Must be those years in the fashion industry."

Carissa wondered what he was going to say.

"And that is?" Obviously, Johannsen wondered, too.

"Like she's on a cat walk," Richard said. "She shows off every piece of clothing she wears. And this person was also taking small steps, like the boots didn't fit and were uncomfortable."

"Like they were too small?"

"Yes."

"But this person was strong. Able to push you across uneven ground and then try to push you over the cliff. How did you stop him or her?"

"I locked my brakes. Whoever it was ran right smack into the push handles at the back of the wheelchair. That must have hurt. Then the wheelchair tipped over sideways and I slid out. I guess my attacker either didn't have enough strength to finish the job or was hurting too much from getting jabbed by the wheelchair. Whatever the reason, I'm very glad he or she gave up and left. I don't think I could have put up much resistance to anything else. I was too damned tired by then."

"So, are you're leaning toward this person being a man?"

Richard shook his head. "Maybe I was mistaken, since I was pretty shaken up, but I made a couple of observations. Number one is it certainly wasn't Steve Raymond. He could have picked me up out of that wheelchair and tossed me over the cliff without breaking a sweat. He also wouldn't fit in a woman's coat. Whoever attacked me had small but very strong hands and wore beige leather gloves. That's probably why there were no fingerprints in the car."

"When did you last wear your turquoise coat, Ms. Yates?"

"Not since I came back from New York. I've been wearing a new beige jacket I brought with me."

"We'll need to search your home. Do you want me to get a warrant?"

"No, of course not. Although..." She hesitated. Would William advise her differently? "In view of all that's happened it would make me more comfortable. I'd like William Dansinger to be with me while the police are in my home, too."

"Fine." Johannsen sighed. "More paperwork, but I see your point about protecting yourself. Are you staying here tonight?"

"Yes."

"I'm going to have Ray Watkins stake out the lighthouse."

"All night? Is that really necessary?"

"Any and all measures around these parts right now," Johannsen said. "If your coat was stolen, the perpetrator may try to put it back."

"Now I *really* don't want to go home."

"Stay here as long as you want," Richard told Carissa. He looked at Detective Johannsen. "You're a hard man, and the sheriff's not going to be happy. Ray Watkins will want to quit after tonight."

"He'll be fine." Johannsen rubbed a hand over the stubble on his chin. "I inherited this mess from Detective Giddings. I think he was on the wrong track with this investigation, and I'm determined to get to the bottom of all this. Too much mayhem for any small village. It has to stop."

Richard settled back in his recliner. "Are we about done? I'm really tired."

"I've got enough for tonight, but I may be back tomorrow." Johannsen turned off the recorder and put everything back inside the attaché case.

"I didn't take Richard out to Penwithen so I could murder him," Carissa said. "If I'd wanted him dead, I wouldn't have gone for help."

Johannsen pointed to her boots, drying in front of the fire.

"I'd call those beige leather."

"Size nine. I had them on all day. They're not exclusive designer boots, either. Any woman could go out and buy a pair. I bought them here at the Cove when I first arrived."

"Don't plan on leaving town any time in the near future," Johannsen said.

"I've got a follow-up appointment with my doctor in Bangor tomorrow morning," Richard objected.

"And I was planning to drive him," Carissa added.

"Watkins will drive you instead, Mr. Ebberly." Johannsen got up.

"After spending all night outside the lighthouse? That's inhuman." Carissa got up, too.

"I'll relieve him at midnight," Johannsen said. "Don't worry, Ms. Yates. Under the circumstances, I'll be the one freezing outside in the middle of the night, not Ray Watkins."

"I wouldn't wish that on anyone," she said. But she still couldn't bring herself to give him permission to ransack the keeper's quarters without her being there with William.

"What time does Watkins need to pick you up, Mr. Ebberly?"

"Nine o'clock." Richard looked at his watch. "I think everyone should just go to bed. There are deadbolts on all doors at the lighthouse. No one's going in there, unless they break a window."

"Which happened once before," Johannsen said. "Do I need to remind either of you?"

"No," Richard said.

"Definitely not," Carissa added.

CHAPTER EIGHTY-FIVE

CARISSA DROVE into the Cove to check on Steve the following morning. Pale and hollow-eyed, unshaven and dressed in the rumpled clothes he'd worn the day before, his appearance shocked her. Dot had offered him a donut and coffee, but he'd refused.

"I want this over," he told Carissa. "What's taking them so long?"

"It hasn't even been twenty-four hours," she said. "I'm going to the inn. I can help Hilly while Sally brings you a change of clothes and breakfast." His distress made her feel guilty.

"Don't you let him lay the blame at your door," Dot said as Carissa passed her on the way out. "Steve did this to himself."

"Not everything," Carissa muttered to herself.

Outside, bright-white sunlight sparkled. Shop-keepers had already shoveled sidewalks glistening with run-off from slow-melting piles of snow. Rhythmical dripping came from gutters. Carissa loosened the scarf around her neck. A thaw was definitely setting in. Maybe spring wasn't so far off, after all. She walked over to The Fisherman's Rest, where she found Sally in the dining room.

"Did Hilly call in sick?"

"Nope. She was a no-show yesterday and again this morning." Sally loaded a tray with dirty dishes and limped toward the busing area.

"Did you call her to find out what happened?"

"Do I look like I've got time to chase no-show employees?"

Sally added the dishes to an already-full cart and turned on a vacuum cleaner, effectively cutting off further communication. Hoping for a better reception from Percival Huddleston, Carissa went into the bar. Percival was loading beer into a cooler.

"Did you know Hilly wasn't at work yesterday and didn't come in this morning?" She asked.

Percival closed the cooler. "Yes. We activated the phone tree and mounted a search party yesterday without any results. Her grandmother's worried sick. Hilly's mother agreed with Sally—Hilly's really upset over Steve and has taken off for a couple of days."

"I'm with Hilly's grandmother. I'm really worried. I just tried talking to Sally, but she didn't seem at all interested."

"Sally's overwhelmed. Don't be too hard on her." Percival leaned both elbows on the bar. "She told me she doesn't know what she's going to do about the inn if Steve's gone more than a few days."

"I can help out here today. Ray Watkins is taking Richard to a medical appointment in Bangor, and he's got Nurse Fields with him until the end of the week. I can tend bar or wait tables. I may not do either very well, but I'll try my best. I hope Hilly decides to come home soon. She's invaluable to Steve, isn't she?"

Percival nodded. "Hilly's not only dedicated to Steve and his business, she's in love with the man. But he's never given her a second look." He rubbed a hand over his face. "Maybe I'm prejudiced, but I wish Steve would realize Hilly's a much better match for him than Sally, even if Sally's a lot prettier. That artistic temperament is no myth."

Carissa thought fleetingly of Matthew. "No, it's a bit of a curse. Let me see what I can do to help Sally, even if she doesn't seem to want me here."

The vacuuming had stopped. Sally was laying tables for the noon meal, a cart stacked with white tablecloths and napkins on one side of her, one loaded with dishes on the other. She must have removed everything from the tables, including unused silverware and linens. Carissa wondered why Sally felt a need to overload the inn's dishwashers and laundry as well as herself.

"I can manage," Sally said in reply to Carissa's offer to help out. She pushed the linen cart over to the next table. "You've done enough damage already."

If Carissa was done with anything, it was with being polite. "What the hell is that supposed to mean?"

"Ever since you arrived at the Cove, there's been trouble." Sally fanned out napkins and set them on top of plates before limping toward another table. "You started stupid rumors about your aunt being murdered, you told stories about someone harassing and scaring you, you got between Steve and me, and you slept with Richard. That's quite a track record for an outsider who only arrived last fall."

Carissa felt like grabbing Sally and giving her a good shaking. She resisted, taking a pile of plates and setting them out across several tables while she struggled to regain control of her anger.

"I didn't tell stupid, unfounded stories," she said when she could trust her voice. "My aunt died arguing with Matthew in his New York office. She did *not* fall down the lighthouse stairs. And Blake Ulster confessed to playing scary pranks on me before he died."

Sally pushed the linen cart over to another table. "Thanks to you, Steve's facing a long time in prison." She winced as she put weight on her right side. "And you and I both know you've been using Richard. He deserves to get his heart broken after what he did to me, but you're a real user."

Carissa had no pat answers for those two accusations. She was already giving herself grief over Steve and Richard. Whatever they had done in the past, did they really deserve punishment in whatever form it was about to be delivered. In her opinion, Richard in particular had suffered enough retribution over the last couple of months. Whether Steve had atoned for what he had done to his partner was a lot less certain, although he'd certainly contributed to the local community and kept out of trouble.

Sally brought out silverware baskets. They silently rotated around the tables. Carissa pushed around another cart loaded with glasses, cups and saucers. Sally added condiments and crystal bud vases filled with green ferns and daisies.

"There, we're done. It looks lovely, Sally." Carissa smiled. "Steve would be really happy."

Sally pivoted on her left leg and scowled. "Happy? You think he'd be *happy?*"

"Well, maybe that's the wrong word. Relieved. He'd be relieved to know the inn's running on oiled wheels with you and Percival helping out."

Anger made Sally's face ugly. "You need to leave. Right now. And I'm not just talking about the inn; I'm talking about the Cove." She grabbed a jug of water. "Move out of my way, it's almost time for lunch."

Carissa watched her limp over to a table and fill glasses.

"You outsiders, you always cause trouble," Sally said.

"*You* were an outsider when you first arrived here."

Sally glanced at Carissa, her blue-green eyes flashing fire. "I'm not an outsider. I was *born* here. I left with my family, but I came back and bought a business. I put money into the village. I supported Steve, who showed he loves the Cove as much as the rest of us do. You came to leech. You wanted our friendship and our help, but you weren't willing to give anything back."

"That's unfair. I was prepared to give a lot once I'd settled in. You were one of the people making it harder for me to get accepted."

Sally's hand trembled. Water splashed out of the jug onto a tablecloth. "I don't want to hear your whining. Get out!"

"I was so wrong about you." Carissa stood her ground. It was past time to confront Sally and her jealousy. "I thought you were secure in your relationship with Steve. But you weren't. You're completely jealous of my friendship with him for no reason. I don't want him. He kissed me once. For me, it was like kissing my brother."

Sally whipped around, eyes wide. She lost her balance as she leaned on her right leg. The jug fell, knocking over glasses and spilling water everywhere. "Oh, my God." She burst into tears. "You're such a bitch."

Carissa ran into the bussing station and brought towels to mop up. "I don't *mean* to be a bitch," she said. "Really, I don't. Things just seem to happen around me lately."

"I really hate you," Sally said. She blew her nose on one of the wet napkins. "Why didn't you stay in New York? You got Matt's business. What more do you want here?"

"I came back to take care of a few loose ends, like disposing of the lighthouse and deciding what to do about Penwithen. If I hadn't, well, Steve wouldn't be where he is. I'm sorry about stopping him from escaping to Canada, but if I hadn't, Richard would probably have died."

"I helped Steve escape," Sally said. "I acted like I lost my balance and knocked over the bar stools. They landed on that Bangor detective, and he fell over backwards right onto Ray Watkins. I hurt my hip."

"What a mess," Carissa said, unsure whether she was talking about the dining room, Sally's injury or everything else.

CHAPTER EIGHTY-SIX

SALLY GRUDGINGLY ALLOWED Carissa to help her clean up. Eva could be heard crashing around in the kitchen while complaining in a loud voice about Hilly deserting the inn in its hour of need. Carissa wondered whether anyone would stay at the inn long enough to eat a meal that day.

Percival asked Carissa to visit Hilly's grandmother. He was too worried about Sally to leave her alone at the inn. Carissa picked up a small bouquet of flowers before driving to a modest cottage on the outskirts of town. She knocked several times before an elderly woman opened the door and peered out, her dull brown eyes like two raisins in a white dough face.

"Hi." Carissa tried to sound upbeat. "I'm Carissa Yates. Percival Huddleston asked me to come over to check on you." She held out the flowers.

"I'm Carrie Deavers, Hilly's grandmother. I've heard about you. Come in." Mrs. Deavers opened the door wide. "Percival called and told me you were on your way over." She looked at the flowers. "Those are pretty. Thank you."

"You haven't seen or heard anything from Hilly since yesterday?"

Carissa took off her boots and hung her coat on a rack crowded with many old coats and jackets. She followed Carrie's diminutive figure down a dark hallway.

"No, and I'm really worried." Mrs. Deavers kept one hand on the wall.

"Does Hilly have a cell phone?" Carissa asked.

"No. She can't afford one, and she's either here or at the inn, so we can always reach her."

Not always, Carissa thought. "Why didn't you report her missing as soon as she didn't come home yesterday?"

"I don't like talking to police, even local ones like Ray Watkins. But then Percival called here and told me she didn't go to work. I wondered if she fell. It has to be icy out there. Did you look for her on the way over here? She could be lying in a ditch." Tiny and birdlike, Mrs. Deavers swayed on thin legs encased in heavy elasticated stockings when she tried to look back over her shoulder.

Carissa noticed a walker standing between the kitchen and living-room and wondered why Mrs. Deavers wasn't using it. "I did look, but I didn't see her anywhere."

"Do you think she ran away? Everyone else does." Carrie peered at Carissa.

"I don't see why she should." Carissa wondered why everyone would think Hilly was a runaway. "Did she do that in the past?"

"She did. A couple of times." Carrie tugged down the sleeves of her sweater. "Why don't you sit in the parlor while I make coffee?" She pointed to the left while turning to the right and staggered.

Carissa rushed forward, took Carrie's arm and helped her to a chair beside the fireplace, where a space heater blocked the hearth. "I bet you didn't sleep well last night," she said. "You must be very tired. Why don't I make the coffee, and maybe something to eat, too?"

Tears welled up in Carrie's eyes. She fished a tissue out of a pocket in her flowered apron. "Thank you, dear. You're so kind."

Carissa walked briskly into the kitchen and filled an old-fashioned metal kettle. A jar of instant coffee stood on the counter along with two white cups. Familiar white cups. They were exactly the same as the ones she had seen at the inn. She hoped Steve had told Hilly to take them home, made scrambled eggs and toast, and took them in to Mrs. Deavers on a matching white plate.

She found TV trays beside the couch and bit back a smile at the thought of Hilly and her tiny sparrow of a grandmother eating in front of the six o'clock news. But Hilly would be serving dinner at the inn at that time, Carissa reminded herself. Mrs. Deavers must either manage to get herself a meal or wait for her granddaughter to return after dinner had been served at The Fisherman's Rest.

"What time does Hilly usually get home?" She asked.

"Eight o'clock. On the dot. Mr. Steve usually has someone walk her home. Percival Huddleston often does that."

"Does Percival live close by?"

"One street away. He always tells Hilly she's helping him get his daily exercise." Mrs. Deavers managed a very small smile.

Carissa returned the smile. "Percival's a very good man."

Mrs. Deavers nodded. "He is. But Hilly didn't come home last night." She carefully placed the toast she had been nibbling onto her plate and wiped her nose on her napkin.

Carissa saw a box of tissues and passed them over. Mrs. Deavers took one and blew her nose.

"Percival told me not to worry when I talked to him yesterday," she told Carissa. "He said Mr. Steve had been in some trouble and the police were very busy with that, but he'd try to find out where Hilly had gone." A tear balanced precariously on the edge of Carrie's bottom lid before trickling slowly down one spongy cheek. "He called back later to say Hilly had been missing since Mr. Steve tried to run away from that Bangor detective." Carrie's reed-thin voice wavered, then faded completely.

Carissa thought she should try to lead the conversation away from a potential discussion of Steve's troubles. "Steve told me Hilly's the best waitress."

Carrie swelled with pride, like an old hen plumping her feathers. "He's told me that, too. Going to work for Mr. Steve was the best thing that's ever happened to Hilly. She calmed right down."

A prickle of unrest stirred in Carissa. "Did Hilly get into trouble before she worked for Steve?"

Mrs. Deavers shifted in the chair and poked at her cold eggs.

"Mrs. Deavers, it might help Hilly if you tell the truth," Carissa prompted.

Carrie chewed on her dentures, which clacked like castanets, a jarring sound of which she seemed completely unaware. "Hilly used to go around with some bad boys and girls from Whitstead."

When she didn't elaborate, Carissa asked, "What about later?"

Carrie muttered something into her cup as she brought it to her lips.

"Did you say she got arrested?"

"She was accused of stealing from the register at the Whitstead Tavern when she worked there." Carrie's hand shook as she put down the cup. "Then at the grocery store." Her thin fingers plucked at her well-worn woolen skirt. "She didn't take anything."

"Not even to help out with expenses?"

Carrie continued to avoid eye contact. "I...I don't know," she muttered. "I...I don't think so."

Carissa couldn't bring herself to ask any more questions. What if Sally and Percival found money missing from the inn? Maybe Hilly had taken the opportunity to raid the till while everyone was preoccupied.

"I'm going to put the flowers in water and make you a sandwich before I leave," she said. "You can eat it later, if you get hungry before one of us gets back to you."

"It's not like Hilly," Carrie said. "She'd never leave me alone all night unless she couldn't get home. Her mother works in Whitstead and stays there weeknights."

Carissa went back into the kitchen, where she put the flowers into a chipped china vase, made a couple of peanut butter and jelly sandwiches, sliced up an apple, put the food into plastic containers and brought everything in to Carrie along with a glass of water. She made sure Carrie had everything right beside her, put the flowers on a table opposite Carrie's chair and made sure Carrie's walker was within reach.

. "Mr. Steve would never hurt a fly," Carrie said. "I don't understand why he's in jail."

"I'm sure everything will work out okay." Carissa plastered a reassuring smile on her face.

That was a lie, she thought as she closed the door behind her and got into her car.

CHAPTER EIGHTY-SEVEN

THE LIGHTHOUSE SEARCH turned up nothing other than Carissa's turquoise coat in its usual place beside the front door and a second pair of beige boots in the bedroom closet. Both were bagged and taken away, along with the beige boots she had been wearing. After everything and everyone left, she savored a moment of peace with a cup of herbal tea before calling Richard, who told her Nurse Fields was cracking the whip before leaving that afternoon. Having received clearance to weight-bear on his left ankle, the first thing he had done on the way back to the Cove was to cancel his private duty nursing.

He had meals to microwave, a written list of things he shouldn't do, and had been drilled on when and why he should call 911. He was looking forward to being alone for the first time in three months. He wasn't too thrilled about Carissa being alone at the lighthouse, but she assured him her plan was to pack a bag, make sure everything was locked up tight and drive over to spend the night with him.

She followed up on Hilly by talking to Percival. He reported the scuttlebutt in the village teetered between foul play and embezzlement. Steve had adamantly denied giving Hilly any opportunities to drain either his personal finances or tinker with the inn's bottom line. Percival felt Hilly's disappearance was taking too much of a back seat to Steve's abortive escape attempt and capture, but he had continued to close the bar for periods while scouring ditches, yards and sheds along Hilly's route to work. Her mother had taken time off work to join him, along with a couple of villagers. Percival told Carissa he sadly suspected they would find Hilly's body when the snow melted.

While Carissa packed, she wondered whether her coat and boots could have been used in the attempt on Richard's life. But how would they have been taken from and then returned to the keeper's quarters? She was sure not only her hair but Richard's, possibly Steve's and maybe even some of Matthew's would be found on the turquoise coat. The soles of one pair of her beige boots would contain samples of the same type of gravel and dirt found at Penwithen.

Her beige car coat and second pair of boots had also been bagged and tagged and taken away for analysis. Carissa reluctantly took the old fur coat out of Aunt Jessica's guest room wardrobe. Despite smelling horribly of mothballs, something had been dining on both sleeves and one side of the collar. Unsure when or even if she would get her own coats back, she decided she would have to go coat-shopping yet again. That fur was something she wouldn't be seen dead in, she thought, and then she wished she hadn't chosen those exact words. She hung the coat up in a doorway to try to air it out.

At least she still had the boots she'd bought at the same time she purchased that turquoise coat. She took them out of their box along with the thick hiking socks and removed the labels. It had become increasingly cold in the cottage that afternoon. She'd readjusted the thermostat twice and returned to jack it up a third time. Overhead, something creaked in the rafters, and she swore she heard footsteps on the tower steps. Hairs rose on her arms and a prickle of alarm inched its way up her back.

All Carissa wanted was to get back to New York as soon as possible. But Johannsen had warned her not to leave town. After what had happened to Richard at Penwithen, common-sense told her she needed to tie up her real estate affairs by putting the crumbling family mausoleum on the market. Forget the vacation home and crafting business for the locals. She Googled a realtor in Whitstead to avoid dealing with Al Dyson. He promised to take photos the following day and make sure a short history of Penwithen was included with its listing. She wasn't sure anyone should be living in the lighthouse keeper's quarters, even William, but she decided she should talk that over with him before selling it out from under his memories. When she called him, she got a big surprise.

"Would you consider renting or even selling the lighthouse to me?" William asked. "Living where Jessica made her home all those years would make me very happy."

Carissa wondered whether he'd change his mind after one night of listening to all the creaks, groans and thumps. "I know this has to be a very emotional time for you," she said, trying to choose her words with care. "Maybe you should try out the keeper's quarters for a month or two. Then if you still want to buy, I'm sure we can come to terms."

"Fair enough." William sounded relieved. "I'll sign an agreement as soon as you get it to me, or do you want me to draw something up?"

"If you have the time, that would be wonderful," she told him. She gave him a low monthly figure for the rental and they sealed the bargain with a verbal agreement.

Carissa put on the smelly fur coat and drove over to Whitstead, where she ran into the first store she found selling outdoor gear. An understanding salesperson bagged the offensive coat and promised to dispose of it in a dumpster. Carissa left the shop in yet another down jacket she hoped would last more than a month before it, too, got taken away from her by some traumatic event. She ate a late lunch and returned to pick up her bag and do her final lock-up round of the lighthouse. As she left the rutted track and passed beyond the last of the spindly pines, she jammed on the brakes and stared.

The lighthouse beacon blazed in the watery, late afternoon gloom. Carissa's blood pounded in her ears as her heart hammered a painful tattoo. Two flashes. One, two, three, four, five seconds interval. Two more flashes.

A chill raced up her spine. Gooseflesh rose on her arms beneath her cashmere sweater and new red coat. How could the light be operating? Didn't decommissioned mean unplugged or something?

The beacon went dark and stayed dark, but Carissa *knew*, sitting in the Jeep Cherokee with the engine running and the heater blasting her, that she had seen that light function. The clock on the dash told her it was eight minutes to four in the afternoon.

She put the car into reverse, hit the gas too heavily and shot back. Belatedly glancing in the rearview mirror, she jammed her foot on the brake and jerked to a stop inches away from one of the spindly pines.

Lights twinkled through the trees from the Ulsters' house. Carissa scrambled out of the Jeep and ran to where Quang was trying to fit more boxes into an already over-loaded van.

"I'm so glad you're still here," she said. Did you see the light operating?"

Quang looked puzzled. "What light?"

"The beacon. The lighthouse. It was flashing."

Quang shook his head and returned to shoving a box between two others in the rear of the van. "Blake told me it no longer works. You must be mistaken. Perhaps a ray of sunlight hit the glass. I wouldn't know—I was in the basement. These are the last of my sister's boxes." He got the box into its space and tried to fit in another one.

"The sun couldn't possibly have come out from behind these thick clouds," Carissa said. "I know what I saw, and it was the beacon flashing."

Quang gave up on pushing the box into the back of the van and closed the doors. Holding the box in his arms, he turned to face her. "You've been under a lot of stress."

"I didn't imagine it." Carissa felt defensive. She followed him as he took the box around to the passenger's side of the van and held the door open for him as he made room for it on the floor between several others.

"There's no sun," she repeated. "It's overcast and practically dark."

"I have been in and out of the basement for most of this afternoon," Quang said. "I saw you leave earlier. No one has been at the lighthouse while you were away."

Carissa wondered whether Ray Watkins would believe her if she called him, or if he'd even agree to come over and check the lighthouse for her. She didn't want to worry Richard, and even if she did, what could he do about a flashing beacon at the Bennett Point Light? If Mai Ling's brother believed she was seeing things, so would anyone else.

The lighthouse, barely visible through the gloom, stayed dark and silent.

If Aunt Jessica was trying to send a message, surely it would be for calm, not panic, Carissa told herself. Perhaps everyone around her was correct and she *was* imagining things. Al Dyson had set the tone when she arrived. He'd used the power of suggestion, telling her he thought the place was spooky.

"I will walk through the lighthouse and the cottage with you before I leave." Quang locked the van. "That will make you feel better." He looked at his watch. "I'm late already, but you have been so kind to my sister."

"It won't take long, I promise. I just want to make sure everything's locked up before I leave."

Quang nodded. "Okay."

They walked quickly over to the cottage. The porch was in darkness. Carissa swore she'd left the light on, and the security light over the garage was supposed to be automatic. Had the power gone out again? Had a circuit blown when the beacon flashed? She couldn't seem to get her key into the lock.

"Would you like me to do that?" Quang sounded slightly irritated.

"No, my fingers are cold, that's all." She wanted to tell him he was making her anxious, but she didn't want to risk making him even more irritated. The key suddenly slid into the deadbolt. She opened the door to complete darkness. The power *had* to be off. She knew she had left the hallway light on. She always did.

Quang reached past her and flipped up the light switches, illuminating the porch and the hallway. The security light over the garage suddenly flickered and lit. "Shall we go in?"

A brown out, Carissa told herself. *It had to have tripped all the lights.*

Perhaps that had also made the beacon malfunction, she theorized, although why that would have happened, she didn't even want to hazard a guess. She decided to ask Richard for a more-educated guess.

As she walked down the hallway, she took several deep breaths to calm her jitters. The old place smelled musty. A murky gloom cloaked the living-room. Carissa heard familiar sounds—an ever-present whistling around the eaves, the distant, rhythmic pounding of surf on rocks, the creaking and settling of timbers. All normal. Yet her senses quivered. A feeling of watchfulness pervaded the atmosphere, palpable in its intensity, cloying and even fetid in its odor.

"Is anything disturbed?" Quang sniffed. "Your garbage needs to be taken out." He walked past her into the middle of the living room, bumped into a chair, walked into the floor lamp, steadied it and turned it on.

"I took out the trash this morning." Carissa felt defensive about her housekeeping skills. She saw distaste clearly written on Quang's face as he stood bathed in lamplight.

"It smells like the remains of a tuna sandwich," he said.

"Maybe it's the cat food."

"I don't like cats." He looked around. "Where is it?"

"I'm not sure."

Carissa swore her new cat had been sleeping on the couch when she left. He'd decided Aunt Jessica's afghan was his kitty bed and had rejected the one Carissa bought him.

"Here kitty, kitty," she called softly, but he didn't materialize.

"We should complete our tour of the house," Quang said. "I have to get on the road."

"I know. The cat probably hid because you're a stranger to him. He won't bother you."

She turned on Aunt Jessica's reading lamp. A warm glow made the shadows flee from the living-room, but they remained in the dark kitchen, just as she knew they would be hiding in the bedrooms.

Night shadows, she thought. *Creeping around the cottage. Gliding down the lighthouse steps.*

Where had she heard those words before? *Aunt Jessica's poetry. Something left inside a book.* She remembered seeing a paper flutter to the ground. Picking it up and reading without much thought. Tucking it back inside the pages.

"We should go up to the light," Quang said. "That will calm your fears."

Carissa doubted going up to the lantern room would be soothing, but she nodded. He gave her a flashlight that had been sitting on an end table. She didn't recognize it.

"You go first," Quang said.

Carissa wondered whether the oppressive atmosphere was affecting him. He didn't sound as cocksure as he had before they walked into the cottage, and why would he think they needed a flashlight?

They completed a tour of the keeper's quarters, checking locks on doors and windows. Finding everything secure. As usual, the cottage felt cold. Carissa readjusted the thermostat as they passed.

"You mustn't turn your heat down when you leave," Quang admonished. "Your pipes will crack."

Carissa wanted to tell him she hadn't lowered the heat, but what was the use of telling him the thermostat had a mind of its own? They checked both bedrooms and the bathroom on the way to the tower. Nothing was out of place.

She unlocked the tower door and turned on the lights. Stairs corkscrewed upward. Did she hear something scurrying furtively at the top?"

Nonsense, she told herself. *You're letting your imagination run wild.*

She took the first flight of steps two at a time, the second at a slower pace. By the third set, her thighs were cramping. Carissa stopped at the top to catch her breath. Quang, looking disgustingly well-rested, cruised past her.

"I see nothing unusual," he said after they completed a circuit of the lantern room. "Let's go back down."

Carissa shivered and wrapped her arms around herself. "Even if the sun hit the glass for a while, it couldn't reproduce the flashes. They were sequenced."

"I'm not that well-versed in science." Quang's irritation had returned. "I believe what you saw was due to some natural phenomena. The cottage is locked up tight. I must leave."

"Can't you give me ten more minutes?" She followed him as he walked briskly over to the staircase. "I need to find my cat and get him into his carrier."

"I'm sorry, but I have to go now, so I can access the freeway before nightfall." Quang ran down the stairs ahead of her. "My sister's boxes must be unloaded so the van and I are available for work on Monday morning. I'm already leaving much later than I planned."

"I understand. I've already taken up too much of your time."

By the time she closed and locked the tower door, Quang was on the front step.

"You'll be fine," he told her. "Mai Ling will call."

"I'm leaving for New York in a couple of days," Carissa said. A cold draft blew in through the open door. "Have a safe trip, and thank you."

She walked quickly down the hallway to close the door behind him. She secured the deadbolt and listened to the house creaking and groaning as the wind whipped around it. Despite practically jogging around the cottage and the tower, she still felt cold. She checked the thermostat: 50 degrees, yet again. Frustrated, Carissa turned the dial up to 80 degrees and heard the furnace click on.

Time to find the cat and leave. They hadn't toured the basement. Quang had probably spent more time in his sister's over the last couple of days than he had ever wanted to, which was probably why he hadn't volunteered to go down at the keeper's quarters.

Carissa tried calling the cat but got no response. She was still trying to find a good name for him. She'd tried several on for size, but none of them fit. Maybe that's why he never came when called, although she'd heard cats weren't good about that, anyway. If he could disappear successfully inside the little cottage, how would they find him inside Richard's sprawling ranch when she needed to leave for New York? Maybe Richard would agree to keep him. He didn't need much care, nor did he appear to want it.

In the kitchen, the dry cat food in the long-term feeder remained untouched, but the moist cat food dish was completely empty. She sniffed. No offensive odors. So much for the tuna smell coming from there.

A knock at the front door startled her. Had Quang returned for some reason? Carissa grabbed the poker and slid the chain into place before cautiously opening the door a crack. Finding the doorstep empty, she took off the chain and opened the door completely. A pool of yellow light spilled across the step from the lamp outside, illuminating a vacant path to the picket fence.

Maybe a stray branch hit the door? Surely a gust of wind wouldn't sound like that?

Carissa was tired of rationalizing all the strange noises and happenings. All she wanted to do was find her cat and get out of the place. She started to close the door when something sleek and furry wrapped itself around her leg. She looked down. The cat looked up at her, blinked and gave a soft meow.

"Kitty, you scared me half to death," she told him, closing the door.

Tail held high, the cat purred and wiped himself against her leg.

"What were you doing out there?" Carissa stooped to pet him." "I swore I left you inside."

The cat arched his back. His purring vibrated comfortingly against her hand.

She picked him up cuddled him against her. "It's you and me against the world," she told the little cat, scratching him behind one ear. "I'd thought about giving you to Virginia, but I don't like being bounced from one person to the next. I don't think you'd like it, either." She sighed. "Do you like Richard? You know him already."

The cat tilted his head and closed his eyes, pushing against Carissa's caressing fingers.

"How about eating some more food before you get in the carrier? You could dine on a can of Aunt Jessica's sardines. I'll buy you some more canned food tomorrow and try another brand of the dry. You don't seem to like what's in the feeder right now at all, even though you liked it before."

She set the cat down. He sidled toward the kitchen, his tail continuing to swish. Carissa followed his skinny backside. He still didn't eat much at all, she thought. Perhaps he'd liked the brand they'd given him at the kitty hotel in Whitstead where she'd boarded him while in New York. She'd find out the name and buy him that instead.

Silly as it seemed, she felt less jumpy with the cat for company. She opened the sardines. The cat yowled his approval. He gulped down his treat while she put a filter into the coffee maker. She'd brew one last cup before putting Kitty into his carrier and leaving the lighthouse behind for good. She pulled the coffee canister toward her.

"I like mine black."

Carissa froze, canister in hand.

She turned to see Sally leaning against the wall next to the basement door.

CHAPTER EIGHTY-EIGHT

CARISSA'S THROAT felt so dry, she had trouble swallowing. "What are you doing here?" she croaked. "How did you get in?"

"Coal chute." Sally smiled, looking as relaxed as a friend who had dropped in for coffee. "Well hidden under a ton of ivy. Long ago, the cottage was heated by a coal furnace. The basement's so filled with junk it's not even noticeable. There's still coal dust on the floor." She lifted her foot. "Jessica told me about it."

Carissa saw black on the bottom of Sally's boot. "When did you become such good friends with my aunt?"

"Oh, when I first moved back here." Sally swung a keychain around her left index finger, a rabbit's foot clearly visible.

Carissa's heart contracted. Those had to be Aunt Jessica's missing keys.

"She was still able to get to the village, but it wasn't easy," Sally said. "One day I saw her struggling outside the grocery store and drove her home instead of leaving her to take a cab. She gave me a cup of tea with homemade scones and jam." She smiled in a lazy, insolent way. "By the following fall, Jessica could barely make anything. The jams she'd put up the previous year were in the basement. I volunteered to bring them upstairs. She told me about the chute and warned me not to wander inside the bin by mistake, or I'd track coal dust through the basement and up into the cottage. That's when I saw how easy it would be to get inside if I could get the lock open. Graphite's a great lubricant. Your aunt kept all sorts of handy things like that down there. She didn't mind me looking around when I was visiting. I told her I found the basement *fascinating.*" Sally smiled again, her eyes glittering with amusement.

No wonder I've been hearing noises down there.

"So you've been coming and going as you please?" Carissa could barely contain her anger. "The door of that chute can't be close to the floor. How did you manage to drop down inside? And how on earth did you climb back out of there?"

Sally laughed. "That was a piece of cake most of the time, although I had trouble after the locks got changed upstairs and the ducts were installed. Chuck's work crew moved the step stool and boxes I'd put under the chute. I went sprawling the first time I came after they got through. I was filthy. I had to find everything and put it back in place before I could leave, then go home and take a shower. It took me a while to get that shit out of my car, and I had to throw my clothes away."

"You'll excuse me if I don't feel sorry for you." Carissa didn't even try to hide her contempt. "You stole my aunt's keys."

"I did. I even helped her look for them." She swung the keys around her finger again. "I told her it was okay that her memory was beginning to fade; it happened to everyone as they got older. After a while, I think she began to believe me, and she gave up trying to find them. She had spares, so it wasn't a disaster for her."

"You're really cruel, you know that? My aunt was as sharp as a tack."

Sally shrugged. "What's one more sign you're aging? She was already pretty much homebound at that point. When things started to go missing, she learned to live with it."

"Things went missing? You came in and stole from her?" Carissa's heart lurched.

"Oh, this and that." Sally waved her left hand dismissively. "Whenever I needed to pay some bills and was running a bit short of cash."

"Money, jewelry, or what?"

"A little of everything. I spread it around so she wouldn't notice something like her entire Royal Doulton collection disappearing."

"And you used her keys. You continued using them after I moved in, too. No wonder I thought I heard footsteps and things moving around in the basement."

"I stored things down there until I could get them out of the house, especially the larger stuff, like some of her furnishings."

"She had to have noticed."

"She thought it was the housekeeper. She fired her and then several more. She said they were all untrustworthy. She tried changing agencies. She complained to William Dansinger about them. That's when I had to stop. I don't think he believed she was losing her mind. He became suspicious. She told me he was asking who came to visit her on a regular basis."

Carissa silently thanked William for his astuteness.

"Then she fell, and I didn't want to be caught in here while everything was chaotic." Sally sounded annoyed. "My fingerprints would have been found all over the place. I've been working at getting rid of them ever since you moved in. I haven't taken anything else that was inventoried after Jessica's death. I couldn't take chances. But then Steve fixed the fingerprint problem for me by having Hilly and her mother do some housekeeping while you were freaking out over the cat in the sink. I heard from Dot they'd wiped the place clean of any evidence while they were here."

"You had to start using the coal chute again after I got the locks changed." Everything was beginning to make sense.

"That was inconvenient. I've had to take off my shoes when I leave the basement so I don't track coal dust. Lucky for me, you're a heavy sleeper."

"You've been *watching* me?" Carissa's mind went into five-alarm-fire mode. "Why?"

"Sometimes. But like I told you, usually I've had too much work to do."

Carissa knew she shouldn't be feeling relief, but the knowledge that she hadn't been having paranoid episodes and that she definitely wasn't suffering from hysteria took such a load off her shoulders, for the first time since she had arrived at the Bennett Point Light, she felt vindicated. The lighthouse and its keeper's quarters weren't haunted. Sally Mainard had been playing far more sinister games than Blake Ulster with his clumsy brick and paint can exploits.

"You really should have followed through with getting that security system installed." Sally's laugh was as shrill as breaking glass. "At first I thought you'd leave quickly instead of becoming a problem, but then you got busy involving yourself in other people's lives and stayed. William and Patsy, Virginia...that damned Hubert. I thought I struck it lucky when I saw him outside, but he wouldn't go with me. I hit him with a broom. That got him moving, but the wrong way. He got his fat ass through a hole in the neighbor's fence and got away from me. But since he's never been seen again, I guess he made one hell of a meal for a coyote..."

"Stop it! You're deranged." Carissa didn't want details; she needed to escape. But she couldn't risk running around outside without a coat or boots. She'd left her purse and her smartphone in the bedroom. She doubted she could distract Sally long enough to pick up the cordless and dial 911. And then there was Sally's strength to contend with if she tried fighting her way out of the situation. All the sculpting and woodworking had made her into a formidable foe.

Carissa was fully aware she wasn't in the best physical shape of her life. She'd been too busy working long hours behind a desk. Viable options weren't coming to mind. Quang had left, the police had completed their investigation at the cottage, and until Richard got worried, no one was going to miss her. She could only hope he'd call to find out where she was, and if she didn't pick up, send Detective Watkins over to check on her. However, by then, Sally might have become bored with whatever game she was playing.

"Aren't you going to finish making that coffee?" Sally jerked her chin in the direction of the coffee maker.

Carissa silently berated herself. Why hadn't she asked Quang to help her do a thorough search of the basement instead of the tower? Because she hated the basement even more than the tower, she admitted. But if Sally had already been waiting down there, she would probably have hit Quang with something heavy. Many options were available in that creepy spider-nest, and Sally was very familiar with every part of it. Carissa managed to control her shaking hands sufficiently to pry the top off the coffee canister but spilled grounds all over the counter.

"Now there's a waste of money." Sally tsk tsk'd.

Carissa noted Sally kept her right hand behind her back. Since she sculpted wood with a knife, that was probably what she was hiding. A large one, too, which she'd be able to use very creatively. Carissa felt hot, cold and dizzy at the thought of Sally whittling little pieces off her.

She had no choice but to try to buy time, even though it didn't sound useful right at that moment. The longer she kept Sally occupied, the longer she would stay alive, and the longer she'd have to dream up some way to outwit her adversary or distract her long enough to disable her and escape One thing Carissa knew she wasn't about to do was agree to go outside under any circumstances. She felt sure Sally had a thing about throwing people off cliffs.

"Why don't you sit by the fire in the living-room?" she suggested in what she hoped was an off-hand manner. "I'll bring in the coffee as soon as it's finished brewing. Are you hungry? I could make us a sandwich. I've got sliced turkey or peanut butter."

"Now why would I go trotting off and leave you alone out here, right next to the back door?"

Sally's voice was coming from behind instead of Carissa's right side. Carissa forced herself not to turn in an effort to find out where Sally was and exactly what she was doing.

"Where would I run?" Carissa asked. "I'm not dressed for the weather. How long do you think I'd last out there?"

Sally laughed. She was obviously enjoying herself, and as long as she remained in that frame of mind, Carissa hoped she'd stay alive and intact. A chair scraped the floor and she breathed a small sigh of relief— Sally was about to sit at the kitchen table.

Carissa took mugs out of a cabinet while coffee dripped into the carafe. She placed them onto a small tray with a container of hazelnut creamer and a small bowl of brown sugar. The coffee maker beeped to tell her the brewing cycle had finished. She added the full carafe to the tray and picked it up. The carafe slid to one side of the tray, and Carissa almost dropped everything. Silently calling herself an idiot, she put the tray back down and rebalanced its contents before picking it back up.

When she finally around, Sally was sitting with her back against the wall. She had given herself an unobstructed view of anyone who came from the hallway, and had both the basement and mudroom doors clearly in sight. To Carissa, she looked slightly frazzled. The keys sat on the table next to her and she kept running her fingers through her hair as though trying to comb out imaginary knots. Her other hand remained in her lap. Carissa put the tray on the table, sat slowly and tipped the carafe to fill the mugs. Sally's eyes slid back and forth between Carissa, the carafe and the mug Carissa slid over to her.

Keep calm, Carissa told herself. *Don't stare.* "Cream and sugar?" She reached for the creamer.

"Black, I told you." Sally's pupils were dilated.

"I...I'm sorry. You *did* tell me that. I'll put a little creamer in mine."

Carissa tried a reassuring smile, but it fell flatter than a punctured bicycle tire. She splashed creamer all over her hands and had to clean it up with a towel she had left hanging over one of the chairs.

"Can't you just drink the damned coffee?" Sally jerked the tray away.

She had exerted way too much strength. The tray flew across the table and everything disappeared over the edge. The glass carafe hit the floor and shattered, coffee flying. Hot liquid landed on Carissa's jeans, burning through the denim from her knees to her feet.

Having been told in no uncertain terms to drink her coffee, Carissa picked up her mug and sipped, trying to look like nothing was amiss while her insides were turning to ice water and the burns on her lower legs started to throb.

The landline rang; piercing the otherwise silent house.

"Don't answer," Sally said when Carissa started to get to her feet.

Carissa sat back down. "Whoever's calling will think it strange if I don't pick up. Mai Ling might be calling or Richard, who's expecting me at his house." She took a deep breath. "It might even be Detective Johannsen or Deputy Watkins."

Sally lifted her hand from her lap. A knife gleamed, the blade a good eight to ten inches long. "I said, leave it." She placed the knife on the table beside her mug.

Although Carissa tried not to, she couldn't help staring at the knife. Serrated at the edge, the blade looked incredibly sharp. As Carissa thought about the precision of Sally's carved driftwood sculptures, her knees began shaking harder and faster. Her only hope was that the person who called would come over to investigate. Hopefully, that would be Detective Johannsen, armed to the teeth and bringing Deputy Watkins with him.

A knock at the front door was quickly followed by a long push on the doorbell. The cat, immune to exploding coffee carafes, evidently wasn't to doorbells. He materialized from some hiding place in the living room and knocked over the floor lamp before taking off at a dead run. Carissa caught a glimpse of his raised tail disappearing into the back hallway.

"Get rid of whoever it is." Sally pointed the knife at Carissa. "If you don't, I'll find that cat and make you watch while I cut its head off."

"Okay; I get the picture." Carissa got up slowly and walked into the living room. All she had to do was open the front door and start running. She'd make sure whoever was outside ran, too. Since Steve was in jail and was the only person who walked everywhere on foot, there had to be a car in the driveway, and once they were locked inside it, they'd be safe. She was practically running by the time she got to the door. But when she unlocked it and flung it open, her mouth dropped open in dismay.

"Richard!"

"Hello, love." He was leaning heavily on a pair of crutches. "I got cleared to drive, so here I am."

"Oh, my God. How? What did you come in? Your car was wrecked."

"I drove my pickup truck. It wasn't *that* difficult. I'm pretty tired, though. I'd love to sit on that comfortable couch of yours. We could hang out. Watch T.V. Act like a normal couple for a change."

"Oh, you're such a fool." Tears came thick and fast.

CHAPTER EIGHTY-NINE

"Hey, I thought I'd get a better welcome than this," Richard protested. "If coffee's too much trouble, I'll take tea. Any flavor, although I'm not a big fan of chamomile."

A shadow fell across the ground behind him. Sally glided across the little lawn, unnoticed by Richard. Her knife rose, gleaming wickedly in the reflected light from the porch.

Carissa grabbed Richard and held him tight. "Don't," she pleaded with Sally. "Please don't."

"Don't what?" Richard tried to pull away. "If you want, you can drive us back to my house. I'll leave my truck here."

Carissa felt him swaying. His balance wasn't that good, and the porch had become icy. She was afraid they'd fall, but if she let him go, Sally would probably stab him.

"What are you poking into my back?" Richard tried to look over his shoulder. "Ouch, that hurts. Quit!"

"It's not me," Carissa said.

Sally stepped into Richard's line of vision.

"So I see," he said, as though finding Sally there holding a knife was nothing unusual.

Carissa knew they were trapped. Richard couldn't run, even to save his life, and she wouldn't abandon him.

"Get inside. Both of you." Sally's voice sounded more than a little strident.

"Come on, Richard." Carissa stepped aside, but kept a hand on his back.

He stepped into the cottage with the help of his crutches. "This is some reception," he said. "You shouldn't have."

"You've got that right." She rubbed his shoulder.

Sally came in behind Richard, prodded him forward and slammed the door behind her. "Shut the hell up and keep moving."

Carissa hoped she could remain as calm as Richard appeared. "Where do you want us to go?"

Sally hesitated, the knife swinging in an arc. "Living room. No, kitchen."

As they moved slowing down the hallway into the living room, Carissa wondered what she could do to stop Sally. By the time they reached the kitchen, she had thought of and abandoned several ridiculous scenarios, which included her overpowering Sally and hitting her with one of Richard's crutches or the floor lamp, which lay in the middle of the living room floor and had to be stepped over.

"Get some rope and tie him up." Sally waved the knife in Carissa's direction.

"I don't have any rope." Even if Aunt Jessica had a ball of twine as big as a hot air balloon hidden in the basement, Carissa wasn't going to use it. "He's really weak, Sally. He needs to lie down."

"I feel faint." Richard obligingly staggered, almost taking them both down.

"I don't care." Sally's blue-green eyes looked as cold and sharp as her blade. She scowled at Richard. "I was going to take care of you at some later date. Now I'll have to do it today."

"Sally, this is crazy. You're crazy." Richard's entire body was shaking. "Think this through. You'll be on the run. Your business will be ruined. And maybe, just maybe, you'll eventually realize we weren't worth the trouble."

Sally actually snarled.

"Richard, please," Carissa warned.

He shrugged. "She's planning to slice and dice us, so why not talk turkey about the consequences? Detective Johannsen's like a rabid dog with these Cove murders. He'll solve the crimes and Sally'll go to the loony bin. There's a big one in Bangor. Dorothea Dix. Heard of it, Sally?" Richard sat down heavily at the kitchen table. He looked at the mess on the floor. "I see coffee's out. What about a real drink?" He looked up at Carissa. "What've you got around here?"

"Brandy or scotch."

"Scotch'll do. On the rocks. Make it a double. Want one, Sally?"

Sally's eyes widened in astonishment, as though she couldn't believe his gall.

"I'll take that as a 'yes,'" Carissa said. Richard was turning out to be more of a blessing than she could ever have hoped for. His quick wit and repartee were keeping Sally off her game. But how to disarm Sally? Get her drunk and hit her with whatever was within reach at the time?

Richard propped his crutches against the table. "I'm taking off my coat. If you don't like it, tough. I've had enough of all this frightening crap over the last few months. I know Carissa has, too." He peeled off his gloves, ignored a big slit in the back of his coat after one quick look and threw it with his scarf over the back of a chair. "It's even kind of a relief knowing who's responsible."

Deciding a clear head would serve her better than an alcoholic buzz, Carissa splashed a small amount of scotch into one glass before pouring generous servings into the other two. She carefully dropped a small amount of ice into those glasses before adding a lot more into her own. While she made the drinks, she glanced around furtively for any possible weapons.

Unfortunately, Aunt Jessica didn't have a set of kitchen knives to throw at Sally. The only possible missile within reach was the coffee canister. While using it to hit Matthew had proved useful, Carissa didn't think tossing it at Sally would have any effect at all, except to add coffee grounds to everything else on the floor.

She wished she had rat poison or sleeping pills to add to Sally's drink, but nothing that worthwhile sat on the well-worn butcher-block. Feeling a complete failure at self-defense, Carissa gave Richard and Sally their drinks before carefully wrapping her hand around her own glass to conceal the meager serving. Could they really get Sally drunk enough to overpower her? Would she really give them enough time to do that before she started stabbing?

"Thanks." Richard lifted his glass in a toast and smiled at Carissa. "Cheers." He knocked back the drink in a couple of gulps. "How about another?" He held up his empty glass.

"Planning to get drunk?" Sally asked, taking a small sip from her own scotch.

"Hell, why not?" He struggled to his feet and grabbed his crutches. "My back can't handle this chair. I'm going to sit on the couch."

"You stay where you are!" Sally slammed her glass down on the table and waved the knife at him.

"I'm not dying in agony from back pain. You can either stab me while I'm walking into the living room or we can have a civilized drink in front of the fireplace." He walked away.

"*Richard.*" Carissa didn't know what else to say.

"That's my name. Can you bring my new drink in here?"

Unsure what to do for the best she refilled his glass, picked the tray off the floor and wiped it down before placing all three glasses onto it. Sally stood between the kitchen and living room. As she looked from one of her potential victims to the other, her brow furrowed.

Richard sat down and propped his crutches against the arm of the couch. "How's the leg?" He asked Sally in a conversational tone. "I heard you got pretty bruised up creating a diversion while Steve escaped. What an afternoon you must have had. First you got banged up trying to throw me and my wheelchair over the cliff, then you had to give a theatrical performance for the cops." His laugh sounded a little forced. "Where's that drink, Carissa?"

"Coming." Carissa scooted warily past Sally. Reaching Richard with her skin intact, she slowly let out the breath she'd been holding.

As Richard took his drink, he mouthed 'keep her talking.'

Sally was standing beside the coffee table. "Your damned wheelchair really hurt me. The bar stools didn't feel any better. Does that make you happy?"

"No, of course not. I don't get off hurting people, especially those who've been close to me."

"Right. That's why you deserted me and let me pay for my own abortion."

"If you'd told me you were pregnant, I would have done the right thing, Sally, and you know it. You were done with me, and my child was nothing but an inconvenience for you. It would never have been one for me." He paused. Cleared his throat. "If you didn't want it, I would have taken it. Raised it. Loved it." His mouth set into a grim line.

Carissa's heart contracted. She felt his anger, his grief and his disappointment, as she knew Sally must, unless she was too far from rational thought for anything to register except her own rage.

"But all that's in the past, where it needs to stay." His voice was softer but stronger. "The big question right now is what you're going to do about us. You can't get away with killing half the Cove's residents because you've got some beef with us. You *will* get caught."

"Put those crutches on the floor," Sally ordered. She watched him comply before turning her attention to Carissa. She waved the knife toward a chair on the opposite side of the hearth. "Over there."

Carissa held Sally's gaze as she slowly obeyed. It was the single hardest thing she'd done up to that point. She sank onto what had been Aunt Jessica's favorite chair and vehemently wished she hadn't been such a neat-nick. The large bag of knitting Aunt Jessica had left between the stack of firewood and her chair had been stashed in a bedroom closet. Those needles would have come in so handy right then.

Sally held more keys than Aunt Jessica's in her hand. She threw a large assortment onto the hearth. "They're all there. Front and back doors. They'll be too hot to handle real fast." She sneered. "I locked us in. Like it or not, you're both trapped in here with me."

For Carissa, any remaining hope of survival flew up the chimney along with the smoke from the fire. She'd never be able to overpower Sally unless the woman was occupied with murdering Richard, which was unthinkable. Keeping Sally talking was stalling the inevitable. The phone had stayed silent. Detective Johannsen wasn't going to arrive to save the day.

The only remaining question was who Sally would choose to stab first. Trying to get her drunk had failed. She'd only taken a couple of sips from her scotch. She certainly wasn't going to become so tired or bored that she'd lower her guard enough to get hit with the poker, which was on the opposite side of the fireplace, anyway. If Richard had planned to hit Sally with one of his crutches, they were now more difficult to reach.

"Why did you help Steve escape?" Richard asked Sally. "Wouldn't it have been easier to let him take the blame for murdering Dean and Matthew?"

Sally sighed. "It would have been easier. But he needed to be thankful enough to ask me to join him up in Canada. We could have started a new life. Left all this behind." She looked sullen with her lower lip thrust out.

Carissa decided Sally must be delusional as well as homicidal. But how could she have hidden her mental illness for so long? And were there other victims? She'd only been living in the Cove for two years.

"What's the plan now Steve'll end up in prison for years?" Richard asked.

He sounded so calm and conversational; Carissa wondered how he could manage that under the circumstances. He must still be taking pain medication, she decided, and he'd mixed it with alcohol. She peered at him. His eyes did look a little glazed, but when he looked back at her, he almost imperceptibly winked.

"We're not analyzing my future." Sally's anger was back, full-force. Her eyes flashed. "Why don't you concentrate on how much pain you're going to be in before you die?"

The knife made an arc through the air before impaling the embroidered pillow Richard's elbow was resting on. He jerked his arm away, his face draining of all color. Sally pulled the knife free and slid it back and forth level with Richard's chest. The point passed closer and closer while he watched, his breathing increasingly ragged.

Carissa stared in fascinated horror. The rhythmic action brought the blade's serrated edge close enough to catch threads from Richard's thick Aran sweater. The tip pressed into his side on the next pass. Then sweater ripped. Richard gasped and jerked away.

Carissa bit back a scream. She couldn't sit there while Richard was mutilated right in front of her. Richard was right—as long as they'd kept Sally talking, she hadn't done anything but threaten them.

"Where...what...what did you do to Hilly?" She blurted.

The knife stopped moving. Sally came out of her trance-like state. She turned toward Carissa. "What did you say?"

"I asked about Hilly. Where she is." Carissa breathed a sigh of relief. "I...I know you made her...um...disappear."

Dear God, I hope it isn't because she's dead.

Sally left the couch. She came to stand over Carissa, who wondered what Sally was going to do next and hoped it didn't involve sticking that knife into any part of her.

"Aren't *you* the smart one? You should have been the investigator, not those idiot detectives." Sally tossed her head, her pale hair sliding down her back. "Hilly's at Penwithen. That window with the missing board made a great place to push her into the house."

"How...how did you get her to go there?"

"I didn't have to. She came into the bar to confront me after everyone else ran out after Steve and I hit her with a bottle. Dragged her out the back, wrapped in a dirty sheet waiting to be laundered. No one saw."

"When is this going to end?" Richard's voice sounded amazingly strong and calm. "Hilly's completely harmless. How many people do you really need to get rid of before you're satisfied? Anyone who didn't happen to brighten your damned day?"

Sally turned to face him. "Of course not. Even I can't kill the whole town. Someone would eventually notice people like you were gone, Richard. You've got clients. I can't kill them, too, when they come asking why you haven't finished their projects." She left Carissa and went to sit on the other end of the couch. She glared at Richard and waved the knife around again. "I left Hilly inside the house and put the board back in its place. She'll wake up with a headache, but if she doesn't panic, and nothing heavy falls on her, she can probably figure how to get out eventually."

"I doubt you threw a coat or a blanket in there with her," Richard said. "She'll freeze to death."

"That's not my fault." Sally stabbed the knife into the pillow again.

Richard moved as far from it as he could get.

"That stupid girl already knew something was wrong. She'd already seen me lock up the Emporium and follow your car, Carissa, after I spotted you driving Richard through the village. I went to spy on you both, but when I saw how stupid you were, leaving your keys in the car and going around the back of the house at Penwithen, I decided to make your visit a little more interesting. I never expected you to run off and leave Richard. Here *you* are, Richard accusing me of leaving someone to die, like I'm some kind of monster. What does that make *her?*" She pointed the knife at Carissa.

"My own personal heroine," Richard said. "She took off to get help."

"That's so touching, I want to cry." Sally's face contorted into a parody of concern.

"Richard proved to be more resourceful and resilient than you ever dreamed," Carissa retorted before she could stop herself. "He fought you off, despite being in a wheelchair."

Richard had the audacity to grin, which brought the knife into contact with his thigh. It wasn't an outright stab, but blood appeared on his pants. He shot a look at Carissa that plainly told her not to react.

"Hilly asked me why I was limping before I fell over the bar stools," Sally said. "Always trying to do the right thing, she told me, but she wanted to avoid what she saw as maybe unnecessary gossiping. What was I going to do? Risk her deciding she didn't like my explanation and scurrying over to tell that Bangor detective all about it? He's a lot sharper than the other one was. The one who died." She looked hard at Carissa. "No, I didn't rob the damned gas station and shoot the detective, or pay anyone else to do it, either, if that's where your mind's going."

Carissa decided to ignore that train of thought. "Why don't you get in your car and drive up to Canada?" She suggested. "Richard and I won't say a thing, will we?" She looked at Richard. He might have blood on his sweater and his pants, but color had returned to his cheeks. His scotch glass was empty again.

"What a *lovely* suggestion." Sally was back to snarling. "I already decided I needed to do that even before Steve got caught, but first, I wanted to settle up with both of you."

"You already tried to kill me twice." Richard sounded indignant. "Don't I get any points for that?"

"I did not, and no, you don't." Suddenly, Sally looked less angry and out of control. Her mood appeared to be swinging into a more positive arc. "Let me tell you what really happened to your car. It was Matt. He paid Blake Ulster to fix your brakes. He couldn't think of a better way to get you away from Carissa. He was worried that you were actually getting somewhere with her."

Carissa could well imagine Matthew finding one of the two completely unscrupulous people in the Cove and paying him to take care of what Matthew would think was a small problem. "Did Matthew pay Blake to come to the hospital and put a pillow over Richard's face, too?" She asked.

Sally shook her head. "I guess you know your ex-husband better than I thought, but no, Blake didn't drive up to Bangor. I did. It seemed like fun to me. A chance to shake you up and, depending on whether I succeeded in smothering Richard or not, even put you under suspicion. When Matthew told me Blake had gotten out of control and was actually physically threatening you instead of only playing scary pranks to make you go back to New York, I figured I needed to intervene. I made Brownie points with Matt while making you think you were losing your mind. A win-win situation."

"You and Blake Ulster. Scaring me and making me think I was going out of my mind when no one believed me?" Carissa shook her head. "Damn you, Sally Mainard."

"Now, now; don't try to blame me for everything and send me to Hell all by myself. I had help, some of it unintentional. I waved money from my trust fund in front of Al Dyson and used it to convince him I knew someone who wanted to buy the lighthouse and turn it into the center attraction of an amusement park. Blake loved that. He had extensive gambling debts and couldn't get Mai Ling's family to give him any more loans. He was about to put his house on the market to pay off his creditors before he got shot. Trouble was, I kind of tied up my money."

"Which was when you came back here to get all those things you'd hidden in the basement," Carissa said. The cat chose that moment to sashay into the living-room and jump onto her lap.

Sally's face registered disgust. "Get that creature out of here. I told you, I hate cats."

"I think you already proved that when you killed Hubert," Richard said softly. He didn't sound as cheerful and soothing as he had before.

"Poor Virginia," Carissa said, in an attempt to distract Sally before she cut more of Richard. "But if Sally's telling the truth, she didn't actually kill him. She said she hit him with a broom and he ran away, didn't you, Sally?"

"That Virginia's the one I should have cut to pieces," Sally said. "Always interfering and sticking her nose where it didn't belong. She told you I lied about being pregnant with your baby, didn't she, Richard?"

Richard nodded. "I didn't believe her. Now, I'm not so sure."

Sally nicked the end of his nose. "That's for doubting me."

Carissa swallowed the scream rising in her throat and scrambled to distract Sally. "You pushed Dean Halstead over the cliff, didn't you? Why?"

Sally shrugged, as though Halstead's death was inconsequential. "Matt said he'd hired a top-notch P.I. to dig up dirt on all the Cove residents. He told me he couldn't see me because he had a meeting with Halstead at four o'clock. I got suspicious. If Halstead was even half as good as Matt said, he could have dug up dirt on me, too. I followed him up to Penwithen. I wasn't sure what I was going to do." She ran the hand that wasn't holding the knife over her face. "I thought I'd act like I was taking a walk on the cliff and try to find out what he knew. Maybe bribe him. But it was so windy, he couldn't even hear me when I called out his name."

"So you took advantage of him being at the edge of the cliff and pushed him," Richard said.

Sally nodded. "And his death was ruled an accident, so I solved one potential problem. But now Johannsen's back, and he's planning to reopen that investigation, Ray Watkins told me. Someone's going to have to take the blame. It'll either be Steve, or you." She looked at Richard. "The more I think about it, the more I like Steve for Halstead's murder and you for slitting Carissa's throat. It'll mean one more person going off a cliff when I throw you over, but I'm not the most inventive killer, and accidents do happen, especially in snow and ice."

She leaned forward and pointed the knife in Carissa's direction. "You're the one responsible for Matt's death. You weren't man enough for him. He had to come to me to get what he needed."

"Don't get personal, Sally. He demanded things from me that I couldn't give him. Let's leave it at that."

"I gave him everything." Sally's smirk said more than words could ever have done. "Rough as he liked it."

Richard threw up his hands. "Okay, I'm getting more visuals than I'd ever want."

"He didn't just want rough," Carissa said, anger overcoming fear. "He degraded me. He even tried to convince me to do things for other designers, media reps; whoever he thought could benefit the House of Yates. Whatever they wanted." She couldn't elaborate, and seeing the expression on Richard's face, she didn't need to, either.

Richard groaned. "I'm so sorry."

"Save the sympathy," Sally said.

Her knife ripped a gaping hole in the upholstery before sliding under the bottom of Richard's sweater. He sucked in his breath as the blade protruded through the wool at a level with his heart. With a flick of her wrist, Sally shredded the heavy Aran sweater from chest to hem.

"Frightened now, Richard?" She asked.

Carissa couldn't take any more. She had a good pair of legs, and she was going to use them. She moved the cat off her lap and faced Sally head-on. "You're not evil, you're pathetic," she said. "You thought you were the best thing since sliced bread when you arrived at the Cove. First you had Richard, then Steve. When I arrived, that all changed. Suddenly, you had real competition. You couldn't handle that. You were really jealous."

She watched Sally get up from the couch. Richard's expression changed from shock to fear.

"So you thought you'd make me pay by taking Matthew from me," Carissa continued. "And he played along while you amused him. But when you no longer did, he would have thrown you aside like he did everyone else but me, the one person in the world, it turned out, he actually cared about. He left me everything in his will, Sally. Believe me when I say that if Halstead had turned anything up on you, Matthew wouldn't have hesitated to give you up to Detective Giddings. And even if you do murder us today, Detective Johannsen will track you down. You'll never get away with it."

Sally's expression had darkened dangerously. She got up and took a few steps toward Carissa.

"Halstead could have found out I'd been in a psychiatric facility," she said. "When Matt told me Halstead had given him the evidence he needed, I thought he was talking about that. I tried to explain; told him as long as I took my meds, I was okay. Matt wouldn't listen. He called me a crazy bitch. He told me he'd used me to make you jealous but it hadn't worked, so we were through. He told me that while he was mixing a scotch and soda. Then he toasted me, the bastard. I kicked him. He lunged at me. I shoved him. He'd spilled his drink and slipped in it, hitting his head on the corner of the counter. Since he was already bleeding, I finished him off with a hammer lying on the counter. I watched him die. It was interesting."

Sally had found watching Matthew's death *interesting?* Bile rose up Carissa's throat. Richard managed to catch her eye. He shook his head and closed his mouth tightly. He was slowly reaching toward the crutches.

"Men are so stupid," Sally said. "They think women don't have any skills." She rubbed the tips of her fingers together. "And you can learn so many useful little tricks when you've got nothing else to do except hang out in a common room with a bunch of loonies. They tell you what they used to do before they got sent there, and then they teach you how to do all those things. That's where I learned how to use a knife so effectively. We practiced with anything we could find. Mostly rolled-up pages out of books or magazines. It looked harmless to the staff." She sighed. "I took up the woodworking as soon as I got released and found I was just as skilled at that as I was sculpting in clay." She smiled, that time without the anger.

During Sally's revelations, Carissa had finally managed to stretch her arm out far enough to get her hands on the woodpile beside the fireplace. Her fingers closed over the end of a piece of sticky pine, one of the branches she had found lying around outside and brought in to break up for kindling.

"You were never going to get any of these men to hang around long enough to marry you," she told Sally. "They all saw you for what you are...an easy lay with shit for brains."

"Carissa, for God's sake." Richard's voice was hoarse from panic.

"Shut up, Richard." She stayed seated, her muscles straining. *Come on, Sally*, she urged silently. *Take the bait.* "When Steve gets out of prison, guess who he's going to want to be with? He told me he'd never had a better fuck than me." She caught a brief glimpse of Richard's shock and wished there was a better and more dignified way to goad Sally into a complete loss of control.

With a shriek of rage, Sally leaped.

Carissa thrust the branch at Sally's face. Sally instinctively stepped back. Richard swung his crutch, hitting her behind the knees. Sally went down right next to the coffee table. The knife flew out of her hand. Carissa wanted to grab the poker. She lunged for it, but missed as Sally lashed out, the heel of her boot connecting with Carissa's left ankle. Fire radiated up her leg, almost crippling in its intensity, but she refused to give in to the pain. She had to make a run for the bedroom. If she could get there before Sally stopped her, she'd be able to keep her at bay with Aunt Jessica's putter.

But Sally was recovering too quickly; already scrambling to her feet while warding off blows from Richard's thrashing crutch. Carissa pulled over a small table as she ran through the living room. It crashed to the floor, taking a couple of Dresden figurines and a Tiffany lamp down with it. She leapt over the floor lamp, almost got her foot caught on the cord and heard boots crunching over broken china and glass as she ran down the hallway. She realized she wouldn't have time to run into the bedroom and grab the putter before Sally got to her.

The hallway was in darkness, but at the end of it, Carissa saw the tower door was wide open, lights blazing over the staircase. She ran through with barely enough time to slam it in Sally's face. While she leaned against it, hearing pounding and kicking from the other side, she wondered how the door had opened itself. But she couldn't waste precious time on that issue when she had to figure out what to do next. Sally was much stronger and would push that door wide open in a few minutes. Unless Richard got the cordless phone and locked himself in the bathroom, they were still in very serious trouble.

Her back was rubbing against something that didn't feel like the door's key hole. She slid away from it and glanced down. For the first time, she realized there was a bolt on the inside of the door. She had no idea why. Perhaps Aunt Jessica had been clairvoyant, or one of the keepers had put it there for an unknown reason. Carissa hoped Richard had been able to make that call. She secured the bolt and stepped away from the door. Sally continued her assault, the bolt shaking and straining with every push. It was old, rusty and nailed into the door instead of screwed. The nails were already loosening. Carissa started running again, this time up the stairs.

She knew if she continued to take the stairs two at a time she would fatigue by the first landing, take one step at a time to the second landing, and need a rest before she tackled the last flight of those 125 stairs, but she had no choice. There were tools in the cupboards, and she'd have to use them to fend Sally off until help arrived. Even if Watkins and Johannsen responded immediately, it would take them at least 10 minutes to get to the lighthouse. By then, Sally would have killed and filleted her before going in search of Richard. She kept a snow shovel in the mudroom, if he could even get inside, since Sally had locked all the outer doors and heated up the keys. His crutch might still be a better choice.

Carissa charged up the stairs. She heard the tower door crash back as she passed the first landing. Sally's footsteps rang out on the iron stairs behind her. Carissa's breath scorched her throat as she passed the second landing. That last flight of stairs suddenly felt more like 500.

Despite her frantic efforts to speed up, her steps slowed. Her thighs ached and her knees wobbled. She tried to ignore her fatigue by concentrating on placing one foot in front of the other. She made herself resist looking up for the last step. She didn't dare glance back and risk tripping, despite hearing Sally's clattering footsteps grow ever closer. Carissa's calf muscles knotted. She tasted salty blood and realized she had clamped her teeth down so hard, she'd bitten her bottom lip.

The top step suddenly loomed into view. And then, just as suddenly she felt Sally's hand grab her right ankle. Carissa couldn't shake her off. She fell, knees, elbows and chin striking the floor. It took every ounce of her willpower to ignore the pain and lash out with her left foot in the hope she could break free. She felt the impact as her foot connected with something solid.

Sally screamed and let go, but the white-hot tip of her knife sliced into Carissa's right calf. It was Carissa's turn to scream as she jerked her leg away. If she didn't get up, she was going to die right there.

She forced herself onto her knees, then onto her feet, catapulting herself into the lantern room. Her momentum sent her crashing to the floor, right in front of open cabinets she knew Quang had closed before they left the tower less than an hour before. On a dusty shelf within reaching distance lay the flare gun, already loaded. She grabbed it.

If it misfired, it would explode and probably kill her, but that was the least of her worries with Sally coming at her. Rolling onto her back, she raised the gun right as Sally lunged at her, knife poised and face filled with hate. The sound deafened Carissa. Ears ringing, she closed her eyes in a belated attempt to shut out the kaleidoscope of horror. She dropped the gun and crawled out from under Sally's body.

And then she ran, ignoring the pain in her legs, holding tight to the bannister all the way back down those 125 stairs, right into Richard's arms.

CHAPTER NINETY

WITHIN HOURS of Sally's death, another detective arrived from Bangor. Detective Sergeant Malcolm Jennings was a very different man than his subordinates. He radiated warmth and understanding, confidence and maturity. He wore a dark gray overcoat with lightly frayed cuffs. His close-cropped black hair, graying at the temples, and mellow brown eyes contrasted strongly with Giddings' flash and dash or Johannsen's sharp edges.

He listened to Carissa and Richard's sometimes garbled statements. He treated everyone with respect and dignity. Sally's body was eventually removed and Carissa returned with Richard to his home. The following morning, she drove the Jeep down to the Cove over hard-packed snow to look over and sign her typed statement. She passed Detective Johannsen in the parking lot.

"I'm taking Mr. Ebberly's statement over to him," Johannsen told her. "Detective Jennings wants to meet with you separately."

Carissa wasn't sure whether she was going to have handcuffs clapped onto her wrists until Dot gave her a cup of coffee and a pastry from the Brickley House Tea Room and ushered her into Sheriff Crosby's office, where Detective Sergeant Jennings sat behind the desk with his own pastry and coffee.

"I'm so sorry all this happened," Jennings told her as they both sipped coffee. "This investigation was too piecemeal for my liking. Detective Giddings' unfortunate death resulted in a suspicious accident going uninvestigated for months, by which time another supposed accident had occurred."

"Which Sally confirmed wasn't an accident at all," Carissa said. "I couldn't see Matthew slipping and hitting his head so severely when I was first told how he'd died."

"The local coroner doesn't usually have to deal with anything other than accidental deaths," Jennings said. "Giddings evidently viewed all the crime-scene photographs and agreed with the coroner's findings. I already spoke at length with Johannsen, who told me Detective Giddings refused to consider the extra set of footprints or all the disturbed snow around the area where Mr. Halstead went over the cliff. I firmly believe he tried to grab the railing to save himself, but it came away in his hand. I've ordered a second investigative team to determine whether the support for that rail had been tampered with, but now months have passed and it may be more difficult to establish that. In any case, Sally Mainard confessed to pushing him as well as killing Mr. Yates. Your statement was corroborated by Mr. Ebberly. We're thoroughly investigating Ms. Mainard's background to determine whether she can be linked to any other suspicious deaths before she moved back to Treacher's Cove."

Carissa shuddered. "She said she'd been in a psychiatric institution for some time. Hopefully it was long enough to keep her from harming anyone else."

Jennings nodded. "According to other residents we've interviewed, Ms. Mainard was here for two years without incident."

"Until I came along." Carissa pushed the remains of her pastry around the plate, unwilling to look at the detective while she thought about absorbing the guilt that had wracked her after Sally's accusations.

"I feel I have to accept some responsibility for those two deaths. My involvement may have been unknowing, maybe, but that doesn't let me off the hook. I got into a relationship not only with one of Sally's past lovers but on a much less intimate basis with her current boyfriend, Steve Raymond—Steven Tanner as you know him. Steve became too friendly. He wanted more out of our relationship, and although I told him I wasn't interested, Sally became really jealous. It must have triggered her mental illness again."

"You can't take the blame for anything that happened here, Ms. Yates. Sally Mainard was deluded and dangerous. She hadn't renewed her prescriptions for months."

Carissa managed a small smile to reassure him. "I'm going to work through all of this," she told him. "But it'll take time."

He nodded. "Remember, you're one of Ms. Mainard's victims. One of the luckier ones, since you're sitting here talking with me, but you and Mr. Ebberly have a lot of healing ahead of you. I suspect his will be more physical, yours more mental. He told me he's ready to move on with his life."

Carissa felt Richard's healing would take place a lot faster if she wasn't around. "I need to go back to New York as soon as you tell me I can leave," she said. "I'll be too busy and probably too tired to spend a lot of time thinking about Sally's accusations and the Cove, which will be a very good thing." She took a deep breath. "But can I ask you something?"

"Of course."

"What's going to happen to Steve? He's as much a victim in all this as the rest of us. He was relying on Sally to run his business while he's facing charges."

"All I can tell you is he'll be picked up by New Jersey detectives and returned there for trial."

"Poor Steve." Carissa felt tears slipping down her cheeks. "He's really a good man. Attacking his partner sounds totally out of character for him. He's usually a gentle giant."

Detective Jennings smiled in a way that gave no indication of his thoughts on Steve's guilt or innocence.

"I guess it's true your sins will find you out," she said. "I heard about that cup being found in the back of Detective Giddings' car after it was finally returned to his widow. It was one of my aunt's cups, by the way. But why would Matthew hold back a psychiatric report on Sally? I don't get it. I guess as usual he was trying to manipulate everyone, but that was such a stupid mistake. She told me he confronted her. He should have gone straight to Deputy Watkins instead."

"We could second-guess ourselves and Mr. Yates probably through infinity if we had the time." Jennings stood and held out his hand. "Thank you again for your cooperation, Ms. Yates. You're free to return to New York. If we have any other questions, we know where to find you. As for Ms. Mainard's death—you did what you had to do. Please be at peace with it."

"I'm trying, but it's not easy. I took another person's life in order to protect my own. Sally's going to be on my conscience for a long time. Maybe always."

"Make an appointment with a counselor," he urged. "You need to be able to move forward. From what I've heard, you've got an exciting time ahead of you."

"A challenging time, that's for sure. But I know I'm ready for it." She shook his extended hand.

"Have a good life, Ms. Yates," Detective Jennings said.

She paused at the door. "Am I allowed to say goodbye to Steve?"

"Of course. He should be sitting on a bench outside the station right now as long as Deputy Watkins followed my instructions. I figured Mr. Tanner would appreciate the fresh air before they took him away. The detectives should be here within the next thirty minutes."

"He's chained to the bench?"

"No. Deputy Watkins and Detective Johannsen are both keeping their eyes on him. Dot, too." Jennings' eyes twinkled. "I told him if he moved from there, I would shoot him. I'm pretty sure he believed me."

Carissa found Steve on the bench with his face turned toward the harbor despite the biting wind. Gulls wheeled overhead, their raucous cries filling the air as their bright eyes watched the unloading of the day's catch. Between buildings clustered around the water's edge, masts were visible, dipping and rising with the swell. A familiar tang of salt and fish coasted on the wind.

"I'll really miss this," he told her when she sat next to him.

"I know." She squeezed his hand.

"I hope I can come back some day." His deep voice cracked.

"You will." She squeezed harder as he placed a warm hand over her cold one. "Is there anything I can do for you while you're...away?"

He looked at her then, a wry smile tugging at one corner of his mouth. "You can call it what it is, you know...prison."

"I can't." She blinked back tears.

"When are you going back to New York?"

"In two or three days. After I finish up here, I'll drive to Bangor, spend the night and take the first plane out the following morning, bright and early. Well, early, anyway."

"You can stay at the inn until you leave. No charge. Unless you want to stay with Richard, of course."

"I think it'd be easier for both of us if I didn't stay with him. But I'm going to pay my way if I move to the Fisherman's Rest."

"Hilly and Percival will take care of everything. I already asked them to make sure you're comfortable whenever you come back here...if you ever do. They're going to take care of my place until I get back. They're being too optimistic about how soon that'll be. Two or three years, they're thinking, after talking to William. Me, I'm thinking more like ten to fifteen, maybe longer. But William reminded me I've kept my nose clean here, which may count for something. I still caused Kurt's death though, and then I ran. I was a total coward."

"I think you're a different man now."

"I've tried to be. Although I did slip once, when I hit you." He kept his gaze on the harbor. "And then when I tried to run from here, although you helped me do the right thing and give myself up. Will you keep in touch?"

"Always."

He raised her hand to his lips. "You're a wonderful woman, Carissa Yates. I'm honored you want to stay my friend."

"Do you want me to come and see you, wherever you end up?"

"No; I don't want any visitors. My own punishment for the last two years of freedom."

"You've been a real asset to the Cove," she said. "You provided badly-needed jobs. You made the Fisherman's Rest a safe and welcoming place for residents and visitors alike. And what you did for Richard...you saved his life. No one can take that away from you."

"Jennings said I was a damned fool for running again the other day, but he also said he's going to make sure I get credit for stopping to help Richard. He also told me to man-up and stop panicking. He's right."

"Did you get a chance to talk to Richard?"

"Yeah, he called. They let me talk to him for a while." Steve gave a very thin laugh. "I was way out of line, blaming him for everything. I think he sensed far more about Sally's mental instability than I ever did. And although we may never know for sure, I think Sally lied about being pregnant and never needed an abortion."

"She really loved you in her own way," Carissa said. "I don't think she would ever have hurt you."

"Maybe not, but look what she did to everyone else. Why didn't I see how erratic her behavior was becoming? Mood swings, temper tantrums and outbursts, crazy demands."

His anguish spilled over to Carissa. She sensed how much blame he was placing on himself. A choking amount. She shook his arm.

"Look at me, Steve."

He did.

"You can't blame yourself like this. None of us knew the extent of Sally's illness until yesterday. I even thought poor Hilly might be responsible. I'm so glad that realtor I contacted went to Penwithen to take photos yesterday. He heard her and got her out of the house. If I hadn't called him, things might have ended horribly differently."

"She's so grateful," Steve said. "Would you believe she went to work yesterday evening and brought my dinner over to me?"

"I would." Carissa hoped Steve wasn't as clueless about the extent of Hilly's dedication to him as he'd appeared to be until that moment.

"I don't think Sally hit Hilly very hard," Steve said. "And the board over that window was pretty loose, the realtor told Hilly. I think Sally wanted her to survive."

"I'd like to think that, too. It would make Sally more human. Less insane." Carissa thought about Steve refusing to have any visitors and Hilly's future. "You've been really blind where Hilly's concerned, Steve. She'll be waiting when you've served your time, no matter how long you have to be away."

"I know. I'm not completely clueless. By the time I get out, she'll know everything she needs to about managing an inn. Then I'll have to marry her, so I never have to worry about her leaving my place and opening her own." Steve really smiled that time.

"Time to go, Mr. Tanner." Sergeant Jennings strolled up to them. "The cavalry called. They've reached the outskirts of town."

Carissa got up.

"Take care, love," Steve said.

"You, too." She gave him a hasty peck on the cheek and left quickly.

She glanced toward the harbor before getting into the Jeep. Despite all that had happened, leaving the Cove was going to be very difficult, and she still had more painful goodbyes.

CHAPTER NINETY-ONE

THE LAST BOX had been loaded; the van had left. Carissa took one last walk around the Bennett Point Light's keeper's quarters. Her aunt's beloved home would now be William's. He had told Carissa any spirits would be welcomed, especially if one of them was Jessica. He had asked to rent the furniture as well. Carissa had left most of it, unsure whether disturbing anything in that house would result in some spirit transference with the goods, but she did take her aunt's sewing and knitting supplies, quilting frame and china collection along with many of the photo albums and memorabilia. She left some for William and planned to send others back when she'd had time to enjoy them herself.

"Goodbye," she told the house as she stood in the front hallway. "Don't give William a hard time, and leave the thermostat alone." She swore she felt a gossamer-light touch on her cheek. "And thank you for saving my life. Richard's, too."

She smiled and walked out, locked the door and dropped the keys into the mailbox. William would soon be on his way over, but they had already said their goodbyes. Without looking back, she drove down the rutted track to the road that zigzagged its way down to Treacher's Cove.

The future looked brighter than it had for a long time. She had already set another appointment with the psychologist. They'd have a lot more to discuss after this latest trip to Maine, she thought wryly as she parked in front of Richard's office.

This parting was the most painful of all. Her relationship with Richard had been an unexpected gift of the most precious kind, but it had to end. Their futures led in opposite directions. Helming the House of Yates necessitated she live in New York while Richard's business remained in New England.

She quietly opened the outer door of Ebberly's Construction and Architectural Design, stepping into a small vestibule. Through the etched glass inner door she saw April, Richard's receptionist. April looked up, smiled and beckoned her inside.

"Nice to see you, Ms. Yates. Please go right in. He's been expecting you all morning."

Carissa nodded and walked past April's desk to open Richard's office door. He was working on plans in the north light from the bay window, a cane propped against his desk.

"Hi, 'Rissa," he said before he even looked up.

"How did you know it was me?"

"Your perfume." He turned to face her and a wide smile broke out on his still-handsome face. "You look beautiful. Too beautiful for the likes of Treacher's Cove. You'll put your runway models to shame. I'm jealous of all those men in New York already."

She found herself laughing with him. He always maintained that upbeat attitude. His calm and wit had contributed greatly to saving their lives. Carissa could well imagine how long she would have lasted with Sally if he hadn't decided to get in his truck and drive over to surprise her.

"Have you had any second thoughts about taking over Matthew's business?" He asked. "I made some preliminary sketches on a replacement for Penwithen before you decided to demolish it. I can design and build you a house a little further back from the cliff, with a separate building for you to do any kind of start-up your heart desires. You've got that pattern book your aunt mailed. You could use that as a jumping-off point for your creativity."

"Oh, Richard. You're clutching at straws. The fashion industry's in New York, not New England. I need to be there to manage Matthew's empire. It's my legacy now, and after the initial fright and my doubts over my abilities, I know I can do this. He believed in me and my abilities. I'm going to build on that. I love my work. I don't want to give it up, and I'd put so many people out of work. Good people. We've got so many sales; I know some of it's because of the nostalgia over Matthew, but the new line is really taking off. My line. My work. My beadwork and the enhanced prêt a porter."

She stopped abruptly. She'd been gushing over herself and her work, when what she needed to do was ease into telling him goodbye. It was going to be the hardest thing she'd ever had to do. Even harder than pulling the trigger on that flare gun, she decided as she looked up at Richard and felt an ache that threatened to stifle her.

She forced herself to breathe. "What else are you working on?" She waved toward the sketches on the drawing board.

He kept his eyes on her, a slight frown between his brows. "A shopping mall of a different kind. The online industry has been beating retail into the ground. This one integrates both worlds." He pointed toward a stack of neatly-rolled plans on his desk. "Then there's a supermarket in Whitstead, a museum in Portland, and maybe a new civic center."

"Very ambitious."

"Very late. My accident delayed everything. I'm amazed my clients have been so forgiving. I'm working longer hours and taking stuff home with me. I took Nurse Fields' advice and hired a live-in housekeeper, at least for now. She even found the woman, and she's a dragon. 'Mr. Ebberly,' she says to me this morning, 'I've had strict instructions that you are to eat dinner no later than 6:00 P.M., and you're to get adequate rest. That doesn't include bringing work home with you. Do you want me to call the doctor and tattle on you?'"

"She said that?" Carissa laughed again. "Don't you want to run away from her?"

"That's the plan."

Suddenly, he wrapped his arms around her waist and held her close.

"Richard, stop it. You've got to let me go."

"I love you, and you know it. We can work things out."

"I can't work on anything except putting all this drama behind me and getting my life back together. In New York, not Treacher's Cove."

He released her, and her body instantly yearned for his warmth.

"Too much has happened here," she told him as he stood looking at her, that slight frown now extending to the corners of his eyes and the edges of his mouth. *His very kissable mouth,* her renegade mind told her. She pushed that thought back.

"Neither of us has the time to put into a long-distance relationship. We're too preoccupied with work."

Two spots of color appeared high on Richard's still-pale cheeks. "You're making shallow excuses. You're afraid."

"I am not."

"Yes, you are. But standing here arguing with you isn't going to get me anywhere, is it?"

"No. I'm sorry. My mind's made up. If I was going to stay here, things might be different."

Richard looked like he still wanted to argue his case, but he sat on the stool in front of his sketches. "Your stay here was always going to be temporary," he said without looking at her. "You made your mind up even before you arrived that you weren't going to get involved with any of us."

"But I did." She blinked back tears. "And I came to care very deeply for so many of you. I'll miss you more than anyone else, Richard, but I have to go. You should understand that, after what happened here. I've got to get away and regain some perspective. Some peace. My aunt, Matthew...Sally..."

"I know," he said softly. "You've had a lot to deal with and getting away from the Cove is probably the best thing for you. But leaving me behind, too?"

"Will be the hardest."

He nodded, still without looking at her. He sighed. "So this is really goodbye." He got up from his stool.

"Yes, it really is." If she expected him to protest further or take her in his arms and kiss her, she was sorely disappointed.

"Well, I'm not going to beg, and I'm not going to plead." He guided her back to the front office.

April had evidently decided to take a break. The room was empty. As empty as Carissa's heart.

"Richard..."

"Don't say it." He held up his hand.

"Who's being the hard-nose now?"

"Take the utmost care of yourself." He kissed her forehead, his lips warm and gentle.

Carissa closed her eyes and felt the tears slide from beneath her lids. He kissed her temples, her cheeks, and finally, and only lightly, her lips.

Her skin felt as though it was on fire wherever he touched her.

"Stay out of trouble," she said, wishing she could think of something far more profound. "Call me if you ever get to New York and want to catch up."

She ran out the door before she broke down completely.

Richard watched Carissa leave. He watched her distinctive graceful walk and her long legs as she tucked them into the Jeep. He remembered every moment with her. Savored every memory as he watched her drive away.

When he turned, he found April had returned from wherever she was hiding. Without either of them saying anything, he walked back into his office and closed the door. He'd failed to keep the love of his life. Richard knew Carissa ached for him, but it hadn't been enough.

CHAPTER NINETY-TWO

OVER THE FOLLOWING MONTHS, Richard worked long hours, slept fitfully, and completed all the projects that had been delayed. Finally, those came to an end as May roared in like a lion with gale-force winds instead of spring flowers. It had been three months since Sally's death. Three months since Carissa had left the Cove for good.

Richard had no idea what he was going to do next. Nothing appealed. William had settled in at the lighthouse, his devoted companion Carissa's once-stray cat. A young family had bought the Ulsters,' which had been turned into a small farm with a cow, a couple of pigs and several chickens. William said he enjoyed visiting his new neighbors. He bounced their two small children on his knees, fed the chickens and sneaked treats to the cow whenever she hung her head over his wall. He'd even warmed to the pigs. So much so that he told the family he would buy either or both of them if there was a question of butchering.

Penwithen had been leveled, but so far, no one had made an offer for the land. Its stark location would look more appealing in the summer months. Richard thought a bed and breakfast might do well there, constructed as a replica of the original but without the drafts, narrow hallways and rabbit-warren servants' quarters. He had bought the columns, the tiles and that wrought iron staircase. All were stored in one of his warehouses, awaiting the right project to find new life.

He poured coffee and sipped as he stared out the window. Leaving his cup on the sill, he sat down and started flipping through his appointments calendar. He paused when he saw a phone number, his mind racing at the consequences of calling the person attached to it.

He pulled out the preliminary plans for the civic center and pressed the intercom: "Get me Gary Greenwood in New York, will you, April?"

"Yes, boss. Do I get to go with you?"

"Where I go, you go. If I firm up this deal, you can start packing immediately."

She let out a whoop before hanging up.

While he waited for the call to go through, he poured himself a small glass of brandy from the wet bar and raised it in a toast.

"To the future," he said, swirling the amber liquid around the glass. "Here's to a highly successful civic center, and an even more highly successful merger of the House of Yates and Ebberly Architectural Consultants."

"Your call, Richard," April said over the intercom.

He picked up the phone. "Hi, Gary. How are things?" He listened while Greenwood told him everything was shit because he needed an architect with vision. "You can stop worrying, Gary; I'm coming on board," he said.

"When?" Greenwood asked. "I need you here ASAP."

"My assistant and I will be on the next available flight." Richard hung up. "April?" He called.

She appeared in the doorway, her face radiant with expectation. "Yes?"

"We're heading for the Big Apple as soon as you get us on a flight. Put in a forwarding address with Nancy Burton after you've completed the rest of the travel arrangements, and please send a dozen red roses to Carissa at the House of Yates."

April dimpled. "What do you want on the card?"

"Picking you up from work at seven. Dinner's at Delmonico's." He paused, looking at April's radiant expression. "That's if you can make the reservation."

"Consider it done." She paused in the doorway. "How do you want the card signed?"

He smiled to himself. Carissa didn't want love, but given time, he'd get her to change her mind. He could be very persuasive when the stakes were high enough, and they most definitely were.

"Just sign it 'Richard,'" he said.

THE END

ACKNOWLEDGMENTS

Thanks as always to The Pacific Online Writers Group (POWG) members, currently Bonnie Schroeder and Miriam Johnston, for their continued support as well as their careful and insightful critiquing. They make my writing better and keep me striving to do my very best.

To Paula Johnson, who always ensures my website looks sharp, is easily navigated, remains updated, and reflects who I am, as always, a big thank you.

To Jenn Oliver for saving me from having to tackle formatting my own books.

Lastly, but absolutely far from least, to my readers: Thank you for taking the time and giving me your support. It's always much appreciated.

ABOUT THE AUTHOR

Heather Ames knew she was a writer from the time she won first prize in a high school novel contest. An unconventional upbringing gave her opportunities to travel extensively, leading to nomadic ways and an insatiable desire to see the world. She has made her home in 5 countries and 7 states, learning a couple of languages along the way. She is currently pitching her tents in Portland, Oregon, and after a long career in healthcare, made her dream of writing full-time come true.

Heather is a current board member of the Harriet Vane Chapter of Sisters in Crime and member of Toastmasters International.

Visit her website at
www.heatherames.com

ALSO BY HEATHER AMES

Mystery / Suspense series

Indelible (Book 1)

A Swift Brand of Justice (Indelible—Book 2)

Romantic Suspense

All That Glitters

Contemporary Romance

The Sweetest Song

Upcoming Books

Swift Retribution

(*Indelible* mystery / suspense series—Book 3) *2018*

www.ingramcontent.com/pod-product-compliance
Lightning Source LLC
Chambersburg PA
CBHW051928020726
47501CB00001B/34